WIRED

A Novel by Ronson Duncan

An Old Line Publishing Book

Printed in the United States of America

ISBN-13: 978-0-9846143-5-6

ISBN-10: 0-9846143-5-4

This book is a work of fiction. Any references to real people, events, establishments, organizations, or locales are intended solely to provide a sense of authenticity and are used fictitiously. All other characters, incidents, and dialogue are drawn from the author's imagination and are not to be construed as real.

Old Line Publishing, LLC
P.O. Box 624
Hampstead, MD 21074
Toll-Free Phone: 1-877-866-8820
Toll-Free Fax: 1-877-778-3756
Email: oldlinepublishing@comcast.net
Website: www.oldlinepublishingllc.com

AUTHOR'S NOTE

This novel has been a "work in progress" for a longtime. When I first started it, Bill Clinton was President and my wife and I lived in Chattanooga on Signal Mountain. The first draft was 65 pages. Then we moved back to Clearwater Beach. After that we moved to Wake Forest, NC. Then we moved back to Florida. From the book's start to finish, I held five different jobs and we moved seven times for one reason or another. In the course of all this, I plugged away on my novel an hour here and an hour there whenever I could find the time, mostly in the wee hours of the morning before work.

This novel is a work of fiction. Clearwater, Florida is a real place, faithfully described, but used fictitiously in this novel. Names, characters, places, cities, marinas, restaurants, and all incidents and actions pertaining to the United States Coast Guard are either the product of the author's imagination or used fictitiously. Any resemblance to persons, living or dead, or to actual events or locales is purely coincidental. However, the Mexican paramilitary drug-traffickers known as 'Los Zetas' are factual and they pose a genuine threat to America. According to the Justice Department, the Zetas have blended in with the Latin community and now operate from safe houses in Texas, California, Oklahoma, Tennessee, Georgia, and Florida.

I would like to dedicate this book to my friends and family out there (you know who you are) and to my former SEA-TOW pals, with a special shout-out to Bob Kirn—the real-life Captain Brillo. I would also like to dedicate this book to my incredible wife, Kathy. During our 20 years of marriage, I have dragged her all over the country in the pursuit of dreams and making a living. In between jobs and moves, my nose has been buried in this book, which oftentimes stretched her "for better or worse" vow to the nuptial limit.

However, now that "WIRED" has been published and I am semi-retired, I suspect she may encourage me to start another. One must be careful what they wish for.

AUTHOR'S BIO

Ron Duncan is a retired businessman who resides on the Gulf coast of Florida. In the mid-90's he owned and operated a Tampa Bay boat towing business called SEA-TOW, where he worked hand-in-hand with the Coast Guard in rescuing stranded boaters. It was the product of his experiences there that inspired this book. He is an avid reader and this is his first novel.

TABLE OF CONTENTS

PROLOGUE

Monday 23:00 Hours - The Gulf of Mexico

With his bleary eyes transfixed on the heavenly light, Cal wondered if he was dead.

Was that the bright light everybody talked about? The one you were supposed to walk toward?

With his mental faculties scrambled, nothing was clear in his head. Yet the harder he tried to concentrate, the more his mind seemed to slip. Obviously the loss of blood was affecting his thinking.

Loss of blood?

Lying flat on his back, he studied the intriguing light. His mouth was bone dry with a faint taste of blood and both ears were ringing. His hearing was hollow and muffled, as if submersed underwater.

What was happening? Where was he? Is this what it felt like to die?

But he was too young to die. He had more living to do—a whole lot more.

His mind was struggling to make sense of things when a rope ladder magically appeared and lowered itself through the divine light. This curious phenomenon piqued his interest and he dwelled on it for an inexact time.

Was that the way to heaven?

In his disoriented state the line between seeming and being was vague, straining against reality.

Thinking that God should be able to do better than that, he debated whether to get on the ladder or not. After all, he hadn't exactly been a saint during his lifetime on Earth. It could take him the opposite direction and that wouldn't be so hot. Or maybe it would. It brought to mind the bumper sticker he had seen earlier on that pickup truck, the one that read: "**WHERE ARE YOU GOING TO SPEND ETERNITY—SMOKING OR NON-SMOKING?**" For all he knew, the ladder might carry him to the smoking section.

No, this was a big decision and he wasn't going to be rushed. Obviously he had a choice in the matter or a spiritual entity of some kind would be telling him what to do. He had always heard that a dead relative was supposed to meet you when you died, to help guide you to the other side. Well, so far, he hadn't seen anyone, not even a cherub.

With a giddy grin, Cal pictured a cherub with a stubby cigar climbing down the rope ladder and saying in a gruff voice: "Better hop on, pal. Ladder leaves in five minutes. Next one in fifty years."

No, for the time being, he was going to stay put right here—wherever that was—while he thought more on it. After all, there was no hurry. He had all eternity to make up his mind. And it wasn't so bad here. The floor under him was a bit cold and the wind was rather raw, but it wasn't too terribly uncomfortable.

While marveling at the light, his head began to clear and a sliver of logic pierced his mental fog, questioning the absurdity of it all.

Ladder to Heaven!!?? Smoking Section!!?? Cherubs with Cigars!!??

Cal emerged from his delirium to find himself still alive and breathing. Along with his resurrection came sound and sensation—the thundering whirl of a helicopter and crucifying pain. A Coast Guard Jayhawk helo was hovering directly overhead and a rescue ladder had been lowered. A familiar voice was blaring from the hailer horn, ordering everyone to evacuate. The rope ladder was his ride off this Godforsaken ship and away from those schizoid Zetas. Somehow or other, he had to get on it.

But his limbs felt heavy, as if sheathed in lead, and his entire being was weighted with fatigue. Straining against exhaustion, he raised his head and took stock of his battered body. The bullet wound in his shoulder had stopped bleeding but he'd clearly lost a lot of blood. He was scraped and bruised all over and his swollen testicles felt the size of basketballs. Everything he had hurt.

Cal relaxed his head on the deck and gazed at the spotlight through stringy sweat-soaked hair. It was no use. He was too weak. Whatever fate awaited him, so be it.

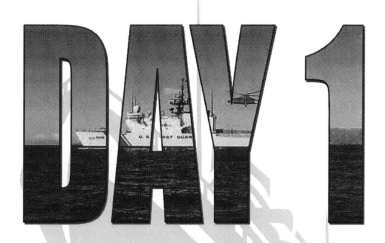

"THE TAKEOVER"

"First we kill all the subversives; then, their collaborators; later, those who sympathize with them; afterward, those who remain indifferent; and finally, the undecided . . ."

General Iberico Saint Jean, Argentine soldier, politician, governor of the province of Buenos Aires during the military rule in Argentina.

"Evil is unspectacular and always human,
And shares our bed and eats at our own table."

W. H. Auden (1907-1973), Anglo-American poet

"He that is taken and put into prison or chains is not conquered, though overcome; for he is still an enemy."

Thomas Hobbes (1588–1679), English philosopher

WIRED

It was the height of tourist season and traffic heading for the beach was bumper-to-bumper. The spring-breakers—or *snowbirds* as northerners were locally called—were out in full force, honking and weaving their way westward along Gulf to Bay Boulevard.

Stuck in the hubbub, the beach residents tolerated the crowding by knowing full well that the local economy depended on it. It was an annual inconvenience, but taken in stride and considered a small price to pay for living in paradise. Besides, they all knew that in the hot and humid summer months ahead, the motels would be mostly vacant and the streets sparse with traffic. Then they would reclaim their island once again until next season.

It was a balmy 78-degrees and one of those picture-perfect days. The midday sun was a bright buttery ball dangling high overhead against a cloudless blue sky. As the sun's rays reflected off the Gulf of Mexico's quartz crystal seafloor, the aquamarine waters took on a phosphorescent radiance that seemed to glow from within. Palm trees and lush tropical foliage adorned the sugar-white sand shoreline, swaying in tempo with a gentle onshore breeze. Along the water's edge, Great White Herons and long-legged Snowy Egrets leisurely waded the shallows, stabbing the water every so often for fish. Dotting the heavens above were white-feathered sea gulls and pinwheeling terns, scouting the seascape for sustenance. As they squawked and screeched in their winged quest for food, the more placid pelicans perched on their favorite dock piling and scoured the water beneath them for a free fish dinner.

Unlike the busier weekends, today's boating activity was relatively light. But from time to time a sailboater would show up at the Memorial Causeway Drawbridge and radio the bridge tender for an opening.

The four-lane bascule drawbridge was built in 1963 to replace a two lane concrete bridge built in the 1920's. It was the only land link between downtown Clearwater and the barrier island of Clearwater Beach and it halted traffic in both directions whenever it rose. But despite everybody's rush to get to the beach—or wherever they were going—most folks didn't really seem to mind. As the tall ships sailed through the bridge's raised spans, the locals waited uncomplainingly while the tourists gawked with wonderment, sometimes hanging out their car windows for a better view.

Indeed there was something majestic about a sailboat gliding across the water—its brilliant white sails billowing with air, its stainless rigging glinting with sunlight. Yet, in spite of their magnificence, nearly one and all seemed more stricken by the regal old drawbridge that gave them passage. Kids would giggle and point excitedly at the rising bridge while the adults marveled at the mechanized structure, often snapping pictures. Young or old, tourist or local, there was a shared admiration for the old drawbridge.

For children, the whole process was just too cool—the gates lowering to halt traffic...bells ringing...lights flashing...metal creaking...the rising span splitting to become two halves. For adults the drawbridges had a sentimental appeal because they were fast becoming extinct. The Memorial Causeway Drawbridge itself was high on the endangered list and destined to join the ranks of her bygone sister bridges. In the name of developmental change it was slated for destruction in favor of an "arched bridge" with a soaring 74' vertical clearance to allow boat passage beneath without an opening.

There were only two land routes serving Clearwater Beach: the Memorial Causeway Drawbridge spanning east-west over the Intracoastal Waterway and the Clearwater Pass Bridge giving southerly passage to Sand Key and a string of island communities beyond, ending up at St. Pete Beach. The Clearwater Pass Bridge was one of the newer-variety arched bridges that replaced the former drawbridge a few years ago.

This left the Memorial Causeway Drawbridge as a final remnant of a fading era. Although it was tired and known to breakdown from time to time, and although its openings snarled traffic, beach residents revered the old landmark. Progress may be practical but it wasn't always popular and there were several local movements to save it from extinction.

Petitions sponsored by various citizens groups and yacht clubs were being circulated at shopping malls, beach restaurants, and marinas. "SAVE OUR BRIDGE" ads were being run in local newspapers and the signatures were mounting. Nevertheless, the $70 million project had already been funded and the city planners refused to back down. As a countermove they published full-page ads of their own with graphs and illustrations

WIRED

detailing the necessity of a new bridge and how it would alleviate congestion.

In rebellion, three errant senior citizens physically chained themselves to the bridge and tossed the key in the waterway. Traffic was halted for nearly two hours while the Fire Department torched the chains and the Clearwater Police hauled them away. The local newscopters provided live coverage of the event, which sparked further demonstrations. It was a real circus.

Two hundred yards north of the drawbridge was the Clearwater Bay Marina. Moored there was the *Majestic Star*, a local day cruise ship that sailed the Gulf of Mexico for legalized gambling. As paying passengers embarked for the noontime excursion, Captain Jason "Skip" Myles and his crew stood by the gangplank in their sparkling white uniforms.

"Welcome aboard," Skip greeted the passengers filing past him. "I'm Captain Myles. Hope you enjoy the cruise. Good luck in the casino."

The reception line was Skip's favorite part of the job and he never tired of it. This was *his* ship and *his* crew and he was exceedingly proud of each.

Skip was a "people person" and his warm nature came across as genuine. Patrons largely responded in kind with broad smiles, friendly handshakes, or playful salutes. When a youngster came aboard, Skip would dip his head and give them a snappy salute from the black bill of his white hat. Then he would present them with a paper sailor's cap and proclaim them his honorary *First-Mate-For-The-Day*. The ceremonial act always elicited beaming smiles and Skip enjoyed watching them giggle up the gangplank wearing their hats proudly. The doting parents also delighted in the fun, flattered by the captain's fawning over their oftentimes-bratty children.

"Looks like we have a pretty full boat this trip, Neal," Skip muttered out of the side of his mouth. "Better advise the kitchen."

Standing in line next to Skip, Neal jokingly snapped to attention. "Aye-aye, sir!"

When Skip gave him one of his enough-is-enough looks, Neal grinned and hustled off in the direction of the dining room. As Skip watched Neal fade into the crowd, he shook his head and smiled. He and Neal had worked together for over twenty years now—from smelly fishing boats to tugs and barges—and the decades had left them good friends. Neal was caring, competent, and conscientious—epitomizing the sort of officer that Skip wanted representing his ship.

Skip believed that you could pay someone to do a job, but you couldn't pay him or her to care. Either they did or they didn't. As well as being capable, Neal cared, which Skip deemed invaluable. So, eight weeks ago, right after landing his captain's position aboard the *Majestic Star*—the undisputed pinnacle of his twenty-five year career—Skip was thrilled to have offered Neal the esteemed position of First Officer.

Thursday 11:55 Hours – Clearwater Bay Marina

As a few last-minute passengers raced up the gangway, Skip made his way toward the wheelhouse, smiling and making small talk along the way. He loved his new job and he took great pride in being in command. Being an ex-Navy man, he ran a tight ship and carried a no-nonsense reputation amongst the crew. But Skip was a *leader*, not a *boss*, and led by example. In between excursions he had chipped paint and swabbed decks alongside the crewmen in order to bring things shipshape. Seeing the *Old Man*—as captains were called—join in on the grunt work promptly earned him the respect of the crew.

Skip walked into the wheelhouse looking at his watch. "Okay, Neal, time to shove off."

As the moorings were cast off and the gangplank was withdrawn, Skip picked up the handset of the ship's PA system. After welcoming everyone aboard, he announced that the dining room would begin serving as soon as they were underway and the casino would open in approximately thirty minutes upon reaching international waters.

The *Majestic Star* made two four-hour excursions per day, seven days a week. The first departure was at noon and the evening departure was at 19:00 hours, or 7:00PM. Although Skip's employer gave him two days off each week, he had worked every single day since taking the job. But the constant pace was catching up with him and he planned to take off this coming Sunday and spend it with his wife. Kathy had been a real trouper about his long hours away from home and he intended to make it up to her.

WIRED

Neal sounded the air horn and began backing the ship into the Intracoastal Waterway. Calling on years of experience, he simultaneously manipulated the throttle, the bowthrusters, and the steering wheel with masterful efficacy.

As the giant twin props vibrated rearward, Skip thought of the front row tickets in his wallet for *The Eagles* concert. It was the rock band's first tour since the release of their *Long Road Out of Eden* album and Kathy would be totally thrilled. A devoted fan, she had been flocking to their concerts since the eighties. After the performance he planned to treat her to a romantic late-night dinner and then go for a moonlight walk on the beach. After years of scrounging to pay the bills, he couldn't wait to surprise her. Through good times and bad, they were still very much in love.

As the *Majestic Star* approached the opened-and-waiting drawbridge, Skip spied a group of protesters atop the bridge. Smiling, he raised his binoculars to see what the picketers were up to. They were toting "**SAVE OUR BRIDGE**" signs and marching single file along the pedestrian walkway. As Neal threaded the ship through the drawbridge's narrow opening—scarcely leaving two yards of clearance on either side—Skip blared the horn and waved at the demonstrators. This show of support sparked a big round of cheers and added more fervor to their sign waving.

Like most of the locals, Skip, too, cherished the aging old bridge. In order to reach international waters for lawful gambling, the *Majestic Star* traversed the drawbridge four times each day. Sometimes it was a pain in the backside waiting for an opening, but that was okay. The old bridge was a classic and the elderly bridge tender was a first-rate fellow. After thirty years of opening bridges, Skip hated to see the old guy thrown out of work. He had a sick wife at home and a heap of medical bills to pay.

The tender was a colorful old character nicknamed Pops and he reminded Skip of his grandpa. Most bridge tenders stayed tucked away in their air-conditioned shacks and remained relatively anonymous; but not Pops. Instead of being an obscure voice on the radio, he was always visible through open windows and he was never too busy for a warm smile and friendly wave.

Pops always wore a ball cap of some kind that caged his downy white hair. Skip figured he must own hundreds of them because each day they were different. Today he was sporting a politically correct *Save Our Bridge* hat. Yesterday, his cap read: *Tampa Bay Buccaneers - Super Bowl Champions*. The day before that he'd worn a *New York Yankees* hat.

Skip made a mental note to give him a *Majestic Star* cap on his way to work tomorrow. Not because Pops needed another cap—though he'd probably fancy one for his collection—but because Skip regretted the raw deal he was getting and wanted him to feel appreciated. Over the decades Pops had become a local fixture and the maritime community would sorely miss him.

Four minutes later, the *Majestic Star* sailed under the new Clearwater Pass Bridge and entered the gleaming Gulf of Mexico. Clearwater Beach was lying off the starboard bow and Skip raised his binoculars to pan the beach goers. It was spring break season and the one-mile stretch of powdery white sand was jam-packed with oil-slick bodies.

"I ain't seen this much white meat since Thanksgiving, Neal."

As Neal chuckled, Skip scanned the multitude of swim-suited sunbathers. Most were snowbirds from up north, thawing out in the Florida sun—lounging on spread blankets and beach chairs...collecting souvenir shells...building sandcastles...sailing colorful kites. A handful of the more thick-blooded vacationers were braving the cold surf. Canadians, Skip figured.

When Skip spotted a group of teenagers playing sand volleyball, he paused a moment to watch the action—smiling when a skinny kid plowed face-first into the sand while trying to return a tricky serve. As the skinny boy got up spitting sand, the opposing team razzed him and celebrated the point with high-fives. They were all so young, so full of life, and Skip envied their youthful vitality. He was 56 now and, after the long hours he had put in lately, he felt every year of it.

When the ship cleared the #1 Bell Buoy and entered open sea, Skip decided to check on things below. "I'm goin' on a walk-through and mingle awhile, Neal. When I get back, you can break for some chow. How's that sound?"

"Scrumptious." Neal let go of the ship's wheel and patted his belly. "I could eat a horse."

"Sorry, but we're fresh outta horsemeat." Grinning, Skip turned for the door. "Guess you'll have to settle for lobster and crab legs."

WIRED

When Skip walked outside, he lingered on the catwalk awhile to take in the sunshiny day. There wasn't a cloud in the sky and the aqua-blue water was resplendent with sunlight. Mother Ocean had always afforded him great pleasure and he never tired of her infinite splendor. Filling his lungs with salt air, Skip removed his hat and let the tropical breeze rustle through his hair. Then he closed his eyes and turned his face toward the sun. As its solar warmth basked his upturned face, he thought about how good it felt to be alive.

Skip wasn't a church going man, but he couldn't believe all this earthly grandeur happened by accident. Somewhere up there, he was convinced, there had to be someone pretty "Almighty" looking after things.

After soaking up a few rays, he put his hat back on and delighted in the seascape once more. He could have stood there all day but duty called. For Captain Skip Myles, though, it was a labor of love and he was actually getting paid for it. He was one lucky old seadog.

Feeling blessed, Skip shot a thankful salute toward the heavens—just in case the "supreme" Commander-in-Chief happened to be watching—then he whistled his way down the bridge deck.

Thursday 12:14 Hours – Gulf of Mexico

With his deck shoes squeaking against the sundeck's white enamel paint, Skip threaded his way through the festive crowd. The reggae band was in full swing and smiling passengers were crowded in front of the stage, swaying with the tropical beat.

When Skip hired on, the ship employed a boring folk singer that sat on a stool and played old James Taylor and Jim Croce tunes. Skip didn't have anything against *Bad, Bad, Leroy Brown* but he wanted to liven things up a bit—something with a tropical flavor. So, after pleading with the company bean counters for a larger entertainment budget, he hired a genuine Jamaican reggae band with dreadlocks and all. They were an instant hit with the passengers and kept the six-dollar umbrella drinks flowing—eight bucks if they kept the glass.

Cha-ching!

After dodging some partiers doing the limbo, Skip headed for the casino on the next level down. Before going downstairs, he unhooked the "CLOSED" chain stretched across the stairwell entrance and then reattached it behind him. Passengers weren't permitted inside the casino until the ship was outside territorial waters and the chain served as a reminder.

When Skip entered the casino he found the bartenders, waitresses, and blackjack dealers diligently making last minute preparations. This is where the real money was made. The $35.00 excursion fee barely covered the food and fuel. Satisfied with what he saw, Skip continued down the staircase for the dining room on the main deck.

While descending the steps the clamor from below grew increasingly louder—sounds of mixed chatter...scattered laughter...the chinking of silverware and tinkling of glasses. By the time he rounded the mid landing, the mouth-watering aroma filled his nostrils. When he reached the last step, Skip found the dining room teeming with hungry seafood-loving passengers.

During a typical walk-through, Skip would randomly stop by tables to inquire about the food. After listening to their anticipated raves, he would thank them for sailing with him and move on to the next table. As Skip made today's rounds, he stopped by a table occupied by two Hispanic gentlemen. Upon making his standard inquiry, a man with a gold tooth grinned up at him and praised the lobster bisque in broken English. Since this was another change Skip had made during his short tenure, he was pleased to hear that it was working.

Instead of a steam table laden with dried-up meatloaf and vegetables, Skip had insisted upon a nice seafood buffet. After all, this was a cruise ship and he argued that passengers naturally expected seafood fare. He also cited that if the ship offered tastier cuisine, it would attract more locals, which would help cover their expenses during the off-season. Tired of battling the contentious new captain, the bean counters gave in and agreed to give it a ninety-day trial.

The next day Skip hired a Cajun cook from New Orleans. Over the weeks that followed, the word spread quickly and now many locals paid the $35.00 boarding fee just for the flavorsome buffet. They didn't gamble as much as the tourists, but they consumed a fair share of beer, wine, and liquor—all of which fell to the bottom line. So, much to the chagrin of the company accountants, Skip's *New Orleans Seafood Buffet* was a smash hit and a real moneymaker.

As Skip worked his way toward the galley, he ruffled the red hair of a freckle-faced *First-Mate-For-The-Day* standing in line at the dessert bar. Just before entering the kitchen, Skip noticed a corner table in the back piled high with discarded crab shells. With his palms frozen against the stainless double-doors, he studied the group of men as they devoured their food. With cheeks bulging with crabmeat, they were talking excitedly between themselves and licking their fingers like they hadn't eaten in weeks. They reminded Skip of a bunch of feasting pirates in an old Erroll Flynn movie.

Annoyed by their obvious abuse of the "only-one-trip-through-the-buffet-line" rule, Skip decided to put a stop to it. Putting on a casual face, he wandered over to their table and asked them in passing if they were enjoying the seafood.

Taken aback by the intrusion, the men quit eating long enough to gawk up at him, shrug at each other, and nod ignorantly. It was patently clear they didn't understand English. Most of them looked Mexican except for a big bearded man with a strange tattoo, who looked Middle-Eastern. As Skip looked them over, one of the Hispanics wiped his greasy chin on a shirtsleeve and spoke in a pidgin of Spanish and English— *Spanglish.*

"Yes, Capitán—Bueno." The man held up a half-eaten crab leg and smiled with food stuck between his teeth. "No habla Inglés."

Skip knew that *"bueno"* meant *"good"* and that the man was obviously referring to the food. Apparently he understood some English but wasn't fluent. Unable to speak Spanish himself, Skip stared longingly at the mountain of crab legs and simply smiled. In view of the language barrier, he decided to forget about it and move on. Making a scene in front of the other passengers and coming across as a hard-ass wasn't good P.R. Before leaving, he grudgingly told them to *"enjoy"* and headed for the kitchen.

As Skip passed through the galley doors, the Arab's unusual tattoo stuck in his mind. For some odd reason it seemed familiar to him. He had seen one like it somewhere before, but he couldn't recall where or on whom.

WIRED

Skip's thoughts were harshly interrupted by an earsplitting crash of plates. Turning toward the racket, Skip glared at the newly hired busboy and then frowned at John-Renée, the Cajun chef in charge. With a what-do-you-expect-for-minimum-wage look on his face, John-Renée shrugged at Skip and rolled his eyes.

Fully aware of the help problem in Florida, Skip shook his head in exasperation and went inside the storeroom to check on provisions for the upcoming weekend. On his way back, he deliberately stomped through the shattered debris of plates to show his displeasure. Upon entering the dining room, he shot an angry glance toward the corner table to find the feasting crab-lovers gone. Glad of it, he checked his watch and started back for the wheelhouse.

Thursday 12:33 Hours – Gulf of Mexico

When Skip entered the wheelhouse, Neal was still manning the ship's wheel.

"Okay, Neal, go grab some chow. I'll take over."

"Thought you'd never ask." Neal stepped aside and gave Skip the helm. "You want anything?"

"Not unless you know where I can get some competent kitchen help." Skip's voice was full of irritation. "On your way down, tell the casino they have about five minutes. Okay?"

"Will do." Neal pocketed his sunglasses and slunk toward the doorway. When Skip had that *look* on his face, it was best to make yourself scarce. "Be back in a few."

When the *Majestic Star* reached international waters, Skip throttled back to conserve fuel and set the autopilot for a wide looping course. After circumnavigating the area for the next few hours, he would close the casino and return to port.

"Attention! The casino is now open," Skip announced over the PA system. "Good luck to you all." In hanging up the handset, he muttered under his breath: "But not *too* much luck."

When Neal returned from lunch, Skip gave him the helm and headed for his cabin. During the hourly gambling period, Skip generally went to his quarters to do some paperwork and rest up for the evening cruise. It

WIRED

was usually midnight when he got home at night, making for a very long day.

At entering the cabin, Skip hung his hat on a hook by the doorway and stripped down to his undershirt to get comfortable. He was hanging his starched uniform shirt in the closet when he noted a piece of lint on one of the black shoulder epaulets. Like the gold leaf on the bill of his Navy dress hat—a.k.a. scrambled eggs—the epaulet denoted him as ship captain. A stickler for neatness, Skip picked it off meticulously and flicked it into oblivion.

Before getting down to business, Skip ducked into the head to freshen up. It was muggy for March and the cool water felt refreshing as it splashed over his face. As he straightened up to towel off, he studied his reflection in the medicine cabinet mirror.

A lifetime of outdoor work had left his tanned face a bit leathery, but not so much so. He had crow's feet around his eyes from years of squinting into the sun, but that was okay. The lines added a little character. Boat captains were supposed to look a little weathered. And they weren't really that noticeable unless he spent all day in the sun, leaving white streaks jetting from the corners of his steel-gray eyes.

Standing taller, Skip squared his shoulders and evaluated himself further. His wispy brown hair was woven with gray strands and thinning a little at the crown, but it looked okay with his matching gray-flecked beard. Actually, the look suited him just fine—he looked like a boat captain. And at 6' 2" and 195 pounds, he was still lean and muscular from years of working on the docks. Kathy had always bragged about his "bearish charm" and that's all that mattered to him. He would never admit it, but he loved it when she described him to others as the handsome, rugged type.

"That's me, all right," he chuckled, hanging the towel to dry. "Me Tarzan—you Jane. Jeez!"

Shaking his head at the thought of him wearing a silly Tarzan outfit, Skip sat down at his desk and opened his laptop computer. Thirty minutes later the report was done and he clicked the e-mail 'Send' button. Obeying the command, the upload bar progressed to 100% and the ship log was magically dispatched to his corporate headquarters via satellite. Skip didn't understand how the whole cyberspace thing worked, but he was genuinely impressed with the technology.

With a yawn, Skip leaned back in his chair and checked his watch. There was enough time left to stretch out on the bunk awhile and recharge his batteries. He closed the laptop and was about to rise when Kathy's photo caught his eye. The picture was taken four years ago on her 40th birthday. She was sitting on the sundeck of their waterfront condo holding her prized possession, Toby—a black terrier he had bought for her birthday.

Smiling, Skip picked up the picture frame and gazed at it fondly. Kathy hadn't changed much but Toby was full grown, of course. It was amazing how attached they were. Wherever you saw Kathy, you saw Toby. The dog wouldn't let her out of his sight. And he was insanely jealous of her. Skip couldn't even kiss her goodbye without him jumping between them and licking his face. Not licks of affection either; big slobbery licks of jealousy to drive him away.

Grinning at Toby's image, Skip shook his head. "The crazy mutt thinks *he's* the husband. Doesn't know he's just a freakin' dog."

Then Skip's eyes shifted to Kathy. At age 44, fewer than 30 years could be read in the pretty face framing her big brown eyes. She was still slender and petite with thick honey-blond hair flowing past her shoulders. But best of all was her infectious hundred-watt smile. She had the cutest dimples in all the Seven Seas.

Skip was tracing a finger across her lovable face when the sound of firecrackers startled him back to reality.

"Firecrackers?" He stiffened in his chair and cocked an ear toward the door. "What the hell?"

While listening more intently, his eyes roamed the cabin ceiling. Was it his imagination?

Suddenly worried, Skip set the picture frame down and sprung from his chair. Then he froze at hearing more popping sounds followed by muted shrieks and screams. It sounded like gunfire, automatic gunfire. But the sound was so unnatural aboard his ship, so out of place, his brain couldn't associate the two—couldn't grasp it. It was too inconceivable.

Then the realization of it struck him full force—it *was* gunfire.

Startled by the revelation, his blood surged and the flesh crawled on his back. Afraid to look, but more afraid not to, Skip was racing for the cabin door when the doorknob rattled from the other side. An instant later the door swung open and banged violently against the inside wall. Clinging to the doorframe was Neal, panting with panic and visibly shaken. His face was slick with sweat and strained with fright. He looked scared out of his wits.

"We got a serious problem, Skip!" Neal's words came out in heavy gasps and he was rubbernecking up and down the deck as if anticipating danger. "A real God-awful problem!"

DAY 2

"THE UNCERTAINTY"

"Where does one go from a world of insanity?
Somewhere on the other side of despair."

T. S. Eliot (1888–1965), Anglo-American poet, critic.

"I turn and turn in my cell like a fly that doesn't know where to die."

Antonio Gramsci (1891-1937), Italian political theorist

"Between the conception,
And the creation,
Between the emotion,
And the response,
Falls the Shadow . . ."

T. S. Eliot (1888–1965), Anglo-American poet, critic.

WIRED

Friday 06:30 Hours – Detroit, Michigan

The clock radio blasted to life at precisely 6:30AM and the sound of *Kokomo* by the Beach Boys nearly knocked him out of his bed.

On most mornings Cal would have slam-dunked the snooze button and rolled over for a few more winks. But with this particular song, he simply lowered the volume, bunched the covers up under his chin, and lazily soaked in the soothing sounds of the steel drums. As they resonated their distinct tropical tones, he was transported to another place and time...a sunny place where he grew up...a place where he longed to be.

As *Kokomo* gradually faded *(Aruba, Jamaica, o-u-u I wanna take ya . . .)* the oldies station disc jockey did his 60's, 70's, and 80's best to hopelessly brighten another shitty March day. In a booming baritone, he reminded his listeners to: *"STAY TUNED FOR THE UPCOMING BEACH BOYS BASH WEEKEND!"* Then on a less boisterous note he announced it was time for the local weather and early traffic report.

Cal was still under the song's tropical spell when the meteorologist spoiled his serenity. A Canadian cold front was moving southeast across Lake Michigan and there was an eighty percent chance of it dumping six inches of snow later today.

Like Detroit life in general, Cal found the forecast depressing. He didn't care how many surfing songs they played; this was Motown—not Bermuda, Aruba *or* Jamaica—and the weather around here was going to be cruddy until April or May, if they were lucky.

Following the weather forecast, the *Eye in the Sky* traffic copter began reporting the latest traffic delays. Cal generally took sardonic pleasure in listening to the commuting problems because he escaped the road-rage drudgery by walking to work. He had planned it that way, of course, when leasing his downtown studio apartment. Still, after hearing today's snowy forecast he didn't feel much like gloating. He would be trudging through the white stuff while the commuters stayed toasty-warm in their cars.

With that bone-chilling thought, Cal turned off the radio just as the oldies station launched into its daily bombardment of crass commercials for hair loss, erectile dysfunction, osteoporosis prevention, enlarged prostates, and other irksome messages directed at the aging baby boomers. On top of today's lousy weather report, Cal didn't need their underlying truths dragging him further down.

Being acrimonious by nature, he made a mental note to put the tire chains on his wheelchair before leaving for work. After all, he wouldn't want to slide off the snowy sidewalk and end up facedown in the street like some old codger in a TV commercial.

Help!...I fell down and I can't get up!

Maybe he *was* an old hippie, and maybe he *was* struggling with his own mortality, but he still had trouble accepting that any hardcore Beach Boys fan would have an erection problem. Why, that was unthinkable and simply un-American. And *he* certainly didn't have any problem in that area—no way. Viagra wasn't needed in Cal Stringer's bedroom.

With that macho thought, he rose up on one elbow and slapped his bed partner on her gorgeous backside. "Rise and shine, sweetcakes. How about putting on the coffee while I take a shower? Don't want to be late for work, you know."

His sleepy bedmate stirred and murmured something indistinguishable, then rolled over and cuddled up against him. As she lay there with her eyes closed, she looked simply stunning in the muted morning light—long raven hair draped over one breast, high cheekbones, full sensuous lips, the kind of brick-house body that would make any man write bad checks for. On a scale of 1 to 10, she was a solid 10 and Cal felt blessed to possess such a lovely creature.

Despite his intention to get to work on time, the warmth of her silken skin was too inviting on such a frigid morning. Succumbing to the sumptuous feel of her flesh, he pressed the snooze button and curled up against her. What the hell—it was Friday.

The movement disturbed his bedmate, who rolled away from him and pressed her voluptuous buttocks against his groin. Savoring their luscious feel, Cal cozied up to her backside and slipped his arm around her waist, molding himself to the contour of her body. Her feel and fragrance stirred the lust in him and he suddenly felt hot blood moving to his loins. With heightening sexual desire, he nestled his nose against the wispy hairs on back of her neck and kissed the pulse of her throat. When she moaned in delight, he kissed her again and then made himself stop. An early-morning quickie while she was still half-asleep would be selfish of him.

WIRED

Besides, there would be plenty of time for that sort of philandering over the weekend. Being snowed-in with a ten had its fringe benefits.

To help resist the temptation, Cal twisted away from her and sprawled flat on his back. After fantasizing a moment about his X-rated weekend, he rolled over opposite her with a lecherous smile. "I can dig it," he sighed dreamily into the pillow. "Let it snow, let it snow, let it snow."

A minute later he drifted off to sleep with the lyrics of *Kokomo* still playing in his mind. In his dreamful state he was Humphrey Bogart with Ingrid Bergman lying at his side. They were at a tacky but tropical no-tell motel that could have been in Casablanca or perhaps Key Largo. They had just made passionate love and were now lying together, basking in the warm afterglow of lovemaking. Ingrid was clinging to his shoulder with her head resting on his hairy chest. Bogey was smoking a Camel and coolly blowing smoke rings toward the ceiling.

The dream was pictured from overhead in black-and-white with the soft-filtered-lens look of the old 40's movies. The view was from right above the slow-turning ceiling fan. They were lying in a bleached rattan bed with white linens—their nude bodies slick with mingled perspiration, the air around them thick with the sensual scent of post-passionate lovemaking. As the fan blades circled, they sliced through the scene ever so slowly, scattering the rising smoke rings spiraling upward.

Suddenly the falsetto sound of *Big Girls Don't Cry* interrupted Cal's dream and jolted him awake. When his eyes popped open, he was letdown to find himself back in his own bedroom. Wondering how long he had been asleep, he eyed the clock radio while turning down the volume. Noting that ten minutes had passed, he was about to roll over and resume his sultry dream when he remembered his ten o'clock court case.

"Damn!"

Dreading the workday ahead, he sat up in bed with his back against the headboard. At his age he should be slowing down. He had paid his dues and it was high time for the simpler pleasures in life. *Right on!* Like sleeping-in late, a martini before noon, sand between your toes and all that stuff. Besides it was colder than hell outside.

With a groan Cal threw back the covers and slung his legs over the mattress edge. As he raked his fingers through his tangled dark hair, he wondered if anyone still said: *"Right on."* After thinking on it, he more or less doubted it and vowed to never say it in public. There was no use showing your age.

When he reached for his cigarettes on the nightstand, it furthered his petulance. There were none. He had quit a week ago as a testament to his upcoming 55th birthday—the dreaded double nickels. But kicking the habit wasn't easy and Mr. Nicotine still courted him on a daily basis. Trying to neglect the craving, he looked out his bedroom window only to find the panes frosted so thick he couldn't see out.

"Lovely," he humpfed. "Another freaking day in paradise."

He was wondering how long the nicotine withdrawals would last when he remembered the Bogart dream. Interestingly, the dream had been recurring a lot lately and he couldn't imagine why. Had the *Kokomo* song triggered it? Or perhaps his craving for cigarettes?

After considering it, he thought not. Neither the song nor Bogey's non-filtered Camels had anything to do with it. He was pretty sure of that. Was his upcoming birthday at the root of it? Causing some sort of male-menopause thing? Subconsciously urging him to flee everyday life for some imaginary place full of mystery and intrigue, like an old classic movie? Maybe.

Come to think of it, he *was* having a harder time getting out of bed lately. And he honestly *did* enjoy the dream. Inexplicably, he was comfortable there. Was he hiding in his dreams from everyday life, or was it something else? Fifty-five perhaps. He *had* been dwelling a lot on his birthday. It was another milestone. *(tombstone?)*

While taking this into account, Cal stepped into his pajama bottoms and pulled them up by the elastic. "Hell, fifty-five ain't old, dude," he muttered. "Not old at all." Suddenly one of his knees cracked bringing a frown to his face. *Or was it?*

Wondering if anybody said: *"dude"* anymore, Cal reached for his cigarettes a second time. Coming up empty-handed, he scowled and padded barefoot into the bathroom. While urinating he hashed over things that could possibly be bothering him.

Turning fifty-five was nagging at him—true. It was a wakeup call. The next he knew, he would be facing the Big Six-O. *Whoa!* At his age birthdays weren't celebrated—they were dreaded. They were jolting reminders that life was short and his time on planet earth was running out.

WIRED

Still, Cal realized he had deeper issues than that. Somewhere along the line he had lost his place in life. He no longer cared about his law practice and he was fed up with his rat race existence. He subconsciously yearned for a more satisfying life while he was still young enough to enjoy it, where the rigors of life weren't so mundane.

He needed a change...a new place to live...a place where it was warm.

"Yeah," he poked fun at himself, "a place where there's romance and adventure in the air!" Flushing the toilet, Cal furthered his foolery. "Bogey wouldn't worry about his insurance rates going up due to a lousy speeding ticket. No sir. And he'd *never* go to freaking traffic school—not Bogey. He'd simply tell those dirty coppers to scram and flip a Camel in their face. Then he'd speed off and go on the lam—hide out at some sexy dame's place or cool his heels in the back room of an exotic bar. And Bogey would certainly never freeze his ass off in Detroit, Michigan. Hell no—not Bogey!"

Chuckling at himself, Cal filled the sink with hot water and retrieved his safety razor. He needed to stop overanalyzing things and chill out.

As the razor glided across his face, Cal studied his reflection in the bathroom mirror. He didn't look too bad—for an old hippie. He had the beginnings of crow's feet around his ice-blue eyes, but he still had a thick head of black hair with a touch of gray at the temples. And, at 6'1" and 200 pounds, he was solidly built.

Cal stepped back for a better view and frowned at the slight development around his waistline—*love handles* they were so quaintly called. He had obviously gained a few pounds over the winter months and on top of the age issue it furthered his discontent. He had always prided himself on his lean-machine look and he wasn't about to let his mid-fifties change that. No way. Getting the middle-age spread was *not* an option.

Cal pulled up his pajama pants to hide the excess belly flab and twisted side-to-side. After some scrutiny he decided he carried the extra weight okay. In fact, he looked pretty darned good. On a wild and zany lark, he laughed off the matter by grabbing his crotch and making a vulgar face in the mirror. "Hey, I got your love handle right here, baby!"

Smiling at his silly self, Cal stepped in the shower and turned on the custom showerheads. As the high-pressure jets pelted his skin from six angles, he lowered his head into the stream and flattened his palms against the wall tiles, moaning with delight. Life was good.

As the pulsating water cascaded over him, the shower door opened and "she" appeared naked within the steam. She looked like a *Goddess* coming at him through a foggy mist—an ethereal apparition. But as she handed him his coffee cup, her come-hither eyes reminded him of a sultry *She-Devil* on one of those old 50's horror movies.

He couldn't decide if she was a goddess or a she-devil until she began kissing him. Starting with his neck, she kissed her way slowly down his chest, then to his stomach, then beyond. As raging goose bumps engulfed his body, his arms wilted in erotic pleasure and his coffee trickled down the drain. She was a she-devil all right and he was darned glad of it.

In years past Cal had dated a goddess or two and was turned off by their prissy attitudes. They were high-maintenance, inappreciative women, who yammered too much and made their men work too hard. It was all about me, me, me.

At the height of his ecstasy, the she-devil unexpectedly rose and pecked him on the forehead. "Can't be late for work!"

When Cal begged her to stay, she reminded him that her boss was a real prick and she had to get a move on.

"Well, he might be a real prick," he complained over the hissing water, "but that's better than being a real prick teaser!"

"Sorry." With a puckish grin, she closed the shower door. "Gotta run!"

Now really hot and bothered, Cal adjusted the water temperature to cool down his sexually frustrated body, fussing at himself for not taking the quickie.

"See, Cal, that's the thanks you get. You try to be a considerate, unselfish lover, and you end up gettin' nothing—zilch, zero. Left high and dry." Peering down at his manhood he gloated, "Well...maybe not dry, but *high* is certainly an accurate description."

(Yeah, and, at your age, old-timer, that's something to brag about—right?)

Ignoring his smart-alecky alter persona, Cal finished his shower and dried his hair. Then he entered his walk-in closet with a bath towel cinched around his waist. Inherent to his fastidious nature, one side was neatly lined with suits, ties, and dress shirts, while the opposite side displayed his casual wear. With his court appearance in mind, he selected a powder-gray pinstriped wool suit, crisp white button-down shirt, and bright red power tie.

After taking a final swig of coffee, Cal donned his overcoat and grabbed his briefcase. As he walked for the elevator, he wasn't looking forward to facing the freezing weather. He was tempted to take a taxicab but the "love handle" matter was still nagging at his vanity.

When Cal stepped outside, he was met by a blustery blast of cold air that whipped the lower flaps of his overcoat. As he tightened his neck scarf and stooped into the wind, he asked himself why he had moved to this hellhole in the first place. He should have set up practice in Florida after graduating from law school instead of taking that lousy job up here. Instead of freezing his gonads off, he could be strolling down Duvall Street in Key West right now wearing shorts.

As Cal trudged down the sidewalk his ears began to ache, so he pulled up his coat collar to shield them from the wind. In doing so, he made a mental note to buy some earmuffs. Or perhaps one of those Russian fur hats with the fold down earflaps. That would do the trick.

"Never mind the crackheads and muggers. Even they've got better sense than to come outside in this crap! If anything's gonna be the death of me, it'll be this freaking Detroit weather!"

Friday 07:54 Hours – Clearwater Beach, Florida

Kathy Myles was sitting on her leather sofa, watching the morning rain trace down the sliding glass doors. She had spent a long sleepless night smoking cigarettes and pacing the living room floor, waiting for her husband to come home. Now, overwrought with worry and convinced that something awful had happened, her imagination was running rampant—awash with images of wreck and ruin.

Early on in their marriage Skip had oftentimes drank too much and staggered home in the wee hours of the morning. Occasionally, on his poker night with his fishing buddies, he would get too smashed to drive and, peevishly, she would go pick up his drunken butt and put him to bed. But he always came home sooner or later, or at least someone called.

Besides, that was over ten years ago and Skip had since given up the hard stuff for beer. Something wasn't right. Something terrible had happened. She could feel it in the hollows of her bones.

Unless there was a problem aboard the *Majestic Star*, Skip was generally home by midnight. If he worked any later than that, he always called her out of consideration. She was a worrywart and Skip knew it. Since his new job required him to work late hours, he had asked her repeatedly not to wait up for him; but his words had fallen on deaf ears. She would not—*could not*—go to sleep without him and that was that. Not because she didn't trust him, because she loved him.

When Skip wasn't home by one o'clock, Kathy was concerned. When he wasn't home by two, she became alarmed. Since the ticket office closed after the 7:00PM departure, there had been no one for her to call. When the clock struck three she jumped into her car and drove to the marina, but the gates were locked and she couldn't get in. Upon returning home she was tempted to call Neal's house, but she didn't want to wake anyone at that late hour. Besides, her calling Skip's employees in the middle of the night might be embarrassing for her husband—like she was checking up on him or something.

So, after phoning the Coast Guard, the hospitals, and the local police, she'd smoked cigarettes in the dark and drank black coffee—coping with the chaos of her own mind. Then at long last the sun lit the eastern horizon and her seemingly endless night came to a merciful end.

Friday 08:07 Hours - Detroit, Michigan

As he shivered along, Cal realized just how much he missed Florida—the beaches, the ocean, the laid-back lifestyle. He even missed watching the tourists make fools of themselves by feeding the seagulls—a telltale sign of an out-of-towner. The recollection of it struck an amusing chord, bringing a grin to his frozen face.

Tourists would innocently feed one seagull and then suddenly find themselves engulfed by other squawking gulls, as they too demanded food. The besieged adults would generally defend themselves by covering their heads and flailing their arms. The children would either stare at the gulls totally mesmerized, or run amok while bawling hysterically. The

WIRED

locals, who *never* fed the seagulls, found it entertaining to watch.

It amazed Cal how quickly the seagulls had evolved into skilled beggars. Over an incredibly short span, these wild creatures had forsaken their natural diet in favor of bumming Doritos and french fries. It reminded Cal of today's society; and the more he thought about it, the more parallels he drew. He couldn't really blame the seagulls, though, because they were just a bunch of stupid birds looking for a handout. At least they didn't expect him to support them like some of the sorry-ass Homo sapiens.

They can't find work *(yeah, right)* so they get a government check. They have a bad back *(yeah, sure)* so they collect disability. They can't afford school lunches *(yeah, but they can always afford those $150 pump-up-and-fly-in-your-freaking-face basketball shoes)* so they eat free at taxpayers' expense.

Cal looked both ways and stepped into a blustery crosswalk. While plodding between the white lines he pictured the poor unemployed and disabled, all warm and snug in their beds right now. *Their* eyes weren't watering and *their* teeth weren't chattering. No siree. They were worse than the seagulls, he thought. They were vultures—bum-sucking vultures.

But, in all fairness, wasn't this the system our vote-seeking-chicken-in-every-pot government created for its electorate? The so-called American Way? The one that says: Don't work if you don't have to...beat the system if you can...screw them before they screw you?

As a taxpayer the socio-slackers peeved him royally. As a lawyer, he represented them. Ashamed of his own profession, Cal walked on, seriously thinking about getting out. He hated the system but earned a handsome living from it. So, in the end, was he any better? Wasn't he just as pathetic?

In his younger days it hadn't bothered him. He'd once won a lawsuit because his elderly client tripped over her own feet while scurrying to a blue-light-special. "After all, your honor, those large department stores should allow more time for the old and feeble senior citizens." And he had won a multi-million dollar suit when a soda machine fell on a teenager, who later died in the hospital. Never mind the fact that the punk was shaking it down for loose change. "Those top-heavy machines should be bolted down, your honor. It's negligence, pure and simple."

34

WIRED

At the time, he hadn't felt the least bit guilty. He was young, ambitious, and too caught up in the game of winning. Right or wrong wasn't an issue. But over the years he had grown tired of representing the mooches of the world who were always looking for something for nothing. He was also tired of suing businesses just because they had deep pockets. In fact, he was sick of it all. Like the truism went: *99% of all lawyers give the rest a bad name.*

"If it weren't for lawyers," Cal admitted, "the world wouldn't need lawyers. That's a fact."

A blast of air whistled through the alleyways and a flurry of old newspapers sailed into the streets. While squinting against a powerful wind gust, Cal nearly tripped over a rolling garbage can powered by Mother Nature. Meanwhile, overhead, the snow-laden clouds were a deeper gray and moving in with greater haste. It wasn't looking good.

Cal was thinking about the Russian fur hat again when a carload of high school kids sped by, showering him from the knees down with icy slush. As he stood there dripping, he yelled after the car in a wasted attempt to make his voice heard above the ear-bruising bass of the music.

"And I'm sick and tired of spoiled-ass brats driving fancy cars while their parents drive the ragged-out old station wagon!"

His angry outburst attracted the attention of two passersby, who'd stopped to stare. A tad embarrassed, Cal glimpsed sidelong at them while brushing off his pant legs with a gloved hand. Then he tightened his neck scarf and huffed off indignantly, all the while wondering what the country was coming to.

Today's youth didn't show much respect for anything and that really rankled him. In their impudent little world "respect for your elders" was ranked somewhere between milk carton recycling and saving the woolly worm.

Every generation had its proverbial "gap," but was it asking too much for just a shred of respect? Or was he the problem? Had *he* become the crotchety old man who kept the baseball when it landed in his yard? Was that possible? While staring down at his slush-covered wingtips, Cal pondered the plausibility.

Maybe he *was* struggling with the age issue more than he thought. After all, he wasn't used to being the older generation just yet. He hadn't had time to adjust. Just yesterday, he was cool and very hip if he did say so himself.

Unlike the current generation, he didn't care for video games, hip-hop music, tattoos, or body piercing. Cell phones were useful but he didn't like the ones that played those cutesy little tunes instead of ringing like a normal phone. Outside of that, he was a today's man. Well, except for his dislike of the whiny women's groups, gay groups, minority groups, and all the other I'll-moan-and-groan-until-I-get-my-way groups. They got under his conservative skin. He also disliked the way today's youths rapped their knuckles together instead of shaking hands. That was goofy and needed to go. It might be "old school" but he still believed in a firm handshake while looking the person in the eye. He couldn't see two lawyers clacking knuckles together before going into negotiations. And, of course, today's musicians really sucked, unlike the great rock groups of the seventies. Other than those few things, he was pretty hip...for his age, anyway...sort of.

As he plodded along, Cal switched hands with the briefcase and wondered if anyone said *"hip"* anymore.

Friday 08:26 Hours – Clearwater Beach, Florida

When her brother's answering service picked up again, Kathy broke the connection and cradled the phone. She had already left two messages and had been told rather rudely the last time that his office didn't open until nine o'clock. In spite of her urgency, two messages were enough. There was no point in appearing as a *total* blubbering female alarmist.

For the sixth time in so many hours she called the police to see if anything regarding Skip had been reported. After receiving a polite but indifferent don't-call-us-we'll-call-you, she checked once again with the hospitals and Coast Guard. With no news there, she dialed the ticket office, hoping that a worker may accidentally arrive early. The office opened at ten. When she got a recording of the ship's ticket prices and departure times, she hung up the phone and resumed her nightlong ritual of pacing.

With her mind going in circles she wandered about aimlessly, stopping occasionally to touch something or pick something up. After two or three laps around her townhouse, she ended up at the sliding glass doors, staring out at the blurry world. The drizzle had now become sheets of slanting rain and it was gusting in great swathes across the glass. Feeling heavyhearted and wrung out, she folded her arms across her chest and touched her forehead against the cool glass.

"Skip Myles, I'll absolutely kill you if you've been out with the guys. You know how much I worry."

Wishing that were the case, she turned her back on the rainy world and leaned against the glass. If Skip staggered shitfaced through that door right now, nothing would make her happier. She would give him the tongue-lashing of the century and then put her sailor man to bed where he belonged. But Kathy's intuition told her different. Skip didn't do that anymore and that's what frightened her so. Something was wrong. She could feel it. *But what?*

Overcome by a sense of despair, a lump rose in her throat signaling imminent tears. Stubbornly, she had been holding them back all night. In a step to stifle them, she took long even breaths but it was no use. The weight on her chest was crushing, as if she were sinking into a deep-sea abyss and an ever-mounting volume of seawater was pressing down on her.

With tears spilling down her cheeks, she slid down the glass doors until her seat met the living room carpet. There, sitting against the glass, she drew her legs into her chest and hugged them with both arms. Then she cried until there was not a tear left in her body, until she thought something inside her might break if she didn't stop. It was a good cry, a cleansing cry, leaving her drained yet oddly contented.

Peeved at her feminine side for being such a crybaby, Kathy rose on flimsy legs and blotted her smeared face with a tissue. In times past she had used physical exertion to dispel her anxiety. If it weren't raining outside, she would run it off—run until she dropped.

Unable to wait another second, she redialed her brother's office through bleared eyes. If she got lucky, maybe he would get to work early.

"Come on, Cal. Answer." As the phone rang in her ear, she sniffed and wiped her runny nose with a tissue. "Please don't be in court this morning. I need you."

WIRED

With his soggy pant legs beginning to freeze, Cal rounded a corner to see *Shorty's Diner* in all its rundown neon glory. By now, he was chilled to the bone and the neighborhood restaurant looked like *Caesar's Freaking Palace*.

The diner was set in a row of ancient yellow-brick storefronts and flanked on either side by a pawnshop and junk furniture store. Though a bit ramshackled on the outside, the diner was always clean and smelled of fresh coffee and bacon grease. Its usual clientele was an amalgamation of blue-collar workers, street people, and low-level clerical workers.

On most mornings Cal would stop by the restaurant on his way to work and buy two coffees to go. But today he would sip his coffee at the counter while his frozen pants thawed out. His legs were numb from the knees down and his ears felt like they were going to break off any second.

When Cal first began frequenting the diner, everybody in the joint eyeballed him suspiciously whenever he came in. One morning, after giving him the once over, he overheard one of the scraggily patrons refer to him as a "suit." He wasn't sure at the time what *suit* meant, but, judging from the surly way it was said, he knew it wasn't flattering.

After thinking it over, Cal'd theorized that their mistrust was predicated on the misguided belief that he was a plainclothes cop. When he later told Shorty—in a voice loud enough for the patrons to overhear—that he was an attorney, the room fell quiet and they regarded him with even more suspicion. Apparently, in their book, lawyers were rated somewhere below rats with rabies and root canals. In any event, the regulars were now familiar with him and paid him little mind—although they still kept their distance. Even street people had certain standards and would only stoop so low.

In between sips of hot coffee, Cal cradled the ceramic mug between his palms near his chin. Its contents radiated warmth to his hands and the rising steam helped thaw out his ruby-red nose. While watching Shorty pour pancake batter on the griddle, Cal mused over the inglorious way the 6'3" man had earned his nickname. When he had asked Shorty in passing one day, his wife, Lorena, emitted a cruel laugh and Shorty huffed off testily without answering. By chance, a while later, Cal happened to overhear some sniggering table talk about Shorty's "accident." He didn't catch all the details but supposedly while in the Navy, Shorty was standing night watch alone in sub-zero weather when he had to urinate. While discreetly relieving himself, his dingus somehow got stuck to a metal pole and it was either use his knife or freeze to death. After making the painful decision to "downsize," his then young bride dubbed him "Shorty" and the shameful moniker stuck—the poor bastard.

Shorty was also the neighborhood nicotine pusher, who sold cigarettes one at a time to street people and poor souls trying to quit. For a bargain price of fifty cents each, you had a choice of Camels or Kools.

After draining his second mug of coffee, Cal left a buck on the counter and buttoned up his overcoat to the chin. Then he lit his Camel *(it's okay to cheat a little, Cal, go ahead)*, grabbed his order-to-go sack, and picked up his briefcase. Once all set for the cold, he nodded goodbye to Shorty and traipsed out into the arctic weather.

Six months ago Cal had given up Shorty's homemade donuts—called *dog-nuts* by Shorty—and pledged to walk to work everyday rain or shine. In the summer months he enjoyed the walks. It was good exercise and it gave him time to think. But in the wintertime, it was a self-imposed, bone-chilling drudgery.

"This business of getting old really sucks." He took a big drag on the Camel and coughed. "Can't even have a dog-nut anymore without feeling guilty—*or* a stinking cigarette!"

His office building was located in a rundown business district of downtown Detroit. Half of the time the elevator didn't work, but the rent was cheap and it was near the courthouses. It wasn't surrounded by adult bookstores or massage parlors yet, but day-by-day the disease took another bite of healthy tissue.

As Cal neared the entrance, he flicked his cigarette butt into the gutter and squirted a blast of breath freshener into his mouth. Looking forward to some warmth, he entered the building stomping icy sludge from his shoes as he walked. When he reached the elevator he found an **OUT OF ORDER** sign taped to its archaic double doors. Unsurprised, he snorted at the sign and headed up the stairs for the third floor, thinking about how pissed off the guys on the tenth floor would be.

As Cal approached his office, the door read: **"CALVIN H. STRINGER,**

WIRED

ATTORNEY AT LAW." But it should have read: "CAL STRINGER, MIDDLE-AGED MALCONTENT, SYSTEM-HATER, RAT RACE-HATER, COLD WEATHER-HATER, BOSSY WIFE-HATER, SPOILED BRAT-HATER, MOOCH-HATER, LIFE-IN-GENERAL-HATER, AND WANNABE BEACH BUM."

When he entered the office, Cindy was seated at her desk opening the morning mail. She was 36, divorced, and sleeping with her boss.

Cal knew it wasn't wise to "dip your pen in company ink" but at this stage in his life he didn't give a big hairy crap. After two divorces and a palimony suit, he didn't have much to lose anyway. He'd been cleaned more times than some of the overcoats hanging in his closet. Besides, Cindy had come on to him first and she was way too hot to ignore.

"Good morning, Miss Prick Teaser." With a pouty air, Cal placed a styrofoam cup on her desk.

"Good morning, Mr. Prick." She smiled up at him. "Did you have a nice shower?"

"It was getting interesting." He gave her a flat grin. "Any messages?"

"On your desk."

It was Friday—casual day in the yuppie business world—and Cindy was sporting her sexiest, tightest jeans along with a low-cut purple sweater that revealed some hellacious cleavage. Whenever she dressed in her business suits, she wore her long hair up. But today her raven-black hair was flowing halfway down her back and neatly tied off with a ribbon. She looked simply stunning and she would be a major distraction while he tried to concentrate on his work—especially after the hung-out-to-dry shower incident.

As far as Cal was concerned, casual Friday was just another excuse for females to flaunt themselves and drive their male co-workers crazy. Millions of guys across the country were ogling away right now, but afraid to say a word. No-o-o. That wasn't allowed. These days that was serious business—business called sexual harassment.

It was wrong for horny male employers to pressure female workers for sex, but Cal felt it was just as wrong for women to jiggle around the office with everything about ready to fall out. Even if a poor innocent slob didn't say anything, he could get called on the carpet for breast-staring on company time.

After hanging his overcoat in the closet, Cal sat down at his desk and removed his coffee from the paper sack. While opening its plastic lid, he posed a question to Cindy in the outer office.

"Hey, Cindy. Why is it that when a man talks dirty to a woman, it's sexual harassment? But when a woman talks dirty to a man, it's $3.95 per minute?"

"Because women rule and men drool," came her reply. "That's why."

"I can't argue with that—your highness. Go figure."

Smiling, Cal propped his size-12 wingtip on the edge of his desk and opened the newspaper. This was his morning ritual and he refused to take any calls until he was finished. It was his well-deserved quiet time, a brief respite before combating worldly injustice, the proverbial calm before the legal storm.

On the newspaper's front page, the bold headline read: *"DRUG KINGPINS FACE FEDERAL CHARGES IN MIAMI."* The article went on to say that Juan Carlos Alvarez—drug boss of the notorious Cali Cartel in Colombia—and Cesar Gonzalez—kingpin of Mexico's infamous Gulf Cartel—were taken into custody during a DEA raid of a high level narco-summit. By way of bribery and corruption, the drug lords had successfully eluded U.S. extradition for years and both now faced a long list of indictments for trafficking, money laundering, extortion, and murder. By virtue of the drug cartels' well-known business ties with Al-Qaeda, the Department of Homeland Security was currently investigating a possible link between the DEA arrests and recent U.S. terrorism.

Peering down at the newspaper, Cal emitted a low whistle. "Man, I'd give my left nut for a case like that. I'd charge big buckaroos and then head south for good. I'd be outta here in a Detroit minute."

While scanning the rest of the newspaper, his face clouded with concern. **"CAR BOMB SHATTERS WINDOWS AT DEA HEADQUARTERS IN VIRGINIA"** one article said. **"FEDERAL JUDGE KILLED IN LOREDO BY SNIPER"** another headline read.

Cal dropped the newspaper into a wastebasket and strolled over to the third floor window. As he took in the decaying landscape, he contemplated the dramatic rise in stateside terrorism.

Could Alvarez and Gonzalez be behind it all? Were they that all-powerful? Or was Al-Qaeda up to their old tricks again, making American life as miserable as possible?

WIRED

The crime happenings in Detroit used to dominate the headlines, but not anymore. The murder capital of the world was now Iraq or Afghanistan and local stories of neighborhood shootings, carjackings, and armed robbery were buried in the back section of the newspaper.

As Cal took in the gray and grime, he asked himself why he was here. Detroit was a city crawling with despair. Where hopeless people went to hopeless jobs and hoped that life got better. Where the relentless wail of sirens announced Motown's latest victim-of-the-day.

"Florida's the ticket for me," he murmured at the glass. "Back home."

Cal knew that Florida had changed too since leaving there—with the invasion of the Cubans, Haitians, Mexicans, boat people, and the god-knows-who-else people—but at least it was warm. Someday he planned to return there and buy a place on the water. Or maybe live on a boat—a big boat. In fact, he already had a name picked out for it: "NO-MO-SNO." Once he escaped from Motown, he never wanted to see another flake.

Deciding it was time to get down to business, Cal sat down at his desk and flipped the page of his day-planner-combination-trivia-desk-calendar. Being that he was a trivia buff, Cindy had purchased it from the neighborhood office supply store two blocks over—the one with iron bars guarding every possible entry.

Reading that *"80% of people put on their left sock first,"* Cal tried to recollect which sock he donned first. Not sure, he dismissed it as a moot point and pored over the day's appointments. He had a court hearing at ten this morning, a divorce case at three o'clock, and nothing in between.

"Slow-ass day," he swore under his breath. "A lawyer could starve to death handling divorces and personal injury claims."

With a glance at his watch, he began leafing through the pink "**WHILE YOU WERE OUT**" messages lying next to his phone. When he saw two messages from his sister in Clearwater, it rather alarmed him. Kathy seldom called him at work and Cal instantly thought of her hotheaded boat captain husband. Skip was a hell of a guy but his short temper had landed him in trouble on more than one occasion, especially when he'd had too many beers.

Cal was dialing her number when Cindy announced that Kathy was holding on the other line. With a mischievous grin, he cleared his throat and punched the blinking button.

"Cal Stringer here," he intoned in a grating, singsong voice. "Attorney at Law. Marriage is grand—divorce is a hundred grand. May I help you?"

"Cal, this is Kathy and that's not funny. How've you been?"

"'Tis the Season for Freezin', but I'm still kicking. How about you, Sis?"

"Well, not so good. I'm really worried about Skip. He took a new captain's job a few weeks ago on the Majestic Star. It's a day cruise ship that sails out of Clearwater. Goes out into the gulf twice daily so passengers can gamble and stuff. Anyway, it's a great job and Skip loves it, but he left home yesterday for the noon excursion and I haven't heard from him since. He usually comes home between trips to eat and rest up for the evening cruise, but not yesterday. Besides that, the evening cruise ends at eleven and he's always home by midnight. I'm worried sick."

"Well, you know how boat captains are," Cal cracked, playing down the situation, "especially our Captain Jason. He probably ran into some old fishing buddies and they're whooping it up at Frenchy's."

"Oh come on, Cal!" Kathy snapped. "You know he doesn't do that anymore. And don't call him Jason—you know he hates being called that. This is serious shit and I'm worried!"

She was genuinely upset and in no mood for kidding; Cal could hear it in her voice. "You have every right to be worried, Sis. Sorry. Have you talked to the employees at the cruise line?"

"Not yet. I'm going over there after we hang up. The ticket office opens at ten."

"Well, I suppose you've already called the police and local hospitals. Right?"

"Yep, no luck there. And I also checked with the Florida Marine Patrol and the Coast Guard. I'm going crazy down here, Cal. Something bad has happened to him. I just know it. Skip would never stay gone this long without a phone call." She was close to tears and her voice quivered. "You're the only family I have left, Cal. If I don't hear from him soon, could you come down? I hate to ask you, but I don't know what else to do."

"Sure I will, Sis—anything for you, you know that. Listen, I know it's hard, but try to remain calm. Getting all worked up won't solve anything. If you don't hear something by this afternoon, call me back. Matter of fact, call me back either way. Skip's probably okay, but I'm concerned too. I'll wrap up some things here and check with the airlines. If you don't hear from him, I'll catch a flight out of here tonight. Besides, it would be terrific seeing you again and Lord knows I could use a break from our rotten weather. There's not much I can do from Detroit, you know."

"I know," she sniffed. "I just didn't know who else to call."

"And I'm glad you did. Look, I'm running late for a court hearing. Check with the ticket office and call me back later. Okay?"

"Thanks for being so understanding, Cal." Relief was in her voice. "I'll call you later. Love you. Bye."

Cal hung up the phone and pushed back in his chair with mounting concern. Kathy was right: this wasn't like Skip. In his younger days it wouldn't have been too out of character for him. Skip was raised on Georgia moonshine and sometimes went on a bender. But that was years ago, early in their marriage. Skip had settled down a bunch since then.

In those days Kathy blamed their troubles on his "beer-drinking-fishing-buddies." But Cal knew better. Skip was a free-spirited guy who spent his idle time between jobs doing what he does best: hanging around marinas, swapping tall tales, and drinking lots of cold beer.

But sometimes Kathy worked two jobs to support them, giving her a different outlook. Although Skip made extra money from selling his catch, she viewed his "beer-drinking-fishing-trips" as partying with his pals while she slaved to pay the bills. Skip's position was the opposite, naturally, claiming the extra cash he earned while looking for steady work was better than nothing. So they argued.

Cal saw both sides of the argument and stayed out of the middle. This was his sister and best friend and taking sides was a losing proposition. Besides, he knew they would eventually work things out because they always did. They were still very much in love.

As Cal donned his overcoat he pictured Skip's bearded face and smiled fondly. Though Skip was far from perfect, the big lug was as good as they come. Still, in many ways he and Kathy were total opposites and Cal oftentimes wondered why she married him to begin with.

WIRED

Thinking Skip must be fishing with a mighty long pole, Cal scolded himself for having such indecent thoughts about his sister.

"Well," he defended himself out loud, "something keeps her coming back for more." He picked up his briefcase with a naughty grin. "It's sure not for his big fat bank account."

Friday 12:17 Hours – Detroit, Michigan

After the court hearing Cal hopped a taxicab back to his apartment to grab some lunch and pack an overnight bag. After settling on the couch with a ham on rye, he turned on the TV to catch the noon weather report—now calling for up to a foot of snow. Thinking Florida was sounding better all the time, Cal was poised to turn off the television set when breaking news of another U.S. car bombing appeared on the screen.

This time the tragedy occurred in downtown Orlando near the Federal Building, killing fourteen people and injuring twenty-two. As the newscaster gave the grisly details, filmed footage of the carnage played on the screen. For the second time this week, American blood had been spilled on American soil at the hands of terrorists.

Following the car-bombing story the news network switched to live coverage of the Miami arraignment of Juan Carlos Alvarez. A cyber-second later the Colombian's craggy face filled Cal's flat-screen TV in high definition. He was a rather tall, dark-complected man with black slicked-back hair and matching mustache. He bore a striking resemblance to Saddam Hussein before the Iraqi was caught hiding in a spider hole and later hanged. Alvarez's wrists and ankles were shackled and attached to a belly chain, forcing him to take baby steps while shuffling past the cameras. He was surrounded by a veritable army of watchful lawmen, two of which were escorting him by the elbows.

When Alvarez looked into the camera, Cal felt a shiver. His eyes were as black as coal and filled with hate, as if he wanted to jump through the camera lens and butcher anyone watching. Something evil was living behind those eyes, Cal thought, something malignant. Seconds later, Alvarez vanished behind closed courtroom doors, leaving reporters behind to commentate on his impending trial and his alleged connection to Al-Qaeda and the car bombings.

45

WIRED

As an attorney, Cal found the case intriguing and he would follow the trial with interest. As a U.S. citizen, he found the proliferation of homeland terrorism darkly disturbing.

Until just a few years ago, America had eluded world terrorism; but now it had come home to roost. The very idea of the good ole' USA—home of county fairs, backyard barbeques, and homecoming games—becoming plagued by Islamic terrorism incensed Cal to no end. As far as he was concerned, Islam could keep their suicide-bombing jihad in their own hemisphere and the drug traffickers could confine their drug wars to south of the border. America had her own share of troubles and wanted nothing to do with either.

Cal poked the remote and the newscaster's face went away. Then he sat there a moment, staring at the dark screen while digesting the upsetting news. Like it or not, our country was under siege and the implications were sobering.

Bewildered by it, Cal picked up the phone and dialed Kathy's number. When he got no answer he packed an overnight bag and then tried calling her again before heading out the door. As the elevator dropped, he eyed his watch and decided to walk back to work. He needed to walk off some steam. This latest assault on America had left him uptight—uptight as hell.

~~~~~~~~~~

Twenty minutes later Cal was rounding the block to his office building when he nearly ran into a homeless person standing on the corner. The scruffy guy was facing oncoming traffic, looking his pitiful best and holding a cardboard sign that read: **"WILL WORK FOR FOOD."**

Cal was familiar with most of the beggars because they were on his way to work. At first he had given them a buck or two despite his contempt for freeloaders. But that was before learning that some of them weren't as destitute as they put on and that certain street corners—or *territories*—were seriously guarded. In their world, if a panhandler infringed on another's territory it was cause for dispute. And since they took in over $200 bucks a day, the disputes oftentimes turned bloody. The whole thing was a scam.

WIRED

In crossing the street, Cal pondered this outrageous profession and the weird lifestyle that must accompany it. He pictured a guy getting up in the morning in a relatively nice home, eating breakfast and then getting ready for work. He skips his shower and shave *(a must for the down-and-out image),* goes to his locker in the garage *(because his clothes smell so bad his wife won't allow them in the house)* and picks out whatever grungy unwashed rags he will wear that day. He kisses the little woman goodbye, hops in his late-model pickup truck and drives to his corner. He parks somewhere out of sight, grabs his **"WILL WORK FOR FOOD"** sign, and meanders pathetically to his corner *(in case someone's watching).* There, he sits or stands all day, staring at the motorists with watery, puppy-dog eyes.

Some of the beggars were truly homeless, but most were shameless scam artists with zero pride and brass balls. Thinking that somebody with some brains ought to organize them, Cal allowed his entrepreneurial mind to cavort.

"Let's see," he daydreamed out loud. "I could offer them protected territories, transportation to and from their corners, a daily bottle of rot gut wine, and let them keep 50% of their take." With the wheels turning in his head, he grinned cleverly. "What a business! I could franchise the whole thing and take it coast-to-coast. I'd call it *Organized Grime* and make a mint. Then I'd blow this stinkin' town for good."

Friday 14:57 Hours – Detroit, Michigan

Killing some time before his three o'clock appointment, Cal was lobbing wadded paper balls into a trashcan across the room.

Since returning to the office he had called Kathy a number of times with no answer, which made him wonder if Skip had shown up and they had gone out somewhere, or if they were having a knock-down-drag-out fight and not answering the phone.

"Three points!" he bragged when one of his shots landed in the wastebasket. "Nothin' but net!"

At that moment Cindy stuck her head in the doorway and rolled her eyes at the paper balls littering the floor.

"Mr. Jordan," she mocked, "your three o'clock is here."

WIRED

Cal was still crawling around the floor picking up his missed shots when his appointment walked through the door—a 40-ish looking woman with a faint black mustache, weighing at least three hundred pounds. After emptying his arms into the wastebasket, he stood up with an embarrassed grin and brushed off the knees of his pants.

"Hard to get dependable janitorial service anymore," he shrugged awkwardly. "Don't show up half the time."

During her free half-hour consultation, the woman charged that her husband had been doing some "ink dipping" at work and she wasn't happy about it. While listening to her allegations, Cal asked the routine questions about household income, number of children, length of marriage, marital assets, and so forth. After jotting down her answers, he asked when she had first suspected her husband of having an affair.

"Hard to say," she said, popping her chewing gum. "For a while, I thought he was bi-sexual."

Now we're getting somewhere, Cal thought, taking notes. "And what made you suspect this deviant behavior, ma'am?"

"Cause he only gives it to me twice a year!" With that, she erupted into hysterical laughter, slapped her fat knee, and started coughing from too many cigarettes. During this exhibition Cal noted a few distasteful teeth that needed the attention of a good dentist. In looking her over, Cal concluded that her husband deserved a medal for doing it *once* a year.

After she calmed down and stopped coughing, Mrs. Brown continued. "Seriously though, I did catch him red-handed coming out of a motel with his little blonde play toy. It was one of those sleazy pay-by-the-hour motels, if you know what I mean? Well, when they got into her car to leave, I blocked them by standing in front of her bumper. I just planted my feet wide and glared at them both, shooting them the finger!"

"Okay," Cal said without looking up, scribbling notes. "What happened next?"

"Well, she eased her car up to me and laid on the horn. Then she yelled: 'Get out of my way you fat bitch or I'll run over you!'"

This is great stuff, Cal thought. "And then what happened?"

"Well, I wasn't gonna be intimidated. After all, I was the wronged party. Right? So I stayed put and flashed them the double finger—using both hands—and I shouted, 'Screw you, whore!'"

WIRED

"Really?" Cal asked, looking up. "Then what?"

When Cal looked up, he swallowed. The lady was reenacting how she had held both fingers at the adulterous couple. Her plump middle fingers were hoisted high in the air and behind them was a face that would scare the bejesus out of any man. She looked like an obese version of the green-faced witch out to get Dorothy; the one that screeched: *"I'll get you my little pretty!"*

"Well, she eased the car up to my legs and gunned the engine, and then she started bumpin' me. Well, after a few bumps, my legs sorta gave out and I fell onto the hood. Then I rolled off and went down on my knees. But I kept my fingers held high enough where they could still see 'em—I made sure of that. I yelled: 'I'll see you in court, Marvin!'" Suddenly her witch face turned pouty. "Then they just sped off and left me there. I coulda been really hurt for cryin' out loud. My leg is still real sore." She rubbed her injured leg. "I still don't know why she just didn't go around me."

Looking at her rotund figure, Cal thought, rather unkindly, that perhaps the car didn't have enough gas.

"Mrs. Brown, I feel you have an excellent case. After hearing your story, I'm sure the judge will throw the book at him. Should I go ahead and file the necessary divorce papers to get things rolling?"

"Nah-h," she shook her head. "I don't wanna divorce Marvin. He really don't mean nuttin by it. I just wanna scare the livin' shit outta him. Make him *think* I'm gonna clean him out. You know—alimony, child support, house, savings, half of his 401k. I do this every so often and it straightens him out for a while. He quits running around with all those floozies at work and pampers me like a queen. Can you do that, Mr. Stringer? Just scare the hell outta him?"

"Well, it's kind of unusual, but I suppose I can write a letter to make him *think* you're going to clean him out. If that's what you want me to do, of course."

Takes all kinds, Cal thought, a little exasperated.

"Great!" she said, blowing a gigantic bubble until it popped. "How much do I owe ya?"

WIRED

Friday 15:38 Hours – Clearwater Beach, Florida

With her thoughts a blur, Kathy pulled into her assigned parking spot and slipped the gearshift into PARK. It had quit raining earlier and the sun was baking the moisture from the ground. The humidity was sweltering and the air was redolent with the smell of dank earth. Uncharacteristic for the gulf coast there wasn't the barest breath of a breeze, making the muggy air feel stickier.

Turning off the engine, Kathy flung her sunglasses onto the passenger seat and climbed out of the car—scarcely conscious of her actions. That's the way she had been functioning lately: in a perfunctory fog. Like she was standing outside her body and watching herself go about her daily life. She fixed her hair, she made coffee, she put gas in the car, but she did it with dissociation; as if the material world was operating at a distance from her.

As Kathy strolled toward her condo, a ribbon of low-flying geese honked noisily overhead in their migration for the warmer waters of the Everglades. But in her deadened state of awareness their honking went unnoticed, as did most everything else happening around her.

Out of habit she stopped by the mailbox cubicle to retrieve her mail. But she was trembling so badly it took both hands to insert the key in the lock. As she continued down the sidewalk, she sorted through the mail with her keys still in hand. Finding it mostly junk mail, she was stuffing the envelopes inside her purse when she noticed a letter from the *"AARP"* addressed to Jason Myles—another throat-catching reminder.

Since turning age fifty, Skip received regular solicitations from them to join their retirement association. But being a stubborn old war-horse who would *"never, ever ask for a senior citizen discount,"* Skip would curse the invitations and trash them. His cranky reaction always amused Kathy and the *AARP* letters had become a running joke between them.

Kathy was twelve years younger than Skip and she never missed an opportunity to rub in their age difference. So, for pure meanness, she would place the invitations under a magnet on the refrigerator. When Skip got home from work, he always headed straight for the fridge for a cold beer. Knowing this, she would wait in the next room for his off-color response. When he would predictably blow his cork, she would laugh out loud and make herself known. Annoyed that she had gotten his goat, Skip would ask her what was so funny and then remind her that she would be fifty someday too—if he didn't strangle her first.

By the time Kathy reached the front door, a sob rose in her throat that she couldn't force back. She was worried sick and sick at heart— heartsick. While fumbling to unlock the deadbolt, scalding teardrops traced down her cheeks. She felt so alone, so empty, like a hollowed out tree filled with dead rot. She missed her husband...her Skip...her soul mate.

When the door swung open, Toby greeted her on the other side with an eager tail-wagging welcome. In desperate need of affection, Kathy scooped him up and nuzzled her teary face against his soft furry body. With Toby in her arms, she tramped up the stairs and headed directly for the living room phone. She needed to talk to her brother.

Sitting on the sofa with Toby stretched across her lap, she dialed Cal's office. When Cindy answered, she asked for Cal while trying to control the tremble in her voice. After being told that he was with a client, she left a message and hung up.

"Call me back, big Brother. Something mighty strange is going on down here."

Kathy made a note of the time and went into the bathroom to freshen up, hoping it would make her feel better. But when she looked into the mirror, she nearly gasped. The crying bouts and lack of sleep had taken a heavy toll on her appearance. Her eyes were puffy and red as a beet and she still had on yesterday's makeup. She looked a fright.

After cleansing her face, she retrieved two ice cubes from the freezer and folded them into a washcloth. Then she stretched out on the sofa and placed the cloth over her eyes. Her eyeballs were so hot and dry that an initial sizzle of steam wouldn't have surprised her. As the ice cooled her bloodshot eyes, she strove to relax but her mind was too crowded with worry. Her suspicions had been right. Something was wrong—very, very wrong.

Fighting the fidgets, she discarded the washcloth and threw an arm over her closed eyes. When she checked the time, she huffed at seeing only five minutes had passed. Giving up on any notion of rest, Kathy sat up on the couch and waited for the phone to ring.

WIRED

Friday 16:02 Hours – Detroit, Michigan

As the corpulent Mrs. Brown waddled out of the office, Cindy told Cal that his sister had called, stating it was urgent. Hurrying back to his desk, Cal dialed Kathy's number.

"Hello?"

Cal's mouth curled at hearing her voice. "Hey, Sis. What's up?"

"Something weird's going on down here, Cal, and I'm scared. After we talked this morning, I went over to the ticket office at the marina. And it was *closed*. It's never closed at that hour, especially before a busy weekend. And the ship is missing!"

"What ship?"

"The Majestic Star for God sake!" Her voice was bordering on hysteria. "What ship do you think I'm talking about?"

"Now calm down, Kathy, and start over. Exactly where is the ship moored?"

"Oh, I'm sorry. I forgot you haven't been down here in a while. The ticket office and ship are both located at the Clearwater Bay Marina. It's on the mainland side of the Intracoastal Waterway just north of the drawbridge. The ticket office is located inside the marina and the ship is moored up behind it. Passengers purchase their tickets, then exit through the rear doors and walk up the ramp whatchamacallit."

"Gangway," Cal interjected.

"Yeah, whatever. But the ship's not there! When I went there last night, the gates were locked and it was too dark to see anything. Where in God's name could it be, Cal? I asked around at the marina and none of the fishermen have seen it either."

"What do the Coasties have to say?"

"Nothing. I drove over to Sand Key and they turned me away at the parking lot. Said they were conducting some sort of military exercise. Then I drove down to the St. Petersburg station but they just gave me the runaround. I'm at my wits' end!"

"How about the owners of the ship; you know, the cruise line headquarters?"

"Skip just started working there and I can't remember their corporate name. Some shipping conglomerate out of Miami, I think. That's where he went for his job interview anyway. They own ships all over. I'll try to find out from the ticket office, if it ever opens."

"Okay. Have you talked to the police lately?"

"Yeah, I just got back from there. There's a waiting period in Florida to file a missing person report—just in case he's shacked up with some broad, I guess. They brushed me off, saying they would notify me if anything came up. It might sound paranoid, Cal, but I've got a feeling that the authorities down here are hiding something. Could you please come down? At least for the weekend? I'm about to lose it!"

"Sure I will, Sis." Cal was deeply troubled, but tried not to show it. Kathy was upset enough. "I know things look pretty weird right now but I'm sure there's a logical explanation. Don't go phobic on me. Skip's probably fine. I don't have any more court cases until next Thursday and Cindy can juggle my appointments for the first part of the week. There's a direct flight that arrives at Tampa International at 8:42 tonight. I'll be on it. Meet me in baggage claim."

"Oh, thank God!" There was an audible sigh of relief. "I don't know what I'd do without you, big Brother. Okay, I'll see you in a few hours. Love you. Bye."

Cal pushed back in his chair and pondered the peculiarities. How could a ship the size of the *Majestic Star* simply disappear? The Coast Guard was bound to know something about it. And what about this military exercise they were conducting? Coincidence? So much was certain: Kathy couldn't be the only relative making inquiries about overdue or missing passengers. No way. Something smelled rotten— rotten as hell.

After dictating a threatening letter to Mrs. Brown's wayward husband, Cal changed clothes for his flight. While suits were a professional necessity, he despised the choking neckties and hard shoes. Glad to be free of the restrictive garb, he slipped on a pair of khaki Dockers, an orange *Florida Gators* sweatshirt, and brown leather deck shoes without socks. With his body screaming free-at-last, he looked into the mirror and smiled approvingly. This was the real Cal Stringer. He didn't have a clue who that other dude was.

All dressed and ready to go, Cal slipped on his overcoat and grabbed his bag. On the way out he stopped at Cindy's desk to say goodbye.

"Well, kid, I'm outta here. I'll be back as soon as I can."

When Cindy rose from her desk all teary-eyed, warning bells went off in his head. He was only going away for the weekend—nothing to cry over.

"Have a safe flight, sweetheart." Her words were scarcely a whisper against his chest. "I hope everything turns out okay for your sister." She reached inside his open overcoat and hugged him around the waist. "I'll miss you." Then she leaned into him and gave him a long, deep kiss.

Cal wasn't prepared for such an emotional farewell and it rather took him by surprise. He wasn't looking for a serious relationship and had been upfront about it from the start. Already a two-time loser, he vowed to never marry again and had told Cindy as much. But lately she'd been getting a little too serious and he was starting to feel hemmed-in. She was a terrific gal but he liked their relationship just as it was—casual. He didn't want to muddy it up with true love and all the associated ills that came with it. At this stage in his life, Cal wanted no complications.

"I'm sure everything will be fine, babe. If I'm still in Florida on Monday, I'll call you first thing." He stepped back and took her by the hands. "The roads are getting slick so be careful driving home. Have a nice weekend."

"I'll try," she whimpered. "But I was really looking forward to our romantic weekend together. I feel bad now about the shower thing." She made an apologetic face. "Sorry."

"Hey, it's okay." He squeezed her hands before dropping them and pecked her on the forehead. "I'll be back before you know it and we'll make up for lost time."

Cindy nodded and gave him a withered smile. Three minutes later Cal was standing outside in the Detroit cold flagging a taxicab.

Friday 16:50 Hours – Tampa Bay, Florida

The United States Coast Guard was founded by Alexander Hamilton on August 4th, 1790 as a fleet of cutters to circumvent smuggling. Since then the duties of the USCG have expanded many fold to include search and rescue, drug and migrant interdiction, oil spill response and environmental protection, boating safety, and the enforcement of port regulations and customs laws. Over and above these tasked responsibilities the Coast Guard regularly maintained lighthouses and navigational aides such as buoys and beacons. Formerly a division of the Department of Transportation, today the Coast Guard operates under the jurisdiction of the Department of Homeland Security, performing regular security patrols on over 90,000 miles of coastline in USA's fight against terrorism.

The U.S. Coast Guard's Seventh District in Miami was responsible for 1.8 million square miles of ocean bordering Florida, Georgia, South Carolina, Puerto Rico, and the Caribbean. Rear Admiral Ray Hanna was D7 Commander and duteous overseer of the district's section office, 4 air stations, 5 group offices, 4 bases, 20 multi-mission stations, 45 aircraft, 150 boats, nearly 50 ships, and 4,600 active duty personnel.

Over his twenty-two year career, Hanna had risen sharply through the ranks by way of a keen intellect and driving ambition. After graduating from the U. S. Coast Guard Academy with a Bachelor of Science degree, he pursued advance studies at the Naval War College where he graduated at the head of his class. After serving as Commanding Officer on two cutters, he was assigned to the Deck Watch Officer exchange program with the U.S. Navy, serving on a destroyer escort. Three years ago he was promoted to flag rank and named Commander of the Seventh District.

Unmarried, the Coast Guard was Ray's life and he took great pride in his work. It was an honorable profession—*Protectors of the Homeland*—and it gave him purpose. He was proud to be in service to his country and dedicated to the Coast Guard motto: *"Semper Paratus"* meaning *"Always Ready!"*

A rear admiral at age 45, Ray was the most eligible bachelor at Richmond Heights. And at 6'1" and 176 pounds, his strapping good looks made him quite a catch. Although twice engaged, he had never married. Ray blamed his relationship failures on many things, but in reality he was married to his career. That was his priority in life and everything else, or anyone else, took a definitive backseat.

As Helo-1 sliced low over Tampa Bay, the Jayhawk's powerful main rotor flattened the seawater beneath it. Tampa Bay was a major shipping lane and the main channel had been dredged to accommodate deep-draft commercial vessels. From Ray's lofty vantage point, the hue of the

WIRED

channel appeared a deeper blue than the turquoise pastels of the shallows.

When Ray spied a northbound oil tanker lumbering toward the Port of Tampa, it conjured up memories of the devastating 1993 oil spill. He had been group commander in St. Petersburg at the time and in charge of the humongous cleanup.

In the early-morning fog of August 10th, two inbound fuel barges collided with an outbound phosphate freighter between Egmont Key and the Skyway Bridge. The catastrophic aftermath left one leaking barge, a burning barge, and one sunken freighter. To Ray, it seemed like yesterday and he still held vivid memories of what 330,000 gallons of No. 6 crude could do to the marine environment. Having the consistency of thick roofing tar, it took millions of dollars and five weeks of round-the-clock work to clean up the oily mess.

In an endeavor to save wildlife, miles of containment boom were deployed around the bird sanctuaries and protected mangrove areas. Boom was also placed near the beaches to help preserve Florida's number one industry—tourism. While it had helped, summer storms and choppy seas washed lots of the crude over the floating booms, fouling many areas. Dead, oil-drenched birds were not uncommon and some of the white sand beaches got soiled with sticky black tar.

Oil skimmers—huge floating rigs that functioned as oil vacuum cleaners—were brought in to siphon the tar and oily film from the sea's surface. But, in the end, despite the nonstop effort, most of the crude sank to the bottom or washed out to sea. All in all, it was an ecological disaster and one that Ray hoped would never happen in Tampa Bay again.

As the Jayhawk's tires bumped the helipad, Ray unbuckled his seatbelt harness and shed his black flight vest. Then he swapped his crew helmet for the ball cap of his Operational Dress Uniform. Coast Guard ODU's were dark-blue in color, consisting of a collared shirt with long sleeves rolled-up-and-buttoned past the elbows and dark-blue trousers bloused above black safety boots.

Bailing out of the cockpit, Ray walked in a stoop toward the stationhouse, holding onto his cap. Following a brisk crossing of the courtyard, he entered the concrete-and-brick facility by way of the rear entrance. Once inside the building, he pocketed his Air Force issue wire-rimmed sunglasses to find the regional hub in a state of organized chaos.

WIRED

Friday 17:10 Hours – Detroit, Michigan

Due to early business closings, the rush hour traffic was light and the cabby was making good time for Detroit Metro Airport. The taxi looked a good twenty years old and the back seat was sticky with what smelled like spilt beer. But the heater worked well and Cal was grateful for that. As it rumbled along, he unbuttoned his overcoat and settled back in his seat.

The snow was coming down heavier now and the snowplows were out, pushing the accumulation onto curbs and sidewalks. Virgin snow had a cleansing effect and it painted a soft wintry scene on the otherwise dreary downtown landscape—all white, fluffy, and clean. Even the alleys and garbage cans took on a certain beauty when topped with fresh snow. But when there was no thaw, the piled-up snow eventually turned a grayish-brownish-ickish color that took on the appearance of frozen muddy water.

And, that, Cal found very depressing—sort of like his two ex-marriages.

As the evening dusk deepened, the cabby turned on the headlamps and a flurry of luminescent snowflakes sprang to life, swirling wildly at the car before bursting against the windshield. As Cal stared trancelike at the onrushing flecks, the cadence of the clacking wipers and the rhythmic thump-thump of the expansion joints had a lulling effect.

Cal was looking forward to seeing Kathy again and soaking up some Florida sun, but Skip's unexplained disappearance robbed him of any excitement. Nothing added up.

Fact: a ship was missing. So why wouldn't the Coast Guard release any information about it? Especially to the relatives of passengers onboard? Why the hush-hush routine?

Cal couldn't imagine what could have conceivably happened to invoke such a shroud of secrecy. Of course, the secrecy in itself made some sort of statement: that whatever had taken place was significant. There was no other explanation. Something serious had occurred, serious enough to warrant an organized cover-up. Whatever it was, it was big. He could feel it in the pit of his stomach.

Deciding to give his brain a rest, Cal purged all thought of it. He would get to the bottom of things when he got to Florida. To divert his attention, he swiped the foggy door window with the sleeve of his overcoat and watched the blurry world whisk past him, trying to think of nothing.

In a snowy field off I-94 was a lighted billboard sponsored by *M.A.D.D. Mothers*. It reminded Cal of the time Skip jokingly phoned him about forming a group called *D.A.M.M.*, standing for *"Drunks Against Mad Mothers."* He said all the guys at the marina supported the idea and they were seriously considering it. He maintained that drinkers had rights too and they were fed up with the *M.A.D.D. Mothers* tea-totaling bullshit. With straight-sounding sincerity, he asked what Cal would charge them to set up *D.A.M.M.* as a legitimate non-profit organization.

Taken aback by the absurd idea and unaware that Skip was kidding, Cal had been at a loss for words when Skip roared out loud with laughter. At realizing he had been duped, Cal called Skip a few choice expletives and hung up on him—with Skip still howling.

As an attorney and right-minded citizen, Cal didn't condone drinking and driving. Nor did be believe in drowning ones troubles in alcohol because that usually made things worse. On the other hand, he saw *nothing* wrong with diluting them a little. Matter of fact, he looked forward to an adult beverage at the end of the day himself. It relaxed him and served as a token reward for enduring another monotonous day. The problem was that amateurs didn't know when to quit.

But according to his first wife, Cal was no amateur—no sir. To her, anyone who imbibed in more than one glass of wine was an alky. As a result she had spent a large portion of their marriage reminding him of his frailties, which also included smoking.

Since Cal had smoked and drank throughout their three-year courtship, he found it inconceivable as to why she suddenly had a problem with it. Then wife #1 enlightened him. She believed that if he truly loved her, he would change his nasty habits once they were married. As it turned out, she was one of *those*—a woman who believed she could mold a perfectly flawed man into prince charming *after* she had him on the hook.

When he had refused to change—more on principle than anything else—she began nagging him about everything. Eventually surrendering to their incompatibility, he ran up the white flag and they divorced. To this day Cal still couldn't understand why women did that—why they married men and then immediately set out to change them; as if it were programmed in their genes to promptly "straighten out" their men, to extinguish all those "wicked" little ways.

If a man's behavior was so darn bothersome, why would a woman marry him in the first place? Was it their mother instinct? Did women believe that all men had to be "house broken" so to speak? If so, were they right? Did males need rescuing from themselves?

It *was* a proven fact that married men lived longer; but Cal wondered if it was it from clean living or because they were so nag-worn by end of the day, they went to bed early for some peace and quiet. Who knows?

It reminded Cal of something a friend used to say. Putting a chauvinistic twist on an old saying, he would proclaim: "Women, you can't live with 'em, and you can't live with 'em!"

Maybe so, Cal mused with a roguish grin, *but how sweet it is!*

~~~~~~~~~~

The taxi wheeled up to the departure level and pulled against an outside curb. Cal paid the cabby and proceeded to the gate, where he upgraded his ticket to first class. A half hour later he surrendered his boarding pass and strode down the drafty jetway to the plane. As he entered the aircraft, a pretty flight attendant greeted him with a smile and helped him remove his overcoat. Then she ushered him to his assigned window seat and asked if he would like a complimentary drink before takeoff.

In his best James Bond voice, Cal looked at her worldly and replied: "Martini—very dry, shaken, but not stirred."

After hesitating a moment, she smiled at him unimpressed and disappeared behind a blue curtain. Duly humbled, Cal's suave smile dimmed. She had obviously heard that one before.

But, in spite of her indifference, Cal was still glad to have a female flight attendant. Being a little old-fashioned, he housed a suspicion that all male flight attendants were borderline fags. He missed the old days when the female attendants were called stewardesses and passengers could smoke on the plane. Back then, all the stews were single and wore tight skirts. Today they wear baggy pants covered by a lousy apron and a guy can't even check out their legs.

While the cabin was being prepared for departure, a harried young lady burst through the door just as the flight attendant was closing it. Out of breath, she was toting a bag in each hand with her boarding pass clamped between her teeth. Acting a bit put out, the flight attendant plucked it from her mouth and directed her to her assigned seat. After puffing her way down the aisle and stowing her belongings in the overhead compartment, she plopped down next to Cal.

She was a stunning blonde who looked to be in her mid-twenties. She was wearing a chocolate brown leather mini-skirt *(with legs that go all the way up to heaven, Cal— if you'll notice)* and a camel cashmere sweater gathered at her svelte waist. The clingy sweater conformed to her bountiful breasts, which reminded Cal of the Grand Tetons. *(double D's at least, buddy boy)* In buckling her seatbelt, she flashed Cal a frazzled smile and his stomach fluttered. Thinking this must be his lucky day; Cal fidgeted in his seat and smiled back. She was a knockout.

When the blonde sat down, her mini-skirt hiked up even further and Cal felt his face getting warm. Trying not to stare at her sexy thighs, he gazed out the window and watched the ground crew de-ice the airplane. Then, in an effort to conceal his nerves, he grabbed a magazine from the elastic seat pocket and pretended to read it. But her shapely legs were like magnets and his eyes wouldn't behave. Flustered, he stuffed the magazine back in the pocket and returned his gaze outside. He was acting like a teenager in heat.

Minutes later came the familiar backward tug and the plane was pulled away from the gate. As the aircraft circled onto the runway, the pilot announced they were number-one for takeoff and gave full acceleration, forcing passengers back in their seats. As the 250-ton plane zoomed bumpily down the runway, Cal felt a clammy hand fold over his and squeeze.

"I hate flying," she said anxiously. "Would you talk to me?" Her hand was trembling and her green eyes were pleading. "Talk to me about anything. I don't care what it is. Just take my mind off things. Please? Are you going to a Gators game or something?"

Cal was puzzled by the question until he traced her eyes down to his orange sweatshirt.

"Well, no, but I am a huge Gators fan. I went to college there and it's stuck with me throughout the years. What do you want to talk about?"

"I don't care!" As the plane vibrated down the runway, her fingernails dug into his hand. "Tell me what you do and where you're going—anything. Okay?"

"Well . . okay . . sure. My name's Cal Stringer and I am an attorney here in Detroit." He was wondering what cool reason he could give her for going to Florida when he recalled the drug lord's trial. "I'm going to Miami to represent Juan Carlos Alvarez in federal court. He's a Colombian businessman that is facing multiple indictments for drug trafficking." Furthering the ruse, he explained away his casual dress. "I always dress like this when flying in on a high-profile case. Sort of throws the press off. I hate it when they all stick their microphones in my face and ask me questions at the same time."

"You're kidding?" She stared at him wide-eyed. "I saw that on TV this morning. You're his lawyer?"

"Well, there are several of us on the case, but I'm his chief counsel—yes."

"Wow! I'm impressed. What did you say your name was?"

Cal sucked in his stomach and fished a wrinkled business card from his wallet. "Stringer. Cal Stringer." After passing the card, he shook her hand politely.

"Well, Mr. Stringer, I guess you're gonna be quite a celebrity when this is over. Right?"

"Oh, I don't know," he said smugly, checking his fingernails. "In Detroit, I'm already quite well known. It's really no big deal."

When the plane reached its cruising altitude, the woman released his hand and began leafing through a *Cosmopolitan* magazine. She was reading an article about body piercing, which made Cal wonder if she had any interesting body parts that were pierced. Trying to take his mind off it, he opened the airline magazine and began working the crossword puzzle.

As he scratched letters into the small boxes, his eyes kept drifting to her creamy thighs. He was fantasizing about running his hand up under her mini-skirt when his pencil lead broke from too much pressure.

WIRED

Frustrated, he closed the magazine and gazed out the window at Cincinnati's sea of city lights. While looking down at Paul Brown Stadium he told himself to calm down, that he was acting like a schoolboy, that he had seen pretty women before. *(That's true, Cal baby, but not like this little hottie!)*

In mid-flight they were served a chicken and rice dinner with a glass of Chardonnay. Knowing a babe like her gets hit-on at least two thousand times a day; Cal made casual conversation and pretended to be sexually uninterested. It was important to his task that he separate himself from the tawdry wolves of the world *(those beasts)* and come across gentlemanly.

They chatted about the weather...their favorite movies...his law career...life in general. After their third glass of wine, Cal cracked a few jokes at which she howled with laughter. During this time he made a point to tell her that he was divorced *(I'm available, baby!)* and, of course, he snuck a peek at her ample bosom every chance he got.

As the plane made its approach to Tampa International, she put her magazine away and peered out the window. "Well, it looks like we're almost there. It's too bad you're going on to Miami for your court case. I think you're quite a classy guy and kinda cute on top of that. I would've enjoyed getting together for a drink—or maybe a nightcap at my place. It's really too bad."

Stricken with panic, Cal thought fast. "Well, actually I'm not going on to Miami until tomorrow. Since I was flying to Florida anyway, I'm spending the night at my sister's place on Clearwater Beach. I haven't seen her for some time and thought I'd mix a little pleasure with business. So, why don't we meet later for a drink?"

"Oh-h-h, I can't," she uttered with a pout. "I just remembered that I have a business appointment with my agent tonight and I don't know when it'll be over. He's the one that arranged my Playboy shoot. He wants to talk to me about some silly movie part or something. I'm really sorry. But if you happen to pass through Tampa on your way back to Detroit, give me a call. Okay? I'll give you my number."

"Playboy?" Cal was altogether stunned.

"Yeah, Miss June, I'm told. I can send you an autographed issue if you want one. My manager says I'll be receiving lots of promotional magazines for giveaways."

WIRED

"Uh-h-h...yeah," he stammered. "I'd love a copy." As Cal crashed inside, he felt both hot and cold at the same time. *(You and your big fat mouth, butt-breath, way to go)*

She opened her purse and withdrew a business card that read: *The Doll House.* She flipped it over and scribbled down her name and number, then kissed it leaving a sexy lipstick mark. She handed it to him with a smile and his stomach sank like the *Titanic.*

"I'm Karol—with a 'K'. If I'm not home, just call the club and leave me a message. I'm the headliner there. It's a gentlemen's club in Tampa. Very classy place, really." She looked at him strangely. "Do you want me to turn on the air vent? You look like you're burning up for heaven sakes."

"Yeah, it's really stuffy in here, isn't it?" Cal fiddled nervously with the overhead vent. "Thanks for your number, Miss June, uh-h, I mean . . ." He glanced down at her card. ". . . Karol. I'll call you for dinner or something when I come back through Tampa."

She wiggled her eyebrows at him suggestively and winked. "Yeah—or something."

The evocative innuendo made Cal flush and he swabbed sweat from his brow with a napkin. By the time the plane landed in Tampa, he totally hated himself. Here he was sitting next to a Playboy centerfold—which was every guy's fantasy to begin with—who had practically invited him into her bed, and *he* had to pretend that he was flying to Miami in the morning. What a blubbering shithead. *(Yeah, Sparky, good job)*

As the plane taxied to the gate, Cal glared out his window and sulked—beating himself up. All he could think of was his missed opportunity with *Miss June* and what a pathetic loser he was. When the captain gave the two-bell signal to deplane, Cal grabbed his garment bag and followed her off the plane into the concourse. Miss June looked even better from behind and he punished himself further by gaping at her perfectly sculpted derriere. And with each sway of her exquisitely rounded hips, he hated himself a little more.

Minutes later they boarded a tram for the short ride to the main terminal. Cal clutched a stainless pole and remained standing while Karol sat down directly in front of him. Hoping his frayed emotions didn't show, he looked away from her and tried to appear nonchalant. Halfway to the terminal, he bent over and viewed the palm trees through the tramcar's tinted windows. Silhouetted against a purplish night sky, their fronds were swaying gently in the breeze. The scene was picturesque and it felt good to be back home in the tropics.

When his eyes returned to Karol, he found her staring into a compact mirror spreading lipstick. The sensuous act was pure torture and while Cal was taking in every lustful detail, she glanced up and caught him leering. But instead of looking away, she kept smearing her luscious lips while eyeing him seductively. The steamy act made Cal blush and he broke her sultry gaze by looking outside. Even so, he could feel her seductress eyes on him, boring a hole straight down to the core of his nervous system. Unable to resist their beck and call, he locked eyes with her once again. While staring at him dreamily she put the lipstick and compact away, then tossed her flaxen hair and crossed her long legs.

Cal's eyes instinctively fell to her gorgeous limbs and he wondered if she was wearing any underwear. As if reading his mind somehow, she grinned at him naughtily and he looked away embarrassed. Feeling caught red-handed, his palms began to sweat and he retightened his grip on the slippery handrail. Grateful when the tram finally rattled to a halt, Cal picked up his bag and faced the sliding doors as they hissed open.

As they started for the escalators, Miss June walked alongside him. She had a graceful lilt in her walk and a gentle swinging of the shoulders and arms—like a model on a runway, or a woman who knew she was being watched. Indeed, most all eyes were upon her—male eyes, anyway—with some guys even turning around to stare.

Being her obvious escort, Cal regarded their ogling as somewhat disrespectful but he supposed the poor lechers couldn't help themselves. In any case, it gave his ego a boost to accompany such a femme fatale. He wasn't going to score with her tonight, but *they* didn't know that.

As they neared the down escalator, Cal's mind raced for some cool departing words to say. Wondering what Bogart would say in a similar situation, he placed a hand on the handrail and stepped onto the moving stairway. Following suit, the comely Karol with a "K" stepped on the escalator directly behind him.

Halfway down to baggage claim, Cal felt something brush against the nape of his neck. Instinctively, he glanced over his shoulder to find her bodacious breasts practically in his face. Shocked and a little intimidated, his pulse quickened and he faced forward. With darting eyes, he swallowed nervously and beads of perspiration popped out on his brow.

While pulling at his collar for air, he felt them again. But this time they remained put, planted firmly against his neck and upper shoulders. Automatically his knees weakened and his heart rate skyrocketed like the Space Shuttle.

Was she doing that on purpose?

Then he wondered if she was wearing a bra, making him sweat even more. Virtually beside himself, his runaway mind was split. Part of him wanted to turn around and grab those puppies while another part wanted to take flight. By now Cal's legs were like rubber and his sweaty palm was slithery on the plastic handrail. After a punishingly long ride down, the escalator reached the bottom and he stepped off. By this time he was so unnerved, he merely wanted to flee.

Getting his goodbyes in order, Cal took a calming breath and turned to face her. "Well, I've really enjoyed your company, Karol, and I'll definitely look you up when I'm back in town."

His words sounded lame as soon as they were out and he inwardly berated himself. *(Is that the best you can do, dip-shit?)* While he grasped for something else to say, she wrapped her arms around his waist and squeezed tightly—once again pressing those "Tetons" against him.

"You'd better, cowboy." Rising on her tiptoes, she whispered in his ear. "If you don't, you'll see what you missed when you get my centerfold in the mail."

On that steamy note she nibbled his earlobe and kissed him lightly on the neck. Then she stepped back and flashed him a tantalizing bleached-white smile.

By this time Cal was intellectually comatose and incapable of a sensible reply. Mindful of the effect she had on men—and largely enjoying it—she winked and blew him a sexy kiss to remember her by. Then she wagged her fingers goodbye and walked away without looking back, leaving him alone to melt.

Now a complete and utter wreck, Cal looked around and grabbed the seat nearest him before his knees buckled. Feeling like an exhausted marathon runner, he painfully watched *Miss June* wiggle out of his life.

WIRED

Friday 20:52 Hours – Tampa, Florida

Cal was still collecting himself when he heard his name being called over the din of the terminal. Recognizing that voice anywhere, he stood up and looked over the heads of the crowd for his sister. When he noticed a hand waving in his direction, he traced it to its rightful owner and there Kathy was—a sight for his sore frostbitten eyes.

While drinking in her warm smile, Cal wondered how long it had been. *A year? Maybe two?* As they weaved their way toward another, he thought Kathy looked pretty good given the circumstances. She was wearing a *Hotel California* T-Shirt, tan capris, and brown leather sandals. Kathy was ten years younger than him—going on 45—but she looked a decade younger.

When the two finally met, Kathy leapt into his arms and grappled him around the neck. With his legs still weak from the *Miss June* experience, Cal staggered back a step under her unexpected weight before recovering. When he dropped his bag to hug her back, the years peeled away and once again she was his little baby sister.

Kathy kissed him on both cheeks while hanging from his neck and raved about how fantastic he looked. Self-conscious about his extra pounds, Cal sucked in his gut and returned the praise while lowering her to the floor. With a big radiant smile, she took his hands and stepped back to take a good look at him. Then she flattered him some more while Cal recovered his garment bag.

Once outside, Cal removed his overcoat and slung it over his shoulder. When he commented on the balmy weather, Kathy boasted that more of the same was in store for the weekend. For the next minute or so they walked along the sidewalk making casual conversation—both hesitant to spoil their reunion by bringing up Skip. After a polite period of small talk, Cal dispensed with the pleasantries and cut to the chase.

"Have you heard anything from the Coast Guard about Skip?"

Halting in her tracks, Kathy's face drained of excitement. "Nothing, Cal, but I know something serious has happened. I drove past Station Sand Key before coming here and they have the whole place cordoned off. You can't even get in the parking lot." Her voice thickened with looming tears. "And there are troops and helicopters all over the place."

WIRED

As the tears built up steam, she yanked a tissue from her purse and sniffed into it. "It looked like a damned war zone or something!"

Cal's eyes filled with foreboding and the joy of being home evaporated. "Well, I admit that doesn't sound good, Sis—not good at all—but we'll get to the bottom of it. That's why I'm here. Now where did you park?"

The pair strode to the parking garage with only the sound of footsteps between them, each lost in their own thoughts. Whatever was happening sounded grave and Skip was smack-dab in the middle of it. When they reached Kathy's red convertible, Cal suggested they crank the top down. He was still basking in the Florida warmth and wanted to savor every BTU of it while he could. With an indifferent shrug, Kathy pushed a button and the white top folded down.

Five minutes later they were motoring west on Courtney Campbell Causeway. The six-lane causeway spanned a ten-mile stretch of upper Tampa Bay, connecting downtown Tampa with Clearwater. The raised road portion of the causeway was lined with beaches, restaurants, and cabbage palms. Midway was an elevated span with a steel arch called "the hump" by locals, giving passage to boaters navigating the upper bay.

As the convertible journeyed westward, both brother and sister rode in silence. Kathy was staring at the road straight ahead with her hair pinned back at the temples and her long tresses streaming in the wind. Lacking expression, Cal rode with his arm extended out the window— twisting and turning his hand to catch the wind.

Under the pale wash of moonlight the causeway's white sand shoreline appeared a soft silvery-blue. The tide was going out and strewn clumps of wet kelp littered the water's edge. The moon was perched low in the sky, playing beautifully off the Tampa Bay water. As facets of rippling waves caught and reflected the lunar light, the bay glittered like sequins on a black evening gown. The effect was mesmeric, reminding Cal of a thousand fireflies flickering off-and-on. As he marveled at the shimmering seascape he wondered if Skip, too, was watching Mother Nature's light show. Then, with a dreadful sinking feeling, he wondered if Skip was even alive.

Peering deeper into the night, Cal spotted a crab boat coasting along the offshore shallows. Looking harder, he made out the silhouette of a

WIRED

man aboard pulling traps, checking his bounty for the day. The scene took him back several years to when Skip was operating a crab boat. It was hard work and long days, but it paid handsomely as long as other unscrupulous fishermen didn't raid your traps.

Once during a Florida visit, Cal tagged along with Skip during his milk run to check the traps. The wooden traps were baited, lowered to the bottom with rope, and then marked with round colored styrofoam buoys called *crab pots*. When crabbers were issued a Florida license, they were assigned a specific color and number in which to identify their buoys. Nevertheless, it wasn't uncommon for a little thievery to take place, so most crabbers carried guns on their boats to safeguard their traps. After all, it was their livelihood.

As Cal watched the crabber, Kathy pushed in the car lighter and fished a cigarette from her purse. Noting this, Cal seized the opportunity to bum a smoke and she obligingly handed him one, unaware that he was trying to quit. At taking his first draw, the nicotine gave him a dizzying head rush. Exhaling delightfully, he looked at Kathy and spoke over the wind.

"Did Skip's friends at the marina have anything new to report?"

"Nothing new." Kathy flipped a red-hot ash into the night air. "Nobody's seen Skip or his ship since yesterday morning."

Cal frowned disagreeably. "The more I think about it, the more nothing makes sense. How could a vessel the size of the Majestic Star simply disappear?"

Unless it sank, he thought, deciding to shut up.

The Coast Guard was bound to be aware of the missing ship and Cal wondered what they were doing about it. Whatever was taking place at Sand Key sounded connected. He was familiar with Sand Key's dinky stationhouse and it was nothing like Kathy had described. It was a substation of St. Petersburg and primarily used for rescuing stranded boaters—equipped with two or three smaller vessels at best.

After rising and falling over Tampa Bay, the causeway ended at Clearwater's easternmost city limit. When Kathy braked for a traffic light, Cal noticed something odd about the ancient red pickup truck stopped in front of them. Its owner had painted out the "F" in **FORD** and replaced it with a hand-painted "L", making the tailgate read: "**LORD**". Painted above it in smaller white letters were the words: "JESUS IS..." On the truck's battered bumper was a faded sticker that read: WHERE ARE YOU GOING TO SPEND ETERNITY—SMOKING OR NON-SMOKING?

For some reason it struck Cal as amusing and he chuckled. At least Hell was warm, he thought, unlike Motown.

Cal flicked his cigarette butt into the street and looked at Kathy sitting behind the wheel. She was staring unblinking at the glowing red stoplight as if under its spell. As he studied her pretty profile, he wondered when she had last eaten. Kathy seldom ate when she was upset because it made her nauseous. Cal was anxious to get some straight answers from the Coasties, but he felt it was equally as important to get some food in Kathy. He had a feeling that whatever they learned tonight, it wouldn't be good, and then he would never get her to eat.

"I don't know about you, Sis, but I'm hungry," he lied. "Let's whip into the next fast-food joint and get a burger to go. It'll only take a sec. My treat. We'll eat 'em on the way to Station Sand Key. Then we'll raise hell until somebody there tells us what's going on. Whattya say?"

"Well—I guess so. If you insist." Kathy eyed the dashboard clock impatiently. "But I don't have much of an appetite."

When the light turned green, Kathy stomped on the gas pedal and zoomed around the red pickup truck. As she whizzed down Gulf-to-Bay Boulevard, she kept one eye peeled for a drive-in restaurant and the other on the lookout for the Clearwater Police. Her brother was hungry and that was understandable. But, to her, eating was unthinkable. Finding out about Skip was vastly more important than wolfing down a stupid cheeseburger.

Was Cal down here to help or was he on a freaking vacation?

When Kathy saw the golden arches two blocks ahead, she mashed harder on the gas pedal. She would whip in, whip out, and then drive straight to Sand Key with no more stops.

As the red convertible streaked down the boulevard, Cal watched the speedometer climb. Kathy wasn't happy about the stop off, not happy at all. His sister's panties were in a wad.

WIRED

Friday 21:29 Hours – Sand Key, Florida

In crossing the bridge from Clearwater Beach to Sand Key, Cal noticed something very different. "Hey, they built a new bridge since I was here last." The revelation caused his neck to turn in all directions. "What happened to the Clearwater Pass Drawbridge that used to be here?"

"They tore it down about a year ago to build this one. It's got enough vertical clearance to let sailboats pass underneath. Doesn't tie up traffic with hourly openings. They're planning to build another one just like it to replace the Memorial Causeway Drawbridge. There's a big stink going on about it."

"Man, I hate to hear that. I like the old drawbridges." There was disappointment in his voice. "There's something special about them. I never minded the wait while they opened and closed. Did you?" Kathy shook her head no. "When we were kids we always got a kick out of waving at the bridge tenders. Remember? They always waved back. Wonder what's gonna happen to those guys? Guess they'll all be out of work someday. That's a shame."

"I know," Kathy nodded. "But, as they say, time marches on. Progress and all that bullshit."

Sand Key was a narrow barrier island with the Intracoastal Waterway bordering its eastern shore and the Gulf of Mexico lying off its west. The Intracoastal side was lined with shops, marinas, and restaurants while the gulf side boasted towering resorts and condominiums. From within the confines of an automobile, one could often see sparkling seawater on either side.

After descending the new bridge, Kathy slowed the car to a near crawl. Station Sand Key was a block on the left and she wanted Cal to get a good long look.

As they cruised slowly past the station, Cal was awed by the scope of military activity. The grounds fronting Gulf Boulevard were lined with orange and white barricades strung with yellow **"DO NOT CROSS"** tape. Behind them troops were posted at regular intervals clad in flak jackets and armed with assault rifles. In the parking lot Coast Guard helos and Navy gunships were staged, some at the ready with their rotors turning slowly. Moored up behind the station was a fleet of cutters, patrol boats, and chase boats. Kathy was right: it looked like a war zone.

Struck by the magnitude of what he saw, Cal told Kathy to turn around. There was a beachfront condominium directly across the street and the stationhouse could be easily surveilled from its parking lot. As Kathy made the U-turn, Cal caught a glimpse of a huge Navy vessel anchored offshore in the Gulf of Mexico. Sitting straight up with interest, he followed the silhouette with his eyes as the car turned around. From the refracted light on the horizon, he recognized it as one of the latest additions to the navy fleet: a Burke Class Guided Missile Destroyer— 510' in length, 66' beam, and laden with the latest warfare technology, including 96 surface-to-surface and surface-to-air missiles. Anchored nearby were the diminutive silhouettes of two naval escorts.

"This doesn't look good, Kathy." Cal's tone was grim. "Something big is happening."

With her palms sweating, Kathy steered into the parking lot and jammed the gearshift lever into PARK. Before the car came to a complete stop, Cal already had his door partway open.

"Wait here, Sis, while I find out what's going on. I'm taking a walk across the street."

But before Cal could get out, four armed sentries surrounded the car. "This is a secure area, sir!" Cal looked to his right to find a petty officer blocking the doorway. He had a firm look on his face and a firm grip on his M-16 rifle. "You must move out!"

Right away, the lawyer in Cal objected. "What do you mean: *secure area*? We're not even on government property!" His voice was indignant. "Look, I'm an attorney and you men don't have any jurisdiction here. This is private property. What's going on here and who's in charge?"

"I'm in charge out here, sir." The Coastie's face hardened and he squared his feet. "Unless you have proof of residence that you live in this building, you must vacate now or you'll be placed under arrest. No civilian sightseers are permitted in this area. I have no time to argue the point."

"Sightseers? Now wait just a goddamn minute!" Cal had finally lost all patience. "My sister here has a husband missing and nobody will tell us jack shit! I demand to know what the hell's going on!"

WIRED

Scowling, Cal nudged the door open with his foot and started to step out. But before his shoe touched the ground, he was met with the butt end of a rifle. As he collapsed backward into the car, Kathy shrieked and reached out to steady her dazed and bleeding brother.

"Are you all CRAZY!" While screaming at the top of her lungs, she cradled Cal's unconscious head between her hands. "This is not Nazi Germany for God sake! All we want is some information about my husband and the Majestic Star! Is that a crime?" She yanked a tissue from her purse and daubed Cal's bloody forehead. "Can't you see that he's bleeding?"

"Sorry ma'am," the sentry apologized, "but you must move out. NOW!"

Lending force to the command, a coastguardsman standing near Kathy's door smacked the car hood with the flat of his hand. The loud noise startled her and she jumped with a squeal. When she gawked up at him, he frowned at her unsympathetically and jabbed his thumb toward the street. When she didn't react fast enough, he smacked the hood again and yelled: "GO NOW!"

After jumping again, Kathy started the engine in a fluster and yanked the gearshift lever into DRIVE. With squealing tires the convertible lurched forward, nearly mowing down a Coastie standing near the front bumper. In a smoke cloud of burning rubber, Kathy jumped the curb and darted onto Gulf Boulevard without regard for oncoming traffic. As horn-blaring vehicles swerved around her, she zoomed ahead with reckless abandon for Clearwater Beach. Cal was out cold, her insides were shaking, and all she could think of was getting home.

When the car veered left out of the parking lot, the centrifugal force pinned Cal against the passenger side door. When it straightened out, his limp body canted the opposite way and he slumped over the floor console between the bucket seats. Now, with his head lying on the padded armrest, Kathy could see the swollen goose egg on his forehead. It was a horrifyingly reddish-purple color with blood oozing from a jagged break at its center.

As the convertible streaked up the bridge incline, Kathy blotted the laceration with a tissue while chewing on her lower lip. But when Cal moaned at her touch, she quit messing with it and returned her shaky hand to the steering wheel. Moments later he stirred with a croaky groan and strained to sit up. But after just rising halfway, he fell back over the armrest. When he made another feeble attempt, Kathy lent a hand by pushing against his shoulder until he sat fully upright. With drowsy unfocused eyes, he mumbled something incoherent and passed out again, sagging against the passenger door with his head drooping outside. This frightened Kathy even more and she mashed harder on the accelerator.

When the car reached the apex of the bridge, Kathy struck the steering wheel with her hand when sighting a solid string of headlights cruising the main strip of Clearwater Beach. Her townhouse was located on the far side of the island, meaning she would have to worm her way through the Friday night traffic in order to reach it.

After merging into the procession of cars, Kathy craned her neck for an upcoming side street to bypass the congestion. When seeing none, she pushed back in her seat and willed herself to settle down. She had been fending off a panic attack ever since that rambunctious coastguardsman clocked Cal with his rifle butt.

It was a pleasant March evening and the weekend nightlife was in full swing. Car radios were blaring different tunes and chattering packs of jaywalking pedestrians paraded the streets and sidewalks. Most cars were loaded with cruising college kids on spring break vacation. Rubbernecking boys were hanging out car windows, yelling and whistling at the flirtatious giggly girls. Amidst the youthful crowd a sprinkling of older folks were wandering in-and-out of restaurants and gazing into the windows of closed shops and galleries.

While chugging along the stop-and-go traffic a fusion of restaurant aromas drifted in and out of Kathy's car—chargrilled steak...seafood...french fries. Ordinarily the savory smells would have made her hungry, but tonight it just made her nervous stomach more nauseous.

When the convertible stopped under a streetlamp, Kathy leaned across the console to check Cal's head. The wind had blow-dried the gash and dried blood was caked along his hairline. She nudged Cal and called him by name, but got no response. After trying again, she gave up and slouched behind the steering wheel. If she didn't get out of this traffic soon, she would suffocate.

WIRED

The driver in front of her unexpectedly hit the brakes and engaged the right blinker, signaling a wait for a forthcoming parking space. In haste Kathy whipped around the blinking car just to be halted again by standstill traffic. Growing ever frustrated, she stood up in her bucket seat and peered over the car ahead to see nothing but a string of glowing brake lights. When the cars in front moved forward a foot, the driver behind her registered a complaint by laying on the horn. Already stressed beyond her limit, Kathy bristled at the honk and spun around in a fit of temper.

"Aww, blow it out your ass!" With balled fists, she glowered down at the driver. "Jerkoff!"

Feeling better, Kathy dropped behind the steering wheel and gunned the engine. Eating up the asphalt, she fishtailed around the car in front and blasted down the wrong side of the road. When she happened upon the first side street, she slid through the turn and raced down the road, relieved to be out of the maddening traffic.

As she sailed past the smaller beach motels, her eyes bounced between the road, the speedometer, and the rearview mirror. She was making good time when the traffic light up ahead suddenly turned yellow. Hoping to beat it, she gripped the wheel tighter and floored the pedal. But it was a short yellow and the light changed quickly to red, forcing her to slam on the brakes and skid to a screeching stop.

With the smell of burning rubber permeating the night air, pedestrians using the crosswalk gawked curiously at the speed demon driver and her bloody male passenger. Some were carrying lawn chairs with kids in tow, obviously heading to Pier 60 for the weekend fireworks.

Ignoring their prying eyes, Kathy stared at the traffic light while drumming her fingers on the steering wheel. As she waited for the green, she envied the normality of her surrounds—the excited chatter...the patchy laughter...the thumping bass of car music...honking horns. For everyone else this was just another carefree fun Friday night. Their loved ones weren't mysteriously missing at sea or practically bleeding to death in the seat next to them. Their freaking lives were normal and she hated them.

When the light turned green, Kathy stomped on the gas and didn't stop again until she wheeled into her reserved parking spot. Now a complete and utter wreck, she crawled out of the car and walked around to the passenger side to fetch Cal. She would raise the convertible top later.

In rounding the car, Kathy thought about how upside down her life had become. For reasons unknown her husband was missing and now her brother had been bashed in the head by the military. What next? The whole thing was surreal, like a late-night *Twilight Zone* episode.

Whatever may be the case, Kathryn Ann Myles had had quite enough of it—thank you very much—and tomorrow she would get some straight answers from some-freaking-body or go to jail trying.

Yanking the passenger door open, Kathy bent over Cal and shook him by the shoulders. He was sunk down in the seat with his chin resting on his chest. "Cal, wake up! Come on, Cal. This is Kathy. Please wake up! Cal!"

After another vigorous shake, Cal opened his eyes but the dizzying effect of double vision forced them shut. Huffing, Kathy pulled down the sun visor and opened the lighted mirror. By its dim light she examined the nasty knot on his forehead, which looked a little better. The bleeding had stopped and the break in the skin had begun to coagulate.

Determined to get her brother inside, Kathy grabbed Cal by his sweatshirt and wrestled him out of the seat. Instinctively he stood, but couldn't maintain his balance. When he faltered, Kathy pinned him against the doorjamb and pulled his arm over her shoulders. Then, hugging him around the waist, she walked Cal inside, wobbling unsteadily under his weight.

After managing to get him on the couch, Kathy fetched the first-aid kit and icepack. She filled the bag with ice cubes and hurried back to his side. After doctoring the wound with antiseptic, she covered it with a gauze patch and planted the icepack on his forehead. Then she covered him with a comforter and knelt on the carpet beside him—staring at Cal's unconscious face and feeling totally helpless.

While holding his hand, a frightful thought popped into Kathy's head—that he could have a concussion, or brain damage for that matter.

Why hadn't she taken him straight to the hospital? Why had she been in such a panic to get home? Why was she such a ditz?

Telling herself to remain calm, Kathy dialed 911 for an ambulance. This was no time to lose it. She had to be strong—strong for Cal and strong for Skip. As the phone rang in her ear, Cal emitted a low moan and sat up groggily. Infinitely relieved to see him awake, her worried face relaxed a notch and she broke the connection.

"What the hell happened?" Cal's voice was croaky and he had a splitting migraine. "I feel like I've been hit by a Mack truck."

"You were clobbered by a rifle butt at the Coast Guard station. Remember? Lie down while I get you some ibuprofen." While hurrying to the medicine cabinet, Kathy spoke over her shoulder. "Maybe we should go to the Emergency Room for some X-Rays. What do you think?"

"Nah," Cal muttered hoarsely. "I only see two of you now, instead of three."

He snickered at the remark, which exacerbated his headache and reversed his cheeky grin. Seconds later Kathy returned with two tablets and a glass of water. After swallowing the pills, Cal tested his forehead with a finger and yelped.

"Ouch! That's quite a lump. I owe that Coastie bastard one—a big one."

"Well, don't worry about paybacks now, Cal. You're out of commission and I'm too tired to think straight. Let's get some rest and tomorrow we'll find out what this insanity's all about."

"Whatever it is, it's serious. Did you see the firepower they've brought in?"

"Yeah, and I know it's got something to do with Skip. But what on earth could it be?"

"No clue. But if Skip's in trouble, I'll be there." Cal curled his head back and held the icepack against his forehead. "We've been through hell and back and I won't let him down now."

"Skip doesn't talk about it much, but I know you guys went through some pretty hairy times in Vietnam. He still has nightmares once in a while."

Cal changed the subject. "Yeah, well, if it weren't for the Navy SEALs, I wouldn't be an attorney right now, would I? Thanks to Uncle Sam and the GI Bill."

"Well, get some rest, Brother." Kathy rose, smothering a yawn. Now that Cal was okay, she was practically asleep on her feet. "We'll get some answers tomorrow."

"For sure." With a sour face, he pointed at the bandage. "This here is bullshit! Somebody's got a lot of explaining to do—a helluva lot!"

Cal's wrath spiked his blood pressure, which made the jackhammer inside his skull pound harder, which riled him all the more, which in turn raised his blood pressure. It was a vicious cycle and his pounding cranium was the loser for it.

Accepting there was nothing he could do for the moment, Cal willed himself to chill out. Maybe he had lost the battle, but not the war. Tomorrow was another day and he would live to fight again. That was a freaking fact.

With sweet thoughts of revenge dancing through his banging head, Cal laid down and placed the icepack on his forehead. Two minutes later the battered brother and stressed-out sister were fast asleep.

DAY 3

"THE REALIZATION"

"Between what I do recognize and what I do not recognize stands myself . . ."

Andre Breton (1896-1966), French surrealist

"Courage is when you have choices."

Terry Anderson, U. S. Hostage

"You are remembered for the rules you break."

Douglas MacArthur, (1880-1964) American General & Field Marshal, WWII

"When you have eliminated the impossible, whatever remains, however improbable, must be the truth."

Sir Arthur Conan Doyle (1859-1930), English author of Sherlock Holmes

WIRED

Saturday 06:08 Hours – Clearwater Beach, Florida

It had been another fitful night for Kathy; the kind that makes one grateful when daybreak comes and the long nocturnal wait was over.

Too troubled to sleep uninterrupted, she had been up-and-down most of the night checking on Cal and worrying over Skip. Though her body ached with exhaustion she found no absolution from her tortured mind. So, for the better part of the night she had lain awake in the darkness, staring at the ceiling, getting up occasionally to smoke another cigarette. When she had dozed off her restless mind stayed on alert, busy beneath the surface—listening, waiting, worrying—robbing her of any beneficial sleep. Then there were the dreams, which inevitably curdled into morbid nightmares; some so frightening they woke her. In desperation she had finally taken a sleeping pill and drifted off in a medicated slumber.

When Kathy opened her eyes they went straight to the clock on the TV cable box. She had stared at its glowing digits for most of the night and she was glad to see it read: **6:08**. Another wearisome night was over.

It was still dark outside and the light from the streetlamp was jutting through the vertical blinds of the sliding doors, creating black and amber stripes across the wall behind her. As she sat up on the loveseat, she averted her eyes from the harsh glare and looked to the couch for Cal. It was empty and the comforter she had placed over him was folded in a neat square.

Standing up stiffly, Kathy looped her hair behind her ears and called out his name. She had a painful crick in her neck and her clothes were a wrinkled mess from sleeping in them. While padding barefoot for the kitchen coffeepot, she tucked in her shirttail to make herself more presentable. Kathy'd been finicky about her appearance her whole life long—finicky to a fault. So much so that it oftentimes maddened her.

Why did she have to be such a girlie-girl? No one cared if her shirttail was hanging out. It was six o'clock in the stupid morning!

With a grouchy grunt, Kathy yanked the shirttail out and walked on. From childhood she had been glorified as little Miss Cutie-Pie with the adorable dimples and curly locks. Well, she was tired of being on a pedestal and tired of living up to everyone's expectations. The continual role-play was too much. She had been brainwashed to the point where she wouldn't even go out to the mailbox without lipstick. Well, she was almost forty-five now, time for Miss Good Ship Lollipop to retire.

Screw 'em all.

When Kathy entered the kitchen, she found a fresh pot of coffee already brewed. The sleeping pill had left her dull and lethargic and she was in dire need of caffeine. In retrieving her favorite mug from the cupboard, she noted that her car keys were missing from the key rack. Wondering where Cal might have gone so early, she filled her mug and staggered back into the living room.

Before sitting down she opened the sliding glass doors to let in some fresh air. After her worrisome chain-smoking night, the room smelled like a back street pool hall and her lungs felt the size of prunes. Skip had been badgering her for years to quit smoking but she had resisted for one reason or another, mainly because of the weight gain. Well, when this ordeal was over and Skip was back home, she would quit smoking and get fat—*obese.*

While sipping from her mug Kathy heard the downstairs door open and close, followed by the thudding of footsteps on the stairway. Seconds later Cal appeared with a sack of donuts and a newspaper clamped under his arm.

"Good morning, big Brother," she smiled. "How's the forehead?"

Without a "good morning" or anything, Cal deposited the donuts on the dining table and sat down heavily. His subdued expression and body language frightened her. Something was wrong.

"Well, Sis, now I know what the fuss was all about at Sand Key last night." He gestured at a chair and dropped his eyes. "Come over here and sit down. I've got something to tell you."

"What is it?" Cal was avoiding eye contact, making her more nervous. "Is it about Skip?"

Cal swallowed. "Fraid so."

With an upwelling of dread, Kathy walked timidly to the table and took a chair across from him. Once seated, she leaned forward and folded her clammy hands on the tabletop, bracing herself for what appeared to be bad news.

Cal looked into her eyes and opened his mouth to speak, but the words stuck in his throat—fearful of her reaction. With no delicate way of softening the blow, his shoulders sagged and he held up the *St. Petersburg Times*. On the front page written in bold black letters read: **"MAJESTIC STAR HIJACKED BY TERRORISTS"**. Under the headline was a black-and-white photo of Skip's ill-fated ship.

Kathy felt herself sway and recoiled from the headline. "Oh m'God!" Gasping, her hand flew to her mouth and she spoke through trembling fingers. "This is awful, Cal. Horrible!"

A wave of nausea suddenly assailed her and she fled into the bathroom. With the bold caption burning in her mind, Kathy retched up soured coffee until there was nothing left to cough up. When the spasms eased she flushed the toilet and rinsed her mouth out with tap water. Her mind was a tempest and a war was waging inside her—her sanity versus the mother lode of all anxiety.

When Kathy rejoined Cal at the table, he was reading the newspaper and didn't look up. He wasn't being cold or insensitive, he simply didn't know what else to say. Skip's situation was dire and any sugarcoating at a time like this would ring hollow. Besides, Kathy hated to be mama-coddled.

Releasing a tremulous sigh, Kathy planted her elbows on the table and rested her chin on her clasped hands. "What else does it say?" Her voice was frail, still not her own. "Is he alive? I can't live without him, Cal." All at once her brown eyes teared and her face crumpled. "He's such an inseparable part of me and ..."

Kathy's words tapered off into a thin screechiness and she burst into tears. In spite of her determination to show courage, she broke down. With her body shuddering, she buried her face in her hands and sobbed miserably.

Offering her what scant solace he could, Cal reached across the table and took her by the upper arms. "The newspaper says the passengers and crew were fine at last report." His voice was low and reassuring, inviting trust. "Skip is safe, Sis." He brushed back a fallen strand of hair covering her face and then shook her lightly to make sure she was listening. "He's okay."

As the meaning of his words sank in, Kathy nodded and wiped her soggy eyes. While she collected herself, Cal read aloud from the newspaper, glancing up occasionally to study the emotions playing across her face. When he was done reading, he folded the newspaper and put it down—deliberately skipping a second article about Alvarez's alleged ties to Al-Qaeda and his suspected role behind the recent wave of U.S. terrorism.

"Okay, Kathy, here's the facts as we know 'em." Cal leaned back in his chair and crossed his arms. "Skip's ship is ten miles offshore and wired with explosives. The hijackers are demanding the release of Juan Carlos Alvarez and Cesar Gonzalez—two cartel drug lords in U.S. custody. There are 218 people onboard the ship including Skip and his crew. So far, nobody's been killed. As we speak, the authorities are negotiating for their release." Cal paused briefly while regarding her. "That's about the long and short of it."

With a gamut of feelings choking her, Kathy sat motionless with her head bowed. Then she rose without expression and strode trance-like to the sliding doors. The eastern sky had brightened and the streetlamp flickered off, but she was too taken with worry to notice.

"Well, at least he's alive," she uttered, swallowing her emotion. "Thank God for that. I suppose things could be worse."

As Cal stared at his sister's back, his heart went out to her. She looked fragile standing there, like a lost little girl. As her elder brother, he felt a natural need to protect her from hurt and harm; but the only thing he could offer her was a pitifully inadequate shoulder to lean on.

Cal crossed the living room and hugged her from behind. "Try not to worry. I'm sure Skip will come out of this thing just fine." As he nuzzled his chin into her crown, Kathy wrested out of his arms and whirled on him.

"Don't patronize me, Cal! This is serious shit! You don't know if he'll be okay or not—nobody does. Don't treat me like a schoolgirl!"

Kathy stormed into the bathroom and slammed the door shut, as if being her final say-so on the subject. Inside, she blew her nose and gazed at her hardened reflection in the mirror. It was a face that was mad—mad as hell. Skip's life was at stake and both the Coast Guard and police had deliberately misled her. She was the captain's wife, by God, and all the lies, cover-ups, and half-truths were inexcusable. She was entitled to know what was happening—she was family.

Well, Kathryn Ann Myles wasn't gonna sit on the couch and rust

WIRED

while waiting for the authorities to grace her with a phone call. They could forget about that! She was going to do something about it—today!

When Kathy emerged from the bathroom, she found Cal sitting outside on the sundeck. He was smoking a cigarette and gazing at the row of boats moored alongside the canal. He looked dejected to her and she felt guilty for venting on him. After all, she had practically begged him to come to Florida and he had dropped everything to be here. Besides, Cal cared deeply about Skip too and he was probably just as worried as she.

Embarrassed by her shameful behavior, Kathy went into the kitchen and poured Cal a cup of coffee. Then she placed some donuts on a paper plate and joined him outside.

"Sorry, big Brother," she said meekly. "Peace offering?" She placed the coffee and donuts in front of him and sat down. "You were only trying to help. I'm so impossible at times. What should we do now, Cal? I've got to get some answers or I'll explode."

Cal cocked an eyebrow and looked at her critically. "I think you already did." The corners of his mouth curled and he crushed out the cigarette in a seashell ashtray. "I was just sitting here wondering what the authorities were doing besides clubbing citizens that get a little too nosy. The drug cartels don't play games, Kathy, or make idle threats. They won't think twice about blowing Skip's ship if Alvarez and Gonzalez are not released. Somehow, we've got to find out what's going on."

"Yeah, I'm gonna kill somebody if we don't."

"Me and you both." Cal ripped the gauze patch from his forehead and probed the lump gently. "It's still real tender but most of the swelling's gone down. I'm going to take a shower and get this matted blood out of my hair. Afterwards, we'll go see what we can find out. Deal?"

"Deal." Then, apologetically, she added: "Thanks for being here, Cal. I'm sorry for blowing up at you like that. God knows it's not your fault. My nerves are just shot, that's all. Forgive me?"

"I guess so. Just don't make a habit of it." He faked a mean look at her. "Or the next time I'll bend you over my knee and give you a good spanking."

Kathy straightened at the challenge. "Oh, yeah?" she grinned. "You and who else?"

"Me, myself, and I—that's who." With each macho word, Cal

thumbed his puffed-out chest. "And don't you forget it."

He rose with a chuckle and ruffled Kathy's hair—like when she was a kid. With mussed up hair, she gazed upward and gave him a slanted grin. Grinning back, he ruffled her hair again to signify their squabble was over. With their peace made, Cal headed upstairs for the shower.

Saturday 06:40 Hours – The "Majestic Star"

The *Majestic Star* was a mid-sized cruise ship featuring a main deck, an upper deck, and a topside sundeck. She was a real beauty, sporting a shiny black hull with red boot stripe at the waterline and two gleaming white decks. The wheelhouse, sometimes called the bridge or pilothouse, complimented the hull with white paint trimmed in black.

On the main level was an elegant dining room with a seating capacity of 250 guests. The tables were draped with white tablecloths and surrounded by red leather chairs to match the plush carmine red carpet. Adding a seafaring flair to the room, the walls were adorned with colorful aqua murals of mermaids, treasure chests, and saltwater memorabilia.

The second level featured a stylish casino equipped with slot machines, blackjack tables, roulette wheels, and craps tables. Staged before the blackjack tables and slots were chrome barstools with upholstered seats and backrests that complemented the royal blue carpet. A neon-lit mirrored bar and cashier's cage were located forward next to the restrooms and near the interior staircase leading either downstairs to the dining room or up to the sundeck.

The top level was a wide-open sundeck surrounded by heavy pipe railing. Scattered around its perimeter were white plastic tables and chairs for passengers to lounge around and sip fancy tropical drinks. A thatched-roof Tiki Bar was located to the fore with an adjoining stage for the reggae band. Next to the Tiki Bar and six steps up was a bridge deck leading to two private cabins and a steel mesh catwalk going to the wheelhouse.

The wheelhouse was the nerve center of the ship, outfitted with state-of-the-art navigational systems and advanced communications. Above and beneath the tinted wraparound bow windows were upper and lower consoles teeming with instrumentation and sophisticated electronics, to include: a weather fax receiver, radiofax and teletype, radarscope, cellular phone, iridium satellite phone, VHF marine band transceiver, depth sounder, GPS, and broadband satellite internet. The centerpiece of the bridge was a commanding wooden wheel mounted on a solid brass pedestal. On either side of it were white leather swivel helmseats with chrome steering wheels and auxiliary helm controls. To the port was a built-in chart table with clamp on red lens light. Aft of the table was a corner deck head with toilet and washbasin. Affixed to the back wall was a white padded bench seat that spanned the breadth of the wheelhouse.

Outside and directly behind the pilothouse were two teak-paneled staterooms that served as the captain's quarters and accommodations for VIP's or seasick passengers. Each private cabin was equipped with bunk, shower, and head.

~~~~~~~~~~

As Captain Myles lay on his bunk, he could feel the anchor chains straining against the tide running under the ship. He had lain awake there all night long—listening, staring at the ceiling tiles, even counting them for distraction—trapped in the bowels of despair. Two days ago his world had come crashing down and except for an infrequent catnap when he could no longer function, he hadn't slept since. Minutes ago, when the sun's first rays peeked through the cabin porthole, he had not only been thankful—he'd been exalted. Hell night was finally over.

Rolling off his bunk, Skip padded stiffly into the head to relieve himself, pulling up his saggy boxer shorts as he walked. The unimaginable shock of losing his ship to armed terrorists—in Florida waters no less; a mere ten miles from port—had left him psychologically stunned. While knowing his situation to be true, he had a hard time accepting it as real. The whole thing so incomprehensible—so unimaginably abstruse—it transcended belief.

Posing as tourists, the hijackers had boarded his ship on Thursday and seized control ten miles offshore. The takeover had been well orchestrated and within minutes the *Majestic Star* was theirs. A newly hired busboy named Mohammad somebody was the gang's inside man. He had evidently smuggled their weapons and explosives aboard the ship sometime Wednesday night after the evening cruise. Skip remembered him dropping a stack of dishes in the kitchen just before the takeover. Skip also remembered where he had seen that unusual tattoo on the crab-loving Arab in the dining room. Mohammad had one identical to it. So, now, in a preposterous twist of fate, the incompetent ex-busboy was standing guard outside his cabin door with an AK-47 assault rifle.

Except for two Muslims, the gang members were all Hispanic. Their leader was the gold-toothed man who had praised the lobster bisque in the dining room. His followers referred to him as *El Asesino*—whatever that meant. He was a loose-built, 40-ish looking man with stringy black hair and an acne-scarred greasy complexion. He was tall for a Mexican, about 5'11". Except for a prominent gold tooth, his front teeth were discolored from decay. He was the cocky sort, sneering when he talked, and he had a lazy eyelid that twitched when he got agitated. He was now sporting a dark stubble of beard and wearing a camouflage-colored headband with flowing tails down his back. Even all scrubbed up the man would look scraggly.

There was a lot of automatic gunfire during the takeover but most of it was directed into the air. Two dissenting male passengers had been roughed up a little when the cell phones and personal electronics were confiscated, but, thankfully, no one had been killed. Once all the passengers and crew were under guard, the ship was wired with bricks of C-4 plastique, the same explosive used to attack the U.S.S. Cole.

Radio negotiations had been ongoing since day one of the hijacking, but thus far no breakthroughs had been made. The talks were largely conducted in Spanish, which Skip neither spoke nor understood. But with each passing day so much was certain: the tone of the talks was getting uglier and Gold-Tooth was growing progressively more militant. After his last radio communiqué, he'd stomped about the wheelhouse for a solid fifteen minutes, ranting in Spanish and giving everyone the jitters—even his own men. If something positive didn't develop pretty soon, Skip feared their war of words would reach a flashpoint and Gold-Tooth might do something rash to show the Americanos he meant business—like killing passengers.

Worsening their plight was the ship's dwindling food and water supply. While the kitchen routinely served meals during the four-hour excursions, it wasn't equipped to feed hundreds of people for several days. Most provisions were brought aboard fresh daily and a large stockpile of food wasn't kept in reserve.

Right after the takeover Gold-Tooth placed Skip in charge of the food and water with orders to make them stretch. Unsure of how long their ordeal would last, Skip began serving two meals per day at 11:00AM and 6:00PM. Up till now the authorities had not replenished their shrinking supplies; but, yesterday, Neal, who understood a little Spanish, overheard the Coast Guard offer food and water for hostages. Be that as it may nothing ever came of it, so there they were.

The *Majestic Star* was designed as a day cruise ship and thereby lacked overnight accommodations for passengers. It featured only two private cabins, presently occupied by Skip and the hijackers. Being captain, Skip was extended the privilege of keeping his quarters as long as he cooperated by keeping the passengers in line. Though as much a prisoner as anyone else, he felt guilty for being afforded this luxury. The passengers and crew weren't so lucky.

There were eight gunmen in all, tasked with guarding the hostages round-the-clock. In order to house everyone in one place, the casino had been gutted to create more room. It was closer to the wheelhouse than the downstairs dining room and it claimed only two exits—a forward staircase and exterior door aft—making it possible for two gunmen to stand watch over all two hundred persons. Once all slot machines and other gambling paraphernalia had been tossed overboard, dining tables were brought up from downstairs to create makeshift bunk beds. Some passengers slept on the hard tabletops, while the luckier ones slept underneath on the plush carpet. It was tight quarters and uncomfortable, but, with no choice in the matter, everyone cooperated.

As Skip donned his captain's uniform, his thoughts were scattered and his spirit low.

What were the authorities doing? What were the terrorists plotting? How many explosives had been planted? Where was the trigger mechanism? Was Kathy aware of his predicament? Was she okay? How and when would this crazy nightmare end?

Logic dictated that Gold-Tooth possessed the detonating device, but Skip couldn't be sure. Rather than risk carrying it on his person, it might be secreted somewhere. Until Skip found that out, he couldn't do anything. One wrong move and *WHAM!*—up she goes. The gang was a murderous lot and capable of most anything.

After slipping on his white uniform pants and matching short-sleeved shirt, Skip screwed on his white skipper's hat by its gold-braided black bill. Now he was ready—for exactly what, he didn't know and that's what worried him. When he opened the cabin door, the startled ex-busboy jumped from the chair and aimed his AK-47 at Skip's midsection.

"At ease!" Skip razzed with a toothful grin. "As you were, raghead."

Unamused by the slur, Mohammad's face reddened and he jammed the gun barrel into Skip's stomach. Not to be intimidated, Skip stood fast and resisted the barrel's pressure by tightening his abs. With their faces inches apart Skip broadened his wiseacre grin, deliberately taunting the scrawny Muslim.

"Since you understand English," Skip said calmly, "I've got somethin' I've been wantin' to tell you." Tact had never been one of his strong suits. "YOU'RE FIRED, ASSHOLE!"

Mohammad's dark Arabic eyes bugged like saucers, then narrowed with pure hate. He wanted nothing more than to kill the uncivil American. Who did this infidel think he was talking to!? His name was Mohammad. His namesake was the sacred *Prophet of God* himself, the *Arab Prophet of Islam*. He was born on September 11th, an omen from heaven above. Allah had greatness in store for him—to be sure.

As Mohammad's rage boiled over, urging him to fire, he prayed to Allah for restraint. The Zeta gang leader wanted the American captain alive. When the infidel was no longer needed, Mohammad would delight in teaching the captain some manners—Islamic style.

As Skip stood his ground, he could feel the gun barrel trembling against his stomach, signaling he had pushed the Arab far enough. Mohammad's self-control was teetering and the molten look on his face said he wanted Skip dead. Had he been wearing a turban, Skip thought it would have surely caught afire.

Declaring himself the winner, Skip gave Mohammad a well-deserved tsk and set out for the wheelhouse, pleased that at least one of the terrorist bastards was as pissed off as him. That was a good start.

WIRED

Saturday 06:52 Hours – Clearwater Beach, Florida

As Cal stood in the shower, he worried about Kathy's fragile state of mind. The landscape of her life had changed dramatically of late—ripped away by the roots—threatening her future and that of her hostage husband. That would be enough to give anyone a mental meltdown.

Kathy was a levelheaded gal, but she was also a bundle of contradictions—a walking talking oxymoron. She could be no-nonsense, but playful. Incredibly giving, yet hardheaded and stubborn. She was a loving person, but don't dare cross her. She was an iron-willed, fiercely determined woman who could be counted on when the chips were down. But Kathy's weak spot had always been Skip—her best friend, her confidante, her lifelong love and soul mate.

Like all marriages, Kathy and Skip had had their ups-and-downs; but she was the rock on which it was built and the rock on which it stood. When other women would have packed up and left during Skip's earlier drinking days, she embarrassed him by dragging him out of bars while his buddies hooted and howled. If he was temporarily out of work, she worked two jobs until something came along. If anyone talked bad about him, they answered to her. If another woman gave him a little too much attention, her fingernails popped out like a stray alley cat. She *made* their marriage work.

Although Kathy and Skip both wanted a family, their marriage had failed to produce children. They'd once checked into in-vitro fertilization at a Tampa fertility clinic, but the procedure was beyond their financial reach with no guarantee of success. Disappointed, they considered adoption but ultimately ruled it out—agreeing that if it wasn't meant to be, it wasn't meant to be.

As a result, Kathy filled the void in her life by immersing herself into her marriage and making Skip her whole world. This suited Skip just fine, of course, who was flattered at being her center of attention. Being the gracious and giving husband he was, he made the personal sacrifice and allowed her to cater to his every whim. Before long he was spoiled rotten and expected Kathy to handle everything.

Skip was a perfectionist at work but he wasn't a ball-of-fire around the house. Being an ex-Navy man, he figured that when he was home, he was "off-duty" and that was that. He wanted to kick back, sip a few beers, and scan the sports channels. Kathy understood this to a point, but she was just as particular about her home as Skip was about his ship. When she wanted something done, she wanted it done right then—not after the game or sometime next week.

Still, after working all day long, fixing a leaky faucet was way down Skip's priority list. And giving up a football game because the car was making a funny *tick-tick* noise was simply out of the question. It wasn't that he was irresponsible, or lazy, because he wasn't—quite the opposite, actually. He just didn't share Kathy's sense of urgency over what he viewed as trivial matters. Unless it was a *real* problem or emergency, it would get done when he felt like it. As a result Kathy gave up trying and hired a local handyman to keep things up. By default, she became overseer of the household.

Cal stepped out of the shower and swiped a towel across the steamy mirror. When it fogged up again, he held a blow dryer against it until his bleary image cleared. Then he leaned over the sink and examined his forehead, which seemed to be healing okay. The purplish lump had shrunk to the size of a quarter and it had a thin scab crusting at its center. After gently dabbing it with peroxide, he covered it with a large band-aid and blow-dried his hair.

Once back in the bedroom, Cal opened his overnight bag and pulled out a yellow tank top and tan cargo shorts. Having spent the past few months bundled-up against Detroit's arctic winter, it felt liberating to don scant summer clothing. But when he stepped into his rubber flip-flops— the ultimate symbol of summer—their cushy feel was near-orgasmic and brought back years of fun-in-the-sun memories.

Feeling renewed, Cal descended the stairs to find Kathy sitting outside on the deck under the umbrella. Toby was lying in her lap and she was reading the newspaper with a knuckle pressed against her teeth. The sliding glass doors were wide open and the television was blaring loudly, tuned to the local 24-hour news channel.

As Cal crossed the living room, Kathy put Toby down and strolled over to the deck railing. Looking out over the canal, she raised the hair off the back of her neck and held it aloft. The dew point was high and the morning air was sticky. After letting her hair fall, she flattened her forearms on the top railing and stared dismally at the water below.

She was scared, angry, worried, frustrated, and ridden with dread. She felt a compelling need to do something without knowing what, heightening her anxiety. All this waiting around crap while Skip's life hung in the balance had her insides stretched as taut as bowstrings. She felt on the verge of snapping.

Cal joined Kathy on the deck and stood mutely beside her, respectful of her sullen mood. It was a spectacular morning and the sun's rays felt warm on his bare shoulders. The tide was low and the herons were feeding on the newly exposed bottom along the seawall. As Cal watched them pluck at the oyster beds, the sound of a boat motor attracted his attention. Looking to his right, he saw a center-console fishing boat putting their way. As the boat idled by, the captain threw up a hand and Cal waved back. Kathy, on the other hand, paid the friendly fisherman no mind. While standing there in body, her mind was long gone.

Cal watched the boat until it passed out of sight around a finger isle. By that time several minutes had lapsed without Kathy so much as acknowledging his presence. After another passed, he broke the prolonged silence.

"Are you ready to go, Sis?" The sun slid behind a cloud and the day went momentarily dull. "I thought we'd start with the local police and go from there. After last night's welcoming committee from the Coast Guard, I don't think they'll tell us anything." When Kathy didn't respond, he pointed at the noisy television. "Unless you'd rather wait around here for the next news update. Either way is okay with me."

"Forget it, Cal," she snapped, staring straight ahead. "While you were in the shower, I called the police, *and* the Coast Guard, *and* the St. Petersburg Times. There's a total blackout during negotiations with the terrorists. No information whatsoever, not even for family members. We're shit outta luck."

"What?" His expression went from baffled to angry. "Now *that* pisses me off!" Cal stuffed his hands inside his cargo pockets and tramped about the deck. "They should at least tell the relatives *something*. What indifference! That's total bullshit!" When the knot on his forehead began to throb, he flopped down in a patio chair and stewed in silence.

"Well, that's the way it is, Brother—your tax dollars at work. But I'll tell you one thing right now. *I'm* not gonna sit around while they play patty-cake with the hijackers. I can tell you that much. I'll go check on Skip myself. Screw 'em all."

"Yeah, right," Cal said cynically. At once *"Kathy Alarms"* went off in his head. When she took a mind to do something, she could be uncompromising. "And how do you intend to do that?"

"Well..." Kathy turned to face him, propping her arms on the railing behind her. "Skip has a lot of fishing buddies with boats. Maybe one of them would take me out there for a look. It's only ten miles offshore."

Cal rose from his chair. "Are you kidding? You wouldn't even get close. The newspaper says they have the ship quarantined. You'd end up getting arrested. Bad idea, Kathy. Forget it."

She considered this a moment. "They couldn't see us at night, could they? Maybe we could go out then."

"What good would that do? You wouldn't be able to see anything in the dark. Besides, the Coasties *do* have radar, you know." Cal waved off the idea. "They'd nail you before you got even close. You can't be serious."

Kathy was undeterred. "Okay then, we could go out during the daytime and pretend to be lost if we're stopped—play dumb. All they can do is run us off. They can't eat us, for heaven's sake. I just can't sit around here wondering what's going on. Can't you understand?"

"Of course I do." Cal empathized with her but hoped to change her mind. "But going out there won't accomplish a thing. As you witnessed last night, the military doesn't take kindly to civilian interference. You'd probably end up with a rifle butt in your face like me—or worse."

"Maybe. Maybe not." She walked up to him and placed a hand on his shoulder. "I've got to do something, Cal, even if it doesn't accomplish anything. Otherwise, I'll go nuts. I know it sounds kinda crazy, but I'd feel better by just seeing Skip's ship, even from a distance."

Sensing defeat, Cal sat back down. It was a nutty idea. Even so, he couldn't allow her to go it alone, even if it meant winding up in the brig with her—which wouldn't set well with the Michigan Bar Association. One way or another he had to talk her out of it. But the emphatic look on her face said it was already too late.

"Look, Kathy, I know you feel compelled to do something. So do I.

But getting locked up won't help anything. I say we stay out of it and let the authorities do their job."

"Why? What's there to lose?" She gestured at the television. "It's a helluva lot better than just sitting around here and watching the same old crappy news reruns. Until the authorities decide to release more information, there's nothing *new* for the media to report. That could be tomorrow, or next week for that matter. You got a better idea?"

Cal heaved a sigh. "Not really." Her mind was made up—case closed.

In reality, though, Kathy was right. With the news blackout in effect, nothing would be forthcoming from the media anytime soon. If they wanted answers, they would have to seek them out on their own.

"All right, then," Kathy said with a jubilant smile. "Wanna go for a boat ride?"

Saturday 07:20 Hours – Group St. Petersburg

The Coast Guard was the first branch of the armed forces to respond to the hijacking and the first to arrive on scene; hence, Rear Admiral Ray Hanna, Commander of the Seventh District, had been the ranking officer in charge of the incident from the outset.

Inasmuch as the perpetrators were foreign nationals, the hijacking was being treated as a terrorist act—falling under the jurisdiction of the Department of Homeland Security and by extension the U.S. Coast Guard. Still, other government agencies sought to self-involve themselves to get a piece of the action. Some high-ranking Pentagon glory-seekers even tried to finagle command of the operation. But, despite their four-star wrangling, it was decided that Rear Admiral Hanna was best suited for the task and would carry on as Incident Commander.

During his Coast Guard career, Hanna had built a reputation for being clever and resourceful. Within ranks he was reputed to be something of a maverick, at times bending regulations and using unconventional methods to accomplish his mission. But, irrespective of his tactics, he was renowned for getting the job done. His knowledge of the drug trade was unparalleled and he was adept at anticipating the drug traffickers' moves, especially the Colombians. And, being a Florida native, he knew the coastal waters like the back of his hand—a distinct advantage should the terrorists attempt an escape at sea using the *Majestic Star*.

"Line five, Admiral," a voice announced over the intercom. "It's Washington, sir."

Ray moaned, plunked down his coffee cup, and punched the blinking button. Since his hectic arrival from Miami yesterday he had spent most of his time in briefings or on the horn with Washington. In D.C. there were an infinite number of bureau chiefs and the volume of bureaucracy was becoming trying. Ray had to keep reminding himself that these were important people with important questions about important matters.

As Ray held on the line for the Director of Homeland Security, he took in the surroundings of his former office. Group St. Petersburg was the regional hub for a cluster of ground and air stations in West Central Florida and he had served as Group Commander here during the nineties. Directly after the hijacking, Ray vacated his Miami office and set up field operations at the St. Petersburg facility to be closer to the action.

As Ray's eyes roamed the room, they landed on a large laminated wall chart of Tampa Bay. In looking closer he saw that it still bore the pinholes where he'd marked the ruins of the freighters that collided in the fog, touching off the disastrous 1993 oil spill. Keeping the phone receiver pinned to his ear, Ray rose and stretched the coiled phone cord to the colored chart. As he ran a fingertip over the old punctures, he found something pleasant about the discovery—like stumbling upon initials carved in a tree from years ago.

The D7 Headquarters complex at Brickell Plaza had its perks but Ray missed the quietude of St. Petersburg. Miami was just too sprawling and metropolitan for his liking, filled with hustle and bustle. Everyone there seemed to be either late for something or in a hurry to get back. In contrast, St. Petersburg was a much more laid-back community.

Years ago, St. Pete was renowned for its honeymooners and retirees. In those days the locals jokingly referred to their fair city as: *"The land of newlyweds and the nearly-deads."* Of course, today, St. Petersburg offered major league baseball and all the amenities of any modern city, but it was still a relatively tranquil place for a town of its size. Ray hadn't realized how much he had missed it until his arrival yesterday.

Station Sand Key was located thirteen air miles northwest of St. Petersburg and ten miles due east of where the *Majestic Star* was anchored. Sand Key was strategically closer to the captive ship, but the comparatively small station lacked the resources to facilitate a field operation of this scope. By contrast the Group St. Petersburg station was a training center built with classrooms and barracks to house transient students assigned there for advanced schooling. It featured an operations center, mess hall, assembly hall, small armory, telecommunications center with satellite uplinks, and a deep draft harborage for medium endurance cutters. In view of these assets, Ray picked the Group St. Petersburg complex to set up his Command and Control Center while utilizing Station Sand Key as a staging area for military aircraft and watercraft.

While additional personnel and materiel were being brought in, a blockade was placed around the *Majestic Star* to both contain the hijackers and to quarantine the ship from the outside world. The Mexican gang leader had demanded a dialogue in Spanish, so a Cuban-American Telecommunications Specialist had been assigned to act as radio translator-negotiator.

Until now the negotiations had gone as anticipated—nowhere. In nearly all hostage situations, early talks were little more than each side probing the other for weaknesses and concessions. But this hostage case was unlike any other that Ray had encountered. Typically, drug traffickers only took hostages when threatened by capture—using them as bargaining chips or shields for escape. When cornered, a show of force generally intimidated them into taking a nonviolent way out. But, in this particular case, the hostage taking had been a deliberate and premeditated act. American captives were being held as human collateral for the release of two cartel kingpins.

The hijacker's radio demand had been loud and clear: *"If Alvarez and Gonzalez were not immediately released from custody, innocent people would die."*

Ray had barely finished talking to the Director for Homeland Security when the Attorney General called. Before answering, he checked the wall clock. Seeing he had three minutes left before his 07:30 briefing, he took a swig of lukewarm coffee and picked up the receiver.

WIRED

It was a spectacular spring day as the red convertible motored for the marina. A mild onshore breeze was wafting from the southwest, giving the inland waters a light glittery chop. Seated behind the steering wheel, Kathy was wearing hot-pink shorts with a matching middy top. Her hair was fixed in a topknot, held in check by a hot-pink scrunchy. Cal was sitting next to her in his yellow tank top and shorts, wearing sunglasses.

As they crossed the Memorial Causeway Drawbridge, Cal took in Clearwater Harbor to his right and left. To the south, powerboats were skimming across the aquamarine water, leaving frothy wakes in their paths. On the north side of the bridge a sailboat was circling in close proximity, obviously waiting for an opening.

When the car reached the apex of the drawbridge the pavement gave way to open steel grating, changing the pitch of the tires to a hollow metallic sound. As Cal looked straight down through the mesh bridgework, he saw a row of pelicans roosting on the wooden fenders under the bridge. Impassively, they seemed to be whiling away the morning by watching the flow of boat traffic parading past them. Turning an occasional beak to another, they almost seemed to be chatting about the human landlubbers and their noisy contraptions.

When Cal looked upward, he caught a glimpse of the bridge tender and waved at him. The elderly gent was wearing a *Detroit Tigers* cap atop wispy white hair and it pleased Cal that he was fellow Tigers fan. When the tender hoisted a hand and waved back, Cal got a good look at him for the first time. He was a spindly gentleman in his late sixties or seventies with bright friendly eyes and a broad good-natured smile. He had a kind and gentle face and it annoyed Cal that he would soon be out of work.

As the car descended the slope for mainland Clearwater, Cal noted two men fishing off the south side of the bridge. On the opposite side was a group of demonstrators marching up-and-down the pedestrian walkway. With determined faces, the protesters were waving picket signs at passing motorists and chanting something that Cal couldn't make out. In more cases than not, like-minded passersby honked their car horns in show of their support.

As Kathy headed north on Fort Harrison Boulevard, Cal removed his sunglasses and closed his eyes. After Detroit's six-month-long winter, his melanin-deprived face eagerly lapped up the sun's rays. He had almost forgotten how good it felt. In temperate bliss, he lolled his head against the headrest and his other senses kicked in—the feel of the wind pawing at his hair...the smell of fresh salt air...the scattered cries of shorebirds...the distant burring of a far-off boat motor.

With his eyes remained closed, Cal heard the faint humming sound of a lawn mower engine. Seconds later the sound grew louder and the scent of freshly mown grass flooded his nostrils. As he inhaled the grassy fragrance deep into his lungs, it was a spiritual experience. No one but a frozen-stiff northerner could fully appreciate its wholesome summery smell.

When the convertible passed through the marina's chain-link gates, Kathy pointed out the ticket office straight ahead. A tropical-colored sign on the building's mansard roof read: **MAJESTIC STAR TICKET OFFICE**. Visible through the plate glass front door was a fluorescent **"CLOSED"** sign. Behind the office building was a concrete seawall rigged with moorings and neatly coiled four-inch dock lines. Affixed to the seawall was an aluminum gangplank winched upright, waiting to be lowered when its ship arrived.

Most daunting of all was the empty berth where the *Majestic Star* should have been. As Cal stared at the vacant expanse of water, he wondered if Skip would ever maneuver his prized ship into her berth again.

Saturday 07:30 Hours – Group St. Petersburg

Ray strode briskly into the briefing room and took his place behind the podium. In attendance was a task force of officers from various branches of the armed forces as well as key representatives from state and federal agencies and law enforcement. There was no press.

After acknowledging the group, Ray removed his ball cap and motioned to a warrant officer. An instant later the fluorescent lights went out and a slide projector came on. On the wall behind him, a silver screen dangled over a jade-green chalkboard.

"Good morning, gentlemen. Let me bring you up to speed."

WIRED

Ray faced the screen in the dim light and pressed the slide projector's remote control. On the screen appeared a grainy photo of the Zeta ringleader aboard the *Majestic Star*. Captured on film while entering the wheelhouse, the gunman was dressed in a wrinkled khaki shirt and wearing a camouflage pattern olive-drab headband. A cigarette dangled from his mouth and an AK-47 was slung over his right shoulder, riding his lower back. He looked dangerous.

"This is Santiago Mendoza, known in Mexico as El Asesino— meaning: The Assassin. He's one of the top chieftains of a mercenary group called Los Zetas. For those of you not familiar with the Z's, I'll fill you in."

Ray changed slides and a group photo of a military combat unit flashed on the screen. The all-Hispanic squadron was dressed like a SWAT Team—wearing helmets, tactical vests, and brandishing automatic weapons and grenade launchers. Staring meanly at the camera, two stocky Mexicans were holding light machine guns with ammo belts crisscrossed over their chests.

"This photo was taken in the 1990's at Fort Benning, Georgia. These are members of an elite paramilitary commando battalion called the *Special Air Mobile Force Group* formed by Vincente Fox of Mexico. The SAMFG was trained at Fort Benning with one purpose in mind: to neutralize Mexico's top three drug cartels—the Gulf Cartel, the Sinaloa Cartel, and the Tijuana Cartel. But some time after returning to Mexico, several dozen deserted the SAMFG and joined forces with the very traffickers they were trained to combat. The cartels paid better."

The slide changed to an aerial photo of some rooftops in a wind-swept desert.

"The Zetas have training camps in Tamaulipas and Michoácan, where recruits undergo a six-week training course in weapons and military tactics. The Zetas now number over 700, with military deserters, ex-FARC soldiers, and former federal police officers amongst their ranks."

The carousel rotated and a photo of a mutilated blood-twisted corpse appeared on the screen.

"Here are some examples of their grisly handiwork." While talking Ray displayed a shocking succession of gory photos. "Since 2006 approximately 18,000 have been killed by the warring cartels and their drug wars have spilled over into the United States. The Zetas have placed a $50,000 bounty on all border agents and U.S. enforcement officials. Last year, 515 law enforcement officers were killed along Texas border towns. If a Zeta member kills an American enforcement officer, their stature rises dramatically within the organization."

Ray changed slides and an embattled town of sun-dried adobe buildings filled the screen.

"This is Nuevo Laredo, across the border from Laredo, where 600 have already died this year in gangland violence. Street shootouts with machine guns and rocket launchers are commonplace. The U.S. ambassador to Mexico closed the U.S. consulate there last month after the chief of police was executed just nine hours after taking office. Just last week, the Zetas beheaded five rival gang members and rolled their heads across the dance floor of a local nightspot. The border cities are war zones and the Z's are feared by everyone."

The next slide was of another besieged Mexican town. "This is the quiet town of Villa Ahumada, Chihuahua, which recently endured a night of terror when forty Zetas took over the town of 30,000. Calls to the police went unanswered because two officers were murdered and the rest were held captive inside the police station. During the spree the Zetas shot up the town, brutalized and robbed citizens, and looted the stores. In the wake of the ordeal, two hundred Mexican Army soldiers were airlifted in to restore order. Since then, the local police force has dwindled from fifteen officers to three because of ongoing threats from the Zetas." The next slide captured the interior of a filthy-looking warehouse. "As you might imagine, body disposal along the border towns has become a lucrative side business. The owner of this warehouse is known as the Soup-Meister, who claims to have liquefied over 300 hundred bodies in his vat of hydrochloric acid."

Appearing next on the screen was a leafless tree somewhere in a dusty desert. Hanging from its bare limbs were multicolored articles of clothing.

"This is another example of the Zetas' cruelty and callousness. It's called a *Rape Tree*. When the Zetas feel like partying, they cull out some of the prettier females crossing the border and rape them repeatedly. Afterwards, just for kinky kicks, the Z's hang their underpants in this tree as a trophy. It's their perverse way of having a good time."

The following slide was of a wiry Arab-looking man dressed in western clothing.

"Thus far we've identified eight hijackers aboard the Majestic Star—six Hispanic and two Middle Eastern. Here's one of the Arabs. We're not sure yet if he's Al-Qaeda, but it's more likely than not. The drug cartels and Al-Qaeda have been collaborating for years. It takes enormous capital to fund a worldwide jihad and it doesn't all come from Mideast oil. As you know the Middle East is a major exporter of opium poppy—especially Afghanistan."

The next slide was of a confiscated semi-trailer laden with bales of marijuana and plastic sacks of white-powdered cocaine.

"The U.S. has a bad drug habit, gentlemen. Nearly 100% of methamphetamine and 90% of all cocaine comes across the 2,000-mile U.S.-Mexican border. The majority of Colombian cocaine comes through Mexico as well. Colombian coke is flown into Mexico by airplane and later transshipped across the border. The Zetas control the drug routes in south Texas all the way to Interstate 35—which runs from Laredo to Canada—giving their drug runners easy access to U.S. cities. According to the Justice Department, the Z's have blended in with the Latin community and are now operating from safe houses in six states—Texas, California, Oklahoma, Tennessee, Georgia, and here in Florida. They have purportedly established ties with street gangs and prison gangs to facilitate their operations within the states. In actuality, the Zetas have become a cartel in their own right."

The next slide was a split-screen image of Alvarez and Gonzalez. Both men were in chains and surrounded by layers of U.S. Marshals and DEA agents.

"This is Juan Carlos Alvarez and Cesar Gonzalez—the motive behind the Majestic Star abduction. Both were arrested recently and face a litany of federal charges from drug trafficking to murder. The Zeta leader aboard the Majestic Star, Mendoza, is demanding their immediate release. Alvarez—the man on the left—is the drug boss of Colombia's most powerful cartel: the Cali Cartel. His tentacles are far reaching and we have good reason to believe that he's behind the recent U.S. car bombings and sniper attacks. Gonzalez heads up the notorious Gulf Cartel—

Mexico's largest. Both are as cold and ruthless as they come. Gonzalez is being extradited to the maximum-security La Palma prison west of Mexico City to stand trial there. This could be a problem for us if Mendoza doesn't believe that. Alvarez, however, will remain here in the states and he'll be our negotiating carrot for the release of the 218 hostages."

Ray pressed the remote and a slide of the *Majestic Star* filled the screen.

"That's what we're up against, gentlemen." In summation Ray stepped into the bright projector light, casting his silhouette on the screen. "The Z's are not wannabes. And they're not your average doper goons with more bullets than brains. They are a heavily armed, ultra-violent army of military-trained narco-killers who unleash bloodshed for whoever pays them the highest price. Needless to say, we've got our work cut out for us."

Ray straightened his shoulders and panned the crowd. "Any questions?" When nobody responded, he nodded and the projector went off and the fluorescents came on. "There'll be further briefings as the situation develops. In the interim, you've all got your assignments. Let's get back to work."

Saturday 07:36 Hours – Clearwater Bay Marina

The covered boat slips were sheltered beneath a rust-patched corrugated metal roof, speckled with years of bird droppings. A long wooden wharf ran its full length with short perpendicular landings making up the divided slips. Most of the vessels moored there were charters with signs displaying their fishing rates by the day and half-day. Some had chalkboards aboard positioned to face dockside. One chalked message read: **NEED 2 MORE FOR 2PM.**

A number of boats had already gone offshore while others were still being readied for the day. Busy deckhands were stowing ice, setting out fishing tackle, and hosing down decks. As the deckhands went about their chores, a procession of pelicans waddled up and down the wharf looking for a handout. Cal chuckled when a deckhand shooed one feathered panhandler away by squirting it with a water hose.

WIRED

Cal followed his sister down the weathered planks until she stopped at a boat named *Sol-Mate*. The *"o"* in *"Sol"* was a bright yellow sun, which Cal thought was pretty catchy. He guessed the boat to be about thirty-six feet long with a fourteen-foot beam. It was gull-white with twin fly bridges and a tuna tower on top crowned by a spinning radar scanner. Four outrigger whips were mounted to the tailfin and two teak fighting chairs were anchored to the aft deck. Rigged for sport fishing, the *Sol-Mate* was a real beauty.

"Ahoy there, Captain Brillo," Kathy called out. "Permission to come aboard?"

"Kathy!" A smiling head popped up from the engine compartment. "Great to see you!"

The 40-ish, clean-shaven, fisherman was holding a quart of motor oil and wearing a cap that read: **A BAD DAY ON THE WATER IS BETTER THAN A GOOD DAY AT WORK.** Standing about six-foot, Brillo was wearing a white T-shirt stretched over a muscular upper torso. His cheery face was deeply tanned and his right cheek bulged from a knot of smokeless tobacco. In virtually one movement, he scrambled out of the compartment, wiped his hands on his pants, and hopped onto the wooden landing. After giving Kathy a burly hug, he held her at arm's length and studied her face.

"Howya holding up, kid?" His bright smile evaporated into seriousness. "We're all worried about Skip too, you know. I tried calling you a few minutes ago. Are you okay?"

"As well as can be—under the circumstances. I haven't heard squat from the authorities yet, so I'm still pretty much in the dark."

Belatedly, Kathy introduced Cal and the two men shook hands. Compared to Cal's office-worker hand, Brillo's callused mitt felt like a pork rind. When Brillo removed his cap to arm sweat off his brow, Cal realized why everyone called him Brillo. He had the kinkiest thicket of black hair that Cal'd ever seen on a white man. Trying not to stare, Cal wondered how he kept his hat from popping off.

"Has anybody here seen the Star yet?" Kathy asked.

Brillo nodded. "Yeah, that's the reason I tried calling you. A fishing buddy of mine spotted her earlier this morning. She's about ten miles west-southwest of Clearwater Pass. He says the Coast Guard and Navy have her completely surrounded. Got buoys floating everywhere wrapped with that yellow '**DO NOT CROSS**' tape. He says that ships and helos are swarming all over the place."

Putting on a casual face, Kathy looked off into the distance and launched her first probe. "How close do you suppose a boat could get, Brill?"

Brillo eyed her a little suspiciously. "Well...I wouldn't have any way of knowing. Not too close, I suppose."

Then came probe number two. "Close enough to see the Majestic Star?"

Brillo shrugged uneasily and his eyes skidded away. "Uh-h-h, I seriously doubt it. My buddy said they're really cracking down on boaters trying to sightsee and all. I guess everyone's read the newspapers by now and are curious. Why do you ask?"

Without batting an eyelash, Kathy sprung her trap. "Because I want you to take us out there today, Brill. I've got to see if Skip is okay."

Squirming, Brillo scrunched his shoulders and stuffed his hands in his back pockets. "I-I-I don't know, Kathy," he said haltingly. "I'd like to help you out, but I can't risk losing my Captain's license. I've got a family to feed and fishing's all I know. Besides, we couldn't get that close in a million years. If you got lucky, you might see something through a good pair of binoculars or a telescope, but that's about it."

"Okay, I'll buy a telescope and you can take us out."

Brillo squirmed some more and toed a weathered plank with his shoe. "Geez, I'd really like to, Kathy, but . . . ."

"Oh, come on, Brillo!" Kathy blurted. "It would mean everything to me. I just want to see Skip's ship. I won't get you into any trouble. Please? You're one of Skip's best friends." Cal could hear the pistons in Kathy's guilt machine firing away. "Skip would do it for your wife if you were being held hostage out there." *That's the clincher*, Cal thought. *He's dead meat.* "What do you say?"

Brillo spat into the water and looked at Cal. "Man! I hate it when they lay that guilt trip on you. Don't you?" While Cal nodded sympathetically, Brillo crossed his beefy arms and stared at his feet. After a moment of thinking he looked at Kathy sideways, squinting into the sun. "Well, you're right about one thing. Skip *would* do it for me." Caught between

Kathy Myles and a hard place, Brillo relented. "Okay, I'll do it."

When Kathy's eyes lit up, he poked a finger in her face. "But only if you behave yourself and do exactly as I say. The fishing grounds lie in that area and since I'm a commercial fisherman, the Coasties might cut me some slack. I'm not making any promises, though. We'll see what happens. I'm not gonna buck the whole Coast Guard fleet. If I see Coasties heading our way, we're outta there. Deal?"

Kathy nodded excitedly and Brillo nodded back, with a lot less enthusiasm.

"I've got a charter this morning, but nothing this afternoon. I'll be back at the dock around one. Meet me here and we'll go out then."

With mission accomplished, Kathy jumped into his arms and gave him a giant hug. "Thanks, Brill!" She mashed her cheek against his, making Brillo's face contort. "We'll be here at one o'clock sharp. See you then!"

Not giving Brillo a chance to change his mind, Kathy released his neck and hooked Cal by the arm. As she led her brother down the dock, she waved goodbye to Brillo over her shoulder.

Saturday 07:43 Hours – Group St. Petersburg

After the briefing, Ray stopped by the radio room to check on the progress of the negotiations or lack thereof. Mendoza and the radio operator had been haggling back and forth since early morning; but, from what Ray'd overheard, the Cuban was negotiating, or trying to, and the Zeta gang leader was mostly yelling. Today marked the third day of the standoff and Mendoza was flat out of patience. An escalation of hostilities appeared imminent.

During the early stages of the negotiations, the Cuban ensign had offered the standard tradeoffs while stalling for time—food and water for the release of all passengers; food and water for the release of women and children; food and water for the release of just about anyone. But regardless of the tactic taken, the talks invariably came back to the initial starting point: *Alvarez and Gonzalez.*

After listening to Mendoza rant a while longer, Ray retreated to the quiet of his office. With Gonzalez out of the picture, he needed to study up on Alvarez. He was the big fish anyway. Cesar Gonzalez was a big man in Mexico but just a drug-trafficking pimple compared to Alvarez.

There was no way of proving it, but Ray was convinced that Alvarez was calling the shots from his jail cell via his crooked American lawyers. In Miami there were only two kinds of lawyers: criminal lawyers and lawyer criminals. The snipers, roadside bombers, and hijacking Zetas were merely carrying out the Colombian's directives.

Ray opened Alvarez's dossier and settled back in his chair. From what he knew about Alvarez's past, the recent mayhem fit his M.O. perfectly. He'd been doing it for decades. To explain how a man like him could have risen to such heights, the report began with a history of Colombia's evolution. The country's decades of bloodshed was a sad story in itself.

Colombia: Political Overview 1819 - Present

Colombia gained its independence from Spain in 1819 and afterward became a cauldron of corruption, turmoil, and civil war. In 1948 the assassination of **Liberal Party** leader Jorge Eliécer Gaitán sparked a nationwide uprising against the conservative government. This period of rural and urban violence, known as *La Violencia,* continued from 1948 to 1958 and claimed 200,000 lives. In 1953, the **Conservative Party** proposed a new constitution modeled after Spain's Francisco Franco. But in 1957, when that totalitarian form of government failed to work, both parties approved a coup d'état deposing the dictatorial regime. In 1958, the two parties formed a coalition agreeing to share all government offices equally. Called the **National Front,** this coalition brought some form of stability to the political scene for the next 16 years. After the coalition ended in 1974, Liberals and Conservatives continued to cooperate, but escalating violence from the guerillas and drug traffickers rocked the country's stability. In 1991, a new constitution took effect providing for a centralized republican form of government. Today, Colombia has a free and open political system with a President elected by popular vote and a Congress composed of a House of Representatives and Senate.

WIRED

Colombia: Peasant/Rebel Movement

The rebel-guerilla movement began in the 1920's and 1930's when peasants organized against harsh working conditions imposed on them by wealthy coffee plantation owners. The use of force in reaction to peasant protests worsened the conflict and by the late 1940's the peasant resistance had evolved into an armed self-defense movement. Government aggression toward this rebellion led to the expulsion of many peasants from their homes and farms. After being forcibly displaced, some of these peasants banded together in self-defense and countered with guerilla warfare. Over time, their resistance evolved into a socialistic-communistic revolutionary force. For years, dozens of rebel groups operated independently—unorganized and poorly armed. When the drug trade exploded in the 60's and 70's, rebels seized the financial opportunity by "taxing" the coca farmers. The **Colombian Army** perceived this drug cultivation as a source of funding for the guerillas and punished the peasant settlers as criminals, eradicating their illegal fields of coca and opium poppies—the raw materials for cocaine and heroin. This action merely pushed farmers deeper into the hands of the rebels, who provided armed protection for their families and farms for a 10% tax on their crops. The millions made from the narcotics trade helped finance the rebels' war effort, providing them uniforms, better weaponry, and modern communications. In time, a number of guerilla groups joined forces to form the Marxist-Leninist army: **Fuerzas Armadas Revolucionarias de Colombia** (Revolutionary Armed Forces of Colombia, or **FARC**). Today, FARC is 17,000 troops strong and controls rural Colombian countryside the size of California, which they defend against the government's war on drugs. The rebels tout themselves as the "Army for the People" fighting for civil rights and change within the country. However, the Colombian government views their narco-guerilla activities as organized crime and considers **FARC** a drug cartel. Government officials also accuse FARC of kidnapping civilians and extorting businesses for millions of dollars, citing that FARC is nothing more than camouflage-clad gangsters and dope peddlers. Spokesmen for FARC vehemently deny these charges, describing themselves as freedom fighters opposed to the corrupt and uncaring Colombian government.

WIRED

Colombia: Illicit Drug Traffickers

While the politicians and guerillas fought for military control of Colombia, the drug cartels flourished by playing both sides. By bribing government officials, the traffickers were left to operate virtually free from prosecution or extradition. By forging business relationships with the guerillas, the traffickers were guaranteed an uninterrupted supply as long as a "fee" was paid for every airplane leaving rebel-controlled airstrips. Through bribery and complicity, drug trafficking proliferated throughout the 80' and 90's with two major cartels emerging—the **Medellin Cartel** led by Pablo Escobar and the **Cali Cartel** controlled by Jorge Luis Ochoa. What the cartels couldn't achieve by bribery, they achieved through intimidation and brute force. In 1982 a car bomb exploded outside the residence of the Colombian Justice Minister. In 1985 drug traffickers and guerrillas joined together to seize the Palace of Justice in Bogotá leaving 100 dead including the president of the Supreme Court and 10 other justices. On August 18th, 1989, Colombian Liberal Party presidential candidate Luis Carlos Galán was killed by drug traffickers at a campaign rally in Bogotá. On March 22nd, 1990, gunmen shot down Colombian Patriotic Union presidential candidate Bernando Jamamillo Ossa at an airport in Bogotà. Later that year two other presidential hopefuls were assassinated. In December 1993, the notorious Medellin Cartel was severely crippled when the Colombian National Police killed their billionaire boss **Pablo Escobar**, leaving Escobar's hatchet man and enforcer, **Juan Carlos Alvarez**, in charge of the shaken cartel. Ultimately a truce broke down between the Medellin and Cali cartels and a bloody war erupted. In the aftermath, thousands of warring gang members and Colombian citizens were killed. By 1996 all Cali kingpins were behind bars and Alvarez seized control of the Cali cartel. After merging both cartels together, he monopolized most all drug exportation from Colombia. Today, Alvarez runs the multi-billion dollar cocaine syndicate from his heavily fortified jungle compound on the outskirts of Cali in western Colombia. Via his global underworld network, he allegedly controls 80% of cocaine and heroin distribution worldwide.

Ray stopped reading for a moment to assimilate the information. Colombia's woes were akin to many Third World countries whose poverty, corruption, and unrest forever threatened to rip apart their fragile framework of society. While the Colombian politicians spent decades warring over self-interests, the needs of the common people had been ignored.

Faced with unemployment and starvation, peasants found themselves either growing poppy crops or joining the payrolls of subversive rebel groups. To help fund their cause, the rebels made pacts with the drug traffickers whose money was plentiful and easy. But their collusion with the cartels tainted their credibility and made them appear as crooked as the politicians whom they railed against. Taking a different direction, the rebels tried their hand at extorting money from business owners and the wealthy, performing an estimated 3,000 kidnappings annually. This provided FARC a stream of income apart from drug trafficking, but it painted them as wrongdoers instead of liberators.

Greed, corruption, and ongoing poverty had spawned violence in Colombia since the country's inception—an endless cycle feeding upon itself. Even today, depending on where one stood, the good guys and the bad guys were hotly contested. So, despite the billions of war-against-drugs dollars poured into Colombia from U.S. coffers, there had been little progress made in terms of the three-way struggle between the government, drug traffickers, and rebel factions.

Nor was there any end in sight for the miserable Colombian citizens caught in the crossfire.

Saturday 07:45 Hours – Clearwater Bay Marina

On their way back to the parking lot, Cal and Kathy passed by an old fisherman dressed in faded dungarees and wearing a dark-blue knit cap. Using gnarled but experienced hands, he was working a cast net from the marina's concrete seawall. The man was slightly bent with a shock of solid white hair and full matching beard—the Norman Rockwell sort. His face was deeply weathered from years of outdoor work and he had bushy-white eyebrows shrouding his crow's-foot eyes.

Unaware of Cal's curiosity, the sailor went about casting and retrieving his net, emptying his catch into a five-gallon pail. Every so often he would remove a larger fish from the bucket and toss it back in the waterway. He was gathering baitfish, Cal thought, probably how he made his living these days—selling bait to the marinas.

After decades at sea, was this the old salt's lot in life? Gathering bait for the weekend fishermen in their fancy $50,000 fishing boats?

Cal was feeling sorry for the old man when he suddenly noticed something. Every time the guy emptied a good catch into his pail, the corners of his eyes crinkled and a vague smile crossed his leathery face. He wasn't unhappy or bitter—quite the reverse, actually. He was still doing what he had devoted a lifetime to doing: making a living from the sea and loving it.

Prior to reaching the parking lot, Cal stopped at a dive boat named *Tanks-a-Lot*. As he perused the air tanks and dive gear aboard, he turned to Kathy with a question. "Do you know this guy?"

"Sure, it's Captain Ernie's boat. One of Skip's poker buddies." She tilted her head to one side and looked at him curiously. "Why?"

"Just wondering." Cal's voice sounded wistful. "I used to love diving—the deeper the better. But I haven't gone down since getting out of the Navy."

As Cal stared at the scuba gear, it brought back a boatload of memories—both good and bad. In a way it seemed like yesterday. In another, it seemed like a millennium ago.

"Cal? Are you okay?"

Kathy's faraway voice interrupted his musing. "Mmm? Oh, sure. Just thinking. Let's go get that telescope."

Saturday 08:15 Hours – Group St. Petersburg

Four phone calls later Ray picked up Alvarez's dossier and went straight to the biography section. In reading it, he hoped to gain some insight into the Colombian's nefarious nature; perhaps catch a glimpse of the diseased DNA that spawned such a depraved monster.

To outwit ones enemy, one had to know their strengths and weaknesses. Ray needed to get inside Alvarez's head—where dark tainted things lurked and bred, twisting and spreading like perverted vines. Although Ray loathed everything about the man, he respected Alvarez's brilliance. He was a racketeering genius and deserving of his *Most*

WIRED

Wanted ranking.

Juan Carlos Alvarez: Confidential Biography

Juan Carlos Alvarez, age 52, was born in the coffee-producing region of Manizales, Colombia, the only child of an upper class Roman Catholic family. As a boy, Alvarez worshipped the Colombian rebels and banditos—heroes of the common class. As a teenager, he was attracted to the glamorous and high profile lifestyles of the wealthy drug barons. At 16, he formed his first gang, stealing cars and running extortion rackets. After several brushes with the law, his concerned family shipped him off to school in the United States. Six years later he received an MBA from **Notre Dame** where his I. Q. was measured at a genius level 153. When returning home from college, Alvarez resumed his criminal career by smuggling arms and contraband. After several years of smuggling, he had accumulated enough money to break into the lucrative drug trade. By that time cocaine was the USA's drug of choice and Alvarez's springboard for building a drug empire. He started out by buying cocaine from the producers and selling it to the traffickers. Later, he cut out the middleman and smuggled the drugs himself. By the time he was thirty, he was charging 35% on all drugs leaving South America. By the time he reached forty, he controlled the majority of cocaine distribution worldwide. Spreading his wealth wisely, Alvarez gave away millions to key government officials. These political bribes bought him certain protection from prosecution and deportation, but not from the **Colombian National Police**. Yet, whenever the CNP did manage to jail him, Alvarez resorted to bombings and assassination to get the charges against him dismissed. In 1997 the Colombian judge he was slated to face was found mysteriously decapitated three days before his trial. In 1998 another was found with his throat sliced from ear-to-ear and his tongue pulled through the gaping throat wound—Alvarez's signature "Colombian Necktie" trademark. In both cases, all criminal charges were inexplicably dropped. To protect his billion-dollar empire from rivals, Alvarez terrorized his enemies in the same brutal fashion. When that didn't work, he killed their families— reputedly slaughtering entire generations of family members including women and children. Police records reveal that many of his male rivals were first tortured by having holes drilled in their kneecaps. Since 1986 an estimated 80,000 people have died violently in the Medellin area alone, 90% of those deaths being young people from ages 12 to 24. By the nineties Alvarez's underworld tentacles had reached global proportions. In the mid-90's he formed alliances with the **Mexican Cartels** to smuggle cocaine and heroin into the U.S. During that same period he established ties with the poppy-producing Islamic leadership in **Afghanistan**. In 1996, the **Taliban** militia overran the capital of Kabul, and the new Taliban regime "officially" stopped producing cocaine. Secretively, however, cocaine was an ongoing export as well as gun trafficking. Via his link with the Taliban, Alvarez was introduced to other fundamentalist groups such as **Al-Qaeda** and **Hezbollah**. This led to Islamic operations in South America, concentrated mainly in Foz do Iguacu, Brazil, Ouerto Iguazu, Argentina, and Cuidad del Este, Paraguay. In the town of **Maicao**, Colombia, 70% of local commerce is controlled by the Islamic community, most of it drug related and under the auspices of Alvarez himself. Until his recent arrest, Alvarez resided with his wife and two children in Cali, 185 miles southwest of Bogotá, behind the walls of a lavish jungle fortress protected 24/7 by a private army of Narco-guerillas. While impossible to verify, conservative estimates of Alvarez's personal fortune tops $5 billion dollars. END OF REPORT.

Ray closed the dossier and stared silently at its cover. Alvarez was a product of his environment. He had been raised in a country where violence was the norm; where parked buses exploded killing hundreds; where decapitated politicians were found lying in their beds; where the poor grew poorer and the rich were kidnapped routinely to beget ransom money for the rebel armies. Where human life was neither special nor sacred.

Ray placed the dossier in a desk drawer and closed it. Alvarez was one of the best criminal minds of the 20th Century. He was also a filthy-rich megalomaniac with a blind lust for power and an unconscionable proclivity for violence.

He was wrongdoing's crème de la crème...iniquity's worst of the very worst...evil beyond the pale. Alvarez was the consummate enemy and would make a very formidable opponent.

WIRED

Saturday 08:28 Hours – The "Majestic Star"

Skip was back in his cabin, stretched out on his bunk with the acid building in his stomach. Something was up. When he had reported to the wheelhouse earlier to relieve Neal, Gold-Tooth was on the ship-to-shore radio ranting in Spanish. Skip couldn't understand what he was saying, but the Mexican was more agitated than usual and unmistakably hostile.

More troubling than that was how Gold-Tooth reacted when he entered the wheelhouse. While still raving like a lunatic, the Mexican waved his arm in a shooing gesture for Skip to leave at once. Mohammad seized the occasion, with gusto, to bulldoze Skip out the doorway until his back struck the catwalk railing. This roughhousing inflamed Mendoza all the more, who swept his arm through the air with greater irritation, ordering them to vacate now. Obeying his boss, Mohammad prodded Skip down the bridge deck with the point of his barrel. Once Skip was back inside his cabin, the Arab planted himself in a chair outside the door, feeling much better for it.

As Skip lay staring at the ceiling, his mind ran in every direction. Clearly, something major was going down or he wouldn't have been expelled from the bridge and confined to his cabin. Something bad was going to happen today—he could feel it in his gut—something very, very bad.

The longer Skip stared at the ceiling, the fuzzier his thoughts became. The prolonged lack of sleep had used him up and the fatigue in his body went to the core. This was no time for a catnap, but he was at the nadir of his biological rhythm and couldn't keep his eyes open.

Whenever Skip caught himself dozing off, he would shake his head vigorously and rub a hand across his sleepy face. But this only revived him temporarily and as more time passed the ceiling tiles blurred and he fell asleep without knowing it.

And for the first time in years, Skip dreamed of the night that forever changed his life.

Mekong Delta, Vietnam – 1974

It was a dark night as his SEAL Team came stealthily ashore in their eleven-man rubber raft. The sky was overcast and the moon was in its fourth quarter, ideal for a night operation. After being dropped at their insertion point, they rendezvoused with another SEAL Team one kilometer away. Once teaming up, they began humping through the dense underbrush and ankle-deep salt mud of the mangrove swamps toward their assigned target.

Their mission was to destroy a riverine fuel depot in the Secret Zone, a free-fire area under total enemy control. Located on the Vinh Long River, the depot was known to be actively supplying gasoline and diesel to the Vietcong sampans and junks. These vessels were the lifeblood of the VC, running the inland river channels at night serving as messengers and transporting troops, weapons, and ammunition. Without fuel the boats would be rendered useless, thus disrupting the VC supply chain—at least for a while.

An hour into the operation the SEALs were crossing a pitch-dark rice paddy. It was an oppressively hot night and the muddy water brought welcome relief to their overheated bodies. Their cammies were already drenched in sweat and they had been eaten alive by the perspiration-attracted mosquitoes and fire ants. Due to the VC's keen sense of smell, the usage of insect repellant and deodorant was strictly forbidden.

The depot was now less than a klick away and the whole operation should have been a cakewalk. But while wading through the waist-high water all hell broke loose. Charlie had somehow found them out and taken up position behind a berm line for a counterattack. In a fraction of a second their protective cover of darkness was replaced by the flickering amber glow of illumination flares drifting aloft from mini-parachutes.

Caught out in the open, the VC were cutting them to ribbons and the SEAL team was taking heavy casualties. With men falling about him, Skip was retreating for cover when a blinding explosion sent him reeling beneath the murky water. As his face sank into the thick bottom mud a numbing sensation spread throughout his body and the blare of battle began to fade. While lying in a dazed stupor, the enveloping water gave him a false sense of security, as if he were safe from the hostilities above. Then the battle noise faded even further until it was altogether removed. Languishing on the bottom in a semiconscious state, his shell-shocked mind regressed to a day five decades past.

WIRED

It was Christmas and flashbulbs were popping all around him as he excitedly unwrapped his gift. While tearing off the wrapping paper, he recognized the box and grinned from ear-to-ear in wide-eyed anticipation. It was a new *Fanner 50* cap pistol and holster. With sparkling boyish eyes, he loaded the pistol with a red roll of caps. Then, with the Polaroid camera flashing away, he pointed the gun toward the ceiling and filled the air with sulfur, firing as fast as he could pull the trigger. *BAM-BAM-BAM-BAM-BAM-BAM-BAM!*

Suddenly his ears were ringing and a piercing pain tore at his temples. As the camera flashed brighter and brighter, the pounding in his head throbbed harder and harder. He closed his eyes to shut out the flashes and covered his ears to suppress the pain, but the hurting refused to desist. When the pain became more than he could bear, he cried out to his mother for solace.

His mother gathered him up and cradled his head in her lap, consoling him as she gently stroked his hair. And with each motherly stroke, the pain lessened more and more until it all but left him. Her tender caresses felt so comforting and soothing that he just wanted to sleep...to close his eyes and sleep...go sound asleep...

Alarms sounded in Skip's head and his eyes popped open in stark terror. The living room was gone and he found himself inexplicably underwater. He strained to see, but the water was dark and his lungs convulsed for air. As his head cleared, the sounds of battle returned and he instinctively remembered where he was. In an adrenaline-boosted panic, he sunk his palms into the squishy bottom muck and pushed upward with all his strength.

Skip broke the surface coughing up muddy water while sucking in as much air as his lungs could handle. Instantly the gooks zeroed in on his position and a storm of bullets came whirring at him—each near miss personifying passing death. Driven by panic, he labored through the waist-high marsh water but its consistency was like liquid lead. Blood was oozing from his ears and his night vision was gone; but he fled anyway, blindly, without knowing where.

When Skip's night sight partly restored, he found himself encircled by a blazing ring of muzzle flashes. His instincts told him to run, to get out of the open, but his disoriented brain couldn't distinguish which way.

114

WIRED

He lacked all sense of direction. Unable to discern friendly fire from enemy fire, he twisted around in the water in a confused circle, enthralled by the starburst muzzle flashes and greenish streaks of tracer rounds. It was if the whole battle now centered on him and his life had become the grand prize. At that instant Skip realized he was going to die and it was enough to make a scared soldier pray.

Then he heard voices—American voices—coming from somewhere behind him. But the thunder of battle had stuffed cotton in his ears and their shouts sounded small and muffled. He spun around and plowed toward the voices with bullets narrowly missing him, some leaving long white tails as they sliced through the water like miniature torpedoes.

While slogging madly through the sludge, Skip tripped over an underwater object and fell facedown into the water. Groping around on the muddy bottom, he felt an arm and realized it was a fallen SEAL brother. He didn't know if the man was dead or alive but felt duty-bound to rescue him all the same.

While underwater, Skip hoisted the soldier over his shoulder and broke the surface in a backbreaking run. As he labored toward the shouts, the water grew shallower and easier to negotiate. By now his night vision had restored and he could make out the grass reeds around the edge of the paddy. The reeds meant the safety of shore and their sight inspired him to push harder. Maybe he wasn't going to die after all. With some luck and God's grace, maybe he would make it out alive.

Maybe.

With just a few yards to go, Skip felt a stinging sensation in his left leg and was surprised when the leg collapsed beneath him. As he and the wounded SEAL fell into the muddy water, his leg exploded in crying pain—the delayed reaction of severed nerve endings winning out over adrenaline. With no alternative but to move on or die, he gritted against the pain and rebounded quickly—using his good leg to propel him forward.

He was almost there now, just a few feet to go. But the burning in his leg was searing and its muscle strength was failing fast. Hoping to reach shore before the leg gave out, he lumbered sideways, taking half steps while dragging the unconscious SEAL by the ammo belt.

Suddenly a tracer round whined past his left ear, so close that Skip felt its phosphorus heat. On the heels of it came an onslaught of enemy fire that sliced and diced the water all round him. Coming to his defense, his SEAL brothers in the reeds returned fire on full automatic, laying down a barrage of flying lead while simultaneously egging him on.

Drawing on his last scrap of strength, Skip crawled out of the water into the tall reeds, dragging the limp-bodied SEAL behind him. Once out of enemy sight he released the man and went down on all fours, retching up foul smelling swamp water. His leg and eardrums were bleeding, he was covered in muck, and his boots were filled with slimestuff.

Altogether used up, he sprawled onto his back and stared up at the smoke from the ground flares marking their pin-downed position. With his chest heaving up and down, he rolled his head toward the fallen SEAL to see the man was still breathing. At least he hadn't risked all life and limb to drag a lifeless corpse from the water.

Minutes later Skip heard the thumpity-thump-thump of approaching helicopters. When a UH-1 medevac helicopter and HH-3E Jolly Green Giant appeared in the night sky above him, he smiled at them through the swirling smoke and wild whipping elephant grass. The 1st Cavalry Airmobile had arrived.

The Huey was taking ground fire from all quarters and both door gunners were blazing away, spitting out tracers every other round to mark their fire. As the M-60 machine guns chased after the scattering VC, Skip propped himself up on one elbow and watched the gook bastards run for it. When his head swooned, he laid back down and watched the M-60's fire away—grateful to be alive. He pictured Charlie beating a retreat in their black PJ's and it brought a feeble smile to his mud-smeared face.

Moments later his head swooned again and the shadows around him turned bright white, then yellow, then a dull orangish-red with dancing white dots. With a flutter of his eyelids, he slipped into unconsciousness next to the soldier he had so valiantly saved.

The next day Skip learned that the SEAL brother had survived. His name was Stringer.

Saturday 10:24 Hours – Group St. Petersburg

When the Cuban complained of sporadic radio interference in the St.

WIRED

Petersburg vicinity, Ray reassigned him to Station Sand Key for resumption of the talks. The *Majestic Star* was riding at anchor off Sand Key's western shore and her radio signal was received much stronger there. This relocation solved the interference problem, but it forced Ray and the ensign to communicate remotely by phone or secure radio. To maintain radio privacy and to prevent public eavesdropping, their radio communiqués were being scrambled. It was an inconvenient and rather cumbersome way of operating but an unfortunate necessity.

After a three-day series of stall tactics, the talks had reached a standstill. Mendoza, who had been vehemently against negotiating in the first place, was fed up with the same old tired excuses: that Gonzalez was in Mexican custody and the Federales would not bring him back; that a number of U.S. government agencies had to grant clearance before Alvarez could be released; that everything humanly possible was being done to expedite the process; that if one hair was harmed on a passenger's head, the release procedure would come to a screeching halt.

In point of fact, many of the obstacles presented to Mendoza were not fabrications at all. There *were* a number of government agencies involved and it *had* taken Ray two days to cut through the bureaucratic red tape for permission to bring Alvarez to St. Petersburg. U.S. Marshals would be delivering the drug czar sometime this afternoon.

Ray had no intention of releasing Alvarez, of course, none whatsoever. But when push came to shove—which Ray believed would ultimately occur—Alvarez could be put on the radio to appease the Zetas. Hearing Alvarez's voice would show Mendoza that the Coast Guard was negotiating in good faith; that Alvarez had been physically relocated from Miami to someplace nearby; that measurable progress was being made in terms of his release.

If nothing else, it would buy more time and that's what Ray so desperately needed. Time to figure a way out of this deadlock; time to save the lives of the two hundred passengers; time to salvage his military career hanging in the balance. *More time.*

Saturday 10:40 Hours – The "Majestic Star"

Skip awoke from his Vietnam nightmare with a jolt, lathered in sweat and sitting straight up in his bunk. Unsure of his whereabouts at first, he panned the room with startled eyes before realizing he was inside his cabin aboard the *Majestic Star*.

Peeved at himself for sleeping at such a critical time, he checked his watch to discover two hours had lapsed. Swearing to himself, he rolled off of the bunk and stomped into the head. The 'Nam dream always left him jittery and its remnants lingered like a hellish hangover. To help expunge it, he splashed water over his sweating face and then held his head under the spigot. He had more pressing matters to think about.

After blotting his face with a hand towel, Skip raked his hair straight back by the fingers. He would have given a week's pay for a hot shower, but, by his order, showers were not permitted. Not because the kidnappers had deemed it so—cause he privately wondered when any of them had last bathed—but because he was conserving the ship's fresh water supply.

Still angry with himself, Skip walked to the cabin's only porthole and looked out. When seeing no activity on deck, he pressed his nose against the glass and strained his eyes left and right. The only visible sign of life was the scuffed work boots belonging to Mohammad in the chair outside his door. Off in the distance there was a 110' island class patrol boat patrolling the perimeter, a big vessel for these local waters. It was one of several keeping tabs on the *Majestic Star*.

While watching the ship glide along, Skip's thoughts crept back to his Vietnam experience. Through some God-given miracle, he and Cal had survived that apocalyptic night. Still, they had witnessed the fall of many comrades—young men who had never left home before; young men with their whole lives ahead of them; young men with troubled wives and anxious girlfriends waiting for them back home. That left scars of its own—invisible ones—the kind that never heal; the kind that makes one feel guilty just for living. Survivor's guilt.

Ever since that fateful night, he and Cal had been spiritually inseparable. There was a bond between them that had strengthened with the passage of time. It was as if their friendship had formed a persona of its own—a third identity, of sorts.

When together, Cal wasn't a lawyer and Skip wasn't a boat captain. Nor were they the young Navy SEAL lads of days gone by. They were kindred spirits...brothers-in-arms...two men that shouldn't be alive. They shared the same pain and fought the same demons. They were two souls hellishly bound by the vestige of spilled blood and carnage, each unable to obliterate its remembrance and both still under obligation to fate.

As the patrol boat vanished from view, Skip thought about how strange fate worked. Had Cal not survived that night, he would have never met and married Kathy.

"There's no tellin' where I'd be right now," he muttered at the glass, backing away. Then, as an afterthought, he added: "But I sure as heck wouldn't be on a hostage ship wired with explosives—that's for sure."

Saturday 11:45 Hours – Group St. Petersburg

"Group St. Petersburg, this is Station Sand Key hailing Admiral Hanna. Over."

Ray was seated two workstations down from the on-duty radio operator, rereading the biography on Alvarez. At hearing the Cuban's voice, Ray closed the dossier and gestured that he would answer the hail. Giving an affirmative nod, the RO stretched his body sideways and slid the desk mike in front of the admiral.

"Hanna here, Ensign. Go ahead."

"Yes, Admiral, Mendoza has just issued a deadline. If Alvarez is not aboard the Majestic Star by 15:00 hours, ten hostages will be executed." Ray looked at the wall clock—*three hours.* "He made no similar demand about Gonzalez, which leads me to believe that he's buying our extradition story. Do we have an ETA on Alvarez's arrival from Miami? Over."

Ray knew this moment would come, but his stomach still churned like an old washing machine. "Negatory, Sand Key. He's scheduled to arrive here sometime mid-afternoon. I'll contact Miami Group and get a precise ETA. Roger?"

"Roger, sir. Please notify this station the moment you get one. Over."

"Will do. In the meanwhile, Ensign, you've *got* to buy us more time. Alvarez *will* be here this afternoon. It's imperative that you make that understood. That we *will not* stand for any executions. NONE! Copy? If nothing further, Group St. Petersburg out."

"I copy, sir, but Mendoza severed communications directly after issuing his ultimatum. All hails since then have gone unanswered. Even so, I will keep trying to raise him. Sand Key out."

Ray released the key and stared into space. His sense of dread and inevitably was here and now. Mendoza meant it this time—he would waste all ten of them.

"Damn him!"

As the storm inside Ray gathered force, he pushed off the console—rolling his chair backwards and toppling the microphone in the process. At reaching mid-room he sprang cat-like to his feet, furthering the chair's rearward thrust. By the time his chair crashed into the wall behind him, he was standing over the cowering radio operator.

"Get Miami Group on a landline. I need an ETA on Alvarez and I need it NOW! There are ten lives at stake here and we're running out of goddamn time!"

Saturday 12:10 Hours – The "Majestic Star"

Skip was hunched over his desk, moving food around on his plate with a fork—more worried than ever. Minutes ago, Mohammad had delivered his meal and left without explanation. Still, the glint in the Arab's eyes and the shifty smirk on his face told Skip that something was up.

Generally, Skip was escorted to the dining area on the sundeck to eat with the passengers. He understood Gold-Tooth's motive for letting him mingle at mealtimes, but went along with it anyway to keep in touch with the passengers. He was their only link to the outside world and they relished his daily visits. Though Skip had little news to share, his mere presence as captain gave them some semblance of order in their now-chaotic lives.

Of course, that's exactly what Gold-Tooth wanted him to do. Skip noticed right away how differently the guards behaved when amongst the passengers. They seldom raised their weapons and often let them dangle casually from their slings. At any other time Skip had a gun barrel in his face or stuck in his back, but not during mealtimes. Recognizing this fundamental change in behavior, Skip had to give Gold-Tooth credit for his obvious cunning. Maybe he was a killer, but he wasn't a stupid killer.

WIRED

Although Skip's daily visits boosted passenger morale, they had the opposite effect on him—adding more guilt to his already guilt-ridden conscience. In reality he was just a figurehead, a token, and an emasculated one at that. His authority as captain had been siphoned off along with his manhood and he was offering little more than false encouragement. He felt like one of those televangelist charlatans on cable TV peddling instant salvation for cash.

Twice each day the passengers would gather around him and ask the same question: "When are we going home, Captain?" And although he wasn't sure if they ever would, he would paste on a counterfeit smile and respond with: "Soon!"

While a little deceit was necessary to calm the masses, the disingenuousness of it still bothered him. Even so, it was important to instill hope. Without hope people become desperate and do desperate things. Passenger welfare was his number one concern and he didn't want anybody getting themselves killed. So, for their sake, he allowed himself to be used.

Skip shoved his half-eaten plate of food away and rose to his feet. He didn't have much of an appetite. For the thousandth time, he walked over to the porthole and peered out. Something was brewing, something that Gold-Tooth didn't want him to see or overhear. He had been physically ejected from the bridge, locked in his cabin, and not allowed to mingle with the passengers. It all added up to no good and he felt heavily pressed to do something. *But what?*

Exasperated, Skip stretched out on the bunk and clasped his hands behind his head. He had to think. In all probability, Gold-Tooth had drawn a line in the sand by issuing some sort of ultimatum. That's why the Mexican had placed him under wraps; so he wouldn't interfere. The negotiations, which had been going poorly in the first place, were probably at an impasse.

Too agitated to remain still, Skip sat up on the edge of his bunk and stared sullenly at the floor. The fear of the unknown was a tormenting thing in itself. Worse yet, was knowing that something dreadful was about to happen and being powerless to prevent it—*totally* powerless.

WIRED

With a high-powered telescope guaranteed to bring in the rings around Saturn, Kathy and Cal wheeled into the marina. When passing through the gates, Kathy spotted a media van parked by the ticket office with its remote broadcast antenna raised high in the air.

"Uh-oh," she muttered, covering the side of her face.

As Kathy drove past the building, Cal observed a female reporter standing prim and proper in front of the *Majestic Star's* empty berth. She was talking into a microphone and facing a shoulder-held TV camera supported by a bearded cameraman wearing baggy shorts.

The last thing Kathy needed was for the local news media to start hounding her wherever she went. She could hear their questions now . . .

"How does it feel to have your husband's life in the hands of international terrorists?"

"What went through your mind when you first learned of your husband's capture?"

"What will you do if your husband doesn't survive the ordeal?"

Kathy dodged a pothole and whipped into a slant parking space next to the covered boat slips. Brillo wasn't back yet from his morning charter, so Cal went inside the ship store to buy a soft drink. Trying to remain inconspicuous, Kathy raised the white convertible top for cover and watched the news crew through her rearview mirror. The cameraman was now setting up a tripod and the girl reporter was smearing on more lipstick.

Kathy was studying the newsgirl in the mirror when something ice-cold touched her neck. She jumped with a start to find a sweating can of cola sticking through her side window. For some warped reason, Cal had always gotten a kick out of practically scaring her to death.

Cal was still chuckling when the *Sol-Mate* pulled into the marina, right on time. Leaning against Kathy's door, Cal waved at the arriving boat and Brillo waved back through the windshield. Once all moored up, the deckhand emptied the ice chests and strung fish side-by-side on a wire clothesline display on the dock. Brillo snapped a souvenir photo of the proud fishermen standing next to their catch and then the deckhand proceeded to fillet them. As he skillfully sliced and diced, he tossed the

122

carcasses to a brood of waiting pelicans that flapped and skirmished after every prize, hungrily swallowing them whole. While this was taking place Brillo strode over to Kathy's car, scoping out the *Channel 10 News* van as he walked.

"Hi, guys. Pretty good catch today." Brillo removed his polarized sunglasses to reveal twin white marks on the bridge of his nose. "Kinda warm out, but the winds are light and the seas are flat. Always makes for nice fishing." He then eyeballed Kathy curiously, who was scrunched down behind the steering wheel wearing Cal's *Florida Gators* cap. "What's up with her?" he asked Cal.

"She's incognito." Cal stifled a grin and nodded at the news crew. "Hiding from the paparazzi."

Kathy shushed Cal with a mean-looking frown and scrunched down further in her seat.

"Yeah, well, maybe we should shove off before they decide to come over here," Brillo said while scrutinizing them. "We don't need any publicity." He looked at Cal and nodded toward the Gulf. "Something's going on offshore. There's beaucoup helos swarming all over the place and I counted four big cutters circling the Star. Besides that, there's a humongous Navy Destroyer anchored off Sand Key, the kind with those Tomahawk missiles. Spooky."

"Oh, m'God!" Kathy exclaimed, sitting up straight. "What's going on out there, Brill?"

Right away, Brillo cringed inside for saying anything to upset her. "Oh, probably nothing. Just a show of force of some kind." He and Cal traded glances. "I'm sure it's nothing to worry about. After we hose down the deck and take on some fuel, we'll put out to sea and have a look. Okay?" Kathy nodded, but sensed that Brillo was hiding something. "I don't know how close we'll be able to get, though. They've got the area sealed off pretty tight." He and Cal exchanged another knowing look. "Did you get that telescope?"

"Sure did, Cap," Cal smiled, concealing his worry. "And it's a real beauty. I'll go get it."

While traipsing toward the car, Cal walked with his head down. "I don't like the sound of this crap," he grumbled at the asphalt. "This thing is escalating and the longer it goes on, the more likely people are gonna

WIRED

get hurt."

Cal reached into the backseat and ripped open a cardboard box. After removing the telescope, he rested it on his shoulder and marched back to the boat slip like a sentinel on guard duty. Five minutes later the *Sol-Mate* was threading the red and green channel markers in its approach to the drawbridge. As Brillo throttled down for the *No Wake Zone*, Cal scaled the ladder to the flybridge and sat down beside him on the bench seat. Kathy was slouched in a teak fighting chair facing the stern, holding onto her can of soda.

When the boat passed beneath the drawbridge, the aging *Tigers* fan stuck his head out the window and waved down at them. Three minutes later the *Sol-Mate* sailed under the archway of the Clearwater Pass Bridge and entered the gleaming Gulf of Mexico. Upon clearing the rock jetty, Cal took in the horizon-to-horizon expanse of brilliant aquamarine water. From high atop the flybridge it was a dazzling sight and he couldn't imagine why he'd ever left it.

Before conferring with Brillo, Cal checked over his shoulder to find Kathy staring impassively at the boat's roiling wake. He'd been waiting to have a private word with Brillo out of Kathy's earshot and the noisy diesels now gave him the chance.

"It sounds like this thing's coming to a head, Brillo. What do you think is really going on?"

"Only one way to find out." With a sly wink, Brillo reached under his seat and produced a new radio of some kind still in the box. "It's a radio scanner with a built-in descrambler. Illegal as hell without a license, but I know where to get 'em. Ever since the hijacking, the Coasties have been scrambling their radio signal for security reasons. They use a voice privacy module that digitizes the voice and encrypts the data being transmitted. Sounds like a bunch of gibberish on my regular radio. But this baby should tell us what's going on. If you'll take the wheel, I can hook it up in no time." When Cal nodded yes, Brillo gave him instructions. "Okay, once you clear the bell buoy up ahead, set a 260-degree course and give her enough throttle to plane out."

The two men swapped seats and Cal steered in the direction of the bell buoy. The sunlight reflecting off the water was near blinding and he was glad that he had worn his sunglasses. Once the *Sol-Mate* cleared the

#1 buoy, Cal turned the wheel until the compass needle pointed to 260-degrees. Then he spun his cap around backwards so it wouldn't blow off and gave the diesels full throttle. Instantly the bow raised and the boat lunged forward. When it reached cruising speed, the bow dropped and Cal adjusted the trim tabs until the fiberglass hull skimmed smoothly across the surface.

Kathy was deep in thought and unaware of the activity going on behind her. Something was up and she didn't like it. She could tell by the way Brillo shrugged at her questions and stammered with his answers. And those secretive little glances between he and Cal had not gone unnoticed on her. Something silent passed between them.

Normally this would have angered her, for she despised being treated like—heaven forbid—a woman. She wasn't a frail little flower for petesake and she couldn't understand the deep-seated male need to shield their women from the truth. But they meant well—trying to spare her worry and all—so she couldn't be too upset with them. Still, she resented the baby treatment.

While Cal stayed the course, Brillo spliced wires and ran antenna cable. Minutes later the scanner was ready to go and Brillo pressed the power button with an impish grin. Responding instantaneously, the digital readout began whizzing through the multitude of preprogrammed frequencies. As it did so, Brillo pointed out its other features to Cal. As well as VHF and military bands, it was capable of picking up UHF bands and police channels.

Receiving an approving nod from Cal, Brillo watched proudly as it skimmed through the frequencies. When it found a channel in use, the scanner locked on it. And if the signal was scrambled, it was automatically unscrambled. However, since there were hundreds of possible frequencies, Brillo cautioned it might take a while to find the channel in use by the Coasties.

Three minutes later, the scanner landed the frequency they were searching for.

Saturday 13:25 Hours – Group St. Petersburg

"Group St. Petersburg, this is Station Sand Key hailing. Over."

"Roger, Sand Key. This is Admiral Hanna. Go ahead."

"I just made comms with the Majestic Star, sir. No extensions—no negotiating. If Alvarez isn't on board by 15:00 hours, the executions will begin. That was the extent of it, sir. Over."

"Well, keep trying!" Ray barked. "You must convince Mendoza that we need more time! Copy? Alvarez will be here soon, but it's going to be close. Buy me another hour, Ensign. ONE HOUR! That's an order. Group St. Petersburg out."

"Roger," came the meek reply. "Station Sand Key out."

Saturday 13:27 Hours – The "Sol-Mate"

Back aboard the *Sol-Mate*, Cal and Brillo were left staring at the radio speaker in disbelief.

"Man, I can't believe it," Brillo said in shock. "Are they insane? If they start killing folks, the shit's really gonna hit the fan." His eyes shifted from the speaker to Cal's face. "God Almighty."

Cal felt a sudden weight in his gut. "Yeah, and thugs from a genetic cesspool like those scumbags are apt to carry out their threats." Cal eyed his watch. "But that's an hour and a half from now. Hopefully the Coasties will negotiate their way out of it. Who knows? They might end up handing Alvarez over to them. The last thing they need is for citizens to start dying."

Cal glanced at Kathy and leaned closer to Brillo. "For now, let's don't mention anything about this to Kathy. There's no need in upsetting her over what might be nothing. Most likely the Coasties will figure a way out of it."

"I hope so." With a worried expression, Brillo looked far away at the horizon. "I sure as hell hope so."

Saturday 13:45 Hours – The "Majestic Star"

Skip heard a loud rapping at his door and it gave him a start. Seconds later the doorknob rattled and the cabin door swung inward, banging against the inside wall. Filling the doorway was Gold-Tooth and he didn't look happy. Coiled around him like a sea snake was Mohammad with his

126

AK-47 pointed at Skip's head.

"Capitán...come!" Gold-Tooth appeared harried and impatient. His lazy eyelid was twitching, which Skip knew to be a bad sign. "NOW!"

Equally confused and alarmed, Skip snatched his hat off the wall hook and hustled out the doorway. Upon entering the wheelhouse he discovered Neal trying to repair the marine radio. Its casing had been shattered and half of the knobs were missing. With worried eyes, Neal looked up at him and then returned his attention to the battered radio.

"Capitán, you have one hour for duties." Mendoza held up one finger *"¡Una hora! No mas!"*

With that curt pronouncement the Mexican turned on his heels and left the wheelhouse. Puzzled as to what was happening, Skip turned to Mohammad for a possible clue, who was sidestepping toward his barstool while keeping his AK aimed at Skip—as if hoping Skip would make a break for it. The Arab had confiscated the chrome stool from the casino because it sat higher than the aft bench seat, enabling him to better watch the backs of the infidels. Without breaking eye contact, Mohammad straddled the barstool and lowered himself onto it slowly and deliberately, taking extra precaution to keep his rifle sights trained on Skip. Throughout his exaggerated journey he had put on his most insidious and menacing face to show the captain he meant business. The American was bound to be scared for his life—to be sure.

Standing with his hands on his hips, Skip was totally unimpressed. Not only was Mohammad a raghead, he was a freaking drama queen. Emitting a disgustful sound between a snort and a grunt, Skip turned his back on the putz and picked up a clipboard holding the food inventory. While pretending to read it, he edged closer to Neal, who was still working on the radio.

"What the hell is happening, Neal?"

"It ain't good, Skip. They rounded up ten passengers about an hour ago and took them downstairs to the dining room. They blindfolded them and ..."

"Oh, Christ!" Skip groaned, rolling his eyes upward.

" ... tied their hands." Neal waited for Skip's eyes to return to him, then nodded at the smashed up radio. "Looks like the negotiations are off, if you know what I mean."

WIRED

Skip's mouth went dry and bile filled the back of his throat. "Yeah, looks like it." With an anxious sigh, he asked: "Can you fix it?"

"Yeah, think so. It looks worse than it really is. I had to splice a few broken wires but it's mostly casing damage. Soon as I tape it up, we'll see."

Skip was rocked by the news but certainly not surprised. Gold-Tooth had grown more militant over the past 24 hours, teetering on the edge of violence. Things were taking a turn for the worse, an irreversible turn that couldn't be taken back. The proverbial: *Point of No Return.*

Dismayed, Skip envisioned the incarcerated passengers downstairs as they awaited their fate—bound...beleaguered...shuddering in aloneness. He visualized their sweat-greased faces as they strove vainly to see through the blindfolds, to see what was happening around them. He could practically feel the chafing of the ropes as they twisted their wrists to free themselves, to escape from the waking nightmare entrapping them, to halt their screaming slide into chaos.

These images weighed heavily on Skip's soul and he felt pressured to act before innocent people died—died on *his* ship and on *his* watch. Ordinary people. People with jobs and car payments and kids in school. People who merely wanted to go home to their families.

Once Neal was through taping the radio housing back together, he plugged it in and pressed the power button. Instantly, the radio sprang back from the dead and Skip heard the Coast Guard hailing his ship in alternating English and Spanish.

The incoming radio signal was digitally encrypted—or scrambled—using a technique called frequency inversion. But like most oceangoing vessels, the *Majestic Star* was equipped with electronic circuitry for sending and receiving altered voice messages while at sea.

Gold-Tooth had banned all use of the marine radio—including his own men—and had issued a shoot-to-kill order if any crewmember were caught even touching it. Nevertheless, with near panic setting in, Skip had almost reached the point of not caring. As the Coast Guard repeatedly hailed his ship, he was bursting inside to grab the microphone and find out for himself what was going on before anybody got hurt.

With his frustration coming through, Skip backed away from the radio and whacked the clipboard against the chart table. The loud noise startled Mohammad, who shot to his feet and regarded the infidel captain with sharp suspicion. Following several moments of prolonged scrutiny, the Muslim settled back down on his stool while keeping his eyes glued to Skip's back.

The hot afternoon sun was bearing down and the wheelhouse was getting stuffy. With all the tension that prevailed in the room, the enclosed space felt like a pressure cooker. To both cool off and do some thinking, Skip walked to an open window and pushed up the bill of his hat.

As captain, he was responsible for those ten souls downstairs and his every thought was consumed with saving them. But what could one unarmed man do against eight mercenaries with assault rifles? Worry as he may, Skip saw no way out of it. Just actions that would make matters worse—like seizing Mohammad by his Arab ears and throwing his rag-ass overboard.

As a practical matter, the situation was out of his hands. There was nothing he could do. The authorities would have to save those ten passengers. As captain of the ship, he was useless. So useless he felt like screaming.

Saturday 14:27 Hours – Gulf of Mexico

When the naval blockade was initially placed around the *Majestic Star*, a one-mile buffer zone was instituted so as not to spook the Zetas. But, now, in view of Mendoza's latest execution threat, all assets had been mobilized and ordered to move in closer—much closer—tightening the noose around the *Majestic Star*. The intent was to intimidate and overawe the Zetas, to pressure Mendoza into rethinking his next step before starting a fight he couldn't possibly win.

Formerly hidden from view, the Navy Destroyer and her escorts descended on the *Majestic Star* like fearsome birds of prey, effectively dwarfing it. With "battle stations" horns blaring, seamen clad in full battle gear scrambled about their decks en route to their assigned stations. As the three warships made their rapid approach, light signals flashed aggressively from vessel to vessel. Not because they relied on this age-old method of ship-to-ship communication, but because it was intimidating and looked militarily impressive.

Closer in, a fleet of Coast Guard cutters and patrol boats circled the *Majestic Star* with sirens wailing. Running an even tighter perimeter were high-speed Florida Marine Patrol chase boats with their blue beacons flashing. Swarming the skies were a dozen Coast Guard helos and Navy gunships, some with snipers visible from open jump doors.

It was an imposing military display and that's what Ray wanted—to show Mendoza he meant business; to remind the Zetas who they were messing with; to scare the living hell out of them.

Saturday 14:33 Hours – The "Majestic Star"

Skip's eyes were transfixed on the military buildup when Mendoza burst into the wheelhouse and made a beeline for the patched-together radio. In a furious eye-twitching frenzy, he grabbed the microphone and began doling out death threats if fired upon.

While Mendoza was screaming over the radio, a helo dipped lowly from overhead and hovered inches above the pilothouse roof. Its deafening noise and downward thrust of air gyrated the wheelhouse and jarred every window, silencing Mendoza in mid-tirade. While everyone in the room gawked upward at the sound, a red laser dot appeared on a wall and began roaming for a target. When the glowing red pinpoint crossed Mohammad's forehead, the Arab panicked and raced outside onto the catwalk. With his backbone curled over the pipe railing, he released a trilling *"YI-YI-YI-YI-YI-YI-YI-YI-YI"* war cry and took aim at the helmeted sniper crouched in the helo's open doorway.

Now sweating profusely, Mendoza shrieked for Mohammad to stand down but his words were lost within the uproar. Without wasting a second he dropped the microphone and tore outside, wrenching the rifle away before Mohammad fired. Then, with his hair and clothes whipping wildly, Mendoza glared defiantly at the helicopter pilot and waved him off. When the flyer didn't comply, Mendoza aimed Mohammad's rifle at the pilot's head and waved him off with more authority. When the pilot still hesitated, Mendoza closed one eye with dead-serious finality as if preparing to fire. Taken aback by the infighting—and under strict orders not to fire even if fired upon—the pilot yanked the nose skyward and peeled off as if obeying his command.

During all of the confusion, Skip shrank away from the window and positioned himself next to the radio. Both sides were playing a dangerous game and he feared Gold-Tooth might start killing indiscriminately. As Skip stood staring at the dangling microphone, he gripped the wooden wheel for something else to hold onto. With his knuckles turning white, he battled an irresistible urge to seize the mike and beg everyone within listening range to take a deep breath and calm down.

Saturday 14:38 Hours – The "Sol-Mate"

The *Sol-Mate* was now three miles north of the *Majestic Star*, still heading westward on its fake course for the fishing grounds.

At first Brillo thought they might get within three or four miles of Skip's ship, if they were lucky. But, now, as he viewed the distant activity through the binoculars, he revised his thinking. The blockade of ships had drawn in much closer to the *Majestic Star*, giving the *Sol-Mate* a wider berth than before. Helos were swarming all over the ship and the huge Navy destroyer was steaming toward the *Majestic Star* from out of the south. Brillo had no idea what was happening, but figured the distraction would work in their favor.

Since the negotiations were being conducted in Español, the descrambler wasn't much help because neither Cal nor Brillo understood Spanish. They were able to distinguish the Coast Guard negotiator's voice from the terrorist's, but that was about it. The Coastie sounded controlled and professional while the hijacker was belligerent and mainly yelled a lot.

Deciding to travel another mile before doubling back, Brillo voyaged westward while watching the radar screen. If it detected anything approaching them, he would hightail it the other way.

As the *Sol-Mate* skirted past the blockade unnoticed, the scanner radio sprang to life.

Saturday 14:43 Hours – Group St. Petersburg

"This is Coast Guard Station Sand Key hailing Group St. Petersburg.

WIRED

Over."

"This is Group St. Petersburg. Go ahead, Sand Key."

"Roger, Group. I have some urgent traffic for Admiral Hanna. Over."

"Affirmative, Sand Key. Stand by one."

Seconds later: "Admiral Hanna here. Go ahead, Ensign."

"Sir, I've just received a message from Miami Group. It will be a negative—repeat, a negative—on getting Alvarez here before the 15:00 deadline. A severe lightning storm en route has temporarily grounded them in Fort Myers. The aircraft will be back airborne as soon as weather permits. Their revised ETA is 15:45 hours, but that could change. Over."

This was a disastrous stroke of bad luck and Ray gritted his teeth to stifle an angry outburst.

"I copy, Ensign, but this is the United States Coast Guard. Our pilots are expected to fly in bad weather. THAT'S WHAT WE DO, FOR CHRIST SAKE!!" Ray took a deep breath and willed himself to settle down. When his crimson face returned halfway normal, he asked in a milder voice: "Any word from Mendoza?"

"Yes, sir. That was my next order of business. He's demanding that we withdraw our forces immediately or he will double the number of executions. He's also threatened to detonate the ship if fired upon. I strongly suggest that we pull back to settle the panic. There's pandemonium aboard ship, sir. Even so, the 15:00 deadline stands. No extensions. Roger?"

"That's UNACCEPTABLE!" Ray shot to his feet and hunkered over the desk mike. "We need more time, Ensign! You MUST convince Mendoza that this is no stall tactic; that Alvarez WILL be here by 16:00 hours. You got that?"

"I will do my best, sir, but he's disregarding our hails. His only communication of late was in sole response to our aggression. But I'll keep at it, sir. Sand Key out."

After releasing the key, Ray's eyes remained fixed on the wire-mesh microphone head—as if he waited long enough a solution would magically spill forth from the airwaves. He had hoped to bully the Zetas into behaving themselves via the massive show of force. Or at least sway them into granting the lousy one-hour extension he requested. But, with only minutes remaining, his gamble hadn't paid off. He was resigned to

132

recalling the ships. By giving Mendoza some breathing room, maybe he would calm down and grant the extra hour. Perhaps.

After giving the order for withdrawal, Ray called Station Fort Myers and left a message for the ace pilot there to call him about a career change. After getting that off his chest, he prowled the radio room like a caged tiger. When he checked the wall clock again, his mouth went dry. Ten minutes to go. The waiting was tortuous, like a sharp sword looming above his head.

With his brain bubbling over, Ray walked to the water cooler and filled a paper cone with water. While drinking from it the Cuban's voice emanated from the speaker behind him in his nonstop bid to raise the *Majestic Star*. As Ray listened to the repeated hails—hoping and praying for a response—he gazed out a window overlooking Bayboro Harbor.

Thirty yards offshore a lone sailboat was cruising past the stationhouse. Sitting low in the cockpit, its captain was manning the rudder with his pretty first mate snuggled against him. As Ray looked on, the sailor tacked hard to port and the overhead boom slammed sideways in a sweeping arc. When the mainsail flapped and fluttered, the captain trimmed it by ratcheting the ropes until it billowed anew with salt air, propelling the sloop eastward. As the lovebirds sipped from their wineglasses, Ray coveted their carefree lifestyle. More than that, he coveted their benign impunity from worry.

To the distant south Ray saw a sinister-looking thunderhead brewing—presumably the same electrical storm responsible for Alvarez's late arrival. Glumly, he shook his head at the cruel irony of it. If the executions did come to pass, it would be something as coincidental as a thunderstorm that sealed the fate of ten human beings—an ordinary springtime thunderstorm.

As Ray gazed southward he could sense the rumble of another gathering storm, one with a wrath and impetus far greater than the mightiest tempest. The ten deaths would rouse the eye-for-an-eye-and-tooth-for-a-tooth ferocity of the United States of America.

Saturday 14:51 Hours – The "Sol-Mate"

When the *Sol-Mate* reached the outer fringe of the fishing grounds,

WIRED

Brillo made a wide U-turn and circled back eastward. His plan was to approach the *Majestic Star* straight out of the west. While steadily advancing on the captive ship, Cal and Brillo took turns watching the military movement through the binoculars. Interestingly enough, after swarming the hijacked ship like bees in a bottle, all military watercraft and aircraft were now pulling away.

"Well, lookie there," Cal said, peering through the binoculars. "They're calling off the dogs."

"What? What is it?" Brillo asked, squinting toward the east.

"They're standing down, Brillo, vacating the area. I guess the Coasties got their one-hour extension."

"That's a relief." The anxiousness on Brillo's face eased. "Had me worried there for a minute."

"Yeah, you and me both." Cal handed the glasses to Brillo. "Here, take a look."

As Brillo peered through the binoculars, Cal climbed down the flybridge ladder to have a word with Kathy. Now that the immediate crisis was over, he wanted her to know that Alvarez was on his way to Sand Key. She would take heart in knowing that the negotiations were producing some positive results. Naturally, he wouldn't say anything about the execution threat, which now appeared to be over with anyway.

While Cal and Kathy sat talking, Brillo steered with his eyes pasted on the distant ships and aircraft. As he watched the task force withdraw, he thought about the relief that Skip must be feeling right now. It was a truly close call and Brillo felt relieved too. But this wasn't the first time the two chums had shared a narrow escape.

Going backward in time, Brillo recalled the time he was offshore and a summertime squall blew up. It had been one of those perfect days for fishing when suddenly the sky closed up and turned pitch black. As luck would have it, the cantankerous engine on his former charter boat had decided not to start that day, leaving him and his paying customers stranded.

As the storm gained strength, the ten-foot swells became twenty-footers and before long it was blowing a full gale. Without engine power to keep the bow pointed into the incoming waves, Brillo's vessel was in danger of capsizing or being swamped. As the wind-whipped waves crested with blowing sea foam, his boat broached to and started taking on water faster than he and his drenched fishermen could bail.

To summon help, Brillo switched his radio frequency to Channel 69—the working channel used by all the local fishermen. He saw no point in hailing the Coast Guard because his boat would never stay afloat that long. His best hope was that another fishing vessel would be somewhere in the area.

As fate would have it, Skip was operating a commercial fishing boat at the time just a few miles away. Because of the squall, he was heading back for the mainland when he intercepted Brillo's Mayday call. Instead of staying his course for safe harbor, Skip relayed Brillo's emergency to the Coast Guard and reversed course back out to sea—right into the brunt of the vicious storm.

By the time Skip got within a mile of Brillo's position, the squall was at its peak and the seas were mountainous. The wind-driven rain was slamming sideways in powerful sheets that threatened to blow out the pilothouse windows. It was extremely slow going and Skip feared that when he reached Brillo's coordinates, it would be too late. Nevertheless, he felt duty-bound to make the attempt. Otherwise, it would spell certain death for Brillo and his passengers.

In spite of rigging a makeshift sea anchor to reduce the pitching and yawing, Brillo's boat began to break up. When he tried to contact Skip again, he discovered the saltwater had shorted out all circuitry including the radio. Realizing that sinking was inevitable, Brillo shot off the last of his flares with hope they would lead Skip to his position—if there was anything left to find.

Incredibly enough, Skip spotted the flares through the pouring deluge and headed straight for their sparkling trails. By the time his boat reached their proximity, seawater was cascading over the gunnels and the deck was completely awash. Floundering in near zero visibility, Skip stood in ankle-deep water while searching the dark churning seas with a rooftop spotlight. Despite a near-mutiny from his crewmen, Skip was steadfast in his refusal to leave, even though his vessel itself was facing serious peril.

Then, against infinitesimal odds, Skip's spotlight illuminated the red bottom paint of Brillo's overturned boat. As it tossed and wallowed within the swirling white foam, Skip saw the bobbing heads of survivors clad in orange life jackets clinging desperately to the hull.

At the risk of collision, Skip maneuvered his vessel in closer while fighting to keep the two boats from colliding. While he manhandled the wheel, his deckhands made several failed attempts to heave the survivors a life ring. With no time to waste, Skip relinquished the helm to his first mate and kicked off his shoes. Then, in one quick motion, he stuck his arm through the life ring and dove daringly into the seas.

Skip was a skilled swimmer from his Navy days but the roiling undertow was stronger than expected. But by fighting it with determined desperation, he exhaustively reached the overturned boat. After placing the ring over the head of the nearest victim, his crewmen hauled out the first survivor. Then the life ring was tossed back out to sea, where Skip was forced to retrieve it. One by one they were all rescued, including Brillo.

Once all survivors were safely aboard, Skip—worn, winded, and waterlogged—was hoisted out of harm's way, just as Brillo's boat took its last breath and sank into the stormy depths.

Saturday 14:56 Hours – The "Majestic Star"

Skip and Neal were sitting on the floor with their backs against the wall and their hands clasped behind their heads. Minutes ago they had been herded into the casino with the other crewmen to join the near-hysterical passengers. After Mendoza ordered everyone to sit still with their arms raised or be shot, he stormed out of the casino, leaving five snarling narco-guerillas behind to enforce his do-or-die command. And from the menacing way they brandished their weapons, nobody in the room doubted they wouldn't.

With edgy gunmen hawking over them, families huddled, couples cuddled, and protective mothers cradled their children. Others prayed. Joined in a silent countdown, all their hearts beat as one. Everybody in the room was terrified and rightfully so. Skip was fearful too, but not so much for his own life as for the lives of his passengers and crew.

Wondering what time it was, Skip strained his eyes sideways and twisted his left wrist to read his watch. When he saw it was nearly 3:00 o'clock, a bitter taste rose from the back of his throat and for the first time he realized that fear actually had a taste.

Why was Gold-Tooth still so agitated? The Coasties were standing down. Was he going to kill the ten hostages anyway? Is he crazy? Something's got to be done before it's too late!

As time crawled by, the climactic wait was tortuous. Although "doing nothing" went solidly against Skip's macho grain, there was nothing he could do. Besides, as captain, his primary duty was to the safety of ALL passengers, not just a few unlucky ones. It ate at his masculinity to accept it, but he had to let it go. Fate would have to run its course. Whatever happens, happens.

To appease his gnawing conscience, Skip lolled his head against the wall and tried not to dwell on it. That's when he felt the roomful of eyes on him. When he straightened and looked around, he found hundreds of eyes staring his direction. Some looked angry...some looked scared...some belonging to worried womenfolk were brimming with tears. All of them bore some degree of expectancy, which made the depths of his lowness plummet further.

What did they expect him to do? Jump up and make the bad guys go home? Fight all five of them barehanded? He wasn't a comic book superhero. And what about the explosives?

The longer the passengers stared at him, the more petulant he grew. The shame of doing nothing was humiliating enough. It was an affront to his rank as ship captain, not to mention a bitter slap in the face of his manhood. Jason Myles had never run from a fight in his life. Ever. He didn't need their puppy-dog stares adding to his already guilt-ridden conscience. Even while dodging their unified gaze he could feel their judgmental eyes on him, tugging like gravity.

In their eyes, he was their leader and by extension accountable. In his eyes, there was nothing he could do. In everyone's eyes there was fright and a fearsome boding of things to come.

Saturday 15:00 Hours – The "Sol-Mate"

When the *Sol-Mate* crossed the one-mile mark to the *Majestic Star*, Brillo decided that was close enough. The visibility was crystal clear and the telescope would zoom in well from this distance. As Cal set up the telescope on the lower deck, Brillo spun the boat about so that the stern would face Skip's ship. Once positioned for a direct view, he cut the engines and dropped fore and aft anchors to keep the boat fast against the crosswind and current.

While Cal adjusted the legs on the tripod, Kathy waited nearby with excitement. After hearing the encouraging news that Alvarez was in transit to Sand Key, she'd halfway permitted herself some hope. She wasn't aware of it, of course, but Cal was more relieved than she for not having to reveal anything about the execution threat. She would have flipped out.

Cal assumed the military received their one-hour extension because it simply made sense. The hijackers had already waited three days, so what was another hour? It would be irrational to spill blood over a few extra minutes. And it would be more irrational for a handful of men to take on the Armed Forces of the United States. In point of fact, it would be suicide.

Once the telescope was all set up, Cal peered through the eyepiece at the distant ship. "Wow!" he exclaimed. "I can almost read the lunch menu from here."

While he played with the focus Kathy bobbed up and down eagerly, waiting her turn. "Do you see Skip yet? Let me look, Cal. Please?"

"Wait a sec. I'll scan the decks for him." Suddenly, Cal's excitement frittered away. "Wait a minute. There's something happening midship...what the hell?" His voice rose with shock. "Oh, no. Don't tell me the crazy sons-of-bitches are actually gonna do it!!"

Through the circular lens Cal saw people in civilian clothing lined up along an opened section of railing. He counted ten of them, all bound and blindfolded.

"Do what? What are you talking about, Cal?" Sensing danger, Kathy's voice rose and she pulled at his arm. "You're scaring me!"

When Cal straightened to face her, his expression said it all. Without a word, Kathy made a play for the telescope; but, reacting quicker, Cal grabbed her wrists and held them as she strained against him.

"Kathy, they've threatened to execute ten people if Alvarez isn't onboard as of . . ." While still gripping her wrists, Cal looked at his watch. "Well," he sighed, "as of right now, actually. I thought the

WIRED

Coasties had bought more time, but evidently they haven't."

"My God, Cal!" Kathy wrenched free of his grasp and glowered at him. "How could you keep this from me? What about Skip? Maybe he's one of them!"

Before Cal could answer, the report of automatic gunfire rumbled across the ocean surface. Startled by it, he peered through the telescope to see the faint splash of bloodied bodies entering the Gulf of Mexico. The unexpected sight was shocking and it rocked him. He had seen bloody bodies before, but not like this. That was different—that was war. These were harmless civilians on a half-day sea cruise.

"Those fuckers!" Cal vented his anger on the lid of a nearby ice chest, beating his fist against it while cursing the killers. "Those . . ROTTEN . . MOTHER . . FUCKERS!"

While Cal was battering the ice chest, Kathy grabbed the telescope and spun it toward the ship. Fearful of what she might find, she pressed her eye against the eyepiece. Like it or not, she had to know if Skip was amongst the ones just killed.

As her trembling hand fumbled with the focus, she began to hyperventilate. The rapid loss of carbon dioxide gave her a fainting feeling, but she kept at it. With one eye closed, she squinted through the eyepiece to find tears blurring her vision. Frustrated, she switched eyes only to find the other eye the same. In haste, she blotted her watery eyes against her bare shoulder and then looked again. But she was unprepared for the revolting sight that filled the lens.

Instantly sickened, Kathy gagged and her stomach clenched. Spurred by reflex, she dashed to the gunnel and retched over the side. After emptying her stomach into the ocean, she crumbled to her knees and wept—her shoulders heaving uncontrollably.

"ANIMALS!" In between convulsive heaves, she coughed and sobbed and spat out bitter tasting upchuck. "GODDAMN ANIMALS!"

For as long as she lived, Kathy would never forget the horrific scene: the aquamarine water tainted by a bloody cloud of rusty-red...fully-clothed, blood-drenched bodies bobbing lifelessly on the surface...and a Mickey Mouse souvenir doll—smiling brightly at the sky as the waves lapped it against the ship's hull.

WIRED

Saturday 15:00 Hours – The "Majestic Star"

Skip flinched at hearing the gunshots and his heart catapulted. Despite his conscious effort to sit back and do nothing, the gunfire ignited something inside him. He snapped.

Spurred by an unseen force, Skip roared at the top of his lungs and assailed the gunman nearest him. Instinctively falling back on his SEAL training, Skip chopped the Latino in the throat and swept his feet out from under him. When the man crashed to the floor on his back gagging for air, Skip pounced on him and grabbed two handfuls of greasy black hair. Then, possessed by a primitive rage, he pounded the Latino's head repeatedly against the floor—oblivious to the spattering droplets of flying blood.

When the unconscious gunman went limp, Skip seized the AK-47 but its sling was bound taut around the man's upper body. With the brute strength of a madman, Skip gave it two powerful yanks and the leather strap snapped. At that very moment a twisted smile crossed his face. The odds had shifted. The weapon was his and he had a fighting chance. Now he could show the terrorist bastards what a real soldier could do.

But as Skip stuffed his finger inside the trigger housing, his peripheral vision detected a dark blur coming from his immediate right. Then, with a crunching thud, everything went dark.

Saturday 15:01 Hours – Group St. Petersburg

"Coast Guard Group St. Petersburg, this is Station Sand Key hailing Admiral Hanna. Over."

Ray had wandered away from the workstation in the course of pacing and hurried back to the microphone. "Admiral Hanna here. Go ahead, Ensign."

"Ten hostages confirmed in the water, sir. Identities unknown. All believed to be dead." Following a respectful pause, the Cuban resumed his report. "I've just received another transmission from Mendoza, sir. At 16:00 another passenger will be executed, then another every fifteen minutes until Alvarez arrives. Over."

This latest caveat made Ray stiffen. "What's Alvarez's ETA? Over."

"It's going to be close, sir. Roger?"

"Radio the transport pilot and get me an exact—and I mean exact—ETA. I'll be standing by."

"Will do, sir. Station Sand Key out."

Wearing a doomsday expression, Ray seemed to grow smaller. "Well, that's that," he sighed. "The die has been cast."

He had been counting on Mendoza ultimately backing down and granting more time—time for Alvarez to arrive and call off the executions by radio. But, instead, the Zeta boss had raised the stakes dramatically by killing ten Americans. And to underscore his terroristic point, the victims had been blindfolded like POW's and gunned down like dogs. Once the press got wind of that, it would be publicized for all it was worth.

The mental image of ten bodies floating facedown in the Gulf of Mexico made Ray's blood curdle. And unless Mendoza was bluffing—which Ray had no reason to believe—the Zetas were prepared to do it again and again until Alvarez was delivered—wherever he was.

Where was Alvarez anyway? Why can't anything ever go right!?

When Ray got ahold of the Group Air Traffic Coordinator in Miami, he was going to give him forty kinds of hell. The U.S. Coast Guard were intermediaries between life and death. A measly thunderstorm wasn't supposed to ground their aircraft. They flew *through* storms, not *around* them. They were accustomed to low-vis flying and feeling their way blind. Coast Guard pilots laughed in the face of thundersqualls and thumbed their noses at killer downdrafts and wind shears. They were trained to perform under extreme conditions that no one else dared. Weren't they?

What's the Coast Guard coming to? The next thing you know, the pilots' wives will be calling me when their hubbies are late for supper. What a bunch of freaking pansies!

Releasing some stored-up rage, Ray kicked over a wastebasket and watched it spew waste along its end-over-end path. Not feeling any better, he refilled his **"SUPPORT SEARCH & RESCUE: GET LOST!"** coffee mug and stormed down the hallway for his office.

Setting the mug down on his gray government desk, Ray walked up to the corkboard and perused the growing collection of surveillance photos. The 8x10's were taken by means of telephoto lens—some by ship, some aerial—capturing an assortment of suspects prowling the ship's decks. Unlike the crewmembers, which were easily identifiable in their white uniforms, the Zetas were hard to distinguish from the passengers. Only the AK's gave them away.

As Ray studied the photographs, he glared bitterly at the eight now-murderers. Obviously they were all quite willing to die which revealed what sort of characters he was dealing with. But why would they die for pariahs like Alvarez and Gonzalez? What was their motivation? Was it purely money or something else? And what about the two Arabs? What was their agenda? Were they members of the Muslim Brotherhood now permeating America? Set on destroying western civilization from within or go to their deaths trying?

Except for Santiago Mendoza, none of the others had been identified. Nevertheless, Ray knew their backgrounds would match the textbook profiles. Mercenaries, terrorists, mobsters—they were all virtually the same. Predictably they would be murderers, thieves, and dregs from society. If they had any family, they had been disowned years ago. They were scums of the earth that only felt at home around other scumbags. In time, the gang itself became their family with the likes of Mendoza serving as clan leader and patron saint. Without him the cutthroat bunch had no finances, no direction, and nowhere to go. Apart from a prison cell, there was no place for them in the civilized world. They were pathetic losers...fallen souls...lowlife miscreants with nothing left for death to take away.

When Ray checked his watch, the tension swelled within him. He had only fifty-five minutes left until the next execution. SEAL Team-3 was on standby, but storming the ship was too risky. Now that the Zetas had spilled American blood, they had nothing more to lose by killing all two hundred men, women, and children. He couldn't sic the SEALs on them until all the passengers were off.

So, if Señor Alvarez didn't arrive in time, what were his options? He was in a box, a Catch-22 box, and it gave him a gross feeling of ineptitude. As Incident Commander he had the full power of the United States military at his disposal. He could send the *Majestic Star* to the ocean bottom with one single command. Yet, despite all this clout, Ray could do nothing but run to the end of his chain and bark.

Like the poor unfortunate hostages, he, too, was suspended in the oblivion of no choice. Only, unlike them, his demise would not be so swift. It would be slower and more tortuous—one of the mind. Ray Hanna's fate was to stand by and do nothing while innocent civilians were murdered every fifteen minutes.

Wearing a bleak expression, Ray turned away from the corkboard and looked outside. The distant gathering of storm clouds was closer now, with lightning firing down at the earth in brilliant blue-white flashes. Instead of moving away like a good little storm front, it seemed to be defying him—flouting itself. And if it persisted in holding up the pilot in Fort Myers, an eleventh victim would breathe their last at 16:00.

As Ray stared thoughtfully out the window, a young lieutenant entered the office with a double-dose of bad news. There had just been a car bombing in downtown Tallahassee and the Commandant was on the telephone.

Saturday 15:05 Hours – The "Sol-Mate"

After getting a grip on himself Cal turned his attention to Kathy, who was still curled over the side with her face buried in a forearm. When he knelt beside her and hugged her shoulders, she turned into him and clutched his neck with a clingy desperateness. Her whole body was trembling and her sobbing face was smeared with tears. While holding her, he could feel their wetness against the bare skin of his collarbone.

As Cal quietly consoled her, he worried about her emotional well-being. She felt as limp as a rag doll and very close to collapse. He wondered if she had any medication at the condo that would calm her nerves. If not, he would take her by the Emergency Room on the way home for a sedative. Kathy was a pretty tough cookie but she would need something to help her sleep tonight. Something to blot out the horror they had just witnessed—something very, very strong.

Letting Kathy cry it out, Cal stroked her hair gently and rocked her to and fro, occasionally hugging her tighter as if trying to squeeze out her suffering. All the while his gaze was fixed on Skip's distant ship. As he stared at the *Majestic Star*, the image of hemorrhaging bodies plunging into the deep replayed in his mind like an assiduous film loop.

143

WIRED

Splash!

Cal tried to banish the hideous images from mind and memory, but the tragedy of it struck him over and over again.

Splash, Splash!

Fortunately, Skip was not among the dead today but there was no reason he couldn't be there tomorrow or the next day. If that happened it would destroy his sister, and it would destroy him too in a different more protracted way.

A lifelong friendship was by definition: lifelong. Skip's death would not release Cal of it. The friendship would endure as long as Cal lived to carry it on. But Skip's passing would give birth to an irreplaceable void in Cal's life; and, like a parasite, this void would strive to consume him bit-by-bit until he was an emotionally empty carcass. Over a passage of time, the burden of bearing this half-friendship would leave him a hollowed-out shell of the friend and brother-in-law he once was. Cal Stringer—good, bad, and sometimes ugly—would never be quite the same.

With his thoughts whipping like a tempest, Cal's brotherly embrace had unknowingly become a crushing bear hug. When Kathy squirmed to gain a little breathing space, he relaxed his hold on her and made a solemn vow.

He would not allow his sister's life to be shattered and he would not stand aside and let his best friend perish...as God was his witness.

~~~~~~~~~~

Brillo was slumped behind the steering wheel with a hand covering his eyes, trying to cope with the mindless split-second horror just forced upon him.

It was all over now—quiet, even—and the stillness seemed a sacrilege somehow. There were no echoes of gunfire, no lasting shrieks from people dying in torment, just the normal sloshing of the ocean against the fiberglass hull of his boat. The silence was unnatural, surreal.

Brillo wondered how such a monstrous crime could be over with just like that. People were massacred in cold blood and minutes later all was back to normal, like nothing ever happened. The tranquility was so incongruous with the atrocity, so at odds, that it made reality hard to grasp. Deeds this vile should have profound repercussions. The skies should cloud over in anger and the seas should swell up in rebellion. The winds should rake violently across the evildoers and banish them to the hellish place where they belonged. *Something should happen.* The stillness wasn't fitting and it deeply disturbed him. He found it disrespectful somehow.

Unable to make sense of his feelings, Brillo put them aside and plotted a mental course back to the marina—a course that would take them well out of the Coast Guard's way. Sitting upright, he straightened the bill of his cap and fired up the diesels. While the engines warmed up, he descended the ladder and weighed the fore and aft anchors. Before putting the boat in gear, he glanced over his shoulder to find Cal still consoling Kathy. Though still very much shaken, the pallor of her face was better and she looked okay.

"Hold on, you guys," Brillo yelled over the engines. "I'm getting underway. We've all had enough for one day. Let's go home."

Saturday 15:55 Hours – The "Majestic Star"

When Skip regained consciousness he had a splitting headache and his arms and legs were tied spread-eagle to the bunk. The pillow under his head was moist with something sticky, and, from the way the back of his skull hurt, he suspected a rifle butt was the cause of it. The last thing he remembered, he was astraddle an unconscious Mexican with an AK-47 in his grasp. Given the foolish try, he was surprised to be still alive. Evidently he wasn't on Gold-Tooth's expendable list yet or he would be a dead man.

Wondering who had tied him up and why, Skip tested the ropes by drawing his arms and legs. When they wouldn't budge he yanked harder, which only served to exacerbate his migraine. With a painful wince he gave it up and relaxed his head on the sticky pillowcase. Then the memory of the executions suddenly popped into his head and his spirit deflated like air fizzling from a balloon. More air fizzled out when he wondered which smiling faces that boarded his ship on Thursday ended up as fish food, never to smile again. Ten passengers were gone—wasted.

After a mournful moment of venerating the dead, reality rushed in and Skip refocused on the present. He had living souls to worry about.

Wondering how long he had been unconscious, Skip tried to read his watch but the wrist restraint held his arm in place. He was hogtied like a freaking animal. Incensed by it, he craned his neck toward the cabin porthole to see daylight still pouring through. Either it was Sunday or he had only been out a relatively short time. His intuition went with the latter, as the blood on his pillow hadn't fully dried yet.

Suddenly sensing another presence in the room, Skip hoisted his head and looked about the cabin. To his amazement Gold-Tooth was sitting silently at the cabin desk, smiling down at his wristwatch. His inexplicable presence and weird behavior gave Skip a start.

As Skip watched him with a wary eye, Mendoza plucked an object from his shirt pocket and raised a miniature antenna. At first Skip thought it was a cell phone, but when the Mexican lifted a hinged cover to expose a blinking button, Skip's heart stopped dead in his chest—the detonator.

"Whatcha doin' in my cabin with that thing?" Skip's mouth was dry and dusty and his voice croaked like a rusty gate. "What's goin' on?"

When Mendoza didn't answer, Skip's temper flared. His head was bleeding, ten people were dead, and the murdering maniac responsible for it all was playing some sort of mind game.

"Haven't you killed enough defenseless people today? Or are you still under your quota?" When Mendoza still didn't answer, Skip pushed harder. "Listen—asswipe—I know you're not deaf, and I know you understand English. So what about it? What the hell's goin' on?"

Skip didn't know what was happening, but the guy was giving him the creeps. Presumably, he was going to blow up *something* or *someone* or he wanted Skip to believe that he was.

"Is that what you yellowbelly spics do for kicks in Mexico? Murder unarmed civilians in cold blood?" When Gold-Tooth still remained silent, Skip raised his voice and strained against the ropes. "Why don't you untie me—you chickenshit bastard—and let's see how brave you are?"

Mendoza's eyes left his watch for a moment to regard the smart-mouthed capitán. The expression in them seemed to be somewhere between annoyance and amusement. A moment later he broke his lengthy silence while still staring at the timepiece.

"Capitán, pick a number."

WIRED

"What?" The weird request took Skip off guard and it threw him.

"Pick number, any number—*uno, dos, tres* . . ."

"I'm not playin' games with you." Gold-Tooth was making him nervous but Skip acted unafraid. "Screw you."

With unhurried movements, Mendoza placed the detonator on the desk and walked over to Skip's bunk. When standing directly above Skip, he bent over with a lewd sneer—exhibiting one gold front tooth with a diamond in it and several teeth nearly rotten to the gums. His breath was revolting, smelling like a mixture of tooth decay and cigarette tobacco.

"Capitán, all peoples die one day—me, you, the Americanos. Some die young, some die old, some die quick . . ." His sneer grew more sinister, revealing more rotten teeth. "Others die slower, with much pain." He produced a large bowie knife and rubbed his thumb affectionately along the blade's razor-sharp edge. "We kill all American pigs before we go, Capitán. All! ¿Comprende? If Alvarez and Gonzalez not released, we kill all pigs. If they released, we kill all pigs. Either way pigs die. ¡Máteles a todos!"

In a lightning quick move that caused Skip to gasp, he pressed the blade across Skip's throat. "But you, Capitán...you mine. Not quick like others." His upper lip curled. "I take time with you for hurting Miguel. "As the blade penetrated slightly, Skip felt blood trickle down the left side of his neck. "You bleed like pig, Capitán?" Sneering, he pressed the blade harder. "Capitán hear of *corbata colombiana*—Colombian necktie?"

Skip knew that a Colombian necktie was the symbol of the Colombian Mafia. After slitting the victim's throat from ear-to-ear, their tongue was pulled out through the gaping neck wound to create a grotesque necktie effect. The disfigurement was both shocking and revolting, which was its intent.

As the blade penetrated deeper, the room went hot and sweat popped out on Skip's face. The pressure of the knife and Gold-Tooth's demented look told him that the Mexican meant business. His eyelid was twitching and his insidious facial expression lent him a convincing deranged look. At that moment, Skip contemplated dying for the second time in his life.

Throughout his fifty plus years, Skip had never been easily intimidated—perhaps even when he should have been. Whenever cornered, he had come out fighting. He didn't want to die, but if Gold-

WIRED

Tooth was aiming to kill him, then Skip wanted the prick to get it over with. This bound-to-his-bunk-torture-chamber-routine was the last straw.

"If you're gonna do it," Skip said through clenched teeth, "then do it, asswad. Get on with it!"

As Skip glared at Gold-Tooth, he suppressed a powerful urge to spit in the man's face; to challenge the eye-twitching freak to either kill him or get the hell out of his cabin. But even while teeming with raw male aggression, Skip knew better than to provoke a proven killer when said killer was holding a finely honed bowie knife against his throat.

As the pair traded threatening looks, the air grew thick with testosterone. Their sweating faces were inches apart and Mendoza's rank breath was making Skip nauseous. At that moment something inside Skip told him to play it smart, to yield to Gold-Tooth's dominance. The Mexican was dangerously unstable and the knife blade was trembling under his hand. If it bore any deeper and nicked a jugular, it would be all over. While loathing the gutless act, Skip forced his eyes away in a feigned show of submission—telling himself a bruised ego was a sight better than a slit throat.

Noting the captain's capitulation, Mendoza lingered over him awhile sneering triumphantly. After savoring the victory he pulled the knife away as if accepting the docile surrender. Then, in a weirdly perverted gesture, he licked Skip sloppily on the right cheek.

"You Americanos taste just like chicken," he hissed in Skip's ear with hot rotten breath. "I think when I kill you, Capitán, I eat your liver first." Then, creepily, he added: "Next I eat your tongue. Tongue and liver are best parts." He straightened with a sordid smile and burst into psychotic laughter, his gold tooth glinting in the dim light.

As Mendoza guffawed, a shiver of gooseflesh ran through Skip's body. He didn't know if the Mexican was kidding about the cannibalism or not and he didn't care to find out. Clearly, the man was a few Coronas short of a six-pack. As a matter of fact, Skip knew of some inkblots the psycho needed to see.

To Skip's huge relief, Gold-Tooth sheathed the knife and sat back down at the desk. But when he picked up the detonator, Skip tensed back up again. While Skip watched, Mendoza flipped up the hinged button cover and placed the detonator on the desk. Then he unfastened his watchband and arranged the detonator and wristwatch side-by-side. The schizo was plainly up to no good and a deepening sense of dread crept into the pit of Skip's stomach.

"Enough about food," Mendoza said, twisting around in the chair to face Skip. "I make myself hungry." He flashed one last psychotic grin and then his features hardened. "It is time, Capitán. Pick a number."

Skip's skin was still crawling from Gold-Tooth's slobbery lick and now the crazy cannibal wanted him to pluck a number out of the air—like he was on some terrorist quiz show.

"Whattya talkin' about?" Skip said sourly. "Whatever you're up to, count me out."

"As you Americanos say: 'humor me'. Pick number, any number."

"Forget it. At the moment, I'm fresh outta humor." Skip's skull was pounding and the fresh wound on his neck was oozing blood. "In case you haven't noticed, I'm bleedin' over here."

Mendoza shot to his feet ramrod straight and gave Skip a blistering look. Then he tore open the cabin door and turned to face Skip. As he stood in the doorway, his guerrilla gang members gathered outside.

"Pick number now or I kill ten more pigs!"

The sudden intrusion of daylight stabbed Skip's eyes and compounded his migraine pain. Whatever Gold-Tooth was up to, he wasn't kidding.

"Okay, you sick freak," Skip conceded. "Twenty-one."

The Mexican hastened back to the desk and put his finger on the blinking button, clearly excited by things to come. Skip could see the exhilaration in his psychopathic eyes. "Wrong answer," he said with a glint of glee.

When Mendoza pressed the button a deafening explosion erupted outside. Skip went rigid at the sound and struggled to sit upright, but the ropes held him down. As he yanked and thrashed in a squirming fit of rage, Mendoza walked over and sneered down at him.

"As I say, Capitán, all pigs will die. *¡Muerte a los Americanos!*"

Saturday 16:00 Hours – Group St. Petersburg

"Coast Guard Group St. Petersburg, this is Station Sand Key hailing

Admiral Hanna. Over."

Seated alongside the radio operator, Ray was bending and twisting a paperclip, trying unsuccessfully not to clock-watch. When the RO slid the desk mike in front of him, Ray looked at it with dread before dropping the mutilated paperclip and pressing the key.

"Hanna here." His voice sounded worn, as if expecting bad news. "Go ahead, Ensign."

"Sir, we've just received a report of an explosion aboard the Majestic Star. I've got a Dauphine checking it out now." The ensign's voice went away for a moment and then returned. "Sir, the Dauphine pilot is hailing me now on our working channel. Stand by one."

The startling news made Ray bristle and he sat straight up. An explosion? What the hell was going on!? One hour ago there had been an explosion in downtown Tallahassee and now another aboard the *Majestic Star*.

"Sorry for the interruption, sir," the Cuban continued, "but I'm afraid the news is grim. The Zetas are now exploding passengers instead of shooting them. Surveillance indicates they have retrofitted the ship's lifejackets with C-4 plastique, similar to suicide bomber vests. One hooded male passenger was just escorted to the bow by one of the Muslims and detonated, sir."

As the ensign reported the shocking event, Ray could hear Mendoza ranting in the background.

"Stand by, sir. The Majestic Star is hailing me on the other channel."

The terrorists were living up to their name, Ray thought. Firing squads were not terrorizing enough, so they had switched to exploding people. Now Ray understood where the Al-Qaeda accomplices fit in. They wrote the book on how to rig suicide bombs. He could see the headlines now: **AUTHORITIES STAND BY WHILE CITIZENS ARE BLOWN TO SMITHEREENS.**

"Admiral, Mendoza has just threatened to detonate another passenger at 16:15 hours. Over."

With his stomach a clenched knot, Ray glanced at the wall clock. "Where's Alvarez now?"

"His helo just landed here, sir."

"Stall, Ensign. I'm on my way. STALL! Group St. Petersburg out."

WIRED

With a face congested with rage, Ray jarred the worktop with his balled fist. "That Colombian sonofabitch is gonna answer to me personally for this shit!"

"A Ready H60 is on the line, sir," the radio operator said. "The pilot is waiting."

"Good!" With a huff, Ray screwed on his cap by the bill. "At least *somebody* around here is on time!"

Saturday 16:08 Hours – Station Sand Key

Eight minutes later the red-and-white Jayhawk put down in Sand Key and Ray stormed inside the stationhouse. He was striding down the hallway, looking at his watch, when he glimpsed Alvarez through the break room window.

The middle-aged Colombian was sitting alone at a wooden table with his wrists still in chains. He was an imposing man with a ruddy Latin complexion, beetled eyebrows, mustache, and coal black hair slicked straight back. He was tall and strongly built, with a thick neck and broad shoulders. He was wearing a yellow cashmere sweater with expensive-looking gray slacks and loafers, presumably the clothing he had been arrested in.

"Well, well," Ray humpfed, barely controlling his anger. "If it ain't Señor Alvarez himself—the Mighty Mafioso...Lord of Latin America...Cream of the Crap...King Shit!"

Ray rounded the next corner and in his haste nearly ran down three U.S. Marshals posted outside the break room door. As a formality Ray gave them a cursory nod, flashed his I.D., and proceeded to go in. But before reaching the door, one marshal blocked his entry while the other two snagged him by the elbows. As the marshal in front apologized for the delay, Ray's eyes traced each elbow-gripping hand to the face of its rightful owner, into which he bitterly glared. The last thing he expected was to be physically detained in his own stationhouse. This was his turf—not theirs.

According to the marshal in charge, their orders were clear. They were to escort Alvarez from Miami to Sand Key and await further instructions. No one was to see the prisoner without proper authorization.

WIRED

A faxed list of those authorized was supposed to be waiting for them when they arrived. When it wasn't they called their office and it should be arriving momentarily.

Ordinarily, Ray would have empathized with the marshals and taken the bureaucratic blunder in stride. But with only seven minutes left to produce a miracle, he had no time for professional courtesy. Blowing his cool, Ray yanked his elbows free and unloaded on the federal officers.

"Look, goddamit! This is a Coast Guard operation and this is *my* jurisdiction!" As Ray reprimanded them, the veins stood out on his neck. "*I'm* in command here and I have a cruise ship out there wired with explosives, with two hundred hostages onboard. And your prisoner's co-conspirators are executing U.S. citizens and feeding them to the sharks. Eleven are already dead and they're threatening to kill again in a few minutes. I'm in charge here and I intend to talk to Alvarez. Do I make myself clear gentlemen?" Ray snapped his fingers and six Coasties with assault weapons surrounded the marshals. "Or do I have to incarcerate you for obstructing a United States Coast Guard military operation?"

~~~~~~~~~~

As Ray cruised past a row of vending machines, he glared in Alvarez's direction. When their eyes met for the first time there was no trace of warmth in the exchange. Without a word, Ray took a chair across from him and placed his SIG P229 .40-caliber sidearm onto the wooden table.

The way the admiral deposited his firearm on the table and sprawled in the chair antagonized Alvarez. He regarded the bullying tactic as rather silly and it struck him amusing. Whoever this Coast Guard official was, he'd been watching too many *Dirty Harry* movies. As the room swelled with tension, Alvarez eased back in his chair and sized up his gunslinging opponent.

Alvarez's snide expression goaded Ray and he wanted to wipe off the man's cocky grin. But, keeping his game face on, Ray stared at him without talk. As the seconds approached one minute, the silence between them became drawn, expectant, waiting to be breached.

"And to whom do I owe this pleasure?" Alvarez finally asked in perfect English.

The Colombian's voice was deep with a husky vibrance. Surprisingly, it sounded more aristocratic than Latino with a stateliness that got on Ray's nerves.

"Fuck you, Alvarez! I'd just as soon shoot you right here and now." Ray leaned across the table. "Let's get to the point—*Drug Lord*. By the way, would you terribly mind if I just called you *Lord*? It's less cumbersome that way."

"As you please." Alvarez's snide expression was gone.

"Good. Eleven people are now dead—*Lord*—and I'm not very happy about it." Ray placed a handheld radio on the table between them. "I demand you contact your paisanos out there and put a stop to any more killings."

"I will be happy to do that for you—Ray. It is Ray, isn't it? It says so on your military ID. I hope you don't mind if I call you by your first name. I'm not a formal person, you know. And, as you say: it's less cumbersome that way."

Though unperturbed on the surface, Ray wanted to choke the presumptuous bastard.

"Look, Ray, give me your word that the Zetas and I will receive safe passage forthwith and you have a deal. Poof! You will never see us again. No more citizens get hurt. No more public outcry. No more difficulties." Alvarez raised his bushy brows and gave Ray a smug smile. "Now, isn't that simple?"

"Yes, except for the eleven dead citizens floating somewhere in the Gulf of Mexico. I don't think their families would appreciate us letting you sail off into the sunset. Do you?"

"Oh, yes, yes...the eleven passengers. That was terrible, indeed. But I believe there are plenty more where they came from—around two hundred or so." Alvarez looked off as if contemplating their plight. "Let's hope nothing unfortunate befalls the rest of them."

Ignoring the veiled threat, Ray held his temper in check. "If I let you and your men go, what assurances do I have that you'll release the passengers unharmed?"

"Well, you have my word, of course." Alvarez leaned forward to emphasize his next words. As he did the chains clunked against the oak

WIRED

table. "And in my world, that carries a *very lot of weight*."

Ray was unimpressed. "Oh yeah, I forgot. When the big kahuna of the cocaine cartels speaks, everybody listens. Right? Like Colombia's Justice Minister, the drug-tainted congress in Bogotá, the Los Zetas, even the Al-Qaeda boys. Right?"

Alvarez went suddenly taut and his voice dropped several degrees. "I have no affiliation with Al-Qaeda. None whatsoever."

"Oh, no? What about in Maicao, Colombia? I understand Al-Qaeda has a large network operating there under your auspices. According to our information they partake in illegal drug smuggling to facilitate their Holy Jihad against the western world. You know, funds for blowing up buildings, embassies, the World Trade Center—little things like that?"

Alvarez shifted uncomfortably in his chair and looked away. His defensive mannerism told Ray that Al-Qaeda was a sore subject.

"I'm a business man, Ray, and blowing up buildings isn't my trade. There's really no money in it. However, I do some business with the Islamic community. You might say we understand each other's...pursuits." Alvarez paused as if considering his next words. "Naturally, if I wanted to exploit our relationship, their extremism could be manipulated into performing certain favors, especially against American interests. They really don't care for you chaps at all. I believe they refer to your lovely country here as The Great Satan."

"Yeah, I bet they'd even orchestrate car bombings in Orlando and Tallahassee if you asked them to. Or explode innocent people with suicide vests."

"Perhaps." Alvarez smiled cagily. "Perhaps even more—if I had a mind to ask." With that caveat his eyes slid away, as if they might mistakenly reveal what he was scheming. "Like I said, Ray, they are not real fond of America or its people."

"Well, most of us Americans don't like those sandmonkeys any more than they like us, so I guess the feeling's mutual. I hear they have this weird obsession about virgins and wine. I suppose both are in short supply in the Middle East." Ray gave him a cheeky grin but Alvarez wasn't amused. "But I digress. Look, maybe your word carries a lot of weight amongst outlaw nations, but it doesn't carry dog shit around here. Got it? Now, what about the explosives? What assurances do I have that you won't blow the ship once your men are off?"

"They will be disabled before we leave, of course. I wouldn't want anyone else to get hurt." Putting on a fraudulent face, he added: "I'm really a very compassionate person, Ray."

The Colombian's false display of sincerity made Ray want to puke. "Yeah, right. I'll tell that to the relatives of the eleven dead passengers. Celebrity killers are always compassionate—*after* they're incarcerated and facing the chair. You're nothing but a goddamn jackal, Alvarez, and you know it. Don't hand me your bullshit."

"Oh, but we're all jackals, Ray. There is a light side and dark side competing in each of us. Don't you know that?" His tone was sermonic. "From the time we first crawled out of the sea, our reptilian consciousness has been within us. The trouble is that people like you try to suppress their primal urges, pretend to be—*civilized*. I, on the other hand, have honored my ancestral genes and instincts by taking what I want, doing what I want, all without remorse. Just like our paternal carnivores from the caves naturally did." He smiled condescendingly. "Why fight it, Ray?"

Ray glanced at his watch and resisted the temptation to chase him in that direction. Sociopaths like Alvarez were incapable of feeling guilt and Ray didn't have time to argue the point.

"Yeah, well, I suppose you're right because I'm having a primal urge to blow your brains out right now." Ray's right hand found the SIG's handgrip. "Guess I should yield to my instincts and do it. Right?"

Alvarez eyed the gun and his brows drew tighter. The executions were still fresh on the admiral's mind and his mobster instincts told him to tread lighter.

"I may be from South America, Ray, but I don't think U.S. admirals are known for executing their prisoners. So let's keep things simple. Just let me go and your world will be back in order. You'll be off the hook, as you Americans say."

"Yeah? What'll happen if I just say fuck you?"

Alvarez blinked twice and his face clouded over. In his world, no one in their right mind talked to him this way—unless they were tired of living.

"Well, Ray, I'm afraid that would create serious problems for your citizenry aboard the ship." He paused, perhaps for drama, then steepled his fingers and stared at Ray over them. "Serious problems indeed."

"Let's cut the horseshit, Alvarez. You know that we're not going to release you, don't you? Might encourage other terrorism and all that crap. Besides, you're quite a catch for our DEA boys. They can parade you around as an example of what happens to drug pushers with a 'reptilian consciousness' in our country. Might even put you on *60 Minutes* or something."

Alvarez pursed his lips and stared darkly at Ray. "I regret to hear that, Ray. That really doesn't fit into my future plans."

"Look, eleven people are dead and you're responsible!" Ray smacked his palm on the tabletop and the unexpectedness of it made Alvarez flinch. "Instead of drug trafficking charges, we're now talking about eleven counts of murder one. In case you're not aware of it, *Lord*, in Florida that means the electric chair—Old Sparky. Wanna go for a ride in it? I hear it's a real blast—if you know what I mean." Ray checked his watch. Two minutes left. "But you might just be able to spare yourself by cooperating with us. I'm sure it would be taken into consideration at your trial. Might even save you from frying. Call off your men and I'll guarantee them safe passage. You have my word on it. The U.S. government doesn't want any more lives lost. Bad for our image. But *you* stay here and that's not negotiable. Got it?"

Alvarez stared at Ray in stony silence, toying with his mustache. His eyes were cold and black, like those of a snake. There was an eternal depth in them that lacked life.

"That's unfortunate, Ray. I don't really like it here in the states. No offense. It's a nice place to visit and all . . ." His voice trailed off. "Besides, I don't believe the Zetas will go without me." His eyes glinted. "Unless, of course, they go out with a BANG—if you know what *I* mean."

At making the veiled threat, Alvarez's cocky smirk broadened and that's when Ray lost it. He'd had all the threats and cold-blooded murder he could hack for one day. In a single bound, Ray seized the P229 with his right hand and grabbed a fistful of cashmere sweater with his other. Then, with a powerful yank, he pulled Alvarez's upper body across the table and shoved the gun barrel into his throat. It all happened so fast

WIRED

Alvarez didn't have time to resist.

"Look, you low-life-sonofabitch, I'm through playing mind games with you!" Ray placed the handheld radio in his shackled hands. "Tell Mendoza you're in Sand Key and negotiating for your release. Tell him that everything is going well. Order him to halt all further executions!"

When Alvarez didn't respond, Ray jacked a shell in the chamber. "DO IT!"

When he still didn't react, Ray fired a slug into the oak tabletop, mere inches from the Colombian's stooped waist. Wood chips spewed from the impact and the smell of gunpowder and burnt wood shavings permeated the air. Within the confines of the small room the gunshot roared like a cannon, startling the three marshals outside.

Ray's features hardened more. "I said: DO IT!"

Alvarez flinched at the gunshot and stared at the scorched bullet hole in incredulous shock. He couldn't believe his eyes. Who did this tyrant admiral think he was!? With his body swelling with rage, he balled his manacled fists and slammed them down hard on the table. As the chains banged loudly, he snarled at Ray like a Rottweiler. "I demand to see my lawyers! NOW!"

Ray glanced at his watch—finding one minute left—and shook the room again by firing a second shot. The bullet whizzed one inch past Alvarez's left ear and shattered the glass front of a vending machine directly behind him, tearing into its metal innards.

The blast peppered Alvarez's face with miniscule grains of hot burning gunpowder and the loud percussion ruptured his eardrum, sending a searing pain through his auditory canal that felt like a hot sliver of glass. Tore between wonder and outrage, Alvarez clutched his injured ear and glowered at Ray with indignation. The ringing in his ears was so harsh and blaring, it drowned out all other sound—including the marshals pounding on the break room door.

With only seconds remaining Ray crawled over the table and grabbed a handful of greasy black hair. As Alvarez's muscular neck opposed the pressure, Ray ground the smoking gun barrel into his temple. "Do it, *Lord*, or say goodbye to your brains 'cause they're going on a fuckin' ride!" Ray's snarling teeth were bared and there was an underlying tremor in his voice. "NOW!!"

WIRED

As Alvarez glared into Ray's seething face, his first urge was to retaliate. Since his arrival moments ago he had been wrongfully manhandled and physically maimed. The hand covering his ear was wet with blood and he needed medical attention. But Hanna's hardcore eyes said he wasn't bluffing, that he would pull the trigger—in fact, *wanted* to pull the trigger. His prominent military rank notwithstanding, the admiral was unstrung and psychologically dangerous.

Going against his will, Alvarez brought the radio to his lips and began talking in Spanish.

"English!" Ray jerked his head back by the hair and ground the barrel harder.

Promising himself revenge and lots of it, Alvarez swallowed his mobster pride and ordered a halt to the executions—in English. For the present time, Hanna had possession of the playing field. But there was still plenty of time left to even the score and there were many ways he could rock this admiral's world—terrorizing ways.

When Mendoza on the *Majestic Star* acknowledged Alvarez's command, Ray snatched the radio from his grasp and stormed out of the break room.

"Lock this piece of shit up!"

Saturday 19:45 Hours – Clearwater Beach, Florida

During the boat ride back to the marina Kathy was quiet and withdrawn, speaking only when spoken to. The accumulation of no sleep, nonstop worry, and severe emotional trauma had drained her dry. Body and spirit, she was all used up—kaput.

As it turned out, Kathy had some sleeping pills at the townhouse, so Cal skipped the Emergency Room stop and drove straight home. After bedding her down, he fixed her a hot cup of chamomile tea and stood over her until she swallowed a double-dose of the sedative. Ten minutes later she was sleeping like a baby.

With Kathy conked out, Cal retrieved his laptop and settled on the sofa to do some research. The executions had put a different light on things and the attorney in him—as well as the ex-soldier within—necessitated more information. He wanted to know what the government was up against and by extension what he, Skip, and Kathy were facing.

After logging on the Internet, he typed in the words: **DRUG CARTELS.** From what Cal had learned of late, there was a three-way connection between the Colombian cartels, the Mexican cartels, and the radical jihadists of the world. When the search results appeared, Alvarez's name filled the computer screen. As Cal scrolled down the page, a tense lump rose in his throat. The fact that Alvarez's name was #1 on all the search engines was revealing in itself.

Cal clicked on a website that chronicled the rise and fall of Colombia's former drug boss, Pablo Escobar. After the Colombian National Police gunned Escobar down in 1993, his trusted henchman, Juan Carlos Alvarez, acceded to the narco-throne. But, unlike Escobar, who was more of a brute mobster, Alvarez used his MBA business smarts to advance his smuggling empire. By the mid-90's he had either bought-up or killed-off most of the other Colombian cartels, placing himself in control of cocaine distribution worldwide.

On another site Cal read an exposé on Islam's tainted history in terms of drug trafficking. Despite avid denials from the Muslim world, it was common knowledge that some Islamic countries—à la Afghanistan—had been growing opium poppy for decades as a means to further their radicalism. In Alvarez's back yard of South America, Islamic cells were actively trafficking in four known countries, suggesting that Alvarez had either sanctioned it or was looking the other way as a favor to a bigger fish in the Middle East pond, perhaps bin Laden himself.

In browsing a website on the Mexican cartels, Cal learned of a group called *Los Zetas*—a paramilitary gang of mercenaries numbering in the hundreds that began operations a decade ago by supplying muscle and armed protection for the big three Mexican cartels. Today, the Zetas controlled the bulk of illegal drugs crossing the U.S.-Mexican border, even acquiring legitimate businesses in the U.S. to launder their drug money. Because of their propensity for violence and reckless disregard for the law, the Z's were feared by law enforcement agencies on either side of the border.

Cal shut down the computer and stared at its darkened screen. He'd had no idea that drug smuggling and terrorism had become such bedfellows. Alvarez wasn't your average drug-pushing punk. No siree.

WIRED

He was a genius-level mastermind with more money than God, who had strong ties with radical groups dedicated to the destruction of America and the Western World. Alvarez was renowned for being vile, abhorrent, perfidious, and evil. He was feared throughout the world and would make a formidable foe, even for a force like the United States.

The way Cal saw it, the U.S. authorities faced a twofold problem stemming from Alvarez's arrest: *Stateside Terrorism* and the *Majestic Star Crisis*. The recent car bombings were at the forefront because the mayhem was being televised into America's living rooms. Politicians lived and died by the ballot box and elections were hard to win when ones constituency was being blasted to bits by car shrapnel—or, in the hostage case, gunned down and fed to the sharks. Adding more pressure was the rash of assassination attempts. DC was in pandemonium up to its political hilt.

As Cal unplugged his laptop, he deliberated on the hijackers. In all likelihood they were members of *Los Zetas*. The gang had a huge financial stake in the continual flow of drugs entering the U.S., and according to the Internet they bore no fear whatsoever of U.S. or Mexican authorities. It was more like the other way around.

Cal put the computer away and turned on the 24-hour news channel. When he learned of the eleventh afternoon execution, his blood ran cold. Without wasting a second, he grabbed the cordless phone and walked outside on the sundeck so that Kathy would not accidentally overhear. After closing the sliding door behind him, he fished a business card from his pocket and dialed Brillo's number from the light of the living room. As the phone rang in his ear, Cal restlessly roamed the wooden deck under a scattering of stars. The night sky was clear and the Big Dipper was dangling directly overhead. When Brillo answered, he got straight to the point.

"Brillo, this is Cal. Did you watch the news? They executed another passenger after we left there today. Blew some guy all to pieces."

"Yeah, I heard. Look, Cal, I can't handle much more today. What's up?"

"Do you know anybody who's familiar with the Majestic Star's layout?"

"Well, I worked on it for a few months while I was saving up for the

Sol-Mate. Why?"

"Brillo, they're going to kill them all—*every one of them.* You realize that, don't you?" When Brillo didn't answer, he continued. "This is no ordinary hijacking any more than Alvarez is a common dope peddler. This is a complex situation involving politics, the military, the drug Mafia, Al-Qaeda—the whole shebang. Alvarez has terrorist ties all over the world, most of whom hate the U.S. They're the ones setting off all these car bombs."

"Maybe so, Cal, but our government ain't gonna let two hundred Americans die out there."

"Don't be so sure. In my law practice I deal with politics everyday and it doesn't always work in favor of the victims—believe me. Our government can't let Alvarez walk, especially now after the killings. If the Coast Guard's hands are tied, which they most likely are, then somebody's got to do something or Skip won't make it out alive."

Cal paused briefly to let him digest the information, then got down to brass tacks.

"Brillo, I need your help. I've got to find a way to get aboard the Majestic Star. Maybe with two hundred people on board, the hijackers won't notice a new face. Skip's my best friend and I'm obligated to help him—or at least try. Will you help me?"

"Sure, I'll help you out anyway I can, Cal. Skip's a good friend of mine too. But I'm a fisherman, not a commando. Besides, do you really think you've got the ability to handle something like this? If not, you're just gonna get yourself killed and maybe Skip too. Those terrorists ain't foolin' around out there."

"I know that!" Cal's reply came across sharper than intended and he instantly regretted it. "Look, I've had more training than those guys ever dreamed of and it's stuff one never forgets, like riding a bicycle. There are many ways to kill, Brillo, and I pretty well know them all. And I can do it if I have to, no problem. I'm still in good shape and I should have a decent chance if I take them on one at a time. They're thugs, not skilled soldiers. And, besides, I don't have a choice. If I don't act, Skip will probably die and Kathy too—on the inside. Do you understand?"

"Yes, I do understand. I still think it's a crazy idea, though. But it's your neck. What information do you want about the Star?"

WIRED

"A diagram of the ship—you know, hatches, doors, and vents, anything that will help me get aboard at sea. And I will need some dive gear. Do you think you can arrange that?"

"Sure, that's no problem. Meet me at the marina tomorrow morning and I'll see what I can do."

"One more thing, Brillo...I'll need a handheld marine radio and a handgun, preferably a nine-millimeter automatic. Any idea where I can get them?"

"Who do you think I am, the Blackbeard of Clearwater Beach?"

"No, but I don't have any contacts around here and Florida has a waiting law on firearms. Come on, Brillo; help me out—for Skip. It's important."

"Well, I've got a handheld radio you can use, and there's a friend of a friend who may dabble in that other sort of thing. Tell you what, I'll make a few calls and meet you in the morning."

"One last thing, Cap. I'll need a ride out to the Majestic Star. Are you game?"

"I figured you'd get around to popping that question on me." Cal heard him release a lengthy sigh. "I might as well. I'm already a co-conspirator in this thing thanks to you, old buddy."

"Thanks, pal, you're a lifesaver. When this is over, I'll make sure Skip and Kathy know how much help you've been. But, for now, don't say a word to Kathy. She would just try to stop me. See you in the morning, Captain. Goodnight."

~~~~~~~~~~

Brillo hung up and began thinking of all the shady characters he had met on the water, which were quite a few. The dive gear, radio, and map of the ship were no sweat. He knew that ship inside and out. But a nine-millimeter? That could be a problem on such short notice.

Then a face from the past popped into his memory and Brillo picked up the phone. Hoping to help save Skip, he started dialing.

~~~~~~~~~~

WIRED

After his talk with Brillo, Cal went upstairs to check on Kathy. Finding her still asleep, he borrowed her car keys and drove straight to the beach hardware store. Twenty minutes later he pulled back into Kathy's parking space and killed the headlights. Two minutes after that he was dumping the contents of a shopping bag onto the glass surface of Kathy's dining room table.

"Ace is the Place," he mimicked with a sly grin.

After sorting out the merchandise, Cal unwrapped a blister pack of wire made for hanging picture frames. It wasn't piano wire, but it would do. Next, he opened two boxes containing replacement pull-starts for lawnmower gas engines. He removed the cable from the hard rubber grips and attached the picture frame wire to each handle. Once done, he gave the grips several solid snaps, smiling with satisfaction.

After that, Cal removed a hunting knife from its nylon sheath and tested the blade's sharpness with his thumb. Frowning at its dullness, he honed it using a whet rock. When it could easily slice through paper, he sheathed the knife and improvised a leg-strap using two Velcro strips.

With that done, he opened the last two packages. One contained a small but powerful waterproof penlight and the other a plastic watertight compass about the size of a quarter. He clicked the halogen penlight on-and-off to make sure it worked and then tested its brilliance by shining it against the wall. Satisfied it would serve its purpose, he placed the penlight aside.

As a final task he fashioned a wristband from Velcro and super-glued the plastic compass to the band. When this was done he placed everything back in the shopping bag and hid it in the downstairs coat closet. Then he went back upstairs to the dining table with pen and paper.

"Think," he coaxed his brain. It had been nearly thirty years, but after concentrating a while most of it came back to him: *dot-dot-dash...dash-dot-dash...dot-dash-dash.*

Cal continued writing until he had listed the entire Morse code alphabet—just about. He wasn't sure about a few letters, but had recalled enough to get by. Once committing the codes to memory, he checked his wristwatch to find it nearly midnight.

Before turning in for the night, he looked in on Kathy one last time and then tiptoed across the hallway to the guest bedroom.

WIRED

Ray leaned back in his chair and propped a foot on the gray government desk, then tilted his head back and rubbed his temples. It had been one hellacious day and he was whipped.

After coercing Alvarez into calling off the Zetas, the executions had ceased. That was the good news—it gave everybody some breathing room. But instead of taking advantage of the temporary cessation to strategize and plan ahead, Ray had spent the remainder of the day on the phone answering for his misdeeds. The only time he could actually think was while waiting on hold for some Washington bigwig.

When word leaked out about the ten executions, the phone calls flooded in. When word got out about the exploding passenger, the flood became a gusher. When the U.S. Marshals tattled to their superiors about Ray's "shootout" in the break room, the switchboard suffered a meltdown. That was the bad news—Washington and Alvarez's attorneys were in a furor over his excessive use of force.

To get the news media off his back, Ray released a prepared statement and relented under pressure to start holding daily press conferences. Tomorrow would be his first face-to-face with them and he wasn't at all enthused about it.

After having dealt with the media, Ray spent the rest of the evening fielding a procession of phone calls. The "pleased as punch" wanted to congratulate him firsthand for a job well done while the "mad as hell" waited in line to chew out his gunslinging ass—like the DEA and Justice Department. On the whole, however, callers were supportive and voiced full confidence in him. Even when the Commandant gave him his "wink-wink" official reprimand, Ray could tell that he was privately pleased. Sometimes the means to an end *was* justified, even when on the radically reckless side.

Some callers had seemed a little bit too accommodating, though, like the well meant but disingenuous way a friend offers encouragement to someone dying of incurable cancer. Their words were sincere, but Ray could hear the I'm-glad-it's-you-and-not-me tone in their voice. And none of them offered any remedial advice in way of resolving the crisis. They all seemed to be waiting for him to wave his magic wand and make the problem disappear.

After all, Ray's military record expounded nothing but excellence. He had graduated summa cum laude from the Naval War College and he was the youngest Coast Guard admiral in active service. He was touted in social circles as Washington's golden boy and a shoe-in to become Commandant one day. He was everyone's "go to" guy—the man—and his peers and superiors had come to expect results.

"That's right, Admiral. You're the man." Ray rose stiffly from his desk and stretched his arms and back muscles. "The man with the plan." He snorted pessimistically while heading for the door. "The man with *no plan* is more like it."

Before retiring to his quarters, duty prevailed upon him to make one last round of the stationhouse, a habit from his old days. As Ray strolled through the outer office, his tattered nerves gobbled up the peace and quiet. It had been a haywire day and now everything was quiet; just the sound of someone pecking on a computer keyboard and a sprinkling of radio chatter—mostly late-night sailboaters hailing bridge tenders. Tomorrow could be another madcap repeat of today—or worse, if earthly possible—and the tranquility was savoring.

After touching base with the watch captain, Ray stopped by the radio room with instructions to wake him right away should anything major crop up. Once satisfied that all was copasetic, he moseyed to his quarters and stretched out on his cot with a grateful moan. He was tired, dog-tired. Not bothering to undress, he kicked off his boots and closed his gritty eyes.

Sixty seconds later, Ray was snoring like a freight train.

Saturday 23:45 Hours – Clearwater Beach, Florida

Too hyped-up to fall asleep, Cal lay gazing at the moon through the skylight above his bed. If everything went as planned, he would be onboard the *Majestic Star* this time tomorrow night. The undertaking would be treacherous and rife with risk; but it was something he must do—for Skip, for Kathy, for himself.

While lying there, an odd exhilaration seeped into him. In an inexplicable way he was looking forward to it. In his Navy days it had been normal to have the jitters the night before a mission—everyone did. But on this particular eve he found himself curiously calm—no fear, no heeby-jeebies, no butterflies in his gut.

Something indefinable had crossed over in him. He didn't understand why, but he felt energized and surprisingly alive; just like the old days. The Cal-to-the-rescue bit excited him—Cal Stringer versus the bad guys...a Navy SEAL blast from the past...bent on snatching Skip from the jaws of death or going down in a blaze of glory. HOOYAH!

He must be crazy. No middle-aged man in his right mind would single-handedly take on eight heavily armed mercenaries. Rescuing a dear friend was an understandably noble cause, but it was still an incredibly reckless endeavor with a high element of risk. So why was he so excited?

Do I have a secret death wish? Or some weirdo hero complex? Could it have anything to do with my middle age? Calvin Stringer's last hurrah before getting too old and decrepit to rescue anyone? Hmm.

Cal hated this self-examining side of him and tried to block it out. If not, he would never fall asleep. Why did he have to dissect everything and analyze it to pieces? Why couldn't he just accept his feelings at face value without getting all-forensic about it?

It suddenly dawned on him that he was self-examining himself about his self-examining fixation and the absurdity of it brought a smile. He was driving himself crazy and he must stop it. The matter was simple: a dear friend and family member was in dire need of help that exacted his intervention. It had nothing to do with his lost youth, his fading masculinity, or because he had pimples in high school.

Exasperated with himself, Cal rolled over and forced his eyes shut. But unsympathetic to his need for sleep, his errant mind drifted back to his younger days.

The NAVY SEALs

The SEALs—from the SEA, from the AIR, from the LAND. The elite maritime counterpart to the U.S. Army Special Forces known as the Green Berets.

The SEALs were the most feared and revered commando forces in the U.S. Military, if not the world. They were highly skilled teams of men

WIRED

who were experts in demolition and covert operations; who packed a lot of firepower and did the seemingly impossible; who regarded pain as weakness leaving the body; who believed that the only thing worse than losing, was quitting.

HOOYAH!

During the 1930's, U.S. Coast Guard divers were known as Surfmen, an enlisted rating equivalent to third class petty officer at a monthly pay rate of sixty dollars. Their naval counterparts were called frogmen or UDT's—Underwater Demolition Teams. In 1962 the Kennedy administration redesignated and commissioned the ex-frogmen to create the Navy SEALs. Their enhanced role was to conduct unconventional warfare and clandestine operations in maritime environments. There was no glory, fame, or public recognition for what they accomplished because most of their missions were classified—executed quickly, professionally, and without fanfare.

When Cal received his training back in the 60's, it was called UDT Replacement Training. Today, the program was known as BUD/s—Basic Underwater Demolition/SEAL—with four phases of training so grueling that only 5% of applicants actually got to a SEAL Team.

During the first five weeks of the First Phase, the trainees—or tadpoles—were taught basic skills and required to meet certain time limits on three-mile soft sand runs and two-mile ocean swims. In addition, a grueling 50-yard underwater swim was mandatory, which proved to be the demise of countless tadpoles. Those who qualified in these areas went on to *Drown Proofing* and *Cold Water Conditioning*.

Drown Proofing was a psychological test to overcome the fear of drowning. The training was simple: with hands tied behind their backs and ankles bound, tadpoles were thrown into deep water without air tanks to sink or swim. These exercises taught them that with the proper training—and if ones life depended on it—one could find a way to swim even when bound.

Cold Water Conditioning was an ongoing part of the training. The cold is a diver's worst enemy. It sucks warmth from the body and drains one's physical and mental abilities. It breaks the weak. So, to prepare for its effect, *Surf Torture*—submersion to the brink of hypothermia—was endured on a regular basis.

WIRED

As part of their cold-water training, tadpoles were made to wade into waist-high water at the surf zone, where incoming waves break before reaching shore. There, they linked arms and sat down in 55-degree water, letting the ice-cold waves crash over their heads. Shivering in unison, they were forced to remain there until on the brink of hypothermia. At this stage they were called ashore to warm up with calisthenics and later ordered back in the frigid surf for further cold conditioning. *Surf Torture* was indeed the appropriate nomenclature, for it was unadulterated, teeth-chattering, bone-chilling torture.

Hell Week occurred during the sixth week of BUD/s training—after 30% of the class had rung out. It consisted of five days and five nights of nonstop training while getting less than eight hours of accumulative sleep during the entire exercise. It was the ultimate make-or-break test, designed to test one's physical and mental limits—and to separate the men from the real men.

The entire time during *Hell Week*, trainees were kept cold, wet, sandy, and exhausted every minute of the day. Grueling exercises consisted of raft paddling for fifteen miles, timed four-mile runs in the sand, timed two-mile swims, low crawls through mud flats, and running obstacle courses while carrying boats over their heads—sometimes filled with water.

Hell Week was nothing short of pure hell. The round-the-clock exertion, punishing cold, wetness, hunger, and lack of sleep took its physical and mental toll on all but the very fittest. For when it was over, another 40% would succumb, bringing the six-week dropout rate to 70%.

The seven-week Second Phase consisted of in-depth diving instruction and the deployment of underwater exploding devices. During this phase the physical training was more intense and the qualifying times more demanding. From launch points at sea, they performed long distance underwater swims to their combat objectives—the trademark skill separating SEALs from all other Special Forces.

Phase Three was a nine-week course pertaining to Land Warfare. There, they learned basic marksmanship skills with a variety of weapons—the M4 Carbine, M14 tactical rifle, M16 rifle, M2 .50 caliber machine gun, M203 grenade launchers, and SIG Sauer .40 caliber sidearm. The training also included infantry tactics, as well as navigation, reconnaissance, demolition, rock and ice climbing, snow skiing, and ambush techniques. During this phase the physical training was increased to fourteen-mile runs and five-mile ocean swims. The FTX—Final Field Training Exercise—was held over a five-day-and-night period where they were broken up into squads to conduct four back-to-back night operations. These military exercises required the collective use of all commando skills learned during the six months of BUD/s training.

Once the surviving trainees graduated, they received parachute training at jump school and were assigned to a SEAL Team for a six-month probationary period. During this time they received more specialized training while performing real-life commando exercises—such as parachuting at night from ten thousand feet into the ocean, then traveling by raft for up to one hundred miles to their assigned target, successfully conducting their mission, and then traveling back out to sea for rendezvous with a submarine.

Once the six-month probationary period was over, the graduates were awarded a SEAL Naval Enlisted Classification (NEC) Code and the highly coveted *Trident*—the Naval Special Warfare Insignia. Following that they served the remainder of their enlistment on a SEAL Team, using their special skills in various parts of the world on whatever covert missions were assigned them, representing a mere 5% of the applicants who had initially enrolled in the SEAL program.

~~~~~~~~~~

As the memory of it all swam through his head, Cal still couldn't believe he had survived it. It had been the most tortuous, agonizing, longest six months of his young life—where the only easy day was yesterday. But when it was all over, he found himself there—bleary-eyed, cut, bruised, blistered, sunburned, and barely standing—but there. Amazingly, he had endured.

Cal's mind suddenly snapped back to the present and he peered at the clock on the nightstand. It was after midnight—Sunday already—and he needed some sleep. Fluffing his pillow with a few sharp punches, he flopped onto his other side and closed his eyes.

After a time of willing himself to sleep, Cal drifted off. But his subconscious mind wasn't quite finished for the night and clung to remembrances of yesteryear.

~~~~~~~~~~

In his dream Cal was twenty years old again, full of piss-and-vinegar and youthful exuberance, with only one sole purpose in life—to become a Navy SEAL. As he tossed and turned, he relived the six months of intense training and witnessed his classmates falling aside in wet filthy exhaustion, unable to absorb the physical punishment.

Then his dream jumped to graduation day. He recalled the immense pride he felt while lined up with Mickey and a handful of others in their dress whites. After 26 weeks of hell, they had made the grade and now belonged to the elite brotherhood of Navy SEALs.

Brotherhood: A union of men dedicated to a common purpose or cause, whose fellowship and shared precepts bind them together in a fraternal bond of kindred spirit.

The brethren of Navy SEALs shared convictions about God and Country—one for all and all for one—and stood ready to defend such beliefs against evildoers worldwide. Their cause was righteous and their purpose just. Each and every one believed they could make a difference.

But Cal's tour of duty in Vietnam had skewed this ideological thinking. There, things weren't so clear-cut and the American soldier wasn't always the perennial good guy. There, Uncle Sam was oftentimes the G.I.'s own worst enemy by politically handcuffing the war effort. From there, over 50,000 KIA's were sent back home to their families in body bags.

At the time, however, even these travesties hadn't shaken his willingness to believe—as blindly naïve and propelled by youth as he now understood it to be. Back then, he had worn the Trident proudly. To him it was more than a symbol of mere training and endurance. It was a mark of distinction, a badge of courage, affirming that he was uniquely special to his country and colleagues. Wherever he had journeyed, the sight of it evoked admiration and respect.

Of course, now, thirty years later, Cal's romantic beliefs had long given way to cynicism and he had no illusions of life. The world was a

WIRED

greedy place revolving around power, money, and personal gain. Outside of family and a handful of friends, nobody gave a damn about you unless it benefited them in some way. The old prophesy that: *"The meek shall inherit the earth"* may come true one day, but Cal suspected the rich and powerful would still hold legal title. In essence, the world was governed by the "unwritten" Golden Rule: *"Those with the gold, make the rules."*

Cal despised how cold and morally bankrupt America had become. It saddened him and he hungered for more simpler times—times when neighbors watched out for another, when you could leave your doors unlocked, when children could play outdoors unattended, when virtually everyone spoke English.

Cal didn't belong in today's world, didn't fit in. Somewhere over the course of time he had lost a step. He coveted the olden days when life was more wholesome and uncorrupt. It was a kinder, gentler world, or so it had seemed, and there was a natural order of things. The fathers went to work, the moms stayed home, and there was always milk and cookies waiting when you got home from school.

Those simpler times were gone for good, of course, but Cal yearned for them just the same. He was spiritually homesick. So much so that he regularly revisited his childhood in his dreams.

~~~~~~~~~~

As Cal fell into a deeper sleep, he was twelve years old again. It was a bright sunny morning and he and his pal Mickey were peddling their bikes toward the corner grocery to buy some baseball cards—a morning ritual during their school summer vacation. Both were avid collectors, having a shoebox each stuffed with cards. Armed with a nickel apiece, it would buy them a pack of five cards and a flat square stick of pink bubble gum.

As they pulled into the store's gravel parking lot, they skidded to a dusty halt and laid their bikes down on their sides—too childishly eager for kickstands. When they entered the store, a bell tinkled from above and the coiled spring from the wood screen door screeched as it stretched taut. Then, as if retaliating for the abuse, the spring contracted and jerked the door shut behind them with a sharp wooden whack.

171

WIRED

The store was owned by a nice elderly couple that always greeted them by name. The floor planks creaked as you walked and there was no air conditioning, but the scattered oscillating fans circulated the summer air nicely. The store had a distinctive odor about it—a mixture of produce and Johnson's paste wax—but it wasn't an unpleasant smell. In fact, young Cal liked it.

Once having made their daily purchase, he and Mickey sat on the plank stoop outside and unwrapped their cards. With mouths bulging bubble gum they riffled through their cards, each hoping to get the prized Mickey Mantle card. That day, Mickey got the second best: a Roger Maris card. His eyes lit up and he smiled sneakily when presenting the card for Cal to see. Mickey already had a Roger Maris and he knew that Cal didn't, which would cost him dearly. And since Cal had two Whitey Ford's and two Yogi Berra's, Mickey knew that one of each would soon be his.

This haggling was part of the fun and it sometimes meant trading two or three cards for one. When Mickey stated his demand, Cal squirmed a while and whined about highway robbery, but agreed to the swap anyway—vowing to get Mickey back with tomorrow's round of cards. Then they both laughed and scoured the backs of the cards for batting averages, home runs, RBI's, and ERA's—most of which they knew by heart. It was a good world—a clean, simple world—and those lost summers would remain with him forevermore.

All of a sudden Cal's childhood dream evaporated and he was yanked back to Vietnam. He was no longer sitting on the sunny grocery stoop, but in waist-deep water under hellacious enemy fire. The night was pitch-black and he was fleeing desperately through a muddy rice field. As he clambered for cover, the world around him was under heavy bombardment, filled with violent explosions, flashes of fire, and shrieks of agony as his SEAL brethren fell. Incoming rounds were whizzing on all sides of him, drilling muddy-white holes in the surrounding water. With each near miss, his heart leapt wildly and he fled through the muck that much faster.

Suddenly a SEAL brother in front of him caught a bullet and was spun around from its impact. Cal grabbed him before he could fall but released him when seeing the man's face was gone. Then a mortar exploded somewhere behind him and its momentary flash lit up the marshy area dead ahead. For a microsecond, Cal caught a glimpse of SEALs returning fire from the reeds at the water's edge. Using their muzzle flashes as a life-saving beacon, he fixed his sights on them and powered in their direction.

Only fifteen yards to go.

Straining onward, Cal labored for air and his chest began to ache, but his adrenaline meter was pegged—keeping him running, running for his life.

Ten yards to go.

By now the jungle air was thick with spent gunpowder and a smoky haze loomed over the field like a death shroud. Hampering visibility all the more was the nonstop deluge of spraying water and dislodged mire. As Cal squinted through the smoke and spray, he spotted Mickey crouched within the tall reeds. He was screaming into a PRC-25 backpack radio with a hand covering his ear. Mickey was radioing the Seawolves for close air support and medevac extraction and Cal wanted to be amongst the living when the helicopters arrived. There would be other times to even the score with the VC.

When Mickey was finished talking, he shoved the radio aside and peered through the smoky haze. When he spotted Cal, his head rose erect with recognition and he began cheering Cal on. His words were lost in the blare of battle, but they summoned up Cal's last ounce of energy. With renewed purpose and grit, Cal forced his disciplined legs to pump harder, faster.

Only five more yards!

Cal's quadricepses were burning but the water was shallower now, easier to negotiate. As he high-stepped through the mire a second volley of rounds whizzed past him and he instinctively ducked while plowing onward in a stooped run. In answer to the enemy fire, Mickey stood up to provide cover, firing his M-16 on full automatic while yelling something over his right shoulder. Seconds later the other SEALs joined in, laying down a fierce barrage of defensive lead.

When Mickey's clip ran empty, he crouched to reload—his worried eyes darting between his M-16 and Cal's progress. After inserting a fresh clip he stood straight up, blazing away with one hand while waving Cal on with the other. When he was all out of ammo, he tossed his M-16 into the reeds and faced Cal with outstretched arms, urging him on with determination.

"Come on, Cal! You're home free! COME ON!"

Then in daring disregard for his own life, Mickey waded out in the open to meet Cal. As he drew nearer, Cal could hear the sucking sound of his boots slogging along the mushy mud bottom. With just a few feet separating them now, Mickey's face was clearer. The whites of his eyes seemed to glow against the dark greasepaint on his face. There was a notable intensity in those eyes; one that contradicted the promising smile on Mickey's face.

With their eyes locked, Cal strained a smile back at him and reached for Mickey's outstretched hand. He was going to make it. In the face of enemy fire, he was delivered. Mickey would not let him die—not here and now, not in a wretched place like this.

All at once there was a thunderous explosion and the deepest dark of the jungle turned blinding white. Simultaneously, shards of searing shrapnel pelted Cal's backside and his legs instantly failed him. While tumbling beneath the watery surface, he heard a faint echo of someone crying out in anguish never realizing it was himself.

As Cal settled on the bottom, a prickling numbness spread throughout his injured body, mercifully commuting the pain. At peace now and pain free, he languished in the muck without awareness or sensation. As Cal's life force ebbed away, he grew more and more disconnected from the mayhem above and his body grew lighter and lighter until feeling weightless, without substance. Then something incorporeal let go inside him—came unanchored—and a strange disembodiment swept over him.

As Cal floated outside his body, the battle noise quieted altogether and he lost all sense of self. Then, as though no longer belonging to life, he faded into nothingness and released Mickey's hand—never aware that he had at last grasped it.

DAY 4

"THE ACCEPTANCE"

"Courage is the price that life exacts for granting peace,
the soul that knows it not, knows no release
from little things."

Amelia Earhart (1897-1937), U.S. aviator, author.

"All that is necessary for evil to succeed is for good men to do nothing."

Edmund Burke (1729-1797), Statesman, author, philosopher.

"Land and sea, weakness and decline are great separators,
but death is the great divorcer for ever."

John Keats (1795-1821), English poet.

"The land cannot be cleansed of the blood that is shed therein,
but by the blood of him that shed it."

Hebrew Bible, numbers 35:33.

WIRED

Sunday 05:58 Hours – Group St. Petersburg

"Admiral," a faraway voice called, "you have an important phone call, sir."

Someone was shaking his arm and Ray protested by pulling away. He was tired and just wanted to sleep. When the shaking persisted, he opened his eyes to find the senior watchstander standing over him—again. He had already awakened Ray three times during the night and the repeated sleep disruption was getting old.

"I'm sorry to disturb you again, sir. The caller won't identify himself, but he says he's a past informant of yours and that you would want to take his call. He claims to have some confidential information regarding the Majestic Star situation."

Nodding, Ray threw his legs over the edge of the cot and sat up sleepily, letting his eyes adjust to the light. If the caller turned out to be a reporter, he would have someone's head on a platter. So far, the media had tried every trick in the book to get a word with him.

After wiggling into his boots, Ray rose with a sigh and lumbered down the hallway with his shoelaces dragging the polished tile floor.

Sunday 06:01 Hours – The "Majestic Star"

Skip opened his eyelids to find his arms and legs untied. Apparently someone had entered his cabin during the night and freed him while he slept. Between his concussion and chronic fatigue, his sleep had been deep—practically catatonic.

Skip checked his watch and started to sit up when the mother of all migraines changed his mind. The slightest movements made his brain throb, as if it were floating around loose inside his head banging against his skull. The only things he could move without some measure of pain were his eyeballs.

After yesterday's maniacal detonator game, Skip had been left alone to languish in his own misery. Tied to his bunk and unable to move, time had run slow—like thick mud—and the minutes crept by at a punishing rate. A prisoner of his own thoughts, his rollercoaster emotions had run full circle—taking him from outrage, to soul-searching despair, back to

176

bitter outrage. During these bouts of enmity and self-pity, he had killed Gold-Tooth in his mind a dozen times. Some time after the porthole went dark, he had drifted off to sleep without knowing when. But it was a twitching, restive sleep and he dreamed of dark disjointed things. Nothing dreadful enough to wake him, but the sort that leaves its gloomy fingerprint after wakening.

Bracing himself for some pain, Skip rolled onto his right side to face the brightening porthole. The migraine punished him as expected but it felt heavenly to be off his aching back. He had lain flat on it for a solid fifteen hours and it was killing him.

It would be daylight soon and Skip wondered if any overnight progress had been made regarding the negotiations. He hadn't heard any gunfire or explosions since yesterday, which he took as a good sign. If the executions started back up again, he would probably get himself killed next time. No matter how hard he tried, he couldn't stand by while innocent people died. He just wasn't made that way. Next time, he was a dead man.

Or, as they would say in Skip's native Georgia: *Dead, slicker 'n shit*.

Sunday 06:02 Hours – Clearwater Beach, Florida

Cal awoke with a start, sitting bolt upright in bed and soaked in sweat. The bed looked like a cyclone hit it and the sheets were twisted around him like a cocoon. Once realizing it was just a dream, that he was safe and sound in Kathy's Florida home, he peeled back the sheets and slumped against the headboard. The 'Nam dream always weirded him out and left him physically drained. Even his insides were shaking.

As reality reasserted itself, Cal snatched up a spare pillow and buried his sweaty face in it. Its coolness brought relief to his overheated skin and the cotton pillowcase gobbled up tiny beads of perspiration. When the pillow lost its freshness, he tossed it aside and relaxed his head against the headboard. He had to get a grip.

But blotting out remembrance of that ill fated night was an imponderable task—the night Mickey died. The night that very nearly claimed his own teenage life.

WIRED

"Admiral Hanna, here." Ray's voice was husky from sleep.

"Ray, this is a friend."

"Pardon me? Who is this?" Running on just a few scattered hours of broken sleep, Ray wondered if he had missed something. "And why are you calling me Ray?"

"We've talked before, Ray. A few years ago I gave you the tip on the big cocaine bust in West Palm. After that, I put you onto the three boatloads of illegals tryin' to sneak into the Keys. Remember?"

"Oh, yes, I certainly do." Ray switched the handset to his other ear and grabbed a pen. "Although I never got your name, Mister..."

"That's not important. Look, you've got a serious situation on your hands—a real-life Mexican standoff. Your hands are tied and I know how flustered you must be."

"Really?" The caller had a gruff northern accent. New York or Jersey, Ray thought. "And exactly where are you getting your information from, Mister...?"

"Does it matter? I get around. Look, I've got another piece of information you might be interested in. Some nameless individual is gonna attempt to save those people aboard the cruise ship. It sounds nutty, but he's supposed to be an ex-Navy SEAL or somethin'. Anyway, he's got a way on the ship and he will be well armed. I know that for a fact 'cause I arranged for the merchandise. Give him a wide berth, Ray. I know you got the ship sealed off tighter'n a drum, but if you want to increase the chances of those passengers living, look the other way tonight. He might make a difference. Whatcha got to lose?"

Ray's reaction was sharp. "Plenty, that's what!" The last thing he needed was civilian interference. "Are you suggesting that I look the other way and allow some lunatic to board the Majestic Star and endanger even more lives? That's ludicrous!"

"Maybe. But I'm told this guy knows his shit and will be carryin' a handheld radio. If he thinks you're on his side, maybe he'll feed you the inside scoop. You know, tell you what's goin' on out there at sea. Might come in handy. That's all I got for you, Ray. Take it or leave it. Chow."

"Wait a second! I need more informat..." Ray's voice trailed off when

178

the line went dead. Perplexed, he asked himself: "Who is this guy? And why does he keep calling me?"

Bothered by this latest complication, Ray rose from his chair and headed for the coffeepot. This was all he needed—a freaking Rambo wannabe.

Sunday 06:09 Hours – The "Majestic Star"

Skip sat up on the edge of his bunk with a grimacing grunt and planted both feet on the floor. The sudden movement made his head swim and the wrecking ball inside it clanged hard against his cranium. When the clanging eased up to a bearable bang, he stood up and was struck by another wave of dizziness. Once he trusted his wobbly legs enough to carry his weight, he tottered into the bathroom to check his injuries.

Latching onto the washbasin for support, Skip looked into the mirror and twisted his head to one side. The back of his head was caked with dried blood and the gash was still sticky to the touch. The entire crown area was swollen and sore but the damage wasn't as bad as it looked. Just a nasty scalp wound. His worst injury was the concussion caused by the jarring blow.

Skip tilted his head back to examine the knife wound on his throat. There was a thin line of clotted blood running crosswise below his beard line. As he ran a finger over it, it evoked raw memories from yesterday and he vowed for the millionth time to get even with Gold-Tooth.

Filling the basin with water, he prepped himself for pain and dipped his head into the warm liquid. Instantly the blood gravitated to his head and his skull exploded in agony. After rinsing the blood from his hair, he straightened with a weave and blotted his wet head with a towel. Then he cleansed his neck with a wet washcloth and applied rubbing alcohol to both wounds—cursing Gold-Tooth as the fiery isopropyl did its job.

Deciding to let the wounds heal without a bandage, Skip turned his attention to his dress whites. His pants were speckled with flecks of red and the back of his shirt had a big bloodstain from his head wound. They needed to be washed. The passengers were already stressed enough and they didn't need to see their captain traipsing around looking like an axe murderer.

WIRED

Skip sat down on the commode lid and removed his pants, being careful not to bend over. He lowered them into the standing water and then removed his shirt to soak. As the tap water turned a cloudy rusty-red, it was a graphic reminder of yesterday's tragedy.

Without posing a threat to anyone, eleven human lives had been snuffed out—exterminated like bugs. The murderous act filled Skip with hate and the vile nature in which it had been committed made his hatred boil. He was especially wroth over the perverse way Gold-Tooth forced him to partake in the explosion of victim eleven. There wasn't enough left of that poor disintegrated soul for his family to even bury.

The raw memory of it reignited Skip's wrath and deepened his thirst for revenge. While rinsing out his pants, he twisted a wet pant leg for lack of an enemy throat to grasp. As the watery-red liquid ran down his muscular forearms, he uttered a solemn vow through clenched teeth.

"There WILL be retribution, by God. Mark my words: those rat bastards will pay!"

Sunday 06:14 Hours – Clearwater Beach, Florida

As Cal sat against the headboard, he couldn't get Mickey off his mind. They had grown up together in the late 60's during the waning years of the Vietnam War. In those days the military draft was in full swing and a foregone conclusion upon your eighteenth birthday. Since the prospect of cringing in a foxhole hadn't appealed to either of them, they both joined the Navy.

At first the Navy recruiter's pitch hadn't persuaded them to enlist. But after hearing all about the adventuresome-sounding SEAL program, they both signed up on the spot—their eighteen-year-old imaginations filled with fantasies of glory and adventure.

The odds of them both completing the BUD/s training was a long shot, more like infinitesimal. If not for their mutual support during those six torturous months, neither would have survived it. Each had wanted to ring out a dozen times but the other wouldn't stand for it. So, in the end, it was as much their friendship as fortitude that carried them through.

On graduation night he and Mickey had gone out on the town to celebrate. After partying until the wee hours, they had ended up in a seedy hotel room with two strippers. Luckily, they were both off-duty the next day, which gave them time to recuperate from their monster hangovers.

That was so long ago, Cal mused. *Younger men in much younger days.*

Following the rice paddy ambush, Cal regained consciousness two days later in a Saigon hospital. Soon afterward he learned that Mickey hadn't survived the firefight and that a fellow SEAL named Jason Myles had saved his life.

Myles, the story went, had been in retreat that fateful night a few yards behind Cal. Following the explosion that took Mickey's life, Myles fished Cal's limp body out of the muddy water and carried him courageously ashore under heavy enemy fire. When Cal was released from the hospital, he looked Myles up to personally thank him and they had been best friends ever since.

As Cal padded barefoot into the bathroom, he felt blessed to have had two best friends like Mickey and Skip. Tragically, he'd lost one dear friend; he wasn't about to lose the other.

After donning a Mickey Mouse tee and khaki pants, Cal started downstairs to brew some coffee. Along the way he peeked in on Kathy, who was still fast asleep. As he studied her sleeping face in the muted light, the years melted away and whisked him backward in time.

After getting out of the Navy, Cal had moved back home to attend college and law school. But things had changed a lot during his four-year military absence—especially his skinny, flat chested, freckle-faced little sister. She had blossomed into a real teenage beauty and he resented the way the local boy-vultures circled her like a meaty carcass to feast upon.

Being a male himself, Cal knew what the boy-vultures were after and that naturally roused his protective instincts. So, true to form, he became the characteristically overprotective brother that hawked over his little baby sister. And to make his self-invited, honor-protecting crusade even more challenging, Kathy seemed to fall in love with nearly every boy she dated.

Kathy was different from the other high school girls and Cal knew it. She possessed a genuine sweetness and a gracious fun-loving personality. Combined with her knockout good looks, it made her enormously popular at school, especially with the guys.

WIRED

It was natural for schoolboys to indulge in the "easy girls" now and again, but, when it came right down to it, Kathy was the kind of gal they wanted to date and go steady with. After all, what respectable guy wanted to be seen in public with a girl who had more fingerprints on her fanny than the freakin' FBI?

So, to help preserve her virtue—needed or not—when Kathy wasn't around, he made it a point to warn her young suitors that he was watching them. And since they had all heard the war stories about her badass Navy SEAL brother, this often caused Kathy problems in keeping a steady boyfriend.

At first Kathy tolerated the interference, telling herself it was just brotherly love. But after a number of beaus mysteriously stopped calling her, she had marched straight into his room and confronted him about it. After receiving a fiery twenty-minute lecture about his unwanted meddling, Cal promised to behave—sort of. After all, he didn't intend to scare off *all* of her boyfriends—just the drooling, hot-and-horny ones.

Later as an adult, though, Kathy admitted being secretly comforted by the fact that he had watched over her during her vulnerable teenage years. She had been flattered by all of his big brother attention and thoroughly convinced at the time that he was insanely jealous.

"Yeah, maybe I was a little jealous," Cal admitted, gazing down at her sleeping face. "And I guess I got carried away with the older brother thing. But you've always been too darn good for your own good." With a loving smile he brushed back a strand of fallen hair covering her eyes. "But that's what makes you my Kathy and I wouldn't change a hair on your pretty head."

~~~~~~~~~~

Instead of a frilly nightgown from *Victoria's Secret*, Kathy preferred an oversized T-shirt to sleep in. So, wearing a wrinkled 3X souvenir tee from the *Daytona 500*, she teetered barefoot down the steps to the sound of Cal noisily fixing breakfast. He was whistling cheerfully and it sounded like he was rattling every pot and pan that she owned.

"Good morning, sleepyhead," Cal smiled. He was standing by the stove beating a bowl of eggs. "You're just in time for my specialty—

western omelet and buttermilk biscuits topped with hot bologna gravy. Just like mom used to fix. Remember?"

"Sure do, Brother." Kathy grinned sleepily at him and patted down her disorderly hair. "But how about a cup of coffee first? My cholesterol can wait a while. I'm not awake yet."

"Probably a little hangover from the sedative. Hungry?"

"Starving."

Kathy sat down at the table where she could watch Cal fix breakfast and picked up a crumpled pack of cigarettes. Yawning, she shook one out, lit it, and exhaled a cloud of smoke at the ceiling. Despite her mental dullness, she did feel better. It was the first time she had slept through the night since Wednesday. The Valium had given her overburdened brain some time off from itself in which to emotionally recuperate; something she sorely needed.

Cal placed a cup of coffee in front of her and pecked her on the forehead.

Kathy smiled up at him appreciatively and blew out a puff of smoke with one eye squinted against it. "Has there been any more news this morning?"

Standing at the kitchen counter with his back to her, Cal froze at the question. When he suddenly stopped whipping the eggs, Kathy's stomach flittered. Something was wrong.

"What is it, Cal? What's going on?" When he didn't answer, she laid her cigarette in an ashtray and straightened in her chair. "Calvin Stringer, don't you dare hide anything from me!"

Cal's shoulders sagged and he released a long sigh at the ceiling. He had hoped to put this off until after breakfast. With Kathy awaiting his answer, he turned around to face her.

"I didn't want to upset you as soon as you got out of bed this morning, but the terrorists executed another passenger yesterday while we were heading back to the marina." Fright registered on Kathy's face and she gasped while covering her mouth. "But it wasn't a crewmember, though," he added to calm her fears. "Skip's okay." When the tension eased on her face, he continued. "According to the TV, there've been no more killings since. The authorities are still negotiating for a peaceful resolution, yada, yada, yada. Same old crap."

WIRED

To avoid upsetting her more, Cal omitted the sadistic way the last victim had been killed. It was the top news story on every TV channel and she would learn of it soon enough.

"Oh, those poor eleven souls," Kathy whimpered with lowered eyes. "And their poor families." Too upset to remain seated, she reclaimed her cigarette and paced around the dining room. "When is the government going to do something? Are they just going to stand by while all two hundred people are selectively murdered?" *Good question,* Cal thought. "Something needs to be done, Cal, and soon."

While standing at the kitchen counter, Cal studied his pacing sister. To spare her worry, he had already concocted a story to cover his absence while on board the *Majestic Star*—assuming he made it that far. He planned to tell her that he was flying back to Detroit for an important court case that couldn't be postponed. But, now, as he watched Kathy pace, he debated whether or not to level with her. She was walking back and forth, berating the authorities and puffing away on her cigarette. *Rant. Puff. Rant. Puff.*

After deliberating on it some more, Cal decided to tell her the truth. If Kathy had been born a man, she would do the same thing. She would say to hell with it and go in for the rescue, regardless of the risk. That's exactly what she'd do.

"Kathy, you're absolutely right. Somebody's got to do something—or at least try." Cal set the bowl down and took a seat at the table. His sister would kick up a big fuss at first, but in time she would come around. He was sure of it. "Sit down." He gestured at a vacant chair opposite him. "I want to tell you something."

Cal's sudden seriousness caught Kathy off guard and she stopped pacing in mid-stride. Something in his tone frightened her. As she edged towards the table, she studied Cal's face but found it unreadable. With her nerves aquiver, she settled into the chair and snuffed out her cigarette.

"Kathy, I think the Coast Guard's hands are completely tied." Cal reached across the table and clasped her hands, finding them cold and sweaty. "With eleven Americans now dead, our government will never release Alvarez—they can't, not after the executions. The public wouldn't stand for it. And if our military storms the Majestic Star, too many innocent people would die—everybody if the ship is detonated. It's a no-win situation, which the terrorists accepted going in. They're mercenaries, meaning they are quite willing to die if it comes down to that. If you think about it, this whole thing's been a suicide mission from the start."

As he spoke, Kathy stared a hole in their clasped hands, as if afraid to look him in the eye.

"Sis, I believe the terrorists are going to blow the Majestic Star no matter what. The drug underworld aims to send a message to our government. In retaliation for the Alvarez and Gonzalez arrests, they've declared war on America. As long as those two drug lords remain behind bars—which they most likely will—their compatriots will keep dishing out the punishment. And they're worthy opponents, even for the combined forces of the United States."

Cal paused momentarily to study her downturned face. Kathy was still avoiding eye contact but she was listening.

"The way I see it, Alvarez will never be released and Gonzalez is already out of the picture. And from a military standpoint the authorities can't do diddlysquat without endangering the two hundred hostages. That means Skip's on his own."

Cal was scaring her and Kathy wondered what he was leading up to. *Was he preparing her for Skip's inevitable death? Was that it?*

Timidly, Kathy looked him in the eye. "I hope to God you're wrong, Cal. It's a hopeless situation, isn't it? Is that what you're trying to tell me?" Her fingernails dug deeper into his palms with each succeeding question. "Are you saying that Skip is going to die and there's nothing we can do about it? Is that it?"

"No, Kathy, that's *not* what I'm saying." Preparing to drop the bomb on her, Cal shifted in his seat. "I've made a decision to board the Majestic Star tonight—to see if I can help Skip."

Kathy's eyes widened and her jaw dropped. "WHAT?" The news was so unbelievable it didn't register right away. At length, she found her tongue. "Like hell you are!" She flung his hands away and crossed her arms in disapproval. "Are you crazy!? You're going to get yourself killed! I've never heard such a ridiculous thing in my entire ..."

"Now wait a minute!" Cal interrupted, rising to his feet. "Hear me out!" The sternness of his voice silenced her. "I'll be armed and dressed like a tourist." He gestured at his Mickey Mouse shirt and Docker slacks.

"Out of 200 passengers, there's a reasonable chance they won't notice me. I'll find Skip and see what's going on. Then I don't know exactly what I'll do, but I'll think of something. If nothing else, I can let the Coast Guard know what's happening out there. Brillo is providing me with a radio."

"BRILLO!? Is he in on this thing too?" Feeling betrayed, Kathy raised her arms in the air and let them drop to her lap. "What is this, a conspiracy? You're both off your rockers!"

By now Kathy had heard enough of this nonsense. She was rising in protest when Cal forced her down by the shoulders.

"Sit down, Kathy. Don't get all gaga on me!"

Kathy shot him a sour look but remained seated. Cal was right—she was getting all worked up. She needed to calm down and reason with him; talk him out of this crazy idea.

"Cal, you're pushing sixty and those men out there are professional killers. What chance do you really have? Please forget this harebrained idea and let the Coast Guard do its job. I couldn't bear to lose my husband and brother too. I don't know what I'd do if . . ."

Cal cut her off in mid-sentence, emphasizing his words by thumping a forefinger against the glass tabletop. "I repeat, Kathy—the Coasties . . ain't . . gonna . . do . . a . . damn . . thing!"

Kathy blinked at Cal's thumps but didn't utter a word. Behind her glistening brown eyes her brain was fast at work, taking everything into account.

"Kathy, it's a deadlock, stalemate, or whatever you want to call it. You saw that for yourself yesterday. Eleven Americans were slaughtered and what did the authorities do about it? Nothing—that's what. They're *negotiating*. I'm not saying it's the Coast Guard's fault. They're just in a helluva spot."

Pausing to let his argument sink in, Cal went into the kitchen to refill his coffee cup. The bologna gravy was burning so he turned off the burner and placed the smoldering skillet in the sink. With that, he sat back down to face Kathy, who still seemed unconvinced.

"The reports say there's only eight guerillas aboard the ship," he continued. "Maybe I can dodge them and stay hidden until I find Skip—I don't know. I can take care of myself, don't you worry about that." He leaned forward. "I'm 54, Kathy, not pushing 60. Don't make me any older than I am." He grinned at her, but she didn't grin back. "Look, if I don't do something, Skip's chances of survival are between slim and none—and Slim just left town. For his sake, I've got to try or he's most likely a dead man. You have to be strong, Sis. I can use your help."

Kathy's eyes dropped and she lapsed into silence. A tug-of-war was waging inside her between Cal's piercing logic and her love for the only two men in her life. Part of her accepted Cal's thinking while another part emphatically rejected it, petrified of the consequences.

Feeling bewildered, Kathy gave up her chair and walked outside. The air was misty and it felt good against her heated face. Leaving the sliders standing open, she crossed the sundeck and lit another cigarette.

The sun was peeping over the Sabal palms across the canal and its orangish glow was mirroring beautifully off the still water. Broadening the splendor, the grass glittered with beads of crystal where the sun's rays touched the dew. Completing the picturesque scene, white seabirds spiraled overhead against a vibrant morning sky. It was a spectacular daybreak.

On most mornings Kathy would have basked in nature's glory and savored the day's new beginning. But, today, she simply wasn't interested. In truth, she dreaded the upcoming day. It promised to be long and empty. She longed to be somewhere else, curled up in a sleepy daydream, where the horrors of the world couldn't reach her.

While staring at the sky, Kathy questioned why it had to be all or none—why she had to risk her only brother in order to save her husband. It wasn't fair. When tears pricked her eyes, Cal's words came to mind urging her to be strong. He was right, of course. This was no time to get sidetracked by maudlin self-pity or by abstract questions that held no real answer.

Cal was also right about the standoff. The government would *never* release Alvarez; meaning those freak-show terrorists would keep on executing people until there were no hostages left to kill, including Skip. Somebody had to do something—fast. Clearly convinced that no one else would or could, Cal was hell-bent on trying. If she were going to do her part to help him, she needed to shed her opposition like an old skin. Her two guys needed her now more than ever.

WIRED

Taking a final puff on her cigarette, Kathy flicked it into the canal and watched the water ripple away from its splashing entry. When it dwindled away to concentric nothingness, she turned for the sliding doors. Since there was no changing Cal's mind, she wanted all the details. His life, and perhaps Skip's too, depended on it.

When Kathy went inside she found Cal sitting pensively at the table, deeply immersed in thought. His hands were clasped before him and his head was slightly bowed, as if he were meditating or perhaps praying. Kathy found this oddly endearing and her heart cracked. He looked like a sad little boy sitting there alone.

What courage he must have, she admired. *Courage forced upon him by circumstances not of his choosing—dire circumstances.*

Cal didn't want to die; she knew that. Yet, there he was—quietly marshaling himself, willing to lay down his life for kith and kin. It brought to mind a passage written by Camille Paglia: *"A woman simply is, but a man must become."*

Feeling blessed to have such a gallant and selfless brother, Kathy went to him and placed a considerate hand on his shoulder. Cal deserved as much support as he could get. Her touch seemed to release him from his trance and he smiled up at her, but Kathy saw no smile in his eyes. There was something cheerless in them—a measure of vulnerability—and it pained her to see him so overburdened with purpose.

"What do you want me to do, Brother?" The former disapproval in her eyes was gone, replaced by empathy. "Since you're dead set on doing this, I guess we should get the show on the road."

Cal's somber eyes brightened a little and he covered her hand with his. "Thanks for understanding, Sis. I really have no choice, you know."

"I know." With watery eyes she tucked Cal's face in her hands and kissed him on the forehead. "I'm sorry for getting so upset. I just can't bear the thought of losing you both. That's all."

"It'll be alright." He patted her hand. "I'll bring him back to you, safe and sound. Promise."

Kathy hugged him and tears spurted. "I know you will."

It was settled then. Tonight, Cal would board the *Majestic Star* and Kathy would help him. With their pact in place, Cal rose to his feet and changed the subject.

"I don't know about you, kiddo, but I'm starved. Let's eat. Then we'll pay Brillo a visit. He's supposed to be rounding up a few items for me. What do you say?"

Kathy looked past him into the kitchen and sniffed. "Okay. But it looks like your gravy's ruined."

"That's okay," he grinned. "I'll make some more—just like mom's."

Sunday 06:50 Hours – Group St. Petersburg

When it was learned that foreign nationals had perpetrated the hijacking, the Department of Homeland Security posted a nationwide *High Condition* orange alert. When the car bombings and sniper attacks began, it was elevated to condition red: *Severe*. From that moment on— by DHS design—a host of other government bureaus were drawn into the case.

As Incident Commander, Ray felt obligated to take all agency calls no matter what time of day. After all, terrorism was not a nine-to-five business. But his body required a minimal amount of rest and his self-imposed 24-hour accessibility was wearing him down. The U. S. government never sleeps and it seemed that every rested-and-bored-night-shift-working-junior-department-head in D.C. was compiling a status report for their respective bosses.

The bureaucratic chain of command was long-and-winding—virtually without beginning or end—and there was no shortage of superiors. Like the dirt on earth, there were layers and layers of them. As rear admiral, Ray had four of them himself—the Commandant, Vice-Commandant, Chief of Staff, and his direct superior: the Vice-Admiral serving as Atlantic Area Commander.

The Vice Admiral—unaffectionately dubbed by Ray as the Vice-Weasel—was a politically motivated glad-hander whom Ray despised. The man was a politician, not a soldier, who spent more time safeguarding his military career than the shores of America. He was a backslapping, scratch-golfing, plastic-coated panderer who delighted in being in the limelight. Not only would the huckster jump at the chance to hold this afternoon's press conference, he would be in his glory. But as long as Ray was in charge, the VW would never represent his district on national television. Never. He would be a discredit to the Seventh.

If Ray had any real choice in the matter, he would have stuck to issuing press releases. He was a military man, not a TV luminary, and he wasn't looking forward to being grilled by the media on live television. Just yesterday the *St. Petersburg Times* broke the story and overnight all the big boys were in town. Broadcast rigs were parked across the street from the station at every possible angle. Emblazoned on the vehicles, the logos of ABC, CNN, and NBC were visible from the stationhouse.

Before tackling his latest stack of messages, Ray decided to shave and shower while things were still relatively quiet. With a psychotic killer like Mendoza at large, anything could happen at any moment and he didn't want to look as rough as he felt during his first televised news conference.

As Ray entered the shower room, he pondered the anonymous caller. Whoever this guy was, his tips had proven accurate in the past, even if his motive remained unclear. Most snitches sought a reward of some kind—or at least a favor—but, thus far, this guy had asked for nothing. Still, Ray knew the day would inevitably come. With these seamy characters it always did.

Ray unzipped his ditty bag and arranged the toiletries on a stainless shelf below the mirror. While brushing his teeth, he studied his haggard reflection. His bloodshot eyes were puffy from lack of sleep and directly beneath them were baggy dark circles making him look a decade older. Complementing his haggard appearance was a dark two-day-old stubble—stylish in Hollywood, perhaps, but certainly not in the military. On the whole he had that dashing death-warmed-over look, perfect for going on national television.

After rinsing toothpaste from his mouth, Ray lathered up his face and began shaving. Three minutes later he was standing in a steamy shower, letting the H2O rejuvenate his sleep-deprived body. After showering, he donned a freshly starched set of ODU's and his dark-blue ball cap, looking and feeling better. Ray could breathe in the utility clothing and greatly preferred it to the dress uniform. Before facing the press corps later today, he would change into his official dress uniform and swap his ball cap for white officer's hat with eagle and gold-embroidered oak leaves. The dress uniform *did* look impressive, adorned with colorful ribbons and medals—a.k.a. chest candy—but, to him, its usefulness ended right there.

Once back at his desk, Ray systematically separated the mound of message slips into two piles. The bulk of calls were from reporters and politicians making inquiries on behalf of their constituents. Apart from those were a number of stirring messages from the relatives of passenger hostages. One frantic father had faxed a photograph of his daughter with: **"IS SHE OK? SOMEONE PLEASE CALL ME"** scribbled along the bottom with his name and phone number.

Ray opened his top desk drawer and raked in the pile from the reporters and politicians. They could wait. Then he picked up the phone and dialed a worried mother in Kentucky. It was an unpleasant task and one that most admirals would have delegated to a junior officer. But given the life-and-death circumstances, Ray felt compelled to speak to the relatives himself. He was in command and it just seemed the proper thing to do.

As the phone rang in Ray's ear, he deliberated on the latest unexpected hitch—the SEAL vigilante. *"Look the other way tonight"* the informant had said. *"Whatcha got to lose?"* As if Ray should actually consider letting some armed whacko board the ship to wreak havoc. The suggestion was not only unthinkable, it was absurd.

"What do I have to lose?" Ray thought aloud. "Oh, not much—two hundred American lives, a multi-million dollar cruise ship, my military career. Just a few things like that." He snorted and looked heavenward. "Hey, will somebody up there please give me a freaking break?"

When the Kentucky woman didn't answer, Ray hung up and peered outside. The sun had risen and crimson spangles of sunlight were pouring through the office window. Weather-wise, it promised to be a decent day. His day, however, remained to be seen. On top of dealing with Mendoza, he now had this SEAL fellow to worry about—whoever he was.

Who is this character and what's his connection with the Majestic Star? Who would even attempt such a thing single-handedly? Either he's a real badass or crazy—maybe both. What's his motive? Was he some glory-seeker looking for his fifteen minutes of fame? Or some shell-shocked war veteran out to save America? Who knows?

Navy SEAL or not, Ray wouldn't tolerate any outside interference. On top of everything else, he didn't need some loose cannon entering the picture. Whoever this Rambo civilian was, he must be stopped.

Sunday 07:15 Hours – Clearwater Beach, Florida

After finishing breakfast, Kathy and Cal climbed into the car to go meet Brillo. As they crossed the Memorial Causeway Drawbridge, Cal glanced up at the bridge tender's shack and spied the elderly man in the open window. When their eyes met the tender stuck out a neighborly hand, but the car streaked by so fast Cal didn't have time to respond. By the time the blurry wave registered in his brain, the convertible was already descending the other side.

Feeling bad for not waving back, Cal scolded Kathy for driving too fast and warned her to slow down before she got a speeding ticket. Aware of his fondness for the tenders, Kathy smiled at the road ahead and ignored his pouty behavior. Two minutes later, they motored into the marina to find Brillo waiting for them on the dock.

"Good morning, Captain." As Cal shook his hand, Brillo's eyes flashed uneasily at Kathy. "It's okay," Cal said, nodding at her. "She knows what's going on. Everything's cool."

Partly relieved, Brillo grinned at Kathy apologetically and shifted his feet, as if embarrassed by being in cahoots with Cal behind her back.

"Well," Cal said, "did you have any luck locating that merchandise we talked about?"

"Yeah—plus some." Brillo smiled proudly. "I have a little surprise for you."

"Oh, yeah? I like surprises. Whatcha got?"

Brillo went into the forward cabin and returned with a beat up backpack. "Here's the sketch of the Majestic Star you wanted. I've marked all the external hatches and entrances. There's a hatch on the starboard side for loading and offloading supplies and waste. It's about three feet above the waterline and can be opened from the outside. That would be the best way to sneak aboard."

While Cal studied the hand drawing, Brillo dug inside the backpack.

"Here's a handheld VHF. The battery is charged and ready to go. Now, for the good stuff." With a sneaky grin, Brillo reached deeper into the bag. "Here's the nine-millimeter you wanted, with a box of ammo to boot. It's a Glock—best there is." He handed it to Cal and went back inside the bag. "And here's a little puppy that you might be able to use."

Cal's eyes widened when Brillo produced a genuine Israeli Uzi 9mm still in the box.

"Wow!" Cal exclaimed. "I can't believe it." He let out a low whistle while admiring it. "Thank you Uzi Gal, wherever you are. It's a real beauty, Brillo. I don't know what to say."

"How about: *where's the ammo?*" Beaming, Brillo handed him a spare clip and two boxes of rounds.

"You're a lifesaver, Brillo—and I mean exactly that. Might save quite a few lives, in fact." Cal reached for his billfold. "How much do I owe you?"

Brillo frowned, looking a little wounded. "Are you kidding me? No way. Skip's my friend too. Now, about that dive gear . . ."

Brillo vanished into the forward cabin again and came back dragging a full set of scuba gear with wet suit. "This ought to fill the bill." He dropped it at Cal's feet. "The air tank's full."

Cal dropped to one knee and examined the gear with an appreciative look. "It's first class, Captain. I owe you one—a big one."

Cal rose and shook Brillo's hand beholdenly. As he did, Kathy expressed her gratitude by hugging Brillo from behind.

"Hey, c'mon you guys. All this touchy-feely stuff is making me blush. It's the least I can do."

"Thanks, Brill!" Kathy gushed. "When this is over, you and Skip can drink all the beer you want. No griping—promise." Then she shook her finger at him. "Within reason, of course."

With a cheesy grin Brillo removed his cap and bowed humbly before her. "I'm at your cervix, ma'am. Uh-h-h, I mean at your service."

Kathy slapped him playfully on the cheek and then gave him another thank you hug.

Smiling at their antics, Cal said to Brillo: "I'll take you up on that boat ride tonight. Unless you've changed your mind."

"Why not?" Brillo held out his arms and gave a what-difference-does-it-make-now shrug. "I'm already an accomplice in this thing, ain't I?"

"Suppose so," Cal admitted, grinning. "What time do we meet?"

WIRED

~~~~~~~~~~~~~

They made plans to meet back at the marina at sunset. Over Cal's objections, Kathy insisted on riding along, arguing she would go crazy if she didn't. Cal understood how she felt but objected all the same, warning her that the Coast Guard could board and even seize the *Sol-Mate* if caught red-handed in restricted waters. Predictably, Kathy sloughed off his concern, claiming he was blowing things out of proportion and that she had a perfect right to tag along. Realizing he was wasting his breath, Cal gave in with fair warning not to blame him if she got arrested.

With that settled, Kathy was in much better spirit—chattering incessantly as she drove back to the condo. It was obvious to Cal that doing something proactive was the best medicine for her.

Not quite as buoyant as she, Cal listened to her enthused babbling while remaining quiet. If nothing else, seeing Kathy smile again almost made the rescue attempt worthwhile—almost.

Sunday 10:42 Hours – The "Majestic Star"

Skip was standing in his boxer shorts with his back to the cabin door. After rinsing out his pants and shirt, he had hung them on a clothes hanger to drip dry. To speed up the process, he was blow-drying them with a hair dryer when Mendoza and two backups burst into the cabin.

The unexpected invasion startled Skip and he automatically spun around to face his attackers. Feeling cornered, he hunkered down and instinctively pointed the hair dryer at them like a gun. When the two Mexicans rushed him, he hurled the hair dryer at them and made a running charge for Gold-Tooth—figuring if they were there to kill him, he would take the gang leader down with him, or at least try. But, reacting swiftly, the men dodged the missile-like hair dryer and snagged Skip's arms as he bolted past them. With a husky Mexican gripping each arm, Skip was forcibly backpedaled until his back smacked solidly against the cabin wall, splintering a section of teak paneling.

"Capitán." Mendoza stepped forward and hooked his thumbs under his belt. "We have problem. People upset over executions. Capitán must calm passengers. Get dressed. We go to sundeck for morning meal."

194

WIRED

"Well, what did you expect?" With a beefy forearm pressed against his throat, Skip's words came out in gasps. "Folks in these parts find mass murder a bit unsettling, especially when they could be next. It kinda puts a damper on your day. You know, fractures the old funny bone."

Ignoring the wise remark, Mendoza snapped his fingers and on cue Mohammad appeared in the doorway holding a whimpering female in a crunching headlock. The girl had gray duct tape across her mouth and a pointed stiletto at her throat. She was no more than sixteen years old, hysterical, and pale with fright. Her face was flushed from being forcibly bent over and there was a timid appeal in her terrified eyes.

Mohammad was leering down at the girl with perverse lust and plying the blade sadistically, twisting it against her soft skin as if he would delight in carving her up. The cruel act infuriated Skip and he attempted to wriggle free, wishing for just one minute alone with the sick freak. He'd take that knife away from him and stick it where the sun didn't shine—*sideways*.

"Señorita will stay with Mohammad while Capitán talk to passengers. If peoples no cooperate, I make girl a gift to mi hombres. Muchacha very pretty—no?"

Smiling vulgarly, Mendoza formed a circle with his left hand and pumped his right index finger in and out—the universal sign for intercourse. In doing so, he traded indecent looks with his men and they all laughed together like lechers.

Mohammad was the lewdest of the bunch, slobbering all over the girl like a sex-craved dog. Skip could practically smell his hormones rage. While eying the Arab in disgust, Skip wondered if he'd ever had a woman. After considering it, he figured not. No girl in her right mind would have the hook-nosed, greasy runt. The only time Mo had gotten a piece of tail was when his finger accidentally slipped through the toilet paper.

Mendoza strolled over to the teenage girl and took a strand of her golden hair. "Then after my men have way with muchacha, I kill girl...slowly." While fondling her hair between his fingers, his eyes roamed the girl's shapely young body, landing on her extended buttocks. The predatory hunger in his eyes was making Skip nervous. He couldn't stomach it if the girl was raped right in front of him.

WIRED

All at once Mendoza ripped the hair from the girl's head, causing her to yelp. A fresh torrent of tears streamed down her cheeks and her waterlogged eyes made a silent plea for help. While bawling she mumbled something at Skip through the duct tape but her words were unintelligible.

As the girl wept and whimpered, Skip panned the faces of the four men. Their disregard for human suffering was only surpassed by their cruel indifference to it. Eleven harmless victims had been slaughtered and there wasn't one ounce of remorse between them. None. Even now, they were swollen with pride as the fraught female cowered before them, as if being so heinously depraved was something to be proud of. Skip hated them all—right down to their craven cores.

"Capitán, we understand another. No?"

From his open palm, Mendoza blew the tuft of hair at Skip with a big exaggerated puff. As it flittered lightly to the floor it inspired another round of catcalls, as if their conquest over a lone boat captain and a helpless female in some way made them real he-men.

As the Zetas rollicked, Skip stared bitterly at the clump of hair on the floor. These men were anomalies—throwbacks in human evolution. Animals. They were blackhearts feeding upon the misery of others. Not only did it make them feel superior and all-powerful, it amused them. Their willing infliction of it served as both their recreation and entertainment.

Unable to withstand their gloating, Skip made a bid to break free with only one purpose in mind: to shove his fist down their jeering Neanderthal throats. But a bruising rifle blow to the solar plexus halted his attempted escape.

"¡Bastantes!" Mendoza commanded. "Enough! Take capitán to casino. "¡Inmediatamente!"

The two Zetas backed off as told, leaving Skip doubled over against the wall. As he coughed and gasped for breath, Mendoza sneered down his nose at him, basking in Skip's misery. Once he had savored enough, he slung his rifle over a shoulder and turned about-face to leave. But before reaching the door, the sound of Skip's raspy voice came from behind him.

"Okay, you Mexican piece of shit. You're callin' the shots. Just leave the girl alone—you perverted prick."

The insulting words stopped Mendoza in his tracks and the throwbacks quit scoffing when seeing their taskmaster stiffen. Standing paralyzed with his right hand gripping the sling, Mendoza silently weighed his options without looking back. The only outward sign of his simmering petulance was a twitching eyelid and the tense way he bounced on his toes.

Such insolence in front of his men would have ordinarily cost the capitán his life. But, for now, the Americano was needed alive. Once he had served his purpose, he would pay dearly for his impudence. Vengeance was sweet and "El Asesino" would have his—unequivocally.

Relishing the many agonizing ways he could kill the capitán, Mendoza swallowed his macho pride and marched on. Halfway out the door he unexpectedly broke out in sinister laughter, startling everyone present. With Skip marveling at him, he cackled his way out the door and down the deck—visions of retribution dancing in his head.

Trailing behind him was his Muslim underling, dragging his virgin prize by the head and drooling like a degenerate.

Sunday 10:49 Hours – Group St. Petersburg

Ray was concluding his conversation with the "faxing" father when the group operations officer dangled a message slip before his eyes. The Commandant was on hold for him and the slip was marked urgent. Ray nodded to the officer, bade farewell to the father, and jabbed the blinking button. Minutes later he slammed down the phone with such ferocity that all personnel in the outer office craned their necks toward the chilling sound.

The news was bad. There had just been an assassination attempt on the Chief Justice of the Supreme Court. It seemed the justice was entering the Supreme Court Building in Washington, when two bullets struck him down. The judge was undergoing surgery now and expected to live. The assassin was taken into custody and identified as a member of an Al-Qaeda sleeper cell based in the DC area. Before the Commandant could say: *"Osama bin Laden,"* the upper echelon was demanding immediate closure to the *Majestic Star* incident. Washington's inner sanctum had been breached and everyone there was in a furor. Who might be next?

After twenty-some years in the Coast Guard, Ray understood how Washington worked. The heat was on and the higher-ups were closing ranks—preserving their fat government paychecks and covering their career-minded butts. Shit rolled downhill and he was standing directly in its political path. By this time tomorrow, he would be up to his eyeballs in it.

But the political fallout wasn't what bothered Ray the most. That was to be expected. What truly irked him was being given a 24-hour ultimatum without options. For all intents and purposes, his standing orders had remained unchanged.

He was to stall the Zetas until they ran out of food and water, and then negotiate a trade: hostages for supplies. If they threatened more executions, he was to put Alvarez on the radio to order them to stand down. If all else failed, he was to send in the standby SEAL team, innocent casualties notwithstanding. Under no circumstances could he deviate from these orders or trade Alvarez for anything—that was final.

From Ray's perspective these parameters were nothing more than a holding pattern. As a counterargument he'd pointed out that Mendoza couldn't be stalled off much longer...that the executions could resume anytime...that the time bought yesterday by forcing Alvarez on the radio would be short-lived when Alvarez wasn't released...that Alvarez wasn't a cooperative part of their plan...that a gun couldn't be held to the drug lord's head every time Mendoza threatened more executions...that since yesterday's gunpoint transmission, Alvarez had refused to speak with anyone except his Miami lawyers, who were now camped out in a downtown St. Petersburg hotel—threatening to sue the government for brutality and violation of their client's right to remain silent.

At one frustrating point during their discussion, Ray posed to the Commandant: *"Why don't they just send me a blindfold and goddamn cigarette?!"*

The Commandant had listened to Ray's plight out of deference for a fine officer, even going as far as to sympathize with him. But the Commandant also made it clear that his personal feelings were neither here nor there. He, himself, had been given 24 hours to end the matter and he was passing down the same order to Ray. If the crisis went beyond that, the Department of Homeland Security would interpose and assume direct control of the incident. Fair or not, that was the bottom line. The political machine was moving full speed ahead and there was no stopping it.

Ray understood the Commandant's position but still resented being set up for failure. He felt trapped—like he was caught on something and couldn't get loose. The whole thing stunk.

"Well, I might be DC's designated fall guy," he griped aloud, "but one thing's for sure: Ray Hanna ain't gonna wait around for his political execution like a dog on a leash—not while Americans are being murdered. They can sure as hell forget that!"

In an ever-darkening frame of mind, Ray scowled his way into the break room. When he found the coffee pot empty, it furthered his rotten mood. On top of everything else he was getting a caffeine headache. Four times today he had poured himself a hot coffee and four times it had gone cold while he put out some fire. He expected disruptions—it came with the territory—but it annoyed him that the world wouldn't permit him one peaceful cup of morning coffee.

While fetching some aspirin from the wall-mounted first aid box, Ray passed by the shot-up candy machine. A cardboard sign had been taped over its shattered front glass with **OUT OF ORDER** inscribed in black marker. Some joker had since altered the sign by scribbling the word "really" on it, making it read: *Really* **OUT OF ORDER.**

After filling a paper cone with water, Ray popped two aspirins and hurled the wadded-up cone into a wastebasket like a Tomahawk Missile. After venting on the trashcan, he wandered aimlessly about the hallways while nursing his troubles. A preemptive strike would end the standoff, but at the risk of too many lives. Washington could scream all they wanted. As long as he was in command, he would not send in the SEAL Team until all the passengers were off.

So what were his other options? He had 24 hours to come up with a miracle—or else.

Refusing defeat, Ray returned to his office and unrolled the blueprints of the *Majestic Star*. If he could stall off the Zetas until their drinking water ran out, maybe he could trade water for hostages—the women and children anyway. That would stave off the Washington lynch mob a while longer and buy him more time.

The *Majestic Star* was designed for short excursions and came equipped with only two 500-gallon potable water tanks. According to the captain's log e-mailed on the morning of the takeover, the tanks were half-full upon departure.

"All right," Ray muttered, pulling on his lower lip, "if strictly conserved, each passenger would require about two liters per each 24-hour day. Five hundred gallons divided by 200 people, divided by a half-gallon per day, equals...roughly five days."

Ray put the pencil down and leaned back in his chair. The backrest creaked as it took his weight. If his calculations were correct, the ship would run out of drinking water tomorrow.

"Okay, Ray-Man," he asked himself, "how can you stall off the Zetas for one more day?" Swiveling his chair around, he studied Mendoza's surveillance photo pinned to the corkboard. "He ain't gonna keep buying the same old we're-still-working-on-it bullshit much longer. That's a fact. Think, man, think."

Sunday 11:00 Hours – The "Majestic Star"

As Skip left his cabin, he corrected the bill of his hat to shade his eyes from the bright sunlight. He had been sequestered for nearly twenty hours now and it felt liberating to be outdoors. The sun had thinned the morning mist and the sky was a perfect powder blue. The westerly winds were light, giving the Gulf surface a sparkling shimmery sheen.

Skip inhaled a deep breath of fresh air and it automatically made him wince. In his zeal over being liberated he had forgotten about his sore ribs, which stabbed him with pain when his lungs expanded. Grimacing, he hugged his rib cage and glared at the two thugs responsible for it. It wasn't every day that he got gut-slammed by a rifle butt and he would not soon forget this one.

Noting the captain's dirty looks; the Mexicans nudged him along by poking him in the back with their barrels. When Skip resisted, they poked him harder and with a good deal more enthusiasm. After giving them another hard look, Skip decided to cut the macho crap before his backbone ended up as sore as his rib cage.

WIRED

As the trio crossed the sundeck for the casino, Skip ogled the steam tables set up alongside the Tiki Bar stage. He hadn't eaten in 24 hours and his stomach-o-meter was on ultra empty.

Since the takeover, all meals were served outside on the sundeck. While passengers ate in shifts, armed lookouts hawked over them from elevated placements on the Tiki stage and bridge deck. All decks below the casino level were strictly off limits except for when preparing food or checking the generators. Even then, armed watchdogs accompanied the crewmen the whole time.

Too occupied in their work to notice Skip and his chaperones, John-Renée and a helper were transferring tubs of prepared food from kitchen pushcarts to the steam tables. John-Renée seemed in a testy mood, as usual, griping about lugging the food up two decks from the kitchen. To him, serving the meals outside on the sundeck was pure madness. What was he to do if it rained? It would spoil his meal and waste precious food. His pantry was in short supply as it was.

When a big bearded Arab reached into a tub to pilfer a potato wedge, John-Renée whacked his hand with a metal serving spoon. Following a loud yelp, the Muslim screeched at the Cajun in heated Arabic and a loud squabble erupted. Not backing down, the fiery Frenchman lashed back with some choice French of his own while waving the spoon over his head as if ready to strike again. When the bilingual war of words ended, the big Arab skulked away rubbing his hand and scowling angrily at John-Renée.

While descending the stairway to the casino, Skip wondered why he was still alive. Gold-Tooth had no qualms about killing people whom he'd never met, much less a crazy boat captain that called him a "Mexican piece of shit" in front of his men. Logic told him that he should be dead right now, but here he was—alive and well—*if* you didn't count the gash on his crown, the cut on his throat, and his black-and-blue battered rib cage. Obviously, he was necessary for some reason, something important enough to keep him alive.

But what? Keeping the passengers in check? Piloting the ship? A getaway by sea *would* require someone experienced to navigate the ship. They were goons, not sailors.

As the three men rounded the landing, the clamor from the casino downstairs grew louder. If the passengers were indeed as hysterical as Gold-Tooth stated, they would require calming down. Panic and rebellion would only elicit more punishment and grief, perhaps more death. For everyone's sake, they needed to behave themselves.

But after witnessing their captain's growling head-banging assault yesterday, would the passengers listen to him? It would be sort of like Charles Manson asking his freaky followers to become model citizens.

When Skip emerged from the stairway a hush fell over the room and everybody stood transfixed...paralyzed with wonder...staring at him as if seeing a ghost. Suddenly it struck Skip that they must have thought him dead. The last time they laid eyes on him, he was lying unconscious on the floor with his head split wide open.

After a moment of silent awe, an older gentleman emerged from the pack and began clapping his hands. One by one the others joined in until applause filled the room. This show of respect caught Skip off guard and it took him a moment to realize they were applauding him. But for what? With nothing else coming to mind, he supposed it was for his failed attempt to stop the executions. While unsuccessful, he had fought his hardest and for that they were applauding him.

Skip had never received a standing ovation before and he didn't know how to react. As the applause went on, he shrugged and smiled self-consciously, then waved at their admiring faces in a clumsy attempt to be gracious—the whole time feeling dreadfully out of place. Once the applause died down, the passengers wasted no time in crowding around him, all shouting at once. The sudden surge was unexpected and Skip shrank back a step before being swallowed up.

"Captain!" a red-faced male shouted. "We demand that you do something—OR WE WILL!"

"What are the authorities doing about the executions?" a 30-ish woman shrieked. "Are they just going to stand by and watch us all die?"

In the blink of an eye the pleasant reception of moments ago had evolved into a near uprising. Everyone was angry and upset and some of the more militant were shouting obscenities. One weepy woman competed for Skip's attention by tugging insistently at his shirtsleeve. "They took my daughter, Madison." Her red-rimmed eyes were pools of grief. "They took my Maddie."

WIRED

Everyone was talking at once and Skip's mind was spilling over. It was mass confusion but their message was the same: they wanted justice and they wanted off this ship—*right now.*

As Skip took in the chaotic scene, he worried if he could control it. The passengers were bordering on mutiny and the Mexican guards were looking more and more skittish. All four had jumpy expressions on their faces and jittery fingers wrapped around their triggers—not a healthy combination. Two were perched atop tables at port and starboard placements and the other two were posted at the casino's fore and aft exits. Skip and his passengers were effectively boxed in, like cattle in a slaughterhouse.

Another complication was the teenager being held elsewhere by the kinky Muslim—Madison, he had just learned. If things got out of control here, she could be brutally raped and murdered.

At that instant Skip's fears tripled when he saw Gold-Tooth enter the casino through the aft doorway. Wearing a nasty-looking scowl, the gang leader skirted the perimeter of the room while studying the unruly mob—like a hawk circling its prey. As he paraded along, the four guards tracked his every movement as if waiting for a signal to open fire. Going mainly unnoticed by the anger-distracted crowd, Mendoza sat down at the bar and deposited his AK on top. With displeasure burning in his eyes, he folded his arms across his chest and glared at the noisy troublemakers. He'd had enough American insubordination for one day.

Thugs like Gold-Tooth worried Skip because they were accustomed to getting their way. And when they didn't, like all bullies, they invariably resorted to violence—beating their adversaries into submission or even killing them. It was their brutal nature, their way of life. In Gold-Tooth's world, murder and mayhem was the norm. In one respect it made him predictable. In another, it made him exceedingly dangerous.

Having seen enough, Skip decided to diffuse the powder keg before something unimaginable occurred. The passengers were flirting with disaster.

"CALM DOWN!" Skip raised both arms for quiet. "LISTEN UP!"

The tumult gradually subsided except for a group of mouthy males in the back. Fearing they would persist in causing trouble, Skip plowed toward them with his sights set on the instigator. When the loudmouth saw the captain coming, he set foot in the opposite direction but not before Skip snagged him by the collar of his flowered Hawaiian shirt.

"Let me handle this, goddammit!" Skip pulled the man face to face. "Shut your fat mouth now or you'll die—along with a lot of others!" Skip gave him a convincing shake. "Got it?"

As the pair traded mean looks, Skip heard the *clack-clack* sounds of munitions being chambered into the breeches of weapons. The familiar sound conjured up unsettling memories and Skip's instincts went on full alert. With his heart pounding, he spun about to face the hostile threat. Using a trained soldier's eye, he quickly sized up the situation to find it precarious at best.

While Skip had been dealing with the agitators, Gold-Tooth climbed atop a craps table near the center of the room. He was now twisting from side-to-side, waving his muzzle over the heads of passengers as if daring anyone to approach. The other gunmen had assumed defensive postures as well, fanning their AK's at the crowd and glancing nervously at their leader. A massacre was in the making.

"HOLD UP!" With his heart leaping, Skip tore through the crowd. "MAKE WAY. I'M COMIN' THROUGH!"

As Skip serpentined his way toward Mendoza, Mr. Hawaiian shirt and friends fell in behind him, still spoiling for a fight. When Skip noticed them tagging along, he spun around and ordered them to stay put. The situation was unstable enough. Relieved when the hotheads obeyed him, Skip resumed his quest for the craps table.

As Skip advanced, Mendoza tracked his movement with the sights of his rifle. He was tired of kissing American ass. If he had his way he would kill them all right now, starting with the cocky capitán. As far as he was concerned, the Americanos were all insolent pigs and deserved to be butchered as such—every one of them. He was a Mafioso chieftain, not a babysitter, and he was sick of their bellyaching bullshit. They were lucky to be alive.

When Skip arrived at the table, he spread his legs wide and stared into the hollow bore of the barrel. From his close-up angle the barrel opening looked like a bottomless pit. Seconds later a wave of jostling passengers squeezed in behind him, bumping and shoving. To gain a little negotiating room, Skip turned around and motioned the crowd back. With a murmuring undertone they shuffled back a few steps, then awaited the face-off with keen anticipation.

Skip hadn't asked for this responsibility and it goaded him to be thrust into this position. What was he doing here? He was a boat captain—not a hostage negotiator. A lot of lives were at stake and he didn't know whether to buckle under or take a stand. But one thing was for sure: Gold-Tooth was a nutcase and apt to open fire anytime.

While undecided on the inside, Skip feigned a bold front. He had a job to do. His first priority was to end the insurrection without anyone getting hurt. If he could tilt things in their favor during the process—say, get the girl back and put an end to the executions—then so much the better. With the passengers backing him and a little luck, he might finagle a concession or two.

Figuring it was now or never, Skip stepped forward and planted his hands on his hips. "What are we gonna do now, amigo?" His voice was low—sotto voce—out of the crowd's earshot. His aim was to come across as a mediator, not an adversary. "I'd say we're in quite a fix, if you know what I mean." Skip gestured at the crowd with his eyes. "As you can see, the passengers have taken all the brutality they're gonna stand for. Most of them are ready to fight right here and now. After yesterday's executions they figure you're gonna kill them anyway, so they've got nothin' to lose. They can die now—fightin' for their lives—or die later like sheep."

As Skip talked Mendoza scanned the sea of mutinous faces, assessing his odds. Then, as if wishing to collaborate, he lowered his weapon and took a knee, then motioned for Skip to approach him. Relieved to have the gun barrel pointed elsewhere, Skip edged up to the table. His good-cop-bad-cop strategy seemed to be working.

"Calm people, Capitán, or I kill all! NOW!" His words were harsh but muffled from the crowd. His breath was so foul that Skip had to resist backing away.

"I might be able to do that," Skip said, "or at least try. But, as you can see, they're pretty worked up right now." He twisted his body to evidence their simmering temperament. "First, bring me the female passenger—as good faith." He paused to let the request sink in. "As you might expect, the girl's mother is hysterical and riling up the other passengers. Bring the girl and I'll see what I can do."

The demand hit Mendoza right between the eyes. The capitán had overstepped his bounds before, but nothing like this. The idea was absurd—laughable.

"Take it or leave it, amigo." Skip shrugged. "After all, you really *do* intend to kill us all anyway. Right? That's what you told me in my cabin yesterday." To jog his memory, Skip pulled down his collar to expose the scab across his throat. "Remember? I believe you said: *máteles a todos*. Maybe I should tell these folks what you really have in store for them."

Spots of color appeared on Mendoza's cheeks and his AK began to tremble. The Americano was coercing him in front of the passengers— blackmailing him. It was *unbelievable*! When his reactionary mind could stand it no more, he jammed the gun barrel against the captain's forehead, straining Skip's neck backward.

"*¡SILENCIO!*" Angry spittle flew from his mouth. "*¡Voy a matar!*"

It all happened so fast, Skip squeezed his eyes shut and waited for the shot. Simultaneously an audible gasp came from the crowd as if all the air had been let out of the room. As Skip stood rooted in place, his adrenal gland flooded his veins with epinephrine, instantly doubling his heart rate. With his heart hammering, Kathy's image flashed before his closed eyes and the thought of dying without saying goodbye to her filled him with regret. There was so much he wanted to say...feelings to express...last wishes...things to caution her about when he was gone. But it was all for naught. Any instant now he would be dead and any parting words would go unsaid.

When the seconds passed and nothing happened, Skip squeamishly opened his eyes and released a pent-up breath. Gold-Tooth was glowering down the barrel at him with sweat trickling from his brow to the darkened stubble on his face. His nostrils were flared like an angry bull and his lips were stretched thin in a full snarl, baring the tips of his rotten teeth. Outwardly he was the epitome of rage, but for some reason he wasn't firing.

Skip knew he was itching to pull the trigger because that's how killers like him settled things. They all lived by the same rule: "*If at first you don't succeed, just kill the bastards.*" Yet, *something* or *someone* was holding him back. Indecision was plastered all over his face.

WIRED

Then it dawned on Skip that he *couldn't* fire. Without hostages, where would that leave him? More importantly, where would it leave Juan Carlos Alvarez? In prison for life? Strapped in the electric chair? Without their human bargaining chips, neither held any leverage. The authorities could simply sink the *Majestic Star* and throw the key away on Alvarez. And it would all be Gold-Tooth's blundering fault—who would likely be sporting a Colombian Necktie himself before the ship went down.

Convinced he was right, Skip decided to make a stand. In spite of everything else, the *Majestic Star* was still *his* ship; and, as her captain, he wanted the teenager back and he wanted a permanent end to the executions. Some ground rules must be set while he possessed some outward appearance of leverage. His passengers and crew deserved civilized and humane treatment. If anybody should be blindfolded and shot, it was Gold-Tooth and his mangy men.

"BRING THE GIRL!"

Skip's authoritative voice ignited the crowd and the passengers surged forward like a tsunami, rallying behind their captain. With a look of surprise, Gold-Tooth shrank back from the aggressors and sprang to his feet with his rifle pointed skyward. The demand for the girl and the resulting passenger backlash went beyond belief. Instead of *him* terrorizing the passengers, *they* were flinging bloodthirsty threats at *him*.

"*¡Trae a la chica!*" Mendoza yelled over his shoulder. The guard posted at the aft entrance responded with: "*¡Enseguida, señor!*" and promptly exited the casino.

"Señorita coming!" Gold-Tooth growled at Skip. He underscored his next words by stomping his heel on the felt covering. "NOW...CALM...PEOPLE!"

Skip raised his arms for quiet and motioned for the man in the Hawaiian shirt. With Mendoza watching curiously, Skip whispered something in his ear and the man scurried back into the crowd. Seconds later the passengers shuffled back a few more feet to give the captain and his adversary more latitude.

While staring up at Gold-Tooth, Skip decided to play out his hand. If he was ever to regain some measure of control over what took place on his own ship, now was the time. It was risky, but a risk Skip felt forced to take—as much for his own dignity as for the lives of those he was charged to protect. Besides, it was too late to turn back now. The damage was done. Gold-Tooth was anything but forgiving and Skip had shamed him twice today in front of his peers. He had to finish it now while he still could.

"Okay, I've moved the passengers back so we can have a man-to-man talk—just you 'n me."

Wondering what the captain could possibly want now, Mendoza gawked down at him incredulously. Their roles were reversed, backwards, inside out.

"While we're waitin' for the girl, you and I need to get a few things straight." Skip crossed his arms assertively and rocked back-and-forth on his heels. "You're on MY ship and you're in American waters. I don't know and I don't care what you raggedly ass bastards do in Mexico—or whatever rock you dicks crawled out from under—but aboard MY ship you WILL NOT harm any more people. Is that clear?"

Mendoza's face went slack and his jaw fell. He couldn't believe such audacity coming from an unarmed man. Captives of *"El Asesino"* were supposed to beg for mercy, grovel for their lives, not fly in his face and make outspoken demands. The capitán was practically daring him to open fire. The gringo was suicidal—¡*loco!*

"In front of all present, I want your word that you won't harm any more passengers." Skip brought a hand to his mouth as if passing a secret. "I know it's a big stretch, but let's pretend your word means something. Okay?" After a wink, Skip continued in a louder voice for the passengers to overhear. "For the record, we're not your enemy. We're just everyday folks that happened to be in the wrong place at the wrong time. We have nothin' to do with drug smuggling, the DEA, or your private war with our government. Do you understand? We demand to be treated like human beings." Skip unfolded his arms and stood straighter. "We ARE NOT cattle to be slaughtered and we WILL NOT stand for it! ¿Comprende?"

The splotches on Mendoza's cheeks were now more pronounced and he licked his lips nervously. He couldn't believe his ears. His side had the weapons; hence he should be in control. That made sense. But here was this mouthy boat captain and bunch of unarmed civilians all but challenging him to a fight, which made no sense at all. The fools were behaving like captors instead of captives. Mendoza's first instinct was to open fire and obliterate the pig bastards, especially the smug-ass capitán. But as his finger tightened around the trigger, a voice from the recesses of his conscious warned against it. Mass murder of the hostages would not set well with his employers. Not well at all.

While Mendoza wallowed in indecision, Skip waited in suspense. However, he knew better than to let the Mexican stew too long because he possessed a shoot-first-and-worry-about-it-later killer mentality. Sensing it was time to switch to his good-cop mode, Skip edged closer in.

"I know what you're thinkin'." His voice was low, confidential. "Do you take control by firing on us or do you make an unwilling concession. Right?" When no answer came, Skip took it as a yes. "Right. That's what I'd be thinkin' right now if I were in your shoes."

With every eye on him, Skip strode an oblong path before the craps table. While pacing, he frowned down at the floor and stroked his beard like a trial lawyer speaking before a jury.

"Let's consider your options," Skip said to the floor. "For starters, you could always open fire and kill a slew of us—maybe fifty or so before the male passengers finally got their hands on you and ripped your balls off." Skip stopped pacing a moment and gestured at the AK. "I know you're packin' a lot of firepower there, but five guys against two hundred?" He shrugged his shoulders. "Come on, you wouldn't stand a chance and you know it. You'd be in hell quicker than you could say Adolf Hitler."

Skip resumed pacing while monitoring Mendoza from the corner of his eye. The Mexican was studying the passengers in detail, as if calculating his odds of survival. Encouraged by this, Skip pressed on.

"Up 'til now, you've been successful at controllin' the passengers because they carried some hope of survival. When you take that away by killin' them off a few at a time, behaviors change—people become drastic and are willing to take risks, even if they're extreme." Skip strode a few paces in silence, adding to the drama. "So you've got a decision to make, amigo. Either try killin' us all right here and now or simply promise to halt the executions." Skip stopped and stared him straight in the eye. "It's your choice."

Mendoza had sweated through his khaki shirt by now, but his face remained resolute. In his way of thinking, giving back the girl had been a relatively small concession to make in order to restore order. But, now, the ballsy capitán was asking too much. Mendoza's rudimentary nature would not allow it. *Never.* It would be a degradation.

Sensing Mendoza wasn't going to capitulate, Skip decided to play his trump card. It carried risk and the fate of everyone would depend on how well it played out. But, barring a miracle, they were all going to die anyway, either by execution or when the ship was ultimately blown.

With his heart beating against his sternum, Skip turned to face his waiting audience. Nothing in his lifetime could have prepared him for this moment. In preparation of his announcement, he removed his hat and clamped it under his arm, then stood erect with chest out. While panning the multitude of trusting faces, he prayed that he was doing the right thing.

"I DON'T THINK THEY HAVE ENOUGH BULLETS TO KILL US ALL!" Skip challenged. "WHAT DO YOU PEOPLE THINK?"

In a roaring show of support, an outpouring of passengers charged in his direction—yelling defiantly, shaking their fists. As they carried on their rebellion, Skip felt the strength leaving his legs. If his bluff backfired, scores of them would die because of his gross misjudgment.

But, for Captain Jason Myles, there was one saving grace: *At least he wouldn't live to see it.* Gold-Tooth would make sure that he got it first— right in the back.

Sunday 11:20 Hours – Clearwater Beach, Florida

After leaving the marina, Cal and Kathy drove back to the condo. With little to do until meeting Brillo later on, they decided to kill the afternoon at *Rockaway's Bar & Grill* on Clearwater Beach. ESPN was televising a sand volleyball tournament from there and Kathy thought it would provide a nice diversion from the dreaded business ahead.

They arrived at the restaurant just before the lunch crowd and nabbed the last outside table having a tournament view. The huge oceanside deck was teeming with rowdy sports enthusiasts, who, in between rooting for their favorite players, were busy gorging upon hot chicken wings and galvanized buckets of longneck beer.

WIRED

The AVP tournament was taking place just a few yards from the deck on the white sugar sand of Clearwater Beach. The play area was enclosed on three sides by temporary bleachers and scaffolding specially erected for the tournament. Inasmuch as *Rockaway's* was a major sponsor of the tournament, its sprawling wooden deck served as the play area's fourth side—providing restaurant patrons with a front row seat. Like the large wooden deck, the stands were jam-packed with spectators and there was standing room only along the sidelines.

Adorning the top of the grandstands were triangular pennants, flapping and snapping in the brisk ocean breeze. Affixed to the scaffolding facing the restaurant was a scoreboard, loudspeakers, and end-to-end banners advertising various tournament sponsors and beer breweries. In the sand beneath the scoreboard stood a skirted table bearing trophies aglitter with sunlight, waiting to be presented. TV cameras were staged at strategic angles surrounding the play area with a tangle of cables leading to a semi-trailer in the parking lot. On the beach next to the parking lot, a three-story inflatable beer can teetered in the wind, straining against its nylon tie downs. In its shadow was a canopied beer trailer with suntanned girls in neon bikinis selling draft beer by the cup. Supplying the musical entertainment was a garishly painted van from a local rock station, blasting music from towering black speakers set up on the sidewalk. The atmosphere was charged with excitement and by local standards it was quite an extravaganza.

Seated under a saffron umbrella, Kathy shucked her straw and planted it in her frozen rumrunner. As she sucked noisily on it, Cal nursed his beer while straining to hear the solo-guitarist perched on a stool in a far corner of the deck. The neglected musician was singing away but the noisy beer-guzzling fans were drowning him out.

Cal enjoyed live entertainment and had fed many a tip bucket to keep the tunes coming. But today wasn't one of those days. He was here to kill time—not have a good time—and neither the tournament nor the singer really interested him. In fact, it annoyed him. He would have preferred some solitude to prepare for tonight's undertaking, not the hoopla of his present surroundings. It was so noisy here, he could hardly think.

During a break in the play action, Kathy shifted her gaze to the gleaming Gulf of Mexico. To her, there was something magical about the sea, something sublime. As the incoming waves crested and collapsed, the sound of lathering surf filled the air, punctuated by a brief silence as Mother Ocean gathered her strength to do it over again. As furrows of milky foam scampered onto the beach and receded, its recurrent rhythm was spellbinding. As Kathy watched the ebb and flow, her mind began to drift and the tournament noise faded. Dreaming with her eyes open, her thoughts turned inward to her missing spouse; the man she loved with the whole of her heart and soul.

Like all true-blue sailors, Skip too loved the sea. Together, they had spent countless hours holding hands and admiring its sheer magnificence. On some mornings before dawn they would carry their coffee mugs outside and sit on the boat dock's weathered planks until the sun rose over the canal, lighting the eastern skyline with lavenders and gold. Kathy treasured those moments and the petrifying thought of never sharing them again scared her back to the present.

As the tournament noise returned, Kathy automatically lit a cigarette and exhaled nervously. She tried to refocus on the tournament but she was too plagued with worry that her life-as-it-used-to-be would never return. A few puffs later she placed her lipstick-stained cigarette in an ashtray and looked back out to sea, as if perhaps Mother Ocean might hold the key.

Cal's mind was also miles away, precisely ten miles due west. Instead of slugging down shooters and leering at the thong bikinis, he was quietly peeling off the label of his beer bottle; an unconscious habit he reverted to when preoccupied.

Cal had never been one for self-delusion or embellishing the odds. *"It is what it is"* was his general take on life. Essentially, he was a realist and not a big believer in fate or karma. To him, fate was merely a culmination of all the choices one made—both good and bad—and it had nothing to do with luck. One had to rely on their instincts and hope for the best.

Right now Cal's instincts were telling him that as Cal Stringer, upstanding law-abiding attorney, his probability of survival was nil. He was too moralistically straight; too soft and cushy to carry out the perfunctory business of bloodshed—a prerequisite of such an undertaking. The present-day Cal would never survive it. He would hesitate at the wrong moment...think a second too long before firing...perhaps catch a fatal bullet in the process.

After twenty-five years of defending law and order, Cal had to lay down his law books and switch sides. He had to revisit the place where he had spent an adult lifetime trying to forget—a place where one killed mechanically, without compunction; a damnable place where survival meant forfeiting all worth for human life. To make it back home alive, he had to pinch off his emotions one by one and force the present-day Cal out.

Mindful of what he must do, Cal closed his eyes and willed the metamorphosis to take place. For one last time he had to revisit the killing fields—where no rules applied and where there were only two kinds of soldiers: *the quick, and the dead.*

With his pulse and respiration steady, his mind traveled inward from the sands of Clearwater Beach to a war torn peninsula in eastern Indochina. As he traversed back in time, the noise of the tournament faded and once again he was in a Southeast Asian world called Vietnam. Here, all the SEAL training came back to him: the guerilla warfare tactics...the infiltration-exfiltration techniques...the dozens of ways to kill a man without a whimper.

In his mind's eye Cal was surrounded by his SEAL brothers in a garrison setting. Young men from different walks of life, making the best of a bad situation—clowning around, playing cards, cleaning their weapons, hunched over notepads writing letters to back home. As Cal's senses sharpened, he could hear their voices and laughter. He could even smell the lingering scent of gun oil. These sights and sounds dredged up dormant memories that he had buried decades ago.

Then, without warning, Cal was whisked to another place in time and the intimate setting melded into the obscene. Gone were the friendly environs of the barracks, replaced by mangled corpses lying twisted in their own blood; mouths hideously agape as if in mid-scream when life deserted their bodies. As Cal pictured the dead and dying, it struck him how so terribly young they were—gangly boys with acne and burr haircuts, mere teenagers.

Like a tragic slideshow, their faces flashed before him one-by-one as if viewing a high school yearbook. Last of all was his friend, Mickey.

Like a slow-motion movie, Mickey was wading toward him in waist-high water. Then, with only a few yards separating them, Mickey did something that Cal would never forget—he extended his hand and smiled. Cal distinctly remembered how so out of place his smile had seemed at the time. Bullets were carving up the water all round them and white-hot tracers were streaking crosswise their field of vision. Exploding mortars and grenades were upheaving bottom muck by the hundredweight and a downpour of brownish slime water was raining down on them like a waterfall. In the midst of all this, Mickey was just standing there...smiling...without the least regard for his own life.

His expression seemed to say: *"Come on, old pal. I'm here for you. You're going to make it."*

This heartfelt image would never leave Cal for the rest of his life. An instant later there was a blinding explosion and that was the last thing Cal remembered.

Mickey, damn him, was gone.

While Cal recuperated in a warm hospital bed, Mickey was flown home zipped in a body bag packed in ice. Not only had Vietnam stolen his best friend, it had robbed him of paying his last respects at Mickey's military funeral. Mickey was dead and buried for months before Cal was discharged and able to visit his Florida gravesite.

Cal had never gotten the chance to thank Mickey, nor to scold him for making himself such a wide-open target. This lack of closure haunted Cal to this day and the bereavement was always there—wounds that had never healed; wounds that left him demoralized, angry, and bitter; wounds that made him want to weep at one moment and break something the next.

Hellish wounds.

But, in order to cross over, Cal needed the pain—invited it. That was his sole purpose in opening the lockbox where he stored his most grievous memories, the box he had buried three decades ago. It was time to release the demons; to allow them to slip their collars and run free; to let them sting his mind over and over again until his spirit hardened, until his thoughts and actions were not his own—basic to a soldier's survival.

As the transformation took place, the modern-day Cal began to ebb away. From somewhere deep within him a bitter voice of denunciation cried out for reprisal, for a settling of scores, rekindling a furor that never left him. Cal embraced this pent-up ferocity and urged it to do its bidding, to consume his moral bondage, to liberate him from compassion, to set him free to kill once more.

With Cal's eyes still closed, a feeling of dejá vu suddenly pervades him and he willingly lets go of the present. In his mind's eye he is walking through the rubble of war behind the sights of his freshly oiled M-16. As he advances death is everywhere around him—it is always there, stalking him like a shadow. He spends every waking hour in a steady state of vigilance. His nerves never rest. He perceives no enemy now, but he knows they are there. The Viet Cong fight a coward's war...lying in wait...secretively watching him...slinking in the shadows like bugs.

As he traverses the smoke and ruin, Cal's senses begin to sharpen—like the honing of a rusty blade. He hears the cries of jungle birds, of something feral rustling through the bush, the buzzing of flies swarming rotten flesh. Riding on the wind is the reek of war—the sulfurous scent of spent gunpowder, the scant gasoline odor of napalm, the putrid stink of burning flesh.

Tainted smells...unforgettable smells...the winds of war.

Also riding on these winds are the screams of courageous men falling in battle—shrieking so shrilly that their voices rise above the thunder of battle. The screams are so real and tormenting that Cal has to restrain his hands from covering his ears. In order to cross over he needs the bloodcurdling screams; he needs the tainted smells; he needs to relive war's wretchedness.

When the shrieking in Cal's head reaches a maddening crescendo and he can stand it no more, his eyes pop open with startling fright.

Disoriented and out-of-it at first, Cal was relieved to find himself back in the present. The volleyball fans were still cheering, the guitarist was still playing, and Kathy was gazing at an open cockpit airplane buzzing overhead, towing an advertising banner for Budweiser. Everything was back to normal—except him.

Cal suddenly felt his mouth dry and took a sip of lukewarm beer. Noting his beer bottle shaking, he set it down and crossed his arms to conceal his frayed nerves. Then he looked around self-consciously to see if anyone was watching. He felt dazed—traumatized—as if someone had just shaken him awake from a horrific nightmare.

WIRED

Suddenly aware that he was perspiring, Cal armed sweat off his brow and picked up Kathy's burning cigarette from the ashtray. With trembling fingers, he took a deep draw and the swooning effect of Mr. Nicotine rushed straight to his head. When he tasted lipstick, he frowned disgustedly at the red-stained filter and put the cigarette out—wiping his lips clean afterward as if he had committed some sort of incest. Then to help calm his wrecked nerves, he lit a fresh cigarette and gazed out to sea.

The unforgettable images rooted in Cal's memory served as a reminder and forewarning—that there will always be evil men in the world and that another friend's life could be lost if the evildoers weren't stopped. To save his best friend, he had to become something he once was: an instrument of death, an unfeeling assassin—a predator.

Sunday 11:22 Hours – The "Majestic Star"

As the passengers carried on their rebellion, Skip stood before them with an unseen bull's-eye on his back—praying that Gold-Tooth and his thugs wouldn't open fire and this huge gamble he was taking wouldn't result in more aimless death.

In the Navy, Skip had heard: *"You never hear the bullet that kills you."* That cringing thought bore on his mind as he awaited his death sentence; for his chest organs to explode all over the passengers before him from a high-velocity exit wound from the rear.

With time dragging by at a snail's pace, one bead of sweat chased another down the crease of his spine. But Skip knew that each second that passed improved his chances of living, of seeing Kathy again. It was a tortuous, climactic wait—one that tested his nerve and fortitude. But he had to brazen it out. Any sign of weakness at this point would give Gold-Tooth cause to stand firm.

Just then, Madison and Mohammad descended the stairway and the decibel level skyrocketed. Celebrating the mini-victory, the passengers stampeded in their direction to observe the girl's release. Fearing all loss of control, Skip held out his arms in an effort to restrain them, but their bodies streamed past him like he wasn't standing there. It was like trying to hold back the sea.

But Skip had no one to blame but himself. He had acted like Wyatt

Earp at the OK Corral instead of a responsible ship captain. He had purposely worked up the passengers and practically dared Gold-Tooth and his gang to open fire—a reckless act that could backfire any second.

When Skip turned around to gauge Gold-Tooth's reaction, he was aghast at finding the craps table surrounded. Some of the male dissidents had skipped the girl's welcome-back reunion in favor of heckling the terrorist leader. The hecklers were glowering up at Gold-Tooth from all sides, peppering him with insults and catcalls. Instead of behaving like meek little hostages, they looked like a lynch mob about to string up one of the bad guys.

In a risky cat-and-mouse game, two males were taking turns lunging across the table, trying to topple Mendoza by the ankle. In jerky self-defense, the Mexican was keeping them at bay by jabbing his gun barrel at them and booting their darting hands away. In between kicks his worried eyes scoured the area around him, as if seeking an alternative getaway route should one be needed. When the ankle-grabbers wouldn't desist, Mendoza cried out in Spanish and his underlings charged in his direction. Not to be left out, Mohammad released the girl's arm and rushed to his rescue as well.

With events rapidly reaching a flashpoint, Skip muscled his way towards the craps table, peeling onlookers away by the shoulder. At reaching the table he took a heated lap around it, shoving the ankle-grabbers away. "BACK OFF!"

While Skip was quelling the troublemakers, the four gunmen bullied their way through the crowd. After joining their leader atop the craps table, they assumed back-to-back positions and aimed their weapons at the yappy heads below. Arriving late, Mohammad climbed atop the table and let out a trilling war whoop, then took it upon himself to fire a burst of rounds at the ceiling. With bits of debris raining down on the crowd, the cowering passengers squealed with panic and scattered in confusion.

In retaliation for the reckless stunt, Mendoza wheeled around and backhanded the Arab—sending him flying from the table. Following an end-over-end somersault of grunts and groans, Mohammad came to rest squinting up at him—rubbing his jaw with a bitter look of surprise.

"*¡Haga lo que digo y siga las órdenes!*" Mendoza growled at him. "*¡Es estúpido imbécil!*"

WIRED

While the sulking Arab got a good tongue-lashing, the hecklers regrouped near the bar and began shouting obscenities at the Zetas. In answer, Mendoza glared at them and fanned his weapon in their direction as if threatening to mow them down. But instead of intimidating them, an object sailed through the air that narrowly missed Mendoza's head. After flinching from it, he took aim in the direction from which it came just as the shot glass shattered against a back wall.

"¡Te mataré!" Threatening to kill the glass thrower, Mendoza set his sights on a rabble-rouser wearing a Hawaiian shirt. He had taken all the guff he was going to take. On top of their nonstop impudence, now the passengers were throwing things at him—as if he were a wimp, a nobody, someone not to be taken seriously. It was time to set an example and show them who was boss.

When Gold-Tooth disengaged his safety, Skip's heart galloped. Someone was about to be shot.

"HOLD IT RIGHT THERE!" Waving his arms over his head, Skip stepped into Mendoza's line of fire. Then he pointed an accusing finger at the provocateurs. "AND THAT GOES FOR YOU JERKOFFS TOO!"

As Skip rounded the table to face the gang leader, he wondered what to do next. He had been forced to intercede but now what? The hijackers were on the verge of firing and the passengers weren't backing off—they were getting worse. With no time to think, Skip decided to play out his original strategy and pray to God it worked. While seemingly cool on the outside, his mouth was as dry as cotton and there was a lump in his throat the size of Rhode Island. It was show time. In his Vietnam days, it was called: *pucker time.*

"I'll ask you one last time, amigo." Skip's voice was mild at first but then ended with a shout. "DO I HAVE YOUR WORD THAT THE EXECUTIONS WILL STOP—OR NOT??!!"

With a spontaneous outcry, the passengers tightened around the table like a noose—yelling...demanding promise...suddenly more physical. Scurrying like a rat, Mohammad crawled between a forest of legs for the safety of the craps table. With their AK's cocked-and-ready, the ring of gunmen were more wary than ever—legs crouched, backs together tight, eyes darting between the angry mob and their leader, waiting for his command.

WIRED

But in stark contrast to his men, Mendoza appeared oblivious to the open rebellion. Standing motionless, he glared down at the cocky pest standing so smugly before him—the brazen ship captain responsible for the uprising. He was so abashed by Skip's demand, so publicly humiliated, that he was struck speechless. He ached inside to shout down the capitán, to decimate him before everyone present. Yet, want as he may, the retaliatory words stuck in his throat—stifled by shock and utter bewilderment.

Even now, with his AK-47 trained between the capitán's eyes, the man refused to budge, choosing to challenge him instead. And defying logic as well, the bulk of surrounding passengers seemed quite willing to follow suit. It was mind-blowing. As far as Mendoza was concerned, the Americanos were an inferior breed with not enough sense to be afraid.

What arrogance!! Just because they were Americans, did they think they were bulletproof? Didn't they realize that their continued existence rested solely with him? That in this room, he was God? To give life or taketh away—at his whim?

If looks could kill, Skip would be a goner. Pure hatred was oozing from Gold-Tooth's pores and fire was shooting from his eyes. His sweat glands were pumping perspiration like an oil well, leaving sopping rings under his armpits. Yet he wasn't firing, furthering Skip's belief that the Mexican didn't have the option to kill him, at least not yet. Otherwise, he wouldn't be struggling so with his animal urge to fire. He would just pull his trigger and be done with it—exterminate Skip without a second thought.

Emboldened by this, Skip crossed his arms and tapped a foot while waiting for his reply. Then, showing a lack of patience, he let out an audible sigh. After a full minute passed, he held up his wristwatch and tapped on its faceplate.

"Well?" With raised eyebrows, Skip tap-tap-tapped on the watch. "We're all waiting."

A bolt of fury shot through Mendoza and hot blood thundered in his ears. The watch-tapping stunt was the last straw, the ultimate indignity. Shaking like a volcano, his face darkened as the magma of mortification reached critical mass. Then, in an explosive release of rage, he sprang through the air—growling like a beast—landing directly in front of Skip.

"YES, CAPITÁN!" He wadded Skip's shirt in both hands and pulled him eye-to-eye. "You have El Asesino's word! NO MORE EXECUTIONS!" While yielding to the demand, his watchdog snarl promised Skip a huge payback. "Now take Americanos to sundeck for meal! *¡Derecho este momento!*"

He released Skip with a powerful push and stomped toward the forward staircase, shoving passengers aside that blocked his path. As if afraid of being left behind, the others hopped off the table and scurried up the stairs after their departing leader. Lagging behind, Mohammad backed up the steps with his sights trained on the crowd, as if anticipating—in all likelihood hoping for—a surprise attack from the rear.

An instant later the Zetas were gone and the drama was over—for now.

Sunday 11:35 Hours – Group St. Petersburg

Since receiving the Commandant's 24-hour ultimatum, Ray had roamed every corner of the stationhouse—thinking, brooding, pondering his predicament—winding up with his hands resting on a window ledge facing the street. As if his situation weren't rotten enough, CBS and FOX could now be added to the growing camp of satellite trucks parked across the street. Pretty soon the entire alphabet would be represented.

Amidst the tangle of vehicles, Ray saw a female reporter standing before a camera. Her back was facing him and she was jabbering into a microphone, using the St. Petersburg Station as a backdrop for her remote telecast. To her left and right, rival reporters were doing the same.

Yackety-yack-yack.

Letting loose a this-is-all-I-need sigh, Ray was turning from the window when he saw a more prominent figure break through the crowd. To his enormous dismay it was Geraldo Rivera followed by two loaded-down cameramen. Toting his own teleprompter, Geraldo was pointing at the station and barking orders to his laden crew. The sight of the flamboyant newshound activated Ray's defenses and put his mental devices on red alert.

"Well, whoop-de-doo," he muttered sourly. "Geraldo is in town." He pronounced *Geraldo* as if it were a disease. "Ray-Man, you've finally made the big time."

When Geraldo melded back into the crowd, Ray closed the window blind and looked at his watch. Now he *really* dreaded his two o'clock press conference. If given a choice, he'd rather have his teeth snapped off at the gums with a bottle opener.

On the way back to his office, Ray had a private talk with himself. "Don't sweat it, Ray-Man. Geraldo's just doing his job. He's here to put his spin on things like everybody else out there. He puts his pants on every morning just like you do. Forget about it."

Ray sat down at his desk and stared straight ahead, then planted his elbows on the desk and rested his chin between his palms. He was fooling himself. Geraldo was going to rip his balls off by the roots and parade them in front of the whole wide world. He ate guys like Ray for breakfast. By the time Rivera got done with him, the entire country would want his head on a platter. He could picture it now: **THE MAJESTIC STAR CRISIS: AMERICA HELD HOSTAGE, WITH YOUR HOST, GERALDO RIVERA.**

Realizing he was overreacting, Ray threw his head back and laughed. He needed to lighten up. "That's right, Ray," he kidded. "Hell, Geraldo's probably already got a hidden camera stashed somewhere in the head so he can televise you taking a classified crap. Christ, next thing you know, his buddy Jerry Springer's gonna show up. Then your ass is really grass!"

Fortunately, all government grounds were off-limits to the press corps, but that didn't stop reporters from hounding station personnel when their work shift ended—running alongside their cars, yelling out questions, poking microphones in their faces. At least the daily press conferences would eliminate some of that, Ray hoped, and help curtail unwanted leaks.

Naturally, he intended to hand the press the official government spiel: that the negotiations were making progress...no further executions were anticipated...Alvarez still remained in custody...blah-blah-blah.

But, in truth, there were no new developments to report—*none*. And therein lies the problem. With his 24-hour window down to 23-and-change, Ray was saddled with the same pathetic options: either wait it out or send in the SEALs—both unacceptable. There *had* to be another angle, something he had overlooked.

With his brain hard at work, Ray's thoughts turned to his anonymous wake-up call. "Look the other way tonight," the caller had said. "He might make a difference."

It was a preposterous idea on the surface but at this point Ray couldn't rule anything out. Had he been too hasty in rejecting the caller's advice? Was this perhaps some quirky opportunity that had fallen in his lap? Toying with the idea, he permitted himself an intellectual foray into the whimsical.

"Okay, Ray-Man, let's say you allow this jerk-off aboard—assuming he can be trusted. If he would stay out of sight and provide you with radio intelligence, that would be a real plus. But you don't need any more floaters in the Gulf of Mexico. That's for sure. Passenger safety reigns supreme. Still, if this mystery man has a cool head on his shoulders and would follow orders, maybe he could be used to your advantage. Off the record, of course."

While dabbling with the theory, Ray's brain snapped back to reality. "People's lives are at stake, Admiral. Forget it. It's a wacky idea and the risk is far too great. You can't look the other way and let some armed civilian get involved. That would be a dereliction of duty. You could be court-martialed and rightly so. What the hell are you thinking?"

This was all true, of course, but the unconventional side of Ray wouldn't let go—recognizing the makings of a slim, yet outside chance of perhaps bettering his odds. With a secret infiltrator aboard, he would have some eyes and ears. He would no longer be working in the dark. And the beauty of it was that he could disavow any knowledge of it should the former SEAL get caught. After all, the Coast Guard would never send a civilian into a situation like this. Right?

Ray swiveled his office chair to face Mendoza's photograph. "Right. Even a murdering scuzzball like you would buy that."

It was an arguably drastic idea, but one that held a scant degree of promise—in theory, anyway—and anything that might favorably tip the scales at this juncture had to be explored. With his wheels turning, Ray checked his watch and tallied the hours until nightfall. According to the snitch, the ex-SEAL was going to board the *Majestic Star* tonight, which would require a transport boat.

There wouldn't be any harm in me intercepting the boat and taking a look at this guy...see what he was made of...what his motives were. He's got to be stopped anyway. Who knows? If this fellow is crazy enough to attempt such a thing, maybe I should let him—assuming he would cooperate and not put the passengers at risk. Hmmmmm.

Sunday 11:40 Hours – The "Majestic Star"

After the Zetas disappeared up the stairway, a hushed shock settled over the room and the casino fell eerily quiet. Now that the suspense was over, everyone seemed lost in a weird voidness—like an invisible switch had been flipped and the wild exhilarating ride they were on had skidded to a screeching halt, creating a mind-numbing shockwave that left everyone psychologically stunned.

Skip was in shock as well, leaning against the craps table for support. He felt like a death row inmate who had just received a last-minute stay of execution. It had been a hell of a close call and the reality of what-could-have-happened was just sinking in, leaving him weak all over.

As the dumbstruck people snapped out of their fugue, they began to stir aimlessly and talk in hushed tones. But it didn't take them long to liven up. Soon their faint murmurings turned to lively chatter followed by noisy celebration. Before long, Skip was surrounded by a drove of supporters, all clamoring to congratulate their hero captain. Some shook his hand, some slapped him on the back, others saluted him or flashed him the victory sign. Everyone was smiling, cheering, and clapping their hands. Trying to keep from being squashed, Skip politely but unenthusiastically received their accolades, feeling unworthy of the acclaim.

"May God forever bless you, Captain Myles," a female voice said from the back.

"Hear, hear!" a male voice interjected.

At the height of their hooraying the crowd suddenly parted to create an open pathway. When two females emerged from the back, Skip recognized them as Madison and her mother.

"Thank you for saving my daughter's life, Captain." The mother's lower lip was quivering and watery mascara ran down her cheeks. "On behalf of Maddie and our shipmates, I want to thank you for standing up to those monsters. No telling what might have happened if you hadn't."

223

WIRED

Before Skip could reply, she grappled him around the neck and clung to him tightly. Her arms were trembling and her face was smeared wet with tears. Though she meant well, her praise and beholden manner gave Skip a huge pang of guilt. Whether the woman realized it or not, he had just played an irresponsible game of winner-take-all poker with the jackpot being the lives of everyone present. And he had done it fully without knowing the outcome—on a hunch. Although the gamble had worked, he felt undeserving of any gratitude. Rather than being proud of his performance, he felt borderline ashamed. His actions had been reckless and in a sense he had betrayed their trust. They could have all been killed.

Breaking the mother's neck hold, two spirited males muscled Skip from behind and hoisted him onto their shoulders. As the men toted him about the room, the onlookers gave him another lively ovation, praising their redeemer once more. Feeling undeserving, Skip gazed down at the applauders and grinned uncomfortably.

All guiltiness aside, Skip didn't want to spoil their fun. After four grueling days of hardship they finally had something to cheer about, something to feel good about. He didn't want this minor victory going to their heads, but he saw no harm in letting them celebrate. For a fleeting moment they were victors instead of victims.

After Skip felt they had rejoiced enough, he instructed the men under him to carry him to the craps table. Eager to oblige, the burly men toted him to the table and deposited him carefully on top. Once standing above the crowd, Skip raised his arms and called for attention. With a *"shush"* here and a *"shush"* there, quiet spread to the far corners of the room.

"Okay, listen up! As you've all witnessed, the Mexican gang leader has promised to halt the executions." This automatically sparked a ripple of applause. "With this fragile truce in place, it's very important that we not provoke them further. Otherwise, we may lose any ground that we've gained today and we certainly don't want that." Everyone voiced agreement, even the hardcore males. "As your captain, I'm asking for your cooperation and ordering you to behave yourselves. We're not out of the woods yet." Skip panned their upturned faces. "I know you all want to go home—so do I—but we've got to be patient. The authorities are working hard for our release and I will keep you informed as things develop. Now, at this time let's proceed to the sundeck in an orderly fashion for the midday meal."

As the passengers herded toward the stairwell, Skip spoke above the commotion. "Remember! Be cool and do what you're told. They're in no mood for further opposition. Your cooperation is crucial. I'll see you topside."

As the passengers filed up the stairway, Skip sat down heavily on the craps table's felt covering. The altercation had left him weak and used up. When the last passenger disappeared up the steps, he leaned back on his elbows, closed his eyes, and breathed a sigh of relief at the ceiling. He felt as though he'd just run the Boston Marathon in the dog days of summer.

For now, anyway, his gamble had paid off. Nobody had been killed and there was a moratorium on the executions—he hoped.

Sunday 12:00 Hours – Clearwater Beach, Florida

Gazing down at his label-free beer bottle, Cal ended his introspection with a final pep talk.

It was kill-or-be-killed time. The odds weren't great, but he had the element of surprise on his side and he had the SEAL training. He knew what to do and how to do it—once a killing machine, always a killing machine. The undertaking would require stealth, guts, and lightninglike speed—just like the old days. And if he didn't survive it, that was the breaks. He had been living on borrowed time since Vietnam anyway, thanks to Skip.

So suck it up, soldier, and give it your best shot. And if everything goes to hell out there, take as many Zetas down with you as you can. HOOYAH!

~~~~~~~~~~

In between bouts of her own self-reflection, Kathy had noticed Cal's sullen mood. She had once thought about interjecting some small talk to take his mind off things, but knew he wouldn't want that. He needed some space, some private time to think. He was playing things out in his mind...plucking up his courage...steeling himself for the unknown ahead.

WIRED

Since Cal's arrival, she had witnessed a dramatic change in him. He no longer joked around and his usual cavalier demeanor had given way to a serious quietude. Nowadays, the look on his face was one of obligation and duty. Whether he truly wanted to or not, he was dead set on rescuing Skip—convinced that if he didn't, no one else would.

Cal's reticence was just fine with her because she didn't feel like chitchatting anyway. Her life was spiraling out of control and she felt utterly powerless to stop it. First, her husband had been taken away from her—kidnapped by mercenaries—and now her only sibling was about to join him. She didn't want to slide further into depression, but the depth of her despair went deep—like a hole in her heart had bored its way down to her soul and drained her of spirit.

She wondered what Skip was doing right then...what his thoughts were...if he was okay. She was plagued with worry that he had been beaten or even killed by the terrorists. He had a serious sense of duty and a dangerously short fuse. She couldn't imagine him standing by while those passengers were executed yesterday—not the man she married.

Kathy tried not to dwell on the terrible, but the prospect of Skip being physically harmed was too likely to ignore. She hadn't mentioned this to Cal because they had made a pact not to hypothesize. Being his logical self, Cal insisted they remain focused on the facts and not let their imaginations run rampant, claiming the distraction would be counterproductive. He was right, of course, but she secretly suspected that he just didn't want to upset her by talking about it. Cal, too, was aware of Skip's keen sense of duty and his hair-trigger temperament.

With frightful imaginings in her head of her husband dead or dying, Kathy prayed for Skip's safety and for the future safety of her brother. More than anything else in the world, she wanted her two men back home safe and sound.

As Kathy prayed, tears welled beneath her closed lids and she squeezed them tighter together. Cal already had enough on his mind and she didn't want to add to his troubles by crying. Besides, if she went on a crying jag, he might change his mind about letting her tag along tonight. Nevertheless, try as she may, one eyelid betrayed her by springing a watery leak.

Annoyed at her sniveling self, Kathy opened her eyes to find Cal staring at his empty beer bottle with an expression of cold composure. She picked up a napkin and gave her cheek a discreet daub, then donned a pair of sunglasses to conceal any future accidents. Under their protection, she folded her hand over his and sipped her melted down rumrunner until the straw noisily sucked air.

Kathy's touch extricated Cal from his pensiveness and he looked over at her with vague surprise. Then, as if sensing her worry, he squeezed her hand and nodded ever so slightly to her, as if to say: *"Everything is going to be okay, Sis."*

Putting on a brave face, Kathy returned the gentle squeeze and nodded back, as if saying: *"Yes, Brother, I believe it will."*

With their feelings and fingers intertwined, they shared a hopeful smile and gazed seaward at the horizon—the indefinable point where the sky melts seamlessly into the sea.

Sunday 12:02 Hours – The "Majestic Star"

Instead of eating with the passengers on the sundeck, Skip weaved his way through the crowd and zipped up the stairway to the bridge deck. At reaching the wheelhouse, he lingered outside the open doorway before going in. Neal was hunched over the instrument panel, tapping the glass faceplate of a cantankerous gauge. The potato-pilfering Arab that John-Renée had whacked earlier was sitting on the bench seat behind him, looking half asleep.

Skip didn't know the big Arab's name but referred to him as "Stan," a slight toward the many "stans" in the Middle East—Pakistan, Afghanistan, Uzbekistan, Tajikistan, Turkmenistan. Stan was a hulk of a man—standing 6'4" and weighing about 300 pounds—with a carbon black beard and flyaway hair. His legs were like tree trunks and his hands were the size of meat platters. A jagged raised scar ran diagonally across his forehead that creased his left eyebrow. If that weren't scary enough, he wore a sheathed jambiya cinched around his waist—an Arab dagger with a wide curved blade. Had it been an axe instead of a dagger, Stan would be a Mideast version of Paul Bunyan.

Stan and Mohammad were the only Arab gang members, but as far as Skip could tell they didn't fraternize all that much. Skip figured their ancestors must've had a falling out somewhere along the line a few thousand years ago—probably over a camel trade or a young virgin. Those Muslims sure knew how to carry a grudge.

After being confined in his cabin since yesterday, Skip found it electrifying to be back on the bridge. The familiar sights and sounds embodied a normalcy that was therapeutic. The radio was alive with crosstalk and a balmy breeze was whisking throughout the cabin. This was his element and Skip felt at home here. Except for the out-of-place Arab hulk, everything was as it should be.

In crossing the threshold, Skip announced his presence. "Steady as she goes, Neal."

At hearing Skip's voice, both men turned to face him. Neal looked surprised at first, then relieved, then overjoyed. Stan stood up grumpily and unslung his AK-47, looking irritated for being disturbed.

"Skip!" Neal blurted excitedly. "I can't believe it—*you're alive!*"

With a big sunny smile, Neal raced to Skip's side and gave him a hearty hug. It was the first time Neal had seen him since Skip got clobbered in the casino and dragged out like a sack of potatoes, leaving Neal unsure if he was dead or alive.

As the reunited shipmates pounded backs, Stan looked beyond Skip for Mohammad, puzzled as to why the captain was roaming the ship unescorted. Baffled by it, the hulk walked to the door and peered down the catwalk. As he gawked outside, Neal demanded a few answers.

"What the hell's going on, Skip? I just about gave you up for dead! I've been worried sick!" Noting the edge in his voice, Neal softened his tone. "How's your head?

"Well, I had a monster migraine this morning, but I suppose I'll live." Skip lifted his hat to reveal the scabbing wound. "Paybacks are hell, though. I'd say Gold-Tooth's pretty pissed off about now. A few minutes ago in the casino, I made him promise to halt all further executions in front of his men and the passengers. It'll probably come back to haunt me, but I think he'll stick by it. For the first time in his mobster life, his bullying backfired on him. The passengers were about to string him up and he damn well knew it."

While Skip gave Neal the rest of the details, Mohammad popped in the doorway short of breath. At catching sight of Skip, the expression in his eyes went from relief, to sour, to squinty someday-I'm-gonna-get-you-sucka slits. His turban was clearly in a wad for having to hunt down the AWOL captain. Reacting to Mo's mean-ass look, Skip pursed his lips and gave him a juicy "air kiss" making a loud kissing sound.

The mockery made Mohammad twice as mad and his face flushed every shade of red in the spectrum. While threatening in Arabic to behead the infidel captain, he lunged forward a step and stomped his boot on the floor, faking a charge at Skip. But if the feigned threat was supposed to scare Skip, it didn't work. The twerp couldn't punch his way out of a wet paper bag.

While still glaring meanly at Skip, Mohammad motioned for Stan to join him outside on the catwalk. Once he did, they began jabbering away while looking in Skip's direction. From the way they were behaving, Skip figured Stan was being enlightened as to recent events in the casino. Standing side by side, the pair was an amusing study in contrasts. Stan stood well over six foot while the pint-sized Arab was about five-foot nothing—Islam's Mutt and Jeff.

"So what's been goin' on here, Neal? Any progress with the negotiations?"

Neal gave him an uncertain shrug. "Gold-Tooth was in here earlier this morning, talking on the radio. He was fairly calm, though. I mean, he didn't scream or bust up the radio like before. I'm not sure, but I think they might be close to making a deal."

This news supported Skip's belief that Gold-Tooth had an ulterior reason holding him back. If a deal with the Coasties was in the offing, it explained why he and his gunmen hadn't made mincemeat of them in the casino.

"I hope so, Neal. If somethin' doesn't give pretty soon, there's gonna be a mutiny. The passengers have had it."

"I hope so too. We're almost out of drinking water." Neal handed Skip a clipboard. "Our food supply is dwindling as well. John-Renée's down to mostly beans and potatoes."

Neal studied Skip's face as he pored over the inventory log. Despite strict rationing, the daily consumption of keeping over two hundred people alive had nearly exhausted their supply. People could go without food for weeks if required, so the food shortage wasn't a major concern.

But drinking water was altogether a different matter. The human body was 70% water and without it dehydration sets in quickly. If Neal's calculations were correct, the ship's potable water tanks would run dry sometime tomorrow.

"Well, Neal, if the terrorist don't shoot us first, we'll all die of thirst anyway."

At that point the Arabs entered the wheelhouse and the two sailors split up. Neal resumed his pecking on the faulty gauge while Skip strode over to the row of bow windows. Some of them were cranked open and the sea breeze felt pleasant against his worried face.

On the southern horizon a tanker was steaming toward the mouth of Tampa Bay—just an ordinary tanker, going to an ordinary port, carrying an ordinary payload and crew. Skip tracked the tanker with envious eyes until it was a tiny lump; all the while wishing he was on it.

Sunday 17:48 Hours – The "Sol-Mate"

As the encroaching darkness chased the daylight into the sea, the setting sun sent long slanted shadows scampering off to the east. The darkening sky was a canopy of deep indigo and some of the brighter stars had emerged from the ashes of twilight. The winds were out of the northwest, ushering in a faint seasonable nip. The inland waters were calm.

The *Sol-Mate* had been underway for ten minutes and had just cleared the Clearwater Pass Bridge. Atop the flybridge, Brillo maneuvered the red and green channel markers with Kathy sitting on the bench seat beside him. In the failing light below, Cal was testing his air tank and underwater breathing apparatus. The tension was thick and everybody was quiet, each dealing with their own apprehensions.

When the boat cleared the rock jetty and entered open sea, a chilly headwind smacked them in the face and Kathy zipped up her windbreaker. A short while later, with the clanging of the bell buoy in the distance behind them, Cal broke the strained silence.

"Well, at least the weather is cooperating. I'd hate to swim two miles in sloppy seas—that's for sure."

When no one replied, Cal understood and went about adjusting his facemask. He was confident in his abilities, yet struggling to maintain his grit. While not consciously dwelling on it, the one-man-against-eight scenario was hard at work in the background, chipping away at his mettle.

Once satisfied that everything was in working order, Cal wrested-on the wet suit over his civilian clothing. If and when he got aboard the *Majestic Star*, he would shed the rubber suit and be clad in tourist-type clothes. During his underwater swim to the ship, his shoes would go in a waterproof plastic bag along with the Uzi, the Glock, and other gear.

"Guess I'll try sending that message now," Cal muttered to himself, zipping up his wet suit. "Let Skip know that The Lone Ranger is on the way."

As Cal climbed the ladder to the flybridge, he prayed that Skip was still alive. Boarding the *Majestic Star* just to find Skip dead would be pathetic. Over and above losing his best friend, he would have risked his neck for nothing. Then what?

When Cal reached the flybridge, he sat down beside Kathy and lifted the microphone from its metal holding clip. It was a long shot, but if Skip knew he was coming, perhaps they could rendezvous and team up. With both of them armed, maybe they could pull off the impossible and get back home in one piece. Maybe.

Sunday 18:14 Hours – The "Majestic Star"

After finishing their six o'clock meal, Skip and Mohammad began the short trek back to the wheelhouse. By now, the western sky was a kaleidoscope of plums and purples and the sun was an orangish-red sliver hanging on the horizon. Skip had heard tales of a "green flash" at the instant the sun dips into the sea, but he had never witnessed it. And having watched his fair share of ocean sunsets, he pooh-poohed the idea as pure hogwash.

At entering the wheelhouse, Skip flipped on the anchor lights and then dropped into his leather helmseat. When he nodded at Neal— indicating it was his turn to go eat—Neal rose and strode toward the exit with Stan trailing behind him.

All afternoon long Skip had watched and waited for some sign from the military, hoping their ordeal would soon end. But to his dismay he had seen nothing but newscopters and outlying reconnaissance crafts. Likewise, he had seen neither hide-nor-hair of Gold-Tooth, which was probably just as well. After their head-on collision in the casino this morning, Skip didn't expect him to be exactly chummy.

Whenever Skip did see him, he still planned to confront Gold-Tooth about the food and water shortage—Coast Guard deal or not. If he were on the fence about trading passengers for supplies, maybe it would sway him into making a trade. Even slimeball terrorists needed drinking water.

Then a troubling thought crossed Skip's mind: that Gold-Tooth might go the other way and resume the executions—thin out the herd, so to speak—figuring, in his own murderous way, that with fewer mouths to feed, the less food and water required. After all, in his gangsterdom workplace, murder was the industry standard for solving most problems.

Skip swiveled his helmseat to see the arrow on the water gauge pointing dangerously close to the E mark. Three gauges away, the arrow on the fuel indicator hovered near the F mark. Since the diesels were only being used to generate electricity, the fuel tanks were three-quarters full. As Skip compared the two gauges, he found himself wishing that humans could drink diesel fuel.

Then his eyes shifted to the battered marine radio. Despite being duct-taped and jury-rigged it was still working, which was nothing short of miraculous. Somehow, he had to warn the Coasties about Gold-Tooth's plan to explode the ship whether Alvarez was released or not; that whatever deal was struck, the passengers must be evacuated first or they would be blown to bits like that poor slob yesterday.

"Capitán, pick a number," Skip grimly recalled. *"Pick any number— uno, dos, tres . . ."*

With temptation gnawing at him, Skip glimpsed over his left shoulder at Mohammad. When his peripheral vision registered the Arab eyeing him closely, he told himself to forget it. It was no use—he was being watched like a hawk. If he got caught trying to send a message, it would be the excuse Mohammad needed to blow his fool head off.

Frustrated, Skip swiveled his helmseat away from the radio and locked his arms across his chest. By now the sun had set and the sea was dark and dim, exactly in line with the way he felt. As Skip stared into the settling darkness, he wondered how this drama would end...how many people would die before it was over...if he and Neal would survive it.

Skip's thoughts were suddenly interrupted by the sound of scratchy static coming from the radio speaker. It was the familiar sound of somebody keying a radio microphone on-and-off. Skip ignored it at first, figuring it was just another idiot boater screwing around with his marine radio. But when the radio interference persisted, it began to annoy him.

Channel 22 was the Coast Guard's official distress frequency and the channel was supposed to remain clear at all times. Although the boater wasn't speaking on the frequency, the sound was obvious to anyone that had worked around radios a while—*static . . no static . . static . . no static . .* and so on. A person unfamiliar with radios would hardly notice it. But Skip had been in life-threatening situations before and had relied on Channel 22 to bail him out of trouble. Hence, he had zero tolerance for anyone interfering with the channel. It was a major pet peeve of his.

In trying to ignore it, Skip noted something familiar about the static. There was a pattern of sorts that piqued his curiosity. *Static . . no static . . static-static-static . . no static . . static.* Its cadence and form reminded him of Morse code that he had learned in the Navy, but he wasn't sure. Trying to be inconspicuous, he leaned closer to the radio and listened more intently.

Yes, he thought, *it is Morse code—definitely. But who would be keying their microphone and sending Morse code?*

Then it struck him full force. *Was someone out there trying to communicate with him?*

With his heart pounding, Skip closed his eyes and tried to recall the dot-and-dash alphabet. Years ago, on boring nightwatches at sea, he would listen to the Merchant Marine frequencies used for ship-to-shore transmissions. To pass the time, he would try to decipher the Morse code messages sent back and forth. Due to their incredible transmitting speed some translation got lost along the way, but he was usually able to decode most of what they were saying.

As Skip mentally unraveled the code, he discovered two things: the message was being repeated over-and-over and the string of dots and dashes spelled out: *July, August, September, October, November.* In between each transmission was a pause and then the message repeated itself: *July, August, September, October, November.* This went on for several minutes before stopping.

What the hell does it mean? It makes no sense. Then Skip had an idea. *Could it be an acronym?*

When communicating over non-secure frequencies, the military would sometimes transmit a series of words that appeared meaningless. But if the first letter or last letter of each word were selected, for instance, the cryptic message became clear. He tried it.

'**J**' for July . . '**A**' for August . . '**S**' for September . . '**O**' for October . . '**N**' for November.

J-A-S-O-N.

Skip was rocked by the revelation and it was all he could do to suppress his surprise.

Is this a coincidence? Or is this message actually meant for me? But nobody calls me Jason anymore, except for a few old family members.

Suddenly a light came on and Skip's eyes twinkled with recognition. There was only one person in the whole world that knew Morse code and who sometimes called him Jason—*Cal Stringer*. It was Cal, for petesake—it had to be.

Well, I'll be damned. Skip looked outside and his heart drummed with excitement. *Cal's somewhere out there.*

As a young lad, Skip had despised his given first name. He thought Jason sounded like a pansy, which was entirely unsuitable for a cool, tough dude like himself. So, early in his teens, he had adopted the nickname *Skip*—a derivative of Skipper from reruns of *Gilligan's Island*. He thought the name sounded both manly and cool. Afterwards, except for close family members, everyone in the neighborhood called him Skip or they were subject to a severe ass-whoopin'.

Kathy had jokingly shared this with Cal one day and Cal had rubbed it in ever since—calling him "Jason" every so often just to get under his skin. And it generally succeeded.

Sunday 18:25 Hours – The "Sol-Mate"

Cal had been keying the microphone for about five minutes, pausing periodically for a hopeful response. When Brillo had once started to ask him what he was doing, Cal quieted him by placing a hand over his mouth—fearing that a voice leaking over the airwaves would rouse attention. After that, both Brillo and Kathy remained quiet while watching Cal go about his peculiar keying.

Cal didn't know if the terrorists knew Skip's real name, or even if they knew Morse code for that matter, but he didn't want to do something stupid to get Skip hurt or possibly killed. So, after doing some thinking, he came up with the bright idea of using the calendar months as an acronym for Skip's first name. He hoped that if Skip happened to be on the bridge, he would make sense of the message and realize who was sending it. And if he weren't, it was no big deal. Chances were the terrorists wouldn't notice a little radio interference anyway.

Cal realized it was a long shot, but one worthy of trying.

Sunday 18:30 Hours – The "Majestic Star"

As Skip scoured the blackish sea, his eyes darted in all directions. Cal was out there somewhere; he just knew it. It made perfect sense, though. He would be the first person Kathy would call in a situation like this.

But what's Cal doing out there? What could he possibly be up to?

When the **J-A-S-O-N** message began again, Skip's pulse quickened. He had no idea why Cal was signaling him—if indeed it *was* Cal—but it boosted his morale just to imagine him close by.

As the radio static persisted, Skip glanced over his shoulder at Mohammad. Now that his belly was full, the dweeb was beginning to nod off. When his eyelids fluttered shut and remained closed, Skip rose quietly and faked a stretch, then shuffled sideways to put his body between Mohammad and the radio. When the **J-A-S-O-N** transmission stopped, he risked another peek to find Mohammad still napping.

As Skip stood poised over the radio, a torrent of tension ran through him. In Vietnam he had seen what an AK-47 could do to a human body and it wasn't pretty. Vacillating, he thought about Kathy and how his death would affect her. But unless Gold-Tooth was bluffing about blowing the ship, everybody was going to die anyway including him.

With his hand suspended in midair, Skip checked behind him one last time. Finding Mo still dozing, he faced the radio and licked his lips. His mouth was so parched he could hardly swallow and nervous sweat traced down his temples into the coarse hairs of his beard.

It was now or never.

Taking a deep breath and holding it, Skip seized the microphone. Deciding not to risk removing it from its holding clip, he squeezed the key frantically while leaving the mike in place. As he soundlessly keyed his Morse code message, his head pivoted between the radio and Mohammad like a tennis fan watching a Wimbledon match.

Gold-Tooth's shoot-to-kill order had been explicit. If the trigger-happy Arab happened to wake up right now, Skip was a dead man.

Sunday 18:36 Hours – The "Sol-Mate"

Cal's hand had begun to ache so he'd decided to give it a rest. He was sitting next to Kathy, sipping coffee from a thermos cup, when he heard something on the radio. Lurching forward, he turned up the volume and craned his neck closer to the speaker.

Yes, he was right. Someone was keying a response.

Spilling his coffee while setting it down, Cal snatched a pencil and notepad off Brillo's dashboard and stuck the penlight in his mouth to write by.

'I-P-H-E-R-E . . S-K-I-P-H-E-R-E . . S-K-I-P-H-E-R-E . . S-K-I-P-H-E-R-E . .'

Smiling down at the translation, Cal mumbled: "Atta boy" and illuminated the paper for Kathy to see. "It's him, Kathy." He nudged her with an elbow. "It's Skip."

Kathy sprang to her feet in jubilation and beamed at the starry skies, latching onto the windshield frame to steady herself. "Thank you, Lord! Thanks for watching over my Skip!" Totally electrified, she plopped back down and grabbed Cal's arm. "You've got to tell Skip what your plans are, Cal. Maybe he can help!"

Happy for them both, Cal's smile broadened. "That was the whole idea, kiddo." Then he began keying a reply.

WIRED

Sunday 18:40 Hours – The "Majestic Star"

Keeping one eye on Mohammad and one eye on the radio, Skip tensely awaited a reply—if there was one. After four days of isolation, he was on the verge of communicating with someone from the outside world, and that someone happened to be his best friend—he thought.

As Skip stood paralyzed before the radio, the buildup of nervous energy was bursting to let go. Any second now the snoring Arab could wake or Neal and Stan could come walking through the door, spoiling everything. The mere prospect of anything, or anybody, getting in his way at a crucial time like this was unthinkable.

As if right on cue, Mo snorted loudly and woke with a spastic jerk. Then he automatically stood as if trying to stay awake. Cringing inside, Skip shrank back from the radio and pretended to check off items on a clipboard. The Arab frowned at his watch sleepily and murmured something indistinct, then plopped back down. As he did, a series of staticky dots and dashes came over the airwaves. With his heart in his mouth, Skip copied down the letters on the clipboard.

"S-T-A-R-B-O-A-R-D-H-A-T-C-H-O-N-E-H-O-U-R-C-A-L."

The message repeated itself three times and stopped. As Skip stared down at the letters, its meaning vibrated throughout his body. He felt stunned...shocked...blown away. Cal was planning to board his ship—in one hour.

Jesus H. Christ!

Trying to act normal, Skip erased the message as if making a wrong entry and then checked his watch to note the time. He didn't know whether to be excited or scared shitless and right now he was a great deal of both. Cal was crazy to attempt such a thing...off his rocker...certifiable.

What if he gets caught? What would Gold-Tooth do? Go on a rampage and start killing people at will? Women and children too?

While his semi-paralytic brain digested the news, Skip tried to act busy by flipping through blank pages on the clipboard. His nerves were shot. Then he heard more radio static and almost jumped out of his skin. With an unsteady hand, he scribbled down the incoming message.

"K-A-T-H-Y-S-A-Y-S-S-H-E-L-O-V-E-S-Y-O-U." After a pause: "D-O-N-T-K-N-O-W-W-H-Y."

WIRED

Restraining a nervous laugh, Skip erased the message until he rubbed a hole through the paper. Then he tore the page from the clipboard and threw it in a trashcan. At that moment Neal and Stan walked through the doorway and it was none too soon. Skip had to get to his cabin before he exploded. He needed some time alone to think, to deal with this madness.

The instant Neal saw Skip, he knew something was up. While imperceptible to the others, it was written all over his friend's face. He was an emotional wreck and Neal wondered why.

Dodging Neal's probing eyes, Skip faked a yawn and told Mohammad he was finished for the night. The overworked Muslim yawned in reply and escorted Skip back to his quarters. Once Skip was in his cabin, the exhausted Arab fell into a chair outside the door to stand watch until later relieved. Inside, Skip paced the length of the room in a full-scale frenzy, ranting at the floor.

"Cal's freakin' crazy for boarding my ship! Is he trying to get himself killed? Maybe all of us? And he's got Kathy with him, for God sake! What the hell's goin' on out there?"

While walking off his mass overload of energy, Skip mentally rehashed Cal's message. The starboard hatch made sense because it could be opened from the outside. But it was three or four feet above the waterline and Cal would probably need some help climbing aboard.

While still pacing Skip checked his watch. "Come on, Skip, you've got less than an hour to come up with a game plan. Think, sailor— think!!"

Sunday 19:03 Hours – The "Sol-Mate"

As the *Sol-Mate* voyaged away from the glowing lights of the mainland, the shades of evening grew deeper and darker. Three miles dead ahead, the gleaming anchor light on the *Majestic Star's* masthead shone like a beacon in the night. As Brillo advanced steadily toward it, his eyes alternated between its distant glow and the radar screen mounted under the dashboard.

"Something ain't right," he muttered at the radarscope, adjusting knobs. "Where's the blockade around the ship?"

Except for a large blip denoting the *Majestic Star*, there was nothing else on radar. By now Brillo had expected to see green dots all over the screen and their unexplained absence gave him a funny feeling. Things seemed a little too easy. To get a broader picture of things, he switched the radarscope to maximum range. At once the screen automatically resized and registered a moving object a mile or so off their stern.

"Uh-oh," Brillo muttered under his breath. "Might be the Coasties."

As the radar wand made another sweep, it confirmed his suspicion. The vessel was on an intersecting course with the *Sol-Mate* and in hot pursuit. Suddenly worried, Brillo looked over his shoulder and studied the horizon behind him. Using skilled seaman's eyes, he visually separated the vessel's red-and-green bow light from the backdrop of city lights. The bow was rising and falling with the seas and gaining on them at an incredible speed.

Twisting around in his seat, Brillo pointed a finger at the bow light. "Looks like we got company!" Down below, Cal was adjusting his rubber fins and Kathy was packing articles into one-gallon size freezer bags. "At its rate of speed, we can't outrun 'em!"

Holding a Ziploc bag in each hand, Kathy squinted in the direction Brillo was pointing. "What are we gonna do, Brother?"

"Hide everything in the cabin," Cal said, shedding his wet suit. "Then act normal."

Two minutes later everything was stowed out of sight and Cal and Kathy were lounging in the teak fighting chairs, appearing cool and relaxed.

"If anybody asks, we're just enjoying an evening boat ride." Cal took her hand. "Isn't that right—honey?"

"Okay, guys," Brillo voiced over the engines, "I've altered our course away from the Star. If it's the Coasties, we'll just play dumb about being in a quarantined area. Hopefully, they'll just give us a lecture and run us off instead of throwing us in the brig."

Cal's chair was facing the advancing boat and his eyes were locked on its bow light. As its glow grew steadily brighter, he detected the shrill sound of high RPM engines. When the Coast Guard vessel finally emerged from obscurity, Cal recognized it as a 25' pursuit boat powered by twin Mercury outboards.

Descending on them in a cloud of white spray, the shrillness of the motors dropped to a low drone and the boat decelerated. Simultaneously the raised bow settled into the surface and an onrushing wake of churning foam sloshed the *Sol-Mate* up and down. Clearly, the boat captain wasn't taking any great pains for a smooth and courteous approach.

Casting Cal a we're-in-deep-shit-now look, Brillo put the diesels in neutral and climbed down the ladder to receive their unexpected company. As the Coast Guard vessel eased up alongside, a Coastie emerged from the pilothouse and tossed Brillo a line. After placing a rubber fender between the two boats, Brillo secured the line to a cleat on the port beam.

As Cal watched all this, four things struck him as odd: the Coastie was in his forties; he was alone; he wasn't wearing a life jacket; and he had not used the boat's siren or flashing lights.

"What's the problem, sir?" Brillo asked, presenting his most innocent face.

"Well, for starters, Captain, you're in a restricted area." While talking, the Coastie panned their faces in the milky moonlight. "Surely you've heard about the Majestic Star situation. Right?"

"Ah-h, yes sir," Brillo sputtered. "On the news. What a bum deal for those poor passengers."

"Yes, it was a bum deal, indeed—to say the very least."

"Well, sir, if we're too close to the Star, we'll gladly move out of the area. Guess we got a little off course. We don't wanna get in the way of a Coast Guard operation."

"Yes, you'll need to vacate the area." The Coastie was studying Cal, looking him up and down. "But since I'm here anyway, I'll need to do a routine safety inspection. It's standard procedure whenever we pull alongside a vessel. May I come aboard?"

"Uh-h, sure." Brillo shot Cal a nonplussed look and scratched the back of his neck. "But I'm in the charter business, so I'm sure you'll find everything in order. Where would you like to start?"

"Oh, we'll start with the routine things: life jackets, flares—your captain's license." The Coastie hopped aboard unceremoniously. "You know the drill. Mind if I look around while you're rounding those up?"

Brillo glanced at Cal for guidance. "Why, no. We don't have anything to hide."

When the Coastie went inside the cabin, Brillo raced over to the others, who were already on their feet. "Did you guys hide the stuff real good? If he finds that Uzi, we're in deep shit!"

Kathy looked at Cal worriedly. "I hid it under the sink in the head. Do you think he'll look there?"

"It's possible," Cal said, watching the cabin door. "He seems pretty thorough. If he does, I'll think of something."

Brillo frowned. "Come on, Cal! How can we possibly talk our way out of having an Uzi and two boxes of ammo aboard a fishing boat in a quarantined area just a few miles from the Star? If he finds them, we're all dead meat and I can kiss my captain's license goodbye—forever!"

"Yeah, you're right," Cal admitted. "We need to distract him before he works his way into the head. I'll handle it."

Cal had always believed that the best defense was a good offense. With no time to think, he barged into the forward cabin with bravado. When he entered, the Coastie's back was turned and he was searching through the cabin's storage compartments and drawers.

Irked by this invasion of privacy, Cal scowled while the man ransacked the cabin. The search method was uncalled for during a routine safety check and Cal took offense to it. Under ordinary circumstances, he would have given the Coastie a blistering education on the Fourth Amendment's search and seizure laws and sent him packing. But, at this point, Cal just wanted to get rid of him. Besides, these were Florida waters—the southeast gateway for drugs and illegal immigrants—and the Coastie was likely operating under a standing order to search all vessels for drugs and contraband.

Venturing further into the cabin, Cal cleared his throat for attention. "Ahem! Can I help you find something?"

Taken off guard, the man straightened and turned to face Cal. "Maybe you can, Mister . . .?"

"Stringer." Cal stepped forward and extended his hand. "Calvin Stringer."

The suspicious-acting Coastie approached Cal in a slow and deliberate manner. When their faces were inches apart, he gripped Cal's hand and held it for an unusually long time before shaking it—his eyes burrowing into Cal's eyes; as if assessing him, seeking to look inside him.

WIRED

The tactless invasion of space made Cal uncomfortable but he stood his ground nonetheless. After what seemed like an eternity, the Coastie released his hand and pointed at the dive gear.

"Going diving tonight, Mr. Stringer? Or are you and your bimbo girlfriend just enjoying the night air?"

The man's provocative attitude instantly annoyed Cal and his first reaction was to snap back. But, instead, he maintained his cool. He was supposed to be at the starboard hatch within the hour and he simply wanted this Coastie to go away.

"Well, for one thing, she's not a bimbo—she's my sister: Kathy Myles. She and the boat captain are friends and we decided to go for a boat ride on the spur of the moment. Is that against maritime law?"

"Well, no." The Coastie turned and wandered away from Cal, his eyes roaming the room. "No law against that, Mr. Stringer. It is a lovely night for a boat ride, isn't it?" He twisted around to face Cal. "Anything else?"

"It's none of the Coast Guard's damned business whether I go diving or not. It's a free country last time I heard. Besides, I thought you were concerned with safety issues—lifejackets and all that. That's what you said."

Ostensibly amused by the response, the Coastie's eyes sharpened. "Oh, but I am concerned about safety issues, Mr. Stringer, for the safety of everyone at sea. That's why I'm here." Smiling at the floor, he began to circle Cal. "Take you folks, for example. Since there's only one scuba tank aboard, it concerns me that someone might go diving alone. That can be dangerous, especially at night." He quit circling when directly in front of Cal and took a step forward, placing them nose-to-nose. The act was intended to intimidate; but Cal didn't budge in spite of his discomfort. "Bad things can happen at sea, Mr. Stringer. Deadly things. I wouldn't want to see anyone slip up and get hurt—maybe killed." He inched closer. "If I were you, I would exercise extreme caution."

The Coastie's words seemed to be weighted, awakening Cal's intuition. "I'll be sure to remember that," Cal answered. "If I decide to go diving tonight."

"Good!" With a satisfied handclap, the Coastguardsman turned away. The unexpected sound made Cal blink. "I'm glad that's settled."

WIRED

After giving the cabin interior a quick once over, the Coastie's eyes landed on the restroom. "I need to get rid of some coffee," he said over his shoulder. "Excuse me while I use the head." Without asking permission, the Coastie stepped inside the head and closed the door.

When Cal heard the lock twist in place, a cold fear struck him—the Uzi. Not wasting a second, he crossed the room and put his ear to the door, hoping to hear what the Coastie was doing. This guy worried Cal. He was no green rookie and he was way beyond suspicious. Given his insinuative remarks and dissecting looks, it was almost like he knew what Cal was up to. But how could he?

Cal's ear was still glued to the door when he heard the latch rattle. Half expecting the Coastie to emerge with the Uzi, he scampered away while his mind raced for a credible explanation for having the weapon.

Without saying a word the Coastie brushed past Cal and sat down at the built-in dinette table. "Have a seat, Mr. Stringer." Acting put upon, the Coastie removed his cap and waved it at the bench seat across from him. "I'd like to talk to you."

The Coastie's demeanor was dead serious and his invitation wasn't a request. Wondering how he could possibly exonerate himself for the Uzi and Glock, Cal took more time than necessary in approaching the table— like an errant student reporting to the principal's office. Trying to appear unruffled, he slid into the booth and folded his hands on the table. That's when Cal noticed for the first time that the Coastie's velcro name tape and rank insignias were missing from his uniform—strange thing number five about this fellow. What *wasn't* missing was the man's official Coast Guard .40 caliber sidearm.

"I'll get to the point, Mr. Stringer. You're acquainted with the Majestic Star predicament. Correct?" Cal nodded. "Well, it's a Mexican standoff—no pun intended—and people are dying. Hostage situations are inherently delicate, especially so when dealing with terrorists. In this particular case the hostage takers are demanding the release of two international drug lords."

"Juan Carlos Alvarez and Cesar Gonzalez," Cal interjected.

"Yes." The Coastie regarded him a moment before proceeding. "To sum it up, the U.S. and Mexican governments won't release them and the military can't attempt a rescue mission without endangering more civilian lives. So, we're damned if we do, and damned if we don't."

Wondering where all this was leading, Cal sat quietly; waiting for the boom to be lowered.

"This morning I learned from a reliable source that some foolish individual will attempt to board the Majestic Star tonight—someone with Navy SEAL training and packing some serious firepower." The Coastie leaned forward. "You wouldn't happen to know the identity of this *individual*, would you, Mr. Stringer?"

"Why...no," Cal lied, trying not to trip over his tongue. He was dumbfounded that the Coast Guard was aware of his plan. "Who would try a stupid thing like that?"

The suspicion in the Coastguardsman's eyes rose like tidewater. "That's exactly what I'd like to know. The situation is critical and certainly no place for amateurs—or mercenaries. Any outside intervention at this point could prove disastrous. The terrorists—or so-called Zetas— are on edge and the least provocation could result in more bad news for the passengers."

"That's right. I understand they're a very dangerous bunch."

"*Very*," the Coastie stressed, "unless one considers rape, beheadings, mutilation, and murder as seemly behavior." He paused a moment while thinking. "But on the positive side—if there is a positive side—it might be advantageous to have someone aboard the Majestic Star to feed us inside information. You know, keep us apprised as to what the Zetas were doing, et cetera, et cetera. Of course, this is assuming this *individual* would be capable of such an undertaking—properly trained and equipped, willing to follow orders, cool head on his shoulders and all that. What do you think?"

At that instant Cal realized what this surprise visit was all about: he was being interviewed. This Coastie had evidently received a tip and he was here to size up the alleged perpetrator. And, depending upon the outcome, Cal would either be arrested on the spot or recruited—more like coerced—into spying for the authorities. Being the said perpetrator in question, Cal didn't like either choice. His plan was to get aboard the ship, find Skip, and get the hell off—not to embark on some long-drawn-out undercover mission.

Does this Coastie really know my plan or is he baiting me? Trying to trick me into confessing? If I admit involvement, will he arrest me? If I don't, will he jail me for refusing to cooperate?

Unsure of which direction to take, Cal played it carefully down the middle. "Well, if this *individual* would radio-in particulars regarding the goings-on out there, it might make sense."

"Yes, I agree," the Coastie stared. "But I didn't mention anything about a radio."

Cal retreated within himself for a split second before responding. He had to watch out for traps.

"You said something about this individual *'feeding you inside information'*. How else could this person communicate with you—smoke signals?"

With an indulgent smile, Ray dropped the subject. Stringer was a fast thinker.

"Let me ask you a question, Mr. Stringer. You seem like a bright fellow." He folded his hands on the table and leaned over them. "If *you* were in my shoes and happened to run across this individual tonight, would *you* allow him to board the Majestic Star?"

Cal gazed thoughtfully at the ceiling as if putting himself in the Coastie's place. In actuality, his cerebral cortex was sorting data like a Pentium processor. This was a loaded question and his answer must be right. He had already flubbed up once about the radio.

If Cal had the Coastie's situation pegged right, it went like this: the authorities were under a lot of pressure to resolve the impasse and this man was exploring every conceivable option, no matter how remote. He was here—unofficially, no doubt—to determine if Cal would be of help or hindrance. Working in the blind had gotten them nowhere and the prospect of having a spy infiltrator aboard the ship—albeit a civilian— was tantalizing. Clearly, this officer was a decision maker of high rank, which explained his shrewdness and the missing insignias on his uniform. "Well, like you said," Cal replied, "if this individual proved to be capable, properly trained and equipped, and had a cool head on his shoulders— why not? What would you have to lose?" In gauging his reaction, Cal added: "Assuming he could get aboard undetected, of course. You certainly wouldn't want him spooking the Zetas and endangering the passengers."

WIRED

The Coastie concurred with a nod but his eyes were still marked by doubt, and understandably so. Permitting a civilian to get involved in a situation like this would be a thorny decision for any military leader. Depending on the outcome, it could be viewed as a bold stroke of genius or a real career-breaker. The soldier across from him was obviously a gambler or they wouldn't be having this conversation. He would have simply ordered his troops to impound the *Sol-Mate* and jail everyone aboard her.

It was time for Cal to disclose his willingness to cooperate, but he had to do so without making any admission of guilt. If it backfired on him, he could end up behind bars.

"Matter of fact," Cal put forward, "this individual could be a real ace in the hole for you. He could be your eyes and ears, let you know what was happening out there at sea; feed you real-time information so you could make informed decisions rather than guessing. In a situation with hostages involved, reliable intel could make a lifesaving difference."

"Maybe," the Coastie grunted, unconvinced. "But it's highly risky and could easily backfire if something went wrong. That would not be good. Lots of folks could get hurt—women and children. Not just anyone could pull this off, Mr. Stringer. It would take a *very* special person."

Cal nodded. "Yes. It would, indeed."

For what seemed like an inordinate amount of time, there was silence between them. While the Coastie pondered Cal's words, he toyed with the bill of his ball cap—shaping it and reshaping it until the curvature suited him. Then, as if coming to a decision, he put the cap down and regarded Cal fully in the face.

"Tell me, Mr. Stringer." His gaze was as direct as a drill press. "Do you consider yourself a special person?"

Anticipating the question, Cal didn't waver. The interview was coming to fruition. "Very," he said, unblinking. "All I can say is that you wouldn't have to worry about me—providing I was this *individual* you're speaking of."

As Cal sat before him, he tried to appear poised and confident. The Coastie was still evaluating him, weighing things out, deciding on whether to lock him up or let him go. At that instant Kathy's head appeared in a window behind the Coastie and quickly vanished.

Obviously, she and Brillo were dying to know their fate. Cal could identify with them because he was waiting to find out himself.

"Yes, Mr. Stringer, you might be special at that." His stare was intent, like a judge pondering a prisoner's fate. "We shall see. Naturally, if the Zetas happened to capture this person, he would be strictly on his own. For obvious reasons the military would have to disavow any knowledge."

"Naturally."

"And Mendoza—the Zeta gang leader?—let's just say he isn't known for his benevolence. They don't call him *'The Assassin'* for nothing. Get my drift?" Cal took the warning with a nod. "Good. Well, I'll be shoving off now. Duty calls and all that bullshit."

The Coastie rose and walked toward the doorway with Cal tagging behind. Abruptly, the man stopped and turned, causing Cal to almost plow into him.

"Incidentally, if you happen to run across this special somebody, tell them to use VHF Channel 12 to communicate with us. It's a Coast Guard channel seldom used anymore. It's not a secure channel but it's better than broadcasting to the maritime world on Channel 16. You never know who's monitoring the airwaves."

"That's a fact," Cal nodded. "Channel 12 would be a good choice, Mister...?"

"Hanna—Ray Hanna. But on Channel 12, I'm known as Bluebird—if you happen to see this individual."

Cal was barely able to conceal his shock. Of late, he had read that name in the newspaper countless times. With his head spinning, he followed the rear admiral outside onto the deck.

"Looks like everything's up to snuff, Captain," Ray said to Brillo, who stood waiting with a load of lifejackets. "I'll be shoving off now."

Before boarding his vessel, Ray turned and extended a hand to Cal. "This person must be discreet and extremely careful not to endanger the passengers." Ray's tone was hushed, confidential. "We don't need any more bodies washing up on our shores. Bad for tourism."

Cal grasped his hand and shook it. "A matter of the highest discretion."

Ray leaned in closer. "I wasn't here tonight, you know."

"Never heard of you," Cal winked conspiratorially.

"Let's keep this between us, shall we?" Ray nodded in the direction of Brillo and Kathy. "I'm at considerable risk by just being here. I don't need any more complications."

"Just a routine safety inspection. Right?"

Ray grinned. "Exactly."

With their rather loose union in place, Ray hopped aboard his vessel and unfettered the nylon line. Following a mighty shove, the Coast Guard boat drifted rearward into the darkness.

"It's a nice night for diving, Mr. Stringer. Be careful, though. Never know what's lurking out there. You might get more than you bargained for."

"Roger that, sir. I'll exercise extreme caution."

"Good luck. Give Bluebird a call later tonight. He'll be expecting to hear from you."

"Will do...first chance I get."

With that, Ray shot him a good-luck salute and disappeared inside the pilothouse. Seconds later the twin outboards gunned to life and the boat sped off the way it came. Left in awe by the encounter, Cal stood frozen in place until the Coast Guard vessel melted into the night.

Sunday 19:38 Hours – The "Majestic Star"

As Skip strode the length of his quarters, his brain was on fire.

What was Cal up to? What were his plans once aboard? Was he coming solo or bringing reinforcements? What was Kathy doing with him? Was he out of his ever-lovin' mind!?

Although Cal's close proximity gave Skip an emotional lift, he already had enough on his plate. He didn't need the added worry of how Gold-Tooth might react if his men caught Cal trying to steal board. But, obviously, his opinion as ship captain didn't matter anyhow. Whether he liked it or not, Cal aimed to board his ship—and soon.

Skip interrupted his nervous pacing to peer out the porthole. Somehow he had to rendezvous with Cal, which meant dealing with Mohammad posted outside his door. Skip couldn't kill him because sooner or later he would be missed. Nor could the Arab be bribed. Muslims weren't motivated by money—virgins and wine maybe—but not money. Besides, Skip only had ten bucks in his wallet, his paltry allowance from Kathy.

Skip was getting discouraged when he recalled how Mo kept dozing off in the wheelhouse. The man was exhausted and had to stand guard duty into the night. With this in mind, an idea bubbled to the surface.

I bet he'd like a nice cup of hot coffee. Skip rubbed his beard and smiled cagily. *Sure he would.*

Skip dashed to the coffeemaker and filled it with a triple scoop of coffee grounds, then added water and pressed the power button. While it brewed, he dashed into the head and opened the door of the medicine cabinet.

"There you are," he said sneakily, plucking a prescription bottle from the cabinet. "Just what the doctor ordered. Dramamine—seasick capsules for our poor nauseous passengers."

Having witnessed the medication's effect on many green-faced landlubbers, Skip knew the pills contained a rather powerful sedative.

"Too many of these babies would put a five-hundred pound gorilla to sleep."

Skip hurried to the desk and began opening the gelatin capsules, humming to himself contentedly as he worked.

Sunday 19:40 Hours – The "Sol-Mate"

Dropping the lifejackets, Brillo gasped with relief. "Man, that was a close call! I thought we were busted for sure." He looked at Cal. "Hey, who's this Bluebird guy he was talking about?"

Cal dodged the question. "It's not important. But, by him delaying us, we're way behind schedule. Skip is expecting me soon, so we'd better get a move on. Resume course for the Majestic Star while I get my dive gear."

"Uh-h, I don't know," Brillo balked. "That Coastie was clear about us being in a quarantine area. If we're picked up on radar again, he might come back and throw us all in the brig."

"That ain't gonna happen, Brillo. Trust me. Now get underway—without your running lights. We don't want to announce our presence."

"Well...okay. If you say so." His expression was still doubtful. "But I don't like it."

While Brillo resumed course, Cal retrieved his dive gear and lugged it back outside. After donning the wet suit a second time, he strapped on the scuba tank and tested its breathing apparatus. Satisfied that everything was in working order, he looked around for Kathy, who was inside the cabin stowing freezer bags of items into a heavy-duty trash bag.

"There!" she huffed to herself, stuffing the last Ziploc bag into the plastic sack. "That oughta keep everything nice and dry."

After their harrowing encounter with the inquisitive Coastie, Kathy was glad for something to do to keep occupied. Her stomach was still in a nervous knot. With all the items finally stowed, Kathy squeezed the air out of the plastic bag and twisted the neck several wraps before sealing it with duct tape. After that she dragged the bag outside to where Cal was waiting.

"This may feel a little cumbersome now, but once you're in the water you'll never know it's there." Kneeling down, Kathy looped the neck of the bag around Cal's dive belt and cinched it with a double-knot. "The freezer bags should keep everything watertight until you arrive."

Kathy was putting on a brave front but her eyes spoke her heart. Since childhood her telltale eyes betrayed her whenever she tried to cover up her feelings. Lacking a dishonest bone in her body, she had never gotten comfortable with deceit. So, now, kneeling before Cal, her true feelings were written in her eyes. She was incredibly, incredibly afraid.

"Thanks, Sis. I don't know what I'd do without you—honest."

Kathy's suffering tugged at his heartstrings but her chutzpah made him proud. She was a gutsy gal. Hoping to brighten her overcast mood, Cal reached down and gave her hair a good-natured ruffle—like he did when she was a kid.

Welcoming some horseplay, Kathy sat back on her haunches and gave Cal a lop-sided grin, then blew her bangs into the air with a crooked lighthearted poof. At this, both brother and sister chuckled, giving them a momentary reprieve from the bodeful business at hand.

WIRED

Sunday 19:43 Hours – The "Majestic Star"

Skip was sitting at his desk, pondering the powdered remains of five empty capsules. The last thing he needed was for Mohammad to OD on the stuff. Scratching his head, he tried to recall how former seasick passengers reacted to the drug. One capsule made them groggy, two pills and it was usually naptime. He figured that three or four pills would do the trick without being toxic.

"Oh, what the hell." Settling his indecision with a broad sweep of the hand, Skip scooped the contents of all five capsules into a **"DIVERS GO DOWN MORE OFTEN"** coffee mug. "If he croaks, he croaks. I don't have time to worry about it."

With that, Skip filled the mug with steaming hot coffee and stirred the concoction until the Dramamine dissolved. Then he added creamer and a large measure of sugar to kill any noticeable taste. Once the solution was ready, he raised the cup to his lips and sampled it. Other than being really sweet, it didn't taste unusual.

Now ready to approach the Arab, Skip checked his watch. It would take ten minutes or so for the sedative to work, scarcely giving him enough time to meet Cal below. With coffee cup in hand, Skip opened the cabin door and stepped outside, whistling casually.

The captain's unexpected emergence startled the half-asleep guard, who shot to his feet and trained his weapon between Skip's eyes. Instead of Mohammad it was a bleary-eyed Hispanic with a ponytail and dirty bandanna tied around his neck. There had obviously been a changing of the guard while Skip was inside preparing his Mickey Finn.

"Hold on there, amigo!" With a winsome smile, Skip nudged the muzzle away from his forehead. "Easy, greasy. I just wanted to see what kinda night we got goin' out here. Okay?"

The perplexed Hispanic frowned and snapped the gun barrel back to Skip's forehead. The language barrier wasn't helping any.

"Hey, c'mon." Flashing a friendly grin, Skip eased the barrel aside. "Relax."

The gunman resisted at first by applying opposing pressure, but then let the barrel move after a tense moment of scrutiny.

Feeling the guard's eyes on his back, Skip moseyed to the rail as if taking in the lovely night. The winds had calmed with dusk and the moon was reflecting off the water like a shimmery white lily pad. As Skip stood there, his steel-gray eyes swept the ocean surface for his longtime friend. Cal was somewhere out there right now, drawing nigh.

Pretending to sip the coffee, Skip chuckled and turned around. "Wow, this stuff is hot! Just about burned my lips off." To help the Hispanic understand, he fanned his lips with his free hand. "Won't be able to drink this stuff until it cools down some, that's for sure."

Skip noted the man eyeing his coffee with want—so far, so good.

"Well, I shouldn't be drinking coffee this late anyway." Skip faked a yawn. "I'm pretty bushed and it might keep me up all night. Guess I'll turn in now." As if an afterthought, he offered the mug to the Latino. "Say, do you want this? If not, I'll just dump it overboard."

Watching from the corner of his eye, Skip acted like he was going to pour it over the side.

"NO!" Skip looked around to see the guard walking toward him with his hand out. "*¡Parada!*"

"Oh, you want it? Sure, help yourself." Skip handed him the mug with an inward grin. "Compliments of Juan Valdez. By the way, do you know him? Lives somewhere in Colombia, I think. Runs around all wired up on caffeine with a little donkey."

When the gunman stared dumbly at him, Skip chuckled and strolled toward his quarters. "No? Oh, well. Catch you in the morning, amigo." Skip opened the door. "Buenas noches, hasta la vista, or some damn thing."

Skip entered the cabin and turned to close the door. But before shutting it, he watched the guard take a drink and then another. With a sly grin, he eased the door shut and waited.

Sunday 19:50 Hours – The "Sol-Mate"

When the *Sol-Mate* was approximately one mile from the *Majestic Star*, Brillo cut the engines and let the boat drift—signaling an end to their nocturnal quest. The sudden stillness told Cal it was time to go and he began making last-minute preparations.

Perched atop an ice chest on the opposite beam, Kathy watched Cal wiggle into his rubber fins. The silhouette of the *Majestic Star* was looming directly behind him and the combined image of the two made the fist in her stomach clench tighter. Once suited up, Cal rose and faced the ship. Using the penlight, he took a compass reading of the magnetic bearing to maintain while swimming underwater in the blind.

With Cal's departure at hand, Kathy whispered a quick prayer and slid off the ice chest.

"Be careful, big Brother." Her smile was reassuring but Cal detected a faint quiver in her voice. "If—I mean *when*—you see Skip, tell him that I love him. Okay?"

"Roger on that, ma'am." Cal grinned in the dark and saluted her off his pushed-up dive mask. "Will do."

Cal was being cavalier, Kathy thought, playing down things for her benefit. But his smile seemed forced and for good reason. The unknown was a scary place and up till now he'd been sitting at its edge, dangling his feet in it. Now he was about to dive into it headlong—both emotionally and physically.

With her heart swelling with emotion, Kathy stood on her tiptoes and kissed him goodbye on the cheek. Then she tried hugging him but the compressed air tank with all of its gauges and hoses were too bulky. So, instead, she clenched him around the neck and squeezed affectionately with a rocking motion.

"You both come back to me—you hear?" While hugging him, the world began to blur. "Life wouldn't be the same without either of . . ."

"I know, I know." Gently, Cal pushed her at arm's length. His nerves were ragged enough and he didn't need a long heart-wrenching goodbye. Kathy didn't either. "I'll be fine, Sis—I can take care of myself. You have to be strong while I'm gone. Promise me you won't torture yourself with worry. Getting all stressed out won't change anything."

"I know. Worrying never helps." She sniffed and raised her chin high. "I'll be fine. I can take care of myself too." Feigning toughness, she punched him playfully on the arm. "It runs in the family." When she smiled at him, standing tears spurted from the corners of her eyes and she scrubbed them with the palm of her hand. "Go give 'em hell, big Brother, and bring my man back to me. I'm sick of this hostage bullshit."

"Me too, Sis." Cal admired her spunk, even if it was fake. "I'll see what I can do."

Following a farewell hug, Cal sat down on the gunwale and put the air regulator into his mouth. Then he lowered his mask and winked at Kathy through the glass. When she smiled and flashed him a confident thumbs-up sign, Cal reciprocated with both thumbs. Then he placed a gloved hand over his facemask and fell backward into the shadowy depths.

Sunday 19:55 Hours – The "Majestic Star"

While waiting for the Dramamine to work, Skip sat down at his desk and plucked a brass compass from its cubbyhole. It had been a gift from Kathy years ago. On the back was inscribed: *"So my sailor man can always find his way back home to me---Love always, Kathy."* Smiling down at it, he ran a fingertip over the inscription and then unscrewed the glass lens. After carefully removing the magnetic inner workings, he retrieved a folded piece of paper hidden inside.

It was a diagram of the ship that he had drawn earlier. Each deck was sketched out in detail and marked with "X's" where he had spotted explosives. Most of the C-4 was located below the waterline, planted there for sinking the ship rather than killing hostages. Skip had spotted them while going to and from the engine room. Twice daily he was escorted down there to check the generators and ventilation system.

Composition-4 plastic bonded explosive, or C-4, was made from 91% cyclotrimethylene-trinitramine mixed with a plasticizer to make it supple like modeling clay. The plastique was a stable yet highly explosive material that required an electrical spark or blasting cap for detonation. If lit with a match, C-4 burned slowly like a piece of wood. In Vietnam the SEALs had actually burned it as an improvised cooking fire. Even shooting the plastique with a bullet wouldn't cause a reaction. But when triggered by heat or shock energy from a detonator, the rapidly expanding gases traveled at over 8,000 meters per second packing incredible destructive power. Just half a kilogram would take out a truck.

Skip folded up the sketch and tucked it in his shirt pocket for later. While screwing on the glass lens he recalled the motto used by the Navy SEALs: *"There's no problem that can't be fixed with the proper application of high explosives."*

"That's true," he muttered, slipping the compass back in its cubbyhole. "Unless the bastards are disabled, of course."

Skip eyed his watch and decided it was time to check on Juan Valdez. Either the drug had worked by now or it hadn't. There was only one way to find out. Carefully, Skip cracked open the door to find the guard out cold—still sitting upright in his chair.

"YES!" he reveled, making a victory fist.

Taking no time to celebrate, Skip tiptoed quietly past the snoozing Mexican. Thirty seconds later he was scampering down the stairwell toward the ship's cargo hold.

Sunday 20:10 Hours – Gulf of Mexico

Cal had been swimming blindly underwater for fifteen minutes now, thirty feet below the surface. The sixty-degree seawater felt like ice water against his exposed face and its perpetual coldness strove to penetrate his wet suit. But the insulating qualities of the neoprene, combined with the physical exertion of swimming, maintained a sustainable level of body heat.

As luck would have it, the current was with him and Cal was making good time. To stay on course he paused at regular intervals to check his compass bearing by penlight. Near the midway point he had surfaced for a visual fix and the sight of Skip's ship gave him the creeps.

From his low sea-level vantage point, the *Majestic Star* towered before him like a mystic Mount Everest. The night sky was thickly seeded with stars except for the ship's solid-black silhouette that eclipsed the starry backdrop. A pale wash of moonlight glinted from the ship's inky outline, giving it an opaque spectral glow—as if something insidious were radiating from it, something evil. To Cal, the ship looked like a black hole in space poised to suck-in-and-destroy anything nearing it. The effect was darkly disturbing.

Once back underwater, Cal tried to shake off the eerie feeling. Skip's ship wasn't a mythical ghostly galleon waiting for its next victim, nor was it some unworldly apparition. It was just a shanghaied ship waiting to be rescued. He was experiencing some pre-mission jitters, that's all, normal under the circumstances. He would be fine once he got aboard the ship.

Convinced it was merely the unknown bugging him and nothing more, Cal swam on with more confidence—grateful that his physical abilities hadn't declined appreciably with age; grateful that time hadn't robbed him of his mettle; grateful for being unselfish enough *(foolish enough?)* to risk his life to save a bosom buddy; grateful that he wasn't scared out of his wits for the first time in his rapidly disintegrating life.

Sunday 20:11 Hours – The "Majestic Star"

Skip arrived at the starboard supply hatch unimpeded and without incident. Since the crew and hostages were confined to the upper levels, no nighttime guards were posted below deck.

With sweaty palms, Skip turned the hatch wheel counterclockwise and pushed against it with his shoulder. As the steel door swung open, the salt-rusted hinges created a loud screeching rasp that reverberated throughout the lower section of the ship. Freezing in place, Skip held his breath with an ear cocked toward the stairwell, praying that nobody above heard the telltale noise. With beads of sweat popping out on his brow, the seconds ticked away without consequence. Able to breathe again, he stuck his head out the opening and searched the expanse of coal-black water.

Although dark, the moonlight reflecting off the water provided some faint visibility. Once his eyes adjusted, Skip knelt down and scanned the watery surface from left-to-right and right-to-left. But, after several 180-degree scans, he saw nothing but empty ocean. Bewildered, he sat back on his legs and frowned at his watch. He was a few minutes late.

Did I miss Cal? Did something happen to him? Am I at the right place?

Since there were no other starboard hatches near the waterline, Skip knew this was the right spot. Growing increasingly alarmed, he poked his head out again and again with still no sign of Cal—his hopes thinning with each turtle-like poke.

Nothing. Either the Coasties had nailed Cal or he had already been here and gone. Those were the only two explanations.

Skip checked his watch again and decided to wait five more minutes.

WIRED

He wasn't sure how long the Dramamine would last and it was imperative he got back before the Mexican regained consciousness. With nothing to do but wait, Skip sat in the open hatchway with his legs dangling outside over the water.

The only source of artificial light was from a glowing red **EXIT** sign above the starboard hatch. As Skip sat under its reddish cast, he listened to the waves lap against the hull. While waiting there, he gazed at the water below with envy. Freedom was only three feet away and the temptation to make a swim for it crossed his mind. He could still swim ten miles if he had to, even in ice-cold water. He'd been trained for it. But that was wishful thinking and Skip knew it. He was ship captain and with that came duty and commitment. To cut and run just to save his own hide would be cowardice. While a far cry from perfect, Skip Myles *was not* a coward. Nor was he a freaking quitter. People were counting on him and he would not let them down.

When five minutes came and went, Skip disappointedly closed the hatch—thinking that for whatever reason Cal wasn't coming. Obviously something had gone wrong. Feeling both cheated and relieved, he twisted the wheel lock clockwise. Cal or no Cal, he had to get topside before the guard came to.

Once the hatch was secured, Skip was about to leave when he heard a hollow tapping sound coming through the steel hull at his feet. *Cal!* With adrenaline pouring into his bloodstream, he spun the wheel lock counterclockwise and swung the hatch open.

"Ahoy there, Captain Jason," a familiar voice hailed. "Permission to come aboard?"

Skip peered downward at the voice and saw a diver's facemask glinting with silvery moonlight. Knowing it was Cal behind the mask, he grinned from ear to ear.

"Cal! You crazy sonofabitch. I don't believe it!" Skip lowered his excited voice and shook his head in disbelief. "You can call me Jason for the rest of my life and I'll never say another damn word. Swear to God."

"Good to see that you're still alive and well, Skipper. I was beginning to wonder. You look like hell, though. What happened to your uniform?"

Skip gazed down at his bloodstained dress whites and shrugged. "Long story. I'll tell you about it over a beer someday." Unable to resist,

Skip razzed: "Water cold?"

"You'll soon find out." Cal pushed up his mask and winced when the rigid rubber brushed against his sore forehead. "Kick off your shoes and dive in. Brillo's boat is less than a mile from here. I'll drop my air tank and we can swim for it."

"Sorry, Cal. I ain't desertin' my ship."

Cal glowered at him impatiently. "C'mon, Skip! Let's get the hell outta here! This is not your fight. Let the military handle it."

"Thanks for askin' but no can do. I got two hundred reasons why not."

"That's bullshit and you know it!" Cal struck the water angrily, causing a large splash. "Kathy needs you too! Now let's get going before those Mexican pricks find us out."

"You have no idea how much I'd like to, Cal, but I'm stayin' put. You would too if the situation was reversed. Give Kathy Ann my love and tell her I'm okay."

"Look, goddammit, I'm trying to rescue you!" Cal's voice was a low growl. "Now come on!"

"Can't, old buddy. I don't need rescuing. But thanks for droppin' by."

Cal had been afraid of this all along. Seeing there was no changing Skip's mule mind, he cursed some more while cutting the plastic bag loose from his dive belt. Then, with a seething scowl, he thrust the bag upward.

"Here, stubborn-ass. Take it."

"What's in it?"

"A present."

Skip grabbed the dripping bag and set it aside while Cal unbuckled his air tank and removed his flippers.

"Now take these and give me a hand."

"What for?"

"I can't tread water all night. I'm coming aboard."

"Look, there's nothin' you can do here, Cal, so go back. I've got enough to worry about."

Cal struck the water again, creating a huge splash. "NO!" His voice was loud enough to echo and Skip cringed. "If you're not leaving with me, then I'm coming aboard and that's final!"

WIRED

"Okay, okay! Just keep your voice down." Skip looked worriedly up the dim stairway. "If those dickbags catch us here, we're dead meat."

Skip placed Cal's air tank and fins next to the plastic bag and reluctantly extended his arm. After locking wrists, Skip hoisted his brother-in-law and best friend out of the icy ocean.

Sunday 20:15 Hours – Tampa Bay, Florida

After leaving the *Sol-Mate*, Ray throttled back the twin outboards and switched the boat radio to Channel 12—purposely dragging out his return trip to St. Pete. It would take Stringer a while to sneak aboard the ship—if he were successful—and Ray was anxiously awaiting his hail.

It was a lustrous star-filled night and, even with the suspenseful wait, Ray found himself enjoying the peaceful ride back. To his port were the glittering city lights of St. Pete Beach. Off the starboard bow, the lighthouse at Egmont Key dutifully winked at him as it had done since 1848. Dead ahead stood the vibrantly lit architecture of the Skyway Bridge—the world's longest bridge with a cable-stayed main span. Spanning 5.5 miles over lower Tampa Bay, its mighty towers and mustard yellow stays stood in striking contrast to the dark nighttime sky. It was an imposing sight.

As the twin Merc's putted at idle speed, Ray could hear the deep-V hull sloshing through the water. After four days of utter turmoil, his frayed nerves gobbled up the peace and quiet. While he wouldn't dare, the temptation to just keep going skittered across his tired beat-up mind. When he got back to the stationhouse—Chaos, Incorporated—he would be pulled in every direction.

As the boat rounded Pinellas Point, the mysterious Cal Stringer dominated Ray's thoughts. He still didn't know Stringer's connection to the *Majestic Star* or his motive for involvement, but Ray was admittedly impressed with the man.

Whatever his cause, Stringer appeared competent, cunning, and in good physical condition. And despite the Uzi stashed under the bathroom sink, he didn't strike Ray as the cowboy-whacko type who would go in blazing away. Stringer was a thinker and way too regimented to go off the deep end. He had military training and the discipline showed.

WIRED

By all accounts Ray had intercepted the *Sol-Mate* to put a stop to Stringer's one-man crusade. At least that's what he told himself during the boat ride out. Granted, he had entertained the idea of having a spy aboard the *Majestic Star* but he had never taken the idea seriously. Or had he?

So what had changed his mind? Was it was Stringer's SEAL training? Or the cool way he had handled himself under pressure? Or was it because the Ray-Man's back was against the wall and he was flat out of options?

Did I want to be convinced of Stringer's usefulness? That he could theoretically help? Was desperation clouding my judgment? If not, why had I removed my name tape and rank insignias before boarding? Why was I allowing a civilian to get mixed up in the matter? Weren't things already bad enough? Am I that hard up?

In truth, Ray wasn't sure about anything anymore. But for some irrational reason he trusted Stringer, which was weird given the seriousness of events and the fact that Ray had just met him. Maybe he *was* grasping at straws, but his gut said that Stringer would be more of an asset than a liability—if Mendoza didn't capture him first and blow him into never-never land.

To Ray's credit, he had commanded thousands of men during his military career and he knew a good soldier when he saw one. At this particular point, that was the *only* thing he was sure of.

Sunday 20:20 Hours – The "Sol-Mate"

In keeping with Cal's instructions, Brillo was holding the *Sol-Mate* steady one mile from the *Majestic Star*.

Cal estimated it would take him twenty minutes of underwater swimming—thirty minutes tops—to reach Skip's ship, equating to a one-hour turnaround time should he be unsuccessful in boarding. However, once on board, Cal wasn't sure if the handheld VHF would pack enough transmitting power to penetrate the ship's steel hull. So, with that in mind, Cal's instructions had been clear. Instead of waiting around for some iffy radio message that he had successfully gotten aboard, Brillo was to return to the marina if Cal wasn't back within one hour.

WIRED

In order to keep the *Sol-Mate's* position fast, Brillo had to periodically reposition the boat to counteract the ocean current, which sought to sweep them toward Skip's anchored ship. As he maneuvered the boat from the lofty flybridge, his eyes alternated between the GPS screen and the radar—using the GPS to pinpoint their latitude and longitude while monitoring the radar screen for the authorities. Thus far, Cal had been right about the Coast Guard's noninterference. Except for the green blip of the *Majestic Star*, the radarscope remained blip-free.

Brillo turned on the dash lights and held his wristwatch within their glow. When noting thirty minutes had lapsed, he turned off the instrument panel and frowned at the shadowy ship, wondering if Cal had made it aboard yet.

To be on the safe side, Brillo decided to wait another forty-five minutes. That would give Cal plenty of extra time. If he hadn't come back by then, Brillo would set sail for the marina.

~~~~~~~~~~

Kathy was slouched next to Brillo in a vague state of awareness. With both of her men now gone, she never felt so alone in her life. Adding to her stinging loneliness was a simmering anger. Above and beyond feeling deserted, she felt wronged—victimized.

To Kathy, this whole hostage business was unconscionable and she, Skip, and Cal, were undeserving of its entanglement. Her family had nothing to do with the war on drugs, nor were they declared enemies of Islam. The very notion of them being drawn into a three-way Armageddon was egregious. Their lives had been extemporaneously uprooted and glaringly violated. As far as Kathy was concerned, the U.S. Government, the drug Mafia, and Al-Qaeda could go settle their jihad somewhere else.

With a set look in her eye, Kathy stared at the moon-glazed silhouette of what had now become her antagonist—the *Majestic Star*. Despite the fact that Skip adored being her captain, and despite the fact that the ship itself was not guilty of any wrongdoing, she felt a deep sense of contempt for it. Her once appreciation of its beauty had vanished and she now viewed the vessel as nothing more than a floating war zone—a wretched place where the fate of her husband and brother would soon be decided.

A sudden shiver coursed through her body and Kathy tightened the zipper of her jacket. But when the cold chill persisted, she came to realize it was emanating from within. Contrary to its benefactor's namesake—*Sun 'n Fun Cruise Lines*—the *Majestic Star* no longer symbolized fun.

It was a death ship and its befouled sight was making her blood run cold—ice-cold.

Sunday 20:22 Hours – The "Majestic Star"

Following a flurry of bear hugs and whacks on the back, the old Navy chums cut their reunion short and got down to business.

While Skip stood guard at the foot of the stairway, Cal quickly shed his wet suit to reveal khaki pants and a T-shirt. After stashing the dive gear behind some wooden crates, he opened the trash bag and removed a terry cloth towel. Moving briskly, he blotted the water from his face, hands, and feet—then tossed the towel to Skip. Upon catching it, Skip hesitated briefly when recognizing it as one of Kathy's guest towels, then began mopping up the trail of seawater from Cal's soggy entry.

While Skip swabbed away the evidence, Cal removed a pair of deck shoes from two Ziploc bags and slipped them on without socks. Within sixty seconds—presto—he was all set. The typical tourist personified. After that he rummaged through the trash bag until finding the freezer bag containing the handheld radio. With Skip watching the stairwell, Cal ducked behind a storage crate in the cargo bay to muffle his voice.

Sunday 20:24 Hours – Tampa Bay, Florida

As the lighted docks of the St. Petersburg station came into view, Ray had still not heard from Stringer. For the dozenth time he double-checked the VHF radio's volume and squelch knobs to find everything in working order—all tuned and waiting.

If he didn't hear from Stringer soon, it would mean one of four things: Stringer had aborted the attempt; he had botched the effort and gotten captured; he had slipped aboard but decided not to cooperate; he had gotten aboard but the handheld radio didn't work.

WIRED

Gliding into the vessel's assigned slip, Ray reversed the engines for a split-second then put them in neutral. When the boat coasted to a gentle stop, bumping the dock lightly, he hopped onto the landing and began securing the lines. He was wrapping the bowline around a cleat when a now-familiar, faint-and-scratchy voice spewed from the marine radio.

~~~~~~~~~~

"Bluebird, this is Stringer. Bluebird, this is Stringer. Over."

With excitation Ray scrambled back into the pilothouse and made a beeline for the radio. Stringer's signal was weak so upon reaching the radio he adjusted the volume knob while keying the microphone.

"This is Bluebird," Ray answered, trying not to sound out of breath. "Go ahead, Stringer."

"Ever wished upon a star, Bluebird?"

"Uh-h-h...roger." The unexpected remark puzzled Ray.

"I'm doing that now—upon the *Star*—wishing for a little luck, that is. Got a feeling I'm gonna need some. Roger?"

The mental fog lifted, bringing clarity to Stringer's message. "That's a big roger—me and you both. While you're at it, make a wish for me. I could use some good luck about now. Copy?"

"I heard that," Cal chuckled into the mike. "Over."

"Well, Godspeed. I trust you'll be vigilant with regard to the innocents. I don't need to be calling any more relatives. Do you copy?"

"Affirmative."

"Good. Glad we're on the same page. Like Billy Shakespeare once said: *The better part of valor is discretion.* There's truth in that, Mr. Stringer. *Only fools rush in.*"

Unable to resist, Cal countered with a cliché of his own. "I'll be sure to *look before I leap.*"

Getting the point, Ray said: "Well, enough platitudes. Proceed with caution and stay in touch—real often. We'll be listening up on this frequency. Copy?"

"Will do."

"And, by the way, soldier—Bravo Zulu. Well done."

"Roger, Bluebird. I'll make comms with you later. Stringer out."

WIRED

When Stringer released his microphone key, there was a scratchy hiss and then open static. With a blank expression, Ray lowered the volume while leaning against the pedestal seat behind him. Despite his confidence in the ex-SEAL, part of him was still surprised that Stringer had actually managed to get on board.

Well, I'll be damned. Stringer did it. He's aboard the Majestic Star.

In mild wonder, Ray pressed on his velcro name tape and cloth insignias and trudged toward the burning lights of the stationhouse, hoping against hope that he had made the right decision.

Sunday 20:26 Hours – The "Majestic Star"

While Cal was behind the crates making his secretive radio transmission, Skip stood watch at the bottom of the stairs, wondering whom Cal was talking to and why. A little more than an hour ago, Skip hadn't given Cal a single thought. Now, here he was—running around the ship like a man on a mission. Everything had all come about so fast it was hard to process.

After making good on his promise to radio Bluebird, Cal emerged from the crates to find Skip standing open-mouthed like a statue about to say something. Noting the rapt expression on his face, Cal took the wet towel from his hand and stuffed it inside the plastic bag, which seemed to release Skip from his state of wonder.

"What the hell's goin' on, Cal? You're crazy comin' here!" Though barely above a whisper, his voice teemed with urgency. "Who were you talkin' to on the radio?"

"Well, believe it or not, it was the Commander of the Coast Guard's Seventh District—Rear Admiral Ray Hanna himself."

"Get outta here," Skip said incredulously, cocking his head. "You're shittin' me—right?"

"Nope. From out of nowhere he boarded us tonight on the way here. At first I thought he was just a regular Coastie checking us out because we were in a restricted area. I didn't realize who he was until he told me his name, which is plastered across every newspaper in the country."

Skip looked confused. "And he's a part of this thing—you comin' aboard, I mean?"

"Well, sort of, in a roundabout way. My guess is that he received a tip about me and decided to investigate things for himself. He pulled alongside us under the guise of a routine safety check. But in truth he was checking *me* out, not the boat. I suppose he wanted to see what I was made of—if I could perhaps better his position without screwing things up for him."

Skip emitted a low whistle. "Wow, I bet you almost shit your britches, huh?"

Despite its untimeliness, Cal couldn't hold back a chuckle. In Detroit one didn't hear too many southern drawls and it had been a while since he had heard Skip's Georgian glide.

"Yeah, I was sweating like a gerbil in a gay bar. Reckon I passed the test, though, 'cause here I am. He's looking the other way and I'm his unofficial forward observer." When Skip looked unclear, Cal elaborated. "In exchange for letting me go, I agreed to provide radio reconnaissance. I guess he feels that having a scout aboard is worth the risk, particularly an off-the-record one. If I get caught, he'll deny everything. I'm just a lunatic and he's never heard of me. End of story."

"Man, that's incredible. So we got a rebel Rear Admiral on our side, huh? That's pretty cool. Officially or unofficially, it's good to have that kind of high-powered help."

"It don't hurt none," Cal nodded. "Now, fill me in. We haven't got much time. What's going on? How many and where are they?"

"First, how's Kathy holdin' up? I've really been worried about her, Cal. Is she okay?"

"She's fine. Worried to death, but fine. She's with Brillo right now on the Sol-Mate." Cal dug into his pocket and handed Skip a folded paper. "Here. I almost forgot. It's a note from her."

Skip's heart leapt at the touch of the paper as if the words written upon it were sacred. Though anxious to read it, he slipped it inside his shirt pocket for later. He didn't want to be rushed. He would read it in the privacy of his cabin with grand anticipation, soaking up every word.

"So Brillo's got a hand in this thing too, huh? I shoulda known." Skip pictured his fishing buddy's face and smiled. "He's a good friend." After a moment of reflection, his face turned serious. "Okay, let me tell you what we're up against."

WIRED

~~~~~~~~~~

When Ray entered the stationhouse the group commander was waiting for him with a priority message from the Cuban. It seemed that during Ray's unaccounted-for absence, Mendoza had issued another deadline—at twelve noon tomorrow more hostages would die.

Now facing two Monday deadlines, Ray hastened to the radio room where he added Channel 12 to the list of frequencies being monitored. He also left a standing order to summon him twenty-four-seven should a hail be received from anyone identifying himself as Stringer. With that accomplished, Ray set out for his office to call the ensign in Sand Key. He wanted every stinking detail regarding Mendoza's latest threat.

As Ray marched down the hallway, telephones were ringing and scores of personnel were scurrying about the stationhouse helter-skelter. That's the way it had been ever since the news networks televised Ray's name and that of the Group St. Petersburg station to every Tom, Dick, and Harry in TV Land.

The press conference had been held in the cramped assembly hall of the St. Petersburg complex. It was Ray's first face-to-face with the press and he had limited the session to ten minutes, which still seemed like a lifetime when being grilled on national television. At first Ray found the solid body of lights, cameras, and newsmen a bit intimidating; but after his stage fright settled, he fielded their questions rather routinely— escaping relatively unscathed save for one minor bout with Geraldo.

True to form, Geraldo upstaged his peers by over sensationalizing the *"poor dead citizens washing up on our beaches"* angle for all it was worth. Backing Ray into a corner, the mustachioed reporter challenged him to look into the TV camera and tell the grieving relatives at home precisely what he and the authorities were intending to do about it. Luckily, while Ray floundered for a response, Geraldo's news brethren inadvertently came to his rescue. Fed up with Rivera hogging more than his share of the limelight, the journalists squeezed him out by yelling over him with other questions. Eager to get off Geraldo's hook, Ray seized the opportunity and moved on to the next question. This circumvention peeved Geraldo royally, who sulked in silence the whole time afterward—openly miffed for being sidelined when he had the admiral squirming in his clutches.

When Ray pictured Geraldo's pouty face, it elicited a cruel smile. Deservedly or not, even prima donna super-snoopers suffered embarrassing setbacks now and then. That was showbiz.

As Ray entered the office, his cruel smiled faded. There was a mound of messages on his desk the size of Pikes Peak. Letting out a groan, he dropped into his chair and began gathering them up. Amongst them were two messages from his Vice-Admiral superior and four messages from Rivera with the **"URGENT"** box checked. With gloating satisfaction Ray scooped those into a wastebasket along with all the other messages from reporters and kooks.

In all likelihood the vice-weasel was calling him to critique his oratory skills, or to lend advice on how to better handle Geraldo in the future. As far as Ray was concerned the sorry excuse for a soldier could keep his silver-tongued advice to himself. Geraldo, on the other hand, was undoubtedly fishing for an interview. Being a celebrity in his own right, he was not accustomed to being relegated to the press corps like some commoner. Having suffered that indignity today, he was most likely pursuing an exclusive to scoop his fellow journalists.

Before tackling the remaining messages, Ray phoned the ensign in Sand Key. After conferring with him regarding Mendoza's latest deadline, he made a quick roundtrip to the vending machines, returning with an energy drink and two candy bars. He had several more hours of work to do and the double-whammy boost of sugar and caffeine would help carry him through.

After finally reaching the worried mother in Kentucky, Ray began working down the stack of messages. But during the process his concentration began to slip, afflicted by a gnawing sense of unease. His thoughts were being commandeered, sucked out to sea, to where the surreptitious Cal Stringer and Santiago Mendoza ever lurked.

Whenever Ray happened to catch his mind drifting, he would reel it back in just for it to drift again. He was thrilled about having a spy aboard the ship, but his lingering reservations spoiled any real feeling of accomplishment. Stringer was a risk, a monumental risk. On top of that were the dual deadlines facing him tomorrow, leaving him scarcely fifteen hours to pull off a miracle. Otherwise more civilians would die and he would be relieved of his command.

Feeling like his head was in an ever-tightening vise, Ray decided to get some fresh air. Things were closing in on him. He would take ten minutes, go for a walk, and give his torn mind permission to worry. Then he would put his sea of troubles aside and get back to work.

~~~~~~~~~~

As if preparing to tell a long story, Skip sat down on the bottom step of the stairway to face Cal. Following his lead, Cal squatted down eyelevel with him and placed the trash bag on the floor between them, giving him an unobstructed view of the rising stairs behind Skip.

"There's eight gunmen in all armed with AK-47's. Six are Hispanics and two are mean-ass Muslims. One was a busboy here on the ship—their inside man. All of 'em would just as soon cut your nuts off as look at you. They take shifts guardin' us round the clock, so they're spread pretty thin. The off-duty ones sleep in a cabin next to mine just aft of the wheelhouse. From all appearances, I don't think they were prepared for an extended stay or they would have brought more men. The ship is wired with bricks of C-4 and the Mexican leader has the triggering device. Don't know his name, but I call him Gold-Tooth. You can't miss the dude—about six-foot, wiry, wears a headband, and sports a gold front tooth with a diamond in it. If they gave honorary degrees for being a slimeball, he'd be a doctor of everything. Watch out for him, Cal. He's a looneytune and he likes to kill."

"Yeah, according to Hanna, his name is Mendoza. He's a chieftain for a Mexican gang known as *Los Zetas*."

"Mendoza, huh? Anyway, he hates my guts and I'm only alive for a reason. Our food supply is low and our drinkin' water will be gone tomorrow. One thing's for sure: Mendoza's patience is all used up. Somethin' bad could happen tomorrow if the Coasties don't hand over Alvarez. All in all, it ain't a rosy picture."

"To say the least," Cal agreed. "Okay, we need a plan of action. Recommendations?"

"Well, there's only two of us against eight of them so we can't tackle 'em head on. Whatever we do, we've gotta keep the passengers in mind and not push Mendoza into a mass retaliation against them. That's my main fear."

"Yeah, and then there's the C-4 to consider. If we screw up, Mendoza might panic and blow the ship. Right?"

"Well, if you can believe the lunatic, he intends to blow the ship anyway, whether Alvarez is released or not. He's certainly capable of it. I can't see him surrenderin' to the authorities."

Cal nodded. "Yeah, I figured as much. It's a rescue and/or suicide mission. If they can rescue Alvarez, they will. If they can't, they'll go out with as much murder and mayhem as they can muster. Either way, they'll get their message across."

Skip scowled. "Yeah, they really get off on media attention. Every time a newscopter flies within camera range, they start screamin' like banshees and firin' their AK's into the air. They're crazy bastards. I wouldn't put it past 'em to blow the ship just for the hell of it—especially if they could do it on camera. That would get them the headlines they're lookin' for, wouldn't it?"

"It sure would, Cap. Quote—*Don't Fuck With Alvarez and the Zetas*—unquote. The Zetas sealed their own fate when they spilled American blood. Once you cross over like that, there's no going back. They've got nothing to lose."

"And that's the most dangerous breed," Skip concurred. "They're playin' for keeps."

The conversation had now reached the point that Cal had been leading up to. If his plan was to succeed, he needed Skip's full backing.

"My sentiments exactly, Skip. You're one hundred percent right. These guys *are* playing for keeps. So, rather than play by their rules, why don't we change the game?"

Skip wrinkled his brow. "Whatcha got in mind?"

"I've got an idea to bounce off you. But before I do, let's reexamine a few things."

"Oh, no," Skip moaned in fun, "not the lawyer cross-examine thing."

Ignoring the crack, Cal rose to his feet and strode in a circle. For some inexplicable reason he focused more clearly when on the move. It helped him collect his thoughts.

WIRED

"From what I've been able to gather, Alvarez is the mastermind behind this whole thing. With that being the case, he was bound to have known from the start—long before he ordered the Zetas to hijack anything—that the authorities wouldn't simply hand him over to the Zetas, no matter how many hostages he took. Right?"

"Right," Skip said, tracking Cal's movements. "But who are these Zetas anyway?"

"Mexican narco-thugs that provide muscle for the major drug traffickers. They're paramilitary trained with lots of heavy firepower. They number in the hundreds and control most of the drugs coming across the U.S.-Mexico border. I looked them up on the Internet."

"Drug mafia, huh?" Skip rubbed his beard. "Hmm."

"Once the Zetas began killing Americans, Alvarez knew our government wouldn't release him—they couldn't at that point—even if they wanted to. Right?"

"Sounds logical."

"So, with that being the case, Alvarez ratcheted up the pressure. You wouldn't know this, Skip, but in the past few days snipers have assassinated a federal judge in Texas and wounded a Supreme Court Justice in Washington. Car bombs have exploded at the DEA Headquarters in Virginia, in Orlando, and Tallahassee. It all reeks of Al-Qaeda and everyone believes Alvarez is behind it. He's flexing his muscles, playing hardball."

"Al-Qaeda? Whoa." Skip wondered if Mo and Stan were Al-Qaeda. "That's bad news."

"Violence is Alvarez's trademark. As long as he's behind bars, he'll use everything in his arsenal to punish and humiliate Washington. Now that he's got this ship and a national TV audience, he can terrorize America every night on the evening news by killing one passenger at a time." Cal stopped pacing. "The bottom line is this: if the authorities don't release Alvarez, his men will end up killing everybody on this ship. And if they do release him, the Zetas will probably blow the ship anyway for the grand finale—as retribution. Do you agree?"

"Sure. It ties in with Mendoza's threats." Skip looked at his watch. "So what's the plan, Cal? I gotta get back to my cabin before I'm missed."

WIRED

Cal nodded. "What if we foiled Señor Alvarez's blow-up-the-ship plan by giving him everything he wants? What if the authorities hand him over to the Zetas along with the Majestic Star to boot, plus enough food and fuel to transport them anywhere they pleased. They wouldn't blow up the ship then. Right?"

"Of course not," Skip answered. "Not if the ship's their getaway vehicle. But I doubt if this slow-ass ship would be Alvarez's preferred method of escape. A jet would be a lot faster. Besides, as long as there are passengers aboard, there's still the risk of him blowin' the ship once they reach their destination."

"No, we couldn't allow them to leave with passengers—or on a jet plane. It has to be an even trade: all hostages in exchange for Alvarez and the ship. It's the only way to guarantee passenger safety. Do you think your Gold-Tooth character would go for that?"

"I doubt it. With no hostages aboard, what would keep the Coasties from sinkin' the ship afterward at sea? They've seen enough firepower in the area to sink a dozen Majestic Stars."

"Good point, Skip. We'd have to leave a few hostages behind as insurance against a double-cross after the trade."

"Okay. So who do you have in mind?"

Cal took a knee and grasped Skip firmly by the shoulders. "You and your crew. They can't navigate this ship without you guys anyway. They're goons, not experienced seamen."

"Oh, thanks buddy. With friends like you ..."

"I don't see any other way out of this mess, do you? Otherwise, this ship is going down with everybody on it, including you and me." Cal released Skip's shoulders and straightened. "I know it carries a certain amount of risk, but do you have a better idea?"

When Skip shook his head no, Cal began laying out his three-prong strategy. "Okay. Time is short, so follow me closely on this. First, I'll have to persuade Hanna that the idea makes sense. Second, Hanna will have to twist some military and political arms to get Alvarez released. Third, Mendoza will have to buy into the whole thing without suspecting a trap or double-cross. All three elements must fall into place or it's a no-go."

While Skip's mind strove to keep pace, Cal continued. "Needless to

271

say, freeing Alvarez won't be a popular decision with anyone, much less throwing in a free cruise ship. It will definitely be a hard sell. But if Hanna can persuade Washington to allow it, then I can pick off the Zetas one at a time once the hostages are gone and we're at sea."

"I don't know, Cal. You're a pretty tough dude but let's face it, the odds aren't real good. What if you get caught? They might take it out on my passengers and crew. They get off on killin' defenseless people anyway."

"Eight-against-one sounds like a long shot, but they'll be easy prey once Alvarez is aboard and they're out of American waters-. Think about it, Skip. They will have just rescued their fearless leader. They'll be celebrating their victory over the evil American empire. Their guard will be down. They'll probably even hooch it up some if there's any liquor left aboard ship. Since there wouldn't be any more passengers for them to guard, they'd be grabbing a little R&R to catch up on their rest. You said so yourself; they're all exhausted. They'd be sitting ducks for me and you know it. Besides, I'd have the element of surprise on my side. They don't know I'm here."

Skip didn't quite share his confidence. "Well, your methodology sounds good. And I suppose with some luck it might work. But, like you said, eight-against-one still ain't..."

"Eight against two," Cal interjected, yanking the nine-millimeter from the waistband under his shirt. "Here's a little present for you." Cal spun it around and handed it to Skip grip first.

"Hot damn!" Skip seized the gun with a greedy grin. "A Glock. Now this is more like it!"

Being proficient with handguns, Skip automatically released the clip, checked it for ammo, and then slammed it home with the palm of his hand. The solid weight of the gun felt pleasantly familiar, just like the old days. With a speedy click-click, he jacked a shell into the chamber.

"Now I can go to the party too, by God." Sneering, Skip twisted the Glock before his eyes. "And I can hardly wait." Then, as an afterthought, he asked Cal: "Hey, where's your weapon?"

Anticipating a big reaction, Cal reached into the bag with more drama than necessary. With Skip watching curiously, Cal extracted three freezer bags containing the broken down Uzi and arranged the parts on the floor.

Then he quickly assembled them and popped in a loaded clip.

"How about this bad boy?" Cal grinned, presenting the finished product.

Skip's eyes bulged. "Jesus Chrysler, son! How'd you manage to get an Uzi? Sa-weet!!"

"Compliments of a kinky-headed friend of ours. Now, about my plan. Are you game?"

"Hell, yeah—especially now that we have these babies."

"It's the only option we have."

"I think you're right, Cal, but do you really think Washington will go along with releasing Alvarez? It seems kinda remote to me. They'd get slaughtered by the press and public opinion."

"Slaughtered is too mild a term, Skip. They'd be crucified. But they can justify it to some extent by hyping the rescue of the passengers. You know, minimizing collateral damage—saving women and children from certain death and all that. After meeting Hanna tonight, I don't think they have much of a choice. According to him there's no viable military option."

"Sounds like a plan to me." Skip closed one eye and aimed the nine-millimeter at an imaginary enemy. "POW! You're dead, you gold-toothed bastard. Sorry it wasn't more painful."

"I suppose Mendoza's the culprit responsible for that scab across your throat. Looks like he was trying to tell you something, Captain."

"Yeah, well, paybacks are hell. He'll regret not finishing the job while he had the chance." Skip blew make-believe smoke from the barrel and smiled. "Like the NRA says: *The only thing that will stop a bad guy with a gun, is a good guy with a gun.*"

While Cal chuckled, Skip suddenly remembered the map in his pocket. "Hey, before I split, here's a diagram of the ship." He handed it to Cal. "It'll help you find your way around. I've marked all the areas where I've seen explosives, but so far I haven't spotted the radio receiver. Most likely it's hidden someplace down here."

"I'll look for it," Cal said, studying the diagram. "But you're the demolitions expert, not me." Cal refolded the map and stuck it in his pocket. "Okay, unless there's something else to discuss, you'd better get back to your cabin. I'll radio Hanna and make my pitch. He won't be

273

easily convinced but I know he'll listen. He's a risk-taker and he's in a bind. Tomorrow morning I'll mingle in with the passengers during mealtime and let you know his response. Be on the lookout for me. What time is chow?"

"11:00 hours, on the sundeck...but that's pretty risky, Cal. What if they notice you? Could blow the whole thing, you know."

"I've considered that, but I've got two hundred people to blend in with and chances are the Zetas haven't memorized every single face. Besides, you can't keep drugging your guard every night in order to meet with me. And I've got to eat too sometimes. What did you think—that I brought groceries with me?"

Though still skeptical, Skip relented. "Okay. Just be careful. It scares me to think what Mendoza might do if you're caught. The passengers are my responsibility, you know."

"Understood."

"Okay, I'll see you tomorrow at chow. Good luck with Hanna." Skip started up the stairs when he stopped and turned. "By the way, have you been to the *Mouse House* in Orlando?"

Cal traced Skip's eyes to his Mickey Mouse shirt and shrugged. "Is it too much?"

"Naw, at least it doesn't have any bloodstains." He gestured at his uniform. "It'll blend in perfect with the other Disney shirts the passengers are wearin'." Skip's smile faded and his expression turned somber. "Thanks for coming for me, Cal. I don't know what else to say."

Playing down the poignant moment, Cal replied: "How about: Let's kick some terrorist ass."

"I'm serious, Cal."

"Forget it. I wouldn't be here at all if you hadn't fished me out of that rice paddy back in 'Nam. Get some rest, pal. Tomorrow's gonna be a big day."

"It'll be interestin' to say the least. Where you gonna hole up?"

Cal pointed to the wooden crates. "Probably behind one of those crates over there. It's a good hiding spot and I can watch the stairs from there. Doubt if I'll sleep much, though. I'm pretty wired. Don't worry about me, Skipper. I'll make do."

"Yeah, well, we've both spent nights in a lot worse places."

"That we have, Captain. At least there are no mosquitoes or fire ants."

"That's true, but watch out for those yellow-bellied Mexican maggots—they're deadly."

With a grin and final wave, Skip stuffed the Glock under his belt and headed up the steps. "Goodnight, amigo."

Sunday 20:31 Hours – Group St. Petersburg

Ray stepped out into the open courtyard and filled his lungs with fresh air. It felt liberating to leave all the commotion behind—albeit temporarily.

At the epicenter of the lighted courtyard was a concrete helipad large enough to stage multiple helos. Radiating outward from it were spokes of intersecting walkways leading to various destinations—the assembly hall, barracks and classrooms, the mess hall, boat anchorage, the armory and one-room brig where Alvarez was being jailed.

Earlier today, Alvarez's hotshot lawyers got an injunction barring the Coast Guard from forcing Alvarez to talk on the radio, citing it violated his right to remain silent. The legal maneuver frosted Ray, who held that Alvarez had no rights at all—zero. He was a criminal, for petesake, and a freaking foreigner to boot. What about the rights of his dead victims?

But, like it or not, America's judicial system protected the rights of everyone in the U.S.—even undeserving bottom-feeders like Alvarez. As a member of the armed forces, Ray was sworn to defend such rights. As an American citizen, it stuck in his craw big time.

Where were the do-gooders yesterday when my coastguardsmen pulled those bullet-riddled floaters from the gulf? Or when innocent U.S. citizens were blown to bits by car bombs? Where were they when school kids across America OD'd on Alvarez's drugs? Probably at some tree hugging, bleeding-heart pep rally—the bunch of bed-wetting crybabies!

Ray had seen it time and again. If the do-gooders showed up at all, they generally showed up too late. And when they did, they often voiced more concern over criminal rights than those of the victim. Lawyers and liberals—he hated them both.

Changing direction, Ray headed for the boat anchorage, away from the hubbub and glaring floodlights. He was getting fired up. He had come outside to clear his head, not to solve America's sociopolitical woes.

When Ray reached the seawall, he sat down on its concrete ledge and let his legs dangle over the tidewater. The latening of day was his most favorite time—when the last light had waned and a sense of calm breathed from the surroundings. A gentle breeze was stirring through the palmetto fans and crickets were chirring harmoniously in the St. Augustine grass. Silvery moonlight was glinting off Bayboro Harbor and stars were twinkling overhead in a serene and untroubled sky. Out here, he could halfway think.

In pondering the delicate situation he was in, Ray scooped up a handful of pebbles. As he dropped them in the water one by one, he wondered what Stringer was doing...what Mendoza was plotting...how the hostages were being treated...how this deadly dilemma would end. He had just dropped his last rock into the drink when he heard someone approaching from behind. Looking over his shoulder, he saw a silhouette advancing toward him. It was one of the watchstanders and his gait was purposeful. Anticipating some sort of news, Ray rose and dusted off the seat of his pants.

When the out-of-breath radio operator reached him, he explained that "Stringer" was hailing "Bluebird" on Channel 12. The man was babbling about looking everywhere for Ray, when Ray bolted past him for the radio room.

~~~~~~~~~~

As Ray entered the stationhouse, he could hear Stringer's voice filtering down the hallway.

"Bluebird, Stringer here. Over." There was a pause. "Bluebird, this is Stringer hailing."

Upon entering the radio room, Ray cleared it of all personnel and snatched up the desk mike.

"Roger, Stringer. Bluebird here. Go ahead."

"Bluebird, do you play chess?"

"Uh, roger," Ray stammered.

"Good. Like you said, you never know who's listening."

"That's affirmative."

"To end the stalemate you must swap evil Black King for all 200 White Pawns. You must also surrender White Ocean Queen and her Worker Pawns to the Black King. After the exchange, you must allow Black King to move White Queen anywhere on the board that he desires. When Black Opponents think they've won the match, undetected White Knight takes out Black King and all his Merry Men. Checkmate. Do you follow?"

There was a pause while Ray absorbed and unraveled Stringer's cryptic message.

"Understood, White Knight, but the judges will never permit the Black King to enter play. It's strictly against game rules. Nevertheless, I'm curious. Why sacrifice the White Ocean Queen and her Worker Pawns? Why not make an even swap and rule the match a draw—Black King for 200 White Pawns?"

"Because the Merry Men have no intention of playing by the rules. They aim to sacrifice all 200 Pawns regardless of who wins the match."

After a short silence, Ray responded. "I see. And surrendering the White Ocean Queen will change this?"

"Affirmative. Black Opponents cannot sacrifice White Ocean Queen as long as it's being used to move about the board. For our game plan to work, all opponents must remain on White Queen after Black King enters the match. White Worker Pawns must also remain in play to move White Queen about the board and to also reassure Black Opponents of no checkmate attempt later in the game. Do you follow?"

"I follow—as insurance."

"Roger."

"But you're suggesting a major rulebook change and permission to swap the Black King won't come easily, if at all. A lot of judges on the panel will strongly object. Copy?"

"I understand, Bluebird, but the swap must take place tomorrow. It's imperative. Roger?"

"I read you, but I can't promise anything. The judges are scattered all over and they will want to confer before yielding a formal decision. I'll do my best. Over."

"If the judges don't comply, some of the 200 White Pawns may not be in play this time tomorrow. That came straight from the team captain. I met with him tonight. Over."

Ray was impressed. "Is that so? That's pretty fast work. It's good to know you have some communication going. Did the captain have anything else to say that I should be aware of?"

"Negative. He just wants to get the pawns off so we can end the game. Over."

"That makes three of us. The captain may not be aware of it yet, but the Black Team ringleader has issued another deadline for noon tomorrow. This is bad news, obviously, but it should give me more leverage when I make my appeal to the judges. Contact me on this frequency at 08:00 hours tomorrow and I'll try to have an answer for you. Roger?"

"Will do—zero eight hundred hours tomorrow. Can I ask a favor, Bluebird?"

"Ask away. Over."

"Will you contact my female teammate and let her know that I arrived here safely and that the team captain is okay. She'll be worried. Over."

Ray had to think a moment before it clicked. Stringer was talking about his sister. "I'll add it to my list." His tone was rather brusque. "Anything else I can do for you tonight?"

"No, that's it. Good luck with the judges. We're all counting on you. White Knight out."

Sunday 20:42 Hours – The "Majestic Star"

When Skip arrived back at his cabin, he found Juan Valdez out cold—still holding onto the empty coffee mug. Once inside, he began looking for a safe place to hide the Glock. On the day of occupation the Zetas had ransacked his cabin in search of weapons and communication devices. Skip didn't expect them to do it again but he wasn't taking any chances.

After contemplating several spots, Skip chose an air duct near the ceiling above the desk. Standing on the desk chair, he removed the metal grill and slid the Glock and box of ammo as far back as he could reach. Then he replaced the grate and hopped off the chair for a look. With his back against the opposite wall, he stood on his tiptoes and stretched his neck long. When the gun wasn't visible from floor level, he breathed his first sigh of relief since hearing Cal's chaos-causing Morse code message. It had been a long time coming.

Until now Skip hadn't given much thought to arming himself, feeling that whatever puny weaponry he might manage to improvise wouldn't do squat against the AK's. But that was before Cal and his Uzi and Mr. Glock entered the picture. Now everything was different and the more weapons the merrier.

Sitting down at his desk, Skip rummaged through its drawers for anything that might serve as a useful weapon. Toward the back of the pencil drawer he found a letter opener stashed under some papers. He eagerly removed it and ran a finger across its edge to check its sharpness. Frowning at its dullness, he checked the point. Not expecting it to be so sharp, his finger jerked back in reflex to its razor-sharp tip. Thinking it may come in handy, he placed it on the desktop. Tomorrow morning he would tuck it under the waistband of his pants beneath his shirt.

While scouring the room for other would-be weapons, a small desk lamp caught his attention. Seizing it, Skip yanked the plug from the wall and ripped the electrical cord from its base. With a sordid grin he coiled the loose ends around his callused hands and snapped the wire taut.

This would cut off the old air supply—yesiree bob. Sneering at it, he snapped it again. *Matter of fact, I'd test-drive it around Gold-Tooth's neck right now if he were here.*

Skip removed his trousers and used the letter opener to pick apart the bottom seam of the right front pocket. Before dressing tomorrow, he would wrap the electrical cord around his upper thigh and tie it off. With the bottom hem out of his pocket, he could access it within seconds if needed.

With no other makeshift weaponry to be had, Skip hung his soiled pants and shirt in the closet. Then he kicked off his deck shoes, removed his smelly socks, and stretched out on the bunk in his boxers. Now that Cal was on board and the Glock was hidden, he could finally relax. It had been one hellacious day and his brittle nerves were in pressing need of respite.

With his hands clasped behind his neck, Skip stared at the ceiling while reflecting on the day. It seemed like a week ago since his showdown with Mendoza in the casino this morning. And then his Uzi-packing brother-in-law came along and made his wild and crazy day even crazier.

For the first time since the hijacking, Skip held some hope—Cal was onboard, they were both armed, and Cal was in radio contact with the Coast Guard. Together, they stood a decent chance against the bad guys. Like Cal said: it was time to kick some terrorist ass.

Well, me and Mr. Glock are ready. And that Mendoza freak is at the top of my hit list.

Suddenly remembering Kathy's letter, Skip slid off the mattress and padded barefoot to the closet. Retrieving the note from his shirt pocket, he scampered back to the bunk and sprawled onto his side to read it. While fumbling excitedly to unfold it, a warm anticipation spread through his body that made his stomach flit.

Scratched in pencil on the backside of a tide chart was Kathy's messy but recognizable handwriting. She had obviously written it aboard Brillo's boat just minutes ago.

> *My Dearest Skip,*
>
> *If you are reading this note, Cal is safely aboard your ship and I thank God for that. I want you to watch each other's backs. You both mean everything to me and I can't imagine life without either of you. Skip, promise me you won't try to be a hero and do something stupid. I understand your strong sense of duty but you also have a responsibility to me, to us. You promised to grow old with me—so don't break it. Come back home to me and Toby safe and sound. We love you dearly and miss you so.*
>
> *Your terrified & loving wife,*
> *Kathy Ann XOXOXO*

Skip read the note twice more through misty eyes. Her words flowed from the page like a song. Even now, Kathy brought him an easy peaceful feeling in his soul.

WIRED

After lingering well beyond the designated cut-off time, Brillo set a course for Clearwater Pass. Typical of Florida's springtime weather, the air temperature had dropped along with the sun—like a rock. It was now in the upper 50's and the cold air pouring over the windshield exemplified every chilly degree of it.

While the *Sol-Mate* made for the marina, Kathy sat slouched next to Brillo with her head down and her feet pressed against the dashboard. Her hair was fluttering in the night air and her hands were shoved deep within the pockets of her windbreaker. Instead of being heartened that Cal was aboard the ship to help save Skip, she now carried twice the worry—the weight of which sought to drag her fragile soul to its knees.

Brillo sensed Kathy's melancholia and steered in silence most of the way back. When he finally did speak, he dispensed with the everything-will-be-all-right twaddle and coaxed her out of her shell by recounting funny stories from Skip's hell-raising days. The amusing tales had a therapeutic effect on her and Kathy soaked them up like a dry sponge. Before long she was laughing and telling comical "Skip stories" of her own.

It reminded Brillo of how folks stood around at funeral homes eulogizing the deceased—how they start off by singing the late one's praises and wind up swapping amusing tales about them. In times of grief there seemed to be a human thirst for humor. It brought levity to grave occasions. Brillo wasn't a college educated man, but he believed that laughter in times of trouble was an emotional safety valve—nature's way of preventing humans from blowing their corks. And, naturally, Kathy was no different.

Though Skip wasn't dead—yet—he was still in significant danger and Kathy felt a natural urge to reminisce, to relive happier times. It was a healthy escape for her and Brillo encouraged it. After the tough day he'd had himself, it was a great stress reliever for him as well. Laughter *was* the best medicine and by the time the boat reached the marina, both were in better spirits.

Once the *Sol-Mate* was in its slip and locked down for the night, Brillo joined Kathy on the dock. They were both drained from head-to-toe and ready to call it a day.

"You gonna be okay, Kathy?" She nodded and offered him a tired smile. "If there's anything else I can do—*anything*—pick up the phone and call me. Okay?"

Brillo's sincerity came straight from the heart and it touched her. Instead of Skip's beer-drinking-fishing-buddy, whom she had sometimes resented, she now held a different view of him. He was a kind, compassionate person, and a loyal friend. She now understood why Skip valued his friendship. To her, Brillo had been a real blessing and she would never forget it.

"Brill, you've already done far more than anyone could ask. You're a true-blue friend and we're all indebted to you. Maybe when Skip and Cal get back home, we can all find a way to repay you. But I don't see how we ever could."

"No need to even try," Brillo shrugged modestly. "That's what seafaring friends are for." He removed his cap and began fidgeting with it. "We mariners watch out for another. That's the way it's been since we got smart enough to build boats."

Even in the darkness, Brillo was uncomfortable with putting his feelings into words. A typical man, Kathy thought.

"Besides," he continued, "I've been indebted to Skip for a while now and I'm glad I could repay some of it back. He pulled me out of the drink a few years back and I'll never forget it—risked his life doing it. Remember that?" Kathy nodded. "He played it down afterward, but I wouldn't be here today if it weren't for him. What little I've done to help him ain't nothing. The way I see it, I still owe *him*."

Brillo put his cap back on and stood erect, as if standing before Mother Superior in parochial school. Kathy smiled at his little-boy backwardness and took his leathery hand, starting them toward the parking lot.

"Well, all the same," she pointed out, "I can't thank you enough. Let's just pray they both come back safe and sound." They stepped from the wharf's wooden planks onto the asphalt. "I don't know if you're a religious man, Brill, but if you would say a little prayer tonight for my two guys out there, I'd appreciate it."

Brillo was watching his feet as he walked, swerving out of his way now and again to kick a loose rock across the pavement.

"I was gonna do that anyway. But, since you asked, I'll say two prayers instead. How's that?"

"That's perfect, Captain. They can use all the prayers they can get." With a grateful smile, Kathy squeezed his hand and gave it back to him, heralding the end of personal talk. Brillo could now relax.

Eager to lighten the mood, Brillo brought up another Skip story. "Hey, did Skip tell you about the time he played strip poker on my boat with me and my girlfriend and we threw his clothes overboard while he was using the head?"

"Is that the night Skip came home in his boxer shorts?" Kathy giggled.

"Yeah," Brillo laughed. "It was a hoot. Let me tell you about it ..."

Sunday 21:15 Hours – Group St. Petersburg

Ray was hunched over his computer keyboard, refining his pitch to Washington. He would only get one shot at making his case, so it had to be good...bulletproof.

As things stood now, none of the cast of characters would buy the idea—not Mendoza, not Alvarez, not a single soul in Washington. The Zetas already had possession of the ship and would be unwilling to give up their passenger shields. Alvarez would thumb his nose at the idea, demanding instead to be whisked out of the country on a jet with a few hostages for good measure. The D.C. bureaucrats would have a cow at the mere mention of releasing Alvarez.

Even so, with a little ingenuity, Ray thought everyone might go for it—except Alvarez.

During the early hours of the crisis, a blue ribbon panel debated the pros and cons of releasing Alvarez and the idea had been unanimously vetoed. Ray had concurred with the decision at the time, even though it meant leaving him with only one course of action—stall, stall, stall— which was textbook strategy for short-lived hostage situations but a piss-poor modus operandi for protracted cases. Sooner or later the good guys run out of excuses, the bad guys run out of patience, and innocent people get hurt.

WIRED

As Ray studied the talking points on his computer screen, he crossed his ankles on the desk. If there were any holes in his strategy, his proposal would be shot down at once. What's more, if not presented just right, he might come across as stonewalling or trying to engineer a flimsy last-minute extension of the Commandant's deadline.

There was still an outside chance of Mendoza trading hostages for water when the ship's tanks ran dry, but Ray wasn't counting on it. Blowing folks to pieces in full view of the media was much more *terroristic*. If the twisted freak got lucky, a blob of guts might splat on the camera lens of a low flying newscopter.

If not for the hostages, Ray would sic the SEALs on them with orders to take no prisoners. But that's what the Zetas wanted: a fight-to-the-death duel before a world audience. They were a deranged band of psychopaths, infatuated with bloodshed and fueled by outside attention. With the cameras rolling, Mendoza would blow the ship and take everybody down with him.

For Ray's strategy to succeed, three obstacles had to be overcome: he had to persuade Washington to release Alvarez; he had to convince Mendoza to give up the hostages; and he had to do it all without Alvarez's participation.

To overcome the last two hurdles, Ray would enlist the help of Master Chief Bloyd from Miami Group. He was a telecommunications specialist and Ray had some electronic trickery in mind to circumvent Alvarez's "right to remain silent".

In terms of petitioning for Alvarez's release, the Commandant would have to be won over first, followed by the military brass and politicians. Duping the terrorists was one thing; convincing Washington to release Alvarez would be quite another. Citizens from coast-to-coast were already clamoring for blood and their outcry would be loud and unfavorable.

Fanning the flames of dissent was the mass media, which had been unrelenting in its quest for culpability—and, of course, higher ratings. Their faultfinding witch-hunts had made the recent bloodshed a political hot potato that had bureaucrats scattering for cover—worsening the usual amount of finger pointing, issue skirting, buck-passing, and politicizing ever rife at the nation's Capitol.

WIRED

In order to secure Alvarez's release, a number of bureaus would have to give sanction—none of which would want to be known as "the" agency that freed the Cali drug boss. Of them all, the DEA boys would scream the loudest. The Colombian was a huge collar for them and letting him skate after a decade of hot pursuit would fly directly in their faces. But, in the end, the DEA would cave-in along with the other agencies. Why? Because when you take out the politics, the tradeoff made sense. People's lives were infinitely more important than pride or public opinion. Everybody would concede to that, except for maybe the military.

Unlike the politicians, the U.S. military operated within its own realm of authority and under its own set of rules. When a threat to national security was at stake—such as terrorism—public opinion wasn't necessarily a key concern. Before consenting to Alvarez's release, the Pentagon warlords would require ironclad assurance that he could not possibly escape. The murdering, car-bombing, drug pusher had already savaged the government's reputation enough and the Pentagon would not risk further embarrassment by him making a monkey out of the military.

With all of these details running through his head, Ray sat up in his chair and lifted the phone receiver. As far as Stringer's participation went, mum was the word—even to his trusted comrade, Chief Bloyd. The subversive act was light years beyond the understanding of by-the-book military minds. That piece of the puzzle would stay put between Ray and the *Majestic Star*.

With the tension rising in him, Ray dialed the Commandant's cellular number. As the phone rang in his ear, he knew what he must do. The higher-ups would never adopt a strategy that lacked a predetermined conclusion—a conclusion with a very definitive finish.

Regrettably, there could only be one ending to this story.

Sunday 21:45 Hours – The "Majestic Star"

The musty cargo hold was typical of many that Cal had seen—haze gray painted floor, gray steel walls, gray ceiling laced with gray pipes and ductwork hanging down. Wooden crates were lined along the portside wall and the bay area was filled with cardboard boxes coated with a fine patina of dust. On the starboard side was an open steel staircase leading

WIRED

up to the main deck and the hatch that Cal had entered by. Aft of the hatch was a freight elevator with sliding wire mesh gate. To the rear of the cargo bay were two storerooms and a stairwell leading down to the ship's deepest compartment: the engine room.

Cal was sitting behind one of the crates within the reddish gloom of the **EXIT** sign. As he studied Skip's diagram using the penlight, the shadows around him seemed to change and move about, threatening to close in on him. With his overtaxed nerves on edge, every creak of the ship's structure or rattle of a loose pipe became a Zeta killer about to swoop down on him.

When Cal'd first unfolded the drawing, he snickered at Skip's notation that read: **YOU ARE HERE**, with an arrow pointing to the starboard hatch. The diagram was in much better detail than the sketch Brillo had drawn. It showed the floor plan deck by deck, including the engine room, interior and exterior stairwells, areas where Skip had sighted explosives, and even where life rafts were stored—the latter obviously marked as a potential means of escape. Printed inside a rectangular box on the second deck was: **CASINO: PASSENGERS HELD HERE**. On the top deck behind the pilothouse, two squares were drawn with: **MY CABIN** and **TERRORIST CABIN**. Aft of the two cabins was an open area marked: **SUNDECK: MEALS SERVED HERE**.

After memorizing the ship's layout, Cal placed the diagram in his pocket and lolled his head against the rough-cut wood. He needed some rest but was too hyped-up to sleep. Now that he was on board and ready for action, he felt like a racecar sitting in stalled traffic. And the more he tried to force sleep, the more wide-awake he became. The adrenalin was interfering with his circadian rhythm.

"Gonna be a long-ass night," he whispered in the dark.

Careful not to make any noise, Cal reached into the trash bag and extracted a pack of cheese crackers and bottle of spring water. While snacking on them he wondered how Hanna was making out with Washington. With eleven Americans now dead they wouldn't be easily persuaded, especially when it came to freeing their prized prisoner. After that, providing Washington approved the exchange, the gang leader upstairs must be convinced. In view of the executions, Mendoza may find it hard to believe that he and his cohorts were simply free to go.

WIRED

After finishing his snack, Cal stowed the empty water bottle inside the bag and illuminated the dial of his dive watch. When seeing only ten minutes had passed since his last look, he wilted against the rough planks. Tomorrow seemed like light years away.

"Time sure flies when you're hiding behind a crate from eight armed terrorists."

It crossed Cal's mind to start looking for the explosives, but he decided against it. It was too dark and he needed to conserve the penlight battery. The C-4 would have to wait until daybreak. With any luck he might stumble across the radio receiver rigged to spark-detonate the plastique. If luckier, he might be able to disarm it. Unfortunately, Skip was the demolitions expert, not him.

So with nothing to do but wait the night out, Cal scavenged up some broken-down cardboard boxes and spread them out flat behind the crate. Then he folded his neoprene wet suit into a pillow and lay down on his back facing the reddish pipes and ductwork.

"Home Sweet Home."

Surprisingly, the makeshift bedding wasn't all that uncomfortable. After lying on his back a while, he rolled onto his side and curled up with the Uzi beside him. Tomorrow was D-Day, so to speak—his date with destiny—and he needed some shuteye, an hour or two at least.

With his eyes closed, Cal tried to picture himself in more pleasant surroundings—anyplace other than a cruise ship being terrorized by the drug Mafia. In wartime, soldiers were capable of sleeping practically anywhere, even under enemy fire. It was a matter of self-will, of switching off your brain.

After a time of lying at rest, Cal's adrenaline dissipated—leaving only the remains of fatigue. As exhaustion settled in, his conscious mind let go and teetered between wakefulness and sleep. Then ever so lightly it floated toward the immaterial world of slumberland—a weightless place where the real and imaginary clash and conjoin to form images from shards of truth and fantasy, melding fact and fiction.

As Cal gently crossed the threshold of sleep, a continuum of nebulous images flowed through his mind—images of people whom he'd met and never met...places he had been and never been...landscapes of meadows, lakes, and forests...of white seabirds rising from flooded wetlands...of warm sand and palms trees and iridescent blue-green water.

When sleep claimed him at last, he dreamt. But Cal Stringer's dreams were never of the innocuous sort that set his soul to rest. Nor were they dreams that evaporated from mind and memory upon waking. When Cal dreamed, he struggled against illusive enemies and battled phantoms of times past; the lingering shadows of which were swept away the next morning with a failed sense of unresolve.

He dreamed of torn souls in torment...of the dead stacked on top of the dying...of a damnable place that had given him his perception of Hell.

Sunday 22:30 Hours – Group St. Petersburg

After receiving Hanna's vitally important phone call, the Commandant pulled some late night strings and arranged an impromptu teleconference with the who's who of Washington's elite. Once the multi-phone connections were made, the Commandant prefaced the conference call by detailing the chain of events from the initial hijacking through tomorrow's noon execution threat. Once the listeners were brought up to speed, it was Ray's turn to make his case.

As the dignitaries listened in silence, Ray unveiled the particulars of his swap-Alvarez-for-the-passengers plan while assuring them that Alvarez could not possibly escape—citing that the beauty of using the ship as a getaway vehicle was its ease of tracking; that with a top speed of twenty-five knots it couldn't go anywhere too fast; that it could even be tracked by satellite.

Aware that his listeners would never adopt a strategy bearing the least risk of escape, Ray then revealed the coup de grâce. *When Alvarez and the Zetas were at sea and out of camera range—destroy the Majestic Star.*

Ray explained that it was their only political way out to both save the passengers and show the world that America would not buckle under to terrorism. That, while deeply regrettable about the captain and crew, the government's image would be restored by the successful rescue of two hundred American lives—many of which were women and children—and by the definitive action taken to punish the terrorists. He added that the public and news media, which had been demanding retribution since the first executions, would be pleased that justice was served and that Alvarez and his thugs were at the bottom of the sea. End of deadlock...end of Americans being murdered and maimed on national television...end of Juan Carlos Alvarez and the Zeta dilemma.

Ray paused at that point to let his unseen audience respond. When he was met by a wall of silence, he took it as a good sign and pressed on with greater optimism—pledging to oversee the entire operation himself; reiterating that it was their only reasonable course of action; that, otherwise, the situation would surely deteriorate and every single passenger would be lost—slowly, painfully, and publicly.

Once again, Ray was met by silence. Then he and the Commandant were placed on hold for a lengthy time while the decision-makers deliberated. Following a tedious wait, they were advised that a decision would be handed down tomorrow morning. Before either he or the Commandant could respond, there was a series of pops and clicks followed by a flat dial tone.

With his phone receiver still in hand, Ray stared off into space. He had presented his case well and he had a strong hunch it would be approved. Now he had to figure a way to get Stringer and crew off the ship before ordering its destruction. But first, he had one last phone call to make.

Sunday 22:42 Hours – Clearwater Beach, Florida

When Kathy got home from the marina, she kicked her shoes off and stood in the center of the living room with her hands on her hips. With everyone now gone, the house felt empty and desolate—just like her—and she didn't know what to do with herself.

After roaming the condo without aim or direction, she took a leisurely hot bath and donned her bathrobe with steam still rolling from her skin. Then she curled up on the sofa with Toby, sipping hot tea and trying to stay awake for the eleven o'clock news. Channel 10 was rerunning a Coast Guard press conference taped earlier today and she didn't want to miss word of it.

As Kathy stared disinterestedly at the television, her thoughts kept straying but she refused to get wrought-up. She'd promised Cal that she wouldn't torture herself with worry and she was too numb from exhaustion to get any more upset. She had worried so much, for so long, that she was all worried out—at least for the night.

When the phone suddenly rang, it gave her a start. When it rang again, Kathy stared at it petrified, unable to react. A call at such a late hour often bore bad news and it frightened her.

"Hello?" There was a timid uptilt in her voice.

"Miss Myles?" the caller inquired. "Kathy Myles?"

"Yes, who's calling?" The man's voice was familiar but she couldn't place it.

"A friend. I visited you on the boat tonight. Your brother gave me your name."

Confused, she had to think for a moment before remembering. "Oh, yes, the Coast Guard officer. You gave us quite a scare out there."

"Yes ma'am. I just wanted to let you know that Mr. Stringer is safely aboard the Majestic Star. We've been in radio contact and he's okay."

"Oh, thank God!" A weight lifted from her shoulders. "And how's my husband? Did Cal mention him?"

"Your husband? I'm not aware of any other individuals accompanying Mr. Stringer."

"He's the captain of the Majestic Star—Captain Jason Myles—but everyone calls him Skip. He and my brother were in the Navy together. That's how we met."

Floored by the news, Ray was at a temporary loss for words. Then he found his tongue.

"I'm sorry, Mrs. Myles, but I wasn't aware that the captain was your husband. According to your brother, they met briefly tonight but I have no other information regarding him. I'll be talking to Mr. Stringer at 08:00 hours tomorrow. I'll find out more and inform you afterward."

"Would you? I would be so grateful!" She was now wide-awake and no longer tired. "Skip and Cal are the only family I have left and I've been crazy with worry. I really don't know how to thank you. Please stay in touch with me, sir. Please?"

"Yes, ma'am. I'll pass on whatever information I can."

"Excuse me, but I didn't catch your name."

"Goodnight, Mrs. Myles. Talk to you tomorrow."

WIRED

~~~~~~~~~~

"Jumpin' Jehoshaphat!" Ray yelped, backing away from the telephone like it was a rattlesnake. "The plot is thickening!"

He was so surprised by the revelation that he couldn't hang up fast enough. Given Kathy Myles' last name, he should have made the correlation. But with so much crap on his mind lately, he had failed to connect the dots. Little did she know that he had just persuaded Washington to blow her husband to hell-and-back along with her Navy SEAL brother.

Ray had actually called her for two reasons: because he promised Stringer that he would and, more importantly, to question her about her brother's motive for boarding the *Majestic Star*. Now, of course, the latter was crystal clear—brother and husband were Navy chums...brother introduces sister to Navy pal...sister and Navy pal get married...Navy pal gets kidnapped and sister calls brother for help...brother shows up with an Uzi and an attitude.

"This whole thing's starting to sound like a freaking Swartzneggar movie!"

Ray intercommed the outer office to requisition the Navy records of Calvin Stringer and Jason Myles, plus a background check on each. There was a hell of a lot riding on these two characters and Ray wanted to know who he was in bed with.

Before talking to Kathy Myles, he had intended to warn Stringer about the ship's destruction, but now Ray wondered if that would be wise of him. If he tipped off Stringer too early, would it spur him into acting prematurely? Perhaps before the passengers were evacuated?

That would screw things up royally.

But to Stringer's credit, it had been his idea to leave the crew behind as hostages. That was pretty sound thinking given that Captain Myles would be one of the key captives.

Too brain-dead to worry about it tonight, Ray yawned and rubbed the back of his neck. His sugar and caffeine buzz had worn off long ago and he needed some rest. This time tomorrow, the nightmare would be over one way or another—perhaps his career right along with it.

With visions of court martial proceedings dancing merrily through his head, Ray turned off the desk lamp and headed for his private barracks.

"Sometimes you get, and sometimes you get got. That's the way it works, Ray-Man. C'est la vie."

"THE RECKONING"

"Death is the king of this world: 'tis his park where he breeds life to feed him. Cries of pain are music for his banquet".

George Eliot (1819 – 1880) English Novelist

"And if any mischief follow, then thou shalt give life for life, eye for eye, tooth for tooth, hand for hand, foot for foot, burning for burning, would for wound, stripe for stripe."

Hebrew Bible, Exodus 21:23

"He who does not punish evil, commands it to be done."

Leonardo Da Vinci (1452-1519) Italian painter, sculptor, scientist, writer

"Revenge is a dish best served cold."

Pierre Ambroise Francois Choderios de LaClos (1741-1803)

"Follow me if I advance, kill me if I retreat, avenge me if I die."

Mary Matalin, U.S. Republican political advisor

WIRED

Monday 05:45 Hours – The "Majestic Star"

The night was pitch-black and Cal was standing in waist-high water with NVA bullets streaking past him from all directions. Yards away, Mickey was crouched amid some tall reeds, shouting something indistinguishable at him and waving him on with fiery emotion.

His words were lost in the blare of battle, but Cal could read his lips as he yelled: *"Come on, Cal! Come on!"*

Heartened by the sight of his old friend, Cal powered his way through the muddy water. But its consistency was like wet cement, heavily impeding his progress. After managing just a handful of steps he was spent and his lungs burned for air. With no strength left in him, Cal shook his head at Mickey with a failed expression that said: *"I can't do it."* This prompted Mickey to yell louder, so loud that it rose above the torrent of small arms fire and earthshaking explosions.

Spurred on by Mickey's rants, Cal set out again but his boots were mired down in thick bottom sludge. With tracer rounds narrowly missing him, he pulled and pulled but his feet wouldn't budge. Now fully fatigued and rooted to the bottom, he stopped struggling and gazed at Mickey with wanting—as if apologizing for his failure and simultaneously bidding Mickey farewell.

Rejecting Cal's goodbye, Mickey sprung into action—leaving the safety of the reeds and slogging toward Cal determinedly. In a compassionate yet reckless move, he waded into the open and extended his arm toward Cal, stepping directly into the path of enemy fire.

Fearing for Mickey's life, Cal waved him back but Mickey kept coming. Now less than ten feet away, Mickey's teeth showed white against the dark camouflage grease paint on his face. In the midst of all the murder and mayhem, he was smiling—motioning for Cal to meet him.

As Mickey stood beckoning him, Cal couldn't believe his eyes. His actions were not only reckless, they were suicidal. Mortars and grenades were disgorging bottom muck by the bucket load and a downpour of muddy water was raining down on them like Niagara Falls. But in defiance of it all, Mickey was just standing there...smiling...wagging the fingers of his extended hand...as if inviting his sweetheart to join him on the dance floor.

WIRED

All at once Charlie zeroed in on Mickey and a blast of bullets struck him full force. Like a string puppet doing an obscene deadly dance, his body jerked and spasmed at each powerful impact. Cal watched in deepening horror as torn chunks of pink flesh flew from Mickey's body, vaporizing into the darkness. But, miraculously, Mickey kept coming, as if feeling no pain—still smiling.

The lead projectiles tore at Mickey's face and blew away clumps of hair until he was unrecognizable—until he was a monstrous, walking, blood-covered, corpse-thing whose carcass had been reduced to a bloody framework of bone and cartilage. As Mickey drew closer in his shredded bullet-torn cammies, Cal recoiled from the macabre sight and tried to take flight, but his mired down boots still wouldn't let go.

Just as Cal released a bloodcurdling scream, Mickey's half-skeletal hand grabbed him by the throat and pulled him face-to-face—or rather face-to-skull. Dark-red slime was dripping from Mickey's mouth and gouts of blood dribbled from his eye sockets. With no lips remaining to cover them, his elongated teeth had grown to hideous proportions.

Fighting for escape, Cal tore at the bony hand while kicking and thrashing, but Mickey's claw-like grasp was fast and unyielding—a hellish death grip. With Cal squirming like a worm on a hook, his zombie friend jerked him close and hissed with slobbering breath: *"It's your fault that I'm dead, Cal, and you damn well know it! It's all your fucking fault!"*

Monday 06:00 Hours – Group St. Petersburg

Ray's slumber was interrupted by a knock at his door. As if attached by an invisible string, his eyelids popped open at the very instant the door opened.

"Admiral, its 06:00 hours, sir."

Still dressed in his ODU's, Ray nodded sleepily at the silhouette in the doorway and turned his eyes away from the glaring hallway light. Military life dictated an early rise whether it was a natural part of one's makeup or not. Fortunately for Ray, it had never been a problem. He had been an early bird since his days of delivering newspapers as a kid.

As Ray's eyes adjusted to the light, he sat up on the cot and pulled on his black steel-toed boots. While lacing them up, the officer told him that the military records and background checks he had ordered were faxed overnight and lying on his desk. Before Ray could ask, the man also reported there had been no word from Washington and that all was quiet on the Zeta front.

Nodding his thanks to the officer, Ray stood up groggily and walked into the head. While standing at the urinal, he murmured at the wall. "The wheels of politics turn mighty slow, Ray-Man, and high noon will be here before you know it."

After zipping up, Ray splashed water over his face and screwed on his USCG ball cap. He would shave and shower later. If he were going to prevent the executions, he had a boatload of miracles to perform before twelve noon.

Monday 06:04 Hours – The "Majestic Star"

Startled awake by the nightmare, Cal sat bolt upright on his cardboard pallet with wild incoherent eyes—hyperventilating...unsure of his whereabouts...trembling like a distempered dog. At recognizing the surrounding crates, he plopped back down on the cardboard and willed his catapulting heart to slow down.

As Cal stared at the ceiling pipes, he armed sweat off his face and took deep controlled breaths. He knew from past experience that it would take a while for the effects of the recurring dream to wear off—it always did.

Although Mickey had died more than thirty years ago, his death was as fresh in Cal's mind as on that tragic night in 1974. Unfortunately for former Special Warfare Combatant Calvin Stringer, there was no statute of limitations on apocalyptic dreams.

Monday 06:05 Hours – Group St. Petersburg

After making a pit stop at the coffeepot, Ray sat down at his desk and plucked the naval records from a basket. One folder was labeled: **"JASON MYLES"** while the other read: **"CALVIN STRINGER."** With his curiosity running high, he settled back in his chair and opened the

"MYLES" folder first.

Jason Myles was born in Atlanta and joined the Navy in 1971. He became a Navy SEAL in 1972, graduating in the top half of his class. He served two tours of duty in Vietnam, where he earned a Purple Heart and Medal of Honor—the latter awarded for "gallantry and intrepidity at the risk of life above and beyond the call of duty while engaged in an action against an enemy of the United States." He took part in covert missions in the Mekong Delta and La Drang River region (a.k.a. Valley of Death), as well as Laos, and Cambodia. Beyond his initial BUD/s SEAL training, Myles received advanced training in high-explosive demolitions, which was his specialty. He was an expert marksman and a seasoned paratrooper with over forty night jumps to his credit. He was honorably discharged in 1975, one month before President Duong Van Minh surrendered Saigon—now Ho Chi Minh City—to North Vietnamese communist forces on April 30th.

Impressive record, Ray had to admit. *Medal of Honor winner. The highest military decoration awarded by the United States government.*

Clipped to Myles' naval record was a background report stamped: **CONFIDENTIAL.** Compiled from the records of various federal, state, and local sources, it gave a personal account of Jason Myles after his discharge from the Navy.

When Myles got out of the Navy he returned to Atlanta and attended Georgia State University for two years. After dropping out in his sophomore year, he relocated to Tampa, Florida to work as a merchant marine on a phosphate barge. In 1979 he obtained his 50-ton Captain's License, which had been steadily upgraded over the years to a 2500-ton license. Spanning his maritime career Myles had operated tugboats, barges, and a host of commercial fishing vessels. At present he was employed as ship captain for *Sun 'n Fun Cruise Lines* based in Miami. His police record showed an arrest in 1985 for assault and battery, the result of a barroom brawl in Pinellas County. In 1986 he was charged with D.U.I. and his driver's license was suspended for 30 days. In 1992 he was audited by the IRS without consequence. Myles was registered as an Independent voter and his FICO credit score was 622. He married Kathryn Ann Stringer in 1984 and in May of 1985 they purchased an Island Estates townhouse at Clearwater Beach, Florida. No record of childbirth was on file. End of report.

Captain Myles ain't no pussy, Ray thought. *If pushed, he could definitely push back.*

Ray gazed up at the color poster of the *Majestic Star* pinned to the wall. Upon his arrival in St. Petersburg, he was told that to captain her was a local status symbol. Being an old salt himself, Ray could certainly see why. She was indeed a magnificent ship.

"Myles must have been ecstatic when he landed the job," Ray said to himself. "After all the years spent on tugs and stinking fishing boats, I can imagine how he felt when he first stepped aboard her as Captain. It had to be the shining crown of his career." Ray closed the folder and shook his head. "Little did he know, poor bastard."

Upon examining Stringer's military record, Ray found it similar to Myles'. Both men had undergone similar training but Stringer had earned higher marks, graduating in the top five percent of his class. After graduation he was assigned to Special Operations—an elite SEAL Team whose members were revered as Ph.D.'s in commando gear. There, he was trained in electronics, submersibles, and technologically advanced equipment specifically developed for SEAL waterborne missions. He also received foreign language instruction and could speak Vietnamese and Chinese. During his tour in Vietnam, he participated in riverine operations in the Gulf of Tonkin and Mekong Delta. In September 1974, he was wounded during a firefight near Vinh Long River and awarded the Purple Heart. He was honorably discharged in January 1975.

Following his discharge, Stringer attended college under the GI Bill, graduating in 1979 from the University of Florida with a 3.8 grade average. After earning his law degree he relocated to Detroit where he worked for two law firms before starting his own practice in 1988. He was a registered Republican and in good standing with the Michigan BAR Association. His credit score was 807 and his police record was clear. He had been twice married with no record of children. End of report.

"Well, I'll be damned—my Uzi-packing partner in crime is a friggin' lawyer." Ray threw his head back and laughed. "If Mendoza knew that, he'd probably surrender just to get away from his shark-ass. Even paid killers have to draw the line somewhere."

Grinning at the irony of it, Ray closed Stringer's file and

contemplated his strange bedfellows. Clearly, Stringer was the more brains while Myles was the more brawn. In either case they were tough, well-trained, highly competent soldiers.

After refilling his coffee mug, Ray sat down at the computer and began drafting two initiatives: *Operation Checkmate* in anticipation of Washington's approval and *Operation Stalemate* in the event it was voted down.

Employing his speedy two-finger typing technique, Ray began pecking away on the keyboard.

Monday 07:05 Hours – The "Majestic Star"

It seemed that Skip had just closed his eyes when a loud rapping at the door jarred him awake.

"Skip, open up!" The voice belonged to Neal and it sounded urgent. "We gotta talk!"

Skip also heard the muted shouts of men in the background and the sounds of a scuffle going on. When he opened the door, Stan and the ponytailed Hispanic were dragging Neal away by the elbows, who was digging in his heels and rebelling at the top of his voice.

The manhandling of his first officer instantaneously riled Skip, who stepped outside to confront the men. "Hey! Let him go! What's goin' on here? STOP IT!"

When the two men halted and looked Skip's way, Neal got his feet back under him and began pushing and shoving. Right away, tempers flared all over again and the scuffle restarted. In the heat of battle, Stan unsheathed his jambiya dagger and cocked it back as if intending to strike. Unbeknownst to Neal, he was about to be sliced and diced.

Acting quickly, Skip bolted toward the tangle of men and grabbed Stan's arm in midair. "I SAID STOP IT," he blared in Stan's face. "NOW!!"

Skip's commanding manner must have triggered some authority-type reaction in their minds because all three men suddenly quit fighting. With Skip glowering at them, the brawlers separated and moved out of each other's reach while eyeing another warily. Neal was tucking his shirttail back inside his pants when he noticed Stan's unsheathed dagger.

"Whatcha planning on doing with that blade? You stinking pile of camel shit!" With clenched fists, Neal started toward him. "C'mon, raghead, I'll show you where to put that knife!"

"That's enough!" Skip snagged Neal by the back of his belt and hauled him backwards until reaching a safe distance. Then he circled in front of Neal and gripped him by the shoulders. "Okay, Neal. What's the meaning of this?"

"Those pricks are at it again, Skip!" Neal pointed accusingly at the men. "A few minutes ago they barged into the casino and rounded up more passengers at gunpoint. Looks like they're starting back with the executions." Raising his voice, Neal flung his words at the Zetas like stones. "So much for their lying spic leader's promise not to harm any more passengers!"

When Stan snorted at him, hot blood rushed to Neal's face and he thrust his middle finger in the air, pumping it up and down at the Arab with a passion. Incensed by the vulgar put-down, Stan charged with his head down and plastered Neal like an NFL lineman, sending Neal airborne through the doorway and sprawling onto the cabin floor.

"I said: THAT WILL BE ENOUGH!" Skip yelled in Stan's face. When it didn't faze him, Skip shoved the hulk aside and stormed inside the cabin. "You two clowns tell your boss I want to see him. NOW!"

The Arab snubbed Skip again by lagging in the doorway and laughing idiotically at Neal, exposing square front teeth with a gap between them. Then his ponytailed accomplice joined in and they laughed together like a pair of hyenas. As they pointed at Neal and jeered, Skip's eyes went to the vent above the desk. With the help of Mr. Glock he could annihilate them both in two seconds flat—*kaboom-kaboom*. No sweat. Knowing this gave Skip enough willpower to keep his temper in check. Every dog has its day.

With premeditated intent, Skip smiled to himself while walking up to Stan in the doorway.

"Neal, call the kitchen and have them send up a can of whoop-ass." After sizing Stan up and down, he added: "Tell 'em to make it a large."

With Neal looking up at him confused, Skip slammed the door shut full force, flattening Stan's nose. When a yelp and crackling crunch of bone came from the other side, Skip sneered at the sweet sound and turned to Neal. "Oops, never mind."

~~~~~~~~~~~

Two decks down and precisely 153 feet aft, Cal was whiling away the time behind his crate. He had a one-hour wait before radioing Hanna and four hours until rendezvousing with Skip on the sundeck. Fortunately it would be daylight soon and he could go exploring for explosives, giving him something else to do besides sitting around in the dark.

To Cal's pleasant surprise he wasn't craving a cigarette, which was the first time he hadn't craved nicotine in many a morning. He couldn't light up anyway for fear of detection, but it felt liberating to be free of Mr. Nicotine's grip. Maybe this time he would quit for good.

Coffee, however, was another matter. Right now, Cal would give a C-note for a hot cup from *Shorty's Diner*—a place far removed from the wicked world he found himself in. At this very second patrons were sitting at Shorty's counter on beat-up barstools, devouring greasy eggs and stacks of buttery pancakes. To them it was just another Monday, with little more to dread than the upcoming workweek—lucky stiffs. Being his acerbic self, Cal made a mental note to pack a thermos of coffee the next time he rescued Skip from the Mexican Mafia.

Forgetting about Shorty's, Cal looked at his watch and wondered how Hanna was doing with the politicians. That's where Cal drew the line. He didn't have any qualms with the military, but he was disposed to doubt when it came to politics and government—a life lesson from Vietnam.

Wars were about power, greed, and misguided egos—definitely not for insuring the *"Domestic Tranquility."* In truth, Cal had never met a soldier on either side that actually had a bone to pick with the other. They fought and killed because politicians told them to fight and kill. Then, years later, the governments would patch up their differences and host each other's ambassadors at fancy cocktail receptions.

"Too bad about our boys that died during our little dispute," one ambassador might say to the other. *"But, as they say: 'shit happens'. Please be a sport and pass the caviar."*

WIRED

Monday 07:10 Hours – Group St. Petersburg

While awaiting word from Washington, Ray put the finishing touches on his two initiatives. Both plans were tactically sound containing timetables, contingencies, and a mandatory conclusion before darkness.

Ray hoped Washington would opt for *Operation Checkmate*, calling for a hostage exchange and destruction of the ship. *Operation Stalemate* was a backup plan that entailed an all-out assault on the ship by Marine commandos and the SEALs. The exercise would be bloody and carry a high probable loss of life. It also bore the risk of Mendoza detonating the C-4 before the *Majestic Star* could be secured, having massive repercussions.

Altogether *Operation Checkmate* would require nine hours to complete; meaning it must commence by 09:00 hours in order to culminate by nightfall. The timetable allocated three hours for swapping Alvarez for passengers, two hours for the transfer of food, water, and fuel, and another two hours for the *Majestic Star* to travel out of camera range so the finishing moments would not appear on the nightly news. The final two hours were earmarked for intercepting the ship and extracting Stringer and the crew in advance of sinking it—if a rescue was possible.

With his computer work done, Ray stretched his back and checked his watch. The "hurry-up-and-wait" routine might be a military tradition, but his patience was all used up. He had less than two hours to launch *Operation Checkmate* or the final rescue phase would be conducted in the dark. Nighttime extractions were tricky by nature and risky for the rescuers. Militarily, it would be more judicious of him to sink the *Majestic Star* and be done with it. But that meant sacrificing the lives of Stringer and company, a call that Ray hoped he wasn't forced to make.

With nothing more to do until receiving Washington's verdict, Ray picked up his coffee cup and strolled to a window. The eastern sky was brightening and wispy cirrus clouds were burning with pastels of rouge and crimson. It brought to mind the old mariner's rhyme: *red skies in the morning, sailor's warning.*

The scenic daybreak was reminiscent of the many Ray had witnessed as a paperboy in Jacksonville. He was raised there by his single-parent mom after his father deserted them at age twelve, leaving young Ray man of the house. It was a weighty responsibility for a young lad but Ray never complained, working after school and during summers to help support them. Instead of playing baseball with his friends, he mowed grass or bagged groceries at the supermarket. Instead of going on dates, he went to bed early so he could rise at 4:00 A.M. to deliver newspapers. When his normal chores were done, he was either off to school or on his way to another part-time job to help make ends meet.

While Ray had been remarkably charitable about being deprived a normal social life, he had never quit hoping that his mother would remarry. When the day-to-day drudgery would drag him down, this hope alone kept him going. He loved his mother dearly, of course, and he wanted her to be happy; but, beyond that, he wanted relief from his premature burden of responsibility. More than anything else, Ray just wanted to be a kid.

His mom had been quite attractive back then and she had entertained various suitors, some of which Ray had gotten quite attached to. But to his mother's disappointment, as well as his own, nothing permanent ever developed and they remained on their own. He had watched them come, and he had watched them go, but nothing ever changed.

By the time Ray reached his mid-teens, this endless string of disappointments had rather soured him on life. At the ripe age of sixteen, he came to the sobering realization that the only real security in life was created, not given, and that his future rested solely on his shoulders and no one else's. And to never, ever, expect anything from anyone.

Ray was wondering how his mother's arthritis was doing, when someone tapped him on the shoulder. When he turned around, a pale-faced lieutenant snapped to attention.

"Admiral, you've got a priority call from Washington, sir."

"Headquarters?" Ray automatically asked, heading for his desk phone.

"No sir," the young officer quaked. "It's the White House."

Ray stopped in his tracks and shot the petty officer an inquisitive look.

"It's the President, sir."

WIRED

Monday 07:19 Hours – The "Majestic Star"

"All right, Neal, start from the beginning and tell me everything that's happened."

Recovering from his spill, Neal rose on rickety legs and sat down on Skip's bunk. "I guess Gold-Tooth's finally fed up with all the waiting around crap." He bent over and crossly scooped up his hat that had fallen off. "I was in the wheelhouse when I heard a bunch of yelling coming from outside. I looked out the door and saw them herding passengers down the midship stairwell. I hotfooted it to your cabin to tell you about it and the big Arab chased after me. When I reached your door, he and the Mexican jumped me. You know the rest."

With the fear rising in him, Skip interrogated Neal rapid-fire. "How many passengers did they take? Were they bound and blindfolded? Were there any females? Was anybody hurt?"

"I don't know how many they took, but I'd say around a dozen or so." Neal swallowed hard and gave Skip a sickly look. "All females."

"Oh, Christ!" Skip groaned as if something gored him in the gut.

"That's all I saw anyway. Like I said, I was on the bridge when the commotion began so there could've been some males in front of the pack, but I didn't see any. It was still pretty dark." Neal flung his hat on the bunk and balled his fists. "What are we gonna do about it, Skip? We can't let 'em get away with this shit! We can't allow them to start killing our women."

"You're right, Neal. And we *will* do something about it." Skip wanted to tell Neal about Cal and the Glock but decided to keep it to himself for now. "But I don't want you or the crew to do anything that might provoke them. Let me handle it. I can't give you any details right now, but something big is comin' down today."

"Yeah, what's up?"

"Can't say just yet. Just pass the word. Tell the guys to follow my lead. Okay?"

When Skip didn't elaborate, Neal dropped his eyes and nodded at the floor. Too agitated to sit still, he rose and walked to the porthole. "God, I hate those bastards." He shoved his hands in his pockets and gazed outside. Dawn was gathering fast off the starboard and the sun was cooking off the morning haze. "I'll do what you say, Skip, but I won't stand by while our women are murdered." He twisted around to face Skip. "If they start that shit, I ain't making no promises."

By now Neal's eyes were glistening and he was visibly shaking. As Skip studied Neal, he decided to level with him.

"I feel the same way, Neal, and we'll have our revenge. I wasn't gonna tell you this just yet, but Cal's onboard. He's armed and so am I."

Neal stared blank-faced at Skip as if not comprehending his words. His dumbstruck reaction amused Skip, who nodded at the air vent. "It's hidden up there—nine-millimeter with a box of ammo. I'm tellin' you this because I trust you and so you'll calm down. We've got a fightin' chance. If those dicks harm one more passenger, they'll pay for it with their lives. But we gotta play it smart and pick the right time. When Cal and I make our move, you and the others need to be ready. Use pipes or anything that makes a good weapon. We'll show the bastards who's runnin' this ship."

"Yeah." Neal's eyes glazed over with vengeance. "You got that right."

"Don't breathe a word of this to anybody. Not a soul. Okay?"

"Of course not." Neal was offended that Skip found it necessary to say.

Skip sat down on the bunk and began putting on his socks and shoes. "If Gold-Tooth ain't here pretty soon, we'll go lookin' for him. He's got some explainin' to do. Hopefully, he's just bluffin' about the female passengers. You know, puttin' on a show for the Coast Guard." With his shoes now on, Skip stood up. "Okay, keep a sharp lookout while I fetch the Glock."

Neal cracked the door open and peeked outside. After finding the coast clear, he poked his head out and looked up and down the empty deck.

While Neal stood watch, Skip climbed atop the desk chair and removed the grate. As he retrieved the Glock, Neal's head swiveled between the deck and the vent opening. Once the grate was back in place, Skip hopped off the chair and handed the gun to Neal. While Neal marveled at it, Skip dashed into the head and returned with a First Aid Kit. After hiking up his pant leg, he opened a roll of first aid tape and taped the nine-millimeter above his right ankle.

"Okay, Neal," Skip said, pulling down his pant leg and standing up. "I'm ready to show that gold-toothed prick who's boss."

Still in mild shock, Neal replied: "I'd say you are, Skipper. You sure as hell are."

~~~~~~~~~~

Following the longest night of his life, Cal emerged from the crates and gazed at his new surroundings. The weak morning light was filtering through the ship's deep-set sidelights, shedding a colorless blue-gray cast over the cargo bay.

While searching for the C-4, Cal hoped to scavenge up some foodstuff from the cartons. He had only two candy bars left and he was saving those in case something unforeseen prevented him from reaching the sundeck for meals.

Deciding to work his way astern, Cal slung the Uzi strap over his right shoulder and set out. As he crept along, he panned the cardboard containers with the penlight, looking for anything edible. To his disappointment, however, the boxes contained nothing but paper products and dry goods—napkins, paper towels, plastic forks and cups.

As Cal journeyed further aft, he detected a foul odor wafting from the storeroom area. Following his nose, the smell led him to a closed door. When opening it the pungent aroma inside hit him full force and he almost gagged. Breathing through his mouth to lessen the stench, he swept the storeroom with the penlight to find dozens of piled up garbage bags—food scraps brought down from the kitchen for offloading when at dockside. Some of the bags were oozing liquid and the fetid smell of fermenting garbage was nauseating.

Cal shut the door and was walking off when his survival training halted him. One of the first rules of survival was to eat whatever you could, whenever you could, and then move on. During his ten days of SEAL survival training, he had eaten some pretty repugnant things including worms, grubs, insects, and reptiles. But this wasn't the jungle and he wasn't *that* hungry. Besides, chow was less than four hours away.

Dismissing the gross thought, Cal started off again when he halted in his tracks.

What if something went wrong? What if he couldn't mingle into the crowd without being spotted? What if he was captured or injured?

Cal's yuck factor told him to eat later but his survival training told him otherwise. Much to his stomach-turning dislike, his training won out.

Monday 07:36 Hours – Group St. Petersburg

Ray was sitting at his desk with his hand resting on the receiver, still in awe over his ten-minute conversation with the President of the United States.

Polite but to the point, the President had expressed a twofold concern regarding Alvarez's release: the first being that it would violate U.S. policy of non-negotiation with terrorists and send the wrong message to other terrorist factions; the second being that if Alvarez managed to escape, the U.S. would be the laughing stock of the world community, which could cost his party the re-election. He was forthright about the latter being politically motivated, but maintained it would be a legitimate concern for any elected official.

Answering the President's first objection, Ray asserted that the message sent to other terrorist groups would be loud and clear: *If you screw with the U.S., you'll end up in the food chain at the bottom of the ocean.* Addressing the second concern, Ray put his military career on the line by giving the President his personal guarantee that Alvarez could not escape and, with such being the case, any reservations regarding it should not be a factor in his decision.

When Ray was done stating his case the President said nothing, testing Ray's intestinal fortitude. Silence over the telephone was awkward in any event and Ray had to restrain himself from saying something to jumpstart the conversation—any kind of babble to break the silence. After all, he was talking to the President of the United States, not some schmuck.

But, mercifully, the President's silence was brief and he resumed the discussion by pointing out the significance of Alvarez's prosecution to the *War on Drugs* campaign. He spoke of the drug-corrupt Colombian government and how the Cali cartel's "political contributions" had effectively stalled his extradition for over a decade. That if Alvarez managed to escape and get back on corrupt Colombian soil, he would never set foot in the U.S. again—meaning he would never stand trial.

The President then addressed the U.S. drug problem and the Chairman of the House Armed Services Committee's plan to build a 2,000-mile fence along the Mexican border—the gateway for drugs and illegal immigrants. After that he complained about the four-thousand-mile U.S.-Canadian border and how it was becoming as bad as the U.S.-Mexican border; that both were sieves for illegal contraband and would-be terrorists; that his administration was working tirelessly to stop the flow and serve notice to the world that the floodgates of America were officially closed.

Without taking a breath the President then switched gears and railed about the proliferation of world terrorism and how our country was a sitting duck by virtue of its under-protected borders. He talked about the World Trade Center tragedy and how it could happen again if Congress and the Special House Oversight Panel on Terrorism didn't tighten security measures and close immigration loopholes. With his voice rising in pitch, he denounced the cowardice of terrorism and vowed that Osama bin Laden and his fanatical Al-Qaeda followers would be hunted down and brought to justice.

Suddenly aware of having gotten carried away, the President stopped ranting and excused himself for allowing his passion to get the better of him. Then, in a calmer more controlled voice, he ended the conversation by reverting to the central issue at hand: Juan Carlos Alvarez.

The President warned that if Alvarez somehow escaped, the consequences would be severe and heads would roll. Not one to pull punches; he explained that the head-rolling process would start with Ray's head and continue up the chain of command. That was how the political system worked. With all the cards laid out on the table, the President then asked Ray one last time: *"Do you still want to proceed with the exchange?"*

Without fear or favor Ray answered yes, reiterating that his plan was foolproof and escape was impossible. He assured the President that in the end—though not by trial—Alvarez would indeed pay for his crimes against America by being dispatched to the bottom of the sea. And while the sacrifice of the crew was deeply regrettable, justice would be served and two hundred American lives would be saved, which would reflect favorably upon his administration and at the polls on Election Day.

Following Ray's final remarks the President put him on hold to parlay with his advisors, whom were no doubt listening the whole time. As Ray endured the nail-biting silence, he nervously tapped a pencil eraser against the desktop while staring at Mendoza's photo. Minutes later the President came back on the line and formally authorized the exchange, then rambled on about the complete faith Washington placed in him and so on and so forth. But by that time Ray's focus had shifted to the task at hand and the President's gratuitous remarks were lost in a vortex of thought. Once the Prez had lavished enough praise, there was a sharp click and he was gone.

As the President's approval sank in, Ray teemed inside with both excitement and dread. He was glad the President found merit in his plan and he was flattered by Washington's confidence in his ability to carry it out. But, by the same token, if something went wrong—which could easily occur in an engagement like this—the President's words still rang in his ears.

"Heads would roll."

Monday 07:45 Hours – The "Majestic Star"

Armed with the Glock, Skip and Neal exited the cabin for the short trek to the wheelhouse. Before going inside they peered through the open doorway to find the wheelhouse deserted except for Mohammad. He was sitting in Skip's white leather helmseat with an AK across his lap, gripping the padded armrests and swiveling side-to-side with a silly grin. To Skip, it looked like the towel-head was playing Captain Kirk on *Star Trek*.

The first time Skip called Mo a *towel-head* to his face, the indignant Arab pointed out that the Muslim headdress was made from linen or a sheet—not a towel. Standing corrected, Skip then dubbed him *sheet-head*, which was made funnier because Mohammad never got the jest of it. Still, from the way the crewmen snickered about it, Mo knew it was a put-down and swore revenge. Someday the infidels would pay for their transgressions, to be sure. Allah himself, the Supreme Being, would see to it. *Allahu Akbar!*

When the Americans barged through the doorway without warning, Mo stopped swiveling and his hands found the AK-47. But before he could get up, the captain was right in his face—demanding to know the whereabouts of the abducted females. Paying the infidel no heed, Mohammad blew him off by screwing the helmseat around and turning his back. In no mood for playing Muslim mind games, Skip grabbed the helmseat and spun it back around, then pressed the Arab harder. When Mohammad still snubbed him, Skip shook the chair and that's when Mo lost it. Flying into a cursing rage, he sprang to his feet and prodded Skip backward with the barrel of his rifle.

Still spoiling for a fight, Neal entered the fracas and a three-way pushing match began. Finding himself outnumbered, Mohammad rammed the gun barrel into Neal's midsection and jacked a shell into the chamber as if going to fire. The trigger-happy move frightened Skip, who was looking around the room for a possible weapon when his eyes landed on Mendoza.

Casting a steamy stare, the Zeta bossman was standing in the doorway larger than life. Behind him were the two gunmen that had jumped Neal outside Skip's cabin. When Skip saw a wad of gauze taped over Stan's nose and the beginnings of two black eyes, he felt a flicker of satisfaction in spite of the fix they were in.

When Mendoza gave the word, the men split up and charged toward the Americans. In one fell swoop Stan grabbed Skip in a crushing bear hug while the ponytailed Mexican bulldozed Neal backwards with the broadside of his rifle. At the same time Neal's back met the wall, Skip was body-slammed against the wall next to him—his hat toppling to the floor.

When Skip bounced off the wall, Stan gave him a bruising get-even body shot to the ribs that curled Skip over. As Skip wheezed for air and hugged his rib cage, Stan straightened him up by pressing his AK across Skip's throat and mashing his head against the wall.

"No more trouble, Capitán!" Mendoza pointed angrily at Stan's broken nose. *"¡No mas!"*

The pressure from the rifle closed Skip's windpipe and his head swam with dizziness. Seconds later his peripheral vision narrowed until Gold-Tooth was standing at the end of a long pulsating tunnel yelling something indistinguishable. As Mendoza's shouting resonated in Skip's head, Stan bared his gapped teeth and pressed harder. In Skip's asphyxiated state, all the leering and yelling and cursing swirled through his half-conscious mind like a runaway carousel.

As Mendoza ranted and raved, a halo of light formed around his head and his actions decelerated like a slow motion movie. Simultaneously his voice deepened like a recording on the wrong speed. Then the corona began to fade and the tunnel contracted smaller and smaller until only encompassing Gold-Tooth's scathing face. His insect eyes looked voracious—like those of a praying mantis—and his nose had blossomed to an outsized proportion. The rest of his face shrank away cartoonishly as if appearing through a fisheye lens.

Skip tried his best to remain lucid but his oxygen-starved brain succumbed. As the caricature of Mendoza's face dissolved into nothingness, his eyelids fluttered shut and he sank into the depths of unconsciousness. Losing all hold on the present, his light-as-a-feather body floated dreamlike to another place and time....

It was a crisp sunny day and he and Kathy were on a sailboat with sails set. Kathy was clad in a colorful nylon jacket and wearing reflective sunglasses. She said something that he couldn't quite make out and then flashed him a bright smile. As she did so, the wind blew a wisp of hair across her face and she smoothed it back with her hand. Then, lovingly, she scooted closer to him and draped an arm over his shoulders. Smiling, he gave her an affectionate pat on the leg and gazed up at the wind-filled sails, then zipped up his jacket against the cool air.

When the boat sliced through a rolling breaker, a spray of cold saltwater sprinkled their faces and they both gasped laughingly at its chilliness. It was a good day and when Kathy smiled at him, his own image grinned back at him in her mirrored sunglasses. He felt warm all over, content, and he lolled his head against her shoulder.

As the sailboat skimmed across the sparkling blue-green water, Kathy toyed with the back of his hair, gently twirling it at the nape of his neck. His scalp tingled with each twirl and his eyes closed in slumberous delight. The sun felt warm on his face and he was incredibly relaxed, wanting nothing more than to cuddle up in her arms and sleep—just quietly go to sleep... .

At that moment Stan released his chokehold and unsheathed the razor -edged jambiya. When Skip faltered forward, Stan drove his shoulder into Skip's midsection and wedged him against the wall. The sudden jolt brought Skip around and his starving lungs automatically gasped for air. As he coughed and wheezed, Stan's image shimmered in and out of focus and the world around him spun like a merry-go-round possessed.

When his coughing fit subsided and his head partly cleared, Skip found himself back on the *Majestic Star* with a curved steel blade pressed against his left cheek.

~~~~~~~~~~

After rummaging through the rancid garbage in the storeroom, Cal managed to pilfer a few leftover dinner rolls and some saltines still in their plastic wrappers—definitely not worth the gagging effort. The rest of the food scraps were rotten and unfit to eat. After finding nothing in the second storeroom, he backtracked toward the cargo bay to fetch the radio. It was approaching 08:00 and he was anxious to talk to Bluebird.

As Cal retraced his steps, the putrid smell of decaying seafood lingered in his nostrils. It was so pungent he could taste it, making his floaty stomach feel even queasier. Fate, it seemed, was not without a sense of irony. The idea of a middle-aged attorney picking through garbage for something to eat struck his alter persona as amusing—like maybe it was a payback for all the scumbags he had gotten off the hook during his thirty-year law career. Karma.

Tired of the same old dead-end job? Tired of being underpaid and unappreciated by your employer? Then call now and Cal Stringer will show you how to go from a successful lawyer to a garbage-picking stowaway in just one week. He did it and so can you! Call 1-800-IAM-NUTS now for more information. Operators are standing by.

Amazed that he could find humor at such a moment, Cal ducked behind the crate and turned on the handheld radio. While waiting for eight o'clock, he unwrapped a twin-pack of saltines and popped one into his mouth. He had always heard that the *soda* in crackers was a useful

WIRED

remedy for an upset stomach. If that were the case, it would take a barrel full of them to quell his right now, which was making peculiar gurgling noises.

Monday 07:48 Hours – Group St. Petersburg

When Chief William Bloyd arrived at the admiral's office, he stopped in the hallway outside and rapped on the open door. The admiral was talking on the telephone and when he looked up, he motioned for the chief to come in. Nodding, Bloyd entered the office, removed his hat, and stood at parade rest in front of his superior's desk.

"Good morning, Chief." Ray hung up the phone and rose. "Your timing is perfect. Washington just gave us the green light for Operation Checkmate."

When the admiral stood, the chief's back tightened out of habit but he held back a salute. Upon assuming command of the Seventh, Ray had officially designated the workplace a *"no-hat, no-salute zone"* so as to eliminate time wasted saluting. He believed there was a time and place for military etiquette, but the workplace wasn't one of them. Chief Bloyd, on the other hand, was from the old school and a stickler for protocol. After decades of military life, saluting came automatic. So to break the chief from it, Ray had embarrassed him several times in Miami by not saluting him back—leaving him hanging with everybody watching.

"Thanks for getting here on such short notice, Chief." When Ray extended his hand, the chief loosened his poker-stiff stance—though just barely—and gave Ray's hand a firm handshake. "How's everything in Miami?"

"Quiet without you there, Admiral." Like any good soldier, the chief carried respect for his commanding officer—especially this one. "All the action's up here."

Master Chief Bloyd was D7's Telecommunications Specialist Chief and he had served under Ray for twelve years. Besides heading up communications for *Operation Checkmate*, his electronic wizardry could be called into play should Mendoza balk at swapping the passengers without first speaking to Alvarez.

"That's a fact, Chief, and the action's about to heat up. We're up

313

against a noon deadline. Ready to get started?"

"Aye, sir." The chief started to put his hat on before catching himself. "Just point me towards the radio room."

Monday 07:49 Hours – The "Majestic Star"

The whites of Skip's eyes bulged as they strained downward at the razor-sharp blade. His head was pinned against the wall and he couldn't budge a centimeter without risking the blade going deeper. When he felt the skin break, he flinched against the sting and glared bitterly into Stan's Arabic eyes.

Skip felt degraded—defiled. Being forced to knuckle under to the enemy was humiliating enough, but getting carved up alive aboard his own vessel was a violation against his very person. He longed to give his captors hell, to curse them a blue streak; but his crushed larynx burned like hellfire and would only eke out a wimpy screech.

"¡No más la desobediencia!" Mendoza yelled in Skip's face. *"¡Comportarse usted!"*

Skip didn't know if it was the tooth decay or the thought of exchanging air with the greasy bastard, but he was instantly sickened. Unable to speak and feeling like he might puke, Skip held his breath and braced himself for more halitosis.

"¡Traiga el americano!" Mendoza ordered, exiting the wheelhouse. "Bring capitán outside!"

Monday 07:50 Hours – Group St. Petersburg

When Ray and Chief Bloyd walked into the radio room, a petty officer was delivering the Marine Broadcast—a daily radio announcement giving sea conditions, tide and weather information, hazards to navigation, and other boater information.

As the Coastie spoke into the desk mike, Chief Bloyd quietly slipped into an unoccupied workstation adjacent to him. Reading from a data terminal, the officer's eyes shifted to the chief's face and then back to the computer screen without skipping a beat. As he recited the day's tide information, the chief perused the stacked reel-to-reel recorders recessed within a vertical storage cabinet adjoining the workstation.

In order to preserve emergency SAR Cases—*Search And Rescue*—for later evaluation, all Coast Guard stations were required to archive 24-hour tape recordings of Channel 16 radio traffic. To comply with this regulation, the station was equipped with two reel-to-reel recorders patched directly into the marine radios.

Being that Group St. Petersburg was a regional hub for West Central Florida, the station was outfitted with the latest telecommunications equipment. In addition to radios, radar, and electronic charting systems, the station had uplinks to NOAA's satellite server and its 1200 global weather stations as well as the National Weather Service's orbiting weather satellites used for storm tracking and predicting aviation weather. The advanced tactical computer system also had uplinks for receiving government-restricted data from a range of military spy satellites.

Chief Bloyd was tinkering with the Doppler DDF600 Direction Finder when Ray tapped him on the shoulder. Knowing the chief's pash for electronics, Ray grinned at the enamored expression on his face.

"Sorry to interrupt you, Chief, but once the petty officer finishes the marine broadcast, I've got a private radio transmission to make. While I'm on the radio, take him for a coffee break and I'll meet you in the break room when I'm done. By then the ensign should be here from Sand Key."

"Aye, sir."

Tearing himself away from the console, Chief Bloyd rose and waited for the officer to finish his broadcast. When the Coastie signed off, he looked up with curiosity at the visiting master chief standing over him. Without explanation the chief nodded toward the exit and motioned for the Coastie to follow. Giving Ray a questioning look, the petty officer rose and trailed Chief Bloyd out the door.

Once alone, Ray settled behind the desk mike and changed the radio frequency to Channel 12. While waiting for Stringer's hail, he debated whether to warn Stringer about the ship's imminent fate or to keep his mouth shut until all the passengers were off.

SEAL or otherwise, the word "expendable" carried ominous connotations, even for the most hardened soldier. It entailed the sort of finality that all fighting men understood but seldom discussed. No combatant, not even the most gung-ho or hardcore, wanted to sacrifice a fellow comrade nor wind up expendable themselves—though that infinite risk came with the profession.

Would Stringer act prematurely to save his hide and that of his brother-in-law?

With doubt still playing on his mind, Stringer's voice came over the airwaves.

~~~~~~~~~~~

"Bluebird, this is White Knight. Do you copy?"

"Roger, Stringer. Go ahead, over."

"What's the game plan? Over."

Ray hesitated while still thinking, then pressed the microphone key. "The officials have approved the match—Black King gets White Queen and her worker Pawns. But there's one catch. White Queen must be sacrificed by nightfall, with or without White Knight and worker Pawns. Sorry, Stringer, but the game's gotta end tonight—one way or the other. There's no other option. Copy?"

There was a pause, and then: "Parameters understood. Do what you gotta do. What time does the game start? Over."

"Soon, but an exact time hasn't been established yet. Once the game starts and two hundred Pawns are off the board, White Knight may enter play—but not one minute before. Naturally, the officials aren't privy to White Knight's entry so that player must remain anonymous. Copy?"

"Roger. Under the radar—all the way."

"When the match is over tonight, I'll do my best to give you and your teammates a *lift* home. But I can't promise anything at this point—too many variables. Roger?"

"Understood. A *lift* would be much obliged, but if you can't make it we'll find another way home...I hope." Cal's voice trailed off. "By the way, Bluebird, the home team here appreciates the straight shooting. Operating in the blind really sucks. Over."

"Well, you gotta know the rules to play by 'em. You *will* play by the rules we discussed. Roger?"

"Roger. White Knight will stand down until two hundred Pawns are out of play."

"Glad to hear it. Anything else new to report? Any more word from your brother-in-law?"

Cal was taken aback that Hanna knew of their relationship. "Uh-h-h, no," he stuttered, "but I'm scheduled to meet with him again at 11:00 hours. The team captain is a little worse for wear, but fit to play. You may want to relay that to his teammate in Clearwater. Over."

"Understood." There was a brief period of dead air while Ray groped for some parting remarks. Under normal circumstances he would have given Stringer some strong words of encouragement before signing off— a military pep talk of sorts. But these weren't ordinary circumstances and nothing encouraging came to mind.

What parting words do you give someone whom you've just possibly condemned? What pleasantries do you offer a person whose head is in the guillotine and you're the executioner—Have a Nice Day?

"Well, good luck with the match today," Ray fumbled. "If the home team prevails, we'll be having a helluva victory celebration tonight. You're invited. Be sure to keep us posted on the game's progress. We'll be listening up on this frequency. If nothing further, Bluebird out."

"See you tonight, Bluebird. I'm buying the beer. White Knight out."

Feeling much older than his years, Ray released the microphone key and pushed the desk mike away. When he stood up, the bones in his back creaked and the stiffness brought a frown.

"And may God help us," Ray muttered. "May God help us all."

Monday 08:01 Hours – The "Majestic Star"

Mohammad and Stan dragged Skip from the wheelhouse, leaving the ponytailed gunman behind to guard Neal. Once outside on the catwalk, the Arabs pinned Skip against an exterior wall a few feet away from Mendoza, who was hunched over the pipe railing facing the bow.

"This is on your head, Capitán!" Mendoza whirled and pointed an accusing finger between Skip's eyes. "YOUR HEAD!"

Skip's body tightened when he saw Mendoza holding the detonator. It tightened more when he saw a writhing female passenger lashed to a stanchion on the foredeck wearing an orange lifejacket laden with C-4.

WIRED

Her wrists were bleeding from straining against the ropes and her cloth blindfold was wet from hysterical bawling. The only identifiable feature Skip could make out was a clump of tawny blonde hair pulled back and clipped in a short ponytail.

The girl's looming death flooded Skip with panic and he made a desperate bid to break free, thrashing his muscular frame to-and-fro and side-to-side like a bucking bronco. He could not—*would not*—allow this to happen even if it meant forfeiting his own life. If he could free up his right hand and reach the Glock, he would kill all three gunmen or go to his death trying.

But, in his weakened physical state, Skip was no match for the stronger men and his flailing went for naught. Exasperating him further was the fact that he couldn't even give them a good swearing. Every time he swallowed or tried to talk, a burning-scratchy-ticklish sensation in his throat brought tears to his eyes.

Once the capitán was brought under control, Mendoza walked the detonator toward him with a cold calculated look. As he drew closer, Stan seized Skip's hand and roughly separated his forefinger from the others, then forcibly dragged Skip's finger toward the flashing button.

At recognizing their murderous intent, Skip pulled to retract his hand but the burly Arab held on tight. Then Mohammad joined in—with obvious pleasure—seizing Skip's other arm and twisting it behind Skip's back until something cracked. A bolt of pain ripped through Skip's shoulder blade and he cried out in suffering, but he was determined not to partake in their maniacal little game.

But, in spite of Skip's resistance and gutsy determination, in the end he was helplessly overpowered. When his straining fingertip met the blinking button, a jarring explosion shook the core of the ship, drowning out his bitter cry of denunciation.

~~~~~~~~~~~

Cal had barely switched off the handheld VHF when a shuddering blast roared through the hollows of the ship, causing his ears to blare with a shrill ringing. Simultaneously the deck tremored beneath his feet and dusty debris sprinkled down from crevices overhead.

318

WIRED

What the hell was happening? Were the terrorists blowing the ship!?

Half expecting a succession of explosions to follow, Cal dropped onto his stomach and covered his head with his arms—awaiting his inexorable fate.

~~~~~~~~~~

When Neal heard the deafening explosion, he deflected the gun barrel aimed at him and seized the rifle with both hands. In a deadly test of strength, he and the ponytailed Mexican pushed, pulled, twisted, and shoved for sole possession of the AK-47.

~~~~~~~~~~

Still pinned against the wall, Skip stared at the mangled aftermath in paralyzed shock. The white paint of the foredeck was now slick with the shimmering red goop of what used to be a human being. When he couldn't bear the sight of it any longer, he tore his eyes away and tried to blot out the after-images. But the flashbacks kept coming—the blonde's hysterical face while squirming to free herself; her shrill screechy scream just before the explosion; the explosive gray cloud of cyclonite laced with the reddish mist of atomized innards; of a woman lost in her prime— disintegrated, blown to kingdom come, murdered before his very eyes.

The monstrous way she had been killed along with its startling unexpectedness had siphoned all the fight left in him. Not only had he been forced to witness her death, he had been an unwilling participant— making him feel guilty, beaten, conquered, subjugated, and terribly sick to his stomach.

When Mendoza gave the sign, the Arabs released Skip's arms and Stan disappeared inside the wheelhouse. Weak-kneed from shock, Skip slid down the wall until the seat of his pants met the steel mesh of the catwalk. With his legs splayed outward, he leaned against the wall with Mohammad's rifle aimed at his head. That's when he felt the vomit coming.

Rolling over onto all fours, Skip puked through the open latticework on quivering arms. Once his stomach emptied, he slumped back against

319

the wall—coughing and wiping his mouth with the back of his hand.

Although the woman's death wasn't essentially his doing, he still felt at fault for breaking Stan's nose. He should have exercised more restraint. The hotheaded act had pushed Mendoza over the edge. As ship captain, his actions had a direct bearing on the passengers. Case in point: the blonde's retaliatory death. It was cause and effect, pure and simple.

In a screwy roundabout way, Gold-Tooth had been right. Her death *was* on his head.

~~~~~~~~~~

While Skip wrangled with his guilt, Stan and the Mexican emerged from the wheelhouse dragging Neal by the arms. After unceremoniously plunking him down next to Skip, they backed away and joined Mohammad with raised weapons. Neal was out cold and the back of his head was bleeding badly from being whacked from behind.

"*¡La vez próxima mato a cinco mujeres!*" Mendoza held up five fingers before Skip's eyes. "Next time five females die! *¿Entiendes?*" With a snide look of superiority, he planted his hands on his hips. "*¡Cinco!*"

~~~~~~~~~~

When no more explosions followed the first, Cal uncovered his head and shot to his feet. Unsure if he should wait there or go charging up the steps, he turned off the Uzi's safety switch and raced to the bottom of the stairs. Standing motionless, he peered upward through the dislodged motes of dust particles swirling in the slanted sunlight.

Deciding to go topside for a look, Cal was taking the steel steps two at a time when Hanna's words came to mind.

"*This person must be discreet and extremely careful not to endanger the passengers*"..."*Lots of folks could get hurt—women and children*"..."*We don't need any more bodies washing up on our shores— bad for tourism*"..."*Once all two hundred Pawns are off the board, White Knight may enter play—but not one minute before*"..."*You will play by the rules that we discussed. Roger?*"

WIRED

~~~~~~~~~~

Once Skip's vocal chords had healed enough to get a few things off his chest, he unloaded on his captors.

"MURDERER!" he croaked at Mendoza. "WOMAN KILLER!" With the same unmitigated disgust, he lashed out at the others. "COWARDS! ALL OF YOU!" He pointed his finger at Mendoza. "*You're* responsible for this, mister—not me! It's on YOUR head and I'm gonna kill you for it. You hear me?"

Pretending to be scared stiff, Mendoza looked bug-eyed at his men while chewing timidly at his fingernails. When all four broke out in bawdy laughter, it added more fuel to the firestorm inside Skip. Their glaring indifference to suffering and their willingness to inflict it subverted every rule that civilized people lived by.

"Go ahead and laugh, assholes, but you're lookin' at the man who's gonna kill you. And I'm gonna do it with my bare hands." Skip balled his fists and snarled at them. "*These* hands!!"

The strain on Skip's larynx proved too much and his voice suddenly went out. While he wasn't done making threats by a long shot, he was forced to give it a rest. As he glared at his antagonists, he was tempted to go for the Glock—to banish the foreign invaders, to protect the tribal women, to kill or be killed. Admittedly, it was a stupid impulse because he had three AKs aimed at his head. If he sneezed the wrong way he was a dead man. Yet, a primal voice from within kept egging him on, emboldening him, proclaiming that with a little luck he could slay two of them before they blew his brains out, leaving two less invaders to threaten the tribe.

Fortunately, for Skip, the beast within didn't override his intellect and his commonsense prevailed. Getting his macho-self killed at this point would accomplish nothing. Still, once his blood got heated, it was slow to cool. And now that he was armed with no civilian bystanders to worry about, it was punishing for him to sit idly by while lives hung in the balance—female lives at that.

This was true, of course, but Skip had something else holding him back—an ulterior reason. The fear that Gold-Tooth might survive a shootout after he got himself foolishly killed. That was a risk Skip wasn't willing to take. Before Captain Skip Myles met his Maker, Mendoza would be sitting next to Satan where he belonged. Skip would personally see to it.

So, as paradoxical as it would seem, Skip's deep-seated hatred for the man was the single most thing keeping both of them alive—at least for now.

Monday 08:05 Hours – Group St. Petersburg

Chief Bloyd and the Cuban were gathered around Ray's desk in a round-table discussion when the group commander barged into the office.

"Pardon the interruption, Admiral, but one of our spotters just reported an explosion aboard the Majestic Star."

The three men exchanged stunned looks, the chief uttered "uh-oh", and Ray sprang from his chair. As the trio advanced down the hallway en route for the radio room, Ray's mind was locked in overdrive.

What the hell was happening? Why was there an explosion with four hours left until the deadline? What was Mendoza up to? Did it have anything to do with Stringer?

Upon entry, Ray relieved the two on-duty watchstanders and ordered the Cuban to hail up the *Majestic Star*. He wanted some answers and he wanted them now.

As the chief and ensign manned their workstations, Ray paced behind them with a fire in his eyes that all but scorched the path in front of him.

Monday 08:06 Hours – The "Majestic Star"

As Neal's limp body sagged against Skip, blood dribbled from his head onto Skip's shoulder. Neal's bleeding didn't overly concern Skip because profuse bleeding often accompanied a scalp injury. What concerned him most was the jarring head trauma Neal had received. More likely than not, he was suffering from a concussion.

When Skip looked up and saw the gleam in Stan's eye, it erased any stray feelings of guilt he may have been harboring for breaking the Arab's nose. Skip felt so much contempt for the man, so much hatred, he wanted

322

to do it again and again until there was no nose left—*slam crunch, slam crunch.* However, Skip knew his revenge would have to wait. For the sake of the other females, he had to put his enmity aside and dissuade Mendoza from committing more murder.

"Look," he said to Mendoza, "you gave your word yesterday that there wouldn't be anymore executions. If you kill any more women, the passengers will revolt and the next time I won't stop 'em. Without hope, Americans will fight back—like the passengers did on United Flight #93. Remember that? The 9/11 plane that crashed in Pennsylvania?" Mendoza nodded yes. "Is that what you want? To martyr yourselves for Alvarez? Why? Do you think he gives a good goddamn about you and your men out here?" When Mendoza didn't respond, Skip answered for him. "Hell no, he don't and you know it."

While Mendoza appeared to be thinking, Skip traced the cut on his cheek with a finger. After examining his fingertip for blood, he shot Stan a dirty look and wiped his finger on a pant leg before resuming.

"We're just about out of food and our water supply will run dry sometime today. We're pretty much up shit creek. If you can talk the Coast Guard into tradin' Alvarez for passengers, you'd better do it. Otherwise there's gonna be a mutiny and a lot of people will die—includin' you. Take my advice: get Alvarez and haul ass. Take this ship to Mexico or Colombia or wherever you want to go. You can have it. ¿Comprende?"

Skip didn't know if the Coasties had offered to trade Alvarez yet, or even if they were going to for that matter, but he wanted to underscore its logic in case they did—to plant a seed that taking the ship and making a run for it with Alvarez was a viable option.

The minute Skip finished talking, the sound of the Coast Guard hailing the *Majestic Star* came through the open doorway. After a brief listen, Mendoza winked at Skip cleverly and strutted inside the wheelhouse with his chest puffed out. After propping his AK against the console, he dropped into Skip's helmseat and clasped his hands behind his head. With the radio beckoning, he swiveled from side-to-side with a self-satisfied smirk. After letting the Coasties stew a bit longer, he picked up the microphone and began talking in Spanish.

While Mendoza sparred with the Coast Guard, Skip shoved Neal's body off him and stood up with the help of the wall behind him. He was still weak and wobbly and his parched mouth tasted of lingering vomit, but he had sat on his backside long enough. Neal was coming around and Skip didn't want him causing any more trouble.

Leaning against the wall for support, Skip put his hat back on and neatened up his rumpled uniform. Like a magnet, his eyes went straight to the viscous red goop now coating the foredeck. The soul-wrenching sight laid his emotions to waste and a streak of guilt ran him through like a samurai sword. A human being had died—a female—and he had been instrumental in her death.

As Skip tore his eyes away, he caught a fleeting glimpse of someone standing in the shadows of the stairwell leading down to the cargo hold— or at least thought he did. *Cal?*

But when Skip looked again, nobody was there.

Monday 08:11 Hours – Group St. Petersburg

While the Cuban haggled with Mendoza, Ray paced the length of the radio room, taking long thoughtful strides. As he walked back and forth, his eyes alternated between the stretch of floor ahead of him and the back of the ensign's head.

The more Ray listened to Mendoza's rantings, the uneasier he felt. Besides coming across as hostile and belligerent, the man sounded unbalanced. At one point during the talks, the ensign rolled his eyes at Chief Bloyd and rotated his forefinger in a tight circle near his temple, suggesting the Mexican was cuckoo. This wound the spring inside Ray even tighter, redoubling his frequency of strides.

A short time later the ensign signed off and swiveled his seat around to face Ray. The brevity of the radio exchange along with the Cuban's somber look told Ray the news wasn't good.

"Mendoza said that one female passenger was detonated as a practice run for the noontime executions."

"FEMALE?...PRACTICE RUN?!" Ray's stomach sank like a cast-iron anchor. "We still have four goddamn hours left!!" He smashed his fist on the laminated worktop. "So now he's killing women, huh? That's BULLSHIT!!!!" As Ray cursed, the image of Stringer and his Uzi popped

into his head. "Did Mendoza mention any other reason for doing it? Anything at all?"

"No, sir. He just kept reciting a saying they have in Mexico. Loosely translated, it means: *it's twelve o'clock somewhere.* You know," the Cuban clarified, "like an excuse to drink alcohol before noon?" The needless explanation annoyed Ray and the look on his face showed it. "Anyway, after that he kept muttering in a gruff pirate-type voice: *'Thar she blows! Thar she blows!'* Then he'd go, *'BOOM!'* and cackle insanely until all laughed out. The guy's a sick twisted freak, sir. A real nutjob."

Monday 08:12 Hours – The "Majestic Star"

After risking a scant look outside, Cal paced the cargo bay with his brain assimilating probabilities like a mainframe computer.

What was going on? Why was someone just exploded? Did it have anything to do with Hanna's offer to trade Alvarez? Could more executions follow? Might Skip be next?

This onrush of uncertainty made Cal pace faster and faster until he was scampering between the stacked boxes like a mouse in a maze—on Prozac. While frenetically navigating the cardboard maze, he sized up the situation as he knew it.

He was facing eight paramilitary-trained killers...the madman in charge was blowing hostages to smithereens...the U.S. military was planning to nuke the ship by nightfall...if Hanna couldn't airlift them before the ship's destruction, he and Skip would have to sprout wings and fly off this mother-freaking tub. If not, they would be dodging Tomahawk missiles from that Navy Destroyer anchored somewhere out in the Gulf.

Reminiscent of soldiers past, Cal had to wonder who the enemy was.

Monday 08:53 Hours – Group St. Petersburg

Ray emerged from the briefing room flanked by a delegation of senior representatives from the Air Force, the Navy's Atlantic Fleet, and the combined forces of the United States Central Command (CENTCOM) headquartered at MacDill Air Force Base in Tampa.

As the task force commanders went their separate ways, each bore their respective assignments for both *Operation Checkmate* and *Operation Stalemate*. Although Ray wasn't in favor of a preemptive strike, he was prepared to order a full-scale amphibious and air assault if another female passenger was lost. Enough was enough.

Chief Bloyd was waiting for Ray outside in the hallway and the two talked privately while walking shoulder to shoulder to the radio room. Their next move would depend on Mendoza's reaction to the pitch he was now getting from the Cuban. If Mendoza readily agreed to the exchange, *Operation Checkmate* could begin right away. If he rejected it, or if he insisted on speaking with Alvarez first, it would mean getting a later start.

Mendoza would be suspicious at first, but Ray was hopeful that the lure of liberating Alvarez would override his doubt. Alvarez was the most powerful Mafioso in the Western Hemisphere and winning his release would greatly elevate Mendoza's gangland status. Would it be inducement enough? Only time would tell. Given the Mexican's bizarre and erratic behavior, his reaction was impossible to predict.

Monday 08:55 Hours – The "Majestic Star"

Back inside the wheelhouse, Skip was perched on Mohammad's barstool sipping water from a paper cone. As he forced small sips over the knot in his throat, Neal was cleansing his bloody cheek with a wet paper towel. While this went on, Mendoza talked into the microphone from Skip's helmseat—swiveling left and right and occasionally full circle.

Skip had doctored Neal's head injury earlier and now it was his turn. But despite Neal's fussing to sit still, Skip kept shrinking away—grumbling it was only a scratch and he didn't need a nursemaid. Luckily, the cut was indeed superficial and had stopped bleeding on its own.

When Neal unintentionally pressed too hard and Skip yelped out loud, Stan rejoiced with a loud snort. Angered by the heckling, Skip's face flushed red and he issued Stan a warning.

"Go ahead and gloat—*Ahab*. Next time, it's *my* turn and it ain't gonna be a flesh wound like this." Skip gestured at his cheek. "When I'm done with your rag ass, you'll be singing Allah's praises in soprano."

Stan snorted again but Skip didn't give him the satisfaction of a response. Instead, he thanked Neal for tending him and slid off the barstool. The strength had returned to his legs and he wanted more H2O. It helped lubricate his tender vocal chords and was soothing to his throat.

Despite his most conscientious eavesdropping, Skip hadn't understood a word between Mendoza and the negotiator except for an occasional mention of *"el Majestic Star."* For the umpteenth time since Thursday, Skip felt like kicking himself in the butt for cutting Mr. Holloway's Spanish classes in high school.

While the nosy capitán refilled his paper cone, Mendoza glanced sidelong at him and spun the helmseat away, then continued to negotiate-bargain-haggle in rapid-fire Spanish. As he jabbered away, Skip glared at the back of his head and wished for something hard to break over it. A short time later Mendoza quit talking and placed the microphone on its hook. As he exited the wheelhouse, he slung the AK over his shoulder and gave Skip a snide grin.

As Skip watched him through the window, Mendoza lit a cigarette and propped his boot on the catwalk railing. Then he threw his greasy head back and expelled a cloud of tobacco smoke at the sky.

He's killing time, Skip thought. *Waiting for a Coast Guard response.*

"Vessel Majestic Star, the vessel Majestic Star. This is the United States Coast Guard hailing. Over." Hearkened by the hail, Mendoza pivoted his head toward the sound. "El buque Majestic Star, el buque Majestic Estrella. Esta es la Guardia Costera de los Estados Unidos. Contestar por favor."

Seemingly uninterested, Mendoza rested his back against the rail and took another casual puff. As the bilingual hail repeated itself, Skip looked at Gold-Tooth, then at the radio, then back outside—wondering if he intended to answer. After letting the Coast Guard sweat a while longer, the Mexican flicked his cigarette over the side and strolled inside at a snail's gait. As he sat down in the leather helmseat, he gave Skip another snide look and swiveled the chair the other way.

Over the next several minutes Mendoza and the Coast Guard quarreled back and forth. At times the talks became heated and Mendoza shouted his point across. At other times his voice sounded strange and creepy, followed by a fiendish laugh. Skip didn't have to know the language to understand he was making murderous threats.

Then, unexpectedly, as if it were his final word on the subject, the

WIRED

Zeta shrieked into the microphone: *"¡Los americanos son cerdos estúpidos!"* and stormed outside. His loudness practically rattled the windows and it startled everybody in the wheelhouse.

With the Cuban's voice ever beckoning, Mendoza fired up another cigarette and squinted at the skyline. In peering closer, Skip detected a subtle smile on the Mexican's lips, as if he were inwardly pleased about how things were going. At noting this, Skip smiled too—on the inside.

The fish was rising to the bait.

Monday 09:15 Hours – Group St. Petersburg

Ray had been standing over the ensign's shoulder for the past twenty minutes with his ear tuned to the speaker. Mendoza was driving a harder bargain than hoped for. While this wasn't terribly surprising, it was a sticking point that would cost valuable time.

Ray's basic strategy had been threefold—to convince Mendoza that Alvarez had already approved the trade-off; to persuade him that Alvarez was adamant about an immediate departure for Colombia; to stonewall, pressure, intimidate, or otherwise trick Mendoza into proceeding with the exchange without the direct involvement of Alvarez. All easier said than done.

Mendoza had been receptive to the exchange but had stuck to his guns about speaking with Alvarez prior to initiating any trade. Anticipating this objection beforehand, Ray had drafted several canned excuses for the Cuban to fall back on during negotiations.

Using canned excuse #1, the ensign told Mendoza that Alvarez had agreed to the exchange and was most anxious to leave U.S. waters. Attaching urgency to it, he added that Señor Alvarez was most emphatic about an early-morning departure—noon at the very latest.

When Mendoza still balked and demanded to talk to Alvarez, the Cuban countered with canned excuse #2: that he was unable to bring Alvarez to the microphone at the present time because he was being held incommunicado elsewhere.

When Mendoza grew more agitated and pressed harder, the ensign fell back on excuse #3, claiming he would make an effort to locate Alvarez and seek permission to put him on the radio, but with all the

WIRED

bureaucracy involved it would consume valuable time that would be better spent refueling and resupplying the ship in view of March's shorter daylight hours.

Mendoza had paused promisingly at this last excuse and for a moment the Cuban thought he might cave in; that the indecision of obeying versus disobeying the express wishes of the implacable drug boss had stretched his nerve to the breaking point. However, the ensign's hopes were dashed when the quick-tempered Zeta swore at the top of his lungs and broke off communication. After a period of trying to reestablish radio contact, it became obvious that Mendoza wasn't answering.

"He's not answering our hails, Admiral."

"Yeah, sounds like it," Ray answered dismally. "What exactly did he say?"

"He said that he and his Zetas had all come prepared to die and they didn't care how many others died with them. That we had until noon to deliver Alvarez or at 12:01 he would detonate another female passenger and one every thirty minutes thereafter—after his men had their way with them."

"*WHAT!?*" Ray's eyes widened and then narrowed, demanding explanation. "So blowing them to bits isn't punishment enough. Now the Zetas are gonna rape them first! Is that it?"

"That's what he's threatening, sir. After that, he started talking in his silly pirate voice again, saying: *'Thar she blows!'* followed by that lewd laugh of his. His last words referred to us as, uh, *'stupid American pigs.'* Sir."

"Oh, really?" Ray stiffened. "Well, we'll see about *that*. Keep trying to raise him." With a scowl on his face, he turned to Chief Bloyd. "Looks like it's time for Plan B. Wait here and I'll be right back."

Ray stamped down the hallway with his rancor on the rise. When he rounded a corner, he nearly collided with a lieutenant coming from the other direction. People were bustling all about the place and every phone in the stationhouse seemed to be ringing. Bad news traveled fast and clearly the word was out about the second explosion.

"I'm not here, people!" Ray reminded anyone listening. "No phone calls. No exceptions."

The ensign had done a commendable job in laying the groundwork

329

for the exchange but Mendoza wasn't budging without speaking to Alvarez, who would *never* go along with it. Nonetheless, there was more than one way to skin a cat. With a little ingenuity and the chief's hi-tech know-how, they may pull the wool over Mendoza's eyes.

Once inside his office, Ray went straight to a row of fireproof file cabinets and removed a gray metal box labeled: "JUAN CARLOS ALVAREZ: PERSONAL EFFECTS." Sitting down, he dumped its contents on his desktop and sifted through the belongings. There was a thick gold necklace, a Rolex, a gold wedding band, a leather wallet, a phony passport, an expensive alligator belt, and a small envelope containing loose change and breath mints.

Ray opened the wallet and counted three thousand dollars in crisp one hundred dollar bills. The only other items inside were two photographs and a forged U.S. driver's license. The wallet was noticeably absent of credit cards, which was of no surprise. When one travels abroad with suitcases full of hundred-dollar bills, it tends to negate any need for credit.

Ray removed the two photographs and studied them front and back. One was of an elderly Hispanic couple—probably Alvarez's parents—while the other was a studio portrait of his wife and two children. On the flipside of the latter, written in a feminine hand was: *Maria, Pablo, and Rosa—We Love You—July 14th, 2010*. Ray jotted down their names and stuffed the paper in his shirt pocket, then he stowed the articles back inside the box. Before closing the lid, he opened his bottom desk drawer and removed a small tape recorder and sheet of paper. After checking the recorder's operation, he placed it in the bottom of the box.

Ray rose to leave when he noticed a new folder lying in his basket. Printed on the tab was: MAJESTIC STAR CASUALTY #12 and the words stung him. Obviously the MI boys in military intelligence had wasted no time in compiling the report.

For nearly a minute Ray stood staring at the folder—vacillating, trying to decide whether to pick it up or not. Inside were details of the woman just blown to bits and he wasn't sure if he should view it just yet, especially just before releasing Alvarez. Although he would have the last laugh by sinking the ship, the mental image of the smug-faced druggie waving goodbye and sailing off into the sunset made the acid in his stomach perk.

Deciding to view the file later, Ray was halfway out the door when an inner voice halted him—exhorting him not to shirk it off until later; telling him that he was obliged to look; that he owed the slain female at least that much.

Already behind schedule, Ray rejected the notion but the voice kept after him—reminding him that he was Incident Commander, that the woman had died on his watch, that he owed her a few minutes of his time out of common respect.

Irritated with himself, but doing it anyway, Ray huffed and set the box down with a clunk. The world would just have to wait. One's sense of propriety didn't always allow for expediency nor did it differentiate between opportune and inopportune times. Still, he had pressing matters to attend to and the holdup was an untimely imposition.

Why did he have to be so darned principled? So morally straight? He wasn't a freaking chaplain. There was no room for sentiment in the military. In fact, it was an encumbrance.

Yielding to the dictates of his conscience—albeit grudgingly—Ray sat down and picked up the folder. He would give it a cursory look, making certain to remain calm and disconnected, and then he would get back to work. The clock was ticking.

Inside the folder was a photo of a barefoot woman sitting on a checkered quilt next to a lake. She was a pretty, lightly freckled, twenty-something girl wearing jeans and a floppy gray sweatshirt. Her quilt was spread beneath a sprawling shade tree and the sunlight sifting through the branches gave her blonde hair a soft golden glow. As she stared into the camera lens, her willow-green eyes sparkled and her bright smile brimmed of life. There was a styrofoam cooler and box of fried chicken on the blanket beside her, obviously a picnic photo.

Ray flipped the picture over to read the adhesive label on the back and his heart dropped into his stomach. Her name was Melissa—*was*.

Feeling his bile stirring, Ray closed the folder but it was already too late. Like a flashbulb leaving its mark, the image of her smiling face was burned into his retinas. But instead of fading away with the passage of time, her imprint would stay forever ingrained—a mental tattoo.

Lacking the power to resist, he reopened the folder and faced his departed accuser. Like silent tongues, her condemning eyes demanded to know what he was going to do about her undeserved death, about the lifetime of picnics she would never attend, about the children she would never bear.

Her image pled: *"I was a person. I existed. Who in God's name will avenge me!?"*

In the folder was a second photo even more disturbing than the first. Taken from a distance by one of the reconnaissance cameras, it was a photo of the blindfolded woman seconds before her death. *Melissa.* From the looks of her rigid posture and contorted face, she was struggling to free herself when the picture was snapped. Seconds later, she was no more.

Ray closed the folder and melted in his chair like a thawing iceberg. Twelve citizens had been slaughtered and he was about to set their executioner free—in front of the whole wide world. He didn't give a flying flip about what the politicians and press corps thought, but he cared a great deal about what the relatives might think.

While knowing better, Ray opened a second folder containing the biographies of the first eleven victims. Four of the dead were locals. The rest bore out-of-state addresses.

Probably here on vacation, he thought grimly. *Little did they know they would end up as chum for the barracudas and sharks.*

Especially upsetting were the photographs donated by friends and relatives for identification purposes—family portraits...graduation pictures...wedding photos. Happy occasions.

At the bottom of three photos "**STILL MISSING**" was stamped in red ink signifying their bodies had not been recovered. Each day their relatives called the station to inquire about their remains and each day they were brokenhearted to learn that nothing had been found. Not so insensitive as to allude to sharks and the like, the official answer was always the same: *"A 24-hour search was being conducted and the relatives would be notified immediately of any recovery."*

While neither party dared mention the carnivorous alternative, Ray knew the family members suspected the worse. They would listen to him politely, often weeping, and then beseech him to find their missing loved one. *"So they can be given a proper burial...brought home where they belong...be laid to rest.*"

And with each heart-rending phone call, Ray hated Mendoza and his Zetas a little more—if that was even possible. If he could, he would send in the SEALs with orders to pulverize the woman-killers until their remains had to be shipped home in sandwich bags—plus some.

In an explosive release of rage Ray swiped the folders from his desk, haphazardly scattering their contents on the floor. But instead of deriving any lasting satisfaction from the impulsive act, it made him feel worse. As he looked down at the strewn photographs, the victims' faces stared back at him, making him feel as if he had grossly dishonored the dead.

Feeling ashamed, Ray got down on his knees and humbly gathered them up—brushing off each photo with respect before placing them back in the folder. Once all were collected, he picked up the metal box and made for the radio room—admonishing himself for the childish tantrum.

Man up, soldier, and get your ass in gear. People are counting on you. You're an admiral—act like one!

Monday 09:36 Hours – The "Majestic Star"

With his ears still ringing from the blast, Cal persisted in his quest for the explosives.

Thus far he had found six separate bundles of C-4 wrapped with duct tape. But they were wired in some oddball sequence using twice the standard number of wires, making him leery of tampering with them. Some of them were no doubt booby traps and he knew better than to jump in and start cutting wires. So, erring on the side of caution, Cal left the explosives alone and began tracing the wires, thinking if he could locate and disable the radio-receiver ignition device, the C-4 would no longer pose a threat.

In tracing the wires, Cal's thoughts turned to the Zeta ringleader with the radio-operated detonating device. He was the same character who had carved up Skip's throat and Skip hated him with a passion. If and when Skip took a notion to even the score, Cal hoped the detonator's safety mechanism would be properly engaged.

If the C-4 happened to go off now, Cal would be toast—burnt toast.

WIRED

Monday 09:40 Hours – Group St. Petersburg

As soon as radio contact was reestablished, Mendoza demanded to speak to Alvarez.

Drawing on another of the admiral's canned stall tactics, the ensign cited that Alvarez was tied up with his attorneys in downtown Tampa where he was being processed for release; that once he was officially cleared to go, he would reclaim his personal possessions and be transported to Sand Key for passage to the *Majestic Star*. Exerting more pressure, the Cuban added that, in the interest of saving time, Señor Alvarez's attorneys had just called ahead to make sure the ship would be refueled and waiting upon their client's arrival and that all women and children would be evacuated in advance.

This bluff led to a dramatic interlude of radio silence, which the ensign took as a promising sign. In the drug world, disobeying a directive from the heavy-handed drug lord could mean a death sentence. As the Cuban awaited Mendoza's response, the admiral entered the radio room carrying a metal box. Once having been brought up to speed, Ray straddled a wooden stool at the chart table and joined the climactic wait.

As the prolonged silence lengthened, Ray could practically hear Mendoza sweat. Santiago Mendoza was a violence-crazed wacko; that was a fact. But Ray felt that even a wacko like him wouldn't want to die on foreign soil if given the choice of going home victorious over the gringos. Within his decadent den of narco-guerillas, he would become a legend. For years to come, he would be hero-worshipped and talked about around hideout campfires throughout Mexico and the jungles of South America.

But, defying all logic, Mendoza dashed Ray's expectations when issuing a non-negotiable flat-out refusal to discuss the matter further without personally speaking to Alvarez.

"Well, that's that, sir," the Cuban said to Ray. "He's not caving in. We've got until noon, sir."

Ray cast an anxious eye at the wall clock and motioned for the ensign and chief to join him at the table. As the pair took separate stools, Ray opened the metal box.

"I want you to memorize these questions, Ensign." Ray handed him a typed sheet of paper. "In fifteen minutes you'll be meeting with Alvarez under the guise of a final briefing. He's already been told that he'll be released today but he hasn't been given any details. As far as Alvarez is concerned, his high-dollar attorneys have cut a deal with the authorities and we're letting him go. If he presses you for more information, just play dumb."

Ray reached into the box and held up the tape recorder. "Leave this in the bottom of the box with the lid open. Don't let Alvarez see it. I've adjusted the sensitivity to record your conversation. Speak to him in Spanish. His response to your questions must be in Spanish. That's crucial. Got it?"

"Yes, sir," the Cuban replied, looking over the questions. "I'll coax him into talking."

"Good. Once we get him on tape, we'll do some creative editing." Ray slid off the stool and handed him the scratch paper. "Here are the names of his wife and kids. Bring them up during the conversation as well." The ensign nodded. "Okay, I've got some things to take care of. Page me if anything comes up. I'll meet you both at the detention area in fifteen minutes."

With time ticking away, Ray headed for the detention room where Alvarez was being fed his farewell breakfast—scrambled eggs, a 24-ounce T-bone, and a vintage bottle of cabernet sauvignon. Earlier this morning, when Alvarez was told without explanation that he was being released today, he had insisted upon a: *"civilized brunch to celebrate my final day in captivity."*

At first Ray went ballistic at the demand, viewing it as a kick-Hanna-in-the-balls-one-last-time-before-I-go Alvarez exploit. But after thinking about it, Ray liked the idea—figuring the 24-ounce concession would perpetuate the ruse of government capitulation. Ray wanted him to feel warm-and-fuzzy about his release; that he had won the battle and he was truly free to go; that his small army of lawyers had done such a bang-up job, that even Admiral Hanna himself—which was especially pleasing—was shamelessly catering to his every whim.

When Ray arrived at the detention cell he stopped in the hallway outside and looked through the wire-reinforced window. Sitting at a table, Alvarez was tucking a napkin under his collar in preparation of his going-away meal. If Ray had his druthers he would have served him a thick grilled filet of camel ass with a generous helping of special seasoning—rat poison. While eyeing the tray of food, Ray fantasized about passing him a pepper mill filled with D-Con. If asked politely, Ray would even grind it for him like a good little maître d'.

Service with a smile—that's D-7's motto.

Wiping off his dreamlike grin, Ray entered the detention room and whispered into the ear of a U.S. Marshal. When the marshal nodded his understanding, Ray proclaimed—in a voice loud enough for Alvarez to overhear—that the prisoner was scheduled for release and that in keeping with Coast Guard regs, a final meeting was scheduled at 10:00 hours where he would reclaim his personal effects.

Checking to see if Alvarez overheard, Ray peeked over the marshal's shoulder to find a self-satisfied smirk on the Colombian's face. So far, the ploy was working.

Monday 09:46 Hours – The "Majestic Star"

Something was brewing and Skip wondered what. After two hours of haggling on the radio, Mendoza was now huddled on the catwalk with his drug-thugs—all smoking cigarettes and jabbering excitedly. At one minute they appeared to be rejoicing while at another they seemed to be getting more worked up, whooping like crazy and stabbing their rifle barrels at the sky. From the crazy way they were acting, it was hard for Skip to tell if they were mad or glad.

Backing away from the window, Skip removed his hat and dropped into the helmseat next to Neal, who was holding a rag against the oozing lump on his skull.

"How's your head?"

"Oh, about the same as yours when you got cold-cocked in the casino—pounding migraine, profuse bleeding, burns like molten rock. Other than that, I'm just peachy." Neal looked at him and snorted. "If we survive this bullshit, we can compare scars over a beer someday."

"Yeah, well, so far I gotcha beat. I got an identical scalp wound on my noggin, plus a scab across my throat, plus a cut on my cheek." Skip shrugged with a crooked grin. "You gotta admit they're pretty good at inflictin' pain. Guess they learned that in Terrorist 101 class."

"Yeah," Neal went along, "I think it's on page 87 of their *Terrorism for Dummies* manual."

While Skip snickered, Neal peered out the window. "What do you think they're talking about out there? Alvarez? More executions? They seem pretty agitated."

Skip joined Neal's gaze. "Hard to say. The whole lot of 'em are one wave short of a shipwreck. I hope they're talkin' about swapping the passengers for Alvarez."

"You and me both," Neal said. "I'm sick of being stuck in hostage purgatory." He eyed the bloody rag and frowned at it. "And I'm sick of worrying about the passengers."

Skip leaned in closer. "I've been doin' some thinkin' on that, Neal. If Gold-Tooth resumes the executions, let's say I take him out with the Glock. If I do it real quick, he won't have time to detonate the C-4. When he drops, you grab his AK and we'll give the rest of 'em a taste of their own medicine. Cal might hear the gunfire and join in. Whattya think?"

Neal shrugged. "It might work here, but what about the passengers? The other gang members might open fire on them."

"That's a risk," Skip upheld, "but we can't just sit here and watch 'em blow up hostages."

"I agree, but we needn't act prematurely and possibly screw up whatever the authorities might have in the works." Neal shot him a serious look. "Unless they kill more women. Then all bets are off."

"Yeah—now you're talkin'." Skip bared his teeth with animal aggression. "Seek and destroy. Maim and mutilate. Take no prisoners and eat the wounded."

Neal marveled at Skip's snarling face and shook his head. "You always were a romantic."

So much was certain. As long as Skip and Neal lived and breathed, the Zetas would never explode another female passenger. Because, at this stage of the game, the only thing holding back the two battered buddies were each other.

WIRED

Monday 09:50 Hours – Group St. Petersburg

With ten minutes to spare before the Alvarez meeting, Ray phoned the station commander in Sand Key. After learning that a fuel barge and two cutters were waiting and standing by, he placed a three-way call to the Clearwater Chief of Police and the Pinellas County Sheriff.

In order to systematically deal with hundreds of arriving relatives, the news media, and the sightseeing public, it would require their combined resources. Ray anticipated a flotilla of pleasure boaters by sea and carloads of curiosity seekers by land—all vying for a celebratory, beer-drinking, front row seat.

After discussing the allocation of manpower for crowd control, the three men reviewed security measures and safeguards against improvised explosive devices, or IED's. In the wake of the World Trade Center tragedy, most U.S. law enforcement agencies had undergone training in this area, which *Operation Checkmate* would put to good use. Inasmuch as Alvarez was allegedly being set free from jail, no acts of terrorism were expected. Even so, car bombs had already wreaked havoc in Orlando and Tallahassee and Ray wasn't taking any chances.

To check incoming vehicles for explosives, the Pinellas County Sheriff agreed to set up roadblocks at key intersections with bomb-sniffing K-9 units. Working in conjunction with the county, the Clearwater Police accepted the formidable task of traffic control and the screening-out of unauthorized vehicles and/or undesirables. The Coast Guard and Florida Marine Patrol would provide air and sea security while the SEALs manned security checkpoints at Station Sand Key to oversee the relatives and passengers during the disembarkation and exodus process.

Satisfied with the cooperative arrangement, Ray thanked the police officials and rang off. All that was needed now was a specific timetable, which depended solely on Mendoza.

With one minute to spare, Ray quickly dialed Kathy Myles' phone number. Though pressed for time, he had promised to call her after talking to her brother. When he got no answer, Ray hung up and hustled toward the detention room.

WIRED

When Kathy opened her front door, the upstairs phone was ringing and she pounded up the steps. But by the time she breathlessly reached the telephone, it stopped. Knowing it was pointless she picked up the receiver anyway and then slammed it down when hearing a dial tone.

Wondering who had called and why, Kathy parked herself on the sofa and waited for it to ring again. In order to pinch a few extra pennies, she had cancelled Caller ID and their Voice Mailbox service a few months ago when Skip was between jobs.

Having just left the marina, she thought the caller might have been Brillo. Going stir-crazy, she had gone there on a whim to see if anybody had heard anything new. But after finding most of the fishermen gone, she was pulling out of the marina just as the *Sol-Mate* was returning from the fuel dock. As she passed through the gates, Brillo spotted her red convertible and sounded his horn at her.

Most importantly of all, Kathy hoped the caller wasn't Admiral Hanna. She had been floored at seeing him on television last night and had tried calling him after the Channel 10 newscast. Now that she knew his identity, she wanted some straight answers about his unexplainable dealings with Cal. But after finally getting through to the station, she was informed that the admiral wasn't accepting calls from the public. When she had identified herself as the ship captain's worried wife, the sympathetic young man took her phone number and promised to pass it on.

As Kathy waited by the phone, she scolded herself for leaving the house to begin with. Hanna had promised to call her this morning after talking to Cal on the radio and like a harebrained fool she had left anyway without a thought. Clearly the sleep deprivation over the past four days was having an effect on her thinking.

After going to bed last night, she had lain awake until the wee hours of the morning with her manic mind running unchecked—Cal collapsing into her car with his forehead bleeding...his sullen but brave face as he fell back into the water...the nosy Coastguardsman who turned out to be an admiral...Brillo's sweet attempt to cheer her up during the boat ride home...of Skip's loving face when he held her tightly in his arms. Even

339

after falling asleep, snippets of memories cycloned through her head all night long, robbing her of any beneficial rest.

Sticking close to the phone, Kathy picked up the remote and turned on the television. The caller could have been anybody, she thought—a telemarketer, or Cal's lonely sexpot secretary from Detroit. The woman called everyday and she was getting on Kathy's nerves. Whoever it was, they would call back if it were really important.

When jerky film footage of the *Majestic Star* flashed on the TV screen with *"Breaking News"* superimposed over it, a knot caught in her throat and she sat straight up.

Monday 10:00 Hours – Group St. Petersburg

When Ray arrived at the detention area, Chief Bloyd was waiting for him in the hallway. To set Alvarez at ease, Ray would not be present at the bogus briefing. There was too much bad blood between them. The Colombian despised Ray and would clam up at the mere sight of him. With any luck, however, Alvarez would identify with the young Spanish-speaking Cuban and open up to him—freely answering the questions that Ray wanted on tape.

While waiting for the ensign, Ray looked through the window with idle interest to find Alvarez still making love to his gourmet breakfast. Fittingly, the black-heart had the appetite of an insatiable carnivore. As he ate, Ray's blood pressure rose with each meticulous little bite—especially when Alvarez politely daubed each corner of his mouth with a linen napkin.

"Well, la-di-da," Ray mimicked with a snooty face. "Aren't we the hoity-toity one?"

Unable to stomach the man's pomposity any longer, Ray was turning away from the window when a familiar sound rang out.

Ping-ping! . . ping-ping!

Instantly recognizing the sound, Ray whirled around to face Alvarez, who was now leering at him through the window while tapping his empty wineglass with a spoon.

Ping-ping!...ping-ping!

As Ray glared at him through the glass, a marshal strode over to the table and begrudgingly refilled the wineglass. Then, with a taunting little smile, Alvarez raised his glass to Ray as if making a toast. With raw images of the twelve dead still fresh in his mind, Ray's tolerance level shot to a magnitude 10 and he charged for the door like a bull in a blind rage with Chief Bloyd close on his heels.

When Ray burst into the room, Alvarez glanced up at him and then looked away with indifference, as if placing no importance on Ray's presence. The slight was deliberate and inwardly Alvarez feasted on the admiral's anger. While smirking, he was raising the wineglass to his lips when Ray grabbed his wrist and held it. As the pair contended for control of the glass, its liquid sloshed outside its confines and dribbled on the table.

"Humph!" Ray grunted gutturally in his face. "Where do you think you are? At the *Steak & Fucking Ale?*"

As Alvarez vied for control of the wineglass, his smirk became a scowl. "I suggest you move your face back where it was, Admiral, and behave yourself." After a few tense moments Alvarez changed direction, as if caught in the unfavorable act of revealing his true self. "Now," he said rather cheerfully, "once I finish my flavorsome meal here that your government has so kindly provided me, I'll be along my way—and out of yours."

When Ray didn't budge, Chief Bloyd placed a hand on his shoulder and squeezed—urging patience. Although grossly disinclined, Ray released the Colombian's arm. The chief was right. This was no time to provoke the prisoner or distance him. The ensign would be arriving shortly and Ray wanted Alvarez to be relaxed and unsuspecting—talkative.

With his dark Latin eyes steady on Ray, Alvarez drained the glass and set it down triumphantly, then began soaking up droplets of spilt wine with his napkin.

"It's a pity to waste good wine, Admiral. Wouldn't you say?" His voice rang of superiority. "I think I'll have another glass of cabernet in your honor."

Snapping his fingers, Alvarez motioned for the marshal to dispense more wine. As the resentful marshal refilled the glass, the Colombian panned their faces with a masterful grin, delighting in his supremacy over

WIRED

the Americanos.

Alvarez's high-and-mightiness galled Ray to no end and it was everything he could do to contain himself. But the drug lord was playing right into his hands which gave Ray the strength to walk away—along with the rewarding thought of blowing his arrogant ass to smithereens once he was aboard the *Majestic Star.*

~~~~~~~~~~

When the Cuban entered the detention room, the admiral brushed past him and slammed the door shut, making the ensign wonder what had happened. But, preserving his cool, he overlooked his superior's behavior and greeted Alvarez in Spanish. Pleased to hear his native tongue, Alvarez returned the greeting in Spanish and offered his right hand. After a cordial handshake, the Cuban took a seat across the table and opened the lid of the metal box.

Ray believed that showing Alvarez his personal effects would lend credibility to the charade and heighten his anticipation over being released. He also felt it would lower Alvarez's guard and make him more talkative—especially to a Latin brother.

Leading up to the loose script Admiral Hanna had laid out, the soft-spoken Cuban reached into the box and removed Alvarez's wallet. With the tape recorder spinning, he handed it to Alvarez and posed his first question.

"I bet you will be glad to see your family again, huh amigo? Maria, Pablo, and Rosa?"

"Sí." Alvarez opened his wallet and gazed fondly at their photograph. "I have missed them very much. But hopefully everything is in order now and it will not be long." He closed the wallet and his doting expression turned businesslike. "When will I be released and under what conditions?"

"Soon, is what I hear. Sorry, but I do not have access to such information. The gringos do not really trust us Latinos very much. Even here in the Coast Guard we are sometimes treated as second class."

Alvarez was fiercely proud of his Latin heritage and the statement was meant to inflame him. As expected, the Colombian erupted.

342

"The American pigs are fools! How can you tolerate this behavior!? Have you no pride, man?"

The Cuban leaned forward and handed Alvarez his passport, playing him like a Stradivarius.

"I have much pride, Señor Alvarez, but I need the money for my family back in Cuba." His tone was confidential. "Castro will not permit them to leave and they have lost everything. They're penniless. I send them all that I can, but it is not enough. What would you have me do?"

"I would demand respect! Latinos are honorable people and should be afforded the same respect as gringos." His voice rose in volume. "No matter how desperately money is needed, one should never sacrifice their honor—not even for family. I would rather die first!"

"Sí. Many times I have been tempted to complain about the injustices, but my family in Cuba depends on me. There's the risk of losing my rank."

"Fuck the risk!" The drug baron jarred the table with his fist. "You are in charge of your destiny—no one else. *You* are in charge!" Following the outburst, Alvarez paused to compose himself. "Look, you are a soldier and being such you must do what you are told. But do not degrade yourself. Nothing is worth that, amigo. Nada!"

Playing up to Alvarez's ego, the Cuban responded meekly. "Yes, I know. But I am not a man of power such as yourself. In your world, you are the boss. People fear you and admire you at the same time. No one questions your authority. You are a man of great respect. Yes?"

"Sí, but it was not given to me." Alvarez leaned forward and narrowed his eyes. "Respect must be demanded. In my country, I give the orders and I expect them to be carried out. *¡Pronto!* Or they pay the price!" He made a throat-slashing gesture with his forefinger. "It is eat or be eaten. ¿Entiendes?"

"Yes, I understand completely." The ensign handed him the Rolex and the rest of his personal effects. "But, with all due respect, Señor, do you feel things will be the same when you return to Colombia? As the Americanos say: '*When the cat is away, the mice will play*'."

Alvarez took offense to the remark and fired back. "That will never happen! My people are loyal to me. I am in control and I dare anyone to question my authority! When I return home, I will find everything as I left it. Be sure of it." Signaling an end to the discussion, Alvarez pushed back in his chair and folded his hands on the table. "Now, I have enjoyed our little conversation and I am grateful for the return of my personal items, but it is time to move onward. I demand to know when I will be released and under what terms."

Ray had been monitoring the conversation from outside in the hallway with the help of a Spanish-speaking lieutenant junior grade. Believing they had enough on tape, Ray barged into the room and answered the question himself.

"You'll be released when I say so, *Lord,* and not a minute before!" With a cat-eating grin, Ray grabbed the metal box and began collecting Alvarez's personal effects.

"What is the meaning of this?" Alvarez grabbed his passport and shot to his feet in protest. "Those are my personal belongings and I insist you leave them with me! I also demand to know the terms of my release!"

"Screw you, Alvarez, and the jackass you rode in on. Or was it a camel?" Ray plucked the forged passport from his hands with a smart-aleck grin. "Let me put it this way: where you're going, you won't be needing a passport. As for the other items, I'll just keep them as a memento of our friendship."

Alvarez's eyes flashed with anger and his face turned beet red. Too upset for words, his body shook like a smoldering volcano on the verge of eruption. When he finally found his voice, he unleashed a spew of Spanish profanities that would make the fallen archangel Lucifer proud.

"Ta-ta!" Ray teased, rubbing it in more.

The taunting farewell elevated the drug lord's decibel level from loud to earsplitting. With gloating satisfaction, Ray strutted out of the room—shutting out the shrieking Spanish when the door closed between them.

Monday 10:22 Hours – The "Majestic Star"

As the Zetas huddled together on the catwalk and conspired against the United States, Skip and Neal kept a sharp eye on them through the window. It had been over thirty minutes since Mendoza's last contact with the Coast Guard and Skip wondered if he was going to trade the passengers or kill them.

WIRED

For the millionth time since Thursday, Skip's eyes went to the marine radio. In order to formulate a game plan, he and Neal needed reliable information. Mohammad was the only one watching them through the glass and that was in between praising Allah and throwing his head back to make shrill trilling noises. To Skip it sounded like a cross between an Apache war cry and an injured *raphus cucullatus*—a dodo bird.

Neal was watching his shipmate from the corner of his eye and he didn't like the way Skip was eyeballing the radio. When Skip's back straightened and he leaned in its direction, warning bells sounded in Neal's head. After crewing together for twenty some years, he could practically read his friend's mind. To prevent Skip from making a fatal mistake, Neal rose from his helmseat and placed himself between Skip and the radio.

When Neal stepped into his line of sight, Skip blinked and looked up to find Neal standing over him with arms crossed and a don't-even-think-about-it expression on his face. Conceding that "Neal-the-Mother-Hen" was probably right—as usual—Skip threw up his hands in a pouty *okay okay!* fashion and spun his chair around to face away from the radio.

~~~~~~~~~~~

Skip and Neal had met two decades ago while working as merchant marines on a phosphate barge. Most of the crewmen were roughnecks and whoremongers who drank like fishes and misbehaved whenever on dry land. But Skip had found Neal quite the opposite. Back then, Neal had been dating a gal named Phyllis and he was undyingly faithful to her.

Being a newlywed himself and very much in love with Kathy, Skip steered clear of the bar scene while away from home so as not to invite trouble. So, instead of going ashore when at port and raising hell like the other guys, Skip and Neal stayed aboard ship drinking beer and playing cards into the wee hours of the morning. As a result they'd struck up a friendship fairly quickly.

Over the years that followed they crewed together on a number of ships and became very close friends. Since steady work on the water was oftentimes scarce, whenever one found a job in need of another hand, they telephoned one another. They jokingly referred to it as their *Starving*

Salty-Dog Pact and they looked out for each other whenever they could.

On Neal's wedding day, Skip was honored to be his best man. Skip would never forget the enamored look on Neal's face as Phyllis walked down the isle in her wedding gown. With a church full of people, Neal could see no other. Advancing arm-in-arm with her father, Phyllis was positively radiant and her adoring eyes never left her bridegroom. With their brand new life awaiting them, their faces gushed with promise and starry-eyed expectations. It was a match made in heaven.

Since tying the nuptial knot, their marriage spawned two lovely children and the bond between them today was stronger than ever. Ditto for the bond of friendship between Neal and Skip.

Appreciative of his old friend, Skip spun his helmseat around to find Neal still guarding the radio. Neal was more straight-laced than he, and at times Skip thought he took life a little too serious; but Neal was a great first officer and an even greater friend—as good as they come. Insiders who knew them called them the *Odd Couple*. When Kathy wasn't around to keep Skip on track, Neal did—or at least he tried.

"Hey, goody-two-shoes," Skip grinned at him. "Thanks for watchin' out for me."

"Yeah, well, somebody's got to," he said. "I'll sic you on the bastards when the time is right."

Monday 10:32 Hours – Group St. Petersburg

While Chief Bloyd copied the mini-cassette recording onto the reel-to-reel, the ensign translated the Alvarez recording onto paper. Ray's task was to predict what questions Mendoza might ask on the radio and then draft a reply using Alvarez's recorded words. After making a list of hypothetical questions, Ray and the ensign pored over the Alvarez translation and drafted ten generic responses to cover most every scenario. The chief's job was to dissect the Alvarez recording and piece together the ten responses in Alvarez's voice.

Under pressure to beat the noon deadline, the three men worked

WIRED

posthaste to craft a convincing soundtrack. Words and phrases were selected from the Alvarez tape and dubbed onto the reel-to-reel, then rearranged to create a patchwork of short choppy sentences. Once the editing was complete, Ray numbered the responses 1 through 10 and the chief cross-referenced them numerically with the digital tape counter on the reel-to-reel.

With their work now done, the group ran through a number of practice runs to hone their skills. The exercises began by the Cuban posing a fictitious question that Mendoza might ask. In turn, Ray would scan the ten selections and hold up his fingers to indicate which 1 to 10 recording to use. In quick response, the chief would fast-forward or rewind the threaded tape to play the appropriate answer.

Ten minutes later they had the cumbersome procedure down as well as possible and the ensign hailed up the *Majestic Star*.

Monday 10:53 Hours – The "Majestic Star"

After dividing the remaining gallons of water by the number of passengers, it confirmed what Skip already knew—the water tanks would be bone dry today after the upcoming ration.

Frowning down at the figures, Skip put the pencil down and wagged his head. If a deal wasn't struck today, he would have a bunch of thirsty folks on his hands. By Thursday, dehydration would set in and by this weekend some of the more frail and elderly could start dying off.

As far as the gang members were concerned, dehydration wasn't a pressing problem. Right after the takeover they confiscated all of the liquor and soft drinks aboard and greedily stashed the booty inside their cabin. From the way their breath usually reeked, Skip imagined they'd already gone through most of the booze. Insofar as he and Neal were concerned, they would likely be provided sodas until their services were no longer needed. Morally, though, Skip had a problem with that. Common decency wouldn't allow him suck down colas while others around him died of thirst.

Hoping it wouldn't come down to that, Skip's dehydration concerns were put on hold when the radio sprang to life.

"Vessel Majestic Star, the vessel Majestic Star. This is the United

WIRED

States Coast Guard. Over."

The radio had been quiet for so long that its resurgence gave Skip the butterflies. As the hail repeated in Spanish, Mendoza stuck his head in the doorway for a better listen.

"La nave Majestic Star. Señor Alvarez es presente y listo hablar en la radio. Responda por favor."

The words *"Señor Alvarez"* caught Skip's ear and the gleam in Mendoza's lazy eye confirmed that something hopeful was in the works.

~~~~~~~~~~

When Mendoza answered the radio, the ensign announced that Señor Alvarez was present in the stationhouse and that permission had been granted for him to speak on the radio. But there were two ground rules. As a security measure that no coded messages could be passed between them, Mendoza was to ask all questions through the Cuban radio operator and the Cuban would in turn ask Alvarez. Then the desk mike would be placed in front of Alvarez where he would be permitted a brief five-second response. The second rule was that, at the Coast Guard's discretion, some questions could be disallowed if deemed irrelevant to the exchange process. Those were the ground rules. Otherwise no communication would be permitted.

Ray hoped the fictitious radio procedure as explained would not paint a suspicious picture. It was the only practical excuse he could dream up for the delay in delivering Alvarez's bogus answers. Even at their fastest, it took five to ten seconds for the three-man-team to translate the question, choose an answer, and fumble with the reel-to-reel to play the selected response.

As Ray awaited Mendoza's answer, a duty officer entered the radio room and handed him a message slip. It was the fourth **"URGENT"** message from the Vice-Admiral since the female passenger's high-explosive death. The weasel was freaking out. After reading it, Ray wadded it up and pitched it in a wastebasket along with the other pink balls.

"Under protest, I accept your ground rules," Mendoza said in Spanish. "Now, put Señor Alvarez on the radio before I run out of

348

patience! I need to consult with him before agreeing to any American offers."

The Cuban interpreted the response for Ray, who nodded his approval.

"Please stand by for Señor Alvarez," the ensign said in Spanish.

"Okay, gentlemen," Ray announced, his pulse rising, "it's now or never. Everyone ready?"

Chief Bloyd straightened in his chair and placed both hands on the tape deck controls. Ray sat down next to him and positioned the legal pad between them. Written on the notepad were the ten responses with their corresponding reel-to-reel numbers. With everybody set, Ray looked at the Cuban and nodded to proceed.

"Señor Alvarez is now present and we are ready to begin," the ensign said. "You may both converse in Spanish. What is your first question?"

"Honorable one," Mendoza began, "the Americanos have offered to trade you for all of the passenger hostages. They have agreed to give us the ship along with fuel and supplies. According to them, we are free to go with the captain and crew as our hostages. Once we reach our destination, we are to release them unharmed. Do you agree to this proposition?"

The ensign quickly translated the question and Ray scanned the legal pad for the best answer. He held up four fingers and Chief Bloyd fast-forwarded the reel-to-reel to generic response #4.

"Sí," the tape said, "everything is in order...be sure of it. "

Mendoza was still skeptical. "But what if we are double-crossed at sea? The Americanos are liars and are not to be trusted. They may well sacrifice their own people for political gain. This proposal could be highly perilous."

After hearing the question in English, Ray held up seven fingers and the chief promptly spun the reel to the corresponding digital number.

"Fuck the risk!...that will never happen...do what you are told...the American pigs are fools!...I am in control! ..."

"I mean no disrespect," Mendoza hedged, "but I fear we cannot trust the military. Should we not appeal to a higher power for additional assurances?"

Upon hearing the translation, Ray held up three fingers and the response followed.

"Have you no pride, man?...I dare anyone to question my authority!"

"Uh-h...Sí, Señor Alvarez. But once we release the hostages, our position of power changes."

Ray held up five fingers.

"That's the way it has to be...¿Entiendes?...I give the orders and I expect them to be carried out. Pronto!"

For the next several moments, total silence reigned in the radio room. Everyone was sitting on the edges of their seats, trading nervous glances. This was it and the tension was electrifying. Ray pictured Mendoza licking his lips nervously; clutching the microphone in a death grip; his eyes darting skittishly as he agonized over the decision.

"Sí, Señor Alvarez! I will personally see to it!" A quiver was in Mendoza's voice. "It will be an honor to see you again!"

Smelling success, Ray breathed a sigh of relief and raised all ten fingers.

"I have enjoyed our little conversation and...it is time to move onward...you are in charge, no one else. *You* are in charge!"

"Sí. At once, Señor! Have no concern. I will see to everything. You can be sure of it!"

After a prudent pause, the ensign spoke into the microphone. "Do you have any more questions for Señor Alvarez?"

"No!" Mendoza blurted. "Proceed with the exchange—immediately!"

Just like that, the ruse was over—leaving Ray and his men staring open-mouthed at the radio speaker. The room was so quiet you could hear a pin drop. They had pulled it off. As the reality of their achievement sank in, their open mouths became broad smiles and their dumbstruck silence turned to lively celebration.

In exaggerated relief, the master chief threw his head back and stretched his arms toward the heavens. "Jeez-Louise!" he wailed. "There is a God!"

This sparked heavier laughter followed by congratulatory backslaps and handshakes. As the buoyant trio paraded from the room, Ray hooked both arms around their necks.

"Great teamwork, guys!" While giving them kudos, Ray squeezed their necks spiritedly. "By God, we did it!"

WIRED

As Mendoza placed the microphone on its hook, Skip's intuition told him something was up. He had heard two distinct Spanish voices coming from the radio and Gold-Tooth had addressed one of them as *Señor Alvarez*. What's more, when conversing with the deeper-voiced man, Gold-Tooth's usual macho tone became noticeably cowed and subservient.

With Skip watching him, Mendoza sneered at the radio and clenched his fist in victory. Then, without so much as a look, he whisked past Skip and out of the wheelhouse. But instead of stopping to smoke another cigarette, he hooked right and started down the catwalk. Something big was brewing and the freakazoid was leaving without explanation.

With mounting anxiety, Skip chased after him. "Hey! Wait a minute!"

The capitán's irritating voice halted Mendoza in his tracks and he turned around with noticeable annoyance. While squinting at Skip's head poking out the doorway, the Zeta gave him an openly disgusted what-do-you-want-now look.

Skip's decision to go after him had been spontaneous and he wasn't prepared with a question to ask. On the spur of the moment he manufactured one about the only topic coming to mind.

"Since you put me in charge of the rations, I need to know what's goin' on. Is the Coast Guard gonna bring us food and water, or what?"

Skip knew full well that the negotiations were about Alvarez, but used it as an excuse to wheedle out some information. When Mendoza didn't answer right away, Skip stepped outside onto the catwalk to further his objection.

"Look, we're gonna to be out of water by noon—that's one hour." He held up one finger. "Pretty soon we're gonna have two hundred thirsty passengers askin' questions and expectin' answers. Now, what did the Coast Guard say?"

For a moment Mendoza said nothing. He just stood there with his trademark shit-eating grin that Skip so despised. Then, with his cocky little walk that Skip despised even more, he swaggered up to Skip and crossed his arms over his chest.

"Capitán, how you Americanos say it?" He cocked his head sideways.

WIRED

"Good News, Bad News?"

While awaiting Skip's reply, Mendoza hitched up his pants and rocked back-and-forth on his heels—clearly full of himself. When some of his flunkies gathered round, he puffed up even more and gave them a knowing wink. Instead of coming across as a badass, Skip thought he looked more like Keith Richards doing a bad Fonzie impression.

Masking his disgust for the man, Skip nodded yes—indicating that *"good news, bad news"* was the correct American term.

"Bueno! Good news is that Señor Alvarez will be here soon. Trade people for Alvarez...trade people for food, water, and petrol. People go home, we go home." His sneer broadened and he cocked his head the other way. "Los Zetas win—Americanos lose."

Although this was exactly what Skip wanted to hear, he pretended to look upset. "Okay," he played along, "so what's the bad news?"

"Capitán going home with us!" Mendoza had scarcely gotten the words out before bursting into unseemly laughter. Then he turned and strolled down the catwalk, belly-laughing so hard that he weaved as he walked.

If Skip hadn't detested him so much, he might have been amused. Not only was the gang leader a sociopath, he was a congenital idiot.

Monday 11:03 Hours – Group St. Petersburg

After pulling off the reel-to-reel caper, Ray immediately sent word out to his key commanders and the local police departments. *Operation Checkmate* was a go and everyone had their assignments. With any luck there wouldn't be any screw-ups. As Mission Coordinator, he would monitor the operation from Helo-1 overhead.

Ray's plan was to deliver Alvarez in a rubber dinghy in full view of the terrorists. The dinghy's bowline would be tossed to the Zetas aboard the *Majestic Star* while the stern line remained fast to a Coast Guard cutter. Once the ship was resupplied and all the passengers were off, the cutter would release the stern line, allowing the dinghy to be hauled to the starboard hatch to receive Alvarez. Afterward, the *Majestic Star* would be permitted to leave American waters unescorted. Then, when the ship got out of media range...BOOM! No more *Majestic Star*, no more terrorists, no more steak and eggs for Señor Alvarez. The only loose end was the rescue of Stringer and the crew.

With *Operation Checkmate* already two hours behind schedule, Ray made haste for the helipad. A minute later Helo-1 was airborne and speeding in the direction of Sand Key.

Monday 11:07 Hours – The "Majestic Star"

After being escorted to the sundeck by Stan—his latest archenemy—Skip stood in the serving line looking for Cal. As he inched forward in line, he chatted with nearby passengers while simultaneously panning the crowd for Cal's face.

When Skip first appeared on the sundeck, he was besieged by a mob of passengers up in arms over the female abductions and unexplained explosion. Hoping to skirt the explosion issue and stave off a mini-mutiny, Skip climbed atop the Tiki Hut stage and announced that a deal had been struck and everyone was going home today including the females. This long-awaited news sparked a spirited celebration that effectively sidetracked them from the explosion question. Skip just hoped their reversal in mood would last long enough to get them off his ship for good.

When Skip finally arrived at the steam table, he found the pickings slim—a scoop of mashed potatoes, a small helping of lima beans, and six ounces of water per passenger. When he looked disappointedly at John-Renée, who now sported a four-day-old stubble, the Cajun gave him a pathetic shrug. Knowing the cooks were doing their best, Skip took his paltry ration and searched for a conspicuous place to sit down. With still no sign of Cal, he perched himself on the Tiki stage letting his feet dangle.

The sea breeze had freshened so Skip removed his hat to let his clammy scalp breathe. The air was getting soupy and the clear skies had given way to high dapples of fleecy altocumulus clouds. Sailors called it a mackerel sky because the cloud pattern resembled the markings of a king mackerel. Oftentimes it was a precursor of wet weather and Skip wondered if rain was in the offing.

Mackerel sky, mackerel sky. Never long wet and never long dry.

WIRED

When Skip swallowed his first bite of beans, he grimaced. His smashed esophagus was still sore and it hurt when food squeezed past the painful constriction in his throat. To help wash it down he took a sip of water, thinking this might be the last water he drank for a while.

While chewing another bite of beans, Skip's eyes flitted from face to face until they landed on Cal. He was standing at the end of the food line in his Mickey Mouse shirt, talking with the passenger in front of him. His open and casual manner fit in perfectly with the others, as if he'd been onboard the whole time. As Skip watched him, the smiling passenger slapped Cal on the back and asked if he had heard the good news. When Cal shook his head no, the man cheerfully told him that everybody was going home today.

After getting his plate of food, Cal locked eyes with Skip briefly and then wandered around a while before sitting down on the stage next to him.

"Nice playactin', buddy boy," Skip teased. "If we survive this, I'm gonna nominate you for an academy award."

"So far, so good." Cal sampled the potatoes. "That was quite a boom I heard earlier. Shook the ship from stem to stern. Scared the hell outta me. Everything okay?"

"That gold-toothed prick was teachin' me a lesson—or so he says. He gets his rocks off by killin' innocent folks." Skip had a flashback of the mutilated blonde and his fork began to shake. "It was bad, Cal. Real bad." He looked at Cal with hurt in his eyes. "Female passenger."

Cal stared at Skip as if struck by lightning. The Zetas were now killing women.

"He'll pay for it, though. His ass is mine." Skip envisioned the white foredeck shiny-red with spattered body tissue and his stomach turned. "I'm too upset to talk about it right now. How's it goin' down below?"

"It ain't. Things down there are way over my head."

"How many wires?"

"Four—in series."

"Whoa. Better watch out. Some of 'em are decoys. Any luck findin' the other thing?"

"Not yet, but I'm still looking."

Just then Stan and a heavyset Mexican plopped down on the stage nearby and began wolfing down their triple ration of food. This stroke of bad luck made Skip cringe inside. Without privacy he and Cal would have to choose their words carefully. Even though the gang members spoke little English, most understood it to some degree—a result of American television.

Cal glanced uneasily at the gunmen and twisted his body away to help conceal his face. "I just heard in the food line that we passengers are going home today, Captain. Any idea when?"

"Not exactly. As soon as they deliver Señor Alcatraz...His Ass-Holiness...the Ayatollah of Rock and Rolla—if you know who I mean. From what I've heard, all passengers will be on dry land sometime this afternoon. My guess is three, four hours."

"That's good news, Captain. Two hundred less worries."

"Thank God." Skip leaned in closer and shook a fork of speared limas in Cal's face. "Once they're outta my hair, we'll see who's runnin' this friggin' ship." Skip gave Cal a decisive nod and poked the beans in his mouth. "Sounds like later today the rest of us will be goin' on a south-of-the-border cruise and I'm not talkin' about a trip to Taco Bell, either."

"Well, it is a lovely day for a *short* sea cruise. Is it not?"

"I guess so," Skip replied, not making the connection. "But I don't think it's gonna be very short for me and the crew."

"Oh, but it shall be, Captain. Very short indeed—in a *Titanic* sort of way." With his eyebrows arched, Cal searched Skip's face for a flicker of understanding—gambling if the Zetas overheard him, they wouldn't be familiar with the ill-fated ocean liner. "Get my drift?"

When Skip finally got the message, a shadow fell over his face. "How short?"

"By dark, Skipper. According to Bluebird, the fat lady's gonna sing by nightfall."

"Oh." Skip dropped his fork on the plate and looked off into the distance. "That puts a different light on things, doesn't it?"

"It sure as hell does, Cap." Clutching his empty plate, Cal slid off the stage and dusted the seat of his pants. "Well, gotta run. It's gonna be a busy afternoon."

"To say the least. When will I hear from you again?"

"Oh, you'll *hear me* alright." Cal eyed the gunmen to find them still engrossed in their food. "And when you do, lock and load. Roger?"

"I'll follow your lead," Skip nodded. "But save Gold-Tooth for me."

"Aye-aye, Skipper. He's all yours. Are you packing now?"

"Wouldn't leave home without it."

"Excellent. Just like the old days—you and me. Devils with the green faces."

"That's what the gooks called us." Skip gave a sardonic grin. "Kicked the shit outta 'em, didn't we?"

"That we did, Captain. That we did."

"Thanks, Cal. I'll buy you a steak when this is all over—a monster-size, kick-ass steak with all the trimmins'. And a keg of beer to wash it down."

"You're on," Cal smiled. "Compared to my early-morning snack anything would be good. Even these beans were delicious and I hate limas. A little on the salty side, though."

"Yeah, the kitchen's been washin' everything in seawater to stretch out our fresh water supply. What early snack are you talkin' about?"

"I'll tell you about it later. Let's just say it was a sinus-opening experience." In parting, Cal looked at Skip solemnly and rested a hand on his shoulder. "Watch your back, Captain."

For a fleeting moment their eyes locked and their true feelings shone through, forcing out all pretense. Each was thinking the same thing and they both knew it—that this could be the last time they saw each other alive. Caught off guard by the sudden openness, their eyes skittered away but rejoined when finding no place to hide. Without their protective masculine veneer, both men felt self-conscious and vulnerable as if standing before each other naked.

Most males were brainwashed from childhood to believe it was unmanly to cry or to show certain emotions. Should one do so, they were persecuted as "sissies" or "wimps." And heaven forbid should a male possess tender feelings for another male, lest they be labeled "queer" and victimized all the more. While misguided, this macho doctrine was ingrained into society. As a result, many adult men found it difficult—even shameful—to show their true feelings.

When Skip's eyes watered up, Cal decided to make tracks before things got mushy. Cal wasn't an overly sentimental guy, but he was on the verge of blubbering himself. So, with no words befitting enough, nor necessary, the two pals exchanged well-wishing nods and smiled goodbye.

Before fading into the crowd, Cal turned and pointed at Skip in a *"You-da-man!"* show of male respect. With a twinkle in his eye, Skip turned his empty plate sideways to hide his hand from enemy eyes and returned the honor by pointing right-back-atcha. Not to be outdone, Cal waved off the gesture and poked his finger at Skip harder still, as if saying: *"No, you-be-da-man!"*

Welcoming some light humor, a battle broke out of whom could pay the most homage. After an impassioned flurry of finger pointing, the mutual praise-fest ended when Cal blended into the crowd.

~~~~~~~~~~

Minutes later Cal was amongst the passengers being herded back to the casino.

By his count there were four Zeta guards escorting them, but they seemed more interested in whispering to another than duly governing the crowd. Judging from their undertone of excitement, Cal figured they were talking about Alvarez's release and their victorious voyage back home. All the passengers around him were equally as excited, all yakking at once and speculating about when they may be released.

As the progression of bodies moved onward, Cal slowed his pace and dropped steadily toward the rear. When the group passed by an open stairwell, he double-checked the Zetas to find them still engrossed in conversation.

With no one the wiser, Cal broke from the crowd and retreated down the stairway steps.

Monday 12:00 Hours – Gulf of Mexico

Helo-1 was hovering eight hundred feet above the task force of ships, flanked on either side by two navy attack helicopters armed with 25mm chain guns and laser-homing AGM-114 Hellfire missiles. From his lofty elevation Ray could see the *Majestic Star* on the western horizon and the sight of it made his pulse quicken. If everything held to plan, the passengers would be evacuated over the next two hours and he could breathe a sigh of relief—at long last.

As Ray peered straight down through the visor on his helmet, his eyes traced the foamy white wakes left behind by the convoy. Held back by the slower fuel barge, the convoy was still five miles shy of its objective. In reality the *Majestic Star* did not need refueling because it would not be voyaging that far before its destruction; but Mendoza and his mangy men didn't know that, so the bogus fuel transfer was a necessary part of the dog and pony show.

"Helo-1, this is Group St. Petersburg. Over."

Recognizing the chief's voice, Ray spoke through the mouthpiece on his helmet. "Admiral Hanna here. Go ahead, Chief."

"I've just picked up a hail on Channel 12, sir. The caller is identifying himself as Stringer. Do you copy?"

Chief Bloyd had worked with Ray long enough to know when *not* to ask questions. Clearly something was up the admiral's sleeve with this Stringer fellow and the chief didn't care to know what. Better for the career that way.

"Roger, Group. I'll handle it. Changing frequencies now. Helo-1 out."

~~~~~~~~~~

The first thing Cal did when arriving back at his hideaway was to radio Bluebird. In order to plan his next move he needed an accurate timeline. There were only six hours of daylight left and the passengers weren't even off the ship yet. Time was running out.

After receiving no response, Cal was turning off the radio when a Coast Guard radio operator intercepted his hail. Moments later, the tinny voice of Admiral Hanna came over the handheld's miniature speaker.

~~~~~~~~~~

"Stringer, this is Bluebird. Do you read?"

The background of engine noise and Hanna's shaky voice told Cal that he was airborne.

"I read you loud and clear, Bluebird. I understand the match is about to begin. Over."

"That's a roger. I'm glad we made comms. I planned to give you a heads-up once we were in closer radio range. Food and water will be brought aboard White Queen by way of starboard hatch. Once delivery is complete and all White Pawns are off the board, Black King will enter play via the same entrance. Roger?"

Cal processed the information quickly. "Understood. What's the ETA? Over."

"About three zero minutes. Do you copy? Three zero minutes."

"Good copy. Approximately how long before White Knight can engage Black Team?"

"Roughly two hours. Again, I must warn White Knight against entering the match until all White Pawns are removed from play. Roger?"

"Roger. But once they're off the board, the black team is fair prey."

"They're all yours. But you'll have to work fast. Because of the game's late start, you won't have much playtime before White Queen gets sacrificed. Roger?"

"I heard that. What about our *lift* home after the game? Is that still on?"

"Can't promise anything, but I'll do my best. The sundeck would be the best spot to *pick you up*. Be watching the friendly skies around dusk. Roger?"

"Will do. Our team would like to leave here before the new opponents arrive—you know, the *Tomahawks*? I hear they're a very *explosive* team. Over."

Ray chuckled into the microphone. "They haven't lost a match yet. Over."

"Well, unless it's a real *blowout* here, I'll see you tonight after the game. White Knight out."

"We'll be rooting for the home team. Bluebird standing by."

~~~~~~~~~~

"Shit! Shit! Shit!" Cal swore, walking in a circle. "They're bringing Alvarez in through my hatch!" With his heart racing, he stowed the radio and looped the Uzi strap around his neck. Then, with the Uzi dangling and his nerves jangling, he rushed over to the hatch area.

To guard against a Coast Guard double-cross, the Zetas would most likely take positions near the hatch to oversee the bringing in of supplies. To check the security of his hideaway, Cal stood by the hatch and faced the crates. Then he walked up the steps and eyeballed the crates from various angles. After looking, he determined he would go undetected as long as he kept to the shadows. Even with the hatch door swung wide open, the outside light wouldn't filter much past the tightly packed boxes in the center of the cargo bay.

To check the reverse field of vision, Cal hastened around the backside of the crates and looked toward the hatch. Peering through a four-inch crack between crates, he had an unobstructed view of the hatchway and approximately six feet on either side.

With nothing to do now but wait, Cal sat behind the crates with the Uzi across his lap—listening to his chest pound. Any minute now the Zetas would be descending the stairway to receive the incoming coastguardsmen.

During his Navy SEAL days, Cal had found the waiting game more nerve-wracking than combat. It gave soldiers too much time to think and came hand in hand with nervous sweats and a jittery gut. Right now, as Cal waited in the shadowy void between the crates and hull, all 60-trillion cells in his body were primed to kill or be killed.

It had been over thirty years since Vietnam and Cal was curious as to how he would react when it came right down to taking a human life. Would he hesitate? Or freeze? After all, he wasn't a callow, preprogrammed, nineteen-year-old anymore that killed indiscriminately because someone of higher rank told him to. The Cal Stringer of today was a freethinker, not a follower, and a steward of the law. It was his profession. But he was also a strong proponent of the death penalty and believed that the punishment should fit the crime.

After mulling it over, Cal knew he wouldn't waver. With twelve civilians dead, one of them female, it wouldn't be murder—it would be justice. In the law world it was called quid pro quo.

Cal checked his watch and peered again through the crack. If he had his druthers, he would pick off Alvarez the moment he set foot on ship. In wartime one rarely had the chance to take out the enemy's key commander and in minutes Alvarez himself would be making his grand entrance. From this distance he and his men would be sitting ducks—more like dead ducks.

But to Cal's bitter disappointment an ambush was out of the question. The Zetas topside would hear the gunfire and might open fire on Skip and his crew. In effect, Cal had no practical choice but to wait for a clash at sea. At that point any logical threat against the Zetas would come from the sea or air—a double-cross by the military. Alvarez and his gang would never expect an assault from within. Why would they?

That's when Cal would make his move. As written in Exodus 21:24: *an eye for eye, tooth for tooth, hand for hand, and foot for a freaking foot.*

Monday 12:30 Hours – "Helo-1"

Now that Stringer was in the loop, it was one less worry on Ray's mind. Had the Zetas or coastguardsmen bringing in supplies taken him unaware, it could have been disastrous.

Ray lifted his tinted visor and squinted at his watch. The snail-like speed of the convoy was putting the operation further behind schedule. Instead of circling overhead like a good little admiral, he wanted to rush full speed ahead and get the show on the road—to put an end to the mother of all nightmares. But nothing could be accomplished without the vessels below and Ray knew it. So, exercising a little patience, he relaxed his shoulders and loosened his clenched jaw. Events would come to pass in their own sweet time and not a minute before.

Looking out his side window, Ray took in the lustrous powder-blue sky encasing his tiny speck of an aircraft. Its sheer magnificence, combined with the rhythm of the rotor and steady vibration of the cabin, had a relaxing effect. As the tension ebbed from his body, Ray began to mellow and his mind drifted to a similar springtime day years ago.

It was his ninth birthday and he was at the Florida State Fair. As a birthday gift, his mother had promised him a hot-air balloon ride and he was filled with anticipation. He had always been thrilled by high places, which was why the Ferris wheel was his favorite ride. On occasion his mother would ride it with him and that was even more fun because then he could scare her.

Full of young boy mischief, he would wait for them to stop on the very tiptop and then rock their seat until it swayed wildly. He loved his mom dearly, but he also loved hearing her petrifying squeals. It was a hoot. Deep down, he suspected that she liked it too—the same way a lot of folks enjoyed a good scare.

Perched way up high, young Ray loved to watch the colorful ants swarming below. Some were red, some were blue—their color depending on the clothing they wore. But they were all just peasant ants and he was king-of-the-world.

When his mother wasn't watching he would invariably lean over and spit. After gathering as much saliva as his mouth would hold, he would let it ooze slowly from his lips and watch it freefall all the way down. If it splattered one of the ants, that was an extra bonus; but if it didn't, that was okay too because he just liked watching it fall in its own bombs-away fashion.

As Ray recalled that special day a nostalgic feeling swept over him. It was all still fresh in his memory—the metallic click-click sound of the rollercoaster being hoisted up the steep track, the shrill squealing as it rushed headlong down the first slope, the blaring calliope music from the merry-go-round, the cracking of .22 rifles from the shooting gallery, the smack of a wooden mallet followed by a clang of the bell, the seedy-looking barkers standing in front of big brown tents calling: *"Hurrrray, hurrray, hurrrrry."*

Then, there were the unforgettable fair smells—the sweet scent of cotton candy, fried cheese steak and onions, corn dogs, funnel cake, animals and hay, spent gunpowder, the occasional whiff of vomit near the rides.

When his mother told the balloonist it was his birthday, the man promised Ray an extra high up-up-and-away birthday ride. With Ray on board, the colorful balloon rose and rose and rose. When it leveled off, the pilot hoisted Ray's head above the basket to view the earth below. With wide-eyed awe, he gawked open-mouthed at the tiny matchbox houses and bug-like cars. He was so overexcited, he remembered almost peeing in his pants. It was a great birthday present, a grand birthday present—his best birthday ever.

WIRED

Out of the blue Ray had an off-the-wall urge to dribble a big spitball on Señor Alvarez. While toying with the thought he looked down at the cutter transporting the infamous drug lord. As Ray gazed down, he pictured how stupendous it would be when the high-altitude, high-velocity, giant globule of saliva crash-landed on Alvarez's slicked-back hair, knocking him flat—*SPLAT!!!*

Relishing the idea, the little boy in Ray grinned with devilment.

Look out below, Señor Dickhead—here it comes. BOMBS A-W-A-A-Y -Y-Y!

Monday 12:45 Hours – The "Majestic Star"

Skip was scanning the eastern horizon when three helos and a small task force of ships came into sight.

"Well, well," Skip said, peering through the binoculars. "Yonder comes the cavalry, Neal. Lickety-split."

Fifteen minutes later a Coast Guard cutter dropped anchor near the *Majestic Star's* starboard hatch while a second cutter maneuvered alongside the port beam to receive passengers. Once both vessels were in position, the starboard cutter launched a dinghy with one person on board.

Focusing the binoculars on the dinghy, Skip saw that it carried a shackled and blindfolded lone male. "That must be him," Skip muttered. "The Prince of Poppy himself."

Once the dinghy floated halfway between the cutter and the *Majestic Star*, its stern line was secured to a cleat on the cutter and the bowline was heaved to a Mexican standing on deck above the starboard hatch. Now each faction had a hawser attached to the skiff. At this, a gangplank was extended between the cutter and the starboard hatch and coastguardsmen began offloading boxes of food rations and bottled water.

While this was taking place the fuel barge pumped diesel fuel and potable water into the tanks of the *Majestic Star*. As the ship's gauges rose toward the FULL mark, large cargo nets were lowered from the sundeck's port railing to the waiting cutter below. Without a moment's delay overanxious passengers began scaling down the nylon netting toward freedom.

Raising his binoculars, Skip panned their faces as folks made their eager descent. He focused on a frightened little girl clinging to her father's neck as he edged unsteadily down the webbing. Moving on, he watched a woman lose her footing and fall into the waiting arms of two seamen below. Some passengers were smiling while others shed tears of joy, all visibly relieved their ordeal was over. And with each passenger that set foot on the cutter, Skip's burden as captain lightened proportionately.

Amazingly it didn't take long for the passengers to disembark. One hour later they were all safely aboard the 270' cutter. As the passenger-laden cutter pulled away from the ship, the second cutter released the dinghy's stern line, allowing the Zetas to retrieve their beloved boss.

As Skip watched the two cutters steam toward shore, he somehow felt free—even though it couldn't be further from the truth.

Monday 14:00 Hours – The "Majestic Star"

Secreted within the shadows of the crates, Cal had watched the Coasties bring in box after box of supplies. Fortunately the boxes were stacked near the hatch opening and no one ventured back toward the crates. Once all goods had been delivered, the gangplank was withdrawn and the Coast Guard cutter pulled away.

The three Zetas that stood watch over the coastguardsmen were now standing in the open hatchway, looking out to sea. The skinny one in the middle was shouting orders to someone up on deck and Cal wondered if he was Mendoza. Though just a dozen yards apart, the outside glare made it difficult to see. The only distinguishable feature Cal could make out was a wad of white gauze on the nose of the bigger man standing beside him.

Then a rope was lowered from somewhere above and the skinny man greedily retrieved it. The other two men laid down their weapons and all three began hauling in the line hand-over-hand. From the way they were babbling and all in a dither, Cal reckoned that Alvarez would soon be making his grand appearance.

WIRED

While the dinghy was being hauled toward the hatch, the gang members topside hung over the deck railing in wild celebration. Some of them cheered and fired their AKs at the sky while others showed their contempt by hoisting their middle fingers in the air and shouting obscenities at the departing ships.

When a Mexican dropped his pants and mooned the departing troops, some of the other Zetas joined in—wiggling their bare rumps degradingly at the ships. As a payback for the offense, an old seadog aboard the civilian fuel barge dropped his drawers and mooned them back, shooting them both "fingers" while doubled over.

Skip was standing on the catwalk during all this, watching the sordid scene through his binoculars. Unsurprisingly, the Zetas were acting like a bunch of high school punks after winning a rival football game. And the more they razzed the Coasties and whooped it up, the more Skip was looking forward to having it out with them.

"And they call *us* infidels," Neal said, looking over Skip's shoulder.

Skip lowered the binoculars and turned his head. "Yeah, they're nothin' but a bunch of heathens. Neanderthals. But if they wanna party, I got their party right here." With a wily wink, Skip raised his pant leg a smidgen to implicate the Glock. "Let the festivities begin."

~~~~~~~~~~

When the dinghy appeared in the hatchway, Cal strained for a glimpse of Alvarez but the gunmen were standing in the way. Then a grungy-looking guy came bounding down the steps, barking harshly at them in Spanish. He was a gangly unshaven man wearing a headband and rumpled khaki shirt. The others deferred to his obvious authority and cleared a pathway to Alvarez, who Cal finally saw for the first time.

Standing in chains, Alvarez was a powerfully built man dressed in civilian clothing. He was blindfolded with a strip of silver duct tape stretched across his mouth. Heading up the welcoming committee, Mendoza removed the blindfold and beamed proudly at his superior—exposing a gold front tooth.

Blinking against the sudden daylight, Alvarez appeared momentarily puzzled and unsure of his whereabouts. While Mendoza tried to delicately peel the tape off his mouth, the Colombian's eyes roamed his new surroundings, taking in every detail. To Cal, his eyes looked as cold and lifeless in person as they did on television. They were black as oil and looked like one solid pupil—like those of a man-eating shark.

Growing increasingly annoyed at his minion's fumbling with the tape, Alvarez frowned at Mendoza and snorted impatiently through his nostrils. This display of dissatisfaction added more pressure and Mendoza's hand began to tremble. When Alvarez snorted again, the stress became too great and he dispensed with the finesse, ripping off the tape in one mighty yank.

The unexpected move took Alvarez's breath away, along with a patch of mustache hairs stuck to the tape. His body stiffened with startlement and his mouth flew open wide, like an overheated marathon runner suddenly doused with ice water.

"You fool! What are you trying to do to me?" His eyes were two molten pits. "Get me out of these chains—now! *¡Prisa para arriba!* The key is in my back pocket!"

"Sí, Señor Alvarez! Right this minute!"

In a panic, Mendoza plunged both hands inside Alvarez's back pockets and began feeling around for the key; and the more he groped, the more perturbed Alvarez's face grew. The drug lord was on the verge of exploding when Mendoza produced the key with a nervous smile. But before unlocking the chains, he grasped Alvarez squarely by the shoulders and kissed him behind each ear.

Witnessing this ceremonial absurdity made Cal want to puke. He'd heard of sucking up to the boss before, but this was ridiculous.

Mendoza unlocked the chains and let them fall freely to the floor. As the steel shackles clanged against the metal flooring, the surrounding men whooped and cheered and that's when Cal noticed that two of the gang members were Arabic. Al-Qaeda, he presumed.

With the chains now lying at his feet, Alvarez stood in poised motionless—head erect, chest out, a stately scowl on his face. Cal hated him already.

He looks like some prize bull standing there. What are they gonna do next—pin a blue ribbon on his chest? Kiss his ring? Anoint him with oil?

The melodrama was sickening enough, but what really irked Cal was

WIRED

the way Alvarez lapped it up with supreme, God-like, self-importance. Any moment now Cal expected the skies to part and a shaft of holy light to spill forth from the heavens, bathing Alvarez's head in a halo of divine radiance—Saint Alvarez.

Pretty proud of yourself, ain't you Señor? I oughta do the world a big favor and take you and your pimps out right now.

By now Cal's self-restraint was razor-thin and a quiet anger boiled within him. He had been in hiding since last night and he was fed up with the waiting game. It would be dark in four hours and he was running out of time. He just wanted to get Skip off this ship and go have a cold beer.

As Cal stared through the crack, his finger toyed with the safety switch. He could take out Alvarez and his entourage in five seconds flat. The dirtballs didn't deserve to live anyway—especially Alvarez. He didn't even deserve to breathe Cal's air.

Alvarez was a deliverer of dope . . a dasher of hope . . a destroyer of lives. He was a death maker. He was a scourge on society, leaving nothing but tragedy in his wake—victimizing and destroying at will for personal gain and power, without a scrap of compunction.

Cal had seen a parade of wise guys just like him in Detroit courtrooms—pushers, thieves, muggers, pimps, pickpockets, killers. They had one thing in common: they were all losers.

While studying the five men, Cal had a flashback of the grisly murders he had eyewitnessed through the telescope—the lifeless bodies splashing into the water...the rust-colored bloom of hot spewing blood mixed with greenish seawater...the way the riddled corpses bobbed upon the waves before slipping under the surface.

Cal ached inside to exact revenge, to kill the warped bastards where they stood. One burst from the Uzi and they would all go bye-bye. Their little praise-a-thon reunion would end with a bang.

~~~~~~~~~

With the task force now specks on the horizon, Skip began to prepare himself for his first encounter with Alvarez. He didn't know exactly what to expect, but assumed that Alvarez would want to get directly underway. So, to both occupy himself and to calm his jitters, he unrolled a chart of

WIRED

the Gulf of Mexico and proceeded to plot a dogleg course taking them west and then due south for the Straits of Florida.

In plotting the first leg, Skip's concentration was interrupted by the sound of an approaching helicopter. Thinking that perhaps one of the military helos had returned, he walked onto the catwalk to spy a *Channel 10 Newscopter* circling overhead. Squinting against the sunlight, he saw a cameraman hanging out its door shooting film.

"Tryin' to get the latest scoop, huh?" Skip said to himself. "Later today, you'd have plenty of breakin' news to film—really breaking."

When the newshounds spotted the captain on the catwalk, the helicopter accelerated and swooped down on Skip like a hawk. Within seconds the copter was hovering eye level with him—its backwash kicking up a whirlwind of air and spraying seawater. Still rolling film, the cameraman was aiming his camera at Skip.

Holding onto his captain's hat, Skip recognized the pretty newsgirl sitting in the cockpit wearing headphones. She smiled and waved at him through the glass bubble and without thinking he waved back and then saluted the camera. After that he flashed them a dorky thumbs-up sign from both hips and his hat blew off, tumbling end-over-end down the catwalk.

As Skip chased after his hat, he regretted the foolish stunt and hoped that *Channel 10* wouldn't air the footage. Given the enormity of the situation, it was a pretty hokey thing for the skipper of a newly liberated hostage ship to do. On television he would probably look more like someone who had just won a new Toyota than a responsible ship captain.

After retrieving his hat, Skip slinked back inside the wheelhouse and peeked out a window. As he did, the newscopter—and incriminating piece of film—whizzed away toward the mainland. If the news channel did happen to televise it, he hoped that Kathy and the guys at the marina wouldn't see it—especially the hat-chasing scene. He would never live it down.

Why am I such a putz? Sheesh!

While still brooding over the goofy stunt, Skip fed their present coordinates into the GPS mapping software. The Global Positioning System was a network of 24 satellites orbiting the earth 10,000 miles in space. The positional system was accurate to within ten feet on earth and much more dependable than the old LORAN navigational system that operated via radio waves using a network of sea buoys.

When Skip keyed in the westerly coordinates, the GPS instantly mapped out a chart taking them from their present position to the point westward. He was entering the southerly coordinates when Mendoza led an unfamiliar person into the wheelhouse—*Alvarez*.

With his muscles tightening, Skip stood erect to receive his new visitor. After five days of captivity and the slaughter of a dozen people, he was about to meet the mastermind behind it all.

Juan Carlos Alvarez was an imposing man with dark Latin features, oily black hair, and a matching mustache. He was tall and his brawny physique was well defined beneath his yellow cashmere sweater. He strode with the confidence of a leader and someone accustomed to getting his way. His presence filled the room.

The Colombian halted a few feet from Skip and dipped his head in salutation. Skip gave him a quick once-over and then stared straight ahead without returning the courtesy. Overlooking the slight, Alvarez edged closer and regarded Skip more fully in the face. His coal-black eyes had a smothering effect.

"Captain Myles, I presume?" His dialect was impeccable.

"That's the name," Skip cracked. "And you must be Señor Alcatraz— I mean Alvarez."

Provoked by the comeback, Mendoza seized Skip by the shirtfront and shook him. "Respect for Señor Alvarez, capitán—or die. *¡Hágalo o muera!*"

Skip snarled his upper lip at Mendoza and wrested loose from his grasp. He'd had a belly full of the Mexican's threats. He wasn't killing anyone—not just yet. Not as long as Skip was needed to captain the ship.

"*¡Bastantes!*" Alvarez shrieked at Mendoza. Then he looked at Skip and his features softened.

"Captain, it appears that we've gotten off to a bad start." Smiling politely, he offered his hand. "I am Juan Carlos Alvarez. I must apologize for my associate's rude behavior."

After some hesitation Skip accepted his hand. Alvarez was a clever man and to beat him at his own game would require patience. Now wasn't the right time. Still, the slimeball was responsible for twelve people dead and Skip couldn't altogether hold his peace.

"You killed my passengers," Skip said man-to-man, pumping Alvarez's hand. "Female included. I don't know about in Colombia, but from where I come from that's very uncool."

"Casualties of war, Captain." Alvarez's expression was stolid. "Of course, when you Americans kill innocents, I believe you call it collateral damage. It's semantics. Sounds less . . *messy* . . that way; but it's all the same." His words were matter-of-fact, without emotional value. "Civilians are often caught up in the throes of war—regrettable, but true. That's the way it's been since time immemorial."

"Well, there's no war going on here, mister, and those dead passengers weren't your enemies."

"I beg to differ," Alvarez corrected. "My world *is* one big war and *everyone* is the enemy."

The Colombian released Skip's hand and wandered about the wheelhouse, casually picking up objects and setting them down. Even in his arrogance there was something magnetic about him.

"Captain, please be so kind as to plot a course due west and then north-northwest for New Orleans. I have friends there expecting me."

Skip looked less astonished than confused. *Why the change in plans? What was going on?*

"Ah-h . . ." Skip stammered, trawling for further explanation, "but I thought we were sailing south for Colombia."

"Eventually. But not on this vessel, I'm afraid." There was a note of reproof in his voice. "I'm a trusting person, Captain, but I really don't think the U.S. authorities will permit it. Do you?"

Skip tried to think fast. "But that was the agreement, wasn't it? That you were free to leave with the ship?"

"Oh, Captain, Captain." Alvarez smiled with cool amusement. "Are you so naïve to think that your government would not sink this vessel with you and your crew on it?" He began circling Skip. "They knew from the start that I would never agree to such an ill-conceived arrangement. That's why they played their little con game on my associate here. Don't you see? They don't intend for me to escape."

Alvarez was right on the money and Skip felt pressured to dissuade him. "Well, why not? The government rescued the passengers, didn't they? That will score a lot of points with the American public—take some of the heat off. The Coasties will keep their word."

Alvarez's chicken hawk circling was making it hard for Skip to think. His words were hurried and stumbled and his bluff was sounding more and more unconvincing.

"My dear Captain, indulge me a moment." Alvarez stopped directly in front of Skip. "What about the passengers that didn't get saved? Twelve in all. Do you think the media will forget that? Do you think their families will forget that? Do you think the American authorities will forget that? Certainly, Admiral Hanna will not forget it; that I can assure you."

Leaving the questions hanging in the air, Skip fell silent and stared at the floor. He was fresh out of arguments.

"That's what I thought, Captain." He looked at Skip with amused pity. "I'm glad we're in agreement. Please proceed due west for one hour and then plot a direct course for New Orleans. Do you understand?"

"Yeah," Skip muttered, feeling defeated.

How about a direct course up shit creek? he wanted to say.

Monday 15:16 Hours – Station Sand Key

As Helo-1 made its approach to Sand Key, Ray took in the gridlock below.

The mass convergence of emergency vehicles, media trucks, incoming relatives, and nosy spectators had the streets clogged in every direction. The Intracoastal Waterway behind the station was similarly congested, teeming with pleasure boaters, wave runners, Coast Guard vessels, and the Florida Marine Patrol—all zigging and zagging. Adding to the bedlam on the ground was a sky full of military aircraft, police copters, and newscopters swarming overhead like killer bees. Topping off the circus-like atmosphere was the ringmaster himself: Geraldo Rivera. The news icon's semi-trailer was now parked across the street from the Sand Key stationhouse with its rooftop microwave dish poised for telecast.

As arranged beforehand, police roadblocks were set up at major intersections made up of bomb-sniffing K-9 units. Authorized vehicles were searched for explosives while unauthorized vehicles were turned away. Coast Guard sentries were stationed along the perimeter of the grounds and the SEALs manned designated checkpoints for incoming relatives. From what Ray could visibly determine from the air, the collaborative effort appeared to be working.

But contrary to Ray's best-laid plans, when Helo-1 touched down the waiting newspeople burst onto station grounds like the Green Bay Packers. Before Ray could shed his Mustang life jacket, a horde of journalists engulfed the helipad and surrounded the red-and-white helicopter.

Thinking, *so much for my top-notch security*, Ray swapped his crew helmet for a ball cap and opened the cockpit door. Right away reporters bombarded him with questions but the roar of the decelerating engines drowned them out. As the gas turbines wound down to a low whistle, Ray held up his arms for quiet. Anticipating a late-breaking announcement, the rival reporters all crowded around him, pushing and shoving for position while poking their microphones in his direction.

"I don't have time for a full-blown news conference," Ray began, "but I'll be glad to answer a few questions after I make a brief statement." He paused while the reporters readied their cameras and recorders. "After lengthy negotiations with the terrorists, we have secured the release of all passengers aboard the Majestic Star. They have been successfully evacuated and will be arriving here shortly to join their loved ones. They're a little worse for wear, but I'm happy to report they're alive and well." There was a ripple of approval. "In exchange for the lives of the passengers, the courageous crew of the Majestic Star will transport the terrorists out of American waters. When the ship reaches its final destination, Captain Myles and his crew will be released unharmed."

Chomping at the bit, a half-dozen reporters chimed in at once. "What's their destination?"

"Sorry, but for the time being that's classified." At dodging the question, Ray pointed to a local TV anchorman waving his arm. "Yes?"

"Admiral, our sources indicate that Juan Carlos Alvarez was also included in the trade for the passengers. Can you elaborate on that?"

Ray cringed at the question, but knew it was one that would be asked. In his morning press release, he had purposely left that piece of information out.

"Yes, that's correct. Washington believes that the lives of two hundred citizens are of much greater importance than the immediate prosecution of one drug-peddling criminal."

Just then, someone shouldered their way through the crowd, raising a rash of complaints from the other reporters. "Admiral Hanna! Excuse me! Admiral Hanna!"

When Ray looked toward the voice, he saw Geraldo and his stomach gurgled.

"With all due respect, sir, isn't that glossing over the truth somewhat?" When Geraldo saw the TV cameras zoom in on him, he straightened his tie and assumed a more dramatic demeanor. "Not only have you rewarded a Mafioso kingpin by giving him his freedom and a multi-million dollar cruise ship, you have in fact allowed him to get away with murder. As we speak, Alvarez is somewhere off our shores with his armed band of compatriots and once again a menace to society. Isn't that the bare truth, sir?"

As the mustachioed journalist awaited his answer, Ray eyed him up and down—convinced that Geraldo's lineage would trace back to the 1591 Spanish Inquisition. All reporters sensationalized the facts now and then, but Rivera was a grandmaster. There *was* a hint of truth in what he was saying, but Ray couldn't let him get away with taking potshots at him or making a laughingstock of the military.

"No, Mr. Rivera. That's not the bare truth—at least not entirely."

Ray directed their attention by pointing to a Coast Guard cutter just mooring up behind the station. Jubilant passengers were leaning over the railings and waving ecstatically to waiting relatives onshore. Some fathers aboard were toting children on their shoulders for a better view of the crowd below. Joyous friends and family members on the dock were yelling names and waving their arms excitedly for attention. One and all were celebrating the reunion and either smiling or crying or hugging or clapping. It was a touching, emotionally packed scene. After five terrifying days of captivity, their ordeal was finally over.

"The bare truth, Mr. Rivera, is that those children will sleep in their own beds tonight—safe and sound. There will be no more threats...there will be no more eyes brimming with terror...there will be no more murder." Ray's voice was scolding, rising in pitch. "The *bare truth* is that our government won't rest until Mr. Alvarez is back behind bars. He will pay for his crimes against America, that I can assure you. Mr. Rivera, I suppose the *bare truth* is that you'd rather see those children die of dehydration than have your government yield to one or two terrorist demands. That would give you plenty to report about, wouldn't it? *'CHILDREN DIE OF THIRST WHILE AUTHORITIES FLOUNDER.'* The Majestic Star was completely out of drinking water, Mr. Rivera, or didn't your sources tell you that?"

Publicly embarrassed and at a rare loss for words, Geraldo glowered red-faced at Ray while slowly lowering his microphone. Relishing Geraldo's hangdog expression, Ray brushed past him while heading for the stationhouse, followed by a trail of question-filled reporters.

One 510' guided missile destroyer: $410-million dollars. One Sikorsky Jayhawk helicopter: $10-million dollars. Spoiling Geraldo's wet dream on live television: priceless.

Monday 15:24 Hours – Clearwater Beach, Florida

As the television cameras followed Admiral Hanna inside Station Sand Key, Kathy turned off the television and smashed the remote control against the wall.

"What the hell's going on here!? This wasn't supposed to happen!"

Feeling betrayed and deliberately misled, she seized the telephone and jabbed in the numbers for Sand Key. She was half-past furious and going on rabid.

"This is bullshit! No one said Skip would remain a hostage!" As the phone rang in her ear, she stomped around the living room, cursing the admiral under her breath. "Hanna's got a lot of explaining to do—one helluva lot!"

Monday 15:26 Hours – Station Sand Key

As soon as Ray entered the stationhouse, the Cuban telecommunications specialist snagged him by the elbow and pulled him aside.

WIRED

"Excuse me, Admiral. While you were busy with the press, your acquaintance—Mr. Stringer—hailed for you on Channel 12. I intercepted the hail and instructed him to stand by. He's waiting for you now on the radio, sir."

Nodding, Ray commended the ensign for his discretion and made tracks for the radio room.

~~~~~~~~~~

"Stringer, this is Bluebird. Over."

"Roger, Bluebird. I've got an update for you. Black King has joined his Black Pawns topside and White Queen is currently heading due west."

"Roger. When is White Knight planning to enter the game?"

"Once things settle down just a bit. Roger?"

"Is your brother-in-law planning to enter the game too, or remain a spectator?"

"He's ready to play and will follow my move. Over."

"Is he equipped to play?"

"Roger."

"Glad to hear it. Is he also aware of when the game must end?"

"Affirmative."

"Good. Then everybody understands the rules."

"Roger. We definitely know the score."

"Excellent. Keep me posted on the game's progress. Assuming the home team prevails, I'll see you tonight after the match. If nothing further, Bluebird out."

"Catch you later—I hope. White Knight out."

~~~~~~~~~~

As Ray exited the radio room, a message was handed to him that made his stomach sink. Kathy Myles was holding for him on the telephone and refusing to hang up until she spoke with him. The message slip quoted her as saying: "Even-if-I-have-to-stay-on-hold-for-the-rest-of-my-entire-miserable-freaking-life!"

Ray groaned, thinking: *Great...just what I need...she must've just seen me on TV.*

Not looking forward to the conversation, Ray found an empty desk and sat down. After thinking for a moment, he pasted on a smile and picked up the receiver.

"Mrs. Myles," he answered brightly, "this is Ray Hanna. I was just getting ready to call you."

"Yeah, I'll bet you were!" she snapped. "What the hell's going on, Hanna? Why was Skip left out there to rot aboard the Majestic Star?"

Guilty for not being upfront with her to begin with, Ray endured the scolding. He deserved it.

"It was the only way the terrorists would release the passengers, Mrs. Myles. I can only say that if all goes as planned, your husband and brother will be home sometime tonight."

"That's a crock! It's not what you said on television a few minutes ago."

"That's correct. But, then again, we can't tell them everything, can we?"

Kathy calmed down a notch. "Well, if that's true, you won't mind me coming to the station and waiting for them there. I'm going stir crazy sitting here alone."

"Sorry, ma'am. I'm afraid that won't be possible until the roadblocks are lifted." While talking Ray peered out a window at the departing passengers. Their tired but grateful expressions lent him a good feeling. They were safe and going home. But the feeling fizzled when he spotted Geraldo interviewing a woman passenger. "But you have my word that I'll contact you the moment I get an ETA. Then you can pick them up. How's that?"

Kathy was still skeptical. "Well...okay...I guess. But I still don't like it. If anything changes—*anything*—do you promise to notify me immediately?"

"Promise. Hang in there, Mrs. Myles. It'll be over soon. I'll contact you later. Goodbye."

As Ray cradled the receiver, he felt a twinge of guilt for getting her hopes up. After all, in just a few hours he was going to sink her husband's ship whether he was on it or not. Ray just hoped that Myles and Stringer could in fact be rescued. If not, his next conversation with Kathy Myles would not be so civil. She would rip his head off and crap down his throat.

Curious as to what Geraldo was doing, Ray raised in his seat for a better look outside. The woman he had cornered was one of the females singled out for execution this morning. With the cameras rolling, the newshound was interviewing away with a dramatic up-close-and-personal look on his face. As Ray twisted the window blind closed, he imagined Geraldo's lead story: **"BLINDFOLDED AND BOUND---WAITING FOR DEATH."**

Forgetting about Geraldo, Ray walked over to a large wall chart of the Gulf of Mexico. It was time to focus on his next task: the destruction of the *Majestic Star*. While studying the laminated chart, he absentmindedly tapped a black grease pencil against his front teeth.

The ship's cruising speed was twenty-two knots, twenty-five if pushed. Stringer had just confirmed the ship was sailing due west. In all probability Alvarez's destination would be the Colombian seaport of Cartagena, 916 nautical miles southeast of Cancun. Mexico would be much closer, obviously, but the *Policía Federal Ministerial* would be waiting for him when he arrived. The PFM was a federal agency created to combat the Mexican drug cartels and they had enough arrest warrants on Alvarez to fill a suitcase.

Sticking with the Cartagena premise, Ray plotted a hypothetical course taking the ship west of Florida until picking up the southerly flow of the Gulf Stream—the shipping lanes—then on a course south-southwest for the Yucatán Channel. By factoring in the *Majestic Star's* cruising speed, he projected the ship's offshore latitude to be somewhere between Sarasota and Fort Myers by nightfall. To confirm this he would have Chief Bloyd maintain visual verification via satellite.

Ray marked a big 'X' on the chart and circled it. That's where she was going down. The Guided Missile Destroyer would be waiting for the *Majestic Star* there.

Monday 15:54 Hours – The "Majestic Star"

When Cal checked his wrist compass, it read 270°—confirming they were still on a heading due west. If Alvarez's destination was South

WIRED

America, Skip would soon be altering course to the south. That's when Cal decided to make his move.

Like a lion stalking its prey, he would single them out and pick them off. But, unlike a herd of wide-eyed stampeding animals fleeing from a heel-snapping predator, when the Zetas became aware of *this* predator's presence, it would be too late for escape—way too late.

~~~~~~~~~~

Following Alvarez's abrupt introduction to the captain, Mendoza took him for a tour of the ship, leaving Stan behind to watch Skip. Mohammad was down in the engine room with Neal, who was helping a crewman change out a leaky valve. Under orders to cruise at top speed, the diesels were wound up to maximum RPM and the strain was already showing. On a typical four-hour day cruise the engines seldom exceeded half-throttle.

As Skip steered the ship into the late afternoon sun, glaring rays of orange and gold poured through the bow windows. As it shone directly into their faces, Skip could clearly see just how jet-black Stan's swollen eyes had become as a result of the broken nose. The wad of gauze was now gone and the hulk resembled a football player with black greasepaint under his eyes, or a zombie extra in a low-budget horror movie. Though he didn't dare let on, Skip found it hilarious.

Some minutes later Neal and Mohammad entered the wheelhouse and Neal joined Skip's side.

"You missed it, Neal," Skip said without turning his head. "Alcatraz just left here. Gold-Tooth's showin' him around the ship like he owns the place. Guess in his eyes, he does."

Since unnecessary talk was forbidden on the bridge, Neal checked over his shoulder before answering. "What was he like?"

Facing straight ahead, Skip removed his sunglasses and rolled his eyes toward Neal. "Cold. Dangerous. Wants to go to New Orleans."

"New Orleans!?" Neal said a little too loudly.

Overhearing the remark, Mohammad shot to his feet and pointed at Neal. "Silence!"

Not caring to provoke the scrawny hothead, Neal backed away from

Skip and pretended to wipe his greasy hands with a rag. The New Orleans revelation was a real shocker and it bummed Neal out. When he had learned of Cal's presence and seen the Glock, it gave him a newfound feeling of optimism—a feeling that maybe he *would* live to tell friends and family all about it. But, now, as he watched Skip alter their course northward, he couldn't fathom what sort of fate awaited them. With his hopes thinning, Neal pitched the rag down and stared longingly at the changing compass needle.

Skip knew exactly what Neal was thinking because he was thinking the same thing—that the Coasties wouldn't be expecting a getaway to the north and that each rise and fall of the bow could be taking them further away from rescue.

As the rudder answered the helm and pointed the ship west-northwest, Skip switched the radar scanner to maximum range. As he watched the wand make a full revolution, it confirmed his suspicion. For now, anyway, they were on their own—just them, the deep blue sea, and darkening skies to the north.

In his mind's eye, Skip visualized the Navy Destroyer that Cal had described—a little unknown fact he hadn't shared with Neal yet. The name in itself expressed its sole purpose in life—to destroy. Skip was keenly aware of the massive destruction a missile destroyer could inflict. Just one cruise missile below the waterline would sink the *Majestic Star* in a matter of minutes. Any hit above the waterline would blow a gaping hole through the entire ship.

That was one navy vessel Skip didn't want to see making its approach. While Neal danced around in ignorant bliss and celebrated their rescue, Skip's sphincter would be puckered up so tight that a greased BB couldn't slither past.

Monday 16:14 Hours – Group St. Petersburg

Ray was back in his St. Petersburg office standing next to Chief Bloyd.

"They should be here about now, Chief, and preparing to alter course to the south." Ray jabbed a pushpin into the wall chart. "Is my helo ready?"

WIRED

"Fueled and waiting, sir. Your pilot will be Lt. Commander Henninger. One of D7's best."

"Good. Keep close tabs on the ship's progress via one of the keyhole-class reconnaissance satellites. I'll make comms with you once we're airborne for Fort Myers."

"Aye, sir. Will do." The chief went rigid and nearly saluted before catching himself. When his eyes dropped self-consciously, Ray grinned and pretended not to notice.

During his short walk to the helipad, Ray rehashed the standard Coast Guard methods used for rescuing stranded victims at sea—namely Stringer and the crew. In a perfect world the Zetas would all be dead when the rescue attempt took place, making the whole thing a breeze. But if they were still alive and lurking, lowering a horse-collar sling or heli-basket would be too dangerous under fire. The electric hoist was relatively slow and only had a 600-pound capacity, meaning it would take a series of lifts to get everyone off—too risky for the aircraft and rescue crew. The rescue of Stringer and company was a high-priority with Ray, but not at all costs. The lives of the rescuers were of equal importance.

This situation called for a method that would get the rescuers in and out quickly—wham bam, thank you ma'am. A standard rope ladder would be safer, quicker, and more efficient. Simply drag it across the deck and let everybody hop on. Then, once at sea and out of firing range, the survivors could scale the ladder and climb aboard the rescue craft. Another option would be to drop a rubber raft and let everybody swim for it. The sixty-degree water would feel like ice water and some may not survive it, but it was still better odds than going down with the ship.

With his brain abuzz, Ray climbed into the cockpit and strapped himself in. While donning his crew helmet, the turbines accelerated from a low idle to a gyrating roar. As the swirling 54' rotor built up velocity, a helmeted Coastie appeared in the pilot's side window and slapped the door, signaling the aircraft was ready for departure.

Nodding back, the pilot wagged the control stick and the Jayhawk ascended straight up, then sliced low across the courtyard in the direction of Fort Myers. As the reverberating thumps echoed off the pavement below, Ray's mind groped for a better rescue solution but there were none. If the rope ladder didn't work, he would drop them an inflatable raft equipped with EPIRB for tracking and wish them luck.

If Stringer and Myles were even alive when he got there.

Monday 16:05 Hours – The "Majestic Star"

As the *Majestic Star* entered deeper ocean, the turquoise hue of the shallows gave way to a grayish-blue indigo. Now, instead of muscling its way through choppy swells, the sleek black hull raised and flattened in lazy rhythm with the rollers.

After being dead in the water for what seemed like weeks, Skip was thrilled to be back underway—to feel the wheel's polished spars in his grasp, to feel the familiar thrum of the engines beneath his feet. While both helmseats were outfitted with chrome steering wheels for piloting the ship, Skip preferred to stand and steer the old fashioned way. After decades of captaining tugboats and the like, he could never man the helm while sitting on his rump like some pantywaist office worker. To him, it just wasn't nautical-like.

Though a far cry from the truth, being underway gave Skip the illusion of freedom and it had a euphoric effect on him. On a whim he gave Neal the helm and cranked open all the windows, inviting the salt air to rip through the wheelhouse. As papers and charts fluttered from the intrusion, the suspicious Arabs rose to their feet and eyeballed the unpredictable captain.

Paying them no mind, Skip walked to the open doorway and leaned a shoulder against it. Wearing a contented look, he crossed his arms and took in the sweeping seascape. Having spent a good deal of his adult life at sea, he was something of a stranger on land. Inhaling deeply, he removed his hat and let the wind rustle through his hair. Then, on a whim, he flung the hat outside by its shiny black bill. The round flat portion of the hat caught the wind and it sailed through the air like a Frisbee before splashing into the sea. If everything went right and God was willing, he would see Kathy tonight—*tonight*.

Skip envisioned her dear face and smiled. It seemed like months since he had last seen her. He wondered what she was doing right then, how she was holding up. For her sake, he hoped she could cope with the outcome should fate not be sympathetic to them. In talks past he had made his wishes known about her moving on and remarrying should something happen to him. With no children to care for her, it upset him to imagine her in a nursing home someday as a forgotten old woman.

A wistful look crossed Skip's face as he recalled the silly game they played on some lazy mornings. While the coffee was brewing, both of them would mentally pick a number from one to ten. Then they would take turns guessing at each other's secret number. Whoever guessed the closest got to stay in bed while the other one fetched the coffee.

While musing on it, Skip gave a ridiculous chuckle. Here he was...standing on the precipice of life-or-death...up to his white ass in alligators...and he was daydreaming about drinking coffee with his wife. Adversity, it seemed, sure had a way of rearranging ones priorities in life.

If I get out of this mess alive, I'll never take my marriage for granted ever again. No siree. For, in the end, nothing else truly matters—I just thought it did. And if I don't survive it, so be it. Kathy deserves better than the likes of me anyway.

A jagged streak of lightning flashed brightly to the north, bringing Skip's awareness back to the present. While he had been daydreaming the seas had grown rougher and the bow was slapping harder against the head swells. Standing taller, he scanned the dark nebula of clouds dead ahead. A thunderhead was brewing and the magnitude of it covered the entire horizon.

Respectful of any approaching front with an "N" in it—from the North, from the Northeast, from the Northwest—Skip hastened to the radio facsimile and pressed a button. Seconds later the Furuno Weather FAX408 spat out a high-resolution satellite image of the central Gulf of Mexico. After tearing off the thermal paper, Skip studied it with a frown.

On top of everything else, they were sailing into the path of a freak springtime squall.

~~~~~~~~~

When Cal checked his compass he was shocked to find the ship on a northwesterly heading. Wondering why the change in course, he hailed Bluebird on Channel 12 to alert him. After several failed attempts, he broke Hanna's cardinal rule and hailed the Coast Guard on Channel 22.

When he still got no answer, he tried Channel 16 to receive nothing but static.

Then it struck him. With the ship moving steadily away from the mainland, his portable radio was now out of range. Even the high site antennas of the Coast Guard couldn't pick up his minuscule signal.

With this realization Cal switched off the radio and picked up the Uzi. He was on his own—time to lock and load. With a flutter in his belly, he clicked off the safety and headed up the diamond-tread steps.

~~~~~~~~~~

"What's our heading, Captain?" Alvarez quizzed, strutting into the wheelhouse with Mendoza.

Sighing with dislike, Skip said: "315° west-northwest."

"Yes, that sounds about right." Alvarez walked over and checked the compass for himself. "And what is our ETA to New Orleans?"

Alvarez's superior attitude was getting under Skip's skin. "Well, from here, it's about 325 miles to the South Pass entrance, and then it's another 73 miles up the Mississippi. At this speed, our ETA is approximately 10:00 hours tomorrow morning, depending on the weather." He pointed at the sky. "We got some bad weather moving in from the north."

Alvarez eyed the horizon unconcerned. "Yes, I dare say you're right. But I'm sure it's nothing this capable vessel can't handle. Would you like to break for some food, now? I have a nice Colombian stew being prepared below that I'm sure you would enjoy."

Skip was disinclined to take any favors from the mobster, but in this case he thought it wise to accept. The ration of limas and potatoes had worn off long ago and this would be his last chance to eat before things hit the fan. "Yes, that would be good about now. My first officer here can take the helm."

"No need, Captain." Alvarez extended his hand at Mendoza. "Santiago, here, can man the helm while you both eat. He is quite capable of keeping us on course. I will have two hot bowls brought up as soon as the stew is ready."

Mendoza beamed with the compliment, prompting Skip and Neal to roll their eyes. Even his gold tooth seemed to have an extra sparkle to it.

"That will be fine," Skip said. "Thank you—I suppose."

"Not at all, Captain. We Colombians are very civilized people, you know." His tone was laced with arrogance. "Quite benevolent, actually." On his way to the exit, he turned and leveled an arctic stare. "Just don't fuck with us." A dark force seemed to emanate from his eyes. "Ever."

Skip Myles feared no man alive on Earth. Nevertheless, a chill trickled down his spine. Beneath Alvarez's artificial politeness and gentlemanly facade, there was something infernal about him, something soulless—like Satan himself.

~~~~~~~~~~

As Cal climbed the outer stairs to the main deck, a downdraft of wind whisked through the hollows of the stairwell creating a low moaning sound. In the sky above the stairwell opening, he could see heavy rain-laden clouds scudding in from the north. Then, as if the gods were angry, a cannonade of thunder rumbled across the heavens and a lance of blue-green lightning tore across the darkening skies. Seconds later a rolling clap of thunder boomed and it began to sprinkle. This was a grossly inopportune time for a thunderstorm and Cal cursed the inclement weather.

Taking the steps two at a time now, he kept one eye on the sky and one eye on the flight of stairs before him. As he scaled the heights his darkish path was illuminated by intermittent cracks of lightning. At reaching the top, Cal stopped short of the opening and crawled up the remaining steps on his belly. Then, like a timid turtle, he poked his head out between the railings and peered up and down the deck.

Several yards astern, Cal saw two Mexicans sitting in white lounge chairs with their backs facing him. Their AK's were lying flat on the deck between them and they were sharing a six-pack of beer. One of them sported a backwards ball cap and the other wore a plaid lumberjack shirt with the sleeves cut out.

Letting the Uzi dangle from its shoulder strap, Cal slung it behind him to ride his lower back and raised his pant leg to extract the hunting knife. After slipping the knife under his belt buckle, he removed the lawnmower grips from his pant pocket and stretched the wire taut.

WIRED

Now ready to strike, Cal crept in silence toward his unsuspecting prey.

Monday 16:40 Hours – "Helo-1"

As Helo-1 cruised 3,000 feet over Sarasota, Ray radioed ahead to Station Fort Myers with his revised ETA. He would be arriving a few minutes late for the task force meeting.

If everything held to plan, the *Majestic Star* would reach the northern sector of the blockade area at dusk. When given the command, a detachment of naval warships would converge on the *Majestic Star* and destroy her. The purpose of the scheduled briefing was to finalize the logistics and implementation of the synchronized strike.

Ray had just signed off with Fort Myers when Chief Bloyd's voice came over his headset.

"Helo-1, this is Group St. Petersburg hailing. Over."

"Roger, Chief. Hanna here. Over."

"We've got a problem, sir. Dense cloud cover has moved into the Gulf of Mexico from the Florida panhandle. It looks like a squall—northern cold front colliding with our warm tropical air. It's moving into our theater of operations now. The impenetrable cloud cover will obscure optical satellite imagery until it blows through. Over."

Ray didn't like what he was hearing. Without the ability to track the *Majestic Star* by satellite, they had no means of knowing where the ship was or when it would reach the blockade zone.

"That's bad news, Chief. It's imperative we maintain a fix on the Majestic Star. Did you try one of the radar-imaging satellites capable of penetrating cloud cover?"

"Not yet, sir. The radar-imaging and near-infrared radiation satellites are not geostationary. Most are in polar orbits. There are none over our region at the present time. The multispectral satellite used for gathering Cuban intelligence will be in position in roughly three hours. I can check then, sir. Over."

Ray wanted to curse but held his tongue. The news was upsetting and he was unstrung by it. As part of the negotiations with Mendoza, he had granted the Zetas unconditional free passage devoid of chaperones. With the surveillance technology available to him, he didn't believe the concession mattered at the time. Obviously, he'd been remiss.

"We can't wait three hours, Chief. What was the ship's last known position? Over."

"Thirty-three miles west of Sand Key on a course due west, sir. That was about a half-hour ago. I have reprogrammed the computer for continuous real-time satellite downloads. I've also got TISCOM in Alexandria and the National Imagery and Mapping Agency working on it. NOAA, too. We're all monitoring the situation closely, sir. Over."

Ray suddenly felt warm all over and he raised his visor for some fresh air. At a top speed of twenty-five knots the *Majestic Star* wasn't going anywhere too fast, but losing visual contact was disconcerting.

"Roger. Well, maybe there'll be a break in the cloud cover and we'll get lucky. How long is the storm predicted to last?"

"The front is heading south-southwest with clear skies behind it, sir, but it's a slow mover. At its present speed, we should be clear of it in four to five hours—unless it stalls out. Copy?"

"Well, let's hope *that* doesn't happen." The dissatisfaction in Ray's voice was unequivocal. "All right, Chief, one last thing. Change frequencies to Channel 12 and hail Mr. Stringer. I'm too far away or I would do it myself. If he answers, get a compass reading from him and report back to me. Roger?"

"Affirmative, sir. Will do. I'll notify you of any response. Over."

"Good. Find the Majestic Star for me, Chief. I'm counting on you. Helo-1 out."

Ray twisted his mouthpiece away and pushed back in his seat. His airtight operation had just sprung a leak. If the Commandant found out that he had lost track of the ship, he would be cleaning up oil spills for the rest of his career—his incredibly short career.

The only option now was to send in a spotter aircraft, but that carried risk. Due to the low ceiling of clouds, a visual fix would necessitate an even lower flyby. If the aircraft was sighted, it might look like a double-cross and screw things up royally.

Congratulations, Ray-Man. You've been racking your brain for a graceful way out of this mucked up mess and now you don't even know where the godforsaken ship is!

WIRED

Monday 17:02 Hours – The "Majestic Star"

Lightning flashed across the sky in a brilliant blue arc followed by a bellowing boom of thunder. Simultaneously scattered raindrops began to fall intermixed with pea-sized hailstones.

As Cal neared the gunmen from behind, the Mexican on the right said something in Spanish and the other man's eyes climbed skyward. Then the two began gathering up beer bottles as if moving to a drier place.

Now ten feet away, the pounding of Cal's heart thundered in his ears like a drum. He had to make this quick. The pair could turn around any second and one shout would bring the entire mob down on him.

With time slowing down to a crawl, Cal vaulted through the air and landed behind the Zeta on his left wearing the ball cap. In a slow-motion flurry he looped the wire around the man's throat and shoved a knee between his shoulder blades, then pulled back powerfully. When the wire met resistance, Cal gave it a vicious yank and the tough gristle of the trachea gave way, spewing a sickening effusion of hot blood down the Mexican's chest. Gurgling with his tongue sticking out, the bug-eyed man tore desperately at the wire while flailing his legs like a puppet doing a spasmodic tap dance.

Without letting up pressure, Cal switched both lawnmower grips to his left hand and extracted the hunting knife with his right, then turned to deal with the Zeta wearing the sleeveless shirt.

In paralytic disbelief, the other man was gaping up at Cal from his chair, still holding onto the beer bottles. When his lips parted to scream, Cal reacted with lightninglike speed and brought the knife down in a sweeping arc, embedding it in the gunman's throat. As the steel blade severed his vocal cords, ropes of slime shot from his mouth and the brute force caused him to topple backwards in the chair. With beer bottles scattering, he writhed about the deck in a stifled frenzy, emitting wet grunting noises while pulling hysterically at the knife handle.

Realizing the man was finished, Cal refocused on his first victim, who had ceased struggling and gone limp. With both men either dead or dying, Cal uncoiled the wire and let the Mexican fall to the deck. The lifeless man sprawled onto his back and droplets of rainwater sprinkled his bronze face. When Cal checked again to his right, the other man's legs spasmed a final time and stopped. Though he was dead, his hands still clung to the knife handle and tiny bubbles percolated from around the embedded blade. His teeth were red with fresh blood and pinkish drool leaked from one corner of his gaping mouth.

As blood and body fluids pooled beneath both victims, its stench rose on the damp air. While seemingly much longer the entire skirmish had lasted less than a minute.

After searching both men for the detonator, Cal dumped the first body overboard. Then he pried the Mexican's fingers from the knife handle and used the knife to cut off his sleeveless shirt. After rolling him overboard as well, Cal mopped up the bloodstains with the shirt and stuffed it in a trashcan along with the ball cap and empty beer bottles. Then he hid the two AK's in a storage locker under some lifejackets, thinking they might come in handy later.

Not letting the lawyer in him dwell on the double homicide, Cal armed rainwater off his face and chugged the only remaining beer. By this time the waves were whitecapping and the wind was blowing at least 50 knots. Just then, thunder boomed like a bombshell and cold rain pelted him sideways. Simultaneously the ship listed to port causing him to temporarily lose his balance. After regaining his footing, Cal turned his face away from the driving rain and staggered blindly toward the dining room entrance. He would search the dining room first and work his way up.

As Cal opened the door, he tallied: *Two down. Seven to go.*

~~~~~~~~~~~

As the *Majestic Star* entered the outer bands of the thundersquall, torrential rain peppered the windows like buckshot and a fitful wind howled through every crack and cranny of the wheelhouse—ranging in sounds from a shrill whistle to a low moaning ghost-ship sound.

While the storm raged outside Skip and Neal sat the chart table, hunkered over their bowls of sloshing stew. As Skip chewed his food, he took stock of the gang members in the wheelhouse.

Gold-Tooth was manning the helm with a death grip on the wheel and a terrified look on his ashen face. Funnier still were Mo and Stan, who were sitting poker straight on the aft bench seat, bracing themselves like a couple of frozen-stiff airline passengers making their first flight. All three were taken in by the storm, making them easy and unsuspecting targets.

I could take all of 'em out right now, Skip thought. *Pow, pow, pow. Piece of cake.*

Skip had been held hostage long enough. He was ready to go home—way past ready. Pushing his empty bowl away, he checked his watch. It would be dark soon. At 18:00 he would make his move. Cal or no Cal, that was long enough.

Monday 17:08 Hours – Station Fort Meyers

As Helo-1 touched down in Fort Myers, Chief Bloyd's voice came over Ray's headphones. Hoping for some good news, Ray hung onto his words just to be disappointed. Attempted comms with Stringer had failed and there had been no appreciable change in the cloud cover.

With the unfavorable news gnawing at him, Ray unbuckled his seat harness and strode inside the stationhouse. Already assembled in the briefing room were top-ranking commanders from the Coast Guard, Air Force, and Mayport Naval Station. Upon entering the room Ray gave the task force members a respectful nod and spread out his chart on the conference table.

"Okay, gentlemen. Time is short, so let's get down to it." While everyone gathered around, Ray pointed to the X's marked in grease pencil. "Here are the designated positions for Destroyer Squadron Fourteen. I want the destroyer USS Farragut here and the guided missile frigates Halyburton and Taylor here and here." While talking, he thumped his index finger on each mark. "I want the Island Class patrol boats posted at five-mile intervals along this longitudinal line to make up the western enclosure. That will comprise the blockade. Here are the lats and longs." Ray divvied out sheets of paper from his briefcase. "Pass these coordinates to the respective vessels. Once they reach their assigned positions, tell them to stand by for further orders. The Majestic Star should reach the blockade area around dusk. That's when the Farragut will take her out. As a backup, a squadron of F-16's will be standing by at MacDill in the event they are needed." An Air Force colonel nodded affirmatively. "I'll be monitoring the operation from Helo-1 overhead. Our working channel will be Channel 12. No one is to fire upon the Majestic Star without my express command. Is that understood?" As Ray checked their faces, everyone nodded. "And this is imperative—inform all personnel to notify me at once if a radio communication is intercepted from anyone identifying himself as Stringer."

With the task force commanders still looking down at the chart, Ray stood up to leave—his chair screeching backward in his anxiousness to get airborne. He had decided to perform the reconnaissance flight himself. Someone had to find the *Majestic Star* and he couldn't risk some hot-dog pilot screwing things up. The search would have to be discreet—just a peek.

"Pardon me, Admiral," the colonel spoke up, ostensibly puzzled. "Is this Stringer individual an integral part of our operation?"

"You could say that," Ray answered without explanation. "Just pass it on."

Monday 17:11 Hours – The "Majestic Star"

With his hair a wet clump and rainwater dripping from his clothes, Cal prowled quietly through the unlit gloom of the dining room. As he crept forward, strobes of lightning flashed through the outer windows giving him an on-again-off-again glimpse of the room's interior.

To his left was a mirrored liquor bar and on his right was a corner bandstand with small dance floor. At the far end of the room were long steam tables, a dessert bar, and stainless double-doors leading into the kitchen. Adjacent to the galley were restrooms and an interior staircase leading up to the casino on the second level.

Just as Skip described, the room was empty of tables. Having been pillaged, the once charming room looked like a cyclone had blown through it—littered with upset chairs, scattered silverware, ketchup bottles, strewn salt and peppershakers, and countless packets of sweeteners. The floor was so cluttered that Cal had to look carefully before setting each foot down. With the Zetas lurking about, the slightest noise could have deadly consequences.

After making a clean sweep of the dining room, Cal advanced silently toward the kitchen. In drawing nearer he detected the tinny rattle of pots and pans and the smell of food being cooked. When he reached the swinging double-doors, he peeked through one of the oval windows to see a man standing at a stove wearing a cook's apron. His back was facing Cal and he was stirring something in a big pot. His AK-47 was propped against the kitchen counter approximately five feet to his right.

Sidestepping to the other door, Cal stretched his neck and peered through the glass. As far as he could see the man was alone.

Without a sound, Cal backed away from the doors and rested the Uzi on the floor. He would have to make this quiet and quick. Deciding against the knife, he withdrew the bloodstained wire. After peering through the window a second time, his instincts told him to make his move. With a grip in each hand, he nudged the swinging door open with his left shoulder and entered the kitchen.

As Cal stalked him from behind the clueless cook tasted the contents of the pot, added salt, and then stirred some more while humming to himself. Now just seconds away, Cal was set to strike when he accidentally kicked a metal spoon left lying carelessly on the ceramic tile floor. As the utensil screeched loudly across the hard surface, the startled cook spun about and hunkered down in anticipation of an assault.

Crouched eye-to-eye a mere six feet apart, the cook wavered a split-second before going for his weapon. Reacting just as fast, Cal dropped the wire and dove through the air in a do-or-die challenge to head him off. Cal slammed into him with the full force of his bodyweight, pinning the cook sideways against the hot stove. The man whimpered at impact and fought back to shove Cal off him, spilling stew down into the gas burner during the struggle.

With the smell of burnt stew flooding the air, the Mexican elbowed Cal in the chest and unleashed a roundhouse swing that barely missed Cal's jaw. Then he cried out for help, forcing Cal to smother his scream with the palm of his left hand. Suddenly finding himself in a hand-to-hand -face-to-face duel, Cal seized the man's throat with his right hand and squeezed with all his might. The vise-like stranglehold purpled the cook's face and his eyes bulged twice their natural size. On the verge of choking to death, the Mexican chomped down hard on the heel of Cal's hand, shaking his head side-to-side like a wild beast.

WIRED

The pain was excruciating but Cal's discipline kept his hand in place. Seconds later blood dribbled down the man-eater's chin and Cal realized it was his own. When the mounting agony transcended his threshold of pain, Cal released the cook's throat and grabbed his hair, yanking the man's head toward the gas flame.

The Zeta flexed his neck against the pressure and arched his back in opposition, but without any leverage he began to weaken. As his head neared the gas burner, his nostrils flared wider with rising panic and his eyes darted frantically between the flame and Cal's snarling face. When the smell of burning hair suddenly filled the air, he emitted a stifled squeal and squirmed away from the flame—rolling his wiry frame lengthwise along the countertop, taking Cal with him. After a few twisting turns their legs entangled and the cook tripped to the floor, dragging Cal down by his lockjaw teeth.

Now balled up in a flailing knot, the fighters somersaulted across the kitchen floor—crashing into a pushcart of dishes. . grunting. . groaning. . trading jabs and blows. As the Zeta crawled toward the AK with Cal's hand clenched in his mouth, Cal delivered two bruising body shots and rolled him onto his back. After another squirming bout of flinging and flailing, Cal maneuvered himself on top and straddled his writhing opponent. But by now he was sweating profusely and beginning to tire against the younger man.

Pressed to end the skirmish before running out of steam, Cal groped for the ankle knife with his free hand; but due to his straddled position the pant leg was bound tightly around the knife handle. Every time Cal tried to loosen the cuff, the Mexican bucked wildly to throw him off and clawed savagely at Cal's unprotected face—forcing Cal to thrash his head side-to-side like a wild horse to evade the slashing fingernails.

While Cal was fumbling blindly for the knife, the cook emitted a psychotic growl and clamped down with a vengeance, burying his fangs deeper into the tendons of Cal's hand. Then he gnashed his teeth grindingly, driving Cal to tear harder at the constricted trouser leg. Just as the cook's fingernails sank into Cal's cheek, there was an audible rip and Cal felt the pant leg loosen. Unsheathing the knife with lightning speed, he fell eye-to-eye upon his opponent and buried the knife just below the Mexican's breastbone.

WIRED

The cook's eyes bulged at its entry and his body went rigid, but his teeth stayed clamped around Cal's hand. To finish the job, Cal twisted the knife and ripped the blade upward toward the man's heart. The cook shuddered in response and his knuckles flailed violently against the floor, but moments later he quit thrashing and a peculiar peace settled over him. Lying still in a filmy sweat, the man gazed sorrowfully into Cal's eyes—the eyes of his executioner.

It was a familiar sight to Cal; one he had witnessed on the battlefield. The docility was a sign of surrender—of acceptance. The Mexican knew he was dying and had reconciled himself to it.

All at once the cook's eyelids fluttered shut and Cal felt the teeth relax, bringing sweet relief at last. But as Cal withdrew his hand, the man's eyes reopened and he craned his head to the left. With a glimmer of recognition on his face, the cook extended his arm as if reaching out to some imaginary figure. Then, with a faint smile on his bloody lips, he mouthed a few words but nothing audible came out. Moments later the mouthing stopped and he sucked in a mighty gasp of air. As his last shuddering breath escaped him, his outstretched arm dropped heavily and the full weight of his body sagged on the floor.

As Cal stared into his waxy whites, the man's life energy ebbed away as quietly as the tide.

Winded and altogether used up, Cal rolled off the dead man and sprawled on his back. The coolness of the ceramic tile was a welcome relief to his overheated body. While gasping for breath, he stared up at the kitchen lights in steamy wet clothing. As hot blood pulsed against the back of his eyes, the fluorescent lamps strobed bright-and-dim in systaltic rhythm with his heart.

Cal's mouth was dry as tinder and his face was slathered with sweat. His hand and cheek were bleeding and there was a sharp catch in his right side. But it could have been worse, much worse. At least he was alive.

~~~~~~~~~~

As the *Majestic Star* bore the brunt of the storm, it rose skyward on mountainous waves before crashing headlong into churning troughs, repeatedly awashing the foredeck with swirling foam. Veins of lightning crisscrossed the nocturnal sky and thunder rolled overhead like boulders, vibrating the innards of the wheelhouse. The torrential rain and encroaching darkness made for near zero visibility and the heavy seas and buffeting winds competed for control of the ship.

Skip was back at the helm with a steady grip on the wheel and a toothpick dangling from his mouth. After he and Neal finished eating their stew, Mendoza gladly surrendered the helm and joined his boss for a bowl of "victory stew" in Skip's quarters, which Alvarez now claimed as his own. Neal was presently outside with his watchdog Stan, doing an emergency fix on a rooftop antenna loosened by the wind. This left Skip and Mohammad alone in the wheelhouse.

Mo was perched on the bench seat behind Skip, cleaning his AK-47. He had rags scattered everywhere and a small can of oil sandwiched between his boots. From the jumpy way he was acting, Skip figured he was just trying to keep his gay monkey brain off the stormy weather.

The storm posed no real threat to the ship, of course, but that was unbeknownst to the landlubbing camel jockey. So, for a little payback fun, Skip would peer down at the radar screen, murmur a concerned "uh-oh," then bend over and cast a worried eye toward the heavens.

Whenever he did this, Mohammad's black eyes darted worriedly between Skip's face, the radarscope, and the threatening skies outside. And the more nervous he got, the faster he rubbed on his AK, bringing Skip that much more inner satisfaction.

~~~~~~~~~~

Cal was still sprawled on the kitchen floor, catching his breath. By now his blood had re-oxygenated and his redline heartbeat had slowed to a more natural rhythm. While not fully recovered from the skirmish, he felt pressed to move on before being discovered.

Rolling onto his belly, Cal drew his knees up under him and pushed against the floor with his palms. Rising on rubbery legs, he latched onto the countertop for support and drank thirstily from the spigot. Then he held his sweaty head under the running stream. The cool water felt fabulous and brought blessed relief to his boiling body temperature. After cooling down to some extent, he straightened and shook water from his hair, then held his chewed-up hand under the spigot.

"Christ it hurts!" he growled, flinching from the watery sting.

Once the blood was rinsed off, Cal examined the throbbing bite wound. On each side of his hand near the fleshy part of the heel was a bloodied arc of teeth-marks. In peering closer, he noticed a gap in one of the imprints, obviously due to a missing tooth. Wincing, Cal made a fist to check for muscle damage. Finding the hand more sore than injured, he wrapped it with a dishrag and tied it off using his right hand and teeth. Then he cleansed the fingernail gouge on his cheek and took another long drink of water.

Feeling his strength returning, Cal bent over the dead man and went to work. After removing the knife from his chest cavity, Cal cut off the apron and dragged the body to the walk-in freezer. When he opened the freezer door a frosty vapor of cold air drifted past him and he paused a second to savor its coolness. Inhaling deeply, he stepped inside the cooler and hid the corpse behind a stack of frozen boxes. At that, he turned off the gas burner and used the apron to tidy up the stovetop and bloodspot on the floor. Once all was wiped clean he reentered the freezer and tossed the apron and AK next to the dead body. Then he locked the freezer door and stuffed the key in his pocket.

Before leaving, Cal recovered the wire grips and surveyed the empty room. Satisfied that everything looked back to normal, he peered through the double-doors and exited the kitchen.

Three down and six to go.

~~~~~~~~~~

With twilight setting in, Skip checked the radarscope to see if they had any company yet. Nothing. Not even a lousy shrimp boat. Obviously, Hanna and his men were on a wild-goose-chase somewhere south of them. Otherwise they would be making their approach by now to get within firing range.

Skip viewed the snafu as a double-edged sword. If Hanna didn't know their whereabouts he couldn't very well sink them, thus giving he and Cal more time to kill off the bad guys. On the other hand it meant they were totally on their own—win, lose or draw—with no prospect of outside help or rescue.

Skip's eyes shifted from the radar screen to the marine radio. If he could use it for just ten seconds, he would blurt out "Mayday, Mayday" and transmit their latitude and longitude to the entire listening world. That was altogether out of the question, of course, but it spawned another idea that could conceivably signal their position—if Skip could pull it off.

Skip switched the toothpick to the other corner of his mouth and glanced over his shoulder at Mohammad. As he did, the ship listed hard to starboard and Mo's oilcan slid away from him, scooting across the floor. Muttering something profane-sounding in Arabic, Mohammad threw down his rag and chased after the can. Just as he sat back down, a booming clap of thunder jarred the wheelhouse and the faintheart almost jumped out of his skin. Spewing more native vulgarity, he snatched up the oily rag and began wiping away with a passion.

Looking straight ahead, Skip bit down on the toothpick and broke off a sliver with his fingers. Then he shuffled his body sideways to block Mo's line of sight to the radio. With a flutter in his gut, he looked over his shoulder one more time to find Mohammad still wiping away. He had to make this quick. If he got caught messing with the radio, the Arab would shoot him on the spot.

Deciding to go for it, Skip squeezed the transmitter button on the side of the microphone and wedged the piece of toothpick between the button and plastic housing. Then, with his two-second mission accomplished, he returned his hands to the ship's wheel and acted normal. In scrutinizing his handiwork, Skip noted that the inconspicuous toothpick was holding the transmitter button in the depressed "TALK" position. The microphone was now permanently keyed, transmitting a streaming squelch-hiss to anyone listening within radio range.

The Coast Guard referred to them as *"open carriers"* and they severely interfered with radio reception. If the open carrier—usually a stuck microphone key—happened to be in closer range to a Coast Guard antenna than an outlying ship at sea, its stronger radio signal would block out the weaker signal from afar. Since this posed a serious threat for offshore vessels seeking emergency assistance, the Coast Guard routinely policed Channels 16 and 22 for unauthorized talk and open carriers.

The procedure for locating an open carrier was the same method used for finding lost boaters at sea: an electronic device called a Radio Direction Finder. The DF's worked by locking onto an incoming radio signal and displaying a compass bearing back to the signal source. However, Direction Finders were only capable of interpreting the *direction* of the signal, not the *distance*. To figure the distance, two or more DF's were activated from multiple Coast Guard stations. Because the stations were located miles apart, each DF reading gave a different bearing to the emanating source. To pinpoint the origin, each bearing was plotted on a chart and where the lines intersected revealed its exact location.

Skip hoped that a vessel within hearing range would notice the radio interference and report the open carrier to the Coast Guard. At this stage of the game, anything was worth a try.

Monday 18:00 Hours – Gulf of Mexico

Since departing Fort Myers, Helo-1 had covered a widespread area of coastal waters with no sign of the *Majestic Star*.

The sun had set by now and the fiery-red western sky had softened to silken wisps of luminous gold. On the skyline to the distant north an ominous gathering of clouds loomed; the leading edge of the squall Chief Bloyd warned about. In the irradiant afterglow of dusk, the storm clouds looked like smoldering embers of cinder and ash, making Ray squirm in his seat. It would be dark soon and if he didn't locate the missing ship, *Operation Checkmate* could wind up a big fat embarrassing bust.

Since optical satellite imagery was useless at night, it left only infrared technology to locate the ship. But unlike optical satellites, which could be zoomed-in to identify daytime objects as small as six inches, near-infrared satellites merely detected the heat emanating from objects— like a running combustible engine. And from high overhead many heat signatures appeared the same. Since ships the size of the *Majestic Star* were plentiful in the shipping lanes, a positive identification would be impossible without visual verification.

Growing more anxious by the minute, Ray double-checked his computations to arrive at the same conclusion: if the Majestic Star was indeed heading south, it should be in this vicinity. Nevertheless, with nothing but empty ocean stretched before him, Ray had to accept the harsh fact that it wasn't. He had made a serious error.

So, if not south, which way was the ship heading? With the peninsula of Florida lying to the east, it meant the *Majestic Star* was traveling either west or north. Could Alvarez be heading for Mexico? In spite of the Mexican authorities and the PFM? Not ruling anything out, Ray rehashed the known facts.

FACT: the last satellite telemetry showed the ship on a westerly course. FACT: Stringer had verified this by radio. FACT: Alvarez had close underworld ties with the Mexican cartels. FACT: the *Majestic Star* carried enough fuel to cross the 1,000-mile Gulf of Mexico. FACT: Mexico would be a logical choice if Alvarez could slip in undetected. A straight shot across the Gulf and he's in a friendly but corrupt Spanish-speaking country—his kind of place.

After some deliberation Ray ordered his pilot back to St. Petersburg. After refueling, he would personally lead a systematic search beginning with the ship's last known position.

As Helo-1 sped northward through the dying light, Ray hailed Station Fort Myers and recalled the blockade of warships. Much to his discredit, the *Majestic Star* wasn't out there.

Monday 18:10 Hours – The "Majestic Star"

As Cal climbed the connecting staircase between the dining room and casino, his left cheek was oozing blood and the bite mark on his hand throbbed in unison with his heart.

"I'm getting too old for this hand-to-hand crap," he growled under his breath. "The next guy that even smiles at me is gonna get shot on the spot—noise or not. If I see teeth, they're a freaking dead man."

When Cal rounded the landing, the dim ceiling of the casino came into view above the stairwell opening. Pausing a moment, he cocked his ear for a listen. At hearing nothing but the howling wind, he continued up the stairway and stopped again when at eye level with the carpeted floor of the casino.

The casino was pitch black inside but intermittent flashes of lightning revealed split-second snapshots of its interior. The room was crammed with dining tables brought up from below, some stacked on top of others to create makeshift bunk beds. Crumpled white tablecloths were scattered about the tables and floor, evidently used for blankets. The room was absent of life.

Sensing the casino was safe to enter, Cal stood more erect and clicked on the penlight, careful to keep the beam away from the portholes. Just like Skip described, all gaming equipment had been removed to make room for the tables. Except for two leftover craps tables and a banner that read: **"Sign Up Here for Our $5,000 Slot Tournament,"** the room held little semblance to a casino.

As the penlight swept the room, it revealed other scraps of humanity left behind: a paper sailor's cap...a souvenir lei...a doll's head...plastic water bottles...scattered belongings. While panning the litter Cal pictured the two hundred folks confined here for five long days, crammed together like sardines—terrified and morose.

Although the passengers were long gone, Cal could still sense their presence within the walls; as if their suffering had left a lingering imprint of sorts, the essence of which he found bleak and depressing. Even more depressing were the luckless passengers that had not survived to go home, the ones Cal had seen through the telescope.

The flashback angered Cal and negated any leftover feelings of guilt perchance lingering in his subconscious for cold-bloodedly killing the three Mexicans. The spic bastards deserved it. They had condemned themselves two days ago when spilling first blood. He was merely carrying out their self-imposed death sentence.

Cal took no enjoyment in playing executioner, but he had a job to do. He couldn't let himself get sidetracked by matters of right-and-wrong or if he was any less of a murderer. There were six other evildoers in need of elimination; other waxy whites waiting to stare back at him.

A fine spray of mist unexpectedly sprinkled Cal's face, interrupting his thoughts. He looked in the direction of it and noted a porthole left standing open. For no particular reason he closed the window and then headed for the rear exit. Halfway there, something crunched underfoot and he illuminated the floor to find a scattering of plastic gambling chips.

Knowing it was silly, but doing it anyway, Cal picked up a thousand dollar chip and tucked it in his back pocket. Armed with his good luck piece, he exited the casino and stepped out into the darkest shadows of night.

~~~~~~~~~~

By now the *Majestic* Star had reached the outer fringes of the squall, leaving the severest weather behind. Instead of rain slamming against the windows in sidelong sheets, it was now coming straight down in a steady drizzle, drumming heavily on the wheelhouse roof.

When Skip spotted a purple patch of evening sky up ahead, he was elated. He was tired of wrestling the rudder and being pounded by the surf. He was also tired of waiting. He had delayed his 18:00 deadline so as to navigate the storm and he was anxious to be rid of it. At the ship's present speed, he expected to run clear of the squall within the hour—thank God.

Neal and Stan were back inside the wheelhouse, still wearing their yellow foul weather gear. Sopping wet, Neal was staring down at the latest weather fax report with water dripping from the tip of his nose. Stan was sitting next to Mohammad with rainwater pooling at his feet. Finally done with his gun cleaning, Mo was inserting his freshly oiled clip into the AK-47.

Skip checked the toothpick to find it still wedged in the microphone housing. That was all well and good, of course, but the further offshore they sailed, the less likely somebody would report the open carrier, especially in view of the storm which always interfered with radio communications anyway. Unless a stray freighter happened to complain to the Coast Guard about it, it would likely go unnoticed.

As Skip watched the wiper blades scrape vainly at the bow windows, he wondered what Cal was doing—or not doing. The ship had been underway for several hours now without as much as a peep from him. What the hell was Cal waiting for? Had something happened to him?

Bewildered and flat out of patience, Skip made a decision. Once clear of the storm, he would excuse himself to use the head. When he came out, he would kill the two Arabs. The Glock would make a lot of noise and attract the others. When they came to investigate, he and Neal would cut them down with the AK-47's.

400

WIRED

Cal or no Cal, he wasn't waiting any longer.

Monday 18:42 Hours – Group St. Petersburg

While Helo-1 was being refueled, Ray hustled inside the stationhouse to meet with the Air Tactical Group pilots assembled for the search.

Ray's first order of business should have been to alert Washington of the ship's disappearance, but after browsing the succession of messages lying on his desk—first asking him, then urging him, then ordering him to call headquarters or else—he didn't see the need. The Vice-Admiral's last message was more of a written reprimand, accusing Ray of insubordination and knowingly circumventing the chain of command.

Ray understood the consequences, but what could he really tell the weasel? That Alvarez was nowhere to be found? That he had evaporated into thin air? That he had managed to escape and make a mockery of the U. S. Coast Guard? That a mere thunderstorm had rendered their surveillance technology useless? That as Incident Commander he was a fool for letting the Majestic Star sail unescorted?

"Well...at least everyone would agree on that last one," Ray muttered under his breath.

He was dodging Washington because he didn't have any concrete answers yet—that's all. He would appear as a buffoon, which, of late, was a reasonably accurate account. In any case, he wasn't ready to admit defeat yet. The *Majestic Star* was out there somewhere and he would find her. The ship wasn't missing; it was just AWOL. When he located it, he would personally contact the Commandant and square everything away.

Screw the VW and the golf cart he rode in on!

Ray entered the ready room without ceremony and motioned for the pilots to scoot-in closer, then spread his chart out on the table.

The *Majestic Star* had been underway for approximately four hours at a top speed of twenty-five knots. Given this, Ray had drawn a circle on the chart delineating a hundred-mile radius from her last known position. Then he had divided the circle into four quarters, or quadrants. Helo-1 had already explored the southwest quadrant in proximity to Fort Myers, so that sector had been eliminated. Mainland Florida itself blocked the northeast and southeast quadrants, exempting them as escape routes. That

WIRED

left only the northwest quadrant to search. Still, by using the formula *"pi r squared"* (πr^2), it meant that a whopping 7,854 miles had to be explored.

To first rule out Mexico, the search team would start off by flying due west and then sweep north-northeast along a 90° arc in the direction of New Orleans and Mobile. Ray had divided the quadrant into radial sectors with individual search assignments based on air distance capability. Short-range helos would be restricted closer to the mainland while the *HH-65A Dauphines*, having a 400-nautical-mile range, would scout the intermediate sectors. The longer range *HH-60 Jayhawks* would reconnoiter the farthest reaches of the quadrant.

As Ray detailed the search procedure, he noted the pilots looking askance at one another. He pretended not to notice but knew what they were thinking: that locating a relatively small ship in such a huge area, at night, and in bad weather, was a tall order—especially if the *Majestic Star* was running without lights, which was probable. Regrettably, the pilots were right.

Upon adjournment, the pilots exited the room with their respective search assignments. Their orders were clear: locate the ship and stand by for Admiral Hanna's command. When he gave the order, unload their missiles below the waterline and sink the *Majestic Star*. If they weren't carrying armament a navy gunship would be dispatched to perform the task. If none were within range, an air strike would be launched from MacDill Air Force Base in Tampa.

After the room emptied out, Master Chief Bloyd walked in carrying a stack of aerial photographs and radar images. Following a curt smile and respectful nod, he took a seat across from Ray and arranged the images side-by-side on the conference table.

"These are time-lapsed Doppler images of the storm, sir. When the cold air mass plowed southward into the Gulf and clashed with our warm tropical air, it created a rapid build-up of energy." He leaned over and placed his index finger on the NOAA weather map. "Right now the frontal boundary of the storm is here, west of us and moving south. The storm has a lot of upper level disturbance and convective activity, so I wouldn't rule out a waterspout. Your search team will experience lightning and severe storm cells with winds upward of fifty knots. The dense cloud cover will restrict visibility above one thousand feet.

402

WIRED

Altitudes much higher than that will require clearance to fly Instrument Flight Rules. Your pilots could get the leans."

Ray knew all about the *leans*. It was a condition brought on by flying in the blind using instruments only. With no visual references to rely on, one's equilibrium gets out of kilter and the brain's gyro tells the pilot that certain things are happening even when they're not—such as making one feel like they are turning or leaning one way or another when actually not the case.

"At any rate," the chief continued, "it will be a helluva rough ride, so I would recommend sweeping the northern sectors first until the brunt of the storm passes."

Ray frowned. "How long before the near-infrared satellite is in position?"

"Another hour, sir. Now that it's dark, it's our only option."

"Afraid so." Ray looked worried. "How many FLIR equipped aircraft do we have available?"

"Three, sir. Two helos and a Hercules hangared at Air Station Clearwater."

"Okay, let's get them in the air. Their FLIR range will be limited, but maybe we'll get lucky. Have them fly at twelve hundred feet and shoot through the cloud cover. Start them out on a westerly course and then work them west-northwest one radial sector at a time. If they detect anything on the surface that appears promising, radio me on Helo-1 and I'll have it checked out."

The *HC-130 Hercules* was a long-range, fixed-wing, four-engine turboprop surveillance aircraft. In addition to other sophisticated electronics, it was equipped with *Forward Looking Infrared Radar*—or FLIR—the same device used by law enforcement for tracking criminals. At nighttime, thermal objects on the FLIR screen appeared as white heat-generated video images. A skilled FLIR operator could distinguish one-tenth of a degree Celsius at a range of 300 meters.

"Aye, sir. Will do."

Ray checked his watch and rolled up the chart. "I realize the weather's a lot nastier to the south, but I want to begin the search there anyway. If Alvarez is hightailing it for Mexico, we've got to sink the ship before it reaches Mexican waters. On top of our other screw-ups, we

403

don't need to spark an international incident." Ray stood and handed him the chart. "Here's a detailed chart of the search area. I'll spearhead the search from the air while you coordinate the mission from here and direct communications. Time's running out, Chief. Find the Majestic Star for me. I'm counting on you."

Chief Bloyd stood up confidently—chest out, chin up. "Don't worry, sir. I'll find the sonofabitch."

"That you will, Chief. I'm sure of it." Ray gave him an appreciative grin. "By the way, if headquarters calls———"

"You're out of radio contact. I'll handle it, sir."

Ray's grin broadened. "Chief, what would I do without you?"

William Bloyd was unprepared for the compliment and his cheeks blushed self-consciously. Unable to express himself in words, he snapped to attention and gave Ray a spontaneous salute. Despite his infringement of the no-saluting-inside-the-stationhouse rule, Ray took one step back and indulged him with a return salute.

"Thanks, Chief. You're one in a million."

When Ray extended his hand, the chief accepted it with eye-squirming uncomfortableness. Following a quick handshake, Ray slapped him on the back and headed for the helipad.

Monday 18:32 Hours – The "Majestic Star"

The mixed sleet of earlier had softened to a cold rainy drizzle and Cal was shivering wet. After a thorough search of the sundeck he had sought refuge beneath the Tiki Bar's thatched roof. It was situated by the steps leading up to the bridge deck, making it an ideal place for a stakeout. From within its shadowy confines he could monitor all comings and goings to the wheelhouse.

Cal had seen neither friend nor foe since his hand-gnawing encounter in the kitchen. But there were still six gunmen holed up somewhere and the process of elimination left only the wheelhouse and private cabins.

In the night sky up ahead a few stars were visible, telling Cal that the storm would be over soon. Once the rain tapered off, he would probe the cabins first and then strike the wheelhouse. With any luck, Skip would be locked-and-loaded and ready to rumble.

WIRED

Monday 18:45 Hours – Group St. Petersburg

Ray had one leg sticking inside the cockpit when he heard his name called over the engine noise. Looking toward the voice, he saw Kathy Myles marching tenaciously toward him. On her heels was a troubled looking Coast Guard sentry striving to keep pace with her.

"Oh, great," Ray groaned, withdrawing his leg. "This is all I need."

"She said you were expecting her, sir," the harried sentry explained.

"Its okay, Seaman." Ray sighed and waved him off. "Go back to your post." As the relieved Coastie scooted away, Ray closed the helo door. "What are you doing here, Mrs. Myles?" His tone was curt and impatient. "I don't want to be rude, but I promised to keep you apprised of things and I will. But I'm much too busy to talk to you right now. Please go home and wait."

"Please don't be upset with me." Kathy's hair was flying on end from the downwash. "I just couldn't sit by the phone any longer. I thought Skip and my brother would be set free by now and I was worried. It's been over three hours since you told me that. Remember?"

When the admiral didn't respond right away, Kathy grew more assertive. "I deserve to know what's going on, don't I?" The feeling in her voice rose. "Everybody I love is on that ship and I don't know what I'd do if something happened to them." Tears swam in her eyes. "For God sake, man, tell me what's going on. Please!"

Ray looked at her puckered face and began to melt. He couldn't stand to see a woman cry. While growing up in Jacksonville, he had watched his mother weep all too often and it really got to him. Against his better judgment, he decided to tell her the truth.

"Look, Mrs. Myles, I'll level with you. We don't know exactly which way the Majestic Star is heading right now, but we think she's steaming west. We're going out to search for her right now. So, if you will excuse me."

Leaving Kathy with disappointment on her face, Ray turned and opened the cockpit door. But before he could climb in, he felt a tug on his arm.

"Could I go too? I promise not to be in the way or anything. Don't leave me standing here to wonder if they're dead or alive. Please?"

By now her chin was trembling and tears were streaming down both cheeks. And the rough-and-tough Ray-Man was weakening fast.

"Mrs. Myles, if you want me to find your husband and brother, I've got to go now." His right hand found her shoulder and he spoke with sincerity. "I'll keep you informed. You have my word on it. Now, please let go of my elbow."

"NO! There's room in the back seat and by God I'm going!" Her words were cutting, like sharp pieces of glass. "Unless you'd prefer that I stay here and call your superiors in Washington. I'm sure they'd be interested to learn that you knowingly permitted my civilian brother to board the Majestic Star!"

As Ray eyed his blackmailer, his forehead wrinkled. "Well, well. Playing hardball are we?"

"Damn right!" She seemed to grow taller. "If I have to!"

If looks could kill, Ray would be dead. Fire was shooting from her eyes and her jaw was set with determination. Her respiration was deep and her balled fists were planted firmly on her hips. From head-to-toe her body language read: *Don't you dare mess with me, buster!*

As Ray sized her up, he knew she wasn't bluffing. If left behind, she was distraught enough and certainly spiteful enough to report him to Washington. Utterly bewildered, his shoulders sagged. This was all he needed—a madder-than-hell civilian housewife tagging along.

"Okay, okay!" Scowling, Ray stepped aside and opened the door for her. "Take the seat behind the pilot." He placed a hand on her back, half-guiding, half-shoving her aboard. "I might as well break another Coast Guard regulation. The firing squad can only shoot me once."

Ray climbed in after her and slammed the door shut with more force than needed. "Just don't make me sorry," he growled at her. After buckling up, he barked at his pilot. "Let's go!"

Monday 19:00 Hours – The "Majestic Star"

Skip was turning on the ship's running lights when Alvarez and two narco-guerrillas walked into the wheelhouse.

"No lights, Captain!" Alvarez's oily black hair was beaded with raindrops and his cashmere sweater was dotted with wet rain. Figuring it was a good try, Skip flipped off the navigational lights and returned his hand to the ship's wheel. "Captain, is there any other person aboard this vessel other than your crew and my men?"

Skip's body went taut and a chill raced down his spine. The question sounded more like an accusation. "Not that I know of," he lied, trying to act normal. "Why?"

"Well, it seems that we can't locate a few of our associates." While talking, Alvarez blotted raindrops from his face with a handkerchief. "My colleague who prepared the Colombian stew is nowhere to be found and two others are missing. They seemed to have vanished into thin air. Don't you find that interesting, Captain?"

Skip immediately thought of Cal. "I don't know what you're talkin' about. I've been here the whole time. How the hell would I know?"

"Yes, Captain, I realize that. However, if there *is* someone else aboard this ship and I find that you have lied to me, it will not bode well for your crew. I will have them executed while you watch. Do I make myself clear?"

Alvarez was pacing back-and-forth, making Skip nervous. "Perfectly."

"I will execute one member of your crew for each person I cannot locate. Do you understand that, Captain?"

"YES!" Skip was feeling the pressure. "But I still don't know what you're talkin' about."

"Are you sure, Captain?" Alvarez stopped pacing and gave Skip the full glare of his shark eyes. "Last chance."

With his eyes darting nervously, Skip tightened his grip on the spars. It sounded like Alvarez was on the verge of springing something on him—but what? Did he know about Cal? Was it a trap? Skip decided to play it safe. "Positive."

With a sadistic smile, Alvarez inched closer to Skip. When delivering his next words, he wanted to see the captain's eyes. Like most beasts of prey, he enjoyed toying with his quarry.

"Very well, Captain. Since I have three men unaccounted for, I have ordered the immediate execution of three crewmen."

"WHAT!?" Shock registered on Skip's face. "You can't do that! I won't let you to do that!"

WIRED

Skip made a lunge for him but the two Zetas intervened and slammed him to the floor. In the same instant Mohammad and Stan restrained Neal by the arms. Following a brief but heated fracas, Skip ended up facedown on the floor with his arms drawn tightly behind him.

Standing over Skip, Alvarez leered down at him. "Would you like a front row seat, Captain?"

Skip flexed his body and strained to get free, but it was no use. He was pinned down so hard he could barely breathe. With no other means of showing his contempt, he glared up at Alvarez and spat on his shoe.

"I think he does, gentlemen." With a fiendish grin Alvarez wiped his Italian loafer on the sleeve of Skip's shirt. Then he pointed at Neal. "You! Take the helm and maintain our course." He motioned at Mohammad and the two Zetas. "You three bring the captain to the sundeck. The rain seems to have stopped for the moment."

The men righted Skip roughly and sat him down hard on Mohammad's barstool. With Skip squirming and cursing, they cinched his wrists behind his back and coiled a rope around his chest and stool backrest. Once Skip was fettered tight, the three hoisted the barstool in the air to carry him outside.

~~~~~~~~~~

Cal was creeping along the catwalk when a cabin door suddenly flew open a few feet ahead of him. An instant later a group of dark figures came streaming out, scaring the bejesus out of him. As Cal retreated for the Tiki Bar, sounds of a major scuffle floated out of the darkness behind him—heavy stamping of feet...grunting-and-groaning...pushing-and-shoving...the heated exchange of profanity in different languages. It sounded like a multicultural free-for-all or a liquored-up lynch mob from an old Western movie.

Just as Cal ducked down behind the bar, the boisterous blob descended the stairs to the sundeck and tramped past him in the direction of the stern. Amidst the wrangling and vulgarities, someone yelled: *"Get your damn hands off me!"* telling Cal that Americans were involved. Whatever was happening, it didn't sound good.

When the commotion grew fainter, Cal rose to one knee and peered above the polyurethane bar top. The mob was now across the sundeck near the portside, but he couldn't make out what they were doing. While on the lookout for Skip, he tried counting the silhouettes but it was too dark. It didn't matter anyway because he couldn't tell the good guys from the enemy.

Seconds later the wheelhouse door slid open and another obscure cluster of men barged outside. Before ducking down, Cal scoured the darkness for Skip's face but it was no good. All he could make out was a faceless mass of humanity advancing toward the sundeck. But when the group passed by the private cabins, the backlight from an open door revealed something—or someone—being carried overhead by the others. When Skip's voice rose above the clamor, cursing his captors at the top of his lungs, warning bells sounded in Cal's head.

Skip's life was in danger.

With his pulse pounding, Cal crawled rapidly on all fours toward the bottom of the adjoining stage. In the face of exposing himself, he needed more elevation to see what was happening. Soon after the groups came together, Cal heard a blast of automatic gunfire intermixed with shouts and screams. Cold fear flooded him and he rose up on his knees.

Skip!

Frightened of what he might discover, but acting just the same, Cal scrambled atop the stage and faced the dark mass of trouble.

Monday 19:23 Hours – "Helo-1"

When the helicopter hit another pocket of air turbulence, Kathy lost her stomach and suppressed a startled squeal. Thus far the ride had been exactly as Hanna had forewarned—*bouncy as hell*—and she had clung onto her seatbelt harness for dear life.

Fortunately the leading edge of the storm had slid southward, taking most of the splintering lightning and jackhammer headwinds with it. The drenching rain bands had lessened in severity and were now spaced further apart. Instead of a heavy downpour, the red-and-white Jayhawk was carving through a steady gray drizzle.

Seated behind the pilot, Kathy peered out her rain-streaked window, wondering how *anyone* could find *anything* in this godforsaken weather.

WIRED

Visibility was near zero and the dark ocean swells looked like mountains of landsliding water. Given these abysmal conditions, she worried about what the Coast Guard might find if-and-when they did locate Skip's ship.

Kathy believed Skip to be alive as long as he was needed to captain the ship. But would the terrorists kill him at reaching their destination? Throw his body overboard like leftover food scraps? After all, they were nothing more than a crazed bunch of psychopaths. They would probably take pleasure in it. And what about Cal? What were his true odds of survival against eight mercenaries? Thirty percent? Twenty percent? *None?*

Feeling that familiar weight on her chest, Kathy bit down on her lower lip to stop it from quivering. She was on the verge of a crying jag. Fearing tears to follow, she gazed self-consciously at the men around her working within the lambent cockpit lighting.

Strapped in the rear seat next to her, a young flight engineer was peering out the jump door window. He was wearing one of those weird night vision thingies that gave off a green glow around his eyes. Directly in front of her, the pilot was busy at the controls and next to him Admiral Hanna occupied the co-pilot seat. Hanna was talking on the radio through the mouthpiece on his helmet while scanning the watery surface below.

The entire nose of the cockpit was taken up by a dashboard infested with switches, screen displays, and complicated clusters of reddish gauges. A ceiling panel overhead housed more of the same and the floor console between the pilot and Hanna was a collage of toggle switches and electronic gadgetry. The cargo area between her and the cockpit was rather Spartan, equipped with flotation devices, flares, and assorted pyrotechnics strapped behind the pilot's seat.

What couldn't be seen was the survival gear and rescue equipment packed in the rear of the aircraft—rafts, dewatering pump, first-aid pack, collapsible litter, oxygen bottle, backpack trauma kit, IVs and intubators, and a Lifepack multifunction monitor with automatic defibrillator. In short, anything one would expect to find in a big city ambulance.

As Kathy gazed at the heaving seas, she pictured Skip somewhere down there fighting the helm with a gun held to his head. The fearsome image struck a panicky chord that made her throat tighten. But this was no time to get emotional and all weepy. She was an unwelcome guest in

410

the first place and if she started bawling, Hanna would dump her off the first chance he got—and she wouldn't blame him.

So telling herself to calm down, that it would be over soon, Kathy amassed enough strength to stave off the tears.

Soon, she kept repeating to herself. *Soon.*

But in a dread-filled way, that's exactly what she was afraid of.

Monday 19:25 Hours – The "Majestic Star"

Still tied to the barstool, Skip sat slumped in a deadened state of shock. His face bore the hollow look of a prisoner-refugee staring from the gates of a death camp. The bullet-riddled corpses lying at his feet were longtime friends of his that he had just hired weeks ago.

As Skip stared at Ron and Ivan's remains, his mind went back ten years ago. They had met while working on a rundown fishing trawler owned by a seafood restaurant on Treasure Island. Each morning at dawn they would motor out John's Pass to fish for whatever was biting that day, and every evening they returned with the *Catch of the Day* to be served fresh at the restaurant the following day. It was long twelve-hour days but Ron and Ivan's enjoyable companionship made the grueling workdays bearable.

Then Skip's eyes shifted painfully to his other friend, Pete Sullivan. Sully was married to Gabriela, or *Gabby* as he fondly called her, and they had two children. Gabby was from Czechoslovakia, where Sully had met her during his days as a merchant marine. It was love at first sight and they married two months later. Before meeting Gabby, Sully drank like a fish and partied all night long. But soon after their marriage, he gave up drinking and started going to church. The other guys teased him about it, but Sully didn't seem to mind. He claimed they just hadn't gotten "it" yet and when they found "it" they would understand.

Out of the blue Skip wondered if Sully ever bought that life insurance policy he was talking about. He had been worried about making the monthly premiums on an on-again-off-again seaman's wage and had approached Skip a few weeks ago about the security of his job. Skip recalled smiling at the time and saying: *"Sully, as long as I'm ship captain, you've got a job for the rest of your life."* Sadly, Skip had no

WIRED

idea how prophetic those words would turn out to be.

As Skip stared at the bloody remains, his eyes registered the carnage but his brain rejected it as real—retreating within itself for sanctuary; denying that this mangled mess of oozing flesh had any connection with his friends. But while a part of him wanted to cling to this self-delusion, another part cried out for reason, arguing that these murders were in fact real and that these butchered carcasses were indeed his former friends.

As the shock gradually wore off, Skip's denial wore off with it—leaving him face-to-face with the harsh truth. And with this painful acceptance came anger—raw, rampant, anger. It was as if his friends were nothing more than garbage. They weren't human beings to these captors—they weren't men...fathers...husbands. They were pieces of shit—something to be swept away and discarded, their blood later hosed from the deck like leftover fish guts.

"Release him!" Alvarez commanded. *"¡Desatar el hombre!"*

Mohammad cut the ropes with his stiletto and backed away with his rifle raised. Oblivious to the outside world, Skip remained perched on the barstool without expression, staring trancelike at the mutilated bodies. But while seemingly calm on the surface, inside him was a festering rage. As the storm boiled blackly within him, blood lust shone in his eyes and his hands began to shake. His friends didn't deserve to die—not like this—not like dogs shot down in the street.

"Get up!" Losing patience, Mendoza jarred the barstool with his boot. *"¡Vamos!"*

When Skip didn't react, Mohammad poked him in the chest with his gun barrel. When he still didn't respond, Mo poked him harder and shouted something Arabic in his face.

As Alvarez and Mendoza turned to leave, they heard a low glottal growl come from behind them. Spinning around, they were startled to find the sound coming from the captain. They were startled more when Skip sprang cat-like from his stool and seized Mohammad by the skull with both hands.

Like a wild beast, Skip growled savagely from the back of the throat while thrusting his thumbs into Mohammad's eye sockets. As the Arab wailed in soul-wrenching agony, a grotesque milky liquid oozed thickly around Skip's sunken thumbs. Hysterical with pain, Mohammad backpedaled blindly to break the insidious grasp, tripping over his own feet and falling onto his back. Refusing to let go, Skip piled on top of him and plunged his thumbs even deeper. The pain was unbearable and Mohammad emitted a shrewish howl while flailing his legs uncontrollably. But despite his frantic tugging at Skip's wrists, he could not expel the invasive thumbs. Now on the verge of unconsciousness, all he could do was emit blood-curdling scream after scream after scream.

Shocked by the captain's eye-gouging assault, the Zetas on either side of Alvarez took aim at Skip's back. But, reacting fast, Alvarez deflected their muzzles into the air before they could fire.

"Don't kill him, fools! We need him to navigate the ship. Pull him off! *¡Ahora!*"

Fixated on revenge, Skip was unrelenting in his punishment. The Arab deserved to die—for Ron...for Ivan...for Sully...for the other twelve lost.

Growling maniacally, Skip sunk his left thumb up to the bottom knuckle and wrapped his remaining fingers around Mohammad's right ear. The Arab screeched shrilly at this and his body went rigid, then limp. Clutching Mohammad's head in this hideous fashion, Skip pounded his face furiously with his right fist. The repeated punches landed with a wet fleshy sound and droplets of blood spattered into the night. The milky ooze around Skip's thumb was now a dark-red goo and beginning to puddle under the unconscious Arab's head.

Coming to Mohammad's rescue, the two Mexicans seized Skip's arms and yanked mightily to pull him off. But, with superhuman strength borne of fury, Skip held onto Mohammad's ear and pummeled away without mercy. In defeat, one of the Zetas gave up yanking and raised his rifle to bash Skip from behind. But just as he was set to strike, his body convulsed in synch with rapid-fire gunshots that came from somewhere behind.

When the salvo of rounds struck the Zeta's upper body, they stood him up and knocked him down, shocking everyone present. As the bullet-riddled man collapsed to the deck, the other gang members scattered for cover, leaving Skip alone to batter away.

Mendoza dropped flat onto his stomach and scoured the shadows for the unidentified shooter. When the shooter fired again, Mendoza caught a glimpse of the muzzle flash and zeroed in on it. The gunman was crouched behind a metal trashcan next to the Tiki stage.

Rolling onto his side, Mendoza pointed a finger at Cal's silhouette and ordered the man lying next to him to attack. Obeying the command, the ponytailed Latino sprang to his feet and charged toward Cal's position. In a screaming rampage, he shrieked at the top of his lungs while spraying lead on full automatic. As the AK-47 spat out round after round, bright starbursts flashed from its muzzle and ejected shell casings sailed into the night. As the spewing brass casings pinged off the steel deck, their thin metallic tinkling noise sounded oddly like wind chimes. Cal had barely ducked down when the deadly barrage ricocheted off the trashcan shielding him.

In answer to the assault, Cal stretched his arm around the trashcan and blindly unloaded the remainder of his clip in the direction of his assailant. Once the clip was spent, he risked a peek to find the man still charging full force. When the gunman spotted Cal's head poking out, he unleashed another fierce volley on the run, shredding the upper portion of the trashcan and showering Cal with metal shavings and shrapnel.

With his attacker closing in fast, Cal had no time to change clips. In pressing need of escape he dove onto the deck and rolled for the midship stairwell with as much speed as he could muster. As he twisted and turned for all he was worth, lead slugs sparked off the deck on all sides of him before zinging off into the darkness with glittering white trails. When Cal reached the stairwell opening he plunged end-over-end down the non-skid treads, leaving vestiges of skin behind from his knees and elbows. As he cascaded downward, his body careened uncontrollably from wall-to-wall, absorbing a profusion of punishment. His bruising descent finally ended when his battered body sprawled on the landing in a crumpled heap.

Expecting the gunman to appear above him any moment, Cal scrambled to his scraped knees and removed the spent clip. He had to reload quickly or die. With his eyes glued to the stairwell opening above him, he reached for the spare clip in his back pocket and his world suddenly stopped. It was gone. It had evidently fallen out during his spill down the stairway.

With his heart in his throat, Cal went down on all fours and began searching blindly for the missing clip. He was feeling around in the dark when the out-of-breath gunman appeared above him. The Latino was panting for air and blinking against sweat trickling from his brow; but his AK was rock steady and aimed right between Cal's eyes.

For a fleeting moment Cal thought about going for the hunting knife, but ruled it out. The Zeta had a bead on him and he would never get it out of its sheath. Forced to capitulate or die, Cal dropped the Uzi and raised his arms, praying that Alvarez wanted him taken alive. As Cal stared intently into the bore of the AK-47, the Latino gave him an ugly sneer and closed one eye. He was going to fire.

As Cal drew back in self-defense, he heard a crackling *POW! POW! POW!* and the gunman arched his back. When the Zeta spun around to face his assailant, there was another *POW! POW!* and he staggered backward a step before dropping his weapon. With Cal watching, he clutched his stomach and fell to his knees, then aimed his voice at the sky and released a great agonizing bray. With that final lament he collapsed backwards and slid down the stairway washboard-like on his back, stopping at Cal's feet. As Cal stared down at him, the Latino's face went slack and the light of consciousness drained from his eyes. Another Zeta was gone.

When Cal looked up, he saw Skip standing at the top of the stairwell. The front of his white uniform was glistening with blood and he was holding the nine-millimeter in his right hand. His fine-spun hair was whipping wildly in the wind.

"You can lower your arms now," Skip said matter-of-factly. "The bad guys are gone."

Forgetting his arms were raised, Cal lowered them and scurried up the steps to join his friend.

"Where are you hit, Skip?"

"Huh? Oh, I'm okay—I guess. You should see the other guy." Skip attempted a smile, but couldn't. "Here, take this. You might need it." He handed Cal the spare clip and walked down the steps. "Watch our backs a minute while I sit down."

Now that the fighting was over, Skip's legs were like spaghetti. Midway down the stairwell, he sat down heavily and rested his forearms on his knees. He was all washed-out and emotionally wasted.

"Looks like you just slaughtered a pig or something," Cal said.

Skip pictured Mohammad lying in a pool of his own blood. "I guess you could say that."

While Skip took a breather, Cal crouched down near the stairwell opening to keep a lookout. As he reloaded his spare clip, the cold wind sent an icy shiver through him. The temperature was dropping fast. "Why did they kill your crewmen?"

Staring between his knees, Skip was a picture of dejection. "Retribution. An eye-for-an-eye thing for the three asswads you killed earlier. It's their way of settling things. If somebody crosses you, you kill 'em. If your coffee doesn't taste just right, you kill 'em. Keeps the local population down." Skip held up the nine-millimeter. "But they weren't expectin' Mister Glock."

As Skip spoke, Cal counted the bodies in the dark. "Looks like two of 'em got away—Alvarez and Mendoza. Did you see which way they went?"

Skip shook his head. "Naw, I was too busy with Ahab there. Guess they got outta Dodge during the shootout." With the loss of his friends fresh in his mind, Skip bowed his head and exhaled long and slow. "Look, Cal, gimme a minute. They were good friends of mine. Know what I mean?"

"Yeah, sure." There was anguish in Skip's voice and Cal empathized with him. "Sorry."

While giving Skip some time, Cal belly-crawled across the sundeck and turned over the dead bodies. While searching each for the detonator he recoiled at the sight of Mohammad's corpse, whose eyeless head was battered beyond recognition. After confiscating the weapons, Cal crawled back to the stairwell, dragging the rifles by their slings—one AK-47 short.

"No detonator," Cal said, descending the stairs. "It looks like Alvarez picked up an AK."

"Yeah, he's too clever to retreat unarmed." Skip was bent over the dead Latino on the landing, searching his pockets. "No detonator here, either. Didn't think so. Gold-Tooth's got it. Let's go find the maggot and finish it."

Cal joined Skip on the landing. "By my count there are three left, including Alvarez. Any idea where they would be?"

WIRED

Skip picked up the Latino's AK-47 and straightened. "Well, the last time I saw the big Arab he was in the wheelhouse guardin' Neal. Alvarez and Mendoza could be lurkin' anywhere."

Wary of an ambush, Cal watched the stairs while talking. "How many crewmen are left?"

Skip's heart sank at the question. "There should be four more around somewhere, countin' the chef. The other nonessential employees went home with the passengers. Neal's probably still in the wheelhouse. The others are probably down in the engine room holdin' the diesels together or locked up in one of the cabins."

"Okay, let's go round 'em up." Cal slung the spare AK's over his shoulder. "We can use all the help we can get. Then we'll go search for Alvarez and Mendoza. Are you up to it?"

"Just try 'n stop me." Snarling, Skip held up the AK with one hand and the Glock with the other. "Their sorry asses belong to me."

Monday 19:45 Hours – "Helo-1"

Once the Air Tactical Group was airborne and running their search assignments, Helo-1 barreled toward Mexico at a dash speed of 180 knots. But after scouting a hundred-plus miles of empty ocean, Ray ditched the idea and ordered the Jayhawk around. Washington's golden boy had guessed wrong—again.

Meanwhile, the search was proceeding at a crawl—impeded by darkness and the unremitting rotten weather. Closest to the storm, the southernmost squadron was experiencing the worst conditions. The northern search team had fairer skies, enabling them to fly higher and perform broader sweeps. But in either case it was slow going. Since the ship was believed to be running without lights, all flight formations were kept ultra-tight lest the shadowy outline of the *Majestic Star* slip past them undetected.

Once an outbound sweep was made, the search team shifted to the next grid of assigned water and doubled back. When that area was covered, the pilots radioed-in their findings and moved onward to the next sector. The process was slow and painstaking, but in near-zero visibility it was the only systematic method for finding a needle in a haystack.

417

WIRED

"Attention all Air Group pilots," Ray spoke into his headset. "Fuel status. Over."

As each pilot relayed their air-miles-until-empty status, Ray logged down the readings. After calculating the results, he concluded that the short-range helos could perform only three more sweeps before refueling. If this shitty weather didn't let up soon, his pilots would be spending as much time refueling as looking for the AWOL ship.

Even using Night Vision Goggles—which merely turned the black rainy night into a pea-green rainy night—it was like searching for a polar bear in a snowstorm. In the world of Night Vision, an 800' tanker, a 40' yacht, and a campfire all looked similar from miles away. Nonetheless, it was all they could do, even if it turned out to be a miserable waste of time.

With a frustrated sigh, Ray hung the clipboard on its hook and rubbed his gritty eyes. Then he swiveled his NVGs into place and returned his eyes to the watery void below. It was destined to be a very long night.

Monday 19:54 Hours – The "Majestic Star"

Their strategy was simple: Skip would stumble into the wheelhouse pretending to be critically wounded. When Stan approached the doorway to investigate, Cal would pick him off with the Uzi. If that didn't work, Skip would shoot him with the Glock tucked under his waistband at the small of his back. Simple enough.

With their plan in place, Skip staggered into the wheelhouse and fell against the inside doorframe clutching his stomach. The front of his uniform was glistening with Mohammad's blood and he moaned out loud as if in severe pain. While Skip playacted, Cal waited outside on the catwalk like a predator with the Uzi cocked and ready. Their trap was set.

When Skip made his dramatic entrance, Stan shot to his feet—his face covered with confusion. And the longer the hulk stood there, the less and less clear he looked.

Who had shot the captain? Where was Mohammad? What should I do?

"Skip!" Neal blurted, bolting from behind the wheel. "Oh, my God! Where ya hit?"

418

WIRED

When Skip had been tied to the barstool and carried out of the wheelhouse, Neal was held behind at gunpoint. Afterward, at hearing automatic gunfire, Neal'd nearly jumped out of his skin and had been crazy with worry ever since. Now, at seeing Skip bleeding and barely alive, Neal rushed to his side.

But reacting swiftly, Stan stepped into Neal's path and plowed him backwards with the broadside of his rifle. While backpedaling, Neal grabbed the AK and a tug-of-war erupted. The rearward momentum carried the struggle across the room until Neal's back collided with the wall. The crushing impact expelled his breath and rendered Neal temporarily defenseless. Quick to take advantage of his vulnerability, Stan pressed the rifle across his throat and pushed with all his might.

As Neal's eyes bulged from strangulation, the pair tested each other's strength—growling...grunting...gnashing their teeth. Their sweaty faces were mere inches apart and their straining muscles quivered from raw exertion. Growing faint from lack of oxygen, Neal was weakening against the bigger man's brawn. On the verge of graying out, Neal unleashed a vicious head-butt that rocked Stan backward, giving Neal possession of the AK-47.

As Neal's lungs greedily sucked in air, there was an earsplitting *POW!* And Stan's face disintegrated—splattering Neal with hot gushing fluids and chunks of meat, bone, and brains. The deafening blast and unexpected splatter startled Neal and caused his knees to buckle. As he slid down the wall, he left behind a clean outline of his upper torso against the wet blood-spattered wall.

Withering down to a sitting position, Neal slumped against the wall in a listless daze—the whites of his eyes staring through a bloody red mask of mucous membrane and cranial goo.

Monday 20:00 Hours – "Helo-1"

After another uneventful outbound sweep, Helo-1 sped back on its return leg toward the mainland. The drenching rains had let up and stars were now visible on the northern skyline—a blessed sight. As the Jayhawk's twin rotors sliced through the soupy air, Ray pressed the stem of his wristwatch to illuminate the dial. According to Chief Bloyd the

WIRED

near-infrared satellite should be in position about now. With any luck it would locate the *Majestic Star* and put an end to this pathetic search in the blind.

"Group St. Petersburg, this is Helo-1. Over." At getting no response, Ray hailed the station again, then again. He was about to try his satellite phone when a faint and scratchy voice crackled through his earphones.

"Helo-1, this is Coast Guard Group St. Petersburg. Over."

Ray adjusted the squelch knob to filter out the static, but it didn't help. "Group, this is Admiral Hanna requesting comms with Chief Bloyd. Do you read?"

"Roger, sir. We have a copy on you, but we're experiencing a strong open carrier in your vicinity. How do you read this station?"

"I read you St. Pete, but your modulation is very weak. Roger?"

"Affirmative. We're trying to locate the source of the open carrier now, sir. Direction Finders have been activated from Yankeetown to Venice. We should have it pinpointed shortly. Stand by one for Chief Bloyd."

Ray almost laughed. How many impediments could one day provide? Not only was he dealing with the black of night, a freak squall, and the satellite issue, now he was faced with major radio interference. What else could possibly go wrong?

Open carriers were not uncommon closer inland; the culprit usually being a weekend boater with a gummy radio key stuck in the TALK mode. But way out here? Ninety miles offshore? Except for bulk freighters and containerships, there wasn't much boat traffic this far out at sea. And since the steamship lines were super-conscientious about their radio communications, Ray all but ruled them out.

Could a stray sailboat be the culprit? Was it just a coincidence? Maybe.

"Helo-1, this is Master Chief Bloyd. Over."

"Roger, Chief. Requesting a weather update and satellite status. Over."

"Aye, sir. The squall has been downgraded to a thunderstorm and it should be clear of our area within the hour. The satellite will be in position momentarily. I'm waiting to receive its telemetry. Over."

"That's welcome news, Chief. Stay on it and keep me posted.

420

Incidentally, I'm curious about this open carrier we've got out here. Besides being strong and from this vicinity, what else can you hear? Can you distinguish any noticeable background noise or conversation? Over."

"I haven't been monitoring it myself, sir. I've got several stations working on it to pin down its source. There's nothing discernible at the present time, but I can check the reel-to-reel recording. Do you want to standby while I replay and analyze the tape?"

"Affirmative. Amplify it and run it through the filters. Let me know if you detect anything intelligible. It's unusual to have an open carrier this far offshore. It's probably nothing, but it's interfering with our comms. I'll stand by. Roger?"

"Will do, sir. Hail you back in a short. Group St. Petersburg out."

It was a little farfetched, but Ray couldn't rule out a potential connection with the *Majestic Star*. Captain Myles was a veteran around marine radios and he would know how to attract Coast Guard attention. Was the carrier coming from a negligent boater or was it being deliberately sent as a homing signal?

On a hunch, Ray twisted around in his seat to ask Kathy Myles a question. When he did, he found her peering out the window through a pair of portable night goggles taken from the seat pocket. When he called her name, it startled her and she quickly lowered them as if caught doing something wrong.

"Mrs. Myles, has your husband ever mentioned anything about radio interference while he was working? You know, weekend boaters talking on the wrong channels or cruising around with their microphones stuck open? That sort of thing?"

Kathy stared beyond Ray a moment while her mind delved into the past. "Well, yeah. It's kind of a pet peeve of his. Skip griped that if a vessel happened to be in trouble way offshore, they wouldn't be able to get through on the radio for help. He thought the FCC and Coast Guard should do more about it. Why?"

"Just curious," Ray said thoughtfully. "Did he mention anything else? Like how the Coast Guard could keep the airwaves open?"

"Yes. He said you guys had a way of locating the violators. Something about tracing the radio signal back to them. But I can't remember exactly how he explained it."

421

As Ray toyed with the idea, the chief's staticky voice came over his headset.

"Sir, it looks like we're onto something." The excitement in the chief's voice prompted Ray to sit straighter. "Most of the tape is unreadable, but I did make out some muffled background conversation. It had something to do with *"associates being missing"* and about *"executing three crewmembers"*. But here's the clincher, sir. Just minutes ago, there was some shouting and what sounded like a gunshot. It looks like our boys. Roger?"

Ray's pulse quickened. "Chief, I need those coordinates as soon as the DFs get a fix. In the meantime, redirect the Herc my way. Have them vector in on my coordinates. Ready to copy?"

Ray pushed a button on the Collins RCVR-3A radio and the built-in NAVSTAR GPS displayed the helo's latitude and longitude, which he passed to Chief Bloyd.

"Once the satellite is in position, Chief, start your infrared search using those coordinates. We've got 'em! Good job. Helo-1 out."

Monday 20:07 Hours – The "Majestic Star"

"Dammit, Skip!" Neal swore. "You scared the hell outta me!" Neal was on his feet now, wiping Stan's bloody remains off his face onto his shirtsleeves. "My ears are still ringing!"

"Sorry about all the gore, Neal, but he was about to run you through with this." Skip held up the dagger. "I couldn't risk hitting you, so I had to take him out point blank."

"Yeah...well...thanks, I guess. Just give me some warning next time. Okay? God, I think I breathed in some of his particles—you know, that vaporized liquid shit?" The sickening thought of inhaling the dead Arab's atoms made Neal gag. "Yuck, I can taste him. I think I'm gonna puke." Neal dashed by Cal standing in the doorway and heaved over the catwalk railing.

Skip motioned at Stan's corpse. "C'mon, Cal. Let's get him out of the wheelhouse."

Cal strode over to the faceless Muslim and grabbed his ankles. "You take his arms. After this, we'll go round up the rest of your crew." Cal twisted his head and spoke to Neal's back. "Neal, alter our course back to Clearwater and radio the Coast Guard. Pass them our coordinates and tell them to contact Admiral Hanna—Admiral Ray Hanna. Tell 'em that everything here is copasetic and to call off the destroyer. Got it?"

Too sickly to question anything about the destroyer, Neal nodded without looking at Cal. Then he bent over and grabbed his kneecaps, inhaling and exhaling mightily as if trying to expel something despicable from his lungs.

"You'd better get in here, Neal," Skip warned. "You're makin' yourself an easy target standin' out there."

With his color returning, Neal nodded and teetered back inside.

Skip picked up Stan's AK-47 and faced Neal. "In case the gunshot draws any unwanted guests, use this. Heads up." Skip pitched Neal the rifle. "Know how to use it?" At making the crack, he gave Cal a wink.

"What, this?" Neal asked naïvely, holding the rifle in front of him. Standing straight, he pinwheeled the AK like a West Point cadet, flipping it end-over-end and inspecting it down the barrel. "You mean this fully automatic 7.62-millimeter gas-operated selective-fire Soviet made Kalashnikov AKM assault rifle with its signature 30-round banana clip magazine? With firepower capability of 600 rounds per minute at a velocity of 710 meters per second? Well, to be honest, it's not quite as good as the newer 5.45-millimeter AK-74, but I guess it'll do."

Duly impressed, Skip and Cal stopped dragging Stan's body to marvel at Neal.

Noting their surprise, Neal explained with a shrug. "Captain...ROTC Honor Guard...Class of '79."

Monday 20:15 Hours – "Helo-1"

While waiting for the Direction Finders to locate the open carrier, Ray conducted an experiment of his own. Instead of running parallel sweeps, he altered Helo-1's flight path to a cloverleaf pattern. By flying in that manner the intensity of radio interference could be measured as the Jayhawk traveled in various directions. As a result, the further north they flew, the more interference they experienced. Likewise, the radio interference was greater to the west than the east. After completing two cloverleaves, Ray concluded that the open carrier was emanating from the northwest.

Unrolling his chart, Ray marked where the interference was the greatest and then drew a line back to the *Majestic Star's* last known position west of Clearwater. Then, continuing along the same plane, he extended the line northward. To his surprise, the hypothetical path led directly to New Orleans. Thinking this must be Alvarez's destination, Ray extrapolated the ship's whereabouts based on an average speed of twenty-knots.

"If they're heading for the Big Easy, they should be here about now." With a diabolical grin, Ray marked a big "X" on the chart and circled it. "Gotcha, asshole!"

Monday 20:20 Hours – The "Majestic Star"

After Cal and Skip left the wheelhouse to find the other crewmembers, Neal went about his assignments. First, he extinguished the cabin lights so as not to present an easy target. Second, he flipped on the exterior running lights to make the ship visible in the night. Third, he spun the big wooden wheel around until the compass pointed south-southeast for Clearwater Pass. Next, he picked up the microphone to notify the Coast Guard of their position.

But when Neal keyed the microphone, it didn't feel exactly right. The "TALK" button was already fully depressed and stuck in place. At first glance, he couldn't see any reason for it. But after looking closer under the faint light, he saw something like a wooden splinter lodged in the plastic housing. It was broken off even with the button and way too short to pull out using bare fingers. Hoping to work the object loose, Neal pressed the button again and again. When it wouldn't dislodge, he grabbed a metal compass from the chart table. Using its sharp point, he began digging at the object with frustration. When it didn't yield, he dug harder.

On top of everything else, he didn't need this aggravation. He was spattered with Stan's remains, his ears were ringing, he had a hammering headache, and there was a sickening taste in the back of his mouth. Now, after five days of pure hell, he was almost home free and something was wrong with the stupid microphone.

Losing all patience, Neal wiggled the point in deeper and that's when he heard it. With a bright *SNAP!* the plastic button broke off and fell to the floor.

He couldn't believe it.

~~~~~~~~~~

Once finding Skip's quarters empty, Cal and Skip carried their search to the next cabin. After a quick listen at the door, they kicked it open and exploded into the room with their weapons at the ready. Startled by the sudden invasion, a bound and gagged crewman was staring wide-eyed at them from the floor. It was John-Renée, the Cajun cook.

When John-Renée recognized Skip, the tenseness left his body and he moaned for removal of the cloth gag. Evidently his life had been spared when Mendoza singled-out three crewmen for execution. While he probably didn't realize it, today was John-Renée's lucky day.

Once the gag was off, the feisty Frenchman blurted out questions faster than Skip could answer them. After learning the fate of his dead shipmates, John-Renée insisted on joining the search for the other crewmen. Skip objected at first, arguing that he should go to the wheelhouse and watch Neal's back. In truth, Skip regarded his combat inexperience as a hazard. Besides being in the way, he might panic and shoot somebody in the back. But when the Cajun refused to accept no for an answer and promised to follow orders, Skip reluctantly agreed to let him come along.

With Cal casting him a skeptical look, Skip showed John-Renée how to operate the Glock and then armed him with it—with the safety switch engaged. A minute later the trio descended the steps to the sundeck and vanished into the night.

Monday 20:44 Hours – "Helo-1"

"Helo-1, this is Group St. Petersburg. Over."

"Roger, Chief." Ray noted the radio interference was gone. "Hanna here. Over."

WIRED

"Sorry for the delay, sir, but it's taken a while to ascertain the exact position of the open carrier. We thought we had it nailed down when it abruptly reversed course, which made us question the data. Then a few minutes ago the carrier vanished altogether. Nevertheless, we programmed the coordinates into the satellite tracking system and we picked something up. I can't be positive it's the Majestic Star, but the thermal signature fits. She's heading south-southeast right now, sir. Ready to copy the lats and longs?"

"Southeast?" This fact puzzled Ray. "Okay, after you pass the coordinates, continue to track her. Do we have any aircraft in that area? Over."

"The Hercules is about twenty minutes east of there, sir. I've already rerouted it. Once they locate the target by FLIR, they'll go in for a low-altitude visual. I'll notify you the moment we get a sighting. Roger?"

"Affirmative. Okay, I'm ready to copy."

The chief's coordinates put the ship in the right neighborhood but it was heading the wrong direction, which sounded like another wild-goose chase. If this unidentified ship was the *Majestic Star*, why the 180° change in course? Had Stringer and Myles already defeated the Zetas and now headed for home? If so, why hadn't they made radio contact? What was going on out there?

These unanswered questions made Ray even more anxious to get there. He fed the ship's coordinates into the NAVSTAR GPS satellite receiver and it computed the air miles to the target, which raised another question—fuel.

Most of the Air Group was already low on fuel and the vessel in question was situated well west of them. Sending the squadron further offshore without refueling first was out of the question. Even Helo-1—a medium range recovery HH-60 Jayhawk—would be running on fumes by the time it reached the mark and returned to Sand Key. On the contrary, if the search was put off until the entire squadron refueled, Alvarez might get away again—also out of the question.

With his choices few, Ray made a decision. He would send the Air Group home except for one other HH-60 Jayhawk. Together, they would fly in and finish the mission—one way or the other.

WIRED

With Skip leading the way, the trio dashed headlong through the winding corridors in their trek to the engine room. The deeper they descended, the narrower the passageways became, some made more claustrophobic by the below-deck maze of conduit, ductwork, and convolution of pipes—some hissing steam from pressure relief valves.

Once below the waterline, the onrushing sound of seawater could be heard whooshing against the hull as the ship bulldozed its way through the water. Every so often the ship would heave and pitch erratically, sending Cal and John-Renée careening toward the opposite wall before regaining their sea legs.

As the men approached the firewall of the engine room, the steady roar of the diesels, gearboxes, and rotating shafts could be heard on the other side. In addition to a low-pitched vibrating rumble, the high RPM demand on the engines gave off a shrill whining noise as if threatening to fly apart. The taxing sound made Skip grimace and he reminded himself to throttle the engines back at first chance.

Before opening the firewall door, Skip motioned for the others to wait. With Cal and John-Renée looking on, he turned the handle until the airtight door cracked open. Then in one fell swoop he shoved the door inward and ducked out of the way. At once the engine noise tripled and a gust of hot air rushed into the corridor, bringing the odor of grease and diesel fumes.

When nothing happened, Skip hooked his arm inside the doorway and shone a flashlight in all directions. When it didn't draw any fire, he peeked cautiously around the edge of the door opening. Except for the faint illumination from an array of gauges, the engine room was uncommonly dark. Someone had turned off the sodium-vapor lamps.

Being careful, Skip directed the flashlight across the room until tragedy stopped him. Ten feet away, two crewmen were slouched against a bulkhead next to the clamoring diesels. Their heads had been bludgeoned by a bloody pipe wrench left lying next to them and their throats were cut from ear to ear. As a sordid caveat, their tongues had been pulled through the gaping neck wound—a Colombian Necktie. The fronts of their blue work shirts were dark and shiny with fresh blood. For shock value, their bodies had been posed against the wall.

Clearly, Alvarez and Mendoza were one step ahead of them.

Shocked and shaken, Skip turned his back on the gruesome scene and meandered slumped-shouldered down the corridor. Finding his knees weak, he leaned against a fire hose box for support. He felt beaten, traumatized. Both crewmen had been murdered and their bodies mutilated—men who had trusted him. Five shipmates were now dead and the accumulation of loss bore down on him like a press. Who would be next—Cal?...John-Renée?...Neal?

Skip's mind suddenly filled with white panic—*NEAL!*

~~~~~~~~~~~~

Neal was standing in the middle of the wheelhouse with a hapless look on his face. He had just finished ransacking the room for a spare microphone and come up empty-handed.

When the Zetas first commandeered the ship, they confiscated all electronic devices and threw them overboard with the exception of the wheelhouse radio. This impound en masse included everything—cell phones, PDA's, laptops, IPODs, handheld radios, satellite phones, and even the factory-installed wall phones used for inner-ship communication.

With the microphone now kaput there was no way of contacting the outside world—an irredeemable setback. As first officer, Neal was duteously embarrassed. He should have exercised more caution when trying to remove the obstruction. In his haste he had been inexcusably derelict and he dreaded facing Skip. He was going to blow a gasket.

While inwardly berating himself, Neal turned off the autopilot and eased the throttle back to give the wound-up diesels a break. As he did, he detected the distant drone of turboprop engines. With an electrifying rush of hope, he raced outside on the catwalk and scanned the night sky, praying that a rescue craft had found them and the busted microphone wouldn't matter.

From out of the clouds a large fixed-wing airplane dropped into view and Neal recognized it as a C-130 Hercules surveillance aircraft. It was flying so low that he could make out the red Coast Guard insignia on the plane's gleaming white fuselage. Rejoicing, he jumped up and down and waved his arms ecstatically at the aircraft. Then he darted inside and signaled the Hercules by flipping the ship's navigational lights off and on. After flashing them a number of times, he dashed back outside and waved wildly at the night sky. The plane was no longer visible, but Neal could hear its turbojets growing louder.

Then the Hercules emerged from the ceiling of clouds and did a second flyby lower yet. This time a blinding spotlight came on and the mighty roar of its four Allison Turboprops vibrated the catwalk in which Neal stood. As the big Herc passed overhead, Neal danced joyously within its spotlight and whistled shrilly at his rescuers. Before disappearing back into the clouds, the pilot signaled Neal by alternately dipping the plane's wingtips.

Hallelujah! The Coasties had found them. Everything was going to be all right. He was going home to Phyllis and the kids!

With Neal beaming heavenward, a hand came from behind him and covered his mouth. Before Neal could react, he felt a cold steel blade at his throat.

~~~~~~~~~~

While rushing headlong back to the wheelhouse, Skip set a blistering pace—forcing Cal and John-Renée to nearly jog to keep up with him. As the three hustled along, Cal silently monitored Skip's behavior. Having handled his share of personal injury claims, he was familiar with *Post-Traumatic Shock Disorder* and Skip was exhibiting some of the classic symptoms.

Physically, Skip was as tough as they come. But despite his macho makeup, emotionally, he was just as vulnerable as anyone else and the accumulated loss of life was having a profound effect on him. At first he had acted lethargic and emotionally numb. When he spoke, his voice had a distant quality. Then he had become agitated and angry, craving revenge. Now he was consumed with grief and obsessing over the lives lost—mumbling that it was all his fault; that he should have done something to prevent it; that he had failed to protect his passengers and crew.

With sleep deprivation added to the mix—a result of the past five days—it was a textbook formula for clinical exhaustion. Skip was skirting on the edges of rational reasoning and Cal feared an emotional crash, especially if something happened to his longtime friend, Neal. Even now, as they approached the glowing red **EXIT** sign, Skip was mumbling something about Phyllis and about helping Neal before it was too late.

As the trio passed through the door marked: *AUTHORIZED PERSONNEL ONLY*, Cal kept a watchful eye on Skip and his other eye on the lookout for Alvarez.

Monday 21:00 Hours – "Helo-1"

"Helo-1, this is Group St. Petersburg hailing. Over."

Detecting a trace of excitement in Chief Bloyd's voice, Ray eagerly keyed his mike. "Hanna here. Go ahead, Chief."

"Good news, Admiral. The Herc just confirmed that she's our ship. Are you ready to copy the Majestic Star's position?"

Elated by the news, Ray jotted down the coordinates. By happenstance the other Jayhawk was only fifteen minutes away.

"Thanks, Chief. I'll contact Helo-2 and we'll converge on the target immediately. Commend the Hercules crew for a job well done. Helo-1 out."

Monday 21:02 Hours – The "Majestic Star"

The trio emerged from the bowels of the ship and started up the stern stairway for the sundeck. As they spiraled upward from landing to landing, the ship's powerful twin screws churned up the seawater below them. In the sky overhead, low patchy clouds scudded southward at a hasty clip, ushering in a cold air mass from the north.

Just before reaching the top of the open stairwell, Cal halted Skip by the back of his belt. In Skip's urgency to reach Neal, he resisted the holdup but Cal refused to let go. Even though it was night, Cal feared an ambush while crossing the wide-open expanse of the sundeck and insisted they cross it one man at a time while the others provided cover. Despite some negative opposition from Skip, it was settled that Cal would go first.

Standing three steps down from the stairwell top, Cal slung the Uzi over his shoulder and nodded at the others. He was ready to make his run. Nodding back, Skip and John-Renée gathered behind him with their weapons aimed into the night. To help launch himself, Cal grasped both handrails and rocked to-and-fro to build momentum. He aimed to make this quick. After several rocks he exploded like a sprinter out of a gate in a zigzagging run for the outline of the Tiki Bar—praying that a stray deck chair wouldn't end up in his path.

At reaching the safety of the hut's solid oak construction, Cal crouched behind the bar to catch his breath. Looking back the way he came, he saw nothing but blackness. Sticking to their game plan, he then signaled the others with a low whistle.

Upon hearing Cal's signal, John-Renée was set to go next. On cue, he stepped onto the sundeck to make his own headlong dash. But, suddenly, from out of nowhere, a single shot rang out and John-Renée fell dead—like a sack of potatoes. Oddly, he didn't make a sound. Not even a groan.

When the Cajun collapsed, Skip flattened himself on the stairway and shouted a warning to Cal. "Sniper! He got John-Renée!"

"Where's the shooter?" Cal yelled back, crouching lower still.

"Don't know! Someplace around the wheelhouse, I think. Must be using a night scope!"

As soon as his words were out, Skip feared even more for Neal's life. If the shooter was in that vicinity, where was Neal? With alarm in his voice, Skip called out towards the wheelhouse.

"Neal! Are you okay? Neal!!" When no answer came, he rose up out of concern. Not thinking, he took a step forward and called out even louder. "NEAL!"

In answer, another shot rang out that creased Skip's scalp, gouging out a half-inch-wide furrow of smoldering hair. Before the delayed pain registered with his brain, his instincts drove him down for cover but his reflexes weren't fast enough. In ducking down, a napalm explosion of pain ripped through his right thigh and the leg folded. Unable to catch himself in time, he toppled down the flight of stairs to the landing below.

The sound of two more gunshots sent an icy chill down Cal's spine. "Skip! Report!"

"I'm winged in the leg!" There was pain in his voice. "I'm on the landing!"

WIRED

Without a thought Cal dashed back through the shadows toward the stern. In the darkness he tripped over the chef's body and fell down. He was checking John-Renée for a pulse when a white-hot round zinged off the deck next to his foot. As the luminous chunk of lead whined off into the night, Cal resumed his zigzag run and zipped down the stairs to find Skip on the landing. His scalp was glistening with wet blood and he was clutching his bleeding leg.

"Bastard . . popped . . me . . twice." Skip's words came out gritty and halted, as if each one hurt. "I'll be okay, though. Just help me to my feet."

As Skip struggled to rise, Cal held him down. "Let me take a look first. You watch out for the shooter." Kneeling down, Cal checked Skip's scalp wound to find it messy but superficial. He then slit Skip's pant leg with the hunting knife and ripped it open to expose the bullet wound. "I've seen worse," he said, shining the penlight over it. "A little muscle damage, but it doesn't look like any bones are shattered. Do you think you can walk on it?"

"Hell yeah, I can!" Skip reared his head back as if there were no question about it. "I've got some unfinished business to settle."

Cal had some doubts about Skip's leg, but there was no doubting his gumption. He had oodles of it. He also seemed to have his wits about him again, which was reassuring. Apparently the pain had driven out some of the shock over losing his friends.

Cal cut off a strip of pant leg and wrapped it tightly above the wound to staunch the bleeding. With the tourniquet in place, he hoisted Skip to his feet and steadied him against the railing. Almost at once Skip's leg buckled under his weight and Cal had to catch him before he fell.

"I don't know, Skip. Maybe you should sit this one out."

"I'll be okay." His face stretched with pain. "Just let me get used to it." Gritting his teeth, Skip shifted his weight from his good leg to the injured one. After a few shifts, he stood unassisted. "I won't be runnin' any marathons, but I think I can get around. But don't let me hold you up, Cal. Go check on Neal. I'm worried as hell."

"Okay, you sit tight here and guard the stern. I'll go down to the main deck, circle around, and come up the midship stairwell by the Tiki Hut. Maybe I can flush out the sniper and you'll get a clear shot."

WIRED

Skip raised the AK and sneered. "One's all I'll need, buddy boy. One shot, one kill."

Monday 21:13 Hours – "Helo-1"

"Helo-1, this is Helo-2 hailing on channel two-two. Over."

"Roger, Helo-2. Go ahead."

"We have the Majestic Star in sight, sir. Requesting rules of engagement. Over."

Being closer in proximity, Helo-2 was the first to arrive on scene.

"Helo-2, we're still about five klicks away. Do not—repeat: DO NOT—engage or fire upon the vessel until we arrive. Reconnoiter the scene and report back to me. I want to know what's going on down there. If you encounter any enemy ground fire, back off. Understood?"

"Will do, sir. Helo-2 out."

Monday 21:14 Hours – The "Majestic Star"

Leaving Skip behind on the landing, Cal descended the stern stairwell for the main deck. While spiraling downward his thoughts were centered on the shooter, who had to be either Alvarez or Mendoza. Whichever it was, Cal was glad that he wasn't facing a schooled sniper. He had met a few snipers during his tour in 'Nam and those guys were a different breed.

Snipers didn't move through the bush, they flowed—seeped. They could lie in wait for hours—silent, unmoving, with one eye peering through the scope and the other squinted shut; waiting for that split-second opening to take out the assigned target; to deliver the 148-grain round resting in the chamber. Skilled snipers squeezed their trigger between breaths, between heartbeats. They were masters at the waiting game, patient beyond patience. They were the consummate predator.

As Cal passed by the dining room entrance and rounded the corner for the bow, he was met with a cold wind whistling down the length of the deck. At once the chilly blast penetrated his Mickey Mouse shirt, giving him the shivers. Striding faster, he tucked his chin into his chest and advanced through the night quietly, staying on the toes of his shoes.

WIRED

When halfway up the midship stairwell, Cal detected the drumming of footsteps on the deck above. Stopping, he listened intently while his eyes roamed the underside of the sundeck. Then he heard the sound of footsteps again. Someone was moving about topside. Was it the sniper? Perhaps Neal?

With the Uzi leading the way, Cal resumed his climb, slithering up the final steps on his belly. When just shy of the opening, he laid in wait. Motionless. Silent. Listening with heightened senses. Breathing shallow. Hoping to catch his adversary off guard. But to his discouragement the footsteps were gone. After a full minute passed, he peeked out between the handrails and panned the gloom for any sign of movement. Nothing.

All at once a lethal round sparked off the pipe railing next to his head, pelting his face with minuscule particles of lead and enamel paint. He had no idea where the shot came from but common sense told him he was an open target. Fearing more shots to follow, Cal pushed off the upper step and slid down the stairway on his belly. During the bumpy facedown slide the non-skid treads balled his T-shirt up under his chin, exposing his stomach and bare chest. As the gritty surface scraped off a layer of hide, another shot rang out and Cal's peripheral vision picked up the flash. It originated from the wheelhouse roof near the masthead and antennas.

Cal's sandpaper slide came to a halt when his feet touched the landing. Simultaneously, the raw skin on his midriff blazed like a bonfire. Moaning, he rose on rusty joints and yanked down his wadded-up shirt. When its cotton fabric brushed against his raw meat, he winced and started up the steps while holding the tee away from his skin. He remembered seeing an exterior ladder mounted aft of the wheelhouse entrance on the starboard side, most likely how the sniper accessed the roof. Was there a matching ladder on the port side? If so, he would flank the ambusher and take him out. He'd had enough bullshit.

Midway up the stairs, Cal sensed the distant thudding of an approaching helicopter, or thought he did. But under his footsteps and heavy breathing, he wasn't sure. Pausing a moment, he listened more intently but the sound was no longer there. It was probably the wind playing tricks, he thought, or just wishful thinking. As he continued up the steps, he wondered if Neal had radioed the Coast Guard. Then he wondered if Neal was even alive.

WIRED

All at once the helicopter noise was back and sounding much closer. Hearkened by it Cal peered up, but from the recesses of the stairwell he couldn't see anything. While he was gawking skyward there was a burst of gunfire followed by the sound of revving engines, as if the helo was peeling away in retreat.

Someone was firing at the helo. *The Zetas!*

With his Uzi aimed at the stairwell opening, Cal forgot about his pains and pounded up the steps—taking them two at a time. From the sound of it, the good guys needed help.

Monday 21:18 Hours – "Helo-2"

"Helo-1, this is Helo-2. We're being fired upon, sir!"

The pilot's voice sounded tense and jerky as if fighting the controls. In the background Ray could hear the straining turbines as the Jayhawk took evasive action. This was no big surprise for Ray, who had expected to take some flak if the Zetas were still lurking. While small arms fire was a hazard to the aircrew, it didn't pose a significant threat to the aircraft.

"Roger, Helo-2." Ray's voice was calm and even. "Have you located the shooter?"

"Affirmative, sir. We have him in our spotlight now." As the pilot spoke, Ray could hear the metallic pings and plunks of bullets striking the cockpit. It sounded like balls of hail spattering against a car hood. "The shooter's a dark male wearing a headband. He's positioned on the pilothouse roof, sir."

Judging from the pilot's description, Ray knew exactly who it was. The image of Santiago Mendoza was forever emblazoned in his mind. Whatever was taking place on the ship right now didn't sound good for Stringer and the crew. Before answering, Ray looked at Kathy and wondered if her relatives were still alive.

"Helo-2, you have my permission to return fire. Take the shot. Over."

"Roger," the pilot answered. "It'll take me a minute to get back in position."

In following the rules of engagement, Helo-2 had fallen back when fired upon and was currently shadowing the *Majestic Star* off her stern, skimming a few yards above the waterline.

435

WIRED

"Let's not take all night, gentlemen." Ray regretted not being there to witness the joyous event, but he couldn't risk Mendoza getting away. "Smoke his ass."

As Helo-1 raced toward the *Majestic Star*, Helo-2 accelerated ahead in the direction of the pilothouse. In narrowing the gap, the pilot kept the nose up so that any ground fire would strike the Jayhawk's armored underside. Once the helo was in position, the pilot matched the ship's forward speed and hovered directly overhead.

At receiving the go-ahead, a helmeted marksman unbuckled his seat harness and grabbed his RC50 laser-sighted .50 caliber Barrett precision sniper rifle.

~~~~~~~~~~~

From within the confines of the stairwell Cal watched the jump door slide open. Then a marksman appeared holding a rifle.

Designated marksmen were used by the Coast Guard to shoot out the engines of smuggling boats from a hovering helicopter. Judging from where the spotlight was aimed, this particular marksman was going to take out the sniper.

Wasting no time, the Coastie took a knee and steadied his rifle against the doorframe. As the sharpshooter peered through the scope, Cal held his breath in anticipation of a shot. But the gunshot never came. Instead, the marksman lowered his rifle and vacated the doorway.

~~~~~~~~~~~

"What do you mean he's gone!?" Ray barked into his mouthpiece. "Where did he go?"

"He ducked inside a cabin aft of the wheelhouse, Admiral." At that instant the sniper reappeared in Helo-2's spotlight. "Wait a minute. There's the target now. We got him, sir!"

With the searchlight trained on him, Mendoza sprinted down the catwalk toward the sundeck carrying a weapon in each hand. With little time to prepare for a shot, the marksman fired hurriedly at the moving target. The round ricocheted off the steel grating next to the runner's foot,

436

prompting Mendoza to run faster. As the Mexican fled at full speed, he kept glimpsing over his shoulder at the blinding spotlight, nearly causing him to stumble.

The marksman fired again and Mendoza spun halfway around—dropping one of the weapons and clutching his wounded shoulder. Still on his feet, but wobbling unsteadily, he staggered down the stairs leading to the sundeck and sat down hard on the last step. As he sprawled onto his stomach, the pilot keyed his microphone to report the good news.

"The target is down, Admiral. I repeat—the target is down, sir. Over."

"Roger that, Helo-2. We're coming up on your eight o'clock now." While pleased to hear it, Ray was sorry for having missed it. "Hold your position until we arrive on scene. Copy?"

"Good copy, sir. Helo-2 standing by."

~~~~~~~~~~

"There they are!" Kathy shrieked, pointing down at the ship. "Over there!" Her exuberant outburst fogged up her window and she excitedly wiped it clear.

As the wayward ship came into view, Ray uttered a small cry of triumph. Lo and behold, there she was—the *Majestic Star*—in all of her infamous glory; carving her way through the black Gulf of Mexico water. After all that had come to pass, it was an imposing sight.

"She's a sight for sore eyes isn't she, Mrs. Myles?"

"That she is, sir!" Kathy's prayers had been answered and she was buoyant. "And for heavensakes call me Kathy. That *Mrs. Myles* stuff makes me feel like my great grandmother!"

Looking over his shoulder, Ray grinned. "Okay, I'll call you Kathy if you quit calling me sir. The name's Ray. Deal?" Kathy nodded. "Good. Now let's go check on your two guys down there. They're not out of the woods yet."

Kathy Myles was unaware of the happenings aboard her husband's ship and Ray decided to leave it that way. Besides, he didn't know what to think himself because nothing made sense. Clearly the Zetas were still at large, hence the ground fire against Helo-2. But if the Zetas were still in control, why the reversal in course? And why was the ship underway

WIRED

with running lights on? That didn't add up. Conversely, if Myles and Stringer were in control, why hadn't someone notified the Coast Guard? The circumstances were ambiguous to say the least.

Then it dawned on Ray that perhaps *nobody* was in control—that opposing forces were still battling it out—which made perfect sense. Figuring he would find out soon enough, Ray rotated his night goggles in place and nodded at the pilot.

"Take us in closer, Lieutenant Commander. Let's crash their little party."

~~~~~~~~~~

When Mendoza was felled by the gunshot he vanished from the marksman's scope. To relocate his target, the Coastie lowered his rifle and scoured the ship's shadows with his bare eyes. At spotting a person sprawled on the sundeck steps, he placed the gunstock against his cheek and studied Mendoza through the scope. Detecting no movement, he lowered his weapon and shook his head at the pilot. The target was either dead or dying. With a hint of accomplishment in his voice, the pilot relayed the good news to Admiral Hanna, whose helo was now into sight.

But when the marksman peered through the scope again, his eyes widened. The Mexican was lying on his stomach, aiming a weapon at Helo-2. At first glance the Coastie thought it was a rifle, which was no big threat. But when he recognized the weapon for what it was, his blood ran cold. Before he could react, there was a bright flash. Mendoza had pulled the trigger.

"Incoming!" the marksman warned his crewmates. "He's got a RPG!"

A white trail of sparks streamed skyward narrowly missing the cockpit. Acting instinctively, the pilot shoved the control stick to one side and gave full acceleration. As the Jayhawk rolled right, the unprepared marksman lost his footing and fell outside the aircraft.

Ray eyewitnessed the hairbreadth escape from aboard Helo-1 and his heart skipped a beat. A rocket-propelled grenade had the capacity of downing an aircraft.

"Helo-2, get out of there!" Ray screamed over the radio. "Now!"

Fleeing for its life, the helicopter labored for higher altitude with the

438

marksman dangling outside from his safety harness. But before the aircraft could make its escape, another trail of sparks rose skyward and struck the tail rotor with a blinding blast, sending the Jayhawk into a wild smoldering tailspin.

"Mayday! Mayday! Can't hold her sir!" The pilot's voice was strained and high-pitched. "We're going down! Mayday! Mayday! May..."

~~~~~~~~~~

The cataclysmic crash upon the sundeck sent a jarring quiver throughout the length of the ship. On impact the 6,460 lbs capacity fuel tanks ruptured, turning the nighttime into a bleached-white supernova of light and flaming debris. As the doomed aircraft skidded sideways across the sundeck, a waterfall of glittering sparks spewed from beneath its pulverized underside, chased by hot liquid plumes of red, yellow, orange, and blue. Accompanying the screeching sound of metal scraping against metal was a roiling black cloud of soot that saturated the night air. As the helicopter plowed a scorched path toward the port beam, it shed a flaming trail of mangled parts and twisted debris. Threatening to skid overboard, the helo ground to a crunching halt when striking the heavy pipe railing surrounding the sundeck. There, in its final resting place, the charred wreckage of Helo-2 belched acrid smoke and burned uncontrollably.

~~~~~~~~~~

When Helo-2 crashed and exploded, the violent shockwave sent Helo -1 careening sideways at a forty-five degree angle. As the rotors struggled to regain draft, the turbines whined shrilly and the laboring engines emitted a low-pitched rumble that shook the entire aircraft.

Nearly blinded by the yellow-green flash, Lt. Commander Henninger twisted his night goggles away and swung into action to keep the Jayhawk airborne, which was losing altitude and yawing severely to Ray's side. As the helo sideslipped earthward at an alarming rate, the dark water of the Gulf of Mexico rushed at Ray through his side door window. He was bracing himself for impact when the helicopter jolted and pitched

WIRED

the opposite way, slewing back over the ship.

When the pilothouse suddenly filled the windshield, Kathy shrieked and bent forward, assuming the crash position. The aircraft was on a collision course and they were all going to die. Although not a Catholic, Kathy crossed herself anyway and prayed out loud for divine intervention, but the blaring cockpit warning alarms drowned out her prayerful plea.

A split-second before impact the helo skirted past the pilothouse, but not before the rotor blade sheered off an antenna and demolished a spinning radar scanner atop the wheelhouse roof. When the radar housing disintegrated, broken pieces of it peppered the fuselage and a large chunk crashed through Kathy's side window, showering her with jagged filaments of polycarbonate safety glass. Now totally scared out of her wits, she unbuckled her seatbelt harness and dove for refuge on the floorboard. Hunkered there with her arms covering her head, the howling wind ripped through the shattered window with hurricane force, adding more commotion to the cockpit chaos.

The damaged rotor caused the aircraft to vibrate rougher and the helo began spiraling downward. With the altimeter spinning wildly, the pilot gave full throttle and nearly yanked the joystick out of the floor to give lift power. Now dangerously close to stalling, the low moaning engines tremored and lugged in RPMs—shaking the entire airframe.

For what seemed like a lifetime the Jayhawk hung suspended in midair—teetering...shimmying...wobbling erratically—as if trying to decide whether to fly or fall. Then, just as Ray thought his time on planet Earth was up, the GE engines sputtered back to full power and the helo began to inch upward.

Favored with a last-minute stay of execution, Helo-1 was finally under control.

Monday 21:37 Hours – The "Majestic Star"

When the Jayhawk crashed, there was a thunderous explosion that sent a fireball in all directions. Cal had only survived the blast by being sheltered within the stairwell cavity when the fireball whooshed by overhead. For the remainder of his days he would never forget the kinetic horror of it—the split-second change of air pressure preceding the jarring

440

concussion; the grinding screech of seven tons of metal against metal; the ripping-shredding-twisting-crunching sound of structural collapse; the choking black smoke and torrent of blistering heat; the hissing aftereffect of liquids on hot metal; the sibilant *whumpf* of spilt fuel igniting into a blue wall of flame. It had all happened in less than a minute, but the powerful assault on Cal's senses would reside within him forevermore.

~~~~~~~~

Cal emerged skittishly from the stairwell and took in the devastation. Under a billowing column of black smoke, the hulk cinder of what used to be a Coast Guard helicopter blazed away against the port railing. The width and length of the sundeck were littered with random fires and smoking patches of strewn rubble. The Tiki Hut and stage had been decimated during the crash and were nothing now but smoldering ruins.

Suddenly remembering Skip, Cal peered through the burning shambles to see Skip's head protruding above the stern stairwell. He, too, was eyeing the wreckage with the same look of shock on his face. Like Cal, he was probably thinking how miraculous it was they were both still alive. In the black of night beyond Skip, Cal could see flaming flotsam and debris bobbing in the ship's wake like burning corks.

Armed with his trusty Uzi, Cal ventured out a little further and looked around. There was no sign of Alvarez or his accomplice and Cal wondered if they had been killed in the blast. The trajectory of the rocket trail suggested that it came from somewhere near the Tiki Hut, which was now a burning heap of wood and ash. It struck Cal how ironic it would be if the hijackers had accidentally self-subverted their coup d'etat and were to blame for their own demise.

If anybody on the helo had survived the crash, it would verge on the miraculous. Still, Cal felt a duty to scour the wreckage for any unlikely survivors. While sidestepping patches of burning debris, he came across a jagged hunk of smoking metal. The heat radiating from it felt good against the chilly air and Cal lingered there a moment to savor some of its warmth. It was a 1662 shaft horsepower General Electric turbine engine, one of two from the wrecked Sikorsky Jayhawk helicopter.

Lying next to the charred engine was a severed leg that made Cal stop in his tracks. It was a shockingly unexpected sight and Cal couldn't divert his eyes from it. The leg was still within the pant leg of a USCG flightsuit and sporting a highly polished boot, which Cal found especially disturbing. Inexplicably, he caught himself looking around for the other boot as if it actually mattered somehow. For a twinkling Cal wondered if the leg belonged to Bluebird, but then forced it from his mind. There was no use dwelling on the leg—or the stupid boot—and he told himself to forget it. He had to take care of business and get the hell off this ship. Whomever the leg belonged to, he couldn't help them now. Perturbed for letting it rattle him, Cal moved on.

Body parts—they affected everyone differently. If a person was mentally prepared for the sight, it wasn't so shocking to the system. Soldiers on the battlefield expected to see them. Police and emergency workers expected to see them. It was a routine part of their job. But when one was unprepared for it, it could be quite chilling—like opening a kitchen drawer and finding a gooey eyeball inside or a blood-caked severed ear.

The *Majestic Star* was a gambling boat, not a battlefield, and this was the Gulf of Mexico, not the Gulf of Tonkin. When on a sea cruise, strewn body parts weren't part of the norm. The leg had simply caught him off guard, that's all, and he needn't get all freaky about it.

Shaking it off, Cal scanned the horizon for the second helicopter caught up in the blast. While down in the stairwell he had watched it fight valiantly for its life and had rooted for its survival. When it grazed the wheelhouse roof and pitched into a tailspin, he thought it was a goner. Yet somehow the skilled pilot managed to get it under control and hightail it out to sea.

If nothing else, Cal was grateful for that. At least one of the rescue crafts had escaped. He just hoped that when it returned with reinforcements, their mission would still be one of *search-and-rescue* instead of *seek-and-destroy*. The U.S. military didn't cotton much to losing $10-million dollar aircraft and sooner or later somebody would pay the piper.

Cal just hoped to be long gone when Uncle Sam collected its due.

~~~~~~~~~~

Fuel that failed to explode upon impact had seeped from the wreckage and spilled downstairs to the level below. Once the casino carpet was saturated with fuel, an inevitable flame found its way down there and a huge fire erupted. Within minutes the room was a fuel-fed blazing inferno and the rapid buildup of heat blew out the glass portholes. Voracious flames were now flaring from their circular openings, reaching skyward for more oxygen to nourish itself.

The good news was that the ship's hull and superstructure were constructed from steel and the ship fire would self-extinguish once all flammable materials burned off.

The bad news was that if the fire spread downstairs to the dining room and then further down into the engine room, the ship's fuel tanks could detonate and reduce everything to nothingness.

Monday 22:00 Hours – "Helo-1"

As the crippled copter flew over open sea, the veteran aircrew acted with sureness under pressure. While the pilot wrestled with the flight controls, the flight engineer silenced the warning alarms and checked the gauges for mechanical malfunctions. As flight commander, Ray supervised the emergency procedures while inspecting the integrity of the aircraft.

As the airmen bustled about the cockpit, Kathy sat with her face buried inside an airsick bag. After her horrifying near-death experience, she had hyperventilated and nearly fainted. If that weren't bad enough, artic air was blasting through her shattered window and it was biting cold.

"Mrs. Myles—I mean Kathy—it's all over now." When Kathy looked up, Ray was standing over her with his helmet clamped under an arm. He was holding a flashlight and his olive drab flightsuit was flapping in the rushing air. "Please calm down."

After what Kathy had just been through, his patronizing manner instantly provoked her. The words: *"please calm down"* sounded like a schoolmarm admonishing her school children—as if she had no rational reason for being upset. Well, where she came from, death was considered a pretty nasty setback.

"Whattya mean it's over?" she yelled over the howling wind. "How can it be over when my husband and brother are still down there? Huh?"

Unprepared with a tactful answer, Ray fell silent and stared at the space between his boots. She was overreacting, of course, but he couldn't argue the point because she was right. This thing wasn't over by a long shot and his remark may have sounded condescending.

Noting his hangdog expression, Kathy emitted a harsh laugh with a trace of hysteria. "Ha! That's what I thought!" With fire in her eyes she plucked a chunk of glass from her hair and flung it at him. "Here's a memento of our quiet little evening together. I hope it was as good for you as it was for me!" She crossed her arms and pushed back in her seat. "Calm down, my ass!"

Ray was in no mood for a chewing-out, but took it in stride and left her alone to fume. After examining her shattered window, he worked his way rearward, checking the airframe for damage along with its miles of wires, cables, and hydraulic lines. When Ray glanced back, he saw Kathy breathing into the bag again—her eyes daring anyone to approach her. That was fine with him, of course. The acid build-up was already eating away at his stomach lining and he didn't want to exacerbate it by quarrelling with a hysterical woman. He just wished he hadn't brought her along.

The loss of the Jayhawk and its four-man crew was a tragic blow and, as Incident Commander and Mission Coordinator, Ray would answer for it. But to make matters worse, Kathy Myles had witnessed the entire event. Now he couldn't engage in a little military coverup even if he wanted to. She might spill her guts to the news media and make a big fat liar out of him and the United States Coast Guard.

Fortunately, Chief Bloyd was heading up radio communications when the Mayday call crossed the airwaves. Instead of reporting the crash up the chain of command, he put a lid on it until checking with Ray first. Had the vice-weasel gotten wind of the downed aircraft, he would have ordered an immediate air strike, leaving Ray without argument. After all, that was the bill of goods Ray had sold Washington. Get the passengers off and then sink the ship with everybody on it. Before you could say: *"Davy Jones's Locker"* a squadron of F-16 Flying Falcons would be scrambled from MacDill with orders to send Majestic Star and company straight to the bottom.

WIRED

After completing his walk-through inspection, Ray backtracked and buckled himself into his seat. Except for the missing window and some minor damage, the airframe was intact. Everything was under control except for the scowling Mrs. Myles in the backseat.

While fastening his chinstrap, Ray eyeballed the fuel gauge with concern. Thanks to his wild-goose chase towards Mexico, their fuel reserves were borderline and the damaged rotor would worsen consumption. By squeezing every last drop from the reserve tank, they barely had enough fuel for a *Majestic Star* flyby and brief hover time—real brief. Otherwise, Helo-1 would be ditching in the wintry Gulf of Mexico a few miles shy of the mainland.

Ray adjusted the mouthpiece on his helmet and hailed Chief Bloyd. While waiting for a reply he lectured himself for the predicament he was in.

This is a shitty mess you've gotten yourself into, Ray-Man, the shittiest in a long time. Serious shit. If this thing ends with an air strike, she'll spill her guts to the media about Stringer for sure—after she physically attacks you in the cockpit and gouges out your husband-killing eyes. You'd better find a way out of this shit or you'll be up shit creek without a paddle. And your career? Pfft! Right down the old shitter.

Ray twisted around in his seat and looked at Kathy Myles, who narrowed her dagger eyes at him while breathing into the bag. The mean-ass look made his stomach clench and he snapped his head around and swallowed.

Aw, shit!

Monday 22:09 Hours – The "Majestic Star"

Peering through the smut and smoke, Skip watched his brother-in-law go up the stairs and disappear down the bridge deck.

Determined to give Cal some needed backup, Skip grabbed the stairway handrail and pulled his battered body up the steps. When he reached the sundeck, he gripped the AK by the gunstock and used it as a crutch to thrust himself upward. But when he tried to stand, his injured leg buckled causing him to fall to one knee. Simultaneously, the barrel tip slipped on the metal surface and the rifle clattered to the deck. Without its support, Skip fell backward onto his buttocks and his spine painfully met the pipe railing.

Now sitting against the rail with a bruised backbone, Skip tightened the tourniquet and decided to take a break. He wasn't going anywhere until the bleeding stopped and he regained some strength. Even with the tourniquet in place, blood squirted in rhythm to his pulse whenever he put pressure on the leg.

As Skip sat alone in the darkness, his concentration began to slip—the flagging effects of blood loss. In an endeavor to remain lucid he shook his head vigorously and slapped himself. If he blacked out now, he wouldn't be able to help anybody.

Wondering if Cal had found Neal yet, Skip peered in the direction of the wheelhouse. He hadn't heard any recent gunfire but that didn't mean a whole lot given Mendoza's proven skills with a bowie knife.

While looking through the black smoke, Skip ran his fingertip over the scab wound on his throat. Since this whole episode began, his throat had been scored; his cheek cut; his skull bashed in; his ribcage battered; his windpipe smashed; his scalp creased by a bullet; and now there was a chunk of lead lodged in his leg. What was in store for him next? The more Skip thought about it, the crazier it sounded and in his semi-delirious state it struck him as funny.

Out of the blue he began giggling to himself, then laughing. The whole thing was bizarre—madcap. The next thing he knew, Gold-Tooth would be poking him in the eyes like *The Three Stooges*. He might even pinch Skip's nose and bonk him on the head with those silly sound effects. The thought of it was hilarious and Skip's belly began to shake. Before long his whole body convulsed with giddy laughter.

While laughing it up, Skip's eyes landed on the sorrowful remains of John-Renée. In all the commotion he had forgotten about his Cajun friend. Exposed to the blazing fireball from the crash, the cook's body had been charred beyond recognition. The rubber soles of his shoes were still smoking.

"Hey, John-Renée, don't you think you're carryin' that blackened Cajun shit a little too far?" Slaphappy, Skip howled like a hyena. Then he had another stroke of wit. "Hey, man, smokin' is bad for ya. When ya gonna quit?" With that, he slapped his good leg and laughed himself hoarse. "Oh-h-h-h, me," he howled at the sky, lolling his head against the rail. "This place is a riot. The fun just never ends."

Once Skip recovered from his laughing jag, he rechecked his leg to find it still bleeding. Deciding to elevate it, he screwed around on his butt to face the railing, then—bracing himself for pain—slung the lifeless leg atop the lower rail. After suppressing a painful outcry, he picked up the AK-47 and lowered himself onto his back. Now lying on the sundeck drenched in cold sweat, he cradled the weapon against his chest and stared up at the heavens.

The moon was encircled by a thin wreath of clouds, giving it a soft misty glow. As its lunar radiance fell upon Skip's face, he basked in its enduring beauty. When a narrow bank of dark clouds scudded past and overshadowed its surface, the moon's luster dimmed and brightened with their passage. Then other gray ribbons followed suit and the stream of broken light was mesmerizing. Yet, there was something lonesome about it as well, turning his thoughts to Kathy.

With Skip's eyelids growing heavier, he envisioned her sweet face and a curl came to his lips. Her likeness, whether real or imagined, brought him great comfort and enriched his bruised spirit. It always did.

All at once the moon lost focus and began to swim before his eyes. As Skip teetered on the edge of unconsciousness, he fought to remain awake but his efforts were for naught. With a final flutter of his lids, he closed his eyes and warm sleep took him at last.

Monday 22:15 Hours – "Helo-1"

When Chief Bloyd's voice came over his headset, Ray told him to switch and answer Channel 12. That frequency wasn't recorded twenty-four-seven like Channels 16 and 22 and Ray wanted to talk off the record. He had already broken enough regulations and the last thing he needed was for some geek in Washington to analyze his taped conversation and later cause trouble.

"Helo-1, this is Chief Bloyd on Channel one-two. How do you read? Over."

Ray had to choose his words carefully. The channel wasn't recorded but anyone with a marine radio could be listening. "Roger, Chief, about

Helo-2...what do you suggest we report to the upper echelon? I need some more time out here."

"That's already been handled, sir. I just got off the horn with the VW. I explained that we had lost comms with Helo-2, which could be storm related, and that you were personally investigating it. I also reported that we had the Majestic Star under surveillance and that Operation Checkmate was proceeding as planned."

The chief's ungracious reference toward the Vice-Admiral brought a smile to Ray's face. The chief, too, held little regard for the pandering worm.

"Uh-h, yes, Chief, but what about the Mayday transmission? That'll be on record. Roger?"

"What Mayday call? You mean I missed a Mayday call? Well, I'll be darned." He was playing dumb and doing it well. The fake innocence in his voice was perfect. "I'll have to play back the tape, sir. I must've been on a landline at the time with the Vice-Admiral. He's been calling here on the hour for a status report. I must apologize for the oversight, sir. The action is inexcusable and I assume full responsibility. Over."

The transfer of blame to the Vice-Admiral amused Ray all the more. "Well," Ray played along, "just don't let it happen again. Missing a Mayday call is nothing short of negligence. I trust you will perform your duties with more diligence in the future. Is that clear?"

"Crystal, sir. I can assure you it won't happen again. Over."

"Duly noted." Ray stifled a chuckle. "Okay, enough about that. We're currently back en route to the Majestic Star. Our fuel level is low, which will restrict our hover time. I'll contact you when we arrive on scene. Helo-1 out."

In the face of the RPG, Ray still felt obligated to make a final rescue attempt. If it failed, he would order an air strike and be done with it. There was no other option. Within the hour, Alvarez and Mendoza would be at the bottom of the sea. The Ray-Man would see to it.

Monday 22:19 Hours – The "Majestic Star"

Cal was slinking in the shadows, prowling toward the wheelhouse, when he felt the ship turning. Stopping, he stared up at the moon to gauge the change in direction. Someone in the wheelhouse was altering course northward. It had to be either Alvarez or his sleazy sidekick, or perhaps Neal with a gun to his head. He would find out soon enough.

At that moment a spotlight atop the pilothouse blazed to life, turning nighttime into day. Suddenly bathed in brilliant light, Cal froze like a deer in car headlights. The assaulting glare on his eyes was blinding and before he could react a bullet ripped painfully into his left shoulder. Then another round split the air next to his ear, missing him by a whisker and tearing into the cabin wall behind him.

In blind self-defense Cal crouched low and fired a salvo of rounds at the light. As the rounds found their mark, the spotlight lens exploded into infinite pieces and shards of tinkling glass rained down on the catwalk. But, for Cal, its destruction had come too late; his night vision was ruined. His world was now an enduring blackness with a circular luminous ghost ingrained at its center. For all intents and purposes he was stone-blind.

Driven by survival, Cal backpedaled toward the sundeck while spraying lead in the direction of the wheelhouse. As the Uzi fired on full automatic, bullets strafed the exterior and blew out the starboard windows. When the clip was empty Cal turned to take flight but didn't get far. Three sightless steps later he stumbled over a chair left outside Skip's cabin door and fell facedown, banging his eyebrow against the bridge deck.

Dazed, disoriented, and expecting to take a slug at anytime, Cal rose up on all fours and crawled for all he was worth—fueled by desperation. Letting the Uzi dangle by its strap, he scurried rat-like through the shadows with one arm groping the air in front of him. In a bizarre twist of fate, he had become an unwilling participant in a hide-and-seek version of blindman's bluff. Except this was no game and the consequences—and bullets—were dangerously real.

When a round ricocheted off the deck next to him, Cal's blood surged and he increased his wriggling to nowhere. Confused as to which way to flee he crawled without direction, head down, his mind desperate for options. From somewhere within a voice told him to turn right and he clambered that way blindly until his knuckles jammed into a solid metal object. When he eagerly grabbed it, its cold roundness told him it was the pipe railing running the length of the catwalk and bridge deck. Keeping the railing to his left, Cal pulled himself toward the sundeck using his good arm. As he drew closer he made out some of the flickering fires, a saving sight. His night vision was restoring.

Using the flames as a beacon, Cal dug in his knees for traction and increased the pace by pulling with both arms. As he pulled hand-over-hand, the gross misuse of his wounded shoulder spewed out molten agony like a volcano. While suffering onward his hand plowed into a welded corner post and the rail changed direction to his right. He followed the pipe two more feet until it ended at another post. He'd found the stairway opening. As he groped blindly for the first descending step, a hot round sparked off the railing just above his head. After recoiling from it, he slithered down the stairs headfirst on his belly to the waiting sundeck below.

Somehow, someway, he had survived the assault—so far.

Lying within the temporary protection of the stairs, Cal rolled onto his back and panted at the night sky. The oval image of the spotlight was still burnt into his retinas but his peripheral vision was able to distinguish some of the brighter stars. Before getting up, he pulled up his shirtsleeve and gave his shoulder a cursory look. It wasn't good, but no bones were broken. The bullet had grazed his ribcage just under the armpit, slicing his left pectoral muscle. Pulsing pain radiated outward from it and it burned like hellfire, but the injury wasn't life threatening. The first chance he got he would immobilize it to stop the bleeding.

Figuring he had better get a move on, Cal inserted a fresh clip and crawled off into the night.

~~~~~~~~~~

When Skip opened his eyes, he was in a muddled state of confusion. *Where was he? Why was he so cold? What was happening?*

When he felt blood trickling underneath his boxer shorts, everything came back to him. His leg was still bleeding and he had evidently blacked out.

How long was he out? Where were Cal and Neal? Had he heard gunfire or just imagined it?

WIRED

The onrush of worry stimulated his adrenal glands and the epinephrine swept away the cobwebs. Now largely alert, Skip rose up on one elbow and peered toward the wheelhouse. At seeing nothing but darkness, he gazed down at his elevated leg. It had finally gone numb and he wasn't looking forward to disturbing it. But in order to help his friends, he had no choice.

Preparing himself for another jolt of pain, Skip pulled his leg off the railing and let it drop. As it jarred against the deck it unleashed a thunderbolt of pain that made beads of sweat pop out on his forehead. When the throbbing slackened to a sufferable level, Skip strained upward to a sitting position. But the sudden change in gravity made his head swim and he had to shore himself up with both arms. Waiting for the dizziness to pass, he shivered in the raw wind, wondering and worrying.

Skip peered toward the wheelhouse again to see nothing. Then he looked down at his bum leg. When its nerve endings quit freaking out and he regained some equilibrium, he would marshal all the strength left in him and go find Cal and Neal. He might die trying, but he would rather bleed to death than to fail his friends in time of need.

That's just the way it was. Skip Myles was coming.

~~~~~~~~~~

Following his narrow escape Cal retreated down the midship stairwell to tend to his wounded shoulder. His direct eyesight was still a dull orange cloud but his peripheral vision had restored enough to get by. Perched on the stairs above the burning casino, he removed his Mickey Mouse shirt and fashioned it into a sling. Then he looped it over his neck and stuck his injured arm through it. Right away the immobilization brought blessed relief.

Luckily—if getting shot could be deemed lucky—Cal had taken the slug in his left shoulder. Being right-handed, he could still operate the Uzi with no problem.

Now a bare-chested one-armed warrior, Cal stood up holding the Uzi. He was ready for round three with the sniper. As he climbed up the steps, an icy updraft whisked through the hollows of the stairwell giving him goose bumps the size of grapefruits. The air temperature was still dropping and the Uzi felt cold in his hand. He was wishing for a warm jacket when he heard his name called from somewhere down below.

"Hey, Cal! What's goin' on?"

Recognizing Skip's voice, Cal peered down over the handrail to find his friend staring up at him. Skip was one flight down, holding onto the handrail and leaning on the stock of his rifle. Exasperated, Cal dashed down the stairwell and scolded him in a loud whisper.

"What are you doing here, Skip? I told you to stay put! Do you wanna bleed to death?"

"I already did. Can't you tell?" With a wry smile, Skip gazed down at himself. "As you can see, I'm on my last leg."

Skip sniggered at the remark, causing his body to weave. His bloodstained uniform was sweat-stuck to his skin and his bad leg glistened with fresh blood. The hair on the right side of his head was matted to his scalp and the ear below it was caked with dried blood. Apart from his crooked grin, he looked like he belonged in the morgue.

Unamused, Cal steadied him by the arm and shushed him up by covering his loud mouth. When Skip nodded that he would quiet down, Cal removed his hand.

"Thought maybe I could lend a hand catchin' Moe and Curly Joe," Skip said in a softer voice. "This is where all the action is. Right? From the looks of that shoulder, you could use some help yourself."

Cal knew it was pointless to argue with him. Skip could be stubborn to a fault and oftentimes exhibited more balls than brains. Nevertheless, Cal had to admire his spunk. Skip had more of it than anyone he'd ever known and Cal had met some pretty gutsy guys.

"Look, Skip, you need to stay off that leg." Kneeling down, Cal examined the tourniquet. "Besides, you'll just slow me down. I can handle these dip-shits myself. Okay?"

"And let you have all the fun?" Skip smiled weakly at him. "Besides, you don't look so hot yourself. You're bleedin' pretty badly there. Let me take a look."

"No time for that, Skipper—just a flesh wound." Cal snugged up the tourniquet and stood. "Hurts like a bastard but it'll be okay." Cal knew that Skip needed to feel involved or he would resist staying behind. "Tell you what, you stay here and guard my back while I do some scouting topside. Then I'll come back and we'll formulate a plan of attack. It'll be faster that way."

Skip pondered the proposition and nodded. "Makes sense. I'd just slow you down. Be careful, Cal. And save Curly Joe for me—the gold-toothed one. I'll be waitin' right here."

Cal was relieved that Skip was cooperating because he didn't have time to argue. As the two embattled men stood in the dark, they each took stock of themselves. Cal was shirtless, his chest and stomach were scraped raw, his pants were ripped at the knees, his eyebrow and kneecaps were bleeding, and his bloody arm was in a makeshift sling. Skip looked like a back-from-the-grave zombie from the *Night of the Living Dead*. From their bruised and beat-up exterior, it didn't appear the two badass Navy SEALs were fairing too well against the Latinos.

"We look like hell," Cal finally said.

"No shit, Sherlock, but looks can be deceivin'." With a snarl, Skip held up his AK-47. "I don't know about you, soldier, but I'm just gettin' warmed up."

"Warmed over death, maybe," Cal kidded.

Shaking his head, Cal turned and started up the steps. For some reason, Skip had never grasped the difference between quitting, and quitting while you were ahead. The man was an animal.

~~~~~~~~~~

As Cal emerged from the stairwell, the voice of a stranger startled him.

"It's a beautiful sight, isn't it? I've always delighted in the scent of burning enemy aircraft."

Cal froze in his tracks and his skin went cold. When he turned toward the voice, Alvarez stepped from the shadows with a high-powered rifle aimed at Cal's midsection. Two steps behind him, Mendoza was holding Neal's head in a squishing headlock with a Colt .45 jammed against his temple.

Mendoza's left sleeve was wet with blood but he appeared strong and alert. Slung across his back was a Soviet made RPG-7 40mm anti-tank grenade launcher. Cal knew the shoulder-fired weapon well. Introduced in the early sixties, it was rugged, lightweight, and packed a lethal punch—the same weapon used to down a U.S. *Blackhawk* in Somalia.

"I don't believe that we've been introduced. I'm Juan Carlos Alvarez." When Cal didn't answer, the Colombian edged closer. "And you must be the uninvited guest who has so skillfully eliminated my men. Mr. Stringer, I am told. Are you not?"

"Maybe," Cal hedged, wondering why he was still alive. Like a cornered animal, his eyes darted between the two men. As his mind raced for what to do next, his finger tightened around the Uzi trigger; but Neal prevented him from firing.

"Don't be modest, Mr. Stringer. The first officer here has told us all about your Navy SEAL accomplishments."

Hunkered over and nearly choking, Neal was gawking up at Cal with clenched teeth. His face was purple from the headlock pressure and large veins stood from his forehead. His little finger was missing and Cal saw that his ring finger had been cut to the bone. Both fingers were spilling huge droplets of blood onto the white deck paint. Neal had been tortured into talking. Why?

"It doesn't matter what my name is," Cal said. "Let the man go before he chokes. Then we'll talk."

"Oh, but it does matter, Mr. Stringer. In my business names are very important. You see, some people are willing to sacrifice themselves when it comes down to it, but not the lives of their loved ones. Take you, Mr. Stringer. You have a sister named Kathy Myles, who happens to be Captain Myles' wife. She lives at Clearwater Beach in a waterfront townhouse. One word from me and she would not live through the night. And her death would be rather unpleasant, excruciating you might say." Alvarez's eyes glinted evilly. "Now that wouldn't set very well with you, would it? It might even convince you to cooperate. So you see names are important. As they say here in your country: information is power."

Cal didn't know what the Colombian was leading up to, but the mention of Kathy's name made the hairs raise on the back of his neck. Alvarez was a diabolical killer and he wouldn't think twice about ordering her death. But it didn't make sense. Why would a fugitive billionaire from South America be talking about Kathy at a time like this? Was Alvarez messing with his mind to achieve some particular result?

WIRED

"Okay," Cal relented, "I'm Calvin Stringer, ex-Navy SEAL. And you're Juan Carlos Alvarez, the ambushing asshole who gave me this little memento." Cal pointed at his shoulder with the barrel of the Uzi. The movement made Alvarez tense up. Blood from Cal's shoulder was trickling down his left side into the waistband of his khaki pants, which was now soaked in red.

"Yes, well," Alvarez countered, "if it's any consolation, you gave me a similar *memento*. So I suppose we're even." Keeping his aim steady, Alvarez twisted his upper body to reveal a bloody hole in the back shoulder of his cashmere sweater. Evidently one of the Uzi rounds had found its mark, which pleased Cal inside. "And your Coast Guard allies have wounded my colleague here. But that was before we shot them down, of course." Alvarez's eyes glazed over at the fond recollection, making Cal wonder if he was having an orgasm. "They won't be bothering us any more, I'm satisfied to say."

Alvarez's stilted bragging about downing the Jayhawk drew Cal's eyes to the severed leg. It belonged to a brave American serviceman killed in action and the sight of it sparked his wrath.

"Neither will your dead lackey friends," Cal hit back. "Whom I might add were all cowards right up till the time I killed them."

Alvarez bristled at the remark and fury streaked across his face. Then putting on a forced smile, he smoothed back his hair with one hand and spoke in a controlled voice.

"Let's not make this too personal, Mr. Stringer. I'm already at the end of my patience and killing you right now would afford me great pleasure." Alvarez was still smiling, but his eyes weren't. "In case you haven't noticed, my associate and I have the upper hand. Like one of your western movies would say: we have the drop on you. So let's forego the wordplay and get down to business. Shall we?"

As Cal stood in silence, the Colombian advanced another step, keeping one eye on the Uzi.

"As I see it, Mr. Stringer, we are facing three problems and it would be in our mutual interest to coalesce. First and foremost, we are all in need of medical attention. If you will notice, the first officer here has also suffered a little accident." He proudly extended his hand at Neal. "Secondly, the Jayhawk that escaped earlier will be back with military reinforcements, and, now that they're aware of our RPG, they'll likely dispense with any formalities and merely sink this ship with everybody on it. Thirdly, someone has disabled the marine radio, which will require repair so that I can arrange for transportation out of here. I understand you possess extensive Navy training in electronics. So I have a proposition for you, Mr. Stringer. You repair the radio and I'll spare your lives. Once we're gone, the ship is yours and you can radio the authorities that I have departed and there's no reason to sink the ship. You go home, I go home. No more bloodshed. What do you say?"

Cal was unaware that the radio was inoperative and the news of it drew his eyes to Neal. Had Neal sabotaged it for some reason? Had a stray bullet damaged its circuitry? Had Neal used it first to notify the Coast Guard? Whatever the case, it explained why he and Neal were still alive.

"If I fix the radio, you'll kill us," Cal reasoned. "Besides, if you have no radio, my sister in Clearwater is safe."

"Are you certain about that, Mr. Stringer? Are you willing to bet her life on it? Nothing is preventing me from killing you both right here and forcing the captain to repair the radio. However, I must warn you that if you put me to that much trouble, your sister will die—extremely slowly." There was an ugly flash in his eye. "I may even do it myself."

At issuing the threat, the orgasmic look crossed Alvarez's face again. Not only was he a narcissistic sadist with a bent mind, he was a psychopathic killer. Cal had once heard that the distance between insanity and genius was often measured by success. With that being the case, Alvarez was a cross between Bill Gates and Jeffrey Dalmer—mega-rich and fiendishly sick.

Riled by the threats against his sister, Cal went on the attack. "The power over life-and-death excites you, doesn't it? That's what you Al-Qaeda boys live for these days, ain't it? Killing defenseless people. Note that I said *boys* because real men stand up and face other men. You terrorists are cowards. You live among us, eat our food, watch our television, and lie in wait. Then you slaughter innocent civilians—women and children. Afterward, you run and hide amongst us like rats in our cellars."

Alvarez's brows pinched together and he exploded. "Don't test me, sir! I am neither a terrorist, nor a coward! I am a prominent citizen of Colombia and proud of it. I am no part of Al-Qaeda."

"Yeah, then what about those two towel-heads I saw earlier? Guess they just happened to be in the neighborhood. Right?"

Alvarez shrugged. "Tag-alongs. It appeases my Islamic clientele. When it comes to waging war upon the U.S., they refuse to be excluded. Besides, they're experts when it comes to rigging suicide bombs." His eyebrows raised and his shark eyes twinkled. "Blowing up those last two passengers was a nice little touch, don't you think?"

Cal's eyes flared, but he held his tongue. Either Alvarez was trying to provoke him or the psychomaniac couldn't help himself.

"Look, Mr. Stringer, I do business with extremists and third world regimes all over the globe. But that's where it ends. We all have our separate agendas. Al-Qaeda hates the U.S. more than they love life. They're religious fanatics who freely sacrifice their lives for their Islam God, Allah. They are brainwashed to believe that martyrdom brings honor and eternal glory."

"Yeah," Cal countered, "they're also brainwashed to believe that if you're not Muslim, you should die. That's pretty radical thinking if you don't happen to be one of the two billion Muslims in the world. The extremists among them are a menace to society."

Alvarez concurred with a nod. "They are paradoxical creatures, to say the least. However, religious fanatics have wrought havoc on world society since ancient times. That's what self-appointed apostles of purity do, Mr. Stringer. *'Believe the way I believe, or die.'* Sectarians are bigots to the highest degree, but they view themselves as fedayeens—defenders of Islam. And, like all extremists, they have strange enthusiasms." His voice was sermonic. "The Moslem spiritual struggle against the infidels has become an obsession and their so-called holy war is little more than hate disguised as religion." Alvarez bent forward, as if confiding. "It's not considered murder, you know, if you kill in the name of Allah." He gave a smug wink. "Their religion justifies it and sanctifies all purpose. I, on the other hand, do not believe in God and I don't hate America. I happen to earn a generous living from your populace. Like I said, Mr. Stringer, I'm a businessman."

Alvarez had gone off on a tangent and Cal was tired of his

sanctimonious rants. It was time to get back on the subject before things got down to the kaka poopie stage.

"Okay, whatever," Cal frowned. "Let's get back to the radio problem. I'm sorry to disappoint you, but the captain is dead. Someone drilled a hole straight through his leg and he bled to death. He's back there on the landing." Cal pointed toward the stern. "If you want the radio fixed, I'm the only game in town and I won't help you without assurances."

"No?" The intensity returned to Alvarez's face. "Then I'll kill your friend right now while you watch." While keeping aim with the rifle, Alvarez held up his left hand and splayed his fingers wide. "FIVE!" he counted out loud.

On cue, Mendoza cocked back the hammer and ground the barrel deeper into Neal's temple.

"Death is permanent, Mr. Stringer, something you can't take back. When I count down to zero, your friend will depart this miserable world forever unless you lay down your weapon and cooperate." The Colombian's stare was cold and uncaring. He wasn't bluffing. "FOUR!" he tallied, folding a finger.

If Cal didn't surrender, Neal was a dead man. If he did, they were both dead men—eventually.

"THREE!" Alvarez closed another finger. "Drop your weapon or your friend dies."

"Don't surrender, Cal," Neal urged. "They'll just kill us anyway."

When Neal spoke, Mendoza tightened his chokehold and Neal's eyes bulged even more. Blood was oozing from around the gun barrel and dribbling down his head. But Neal was right—Alvarez *would* kill them anyway. With nothing to lose, Cal was readying himself for a shootout when Neal's next words sabotaged the idea.

"Cal, if you do make it out of here alive, tell Phyllis I was thinking of her—you know, at the end. That I love her and the kids more than anything." His eyes teared up. "Okay?"

"TWO!" Alvarez counted. "Time is almost up!"

Next to fear, compassion was a soldier's worst enemy and Neal's words skewered Cal right through the heart. Alvarez was right: some people were capable of sacrificing their own lives, while not the lives of others. No matter what the outcome, Cal couldn't stand his ground and watch Neal get his brains blown out. No way.

"ONE!" Alvarez boomed, relishing the mental torture. "Last chance, Mr. Stringer. Throw down your weapon now or the man dies!"

Loathing himself as much as he loathed Alvarez, Cal slid the leather strap from his shoulder and let the Uzi fall. Like it or not, he was a prisoner of his own virtue. As the weapon clattered at his feet the wind suddenly shifted, carrying upon it the thumping cadence of an approaching helicopter. Alvarez, however, was too caught up in the moment to take notice.

"I'm glad you decided to cooperate, Mr. Stringer." Gloatingly, Alvarez kicked the Uzi away. "For a moment, I was beginning to wonder. You Americans are so unpredictable."

As the helo's vibrato grew louder, Cal kept the conversation going to distract Alvarez from it. Mendoza had already detected the sound and was craning his neck skyward.

"Okay," Cal said in a voice louder than necessary, "let's cut the bullshit and go fix the radio." "I'm cold and the sooner you're gone, the sooner we can get the hell off this ship. Lead the way."

Before Alvarez could answer, a helicopter descended from out of nowhere and its 120-knot windblast nearly plastered them to the deck. Simultaneously a spotlight washed them in brilliant light and a voice blared over the helo's loud hailer with authority.

"THIS IS THE UNITED STATES COAST GUARD. DROP YOUR WEAPONS AND SURRENDER IMMEDIATELY!"

Startled by the invasion, Alvarez looked up at the helo, squinting against the downwash and flying specks of debris. While his eyes were diverted upward, Cal pounced on Mendoza and seized the Colt in a last-ditch effort to save Neal. But just as Cal twisted it from his grasp, the gun discharged with a thunderous blast.

As Neal fell to his knees and toppled over, the loose gun followed him clanging to the deck. While both men scuffled to pick it up, Cal unintentionally kicked it away—sending it skidding across the deck's surface. The loss of the handgun temporarily suspended the fight and Alvarez finally got a clear shot at Cal. But before he could fire, Mendoza broke for the gun and Cal gave chase after him, right on his heels.

Winning the footrace by a scant second, Mendoza was stooping over to claim his prize when Cal struck him squarely in the nose with the heel of his hand. The broken nose made a sickening crunch and a thick mess of bloody mucus spewed down the Mexican's chin. Dazed and glassy-eyed, Mendoza reeled back a few steps, inadvertently kicking the pistol toward the railing. As the gun splashed overboard, Mendoza grabbed the makeshift sling dangling around Cal's neck and pulled it toward him. When Cal was drawn within range the Zeta delivered a solid kick to his groin, unleashing a profusion of pain from Cal's testicles to his gullet. Holding his throbbing scrotum in both hands, Cal collapsed to his knees and panted in short rapid gasps, fending off a tidal wave of nausea.

At that moment Alvarez joined the fight, launching into a kicking assault of his own. As both men booted the helpless American, their incoming feet scored repeatedly. Cal tried desperately to defend against the onslaught, but the rain of blows was coming too fast and furious. His shoulder wound had suffered several direct hits and fresh blood was streaming down his side like an open faucet.

As the driving feet punished him over and over again, Cal's world became whiter and whiter. Then a jarring kick landed upside his head and his eardrums resounded with a blaring ring that drowned out all other sound. Now veritably too weak to defend himself, Cal teetered on his knees in a cold sweat with his head drooping, hair hanging. He was verging on collapse when he heard the sound of Skip's raspy voice—or thought he did.

"Say goodnight, asshole!" Skip snarled in Mendoza's ear. "Cal! Get outta here. Hurry!"

Peering through glassy eyes, Cal saw Mendoza being dragged back by the throat. Skip was standing behind him, hopping around on one leg and pulling a wire cord with all his might. As Mendoza stumbled backwards, his fingers dug at the asphyxiating cord but it was stretched too taut across his windpipe. Emitting wet gurgling sounds, his eyes bulged and his mouth was agape in a futile attempt to draw air. Unable to breathe through his broken nose, his face purpled and pinpoints of light danced before his eyes. The Mexican's life was slipping away and the startling realization of it ignited the mother of all panic attacks.

WIRED

Driven by hysteria, Mendoza went berserk—growling like a wild animal and backpedaling as fast as his legs would carry him. As he retreated to the rear his backside crowded against Skip, forcing Skip to hop backward on one leg to keep pace. After a few unsteady hops Skip fell down on his back, dragging Mendoza down by the throat.

As Mendoza fell back on Skip, the RPG got sandwiched between them and its flip-up sight dug into Skip's injured thigh, reaming out the open bullet wound. When Skip emitted a bloodcurdling wail, Mendoza felt the cord relax and he wedged two fingers under the wire. Finally able to breathe again, his chest heaved mightily and the dots before his eyes began to clear. Now more alert, Mendoza raised his right arm and delivered a sharp elbow to Skip's sore ribcage. When the cord slackened, he delivered two more stiff jabs in rapid succession. When it slackened more, he got both hands under the cord and yanked it free from Skip's weakened grasp.

Liberated at last, Mendoza rolled over and straddled Skip's body. With their hair and clothes flapping wildly in the swirling wind, the archenemies traded pounding punches and bruising blows with their bare fists.

~~~~~~~~~~

The 30-million candlepower searchlight was called the *Night Sun* and all Coast Guard helicopters came equipped with one. The ultra-powerful spotlight was so intense, its searing beam had to be kept pointed away from the aircraft lest it blister the paint.

As Ray operated the Night Sun from inside the cockpit, it showcased the battle scene below in striking detail. Appearing a colorless pure-white under the intense light, Ray counted four men fighting with a fifth man lying motionless on the sundeck. Further astern, the twisted wreckage of Helo-2 lay in a smoldering heap. Its skidding trail of smaller deck fires had burned themselves out, leaving behind a checkerboard of scorched patches in the white paint. The casino below the sundeck was in flames, but the fire appeared to have contained itself and not spread further.

For reasons unknown the ship had reversed course—*again*—and was now heading west-northwest. The *Majestic Star's* autopilot was set at twenty knots and its hull was rising and falling with the seas. Lt. Commander Henninger's tricky task was to match the ship's forward speed while maintaining a permissible safety margin between the Jayhawk and fluctuating deck. Adding to his challenge was a strong headwind and the obscurity of night, which tended to obstruct depth perception in any case.

When Ray gave the go-ahead, the pilot maneuvered the helo lower still, bringing the main rotor dangerously close to the hindermost cabin behind the pilothouse.

~~~~~~~~~

"THIS IS THE UNITED STATES COAST GUARD. DROP YOUR WEAPONS NOW AND SURRENDER OR YOU WILL BE FIRED UPON!"

~~~~~~~~~

Sidetracked by the Coast Guard warning, Alvarez quit kicking Cal and squinted skyward with a hand shielding his eyes. The resurgence of the helo so soon after it disappeared was an unplanned surprise. Intent on extinguishing its blinding light, he took aim at the spotlight with the high-powered rifle.

The kicking reprieve gave Cal's head a chance to clear and he remembered the hunting knife. But when he fumbled to unsheathe it, it drew the Colombian's attention and Alvarez buried a size twelve Italian loafer deep into Cal's injured side.

Folding over with the impact, Cal wrapped his arm around Alvarez's ankle and clamped it tight against his side. Caught off balance, Alvarez dropped the rifle and bounced around on one foot while yanking to free his leg. As the drug lord hopped and pulled, Cal held on long enough to extract the knife. Just as Alvarez's foot began to slip from his grasp, Cal plunged the blade deeply into the Colombian's left side. Emitting a howling cry, Alvarez fell to the deck on his back, his bodyweight pulling his leg free.

After planting the knife, Cal sat back on his haunches in sweaty exhaustion. Blood was pouring from his bullet wound and the loss of it was making him incoherent. All at once his head swooned and the world around him flickered in and out. Seconds later he crumpled backwards on the deck with his legs folded under him.

When Cal reopened his eyes, he beheld two celestial lights in the sky above. Then his double vision cleared and the two lights became one. At realizing it was the helicopter's spotlight, he raised his head and traced the shaft of light to its end. With straining eyes he saw Alvarez hobbling off into the shadows with the knife handle protruding from his side. Smiling contentedly, Cal rested his woozy head on the deck. He'd got the bastard.

Suddenly remembering Skip, Cal twisted his head to find him still going strong. He was on top of Mendoza and wailing away with both fists. But his leg was bleeding badly and the deck beneath it was smeared with fresh blood. Both he and Skip needed medical attention before they bled to death.

Seconds later the spotlight became two again and Cal's senses swam. As he melted into unconsciousness, the "whomp-whomp" sound of the helo faded away like an AM radio signal late at night.

~~~~~~~~~~~

In between issuing warnings over the hailer horn, Ray was keeping close tabs on the fighting below. To his giant relief, the RPG was now sandwiched between Mendoza and the deck. Still, it represented a monumental threat and Ray was anxious to get away while the getting was good.

"Take us in closer, Commander. Let's pick up the good guys and go home."

"Roger, sir." Henninger checked the fuel gauge. "We're fast approaching bingo."

Bingo was the point where there was barely enough fuel to return to base, meaning their exodus would have to take place soon. As the Jayhawk descended, Ray nodded at the flight engineer, who unbuckled his seatbelt harness and gripped the handle of the jump door.

"Watch out for Alvarez!" Ray warned over the cabin noise. "He just got away and there's a cache of weapons stashed somewhere."

The Coastie nodded and dropped to his knees, then slid the door open. At once the frosty air swirled through the cabin interior making Kathy even colder. Looking straight down, the man guided the pilot into position and then threw out a rope ladder hooked to an electric hoist. Right away the lightweight ladder flew rearward, flapping ten feet or more above the deck. To remedy the shortfall, the Coastie worked a lever inside the doorway and the hoist drum unreeled more steel cable.

As the man operated the winch, Kathy gawked out her smashed window and chewed on her lower lip. Skip and Cal were directly below her, appearing like ghosts under the blinding light. Moments ago Cal had been fighting a man wearing a yellow shirt but now he was lying flat on his back. Skip was astraddle a second man, slugging it out. Cal was shirtless and Skip's pant leg was missing. Both were bloody messes. But in spite of their ghoulish appearance, her two guys were alive and for that she was thankful. Her prayers had been answered.

So, with the keen wind howling and the hoist motor humming, Kathy bowed her head and whispered a humble prayer of thanks.

~~~~~~~~~~

In Cal's semiconscious delirium, his attempt to save Neal's life replayed in his mind like a slow-motion movie.

When he grabbed the gun there was a thunderous blast and the smell of gunpowder filled the air. Then Neal began to fall slowly with his eyes rolled back, limp as a rag doll. Simultaneously, the loose handgun fell alongside him, eluding the flurry of hands groping for it. As the slow-mo movie played on, Neal was suddenly on his knees. His hair was sticky wet and his head sagged forward with eyes shut. Beside him the pistol continued to freefall, as if it were some malignant race to see which would reach the deck first—Neal or the gun. Then, as if imitating a just-cut oak tree, Neal toppled sideways with his lifeless arms dangling at his sides. As he plummeted in silence, the gun fell along with him—both inanimate victims of gravity.

Neal was almost there now, mere inches from the deck, but the gun was gaining on him. It was going to be close. Very, very close...

WIRED

~~~~~~~~~~

From the outer depths of Cal's mind came the drumming of a helicopter and the trumpeting of a loud hailer.

"ATTENTION! THIS IS THE UNITED STATES COAST GUARD. A RESCUE DEVICE IS BEING LOWERED. ALL U.S. CITIZENS ARE ORDERED TO EVACUATE IMMEDIATELY!"

The far-off voice was intruding on Cal's restfulness and he wanted it to go away. He was in a blissful state and wished not to be disturbed. His pain was finally gone and he was enjoying some much-deserved rest and relaxation.

Go away! Quit pestering me! Let me be!

But instead of it going away the racket continued, as if he were being purposely harassed. On top of the irritating noise, a pinkish light was shining through his closed eyelids, tormenting him even further. Whoever it was, they were begging for a lawsuit.

Didn't they know he was a lawyer?

But when the tireless badgering persisted, Cal opened his eyes to see what the commotion was all about.

Lying flat on his back, he studied the intriguing light. His mouth was bone dry with a faint taste of blood and both ears were ringing. His hearing was hollow and muffled, as if submersed underwater.

What was happening? Where was he? Is this what it felt like to die?

But he was too young to die. He had more living to do—a whole lot more.

His mind was struggling to make sense of things when a rope ladder magically appeared and lowered itself through the divine light. This curious phenomenon piqued his interest and he dwelled on it for an inexact time.

Was that the way to heaven?

In his disoriented state the line between seeming and being was vague, straining against reality.

Thinking that God should be able to do better than that, he debated whether to get on the ladder or not. After all, he hadn't exactly been a saint during his lifetime on Earth. It could take him the opposite direction and that wouldn't be so hot. *Or maybe it would.* It brought to mind the bumper sticker he had seen earlier on that pickup truck, the one that read: **WHERE ARE YOU GOING TO SPEND ETERNITY—SMOKING OR NON-SMOKING?** For all he knew, the ladder might carry him to the smoking section.

No, this was a big decision and he wasn't going to be rushed. Obviously he had a choice in the matter or a spiritual entity of some kind would be telling him what to do. He'd always heard that a dead relative was supposed to meet you when you died, to help guide you to the other side. Well, so far, he hadn't seen anyone, not even a cherub.

With a giddy grin, Cal pictured a cherub with a stubby cigar climbing down the rope ladder and saying in a gruff voice: "Better hop on, pal. Ladder leaves in five minutes. Next one in fifty years."

No, for the time being, he was going to stay put right here—wherever that was—while he thought more on it. After all, there was no hurry. He had all eternity to make up his mind. And it wasn't so bad here. The floor under him was a bit cold and the wind was rather raw, but it wasn't too terribly uncomfortable.

While marveling at the light, his head began to clear and a sliver of logic pierced his mental fog, questioning the absurdity of it all.

Ladder to Heaven!?—Smoking Section!?—Cherubs with Cigars!?

Cal emerged from his delirium to find himself still alive and breathing. Along with his resurrection came sound and sensation—the thundering whirl of a helicopter and crucifying pain. A Coast Guard Jayhawk helo was hovering directly overhead and a rescue ladder had been lowered. A familiar voice was blaring from the hailer horn, ordering everyone to evacuate. The rope ladder was his ride off this Godforsaken ship and away from those schizoid Zetas. Somehow or other, he had to get on it.

But his limbs felt heavy, as if sheathed in lead, and his entire being was weighted with fatigue. Straining against exhaustion, he raised his head and took stock of his battered body. The bullet wound in his shoulder had stopped bleeding but he'd clearly lost a lot of blood. He was scraped and bruised all over and his swollen testicles felt the size of basketballs. Everything he had hurt.

Cal relaxed his head on the deck and gazed at the spotlight through stringy sweat-soaked hair. It was no use. He was too weak. Whatever fate awaited him, so be it.

~~~~~~~~~~

"ATTENTION! A RESCUE DEVICE HAS BEEN LOWERED! ALL U.S. CITIZENS ARE HEREBY ORDERED TO DEPART NOW!"

~~~~~~~~~~

When Cal reopened his eyes he was shivering, making him wonder how he could be so cold while soaked in sweat. Squinting against the bright light, he propped himself up on his good elbow and looked around. Within the confines of the searchlight, he counted three bodies.

Skip was lying nearest him with his eyes closed. On the other side of Skip, Mendoza was sprawled in a bloody heap. Next to the stairwell, where the fight began, Neal was lying motionless with a dark puddle under his head. There was no sign of Alvarez, who Cal had last seen hobbling away with the hunting knife stuck in his side.

With a bruised-and-battered moan, Cal rolled onto his stomach and wormed his way toward Skip. If Skip was still alive, Cal hoped he would have enough strength to climb the ladder. More likely than not, Neal was a dead man. Surviving a point blank gunshot to the temple would be nothing short of a miracle. Even so, Cal would check on him after seeing about Skip.

As Cal drew closer, he saw Skip's chest rising and falling. Relieved, he crawled as fast as his complaining bones would carry him. In reaching Skip, Cal found him unconscious but breathing evenly. Still, he had lost a lot of blood and it would be a challenge getting him up the ladder.

Mendoza was another story. He had been beaten unrecognizable and something metallic was protruding from his left eye socket. If he weren't dead before, he would have died instantly when the object pierced his temporal lobe. Whatever it was, it was planted into his pulverized face as if the planter had wanted to make a statement—the payback of all paybacks.

Remembering the detonator, Cal glanced up at the waiting copter and decided to do a quick search. Crawling over Skip, he rummaged through the dead Mexican's pockets. During the search his eyes were drawn repeatedly to the object jutting from Mendoza's eye. Now that he was closer, Cal recognized it for what it was: a letter opener with an embossed Navy SEAL emblem on the handle. He wondered if Skip had planted it there in self-defense or if it was a crowning stroke of vengeance—a macabre coup de grâce. Whatever the case, Cal didn't have time to ponder it. The detonator was nowhere to be found and he had to get a move on.

While crawling back over Skip, the Coast Guard hailer repeated its evacuation order, pressuring Cal to hurry along.

"Skip! Wake up!" Yelling over the roar of the helicopter, Cal shook him with urgency. "C'mon, Skip, get up!"

When Skip didn't stir, Cal staggered upright and grabbed Skip by the wrists. Barely able to stand himself, he yanked on Skip's arm to wake him. When he didn't budge, Cal jerked repeatedly with more determination—yelling Skip's name. Finally, Skip moaned and looked up at Cal through groggy half-mast eyes.

"Skip! Get up! We've got to climb up the ladder. Can you do it?"

"What? Zat you, Cal?" His speech was slurred and thick. "Whaz th' matter?"

Skip's eyes were unfocused and his lips were pale and parched, making Cal wonder what to do next. He couldn't leave Skip behind but he couldn't carry him up the ladder either. As he wrestled with indecision, Skip's eyes fluttered closed, furthering Cal's anxiety.

"Skip! Don't go back to sleep!" Cal dropped to his skinned knees and slapped Skip's face. Skip's eyes cracked open with the slap and then closed. Frustrated, Cal slapped him again. "Skip! We've got to get out of here and I'm too weak to carry you! Can you walk to the ladder?"

Skip opened his eyes again and this time appeared vaguely more alert. But just as Cal got his hopes up, his eyelids fluttered closed again. Upset and out of patience, Cal reached over and punched Skip in his injured leg—figuring that if a slap roused his attention, a real jolt of pain would work wonders.

WIRED

"OWW-W-W!!" Making a scrunched up face, Skip sat upright and clutched his bad leg. "Jeez, Cal! Whatcha tryin' to do? Kill me?"

The angry rebuke brought relief to Cal's face. "Just the opposite, mate!" He pointed to the rope ladder. "I'm trying to get you off this tub! If you'll notice, our ride's waiting!"

Shielding his eyes from the spotlight, Skip eyed the ladder up and down. His expression was less than hopeful.

"I'll give it a whirl, Cal, but I'm mighty weak!" As Skip yelled over the bluster of wind and noise, the loud hailer issued a final evacuation order. "I can't climb with this bad leg, but I think I can hold on if you will help me over there!" Skip suddenly shivered. "Man! I'm freezin'!"

Calling on his reserve strength, Cal hoisted Skip to his good leg. After steadying him, Cal slung Skip's arm over his shoulder and hugged him around the waist. When all set, they leaned against one another and teetered toward the ladder, looking like two drunken sailors staggering home from an all night bender.

When they got within reach of the ladder, Cal made a grab for it but it sailed away at the last second. Between the ship's forward speed and the windblast from the rotor, the rope ladder was being whipped around like a wet noodle. After several missed attempts, Cal sat Skip down and chased after it, but the elusive ladder kept getting away from him. Finally wising up, Cal stood in one place and waited for the ladder to swing in his direction. When it did, he quickly snagged it and walked it over to where Skip was sitting.

"Here! Get on, Skip!" Cal positioned the ladder in front of him. "I'll help you!"

As Cal steadied the ladder, Skip gritted his teeth and pulled on the rungs hand-over-hand. By the time he was standing, his arms were trembling so much he was forced to stop awhile. While taking a rest, Skip suddenly remembered Neal and looked over his shoulder at Cal.

"What about Neal? We can't just leave him here! He might still be alive!"

"Not a snowball's chance!" Cal shouted in his ear. "He took a bullet point blank in the head. But once you get up the ladder, I'll go check on him anyway. Okay?"

"No!" Skip yelled with conviction. "I'm not leavin' without him!"

Balancing himself on his good leg, he twisted to face Cal. "He's my friend, Cal—and a damned good one! He's got two kids!" Skip handed the ladder to Cal. "Save yourself. I ain't leavin' just yet!"

As Cal stared into Skip's stubborn face, his rescue bubble burst. Here they were, just a step away from freedom, and his pigheaded friend wouldn't leave. *Un-freaking-believable!*

"C'mon, Skip! This is bullshit! Neal's dead. Get on the damn ladder!"

"NO!" Skip's expression was rock hard. "I won't leave!"

Skip's refusal was a maddening setback, but deep down Cal understood. He would feel the same way about leaving Skip behind. Still, Neal was Skip's friend—not his—and Cal wasn't crazy about risking his neck any further for a dead man.

"Okay! Okay!" Cal snapped at him. "You hang onto the ladder with both hands while I go check on Neal. Whatever you do, don't let go of it! I'll be right back."

When Skip nodded, Cal released the ladder and stepped back. After making sure Skip had control of it, he headed in Neal's direction. But halfway there a bullet sparked off the deck between his feet and his mouth went dry.

Alvarez! Cal crouched catlike and looked all around. *That sonofabitch just won't give up!*

Suddenly a second shot rang out and hissed past his left ear. Standing out in the open, Cal dropped onto his stomach and flattened himself to look small. With his heart racing, he searched everywhere for the shooter but it was no use. Everything beyond the brilliance of the spotlight was a solid black curtain.

Realizing they were sitting ducks, Cal looked skyward and waved off the hovering helo. Under the bright spotlight, he and Skip may as well have bull's-eyes drawn on their backs. Luckily the winch operator made sense of the gesture and reacted swiftly. Cal saw him yell something toward the cockpit and seconds later the spotlight was diverted, searching for the shooter instead.

"We gotta go, Skip!" Cal yelled in his ear. "We're being fired upon!"

"No way, Cal!" Skip yelled back. "Not without Neal!"

"Neal's dead, dammit! Climb up the ladder now or we'll be dead too! Think of Kathy—she needs you! You can't help Neal now! Nobody can!"

WIRED

With the darkness favoring their escape, Cal began muscling him up the ladder. Skip was unenthused about it at first but allowed himself to be pushed. But after hauling his bodyweight up only a few rungs, his arms tired out. Letting his injured leg dangle, Skip rested a second and then scaled three more rungs before giving out. Cal stepped on a rung below him and gave him a boost with his upper shoulders, helping Skip up another two rungs. By this time Skip was spent and barely capable of hanging on.

As the flak-jacketed Coastie winched the Americans upward, he was made to dodge round after round of ground fire. When a bullet ricocheted off his helmet, he abandoned the controls and vanished from view. A split-second later the engines revved and the helo nosed over to gain speed, banking hard to the left. With Cal and Skip hanging on for dear life, the Jayhawk peeled away with its tail-mounted strobe light flashing in the night.

As Cal looked up at his injured friend, he wondered how long Skip could hold on. Skip was too weak to climb up the ladder, so that meant holding on until they reached the mainland, which could be a while. To prevent Skip from falling off, Cal climbed up and over his backside and then straddled Skip's body with his arms and legs, effectively pinning Skip against the rope ladder.

"Howya doing, Captain?" Cal yelled into his blood-caked ear.

"Well, I was just fixin' to kick some real ass when you made me leave!"

Cal smiled. "Oh, yeah, I forgot. You were just getting warmed up. Right?"

Skip nodded weakly. "Damn straight!"

As the Jayhawk carried them out to sea, the Night Sun remained fixed on the ship below. When Cal looked down, his heart almost jumped out of his chest. A man wearing yellow was picking up the grenade launcher.

"Oh, shit! Alvarez has the RPG!"

Without answering, Skip cast a baleful smile and removed something from his shirt pocket. Cal looked at the object and couldn't believe his eyes—the detonator.

"A little souvenir from Señor Mendoza." Sneering, Skip raised the button cover and pointed the device at the ship. "You know, Cal, this

471

Alvarez dude is really startin' to piss me off!"

When Skip pressed the button, the C-4 erupted into a fountain of majestic colors and skyrocketing spangles of sparkling debris. A millisecond later the fuel tanks detonated and the former *Majestic Star* lit up the horizon for miles and miles around.

CONCLUSION

Three Months Later – Clearwater Beach, Florida

Sitting on a row of barstools, the rowdy group had been drinking most of the afternoon. As they laughed and swapped stories, the vivacious Miss June listened in with fascination.

Noting his empty glass, Skip registered a complaint to the rest of the group. "You know, this is a pretty nice place but the service around here is really lousy."

At hearing the wisecrack, Cal stopped toweling off the bar and shot Skip an unsympathetic look. With the others looking on, he slung the damp towel over his shoulder and moseyed down to where Skip was sitting. Then, in his best John Wayne, he leaned across the bar on one elbow.

"Okay, mister. What'll it be?"

Closing his eyes and making a dumb face, Skip quipped: "I'll have another draft beer, barkeep!"

After refilling Skip's mug, Cal slid it down the bar until it stopped directly in front of Skip without spilling a drop.

"Hey, I'm impressed," Skip grinned. "You're gettin' pretty good at this."

Eyeballing the others, Cal cracked: "At least I work."

Raising his glass to his lips, Skip said in self-defense: "Well, it's kinda tough gettin' a new job when you have a work history of blowin' up your own ship." Then he sipped the head from his beer in one mighty suck.

"Yeah," Neal added, "and blowing up your help."

Apart from Skip, the whole group laughed out loud.

Wearing a cagey expression, Cal strode down the bar to face Neal. "Well, Neal, let me see if I understand you correctly." Seeing it coming, Skip groaned and shifted on his barstool. "What you're saying is that when an able-bodied seaman signs up to crew on a vessel, being tortured or getting blown to bits isn't generally part of the job description—unless, of course, you sail with Captain Myles. Is that correct?"

Neal nodded. "That's right. If I hadn't latched onto that charred craps table to float on, I'd be on the ocean bottom right now with Alvarez and his banditos." He held up his hand with the missing finger. "And as far as the torture thing goes, let's just say I won't be doing any more Doctor Evil impressions."

While everyone guffawed, Skip sat in silence—smiling into his beer. Having enduring enough at his expense, he blotted his foamy beard on a shirtsleeve and fired back.

"Well, Neal, you've always been full of crap anyway, so most folks feel it was a fitting end to your career as first officer." With that barb, the crowd hooted. "Besides, Cal said you were dead and you were layin' there like a 170-pound paperweight. How could I know the bullet only grazed your head? Of course, if I'd been thinkin' straight, I would've remembered that super-thick skull of yours."

Ignoring Skip's sarcasm, Neal stood up. "Well, at least we saved the ship's wheel." He raised his glass to the wooden wheel mounted as a showpiece behind the bar. Cal's lucky gambling chip was wedged into its center hub. "To the Majestic Star! May she rest in peace!"

Everyone stood and toasted the sunken ship, then took their stools after guzzling more beer.

"Well, maybe I'm unemployed," Skip countered, "but that little divin' expedition we did should tide us over a while. Ain't that right, honey?"

Kathy let out a choked laugh. "Yeah, but we can't keep paying our mortgage every month in silver dollars. I think the bank is getting a wee bit suspicious."

"Ah, yes—our little fishing expedition." Cal gave the group a conspiratorial wink and gestured at Ray with his eyes. "Let's don't brag about that too much. We wouldn't want the authorities to find out about our salvage trip, now would we? Might report us to the insurance company."

The room became still as everyone eyed Ray sitting at the end of the bar next to Skip.

"What are you looking at me for?" Ray shrugged. "I hear nothing...see nothing...know nothing. If you don't believe me, ask Washington. They'll attest to that." While everybody chuckled, Ray changed the subject. "Hey, Cal, I gotta another lawyer joke for you."

WIRED

Having heard a million lawyer jokes, Cal rolled his eyes. "I'm not a lawyer anymore. Remember? I sold my law practice."

"Yeah, but once a shark, always a shark. Right guys?" There was a unanimous murmur of agreement. "Anyway, the joke goes like this. There's a guy in a bar, talking to the bartender. He says, *'I hate lawyers. They're all a bunch of assholes.'* From a table behind him, a guy in a fancy three-piece suit butts in and says: *'Hey, I resent that!'* The first guy turns around and says: *'Why? Are you a lawyer?'* The other guy says: *'No, I'm an asshole.'*"

As the room rang with laughter, Cal shrugged it off and zeroed in on Skip's new gold necklace. It was his turn to laugh.

"Interesting necklace, Skip." With a wry grin, Cal fondled the pendant between his fingers. "Rather unusual, I must say. What is this anyway—a gold nugget with a diamond in it? Looks more like a dentist's worst nightmare to me."

With the room howling, Skip stood and raised his hands for quiet. When the laughter tapered off, he bowed his head ruefully. "Just a little memento from a dear departed friend, that's all." With exaggerated piety, he placed a hand over his heart and shook his lowered head. "I'm sure he would have wanted me to have it."

While the group heckled Skip about his gross-out necklace, Cal poured them all another round. After depositing a foamy mug before each friend, he proposed a toast. "To Captain Brillo—the Blackbeard of Clearwater. Without him, we wouldn't all be here today."

"Hear, hear!" Skip blurted, then chugged his beer in one impressive gulp.

As everyone cheered him, Brillo smiled and dipped his head modestly, then accepted their gratitude with a clack of their mugs.

Scurrying back to his stool from refilling his glass, Skip made a toast. "And here's to Cal's *Silver Dollar Sports Bar*. Where everyone's a winner!"

"Hey, I like that," Cal said. "Just might use that as my slogan."

"But, most of all," Skip furthered, "here's to my beautiful bride." His expression turned serious and he raised his mug to Kathy. "Okay if I tell 'em, honey?" When she nodded meekly, Skip thrust his mug into the air and bellowed: "Who's gonna have me a bouncin' baby boy!"

475

WIRED

The room erupted in noisy celebration with everybody chattering at once. As the excited well-wishers expressed their congrats, Kathy beamed and blushed and gushed with glee. She and Skip were pregnant—finally—after twenty-some years of marriage. The In-Vitro Fertilization had worked. They still couldn't believe it.

Amidst all the rejoicing, Neal muttered to Cal over the rim of his glass. "Oh, no—the legacy continues. A Skip mini-me."

"Yeah, that's all the world needs," Cal joked. "As if one Jason Myles weren't enough."

Another beer later, Kathy and Karol with a 'K' excused themselves to go to the ladies room. Seizing the private moment, Skip leaned across the bar to have a word with Cal.

"Hey, Cal, have you heard anything from Cindy since you sold your law practice? I mean, you guys were pretty tight. Right?"

"Yes, as matter of fact I have. She's moving down here next month to help me and Pops run this place. I'm thinking about settling down, Skip."

"You? You're kiddin'! Uh-h, I mean that's great. But what about Miss Bombshell there?"

"I said I was *thinking* about it. Roger?"

"Roger on that," Skip winked. "From the way *she* looks, I'd have to do some mighty long thinkin'. Her centerfold spread in Playboy was somethin' else!" Caught red-handed, Skip blushed all the way down to his collar and promptly tried to cover the slip-up. "Uh...well...you know, that's what I heard, anyway."

Cal hoisted an eyebrow and looked down his nose at him. "You dog you. Does Kathy know you peeked?"

With a guilty-as-charged look on his face, Skip squirmed on his barstool and quickly changed the subject. "Speakin' of Pops, I'm really glad you hired him, Cal. I was kinda worried about how the old guy would get by and all, now that the new bridge is being built. He'll make a terrific bartender. Everybody loves the old fart."

Cal gave Skip another judgmental look, just to make him squirm, then dropped the centerfold matter—for now. He would have plenty of time to rub it in over the coming months ahead.

"Yep," Cal nodded, "Pops starts next week. I told him he was crazy for not sticking around for his severance pay, but he claims his mind is made up. On July 4th weekend, he's going to raise the bridge one last time, lock up the bridge house, and walk out—snarling beach traffic for miles. He said to me: *'That'll show the ungrateful bastards!'"*

Skip threw back his head and laughed and both men shook their heads at Pops' quirky nature. He was definitely a character.

As soon as Kathy and Karol returned, Cal looked at his watch and decided it was time for some food. A few more drinks with this bunch would mean an all-nighter and tomorrow was going to be a busy day. Fishing a spoon from a drawer, Cal tapped it against his empty glass to draw the group's attention.

Ping-ping! ... Ping-ping!

Ray cringed at the sound and frowned down the bar at the row of faces. "Jeez! I hate it when people do that. Don't you guys?" Then he looked at Cal. "Hey, Cal. Cut out the ping-ping shit, okay? It reminds me of a mutual acquaintance that I'd just as soon forget."

With everyone looking at him confused, Ray half-smiled and drained his glass.

After the chatter quieted down, Cal graciously announced that dinner was on him, which was good for one last cheer. Then he ordered everyone out of the bar—reminding them that tomorrow was his grand opening and he didn't want them messing up the joint.

As the gathering of friends strolled toward the exit, they lagged along the way to admire the slot machines that set the bar's theme. Some of them had been slightly dulled by the corrosive saltwater and none of them actually worked, but the dazzling multi-colored lights made eye-catching décor. Everyone agreed that Cal's sports bar would be a hit with the beach crowd.

Once the congregation filed out, Cal turned around in the doorway for a final look. He was really proud of the place—the sparkling chrome slot machines, the antique bar he had discovered in downtown Tampa, the scattering of flat-screen TV's and colorful neon lights. He particularly liked the custom-made sign hanging behind the bar. The sign featured a likeness of the renowned South American bean-picker and his faithful donkey, Conchita. Above the picture read: **JUAN VALDEZ GO HOME!** Below it, read: **COLOMBIAN COFFEE <u>NOT</u> SERVED HERE!**

After everything he had been through, Cal felt like the luckiest stiff in the world. He was alive and well, and back home in Florida where he belonged with family and friends. He had rediscovered his place in life and he would never lose it again.

With a rewarding sense of fulfillment, Cal smiled to himself and turned off the lights. It was going to be a good life, a slower paced life, and he was looking forward to it. As he backed out the doorway, he flipped over the more traditional sign that read: **SORRY, WE'RE CLOSED. PLEASE CALL AGAIN.**

WIRED

*New Clearwater bridge under construction with
old drawbridge in background.*

New Memorial Bridge Causeway after completion.

From left to right: Captain Bob Kirn and Ron Duncan.

From left to right: Ron Duncan and Captain "Brillo" Kirn.